Richard Laymon wrote over thirty [...] May 2001, *The Travelling Vampire S[...]* Best Horror Novel, a prize for w[...] shortlisted with *Flesh, Funland, A [...]* and *A Writer's Tale* (Best Non-fiction). Laymon's works include the books of the Beast House Chronicles: *The Cellar, The Beast House* and *The Midnight Tour*. Some of his recent novels have been *Night in the Lonesome October, No Sanctuary* and *Amara*.

A native of Chicago, Laymon attended Willamette University in Salem, Oregon, and took an MA in English Literature from Loyola University, Los Angeles. In 2000, he was elected President of the Horror Writers' Association. He died in February 2001.

Laymon's fiction is published in the United Kingdom by Headline, and in the United States by Leisure Books and Cemetery Dance Publications. To learn more, visit the Laymon website at: http://rlk.cjb.net

'A brilliant writer' *Sunday Express*

'No one writes like Laymon and you're going to have a good time with anything he writes' Dean Koontz

'In Laymon's books, blood doesn't so much as drip as explode, splatter and coagulate' *Independent*

'Stephen King without a conscience' Dan Marlowe

'Incapable of writing a disappointing book' *New York Review of Science Fiction*

'A gut-crunching writer' *Time Out*

'This author knows how to sock it to the reader' *The Times*

'This is an author that does not pull his punches . . . A gripping, and at times genuinely shocking, read' *SFX Magazine*

Also in the Richard Laymon Collection published by Headline

The Beast House Trilogy:
The Cellar
The Beast House
The Midnight Tour

Beware!
Dark Mountain
The Woods are Dark
Out are the Lights
Night Show
Allhallow's Eve
Flesh
Resurrection Dreams
Darkness, Tell Us
One Rainy Night
Alarums
Blood Games
Endless Night
Midnight's Lair*
Savage
In The Dark
Island
Quake
Body Rides
Bite
Fiends
After Midnight
Among the Missing
Come Out Tonight
The Travelling Vampire Show
Dreadful Tales
Night in the Lonesome October
No Sanctuary
Amara
The Lake
The Glory Bus

*previously published under the pseudonym of Richard Kelly

Funland

and

The Stake

headline

FUNLAND first published in Great Britain in 1989
by W H Allen and Co Plc

THE STAKE first published in Great Britain in 1990
by HEADLINE BOOK PUBLISHING

First published in this omnibus edition in 2006
by HEADLINE BOOK PUBLISHING

A HEADLINE paperback

1

ISBN 0 7553 3173 7 (ISBN-10)
ISBN 978 0 7553 3173 4 (ISBN-13)

Typeset in Janson by Avon DataSet Ltd, Bidford on Avon, Warwickshire

Printed and bound in Great Britain by
Mackays of Chatham plc, Chatham, Kent

Headline's policy is to use papers that are natural, renewable and recyclable
products and made from wood grown in sustainable forests. The logging and
manufacturing processes are expected to conform to the environmental
regulations of the country of origin.

HEADLINE BOOK PUBLISHING
A division of Hodder Headline
338 Euston Road
London NW1 3BH

www.headline.co.uk
www.hodderheadline.com

Funland

This book is dedicated to
Ann Laymon and Kelly Ann Laymon,
My wife and daughter
My travelling companions
My best friends

With loads of love

Chapter One

He came out of the shadows beside the closed arcade and shambled towards Tanya. He looked like something that had crawled out of a grave in a zombie film – face grey under the moonlight with eyes like holes, head tipped sideways, feet shuffling, ragged clothes flapping in the wind.

Tanya halted. She folded her arms across her breasts. In spite of the chill wind blowing in off the ocean, she was warm enough in her sweatsuit. But now her skin started to crawl as if coming alive and shrinking. A belt seemed to be drawing tight across her forehead. She could *feel* the hair standing upright on the nape of her neck, on her arms.

The man shuffled closer.

Not a zombie, Tanya knew.

Zombies aren't real. Zombies can't mess with you. They don't exist.

This was a troll.

One of the mad, homeless parasites that preyed on anyone – everyone – who ventured near the boardwalk or the beach. More of them all the time. The filthy, degenerate scum of the earth.

This troll, still a few strides from Tanya, reached out his hand.

She took a quick step backwards, suddenly suspected that others might be lurching towards her, and snapped her head around. She saw no one else.

She knew they were watching, though. Trolls. Two, or three, or ten of them. Gazing out from the black rags of shadows near the game booths and rides, from around corners, maybe leering up at her through cracks in the flooring of the board-walk. Watching, but staying out of sight.

1

'Can y'spare two bits, darlin'?'

She snapped her head towards the troll.

She could see his eyes, now. They looked wet and runny in the moonlight. His teeth were bared in a sly, humble grin. Some in front were missing. The wind wasn't strong enough to blow away the sour stench of him.

'Okay,' Tanya said. 'Sure.' She swung her shoulder bag off her hip. Clutching it to her belly, she opened it and took out her change purse.

'Can y'spare a buck, darlin'' He bobbed his head, rubbed his whiskery chin. 'I ain't had a bite t'eat in free days.'

'I'll see what I've got,' she said. Her voice shook. She snapped open the change purse.

'Whacha doin' out here?' he asked. 'Ain't safe, y'know. Lotta *weirdees*, if y'get m'drift.'

'I've noticed,' Tanya said.

'Purty young fing. Weirdees, they sure like purty young fings.'

Instead of coins, Tanya plucked a white card from her purse. She jerked it forward and snapped it across the troll's waiting hand.

'Wha?' He scowled at it.

'Can you read it?'

'Wha-sis shit?'

'It's a message for you.'

He ripped the card and threw it down. The wind flung the pieces aside. 'Wanna buck, free-four bucks. C'mon.' He jigged his outstretched hand. 'C'*mon*.'

Tanya swung the handbag past her hip and behind her, out of the way. She felt its weight against her rump. 'What the card said, you illiterate fuck, is "Dear Troll, Greetings from Great Big Billy Goat Gruff".'

'Wha-sis SHIT?'

Tanya lunged at him. Squealing, he staggered backwards. She grabbed the crusty front of his coat, hooked a leg behind him, swept his legs forward, and shoved him down. His back hit the boardwalk. His breath whooshed out as she stomped on his belly. He rolled onto his side and curled up, wheezing.

Tanya dug inside the neck of her sweatshirt. She drew out the whistle, turned away from the writhing troll, and blew a quick blast.

The ticket booth was a lot farther off than she expected.

If she'd run into trouble . . .

But she hadn't.

They sprang from their hiding place beside the booth and raced towards her: Nate, Samson, Randy, Shiner, Cowboy, Karen, Heather and Liz.

The team.

Tanya's Trollers.

Watching their charge, she felt a swelling of pride in her chest. She smiled and thrust a fist into the air. All of them pumped fists over their heads. Somebody – had to be Cowboy – let out a whoop. Nate cuffed him in the arm to shut him up.

Tanya turned to the troll. He was on his hands and knees, crawling, trying to get away. She hurried over to him and pounded down with her shoe, turning his foot, grinding his ankle against the wood. He let out a shriek and flopped. Keeping his foot pinned, she waited. At first, she heard only the rush of the wind, the distant heavy sound of combers washing onto the beach. Then came the slap and scuff of the approaching team.

In seconds, she and the troll were surrounded.

Nate patted her rump. 'How'd it go?'

'No sweat.' She took her foot off the troll's ankle.

He disappeared under crouched and kneeling bodies.

Tanya stepped back to watch, and Nate joined in.

'Lee me be!' the troll whimpered. 'Lee *go*!'

He gasped and grunted and yelped as blows thumped him.

Turning around, Tanya scanned the boardwalk. She saw nobody. If other trolls were watching – and she was sure they must be – hoped they were – they had no interest in coming to the aid of this one.

'No! Blease!'

Tanya looked down at the troll. Karen had one cuff of his

3

baggy trousers. Heather had the other. They pulled and the pants shot down his pale, skinny legs.

'Oooeee,' Cowboy said. 'This ol' boy's hung like a mule.'

'Sure puts you to shame,' Liz remarked.

'My ass 'n your face.'

'Shut up, you two,' Nate said. 'Come on, let's get him up.'

The naked troll, stretched by hands pulling his wrists and ankles, was raised off the boards. He twisted and jerked. He whimpered. He flung his head from side to side. 'Lee me be!' he cried. 'Lee me be!'

Tanya spread out his coat. Holding her breath, she tossed his shoes and clothing onto it. His shirt and pants felt moist, slick in some places, scabby in others. She gagged once, but went on with her task and wrapped the coat around his other garments. She picked it up. Holding it off to the side, she followed the struggling, spreadeagled troll as he was carried to a lamppost.

Its light – all the lights of Funland – had been extinguished an hour after closing time.

Cowboy slipped a coil of rope off his shoulder. He kept one end. He hurled the rest upward. The coil unwound, rising, and dropped over the wrought-iron arm of the lamppost. The hangman's noose came down. He grabbed it.

'*No!*' the troll cried as Cowboy dangled the noose over his face. '*Blease! I din do nuffin!*'

'He din do nuffin,' Liz mimicked.

'Let's string him up,' Samson said.

'Hang him high,' added Janet.

'*No!*' His head flew from side to side, but Cowboy got the noose around it.

'Gonna stretch your neck,' Cowboy said, leaning over him. 'Gonna watch you do the air-jig.'

'Let's stop wasting time and do it,' Tanya said. Dropping the bundle of clothes, she grabbed the loose end of the rope and pulled the slack out. She strained backwards, tugging. The troll squealed. The group let go of him. Tanya saw his legs drop. He swung down, his rump off the boardwalk, his feet pedalling as he tried to get them under him. His sudden weight yanked the rope. Inches of it scorched Tanya's hands. Then, Samson and Heather and Cowboy joined in.

'Okay, okay,' Nate called.

They stopped pulling. 'Hold on,' Tanya said. She stepped away, leaving the other three to keep the rope anchored.

The naked troll danced on tiptoes, clutching the noose at his throat.

Tanya walked over to him. 'You want to die?' she asked him.

He made sobbing, whining noises. A string of snot hung off his chin, swaying.

'You're disgusting,' Tanya said. 'You're scum. You're a stinking pile of excrement.'

'That means shit,' Liz informed him.

'We don't want your kind creeping around, messing with us. You got no business here. We're sick of it. Do you understand?'

He blatted like a terrified baby.

'Hoist him!' Tanya yelled.

The troll went up, clawing at the noose, back arched, legs flying as if he wanted to sprint on the wind.

'That's enough,' Nate said.

The troll dropped. His heels bounced off the wood. His rump slapped it. His knees shot up, one of them clipping his chin and knocking his head back. Lying sprawled, he whimpered and tore the noose from his neck.

Nate snatched it from his grip.

Looped it around the troll's right ankle, slid it tight.

'Pull,' Nate ordered.

The troll's right leg shot upward.

His body followed.

When his head was a yard above the boardwalk, Cowboy lashed the rope around the base of the post. 'That oughta hold the booger,' he announced.

They gathered in front of the troll. He was swinging from side to side, twisting and spinning, pawing at the boardwalk, which was well out of reach. His loose left leg didn't seem to know what to do with itself.

'Now there's a right pretty sight,' Cowboy said.

'It'd be a lot prettier,' Tanya said, 'if we'd left the rope around his neck.' She crouched and glared at the eyes of the dangling troll. 'Next time, you motherfucker, we're gonna kill you dead! Understand? So you better get the hell away from here as soon as you're down.'

'*Miles* away,' Nate added.

With a giggle, Heather lunged in, slapped her hands against the troll's hip and shoved, sending him high as if he were a kid on a playground swing.

Tanya toed the bundle of clothes towards him. With a small canister of lighter fluid from her handbag, she squirted the coat. She struck a match, cupped its flame from the wind, and touched it to the soaked cloth. The bundle erupted into a ball of flapping fire.

Its glow shimmered on the troll's slimy whiskered face, on his cadaverous, swinging body.

Tanya kicked the bundle.

It tumbled and stopped beneath him. Shrieking, he grabbed his head and jerked as if trying to sit up.

'You nuts?' Nate yelled. Rushing forward, he booted the blazing heap. It rose into the air, falling apart, fiery clothes scattering and flying away on the wind.

The troll clutched the front of Nate's pants. Nate rammed a knee up into his face and staggered backwards out of reach. He whirled towards Tanya. 'What the *hell* were you trying to . . .'

'He looked cold.'

'Jesus.'

'We could've had us a weenie roast,' Liz said.

'We could've had us a murder charge. Judas priest. Come on, let's get out of here.'

They left the troll swinging by his foot above the moonlit promenade, and walked away.

Chapter Two

'Oooo, nice gams. Yum yum.'

Dave glanced towards the voice, saw that it came from the 'mouth' of a green sock on the hand of a beggar woman, and kept walking.

If Joan had heard the remark about her legs, she was ignoring it, just as she usually ignored the appreciative stares, comments and whistles she regularly drew during patrol of the boardwalk.

'Yummy legs. Where was they? Home in bed, dare say, yes. Snug as a virgin's dug when Enoch bit the weenie.'

'She's right,' Joan said. 'You've got gorgeous legs.'

Dave stopped. He looked back at the old woman. She was sitting cross-legged on the bench. Her leathery brown face was turned away as she glared at a young couple strolling by and chattered at them with her sock puppet. The man and woman picked up their pace and didn't look at her.

In spite of the heat, she wore a blanket that covered her head like a hood and draped her shoulders. It hung open, showing the stained front of a T-shirt. There were holes in the T-shirt. A faded skirt was spread across her lap. On the bench beside her was a yellow plastic dish with a few coins in it.

'Go on,' Joan said. 'Give her a buck. She said nice things about your legs.'

'Yours. What was that she said about Enoch?'

'Who's Enoch?'

'I don't know. Something about him biting the weenie?'

'Who knows? Who cares? She's a nut case.'

Dave walked back to her. She glanced at him through greasy cords of grey hair hanging over her eyes, then looked down. But the puppet turned to Dave.

'Weee,' it said. 'Copper legs, here again, gone tomorrow. Copper legs with a Coppertone tan. Fuzzy fuzz legs.'

'What did you say about Enoch?' he asked.

The sock seemed to gape up at him as if startled by the question. Its wide mouth was no more than a tuck between the old woman's thumb and fingers. A pretty sorry puppet, he thought. Didn't even have eyes.

The mouth flapped. 'Curiosity killed the cop, clap killed the twat.'

'He asked you a question, lady,' Joan snapped.

The sock shuddered.

'Christ, Dave.'

Then flipped over as if dead.

'What happened to Enoch?' Dave asked.

'Gone gone gone,' the sock sang. 'Mum's the word. Where oh where was the pretty copper then? Home in bed. Nuff said.' The sock darted, nibbled Dave's thigh and scooted towards his crotch.

With a gasp, he lurched back. The sock-mouth caught hold of the edge of his shorts, then lost its grip.

'Damn it, lady!' he snapped.

Joan cracked up.

Dave rushed off without looking back at the crone.

Joan stayed at his side, laughing, 'First class . . . interrogative technique!'

'She tried to *grope* me.'

'Going for your gun.'

Dave felt a shiver squirm up his back.

'Should we run her in for assaulting an officer?'

'Yuck it up, pal. You'd be laughing out the other side of your face if it was you. Jesus!' He could still feel the damn sock. He rubbed his thigh hard with his hand.

'I'd never get that close,' Joan said. 'Except maybe to cuff her. And then I'd want to be wearing gloves. And a gas mask. And maybe one of those chemical warfare outfits if I could lay my hands on one. Those people suck. I had my way, we'd get rid of every last one of them.'

'Join up with the trollers.'

'Just between you and me, I'd rather join 'em than bust 'em.

8

Not that either's likely to happen. I'm gonna get me a hot dog on a stick. You want one?'

Dave glanced at his hand. It didn't look dirty. But it had rubbed his thigh where the sock had touched him. He was hungry, anyway. They'd been on foot-patrol since the fun zone opened at ten, nearly three hours ago. 'Grab one for me, okay? I want to wash up.'

'Use plenty of soap. It's hard to get those troll-slicks off.'

'Don't get any funnier, Joan. I wouldn't be able to stand it.'

He left his partner in line at the hot dog booth, and headed for the nearest men's room. Funland had two sets of restrooms, one near each end of the promenade. This would be his sixth visit to one or the other.

On park patrol, they made regular stops, Dave looking into the men's, Joan checking out the women's.

'If any shit's going down,' Joan liked to say, 'that's where we'll find it.'

What they often found were loitering bums, folks of various persuasions engaged in sexual activities, and an occasional drug buy. So far today, the only restroom trouble had been a male wino barfing in a toilet of the Ladies' room. Joan had escorted him out, looking as if she'd lost the tan off her face.

Dave entered the men's room with his usual caution. It looked deserted except for a kid of about nine or ten at a urinal. The door of one stall was shut. Crouching, Dave glanced under it. Just a single pair of feet, hobbled by jeans. When he stood up, he saw the kid looking over a shoulder at him.

'You having a good time today?' Dave asked, and stepped over to the sink.

'The Bazooka guns are awful neat.'

Dave smiled. 'I like those, myself. They really blast those tennis balls.' He tugged a few paper towels out of the dispenser, dampened one under the faucet, and started to rub his leg.

'That a real gun you got?' the boy asked.

'A .38 calibre Smith & Wesson.'

'Are you a policeman?'

'I'd better be, don't you think? Guy wandering around packing heat?'

The boy grinned. He zipped up and flushed and walked towards Dave, staring at him.

'See my badge?' Dave asked. With a wet finger, he pointed at the blue shield printed on the chest of his T-shirt.

'Is that a *uniform*? You wear that all the time?'

'Just on park patrol when it's hot out. Otherwise, we wear blues like normal cops.'

'Weird.'

Dave was used to such comments. His blue hat looked like a baseball cap. Instead of a Major League insignia, its front was emblazoned with the gold letters BBPD inside the outline of a star. His white T-shirt bore a similar emblem. His shorts matched the cap. He wore white socks and blue sneakers. Only the black leather utility belt, laden with holster and gun, nightstick, radio, handcuffs, and half a dozen snap-down cases, marked him obviously as a police officer.

'Kinda neat, though,' the kid admitted after a long inspection. Then, he ran his hands under water, pulled down a towel and dried. 'I'm gonna be a policeman.'

'Good deal. Maybe we'll be partners.'

'Naw. I'm from Los Angeles. I'm gonna be LAPD.'

'That's a topnotch outfit, mister.'

The kid beamed up at him, then said, 'Well, see you,' and hurried away.

Dave dried his leg. Then he washed his hands, smiling as he recalled Joan's advice to use plenty of soap for the troll-slicks.

His smile slipped off when his mind did a sudden replay of the old woman touching him.

You try to be civil to those people . . .

Gloria's so fond of them . . . I ought to introduce *her* to the puppet witch.

They're human beings, Dave.

Then why don't they act like it?

Great, he thought. I'm arguing with Gloria, and she isn't even here.

If she had about half the smarts of Joan . . .

Forget it.

He dried his hands and hurried out into the sunlight. He found Joan sitting at a small round table at the edge of the boardwalk. She had one hot dog on a stick and a small Coke for herself. Across the table from Joan were two dogs, a paper sack of French fries, and a larger Coke. Dave sat down in front of the meal.

'Trying to fatten me up?' he asked.

'You're a growing boy. Can't live on bean sprouts and cottage cheese.'

'You should've seen what she fed me last night.'

'Wanta ruin my appetite?' Joan asked. She used her teeth to rip the corner of a plastic envelope, then squeezed out mustard onto the brown coating over her hot dog.

Watching her, Dave's mouth watered. He pulled the paper wrapper off one of his dogs and took a big bite. The crust of deep-fried cornmeal batter crunched. The skin of the hot dog burst. Warm juice sprayed into his mouth. He sighed as he chewed. 'Real food,' he said.

'So, what manner of culinary delight did Gloria prepare for you last night?'

'Something in a wok.'

'That's a bad sign.'

'Stir-fried vegetation.'

'Got any clue as to what it was?' Seeming to smile with her eyes, she took a rather dainty bite of her dog. In spite of her care, a yellow dab of mustard found its way onto her upper lip. It stayed there while she chewed.

'I know exactly what it was,' Dave said. 'Most of it, anyway. Water chestnuts, bamboo shoots, mushrooms, snow peas. The best part was the soy sauce.'

'Mushrooms aren't so bad,' Joan said. She tongued the mustard off her lip. 'Sauteed, they're good with steak.'

'Please, don't mention steak.'

'Sounds like you're in training to be a rickshaw boy.'

'My system is being purified.'

11

'I had a hamburger about yay thick.' Joan held up a hand with her thumb and forefinger spread wide. 'And chili fries.'

'You've got a real nasty streak, you know that?'

'So I've been told. You mind if I put some ketchup on those fries?'

'I thought they were for me.'

'They are.' She used her teeth to rip a ketchup packet, then smothered half the fries and began to eat some.

'Those'll go straight to your thighs.'

'You're the one with the gorgeous gams around here,' she said, and poked more fries into her mouth.

Thanks for the reminder, Dave thought. He could *feel* the sock moving up his leg.

'You think the trollers struck again last night?' Joan asked.

'Sounded like that's what the gal was getting at.'

'Enoch bit the weenie? Sounds like he was killed. The trollers don't kill them.'

'Haven't yet,' Dave admitted. 'Not that we know about, anyway.'

'Bit the weenie usually means bit the weenie.'

'Good thinking.'

'I don't see them killing someone, do you?' Joan asked. 'It's one thing, rousting bums. Murder's a pretty big step from that.'

'Not that big. Look how it's been going. When it started out, they were just snatching the bums and giving them a ride out of town. It's gotten a lot meaner.'

'Some pretty cruel tricks,' Joan said.

'And some rough beatings. They're bound to end up killing someone sooner or later. If they haven't already. And who's to say they haven't? The way these transients come and go, the kids could be nailing them right and left, nobody'd be the wiser till a body turned up.'

'I don't think it's come to that,' Joan said, looking down as she stirred her Coke with the straw. 'It was just a few nights ago they tied that creep to the Hurricane's tracks. They wouldn't have done that if they're already into killing the trolls and disposing of their bodies. Looks to me like they're still into general humiliation and torment.'

'That guy would've been killed the first time the coaster made a run.'

'But these've gotta be local kids,' Joan pointed out. 'They'd know the tracks are walked before the park opens. They just did it to scare the shit out of him.'

'Maybe they went too far with this Enoch fellow.'

'Or maybe that old bird was just pulling your chain.'

'We ought to try asking around.'

'Oh, there's a fine idea.' She wrinkled her nose. 'Spend the afternoon interviewing slugs.'

'Some of them must know the guy. Couldn't hurt to ask a few questions.'

'Couldn't do much good, either. We'd need a translator. You know anyone who speaks Bumese?'

A smile broke across Dave's face. 'Where's your humanity, partner?'

'I save it for the humans I occasionally meet.' She picked up the bag of fries. 'You done with these?'

'I haven't had *any* yet.'

She waved the bag under his nose. 'Go ahead and take one, big guy. They beat the hell out of bamboo shoots.'

When the meal was done, Joan gathered up the wrappers and Coke cartons. She carried them to a trash bin. The seat had left red marks across the backs of her legs. If the French fries went to her thighs, Dave thought, they sure hadn't done any damage.

Put her side by side with Gloria, you'd have an advertisement for the health benefits of the very 'poisons' that Gloria prided herself in denouncing. Joan was a foot taller than Gloria. She had sleek muscle and flesh where Gloria was bony. She had curves where Gloria was straight and flat. Her skin glowed; Gloria's skin was pallid and dull. Joan radiated confidence and power, while Gloria seemed like a wraith animated by nervous energy.

If they were dogs . . . Dave thought.

13

Neither one's a dog, that's for sure.

But if they *were* dogs, Joan would be a golden lab. Gloria would be a poodle.

'You plan to sit there daydreaming?' Joan asked.

'No. Huh-uh. Mind was wandering.' As he got to his feet, he hoped she didn't suspect the direction of the wandering.

They resumed their patrol.

He felt lousy. Cheated and cheating. Ever since being teamed up with Joan, only two weeks ago, he'd been comparing the two and growing more dissatisfied. It was wrong. You don't get involved with your partner, especially when she was already having a relationship. And you don't dump on your gal the minute someone more appealing comes along.

Sure, there were problems with Gloria. But that comes with the territory. You get intimate, you find flaws. The grass is always greener . . . till you get to the other side of the hill and see it close up. Joan's not perfect, either. He'd been on tour with her long enough to see that she was stubborn, hot-tempered, and not especially tolerant. God help anyone who ticked her off.

But she had a neat sense of humour, while Gloria . . .

Stop it, he told himself.

'Officer?'

One glance, and Dave knew that the four men grinning at Joan were sailors. They were out of uniform, but their bristly heads and boyish faces gave them away. They looked as if they were playing hooky from high school and having a great time of it.

'What can I do for you gentlemen?' Joan asked.

'Can we take your picture? Just one picture, okay? With each of us. You'd really be doing us a favour. What do you say? Okay? No funny stuff, just four pictures. We know you're on duty, and all, but we're gonna be shipping out in a couple of days for the Persian Gulf, and . . .'

'Why not,' she said.

Dave couldn't believe it.

Seeming neither embarrassed nor annoyed, she let the leader

of the group stand beside her. He leaned against her, mugging for the fellow with the camera. And before the picture was snapped, Joan put her arm around him. The kid's face blazed scarlet. When his turn was over, he backed away from Joan, blushing and shaking his head, then whirled around and flopped on the boardwalk. 'I've died and gone to heaven, mates,' he announced.

The next sailor was a fat kid with pimples. Joan rubbed his brush cut. He rolled his eyes upwards. She hugged him to her side and the scrawny kid with the camera caught it.

The third sailor was a grinning black giant. He stood beside Joan as if at attention, ramrod straight, chin tucked down. She leaned against him, reached across his back, and squirmed her fingers into his side. He doubled over, giggling like a woman as the picture was snapped.

Then the first sailor tried to take the camera from the gawky kid in glasses who'd been taking all the snapshots. 'Your turn, Henry. Come on.'

'Oh, it's all right.' He shook his head. He made a sheepish smile. 'We've pestered the lady enough.'

'Chicky chick chick.'

'Go on, boy, show some hair.'

'Henry's scared of women.'

'Cut him some slack, guys,' Joan said. She looked at Henry. 'You're not scared of me. Come here.'

The colour went out of his face. But he walked towards her.

His friends hooted and whistled.

He stood beside Joan. He was only as high as her shoulders. Bending down slightly, she tapped a fingertip against her cheek. The kid looked alarmed and delighted. He leaned in to peck her cheek. She turned her head and kissed him on the mouth and the camera clicked.

His friends went silent.

When Joan stopped kissing him, Henry wrapped his arms around her and they held each other. Dave could see his face. His glasses were pushed crooked by Joan's cheek. His eyes were shut, his lips pressed tightly together. He nodded, and

Dave realized that Joan must be whispering to him. Suddenly, a smile spread across his face.

He stepped away from Joan and returned to his friends.

'Lucky sonofabitch,' one of them muttered.

The black giant clapped him on the shoulders.

'Have a good tour, guys,' Joan said, holding up a hand in farewell.

They backed away in a group, waving, pushing each other, calling out thanks. Henry, silent, lifted an open hand and smiled sadly as if he were leaving his best friend.

Head down, Joan unsnapped a leather case on her utility belt. She took out her sunglasses and put them on before turning to Dave. 'Nice kids,' she said.

'You sure made their day,' Dave told her.

'Let's move it. We've got peace to keep.'

Chapter Three

Jeremy Wayne coasted down the hill on his ten-speed Schwinn, smiling into the wind, his open shirt flapping behind him. He felt free and excited.

He was on his way to the Funland boardwalk.

He'd been there last night after a full day of unpacking at the new house, but that was with his mother. 'For a quick look-see,' as she'd put it. And that's all it had amounted to. They'd strolled the length of the promenade, played no games, ridden no rides. 'There'll be plenty of time for that later,' Mom had said.

Later's now, Jeremy thought.

Whipping around a corner, he left the residential neighbour-hood behind. He pedalled past the fronts of gawdy motels, souvenir shops, gas stations, markets and bars and fastfood joints. The cars on the street mostly seemed packed with teenagers, radios blaring. The people on the sidewalks wore swimsuits.

This was too awesome to believe.

He'd been happy to move away from Bakersfield. The place sucked, anyway. The way he saw it, just about anyplace would be an improvement. But this!

This was a vacation place!

And he'd be living here, just a couple of miles from Funland and the beach.

June wasn't even over yet. The whole summer stretched before him, endless days of doing whatever he pleased – exploring the boardwalk, lying on the beach, *looking at girls*.

Incredible.

He pedalled alongside the huge parking lot. With no more buildings in the way, he swept his eyes across the long expanse of Funland. He saw the arch of the main gate topped by the grinning face of a clown; the walls that he knew were merely the backs of the shops, snack stands, sideshow rooms, rides, funhouses, arcades and game booths that faced the boardwalk; the curving, swooping, ghastly high tracks of the roller coaster; the towering parachute drop; the top of the log ride's slide; the upper reaches of the mammoth, spinning Ferris wheel.

Mom, last night, had said, 'It's pretty tacky, isn't it?'

He'd said, 'I think it's great.'

He knew it was no Disneyland, no Knott's Berry Farm, no Magic Mountain. He'd been to some of the best amusement parks in the country, and Boleta Bay's Funland was small by comparison. Small and primitive and pretty darn tacky.

But his.

And all the more exciting because it wasn't like the other places. It didn't seem commercial, pristine, make-believe and *safe*.

Roaming its boardwalk last night, he'd felt a tightness in his chest, heat in his groin.

Anything could happen here.

He felt the same excitement as he climbed off his bike at the front of the parking lot. He chained its frame to the bars of the bicycle rack, and headed for the main gate.

He bounded up the concrete stairs.

He walked right in.

That was another thing about this place. You didn't have to fork out fifteen bucks or more just to get in. Sure, it cost you to *do* things, but you didn't have to shell out a penny to enter.

He would be able to come and go as he pleased – every day.

Though Jeremy had close to thirty dollars in his wallet, he strode past the first ticket booth just for the pleasure of walking in free. On the boardwalk, he knew, there were always booths near at hand for buying tickets. He would just wait until he felt like going on a ride.

He patted his seat pocket, feeling the comfortable bulge of his full wallet. Then he buttoned the pocket flap.

Can't be too careful, a place like this. From last night's brief exploration, he knew that there were a lot of sleazy types around.

Heading down the boardwalk, he started seeing sleazy types immediately. A skinny, dirty guy in a straw cowboy hat that looked as if a horse had stepped on it, crushing its crown. A brown cigarette hung off the guy's lip, and he looked as if he hadn't shaved in three or four days. Jeremy saw a fat, bearded biker in saggy jeans. He was shirtless, wore a faded Levi jacket with its arms cut off, and his chest was tattooed with a skull that had a snake crawling out its eyehole. With the guy was a biker woman, skinny and mean-faced. She wore jeans and a fringed leather vest. The vest was loosely laced in front and she didn't wear a bra or anything else underneath it. Jeremy glimpsed the sides of her breasts through the rawhide lacing, but he looked away fast. He didn't want to be caught peeking. And what he saw wasn't all that terrific, anyway.

This sure wasn't the kind of crowd you saw at Disneyland.

There were a few clean-cut, family types, but he saw a lot of fat, dumb-looking people in drooping old jeans and filthy shirts. Tough guys with sneers and tattoos, many with knives on their belts. Swaggering gals in tube tops and tank shirts. Wild, laughing guys with crew cuts, who pushed each other and whooped and whistled when they spotted a good-looking gal. And bums. This place had more bums than Skid Row.

Jeremy felt some of his excitement slide into uneasiness.

This *wasn't* Disneyland.

Something could happen.

He began to wish he hadn't come here alone. It had been all right last night, when Mom was with him.

Shit, he thought. I'm not a jerk-off kid who can't go anywhere without his mommy. I'm sixteen.

And nothing's going to happen.

Though a lot of the people looked grubby or rough or wild, there were plenty around who seemed normal enough: nicely dressed couples, families with their kids, scads of teenagers wandering around in pairs and groups.

A lot of nifty babes.

They all seemed to be having a fine time. They seemed oblivious to the creeps.

But they aren't by themselves, Jeremy thought.

'Hey, cutie.' The strident voice pushed through the other noises. 'You in the blue shorts.'

I'm wearing blue shorts.

She doesn't mean me.

Jeremy turned his head.

'Yeah, you,' the girl called. She stood inside a game booth, waving for him to approach. Behind her was a platform stacked with pyramids of metal bottles. Both sides of the booth were crowded to the ceiling with brightly coloured stuffed animals. 'Step right over here,' she said. 'Come on, lover boy, don't be shy.' She tossed a softball from hand to hand. One foot was propped up on the low wall at the front of the booth. Her legs looked sleek. A money apron draped her lap like a towel, hiding whatever shorts she must be wearing. Her breasts, loose under her tank top, swayed from side to side as she tossed and caught the ball. 'A dollar buys a throw. Knock the bottles down, you win a prize. You can't win if you don't try.'

Blushing, Jeremy shook his head, mumbled, 'No, thanks,' and hurried away.

Should've tried it, he thought. Shit. Now she'll think I'm a dip.

I could've gotten a better look at her, too. Her face wasn't any great shakes, but the rest of her . . .

'Heya, bud.'

Jeremy stopped fast as a bum sidestepped into his path and grinned brown teeth.

'Heya, bud. Gimme a quarter, huh? You're a good kid, huh? Know what I mean?' He reached out a grimy hand. 'A quarter ain't gonna bust you, huh? Give a guy a break.'

Jeremy felt as if ice had been jammed against his groin. 'I don't have a quarter,' he said. His voice sounded whiny. 'Sorry.'

'Gimme a buck, kid.' The bum's waiting hand jiggled up and down. 'You're a good kid, huh? I ain't had a bite to . . .'

'FUCK OFF, DOG TURD!'

Jeremy flinched and staggered backward as someone lunged past him and whapped the bum in the face with a cowboy hat.

'GET OUTA HERE! GET! VAMOOS.'

The bum, ducking and covering his head, rushed away.

The kid – he looked about Jeremy's age or a little older – frowned and brushed off the crown of his hat. 'Now I've got his fucking cooties on it,' he muttered.

'Sorry,' Jeremy said.

'That's how you've gotta treat these scum-suckers.' He mashed the hat onto his head and swept his hands along the brim to tighten its curl. Smiling, he held out a hand to Jeremy. 'Name's Gibson. George Gibson. My buddies call me Cowboy.'

Jeremy shook his hand. The kid gave it a hard squeeze. 'I'm Jeremy. Jeremy Wayne.'

'Hey, Wayne like the Duke.'

'Yeah. Thanks for getting rid of that creep.'

'No sweat, Duke. Mind if I call you Duke? Jeremy's kind of a wimp name, but you already know that, don't you. Just like George. I hate that name George. You with someone?'

Jeremy hesitated. The kid seemed friendly, but maybe he

was up to something. Maybe he was even in with the bum, and this was some kind of trick they pulled to get money out of suckers. Or maybe he wants to get me off somewhere and mug me. Or maybe he's a fag.

'Hey, you're here with your squeeze, just say the word. She in the can or something?'

'I'm here by myself,' Jeremy admitted.

Cowboy slapped his arm. 'Hot damn, so am I. I'll show you around. You look like a guy who could use a friend.'

'I don't know. I . . .'

'Let's go. Head 'em up, move 'em out.'

Cowboy turned away and started walking, his boots clumping on the boardwalk. Jeremy stayed at his side. Why not? he thought. The guy seems okay. If all he really wants is to be friends . . .

'Where you from, Duke?'

'Well, I live here now. We just moved in.'

'Yeah? Where?'

'Here in Boleta Bay.'

'Yeah? Where?'

Does he want my address? 'I don't know,' Jeremy lied. 'A few blocks from here. Up on a hill.'

'I live on Lilac Lane. There's a wimp name for a street, huh? Lilac.'

Jeremy knew the street. It was one block north of Poppy. This kid was a neighbour. 'Our place is on Poppy.'

'Well, I'll be skinned.' He slapped Jeremy's arm again. 'What grade'll you be going into?'

'I'll be a junior.'

'Hey, me too!'

'Small world,' Jeremy said. He thought it sounded lame. If he wasn't careful, Cowboy might get the idea he was a dork. He'd lived with that image long enough. Here was a chance to start fresh, to leave the old Jeremy behind, to be accepted as a regular guy. 'Shit,' he said, 'I've been hoping I'd find someone to do my homework for me.'

'Haw! Bite my butt. You had one of the waffle cones yet?'

Jeremy shook his head.

'Come on, I'm buying.'

At the stand, Cowboy dug a wad of bills out of his jeans, ordered two 'Super Waffles' and paid for them.

$3.50 each.

'Gosh, thanks a lot,' Jeremy said as Cowboy handed over one of the treats – a cone of crisp, sweet waffle at least twice the size of a normal sugar cone, and packed with ice cream that was drenched with chocolate sauce and topped with whipped cream, jimmies, chopped peanuts and a marischino cherry.

'Can't travel on an empty stomach, Duke.'

'Where to?'

'The dunk tank.'

They headed up the boardwalk, eating their Super Waffles. Though he saw plenty of sleazes, rough-necks and bums, he no longer felt threatened by them. He had Cowboy with him, now. If anyone got funny, he wouldn't have to face it alone.

Cowboy strode along, sometimes calling out to friends he spotted, including a few who were working the game booths. He seemed to know a lot of people – including girls. Plain girls, cute girls, and some who were totally beautiful. And they all acted as if they liked him.

This is great, Jeremy thought. If I can be his buddy, I might meet some of them.

He'd never had a buddy like Cowboy. His best friend in Bakersfield, Ernie, was a skinny, shy kid whose glasses were usually taped together from catching a ball in the face (one that any normal guy would've caught) or a fist (because something about him just *pissed off* every jock in school), and whose idea of a good time was raising Anchorage, Alaska on his ham radio.

A nice guy, but a real loser.

According to Ernie, all the popular guys in school were inane assholes, glandular cases, or throwbacks. The good-looking girls were vapid twits who thought their farts smelled like roses.

With a best friend like that, you didn't stand a chance. With a guy like Cowboy, though . . .

'Hey there, gorgeous!' Cowboy suddenly yelled, startling Jeremy from his thoughts.

A girl smiled at him and waved at him through the bars of a cage. She sat on a narrow platform, swinging her legs. Below her bare feet was a water-filled tank with a glass front.

Even as she waved, a pitched ball struck the bull's eye, knocked back the metal arm, and collapsed her perch. She squealed and dropped, splashing into the deep water. Through the glass, Jeremy saw her descend in a sudden froth of bubbles. Like a wind from below, the water pushed her T-shirt up her belly, lifted her long black hair above her head. She squatted for a moment at the bottom of the tank, cheeks bulging with trapped air, shirt and hair slowly drifting down, and shook her fist at the guy who'd dunked her. Then she stood. Water swirling around her shoulders, she waded to the metal-rung ladder at the side of the tank. She climbed up.

Her wet legs were shiny. Jeremy saw the outline of her panties through the clinging seat of her shorts. Her shirt was plastered to her back, her pink skin showing through the thin fabric. Her hair hung thick and glossy between her shoulder blades, almost long enough to reach the cross-strap of her bra.

Leaning away from the ladder, she raised the shelf. Its braces locked, and she climbed onto it.

'Just a lucky throw, hot stuff!' she yelled.

'Yeah? Watch this!'

'I won't hold my breath.'

Hot stuff threw the ball at the target beside her cage. It missed and whapped the canvas backstop.

She smirked at him and clapped.

Jeremy thought it was too bad about her face. She was one of those gals who looks terrific from behind, slender and shapely, but when you see her from the front she's a letdown. As if God decided He'd blessed her enough from the neck down, so he skimped on her face. She wasn't exactly ugly, but her eyes seemed too close together, her nose small and up-turned and a little piggish, and her mouth too wide. Her front teeth jutted out of her gums like white marble slabs.

Another ball missed the target.

'Don Sutton you're not, Bozo!'

The guy flapped a hand at her, put an arm around his girlfriend, and walked away.

'Come on,' Cowboy said. He stepped over to the man running the concession and passed his Super Waffle to Jeremy. 'Let me have three of those balls, Jim,' he said, handing the man three dollars.

'Couldn't hit the broad side of an outhouse if you were inside it!' she called.

'Get ready to bite the drink, Lizzie!' He hurled the first ball. It slammed the metal target. Lizzie dropped.

Climbing out, she looked over her shoulder at him. 'Nice shot, tenderfoot. Who's your friend?'

Jeremy felt heat rush to his face.

'My pal, Duke. New in town. We just met.'

'Nice to meet you, Duke.'

'Thanks.'

She sat on the platform. Cowboy threw. She hit the water again.

Cowboy smiled. 'Only way to get her clean. She never takes a bath, filthy scrug.'

'Let Duke have a try,' she called as she climbed out.

Cowboy offered the last ball to him. 'Oh, that's okay,' Jeremy said. 'You go on.'

'Don't be a woos,' Lizzie yelled.

With a sigh, he gave the waffle cones to Cowboy, took the ball.

The beginning of the end, he thought. I'm going to miss by a mile and they'll know I'm a dip.

He wound up and fired the ball.

Right on target!

It struck the bull's-eye and bounced off.

Lizzie's perch didn't collapse. She cackled and clapped. 'Tough luck, Duchess.'

Shit!

'You've gotta throw it a little harder than that,' Cowboy

said, smiling and shaking his head. 'Give it another try.' He took out his money.

'No, no. That's okay. Some other time. I'm really wasted today. Been moving furniture, unpacking.'

'Cowboy!' Lizzie shouted through the bars.

'Yo!'

'Give Tanya a message for me?'

'You bet.'

'Tell her about Janet. I want to bring her along tonight. See if it's okay, huh? Give me a call later and let me know.'

'You got it. Adios. Don't get your tits wrinkled.'

She suddenly looked as if she burned to punch out his lights.

Half a dozen people nearby started laughing. Jeremy was too stunned to laugh.

'Let's move out, Duke.'

They hurried away. Jeremy gave a cone back to Cowboy and followed him across the boardwalk. They passed through an open space in the railing, and trotted down concrete stairs to the beach.

Chapter Four

'Somebody sure knows how to pick a banjo,' Dave said. The quick, cheery music was barely audible behind the carnival tunes of the rides, the voices and laughter all around him, the screams of people on the high-swinging Viking Ship, the poomphs of the Bazooka guns.

It seemed to come from somewhere ahead. Dave saw a circle of spectators in the distance, near the north end of the boardwalk.

'Let's check it out,' he said.

'Beats interviewing trolls,' Joan said.

Since lunch, they had approached a total of seven indigents. None could be coaxed into admitting knowledge of a man named Enoch. Asked if anything strange had happened last night, one told of being beamed up into a hovering spacecraft from the planet Mogo, where a creature like a man-sized lizard stuck a tube down his throat and sucked out the contents of his stomach – which the creature drank as it sucked. One said he'd been grabbed by a pair of albinos who tried to drag him under the boardwalk and feed him to their pet spider. A woman had been visited by the Blessed Virgin, who gave her a rough grey stone and said there was a diamond inside. While the woman told her story, she gnawed the rock as if it were a walnut she figured she could crack open with her teeth. One man ranted incoherently. Another simply glared at them and muttered about assassins. Only one seemed fairly rational, and he claimed to have spent a peaceful night sleeping in the dunes.

Joan had spent a lot of time sighing and rolling her eyes upwards. She'd told Dave that it would be a waste of time, questioning the boardwalk's panhandlers.

But it hadn't been a total waste.

After speaking to a few of them, he was half convinced that Enoch 'biting the weenie' had no more basis in reality than the diamond in the rock, the albino attack, or the peculiar feast of the lizard alien.

He heard applause from the banjo-picker's audience. Only a couple of people wandered away from the edges of the circle. Most stayed. Several passers-by joined the crowd. A few people moved inward, apparently to contribute money in appreciation of the performance.

As Dave and Joan approached the group, the next number began. 'When the Saints Go Marching In'. The melody twanged out, strong and lively, with such complex chords and runs in the background that Dave decided there must be at least two banjos. He was listening to a duet, or even a trio of street musicians, banging out a version of 'Saints' so fine that

26

those in the audience who'd been clapping along, at the start, went silent to listen.

Joan stayed at Dave's side while he roamed the perimeter of the group searching for a gap so he could watch the performance.

A couple of grubby bikers, seeing that they were cops, broke away from the circle and wandered off. Dave and Joan stepped into the opening.

Not a trio. Not a duet.

All that music was coming from the banjo of a lone girl who looked no older than eighteen.

She stood straight-backed as if at attention, her weight on one leg, her other leg forward, heel on the boardwalk, toe tapping as she played. The banjo looked heavy, bigger than some Dave had seen, with thick shiny metal surrounding its tambourine-like body. It hung against her belly by a broad, brightly coloured strap. Its neck was tilted upwards at a jaunty angle.

The banjo case, open a short distance in front of her, was littered with coins and dollars. Beside the case rested a backpack.

'Saints' ended. Applause exploded from the audience. The girl bowed her head and dropped her arms to her sides. While the clapping went on, several people (mostly kids on behalf of their parents) hurried forward to toss money into the banjo case. Though she kept her head down, Dave heard her murmur thanks to each of those who contributed.

She looked as shy as a six-year-old on stage at a school show for the parents.

When she raised her head, she stared straight at a kid standing near Dave, wiggled her eyebrows at him, and began playing 'Puff, the Magic Dragon'.

'Damn good,' Joan whispered.

'I'll say.'

Her left hand flew up and down the banjo's neck, fretting and sliding with astonishing quickness. Her right hand hung nearly motionless while its fingers picked the strings. Except for her tapping foot, the rest of her body was rigid and motionless. She gazed straight ahead as she played. Her face seemed blank, as if her mind were far away, but Dave guessed she was concentrating on the music.

All through the song, the pink tip of her tongue protruded from the right corner of her mouth.

To Dave, she seemed very young and very vulnerable.

The backpack showed that she was a wanderer.

He scanned the people gathered around her, trying to spot someone who might be with the girl. Nobody quite seemed to fit the role. That didn't necessarily mean she had no companion, but Dave suspected that she was travelling alone.

Probably hitching rides. Probably sleeping outside.

Sooner or later, a sure victim.

It would be dangerous enough if she were male. The fact that she was female increased the risk tenfold.

From a distance, she might be mistaken for a male. Her blonde hair was cut very short. She had a slim body, and her breasts were only apparent because of the way the banjo rested against her shirt, pulling it taut. Her face hardly looked masculine, but it might be the face of a smooth-cheeked, pretty boy who was short in the hormone department.

On second thoughts, Dave realised, her slender, boyish appearance was a dubious advantage. She might fare worse on the road if the wrong sort took her for a sissy instead of a girl.

She's lucky she made it this far, Dave thought.

Then he wondered what kind of luck that was, making it into Boleta Bay. He doubted that any harm would befall her at the hands of the indigents that were so plentiful in this area. Trapped in their own private worlds of hallucination and terror, they rarely struck out at anyone. But the trollers were a different matter.

She was not a troll. She was a street musician, a roaming minstrel playing for her daily needs.

But the kids might not make such fine distinctions. And she wasn't exactly dressed for a Rotary banquet.

She wore hiking boots, ankle high, scuffed and dusty. Her

faded blue jeans were frayed at the cuffs, and one leg had a rip
that gaped like an open mouth, showing the skin of her thigh.
For a belt, she wore a brightly coloured woven sash that
matched her banjo strap. It was knotted at her hip, and the
ends of it draped the side of her leg and swayed in the breeze.
The sleeves of her old blue shirt had been cut off at the
shoulders. The top buttons were undone. A necklace of small
white shells hung across her chest. She wore big, hoop earrings.
And a red bandana around her head.

Overall, the outfit was what a kid might wear to go trick-or-
treating as a pirate. Or as a hippie.

The teenagers here in Boleta Bay might very well take it as
the costume of a troll.

And act accordingly.

This gal's begging for trouble, he thought as she finished
'Puff'.

While the audience clapped, he made his way forward along
with some others. He took out his wallet and dropped a five-
dollar bill into her banjo case. She thanked him. He stepped
around the case and stopped in front of her.

She met him with calm, questioning eyes. 'Officer?'

'Where'd you learn to play like that?'

'My dad.'

'You're great.'

'Thank you. Is there some kind of problem?'

'I noticed you've got a backpack. Are you planning to sleep
out around here?'

'I thought I might. Is it illegal?'

'We have local ordinances against it, but we generally don't
enforce them. Are you with a friend?'

She shook her head slightly from side to side. Her eyes
never strayed from Dave's.

'Let her alone,' somebody called from behind.

'Goddamn cops,' came another voice.

'She's not hurting anyone.'

'Why don't you pick on somebody causing trouble!'

The girl held up a hand to silence the protests.

'All I want to say,' Dave told her, 'is that we've been having trouble with teenagers running around at night attacking people. They've pulled some pretty nasty stunts. They're after winos and bums, actually. But it isn't safe for anyone to camp out in this area. I wouldn't want you getting jumped by these characters. They . . .'

'Quit hassling her, why don't you!'

'Please,' she called, glancing past him at someone in the crowd. 'He's not bothering me. I'll play some more in a minute.'

'Thanks,' Dave said. 'There are plenty of motels nearby. I think you'd be wise to check into one of them. Can you afford a motel? Some of them are just around thirty-five, forty dollars a night. And there's a Y over on Clancy Street. I'm sure it's pretty cheap.'

'I don't know.' She lowered her eyes. 'I'll think about it, officer. I appreciate your . . .'

'Dave. It's Dave.'

'I'm Robin.'

'Robin.' He liked the name. It seemed to fit her. 'Why do I get the feeling you're not going to take my advice?'

She shrugged her shoulders.

He took out his wallet again. The bill compartment held three ones and a twenty. He slipped the twenty out and held it towards her. 'Take this, okay? Find yourself a room for the night.'

Her fingers slipped around the back of his hand and gently pushed it away. 'I can't. Thank you, though. Really. That's way too much. You already gave me a five, I saw you. And that's fine. I figure that's for the music. But I don't want to take any handouts. Okay?'

'I don't want you getting jumped by a pack of rabid teenagers.'

In the calm of her blue eyes he saw a glint of fear.

'I'll be careful,' she said.

My place, he suddenly thought. She could stay at my place. Don't be an idiot. She'll think I just want in her pants.

'It's up to you,' he said. 'If you won't get yourself a room, at least try to find someplace hidden away. Maybe back in the dunes away from the beach, where nobody'll notice you. And don't come anywhere close to the boardwalk after the fun zone shuts down for the night. That's their favourite place to hit.'

'I'll stay away,' she told him. 'I'll find a good place to hide.' Her mouth slipped into a smile. 'I always do. My pappy didn't raise no fool.'

'All right. Good luck, Robin.'

Nodding, she reached out and brushed a hand against his upper arm. 'Thanks,' she said.

Dave started away. A few people in Robin's audience glared at him as he stepped through the circle.

Behind him, Robin said, 'This one's for Officer Dave.'

Joan looked at him, her eyebrows high. 'What was that all about?' she asked.

Before he could answer, the banjo rang alive. He turned around. Her eyes were on him. Her tongue protruded from the corner of her mouth.

Chapter Five

'Where are we going?' Jeremy asked.

'Gotta see Tanya.' Cowboy said. 'What'd you think of Liz?'

'Man, I don't believe what you said to her.'

'What was that?'

'You know. About getting wrinkled.'

'Oh, that. She likes that kind of stuff. Turns her on.'

'You know her pretty well?'

'Are you kidding? She's my squeeze.'

'Your girlfriend?'

'You got it, Duke.'

He stopped himself before saying 'Wow', which would've sounded stupid. Instead, he commented, 'Not bad. She got a sister?'

'Nope. A cousin, though. Janet. You can meet her tonight, maybe. Her and some of my friends. If you want, I'll check it out with Tanya, see if it's okay with her.'

'Great.'

They were walking over the sand, winding their way among sunbathers stretched out on towels and blankets. Though Cowboy led the way, his route was the same as Jeremy would've picked if he'd been in the lead. One that took them close to girls. Girls lying on their backs, naked except for skimpy swimsuits, their skin glossy with tanning oil. Others face-down, their backs bare, their untied bikini tops loose beneath their breasts. Some were reading books or magazines, some were talking to friends sprawled beside them, some seemed to be asleep. A few were snuggling with boyfriends as if they thought they were alone on the beach.

Jeremy studied them as he strolled along, working on his Super Waffle, listening to Cowboy and sometimes making comments or asking questions. He had a hard time swallowing.

I can come down here every day, he thought.

Man.

Just do nothing but wander around and *look* at them.

Shit, this is *better* than Funland.

Cowboy led him towards a slender young woman lying on a blanket, arms folded beneath her face. Her bikini top was untied. Jeremy could see the pale side of one breast. It bulged as if it were a little bit mashed under her weight. She was bare all the way down to a glossy blue patch of fabric clinging to her rump. The seat of her swimsuit was no more than four inches across at the thin waistband, and tapered to a narrow strip before passing between her legs.

'Hardly enough to cover her crack,' Cowboy muttered.

'I sure wouldn't mind trading places with the guy,' Jeremy said.

The guy was kneeling beside her, squirting suntan oil onto

her back. She shivered as the stream licked her skin. Her smooth buttocks trembled slightly. The guy set the plastic bottle aside, and began to spread the oil around. He wasn't just lending a hand, he was caressing her. Jeremy could almost feel her sun-heated skin, smooth and slick under his own hands.

He hated to leave the scene behind, and Cowboy must've felt the same way. After walking past the couple, Cowboy stopped and looked back. Jeremy, grateful, did the same.

The guy was squirting onto one of her buttocks. The oil, glinting silver in the sunlight, streamed down her cheek. He started rubbing it around.

'Kind of wish she'd turn over,' Cowboy said.

'Yeah, turn over and forget her top's untied.'

Cowboy grinned at him. 'Welcome to Boleta Bay.'

'I do believe I like it here.'

'If you like it now, wait'll you lay your eyes on Tanya.' With that, he started walking again.

Jeremy looked one more time, saw the guy sliding a hand down between the backs of her thighs, then turned away and hurried to catch up with Cowboy.

'Who's this Tanya?' he asked.

'Nate's gal. Wait till you see her. Guys've drowned themselves just so she'd pull them out.'

'Huh?'

'She's a life guard. And head cheerleader at school. You see her bouncing around the sidelines . . . it's a sight to make a blind man juice his skivvies.'

'You got the hots for her?'

'Show me a guy that doesn't, I'll show you a queer. I know *gals* who've got the hots for her.'

'But she's Nate's, you said?'

'The rotten dickhead. I reckon I'd lay waste to him so I could free her up, but he's my best bud.'

'Liz might not approve, either.'

'Well, it ain't about to happen. Nate or no Nate, only way I'd ever stand a chance with Tanya's if maybe I grew six inches and got me a new face.'

'Maybe you could drug her.'

'Haw! Drug her?' Cowboy swept off his hat and whapped Jeremy across the arm. 'Get out of here! You think I'm some kind of pervert? Christ, I don't believe you! Sick! What kind of drug would it take?'

Jeremy walked beside him, beaming. If Cowboy had started suspecting he was a wimp and a dork, the remark about drugging Tanya had put a stop to it. He'd won the guy over, for sure.

'Can't wait to see what she looks like,' Jeremy said.

'Don't have to.' With the last of his cone, Cowboy pointed at a lifeguard station a short distance ahead. It was a white-painted shack on stilts, wooden stairs leading up to a deck on the ocean side. A girl stood on the deck, leaning forward a bit, hands on the railing.

'Is that her?' Jeremy asked.

'You got it.'

They walked closer. Her head was turned away, so he couldn't see her face. Nevertheless, she looked awesome. Jeremy guessed that she must be nearly six feet tall. A lot of gals that tall were skin and bones, but not Tanya. Her bare legs, bronze in the sunlight, looked shapely and powerful. She wore red shorts, and a white T-shirt that wasn't tucked in.

Neither the shorts nor the shirt were tight-fitting. Though the shorts were loose, the way they bulged in the seat told of strong, round buttocks. The wind rippled her shirt against a flat belly and the high, thrusting mounds of her breasts. The oversized garments may have been meant to shroud and conceal, to hide enough so that she might avoid being constantly pestered by guys. But they didn't have that effect. Not on Jeremy. Instead, her body tantalized him like a whispered secret.

Her hair, in a pony tail, shone like gold.

If her face was any match for the rest of her . . .

'Yo! Tanya!' Cowboy called from the foot of the stairs.

Her head turned. She looked down from her high station. She had sunglasses on. They hid her eyes.

But what he could see of her face was even better than

Cowboy had led him to suspect. Not just beautiful, magnificent. Hair like a thick curtain of golden threads drifted and shimmered across her high brow. Her cheekbones and jaw were prominent, as if a sculptor had chiselled them from granite to create a warrior goddess, then relented and rounded off the sharp edges, smoothed and softened them, buffed them to a texture like velvet. And as if to make up for his initial harshness, he'd given her a perfect, feminine nose that was not quite small enough to seem out of place in the centre of such a face.

Her skin was so deeply tanned that her teeth seemed starkly white, almost as if they gave off their own bright light. Her mouth was wide. Her lips, only slightly darker than the skin of her face, were full and luxurious. They looked like the softest part of her. To the magnificent beauty of her face, they added something that seemed both slightly vulnerable and powerfully erotic.

Cowboy's joke (was it a joke?) about guys drowning themselves in hopes of being saved by Tanya no longer seemed farfetched. The promise of being pulled from the ocean by such a woman, of receiving mouth-to-mouth resuscitation from those lips, might drive many a guy to desperate measures.

'Hi there, Cowboy,' she said. Her voice was much as Jeremy might have expected, low and clear.

'Still on for tonight?'

Her head turned slightly towards Jeremy. He felt as if he were melting into warm liquid. He wished he could see her eyes. Maybe better that I can't, he thought.

'Don't worry about Duke. He's a straight-shooter. Fact is, he'd like to come along. I told him I'd have to get your okay. And Liz wants to know if her cousin can come.'

'No.'

Jeremy shrank inside. A lump filled his throat.

Should've known. Everything had been going too good.

I fooled Cowboy, but she sees right through me. Knows I'm a reject. Shit. Shit!

Tanya stepped away from the railing. She strode to the top

35

of the stairs and scowled down at Cowboy. A goddess, beautiful but fierce. 'It's private business,' she said. 'No out-of-towners. You and Liz ought to know that.'

'Well, Duke lives here. He just moved in.'

She took off her sunglasses and looked at Jeremy. The blue of her eyes matched the afternoon sky. They studied Jeremy. Their gaze entered him, probed him. His heart slammed. His legs felt weak.

'No wimps,' she said.

The words froze his mind.

'HEY!' someone yelled at Tanya.

Me. That was me.

'FUCK YOU!' he shouted.

He still had a handful of sodden Super Waffle. The remains of the cone had a swamp of melted vanilla ice cream at the bottom.

He hurled it.

Ice cream flew from the tumbling cone. But not all of it. Far from all of it. The cone struck a golden thigh. White glop exploded.

A large portion of it shot straight up a loose leg hole of Tanya's shorts.

Jeremy blinked. He couldn't believe what he had done. The cone, clinging to Tanya's white-smeared thigh, dropped away as she stormed down the stairs.

'Jesus, Duke,' he heard from Cowboy.

He considered running. Instead, he stood stiff with his arms at his sides.

Tanya grabbed the front of his open shirt. She jerked him up on his tiptoes. Glared down into his eyes. One side of her upper lip lifted, baring her gum. 'You little rat.'

'Fuck you and the horse you rode in on, sister.'

He couldn't believe he'd said that.

She's gonna kill me.

Instead, she yanked his shirt back over his shoulders and pulled it off him. She shoved it into his hands. 'Clean your mess,' she said.

His heart kicked. 'Huh?'

'You heard me.' Grabbing his shoulders, she shoved him down to his knees.

He stared at the dripping front of her shorts, the white fluid streaming down her thigh. He began at her knee and worked his way up, mopping the ice cream with his wadded shirt. He felt the smooth firmness of her muscles. His mouth was parched. His heart punched the air out of his lungs.

He stopped at the hem of the leg hole, turned the shirt to find a dry area, and patted the front of her shorts. Then, he lowered his arms.

'You're not done yet.'

'Huh?'

'Do it.'

Wearing a tail of his shirt like a glove, he slipped his hand up her leg and inside her shorts. The fabric of the shirt quickly went damp. She felt slick and creamy. Nothing in there felt like panties.

'You're just spreading it around.'

He took his hand out, found a dry section of shirt, wrapped it around his hand and went back to work.

Sick with lust. Cramped, tight, burning.

Wiping at his mess. Feeling her. Her leg, and the shallow, slanted valley where her leg joined her torso. If he moved his hand only a couple of inches towards the centre . . .

Oh, man. Man! So close!

Don't do it!

Don't. Christ. Don't. No.

He jerked his hand out. Tilting back his head, he looked up at Tanya.

'What do you say?' she asked.

He shrugged.

'What do you say?'

'Thank you very much,' Jeremy said.

'Haw!' That came from Cowboy.

'Stand up.'

He stood up.

Tanya's lips curled into a smile. 'One o'clock tonight. Under the clown.'

'Does that mean I can come?'

'Yes, indeed.' Her pale blue eyes seemed a little mocking. 'Cowboy, fill him in on the rules. And tell Liz to leave her cousin at home, or stay away herself.'

Chapter Six

Monsters Among Us
by
Gloria Weston

His name is Harrison Bentley. His friends call him Bents. Others among us call him a troll.

A few nights ago, he was beaten, stripped of his clothes, and bound with ropes to the steep downhill tracks of Funland's Hurricane roller coaster. A calling card was taped to his forehead. It read, 'Greetings from Great Big Billy Goat Gruff'.

No, the roller coaster did not race down and crush the life out of Harrison Bentley. No, it was not derailed by the impact and thrown off its tracks, hurtling its luckless riders to their doom. Harrison was discovered in time to prevent such tragedies.

Near death from hypothermia, he was rushed to the hospital emergency room. He had multiple bruises and abrasions. A dislocated shoulder. Two cracked ribs. A broken nose.

The damage to his body will heal, in time. But time is unlikely to mend the deeper wounds – the agony and humiliation of being stripped and brutalized, the terror of being lashed to the Hurricane tracks at a dizzying height above the boardwalk and left there through the long dark hours of the night, knowing that dawn would bring not only the welcome warmth of sunlight, but also the roar of the descending Hurricane.

Such wounds may never heal.

Harrison Bentley has been scarred for life.

Why?

We know why, good folks of Boleta Bay. We all know why. He committed a crime, and he was duly punished for it.

What heinous crime did this man commit?

We all know the answer to that one, too.

He was guilty of being homeless.

He was a 'troll'. And he met rough justice from Great Big Billy Goat Gruff.

He isn't the first victim of the thugs who roam our town, especially our beach and boardwalk, 'trolling', visiting mayhem on the downtrodden of our society. He is only the most recent.

Our local authorities have knowledge of at least twenty incidents in which indigents have been beset by roaming bands of teenaged vigilantes. The earliest attacks, beginning last summer, were mild in comparison to the brutality apparent in the torture of Harrison Bentley. The victims, then, were bound and gagged and driven out of town. They were left miles away, terrified but unharmed. They were left with warnings never to return to Boleta Bay.

Soon, however, the 'bum's rush' ceased to satiate the appetite of the adolescent mob. Instead of a swift ride out of town, transients were beaten senseless and left where they fell – in alleys, on the beach, in the darkness beneath the boardwalk, in the shadows among the rides and game booths of the 'fun zone'. Always with a calling card proclaiming him – or her – to be yet another victim of Great Big Billy Goat Gruff.

But even beatings, as vicious as they were, proved too tame for the pleasures of the brutes who roam our nights. Though the beatings continued, new and perverse elements have now been added to the repertoire.

Four weeks ago, an early-morning jogger found an indigent

known only as 'Mad Mary' handcuffed to the railing of the boardwalk. Like those before her, Mary had been thrashed. Unlike the others, she had been stripped naked. Every inch of her body had been sprayed with green paint.

Biff, the next victim, was painted with red and yellow stripes.

Lucy's buttocks were glued to a boardwalk bench. The plastic bowl that she used for collecting a few paltry coins from passers-by was glued to her face.

James was placed on a carousel horse, hands tied behind his back, a hangman's noose around his neck. Had he fallen during the night or early morning hours . . .

Harrison was tied to the Hurricane's tracks.

It won't stop with him. Our own local band of barbarians will strike again, commit more atrocities, fall with ever increasing cruelty and ferocity on the homeless of our town.

And we are to blame.

We are their accomplices.

We fear the 'bums, winos and crazies' who seem to be everywhere, always with a hand out, begging for change. We treat them like carriers of a dreaded disease, spreading contagion by their mere presence.

They do spread a disease.

The disease they spread, my friends, is guilt.

We *have*. We have homes, families, food, clothes, and countless luxuries. They do not.

We hate them for reminding us of that fact.

And we want them gone.

The trollers want them gone, too. The trollers, our children, react to the 'bums' as the adults do – with fear and loathing. They have seen the revulsion on our faces. They have heard our muttered curses, our derisive laughter. And some of them, perhaps only a handful, chose to do us all the favour of cleaning up the town, getting rid of these hated nuisances. They invented the sport of 'trolling'.

From the beginning, of course, our authorities denounced their activities.

But so many of us were pleased.

At last, something was being done about our 'bum problem'.

Stickers began to appear on car bumpers and store windows: 'Troll Buster' stickers; others that read, 'One Troll Can Ruin Your Whole Day' and 'Billy Goat Gruff For President'. Jokes abounded. 'What bait do you use for trolling in Boleta Bay? Cat food.' And, 'How can you tell if a troll's dead? He doesn't ask for two bits when you step on him.'

We did not condemn the acts of violence perpetrated against the 'trolls', we made sport of them. We applauded them. And with our cynical attitudes, with our approval, we acted as a local Booster's Club for Great Big Billy Goat Gruff.

Will we celebrate, I wonder, when an indigent lies dead on the boardwalk, murdered by our children?

I doubt it.

We'll have the opportunity, though. Tomorrow, next week or next month, they *will* kill.

For us.

The moment is rushing toward us with the momentum of the Hurricane thundering down its tracks.

A troll will die.

A bum, a wino, a crazy. A beggar who talks gibberish, dresses in rags and smells of garbage. And some of us may think that the world is a better place with that troll dead.

But the murderers will be you and me.

And the victim, let us not kid ourselves, will not be a troll.

Not a troll, but a human being – a man or woman who ran out of luck somewhere along the way, who was condemned from birth by a cosmic roll of the dice, or who was trampled beneath the merciless boots of substance addiction. A person, not a troll.

A person. A child, once, who was loved by a mother and father. A child who fought to stay awake on Christmas Eve in hopes of spying Santa Claus. A girl who skipped rope and sped along on roller skates. A boy who beamed when he was given his first bicycle, who cried when his balloon popped, who popped bubble gum and ate ice cream cones.

A child who would've loved Funland with its hot dogs and

cotton candy, with its arcades and game booths and thrilling rides.

This is our troll.

This is our victim.

This is who will die on the moonlit boardwalk, one night soon, with a card taped to his body – 'Greetings from Great Big Billy Goat Gruff'.

Let me suggest a revision in the card's message.

Let it read, 'Greetings From Great Big Billy Goat Gruff *and the citizens of Boleta Bay*'.

Dave folded the *Evening Post* and tossed it onto his coffee table. He lifted his beer mug. He took a drink.

'So, what do you think?' Gloria asked. She was sitting beside him on the sofa, one leg tucked beneath her, an arm resting on the back cushion. She looked at Dave with one eyebrow cocked high, daring him to strike out at her editorial, eager to defend it.

'Nice job,' he said.

'You don't mean that.'

'It sure ought to stir things up.'

'That was the idea. It's a disgrace, what's happening in this town. Something has to be done about it.'

'I agree.' Dave finished his beer and set the mug down. 'Why don't we head on over to the Wharf Rat?'

'You're trying to change the subject.'

'I'm getting hungry.'

'What do you really think about my article?'

Dave sighed. Why not go ahead and get it over with? Tell her what she's waiting so eagerly to hear. 'Wouldn't you rather fight on a full stomach?' he asked.

With kids waiting for Santa Claus, roller skating and popping gum so fresh in his mind, Dave thought that Gloria looked like one who'd just felt a tug on her fishing line.

'I knew it,' she said. 'You're pissed off.'

'Do you have to use that kind of language?'

Now she looked *really* pleased. 'Oh? And Joan doesn't?'

'That's different.'

'In what way?'

'I thought you wanted to argue about bums.'

'We'll get back to them. Tell me, why is Joan permitted to use that kind of language, and I'm not? This ought to be good. Is it because she's "one of the guys"? She obviously is not one of the guys. Or hadn't you noticed?'

'You're certainly feeling your oats tonight. Or your bamboo shoots.'

'Joan was talking like a sailor at the barbecue last week. You never once said boo about that.'

'I don't criticize my guests.'

'But it's all right for her to talk that way.'

'Doesn't bother me.'

'But I'm not allowed to say "pissed off"?'

'Coming from you, it sounds incredibly phony and childish. You sound like a second grader trying to shock her parents.'

Her face went red. Her mouth dropped open.

'You bastard,' she muttered.

Dave knew that he'd gone too far. She had been spoiling for a fight – for a chance to pit her superior social conscience against the cynical cop – but she hadn't expected it to get up close and personal. She hadn't counted on being humiliated.

'I'm sorry,' Dave said. He put his hand on her arm.

She jerked it away from him.

'You asked,' he pointed out.

'Go to hell. Oh, pardon me. Phony, childish me.' She pushed herself off the couch and walked toward the front door.

'Gloria.'

She opened the door.

'Come on, let's forget about it and go to the Wharf Rat.'

She looked back at him.

Her eyes were red.

Good Christ.

'Hey,' he said, 'I didn't mean anything.'

'No. Of course not. Enjoy your dinner.' She left and shut the door hard.

* * *

Joan slid the zipper up the front of her white denim dress and checked herself in the bedroom mirror. A lot of leg showed. This was her first new dress since minis had come back into fashion. She supposed it would take some getting used to.

'Neat outfit,' Debbie said from the doorway.

Joan looked at her sister. 'Do you think it's too short?'

'Looks great,' Debbie said, wandering into the room. 'Can I borrow it sometime?'

'Sure, I guess so.' The girl lacked Joan's height and figure, but the dress would probably fit her. Hard to believe that she had grown so much recently. And a little sad.

'What's wrong?'

'I don't want any of your boyfriends drooling on it.'

'Get real.'

'Your boyfriends don't drool?'

'You ought to know. You see as much of them as I do.'

'Somebody has to watch out for you.'

'Somebody ought to watch out for *you*.'

'What's that supposed to mean?'

'Are you going out with *him* again?' Debbie's upper lip lifted slightly as she spoke.

'He'll be here any minute.'

'It's your life.'

'That's right, it is. There's nothing wrong with Harold.'

'No. Huh-uh. He's perfect. Why don't you marry him?'

'He hasn't asked,' Joan said.

Debbie's eyes widened. 'You wouldn't, would you? I mean, if he asked, you'd tell him to screw off, right?'

'I think I'd be more diplomatic about it.'

'But you wouldn't marry him?'

'I doubt it.'

'Well, at least you're not totally bonkers.'

'Thanks.'

''Cause he's sure no prize. If you ask me, I don't know why you go out with him at all.'

'Did you hear me ask?'

'What do you see in him, anyway?'

'Harold's a nice guy.'

'You could do a lot better.'

'Yeah? Who appointed you Mother?'

The smug smile fell off Debbie's face.

'I'm sorry,' Joan said.

The girl shrugged, but her face had gone pale and for just a moment her eyes looked frantic. She quickly turned her head away. 'Where's Mr Wonderful taking you?'

'A movie. You know, that Summer Film Festival at the university.'

'What a thrill.'

'We might go someplace afterwards. I'll be home by midnight, or I'll call.'

'Don't tear yourself away from him on my account.'

Still regretting the 'Mother' comment, Joan said, 'How would you like to come with us?'

'Oh, that'd be rich.'

'I'm sure Harold wouldn't mind.'

'And I could pick up a few pointers on erogenous zones.'

'I doubt that very much,' Joan said.

'Yeah, he might wilt in front of a spectator.'

'You kidding? He keeps his hands to himself. Spectators or not.'

'Bullshit.' She stared at Joan, eyes narrow. 'He's putting it to you.'

'That's news to me.'

'You're lying.'

'Right. I'm a world-class liar.'

'But that's . . . too weird. You don't let him, or what?'

'Is this any of your business?'

'I'm just curious, that's all. I mean, you've been going with this guy for a month. What's the story?'

'I don't know.' She felt herself starting to blush.

'So it's him, huh? Is he a homo or something?'

Joan shrugged. 'Let's just drop it, okay? I don't know what's wrong, and I don't want to talk about it.'

'Why the hell do you go out with him?'

'I told you, he's a nice guy. So, do you want to come with us, or not?'

'What do you do when you're out with him? Nothing?'

'Come along and find out.'

'Not a chance. Jeez. I knew something was wrong with that guy.'

The doorbell rang.

'See you later,' Joan said. 'Midnight.'

'Yeah. Have a ball.'

Joan grabbed her handbag off the bed and hurried down the hall. She opened the front door. Harold stood on the porch, a few strides back. He glanced at her face as if to confirm who she was, then focused on her chest, as usual. Not that he found her chest special. He just seemed unable to look at her face for any period of time. 'How's my favourite copper?'

'Feeling brassy,' she said.

He smiled and nodded. 'Well, ready to go?'

'Yep.' She pulled the door shut, stepped up to him and took his hand. He squeezed it slightly.

'I think you'll enjoy tonight's film,' he said as they walked towards his Volvo.

'Does that mean it doesn't have subtitles?'

'It's Polanski's *Macbeth*.'

'Really? I thought Shakespeare was the brains behind that one.'

'You're awful.'

'I'm not awful, I'm a wag.'

'Terrible.'

He opened the passenger door for Joan. As she climbed into the car, she watched him. He stood there and never once glanced at her legs.

Typical. But she'd thought that the new dress might spark some interest.

Could've saved my money, she thought as he shut the door.

She looked down. If the dress were any shorter, her panties would be showing. She felt the seat's upholstery against the back of her thighs.

46

Harold slid in behind the wheel.

'What do you think of my new dress?' Joan asked.

'It's very becoming,' he said, and started the car.

'Why don't we skip the movie?'

'But it's a classic.' He pulled away from the curb.

'I've seen it. It can't hold a candle to the Orson Welles version. The height of its innovation is having some gals parade around bare-ass. Is *that* why you're so eager to see it?'

'Don't be silly.'

'Let's go to the boardwalk.'

He looked at her. He looked aghast.

'Have you ever been there?'

'Once. And I assure you, once was enough.'

'I'd like to go. It'll be fun.'

'Joan. You *patrol* the boardwalk. You're there every day. Have you lost your senses?'

'What do you think I do while I'm on duty, ride the Ferris wheel and carousel? You know what I did today? I checked out the restrooms about a dozen times and listened to a bunch of lunatics rant about flying saucers and visits from the Virgin Mary.'

'It's a disgraceful place. And dangerous.'

'Danger knows full well that I am more dangerous than she. We are two lions, whelped by the same . . .'

'And dirty. That park is filthy, and you're wearing a brand new dress – a *white* dress. You'll ruin it the minute you sit down on something. It's madness. Sheer madness.'

'I've seen enough artsy-fart films the past three weeks to choke Renoir. So how about it? Come on, let's go to Funland. Please? I'll buy you a cotton candy.'

'I can't stand the stuff.'

'Party pooper. Okay, never mind. Let's see *Macbeth*. I'll go to the boardwalk some night when you've got a class. Maybe meet a nice sailor.'

Harold drove to Funland.

Chapter Seven

The age guesser said, 'Twenty-three.' Joan showed her driver's licence to prove she was twenty-seven, and he gave her a pencil eraser shaped like a dinosaur.

She tried to get Harold to have his age guessed. He said, 'That'd be pressing our luck.'

The way his hairline was receding and his somewhat paunchy stomach held the front of his sport coat open, she figured he stood a good chance of winning. The guy would probably suspect he was closer to forty than thirty-four. Harold, self-conscious about his looks, no doubt preferred to avoid the embarrassment.

They wandered up the boardwalk.

Joan hadn't been here at night since last summer. It seemed so much more festive after dark: the game booths were brightly lighted; the names of rides and attractions blazed with neon; everywhere she looked, she saw strings of multi-coloured bulbs. The familiar aromas of cotton candy, popcorn, hot dogs, French fries, machine oil, perfumes and after-shave and the ocean all smelled more fragrant and alluring than during the day. The crowd was larger. She felt an aura of mystery and anticipation.

It's like this every night, she thought, and I've been missing it.

If Harold would just get into the spirit of the thing . . .

'What do *you* want to do?' she asked.

'I suppose it's too late for *Macbeth*.'

'There must be something here that you'd enjoy. How about the Tilt-a-Whirl?' she asked, stopping to watch people climb out of the hooded cars. Girls laughing. Couples holding each other and staggering. 'Come on,' she said. 'There's no line. We can get right on.'

'You go ahead. I'll stay here and watch.'

'Oh, that would be loads of fun.'

'No, do it. I insist. I don't want to be responsible for spoiling your fun.'

Joan shrugged. 'Maybe later. Come on.' She took his arm and led him away. 'We'll find something you like.'

'Approximately in the year that Hell freezes over.'

She spotted the hag with the sock puppet. The old crone hadn't moved all day. Her sock was darting out, 'talking' to people unlucky enough to be passing near her. Joan was tempted to steer Harold in her direction.

After all, he was hot to see *Macbeth* tonight, and this gal was certainly a weird sister.

But that would be cruel.

She remembered how the puppet had gone for Dave's leg, and laughed.

'What?' Harold asked.

'One of my favourite bums.' She nodded towards the woman.

Harold looked. 'I don't see anything especially amusing about her.'

'Her puppet nibbled Dave's leg today.'

'Did you read Gloria's piece on trolling?'

'She laid it on pretty thick.'

'I thought she did an admirable job.'

'She ought to get off her high horse. Accomplices, my ass. Typical bleeding heart bullshit. We're *all* guilty?' She flung an arm up, pointing at the high, down-sweeping tracks of the Hurricane's steepest drop. 'Dave and I, we risked our butts climbing that damn thing to rescue that derelict she was rhapsodizing about. Either of us had slipped, we would've been dead meat. Don't tell me about accomplices. She knew we did that, too. But did she put it in her sermon? No way. Her whole point was to make the town – and the cops – look like we're all in favour of trolling. Called us a Booster Club, no less. I don't know how she could look Dave in the face after writing that crap.'

Releasing Harold's hand, she strode over to the Bazooka Guns. She paid the man behind the counter. He loaded the feed trough with five tennis balls. Joan jacked one into the chamber, sighted down the wide barrel, and fired. The first ball poomphed out, rocketed forty feet, and whacked the suspended dummy. The ball caught it in its belly. Its legs flew up and it twirled on the end of its rope.

She glanced at Harold. He looked as if he regretted mentioning Gloria's article.

She blasted another tennis ball at the dummy. This one knocked its stuffed head backwards.

'We might be able to *apprehend* the goddamn Billy Goat Gruff if we got a tiny little bit of cooperation from the victims. They give us nothing. Nothing. Do you know what we've found out so far?'

She shot a ball into the dummy's chest.

'It's teenagers. We've been told they're all girls. We've been told they're all guys. There are anywhere from three to fifty of them, depending on which victim you listen to. The leader is Satan replete with horns and tail, a gorgeous blonde, Mayor Donaldson, a giant black guy, Charles Manson's twin brother, Zarch from the Sixth Dimension . . .'

'I get the point,' Harold said.

Joan missed the dummy.

'Ignorant, self-righteous bitch.'

Her last ball struck the dummy in the face.

Harold put a hand on her shoulder. 'I didn't mean to upset you.'

'Who's upset?'

'Gloria's only doing her job.'

'And we're doing ours, but she conveniently forgets to point that out.'

They wandered into the stream of the moving crowd.

'Want to try the bumper cars?' she asked.

'In your mood, you'd probably hurt someone.'

'My mood's fine,' she muttered.

'Step right in, folks!'

She glanced at Jasper Dunn. The cadaverous old man leered at her. She quickened her pace.

'Don't rush off, Miss Cop. Step right in, you and your handsome beau, and see the amazing, astonishing wonders of Jasper's Oddities. Lead her this way, fellow. Right this way. Don't miss out. See the two-headed baby, the hairless orangutan of Borneo, the mummy Ram Cho-tep, and other rare and mysterious wonders. She'll quiver and shake at the sights. She'll swoon in your arms.'

She kept walking.

'I take it,' said Harold, 'you're not interested in Jasper's Oddities?'

'That guy's swamp scum.'

'Has he done something to you?'

'Just with his eyes. Every time I walk by . . . Fortunately, he spends most of his time inside with his Oddities. Sometimes, I go a whole shift without seeing him. He likes to go in and watch the reactions. And ogle the females.'

'Enjoys watching them quiver and shake,' Harold said. 'Have you ever gone in?'

'Just once. Some gal had fainted.'

'Those oddities must be something to see.'

'I think it was the heat. She was on the floor and her skirt was hiked up around her waist and Dunn was on his knees. I'm not saying he fooled her or anything, but he sure looked startled when the boyfriend towed us in there.'

She stopped and looked back. A couple of teenaged guys with their dates were climbing the stairs, giving tickets to Dunn. One of the girls was husky, but the other was slender and wore a halter top and white shorts. 'Watch,' Joan said. 'He'll follow them in. Goddamn lech.'

Dunn followed them through the doorway. 'I wish the creep would dry up and blow away. He's the guy that owns the Funhouse, you know.' Joan nodded towards the two-storey building that stood adjacent to the Oddities. The dark neon sign above its front door, visible in the glow of nearby lights, read, JASPER'S FUNHOUSE. All the windows were boarded with sheets of plywood. 'I've heard he had a grating in one of its corridors. On the floor. And he used to hide under there and look up the skirts of the women when they walked across it.'

'Charming fellow. Is that why it's closed?'

Joan shook her head. 'A couple of his freaks got loose in it, one night. He used to have a freak show. In there with his Oddities. Some pretty hideous . . . people. That's what I hear. A couple of them got into the Funhouse. This was five or six years ago, I guess. I was still at Stanford. Dave told me about it. He said they jumped a little girl and her grandmother.'

'Terrible,' Harold muttered.

'The old woman keeled over with a heart attack.'

'What about the girl?'

'She wasn't hurt. Some sailors came to the rescue. But the grandmother died. Dunn was forced to shut down his freak show. Then he couldn't afford the liability insurance to keep his Funhouse going, so he closed it. He still owns it, though. Nobody can get him to tear it down.'

'Maybe he wants to reopen it someday.'

'I wouldn't be surprised. He doesn't have a *grate* on the floor of the Oddities place.'

Harold looked at the abandoned Funhouse and shook his head. 'I might've enjoyed that,' he said.

'Right. That's a real shame. The one attraction on the entire boardwalk that you might've enjoyed, and it isn't open.'

'No, I mean it. When I was a kid, I used to go to Riverview in Chicago. I guess Riverview's long gone, now. But they had a funhouse called Aladdin's Castle. Or was it Palace? I don't recall. But I used to love it.'

'Gee, there is hope for you.' She took hold of his arm, and they strolled on. 'So, you used to enjoy amusement parks. In your callow youth.'

'Before I became a stick-in-the-mud.'

Joan smiled. 'Tell me more about your pre-stick days.'

'I was always too timid for my own good.'

She squeezed his arm, said, 'Just a minute,' then smiled and raised her other hand in greeting. 'Hiya, Jim, Beth.'

The two officers walked over to them. Jim looked at her legs.

'Don't you see enough of this place during the day?' Beth asked.

'Dave won't let me ride the Hurricane.'

'Just lets you climb on it,' Jim said.

She introduced them to Harold. He shook hands with them.

'Be careful with her, Harry,' Jim said.

'Is she fragile?'

'She's got a black belt.'

'And I'm not above hitting people with it,' Joan said.

'Don't let her cuff you to the bed. Once she's got you helpless, out comes the belt.'

'Are you speaking from personal experience?' Harold asked him.

'In his dreams,' Joan said.

Beth nudged Jim with her elbow. 'Come on, Casanova. Nice meeting you, Harold.'

'Yeah,' Jim said. He slapped Harold's arm. 'Got one word of advice for you, Harry. Go for it.'

Harold grinned and nodded.

'That was three words, dipstick,' Joan said.

'But who's counting?'

He and Beth ambled away. Before they vanished into the crowd, Joan saw them look at each other and start talking. No doubt discussing her boyfriend. Jim, for one, would not be voicing approval.

'Interesting fellow,' Harold said.

'Rarely.'

At least Jim goes for it, Joan thought. You may not *want* him to go for it, you may have to inflict some pain to stop him, but he's interested enough to make the try.

'Is it true that you have a black belt?'

'I have a black garter belt.'

'Would you like some cotton candy?'

'Sure. That'd be great.'

What does it take to get a rise out of him? she wondered. He bought a cotton candy for Joan, nothing for himself.

She tore off a puffy wad with her teeth, drew it into her mouth, and felt it dissolve before she had much chance to chew it.

'So at that Riverview place,' she said, 'what did you like besides Aladdin's Castle? The roller coaster?'

'They couldn't drag me onto the Bobs. Or the parachute drop. As I said, I was timid.'

'How about the Ferris wheel?'

'I wouldn't go near it.'

'How about the Ferris wheel right now?'

'Oh, I don't think so.'

'I do.' The sign by its gate showed that five tickets were needed. She headed for a nearby ticket booth, Harold hurrying after her.

'Joan, I'm not going on that thing.'

She stepped into line. 'Hold this,' she said, and handed the cotton candy to him. 'Try it, you'll like it.' He looked warily at the confection. He shook his head. Joan took the wallet out of her shoulder bag, and removed a ten dollar bill.

'If you think you're going to get me onto that deathtrap contraption . . .'

'My friend, everyone is afraid of heights.'

'This from the lady who scaled the Hurricane.'

'I was scared shitless. But I did it, anyway, because it had to be done. And you're going to ride the Ferris wheel for the same reason.'

'It does not have to be done.'

'Oh, yes it does.' She bought ten tickets and received five dollars in change.

Harold followed her to the line for the Ferris wheel. He had a nervous smile on his face as he handed the cotton candy to her. 'You don't honestly expect me to go through with this?'

'You'll like it. I promise.'

'I won't like it, because I won't do it.'

'I've already bought the tickets.'

'You may ride it twice. I'll stay right here, safe on the ground, and wait patiently.'

She looked him in the eyes. 'I want you to go on it with me,

Harold. Just the Ferris wheel. I won't ask you to try the Hurricane or the parachute drop or anything else. Just this one ride. It won't kill you.'

'That's because I won't be on it.'

'Harold, please.'

Now, the nervous smile was gone. Replaced by a frown of annoyance. 'I don't understand why you insist on being so adamant about this. For heaven's sake, it's just a carnival ride. It's hardly worth bickering about. It won't make one whit of difference, in the scheme of things, whether or not I go on the stupid thing.'

'It makes a big difference to me,' Joan said.

'Oh, I have to prove I'm a man, is that it? Is this some kind of a test?'

'It didn't start out that way,' Joan told him.

'I'll ride the damn thing if it'll make you happy.'

'Good,' she muttered. She turned away from him. She took a bite of the cotton candy and it melted away in her mouth and she felt like crying.

The Ferris wheel was still going full speed, its lighted spokes spinning, cars rocking, riders squealing as they were swept down from the staggering height. Some of them, she saw, were embracing. She tossed her cotton candy into a trash bin.

'I said I'll do it.' He sounded petulant.

'I heard you.'

'So what are you pouting about?' he asked.

'This was supposed to be fun.'

'I'm sorry.' He didn't sound sorry at all. 'I guess I'm just not a very fun guy. Maybe you should've come here with one of your macho cop friends. I'm sure Dave would be delighted to ride the goddamn Ferris wheel.'

'He wouldn't whine about it.'

'Now, I'm a whiner. Isn't that wonderful.'

'Not especially.'

'Christ.'

'You've never touched me, Harold.'

His mouth fell open.

'Joan, for Christsake.' He glanced around as if fearful that someone might be listening. But the others waiting in line were talking among themselves. The air was thick with laughter and screams, the spiels of pitchmen, the crackle of gunfire from the shooting gallery, hurdy-gurdy music from the Ferris wheel.

He didn't need to worry about eavesdroppers.

'Is it me?' Joan asked. 'Is something wrong with *me*?'

'No, of course not.'

'Then what is it? We've been going together for weeks. We hold hands and kiss goodnight – *I* kiss *you* goodnight. And that's it.'

'I thought you preferred it that way.'

'Then you don't know much about . . .' The miserable look in Harold's eyes forced her to stop. 'You're scared of me, aren't you?' She asked it gently.

'That's ridiculous.'

'I'm . . . like the Ferris wheel. You're afraid of me. Why? Jesus, I'm just a woman.'

'A very beautiful woman.'

'I'm too beautiful for you? You can't look at me, you can't touch me, because I'm too beautiful?'

He lowered his head. 'Something like that, I suppose.'

'Move it along, folks.'

Harold stiffened.

Joan saw that the line had moved forward, that their turn had come to board the Ferris wheel.

'We don't have to do it,' she said.

But he shook his head and went through the gate. The man took the tickets from Joan. They stepped onto a platform and climbed into the waiting gondola of the Ferris wheel. It rocked gently as they sat down. The man swung a metal safety bar across the front and latched it secure.

With a jerk that made the basket tip, the wheel carried them upward. It stopped, and the next passengers boarded.

Harold was clutching the safety bar with both hands.

Joan put a hand on his thigh. He looked at her. He gasped as they were suddenly lifted higher.

'There's nothing to be afraid of,' Joan said. 'The Ferris wheel's safe. So am I.'

'Sure,' he muttered.

'Why do we keep going out together,' she asked, 'if you're so terrified of me?'

'I like you,' he said as the wheel moved again.

'I like you, too.'

'I like talking to you, being with you. You're funny. And you're smart.'

'Then what's to be afraid of?'

'I don't know.'

'Yes you do. Tell me.'

The wheel abruptly lifted them once more. Harold squeezed his eyes shut. He sat there gripping the bar, feet planted on the floor panel, back rigid, eyes tightly shut, teeth gritted.

Joan patted his thigh. 'Loosen up, would you? You're making *me* nervous.'

'I'm sorry.' He managed to say it without moving his jaw.

'Hey, you're not going to capsize us if you open your mouth.'

He sucked in a quick breath as the wheel moved again. When it stopped, they were near the top.

They were damn high.

Joan felt as if her insides had been left at the previous level. 'Jesus,' she muttered.

The boardwalk was *way* down there.

If this damn thing tips over . . .

'I'm not the kind of man,' Harold said, 'who *has* a woman like you.'

'Self-fulfilling prof . . . uh!' She grabbed the safety bar with both hands.

When the wheel stopped, they were at the very top. Their gondola swayed back and forth.

She realized that this position, though higher than the previous one, was considerably less unnerving.

Because, at the pinnacle of the Ferris wheel, the ground was out of sight. She could see the distant, wooded hills of the coastline range, and the headlights of cars on the highway, but nothing of the boardwalk.

Nothing directly below.

Nothing of what she would land on if the contraption fell apart or tipped over.

Not without leaning forward or sideways and peering down.

They started down and she could see the boardwalk again. To avoid the view, she turned her head and looked at Harold.

He still sat rigid with his eyes shut.

The man, she thought, is a coward.

I'm scared, too, she reminded herself.

But not like that.

Though she pitied him, though she felt guilty for making him come up here, she suddenly knew that she had lost her respect for him.

He was no more than an imitation of a man, a counterfeit.

Terrified of harmless carnival rides. Terrified of me.

And she realized she had learned nothing new here tonight. She had confirmed her suspicions, nothing more. Maybe that's why she had brought him here – to take him out of his safe academic world and . . . put him on trial. Not a conscious plan, certainly. But maybe in the back of her mind, that was why she'd insisted they skip the film and come to Funland.

To hold a trial of his manhood.

Not only did all the evidence go against him, but he had even confessed.

Scared of *me*, for Christsake.

He could learn not to be frightened of me, Joan thought. I could teach him. Seduce him. He'd get over his fear in an hour – hell, in ten minutes.

That's how long it would take to find out I'm not laughing at him, not rejecting him. That long, and he'd see that I'm just a woman.

The Ferris wheel moved, dropping them lower. This time, it didn't stop after a few feet. It swept them down close to the ground and lifted them toward the heights and Joan's fear slipped away. They flew over the crest and swung downward.

This is all right, she thought. Just took some getting used to. *I'd just take some getting used to.*

Get him into bed just once, he'll be fine.

Right. Fine. That little piece of him will be fine, the little piece that's scared of me. But what about the rest of him?

She knew that she would never be able to count on him, lean on him, be comforted by his strength. She would have to be the strong one, the leader.

More like his mother than his lover.

I don't need that.

Soon, the Ferris wheel stopped. They were gradually lowered toward the ground. Not until the attendant stepped up to their gondola did Harold release his grip on the safety bar. They climbed down.

On the boardwalk, Joan said, 'You can take me home, now.'

'You're upset with me,' he said.

'No. It's all right.'

'I rode the damn ride.'

'I know. That was very brave.'

'About the other thing . . .'

'That's all right,' Joan said. 'I understand.'

'You're . . . so different from other women I've known. So much more alive and beautiful. I suppose I've just been too overwhelmed, and I didn't want to risk losing you. I was afraid that if I . . . threw myself at you, you might . . . I don't know . . .'

'It's all right, Harold. You don't have to explain.'

'I didn't want to lose you,' he said again.

She took his hand. They walked out of Funland and into the parking lot, and he opened the door of his car for her. She leaned across the seat and unlocked the driver's door. He climbed in without looking at her.

He drove out of the parking lot.

'I knew we should've gone to *Macbeth*,' he said.

Joan said nothing.

'Would you like to stop someplace for a nightcap?'

'No, thanks. I don't think so. I'm not feeling very well. Just take me home.'

'We really should discuss . . .'

'Some other time, okay?'

'Fine . . .'

When he reached her house, he swung to the kerb and killed the engine and turned to her. 'I'll go in with you,' he said. In the dim light from the streetlamps, she saw a nervous smile on his face. 'Now that I know how you feel, I . . . we can make up for lost time. How does that sound?'

Pathetic, she thought. That's how it sounds.

'Not tonight,' she said. 'I really don't feel very well.'

'Joan, please.'

'I'll give you a call.' She patted his knee, sensed that he was about to reach for her wrist, and quickly pulled her hand back. She swung the door open.

'Don't be this way. Please.'

'It's all right,' she told him. 'I'll give you a call.'

She climbed from the car, shut the door, and hurried up the walkway to her house.

Chapter Eight

Robin woke up, and couldn't believe that the movie was over. She had come into the theatre a little late and missed the start of the new James Bond, so after watching the film, she had waited through the intermission and looked at the opening. She'd planned to leave when it came to a familiar scene.

So much for plans.

Apparently, she'd drifted off and slept through the rest of the showing. Now, the auditorium lights were on and people were leaving their seats.

She was glad nobody had ripped her off.

One arm was still hooked through the shoulder strap of her pack, a precaution she must've taken before dropping off. The banjo case still stood on the floor, propped up between her legs.

She moved the case aside, stood up and swung the pack onto her back. Lifting the case, she sidestepped across the deserted row to the aisle.

On her way out, she stopped in the restroom. Nobody was around when she left the toilet stall. She took a few minutes to wash her face and brush her teeth.

The lobby was deserted except for a few workers in the process of closing for the night. Teenagers. As she headed for the door, she heard one of the girls behind the refreshment counter say, 'And he goes, "It won't kill you," and I go, "No way, Jose."' A different girl said, 'I should hope not. Total gross out.'

Robin shouldered open the glass door and stepped outside. The wind was chilly on her bare arms and slipped in through the front of her shirt. Shivering, she hurried up the sidewalk until she came to the recessed entryway of a dark shop. There, she opened her pack. She took out a lightweight nylon parka. She put it on and snapped the front. From a side pocket of her pack, she removed a sheathed knife. She slid it into a seat pocket of her jeans.

Then she shouldered her pack, picked up her banjo case, and walked into the street. She stopped in the middle. No cars were coming. Only a few remained parked at the kerbs. Down near the corner, a man was walking his dog. Otherwise, she saw no one. The lights of the theatre marquee were dark. All the shops and restaurants appeared to be closed for the night.

She crossed to the other side of the street, and headed south towards the boardwalk.

This was obviously one of those towns that rolls up its sidewalks after dark.

It's a lot later than after dark, she told herself.

Still, she thought it strange that a place as touristy as Boleta Bay would be shut down so completely at this hour.

What hour are we talking about, here? she wondered. Must be after midnight.

Which means that Funland's closed, too.

She felt a small tug of fear, and didn't know why. Then she remembered the policeman's warning about a gang of teenagers.

They try to mess with me, she thought, they'll bite the knife.

With each stride, she felt its broad flat blade press against her buttock.

It was her father's hunting knife.

It had saved her many times. Usually, just pulling it was enough to stop trouble.

She'd only cut someone once. That was at the bus depot in San Francisco. A guy came into the restroom while she was washing up, some time before dawn, and slammed her against the wall and ripped her shirt open and was trying to get her jeans down and she shoved the knife between his ribs. He said, 'Look what you done to me!' and fell to his knees.

Though the parka kept her warm, Robin felt cold and tight inside from remembering that night.

Thinking about it was almost like living it again. She *felt* her surprise when the man grabbed her, felt her terror when he tore her clothes, felt the way the knife seemed to be grabbed by his flesh as it slid into him, and the sickness of guilt that came after she fled.

His eyes had looked surprised and betrayed.

'You shouldn't have tried it,' she'd said before running.

She often wondered if the man had died.

She wondered that now, and the chill inside her deepened.

It was self-defence, she told herself. If he died, it was his own damn fault and maybe it was a good thing, besides. He'd probably raped women before. Dead, he would never get another chance at it. So maybe she had done the world a favour.

But Robin hoped he'd lived through it. He probably did, she thought. She didn't get him in the heart. In a lung, more likely.

She wished she knew for sure that he hadn't died. It would

make things easier on nights like this when the memories came back.

What can you do? she asked herself. You live with it. No other choice.

She crossed another street, leaving behind the self-consciously quaint section of downtown. Here, the road wasn't lined with trees. Instead of imitation gaslights, the area was lighted with sodium lamps on metal poles. Gone were the boutiques, tea shops, restaurants, bakeries and bookstores. A Woolworths took up half the block. On the other side of the street stood a gas station, an auto parts store, and the cafe where Robin had eaten a cheeseburger then sipped coffee and worked on song lyrics until she decided to call it quits and go to the movie. All were closed, now. Dim lights glowed inside. The auto parts store had a steel gate across its front.

On the next block, she started seeing bums. One was stretched out on the bench of a bus shelter. Another was curled up inside the dark entryway of a television repair shop.

Robin switched the banjo case to her left hand, freeing her right hand to go for the knife if they made trouble.

Neither of the bums spoke or moved as she hurried by.

Before reaching the intersection, she heard a tinny rattle and knew it came from a shopping cart. It still sounded distant. She quickened her pace. Hurrying past the corner of a closed liquor store, she glanced to the right and spotted a hunched old woman pushing the cart towards her. The cart's wire basket was stacked high with gal's junk. Quickly, Robin looked away.

'C'mere, princess!'

She rushed into the street.

'C'mere! Got a sticky treat for ya! Don' go off!'

Robin didn't look back.

'Blood on ya, then! Blood on ya!'

She bounded onto the other kerb. Glancing over her shoulder, she saw the cart woman stop beside a trash container and lean into it.

She was breathing fast and her heart was pounding.

They're so *creepy*, she thought.

Some of them, like that old woman, hardly seemed human at all. More like . . . creatures from another planet, or something. Lurking in the dark, babbling nonsense, ready to *get* you if you let your guard down.

Shouldn't let them spook me, she told herself. They're just people.

She spotted another one. Even though he was on the opposite side of the street, she felt a chill squirm up her back. He stood straight and motionless, his back to the dimly lighted display window of a thrift shop, his arms at his sides. He wore a dark coat that covered him to the knees. His legs below the edge of the coat were bare and pale. So was his hairless head. And he seemed to be staring at Robin.

That's ridiculous, she told herself. I can't even see his eyes. Just dark holes.

But she could feel his fierce gaze, and it made her shiver. She imagined him suddenly swooping across the street, grabbing her and carrying her away to some secret, foul place.

Man, she thought. I'm sure spooked tonight.

She walked a little farther, and turned her head to keep an eye on him.

So damn many of them.

The town seemed *infested*.

As if they'd been drawn here like flies to a garbage dump.

No wonder the kids are causing trouble. They're scared. So they band together and go after some of these spooks. Who can blame them?

If this place is crawling with bums, she thought, what about the beach?

Maybe she ought to take Dave's advice and check into a motel.

But it might be all right over there. If the kids had been hitting the boardwalk and beach, maybe the bums had scattered. Maybe that's why so many were over here – driven from their lairs, refugees from the danger zone.

At the corner, Robin waited while a lone car approached from the right. It had a rack of lights on top. A police car. It slowed down.

She looked back. The bum was there, halfway down the block, standing rigid, staring at her.

But no longer in front of the thrift shop.

Closer, now.

The patrol car stopped.

'Like to speak to you,' a man's voice called from the driver's window.

She stepped off the kerb and walked to the middle of the street. She bent over, slightly, and peered into the car. There were two uniformed policemen inside. They didn't look much older than Robin. They both had moustaches. The one in the passenger seat had a cardboard cup in his hand. He took a sip from it.

Real people.

But cops. Cops could mean trouble.

Dave had been nice, though.

'Officers?' Robin said.

'It's late to be wandering the streets,' the driver said.

'I just got out of the movies.'

'You see the Bond?' asked the other cop. 'Bitchin' flick, huh?'

'The guy's no Sean Connery,' Robin said.

'Yeah, but who is?'

'Where are you heading?' the driver asked.

'The beach.'

'Not a great idea.'

'I know. I've been warned about the troubles. You know a policeman named Dave?'

'Carson? Sure. He told you about the trolling?'

Robin nodded.

'Climb in, we'll give you a lift.'

'Thanks.' Though her heart was slamming, she opened the back door, tossed her backpack onto the seat, and climbed in. She rested the banjo case across her lap and pulled the door shut.

They seemed nice enough, but who can tell? In the car with them, she was at their mercy. But you don't argue with cops, you do as they say. That was a lesson she'd learned early, and never ignored.

At least they were taking her away from that creep.

The car turned the corner.

'I really appreciate it,' she said. 'All those bums were making me pretty nervous.'

'Most of them are too spaced out to give you any real trouble,' the driver said.

The other cop twisted round and looked at her. 'It's the kids you've gotta worry about,' he said.

'I've had bums attack me a few times,' she told him.

'You been on the road a lot?'

'A couple of years.'

'No way to live,' he said.

'It suits me fine. I figure I've got a whole life ahead for settling down.'

'Some bastard doesn't snuff it out for you.'

'You a runaway?' asked the driver.

'I'm over eighteen, so I guess it doesn't matter, does it?'

'Your folks know where you are?'

'My father's dead. My mother's too busy to care.'

'Shame,' the other cop said.

Robin shrugged.

'So you're what?' he asked. 'A street musician?'

'A boardwalk banjo picker. This week.'

'You're planning to stick around a week?' the driver asked.

'It's nice out at the beach. I don't know. Depends.'

Maybe I'll just hit the road tomorrow, she thought. Put some distance between me and this damned army of bums.

'You've gotta watch out for those trollers,' said the one who was watching her.

'If I run into them, I'll play them a ditty and warm their hearts.'

'Little fucks haven't *got* hearts,' the driver said. Then he added, 'Pardon the language. Not that I've got any use for the indigents, but . . .'

'They make good door-stops,' the other said.

'They have a right to be left in peace.'

'Yeah, there's no excuse . . .' He suddenly turned to the front. Robin realized that something must've come over the radio. It had been crackling, sputtering nasal tinny words while the men talked. 'Fourteen,' the passenger cop said. 'We're on it.'

The car swerved to the kerb.

'Sorry, we've gotta leave you off.'

Robin threw open the door. 'Thanks for the ride,' she said, grabbing her pack and scurrying out.

'Be careful.'

She threw the door shut. The rack on the roof blazed with flashing lights and the car sped away.

On the corner nearby was a Traveller's Haven, a motel with a blue neon vacancy sign, a few cars parked in front of its numbered doors. Across the street stood a minimarket that was not only open, but looked busy. A car was leaving its lot. A man entered the store. Half a dozen teenagers were clustered around a pickup truck at the edge of the parking area, sitting on its hood and bumper, standing in front of it, smoking and laughing and drinking from cardboard cups while music blared from the pickup's radio.

Robin wondered why they were out at this hour.

She wondered if they were trollers.

But she didn't feel afraid.

The part of town she'd left behind had been empty and silent, a cemetery haunted by the shuffling lost. Here, the streets were bright and noisy. Places were open. There were real people. Cars were passing.

She stepped around the corner. Ahead, only two blocks away, stood the dim archway entrance of Funland. Moonlight glowed on the face of the clown.

She walked towards it, passing motels that lined both sides of the street, all-night diners, bars, liquor stores with people coming and going.

When she saw a whiskered bum sitting on the sidewalk with his back to the wall of a closed souvenir shop, she felt no fear.

He lowered his bag-wrapped bottle as she approached. 'Spare a quarter for a cuppa coffee?'

She dug a dollar bill out of her jeans and gave it to him and withdrew her hand quickly, fearing his touch.

'G'bless you,' he mumbled.

Robin hurried away.

What was that for? she wondered. A payoff to ease the guilt of fleeing the others, of fearing them, of letting herself toy with the idea that they were aliens on the hunt?

Regardless of the reason, she felt better for giving him the money.

She looked back. He was still sitting against the wall. In the distance, the kids were still gathered at the pickup truck. The music of its radio was faint.

She crossed a street, and walked alongside the Funland parking lot. Its ticket booths were closed. A few cars remained on the asphalt field. One had a flat rear tyre. She wondered if the others were victims of dead batteries. Or had people abandoned them for other reasons? Or *were* they abandoned.

The windows of a Chevy near the sidewalk were fogged. She looked away quickly, afraid that someone might suddenly rise and press his face to the glass and peer out at her.

Don't be such a dork, she told herself.

Ever since leaving the movie theatre, she'd been letting her imagination run wild, spooking her.

It's this damn town, and its bums, and everybody warning me.

Maybe I should go back, she thought. Check into one of those motels. Just for tonight.

That'd be chicken.

I can take care of myself.

She strode across the street, across the walkway, and up the concrete stairs. The moonlit face of the clown greeted her with a smile.

Chapter Nine

Earlier that night, Jeremy was still at home, sprawled on his bed.

He reached out and lifted his pillow off the alarm clock. Twenty till one. The alarm was set to go off in five minutes. He fingered the stem in, shutting it off.

He hadn't slept at all. He'd tossed and turned, his mind whirling with memories of Cowboy and the boardwalk and the beach and Tanya, with curiosity and hope about tonight, with fantasies about Tanya that made him yearn and ache. He'd trembled. He'd sweated. He'd rolled and squirmed so much that, a few times, his pyjamas had become twisted around him, binding him tightly, seams digging into his armpits and crotch. After a while, he'd taken them off. But being naked had pitched him into a worse frenzy of excitement, so he'd put them on again.

Two hours had never been so long or so delicious.

At last, the waiting was over.

He eased out of bed. He arranged his two pillows lengthwise, and covered them with the blanket so that his mother would at least see more than an empty bed if she should wake up and glance in, maybe on her way to the bathroom.

He took off his damp pyjamas, balled them up, and stuffed them in with the pillows.

Shivering, he sank to his knees. He reached beneath the bed and pulled out the roll of clothing he'd prepared for tonight's adventure. Cowboy had instructed him to wear something dark, warned him that it would be 'colder than a wet butt in a blizzard', and suggested that he bring a knife along just in case of trouble.

The comment about the knife had prompted Jeremy to ask, 'What'll we be doing, anyway?'

'Just having a hoot. But that time of night, you never know. You wanta be ready for anything.'

It was pretty clear that the kids were up to no good. You don't sneak out of your house and meet at Funland at one a.m. just to stand around and talk. He'd wanted to ask more, but feared that Cowboy might think he was worried. Besides, it didn't really matter what they'd be doing. He wanted to be with them.

One of them.

Whatever it was, he planned to join in.

Jeremy slipped into his underwear and dark blue corduroy pants. He patted the front pocket to make sure his keys and knife were still there. He put on his shirt, and tucked it in. He put on his blue windbreaker. He carried his socks and sneakers.

At the bedroom door, he peered down the dark hallway towards his mother's room.

In the other house, when he'd crept out at night sometimes to wander the neighbourhood and look in windows, he'd had to sneak right past her door. In this house, her bedroom was at the end of the hall. A much better arrangement.

Jeremy made his way slowly to the front of the house. He slipped the guard chain off the door. It rattled a little, but not much. The door opened without a sound because he'd oiled the hinges before supper while his mother was taking a bath.

This house had a screened-in porch, another thing that made it better than the last house. His bicycle stood in a corner, ready to go. At the old place, he'd had to keep it in the garage so he'd never bothered to use it on his prowls.

Leaning against the door frame, he put on his socks and shoes. Then, he lifted his bike, carried it to the screen door, pushed open the door with his back, and hurried down the three porch stairs to the walkway.

The neighbourhood was lighted by streetlamps and the moon. Deep patches of darkness hung under the trees. A few of the nearby homes had porch lights on, but most of the windows were dark. He saw no one.

The wind felt chilly on his face and hands. It had a wet fresh smell that made him uneasy with its hints of lonely distances. A feeling of gloom began to smother his excitement, and for just a moment he wished he were still in bed.

I'll be with the kids pretty soon, he told himself. It'll be great.

Shivering, he set his bicycle in the street, pushed it along with one foot on a pedal until it was gliding fast, then swung himself onto the seat. As he coasted down the lane, he checked his wristwatch. Ten till one.

He intended to take back roads, avoiding the main drag since it might still be busy in spite of the late hour. But even with the detour, he thought, he should be able to reach the Funland entrance on time.

He wondered if Tanya was already there. He wondered what she would be wearing. Not shorts. Something warm. He thought about the way she'd looked on the beach in her shorts and T-shirt, and his feeling of desolation faded away. He thought about cleaning the ice cream off her leg, sliding his hand up inside her shorts, and the wind no longer felt cold.

This'll be great, he thought. No matter what the plan is.

He'd had a lot of time to consider what they might be doing tonight. His best guess was that they'd be drinking. Taking drugs was also possible. He'd never done that, and didn't much want to start, but if that was the plan . . .

Whatever.

Even vandalism. He might not like doing drugs or wrecking something, but damned if he would back out and have them think he was a wimp.

This was his best chance, ever, and he didn't plan to blow it.

During his long hours of waiting, he'd ruled out a few other possibilities.

He didn't really think they intended to do anything as drastic as robbery. He sure hoped not.

They might be into witchy stuff. What if Tanya was the leader of a coven, or something, and they met for blood sacrifices (what if I'm it?)? Jeremy had read that such things really go on, and that lots of disappearances (especially kids)

71

are people used for ritual slayings. But that was too far out. He told himself he was crazy for even thinking about it.

Nor could he accept the idea of an orgy. While tossing in bed, he'd tried to convince himself that it might happen. Too much to hope for. And it didn't make sense, meeting at a cold place like the boardwalk for sex. Unless they could go inside. Cowboy had mentioned that Liz's father owned some of the concessions, so Liz might let them into a warm, sheltered place where they'd take off their clothes, and . . . No. A great fantasy, but it wasn't about to happen.

No, it would be drinking, drugs, maybe vandalism. He was pretty sure of that. Nothing as scary as robbery or sacrifices, nothing as terrific as an orgy.

With his mind occupied by such thoughts, Jeremy was taken by surprise to find himself on Ocean Front Drive, pedalling alongside Funland. He spotted a wino sprawled between bushes in front of the wall, but farther up, near the entrance, there was nobody.

Maybe I'm the first one here, he thought.

Or maybe they're gathered on the boardwalk, out of sight.

He glided to the bicycle rack, hopped down, slid his bike between the bars, and chained it there. He walked towards the archway. He trotted up the stairs. Standing beneath the face of the clown, he scanned the darkness ahead. He saw the ticket booth and the boardwalk beyond it, but nobody was there.

He checked his wristwatch. Two minutes after one.

He strode forward, into the shadowed tunnel of the entry-way, past the ticket booth, past the salt-water taffy shop on his right and the souvenir shop on his left. Standing in the middle of the boardwalk, he looked from side to side. He had a clear view of Funland from one end to the other – except where shadows tore out patches of blackness – and he saw no one.

Where are they?

Not here, that's for sure. Unless they're hiding, planning to sneak up and scare me.

Jeremy waited. Nobody appeared.

What if it's a trick? he thought. Suppose they never planned to show up, and this was just a rotten trick to stick it to the wimp?

He leaned back against the main ticket booth. Off in the distance, a seagull squealed. Combers, pale in the moonlight, tumbled onto the beach. He felt cold and small and alone.

Should've known it was too good to be true, he thought.

Probably Tanya's idea to stand me up like this.

Tanya.

Jeremy sank down and hugged his knees to his chest.

Big joke. Set up the nerd. All the time, they were laughing at me behind my back.

Maybe not.

Maybe they really planned to meet here, but had to call it off and didn't know how to reach me.

That was possible. Cowboy knew his street, but not the address, and the telephone hadn't been hooked up yet. They wouldn't be able to let him know about the change in plans.

Jeremy felt better. A little. If they stood him up by accident, it wasn't nearly as bad as if they'd done it to screw him. Still a disappointment, but not humiliating, not crushing. Cowboy was still his friend, and Tanya hadn't turned against him.

Maybe they're only late, he thought.

Sure thing.

He slid up the cuff of his jacket and pressed a button to illuminate the numerals on his wristwatch. Twelve minutes after one.

They *might* be late, he told himself. I'll give it till one-thirty.

He suddenly heard quick, quiet footfalls.

They're here!

His gloom vanished. He sprang up and stepped around the side of the ticket booth, smiling and raising a hand to greet them.

The girl, a few strides away, let out a startled gasp. She lurched to a stop.

She wore a backpack and carried an instrument case that looked as if it might hold a banjo.

Her face was a faint blur in the darkness. But she didn't look short and skinny enough to be Liz, or large enough to be Tanya.

'Sorry if I scared you,' Jeremy said.

Her head turned. She looked to the sides, then glanced behind her.

'The others aren't here yet.'

She faced Jeremy. 'So you're one of *them*?'

Not, *So you're one of us?* He felt like a fool. The backpack and banjo should've tipped him off. She wasn't a town kid. She was a camper or drifter or something.

'Depends who you mean by "them,"' Jeremy said, wondering what she knew.

'The trollers.'

He shrugged. 'I don't know. What're trollers?'

Again, the girl looked over her shoulder. Then she walked straight towards Jeremy. 'Get out of my way, kid.' It was no timid request. It was a command. Jeremy side-stepped out of her path.

She walked past him. She looked to the right and left, but not back to him, and made her way straight across the boardwalk to the open place between the railings. She trotted down the stairs to the beach.

When she reached the sand, only the top of her head showed. Moments later, her shoulders and backpack came into view. She turned around, and Jeremy felt a quick tug of fear. But she didn't come towards him. She walked backwards several paces, then swung around again and strode away in the direction of the shore.

'Bitch,' Jeremy muttered.

Get out of my way, kid. What was her problem, talking like that?

I should've stood my ground and said, 'Yeah? Who's gonna make me?'

And she smiles, oh she's a tough one, and sets down her banjo and swings the pack off her shoulders and takes off her coat. She's wearing a T-shirt. And she pulls that over her head

74

because that's just how she likes to fight, in nothing but her jeans.

Jeremy imagined her, bare to the waist, her skin creamy in the moonlight, her nipples dark. She came for him slowly. Hunched over like a wrestler. Arms out. Circling him, looking for an opening.

'Don't force me to hurt you,' he warns.

'You and what army?' she asks.

Yeah, that'd be something. Wrestling with her, throwing her down. It could get really interesting, then.

Better, though, if she were Tanya.

How about that, wrestling with Tanya?

She'd cream me.

It'd be worth it, though.

Where is she!

A hand clapped Jeremy on the shoulder and he flinched and whirled around.

'Snuck up on you Indian-style,' Cowboy said.

'Jeez, you scared the shit out of me.'

'Lucky it was just me. You gotta be on your guard, you're out here alone. The fuckers'll have you for breakfast.'

'Where're the others?'

'Home in bed, I reckon.'

'What's going on?'

'They called it off for tonight.'

I was right! Jeremy thought. They don't hate me. It wasn't a set-up.

He had a tightness in his throat and a tingling hollow ache between his eyes as if he were very close to crying, but he didn't know whether it was relief or disappointment that made him feel so strange.

'How come?' he asked.

'Damn story in the *Post*. Did you see it?'

Jeremy shook his head.

'Some goat twat reporter did a number on us. Read the dag-blamed riot act. Nate figured the heat might be too much, tonight. You seen any cops around here?'

75

'No.' He thought about mentioning the girl, but decided against it.

'Well, I didn't reckon it'd be a problem. Nate, though, he likes to play it careful. He was afraid they might have the place staked out tonight, or something. Make a big play to grab us. So he got on the horn to Tanya and talked her out of tonight's little hoot.'

'I didn't know,' Jeremy said.

'Why do you think I'm here, Duke? Couldn't have you waiting out here all night, the party called off.'

'Well, thanks.'

'Would've been here sooner, but you know how it goes.'

'Sure,' Jeremy said. 'Better late than never.'

'Hope you didn't think we forgot about you.'

'Naw. I figured it was something like this.'

'Come on, let's get out of here before *we* get jumped.'

Jeremy followed him towards the archway. 'Jumped by who?' he asked.

'The trolls, man.'

He remembered that the girl had asked if he was a troller. 'What's all this troll stuff?' he asked.

'You know, *trolls*.'

'Like monsters that live under bridges.'

'You got it, Duke. Under bridges, under *boardwalks*, on the beach, everywhere. They're like cockroaches. They hide in all the dark places, then they come out and get you.'

'That's fairy tale stuff.'

'You calling me a fairy?' Cowboy elbowed him and laughed.

They trotted down the concrete stairs and Jeremy nodded towards his chained bike.

'We're not talking fairy tale trolls,' Cowboy told him. 'We're talking bums, winos, space-cadets, like the butt-wipe tried to hit you up for change before I came to your rescue.'

'He was a troll?'

'Durn tootin'.'

Jeremy stopped beside his bike and dug into his corduroys

for the key case. There was no other bicycle in the rack. 'How'd you get here?' he asked.

'Walked. You oughta walk, too, next time.'

Next time!

'When'll that be?' he asked, trying to control his excitement and sound nonchalant.

'Who knows? Tanya, she'd be at it every night if Nate didn't keep her in line. So she'll be rarin' to go by tomorrow, I reckon.'

'Count me in, okay?'

'You betcha, Duke.'

Smiling, Jeremy crouched to open the padlock.

'But lose the bike,' Cowboy told him. 'Never know when we might have to vamoos fast. You don't want to be tied to something like that, you might have to leave it behind.'

'I'll walk, next time.' He pulled the chain free, wrapped it around the seat post, and locked its ends together. Then he rolled his bike backwards out of the rack. 'Maybe we can meet and come down together.'

'Sorry, man. You're okay, but you ain't no Liz.'

'Hey, that's all right. No problem.'

They started off, side by side, Jeremy rolling his bike.

'What is it that you do, anyway?' he asked. 'You know, when you meet over here?'

'Have us some fun.'

'Are you . . . trollers?'

'You got it, Duke. They're the trolls, we're the trollers.'

Jeremy nodded. All his guesses, he realized, had been wrong. Even the crazy ones.

'So what you do,' he said, 'you go hunting for them?'

'Fishing's more like it. Trolling, get it? We just put out the bait. We worm the hook. Tanya makes a right fine worm. One of them comes along and bites, we reel him in. Then we have us some fun with him. Or her.'

'You beat them up, or something?'

'Or something.' Cowboy turned his face towards Jeremy. The brim of his hat hid his eyes, but his mouth was a tight line. 'You got a problem with that?'

'Me? No. Fuck 'em.'

The mouth tipped into a grin. 'Figured you'd see it that way, Duke. I can always tell. I saw the look on your face when that scum on the boardwalk went sucking up to you. You damn near crapped your skivvies.'

'Hey, I wasn't . . .'

'Yeah, man, you were scared brown. But that wasn't all. You looked like you wanted to rip his heart out and shove it up his Rio Grande.'

Jeremy smiled. 'Really?'

'You know it, man. And that's how the rest of us feel. Those maggots, they make your skin crawl and they got no right messing with you. They oughta do us all a favour and crawl in a hole and die.'

'But they don't,' Jeremy said.

'Shit no. What they do, they crawl right up out of their holes and get in your face. "Got a quarter, friend?" Cowboy mimicked in a withered, whiny voice. "Poor me, I ain't had a bite to eat in a week. Can y'spare two-bits?" And you just know the creep's gonna *touch* you if you don't come across with the coins.'

That's just how it is, Jeremy thought. That's *exactly* how it is.

'Know what I say?' Cowboy asked.

'Fuck 'em.'

'I say, "No quarter, troll." Do you know what that means, "no quarter"?'

'He isn't going to get any money off you.'

'More than that, Duke. More than that. No quarter.'

Chapter Ten

'Baxter.'

'Huh? Whuh?'

'Wake up.'

Moaning, he opened his eyes. The motel room was dark. He was lying on his side, Kim's warm body curled against his back. 'What is it?' he mumbled.

'Let's get up,' she whispered, her breath tickling the nape of his neck.

'Huh? It's . . . middle of the night.'

'It's a little after three,' she said.

'Jesus.'

'Let's get up and go out, okay?'

'Go *out*?'

'Down to the beach. We'll have it all to ourselves.'

'You're out of your mind.'

'It'll be neat.'

'Neat. Forget it.'

'Please?' She brushed her lips against his neck. Her hand roamed down his chest and belly, caressing him. 'It'll be so romantic. We'll watch the sun come up.'

'Wrong coast,' he muttered.

'It'll still come up. Okay? It'll be something we'll always remember, you know? Watching the sun come up, our first morning together.'

'This isn't the first.'

'The first as man and wife. I want it to be special.'

'We'd freeze our cans.'

'We'll take a blanket. Okay? Please?' Her hand moved lower and gently pulled him. 'I'll make it worth your while, big fella.'

'Yeah?'

'Yeah,' Kim said. 'So how about it?'

'We must be out of our minds.'

79

'You'll love it, just wait and see.'

The mattress rocked Baxter as she rolled away from him and bounded off the bed. Light hit his eyes, stinging them like soapy water. He squeezed them shut. And felt the covers fly off, leaving him naked and chilled.

'Aw, jeez.'

'Up, up, up,' Kim chirped, grabbing his ankles and dragging his legs towards the bedside. He squinted at her. She was bent over, gazing at him through a soft sway of bangs, a rosy suck mark on her shoulder. When she let go of his legs, he sat up.

'Last one dressed is a rotten egg,' she said.

'Consider me a rotten egg.' He sat there and watched Kim prance over to her open suitcase. Her rump jiggled slightly. It had the same golden tan as her back and legs except for a stark white triangle down the middle.

It'll be cold out there, he told himself. But it will be neat. She's right about that. Something to remember.

Kim stepped into baggy grey sweatpants. She hunched over a little as she knotted the drawstring at her waist. Then she lifted a matching sweatshirt out of her suitcase and turned around. 'You just going to sit there?'

'Admiring the view.'

He watched her breasts rise as her arms went up to pull the sweatshirt over her head. They swayed slightly as she searched for the sleeves. Her hands appeared and plucked the front down. 'View all gone,' she said.

'Shucks.'

She took her hairbrush off the dresser, and went into the bathroom. While she was gone, Baxter put on his own sweatsuit. It was the same as Kim's, but not as old. He'd bought it as a replacement after Kim had moved into his condo and started wearing his sweats on chilly mornings. He was tying his shoes by the time she came out of the bathroom.

He went in and brushed his teeth. On the counter beside the sink was the plastic bottle of suntan oil. After rinsing his mouth, he picked up the bottle and slipped it into the pouch-like pocket of his sweatshirt.

Kim was folding the bed's blanket when he returned. He saw that her shoes were on.

At the dresser, he picked up the room key by its big plastic tag that was printed with the name and address of the motel. He dropped it into his pocket with the suntan oil.

She raised her eyebrows. 'What've you got in there?'

He took out the bottle and showed her.

'Well, now. I see you're getting into the spirit of things.'

'Might as well make the best of it.'

He opened the door and they stepped out onto the balcony. The street in front of the motel was well lighted, but no cars were going by and he saw no one wandering about. The parking lot of the all-night market across the street was deserted.

'Neat, huh?' Kim asked. She put an arm around his back and snuggled against his side. 'It's like we're the only people in the world.'

'They're all snug in bed.'

'We'll be snug on the beach.'

They walked to the end of the balcony and down the flight of stairs and across the motel's parking lot. Though Baxter felt her warmth where her body pressed his, the wind seemed to be seeping through his sweatclothes. He began to shiver, and he gritted his teeth to stop their clicking.

'Poor boy,' Kim said. Stopping at the corner, she shook open the blanket. They draped it across their shoulders and pulled it closed in front. That was a lot better. Kim slipped her hand inside the rear of his pants, and that was better still.

They walked past a bum sleeping huddled against a store wall. Kim's hand stopped roaming.

'Guess we're *not* the only people in the world,' Baxter said.

'Poor man.'

'Yeah. He doesn't have you.'

'We're so lucky. It makes you realize how lucky we are, doesn't it? I mean, wouldn't it be awful to live like that? With nobody who loves you, and no place to go at night?'

'We could offer him the use of our room while we're gone.'

She gently slapped his rump. 'It's nothing to make fun of. I think it's awful. I wish we could do something for him.'

'I didn't bring my wallet. The blanket doesn't belong to us. You might give him the clothes off your back. I'd like that.'

'Horny toad,' she said, and gave him another slap.

They crossed the street and walked alongside the Funland parking lot. A few cars were still there. Baxter wondered if kids might be inside some of them, screwing around. This late? Not likely. Even in his heyday of humping in the backseat of his car, he'd never been out past about two.

Nobody's out at three-thirty.

Just us. And some snoozing bums. Maybe a few patrolling cops.

Cute if we got stopped by the cops.

We're not breaking any laws, he told himself. It only *feels* like it, wandering around at this hour.

'Trespassing on the wrong side of midnight,' he said.

'Huh?'

'Just thinking,' he explained. 'It feels illegal, doing this.' They hurried across Ocean Front Drive, climbed the stairs and entered the shadows beneath the Funland archway. In spite of the blanket, in spite of Kim's hand, Baxter began shivering again as they stepped into the moonlight. He looked up and down the boardwalk.

'What's wrong?' Kim asked.

'I just hope it's safe around here.'

She squeezed his rump. 'Don't be a worry-wart.'

They stopped at the edge of the boardwalk. 'Isn't this great?' she asked.

It didn't look great to Baxter. The familiar beach where he'd lazed in the sun, slicked Kim with oil and gazed out at the warm blue Pacific was gone. The beach looked cold and desolate, like a wasteland at the border of an alien ocean.

He didn't want to go down there.

'I'm not so sure about this anymore,' he said.

'Oh really?' Kim slipped her hand out of his pants and turned to him. She swept the blanket open. Holding it at her shoulder, she raised her sweatshirt above her breasts and eased against him. She lifted his sweatshirt. He felt the warm smoothness of her skin. Her hand crept down into the front of his pants and stroked him.

'Why don't we go back to the motel?' he whispered.

'Why don't we not?'

'I don't like it here.'

'*Feels* like you like it.'

He squirmed.

While she caressed him, he stared past the side of her head. The planks of the boardwalk were moon-bleached bone. The black shadows weren't empty. They were hiding-places.

I'm really getting paranoid, he told himself.

And felt his pants drop down around his ankles. The wind wrapped his bare skin.

'Woops,' Kim said.

He bent over. As he grabbed the top of his pants, Kim tugged the blanket off him and whirled away with it and trotted down the stairs to the beach.

'Damn it, Kim!'

She danced on the sand, spinning and swinging the blanket overhead like a giant flag.

Baxter pulled his drawstring tight and knotted it. He descended the stairs. Not rushing. Watching Kim cavort.

He stepped off the last stair. The sand was soft and silent under his shoes. It pushed this way and that as he walked towards her. He wanted to run at her and grab her and carry her to safety. But if he made quick moves, she would flee, laughing.

He stopped. 'Come here,' he said.

She smiled. She draped the blanket over her shoulders. 'What'll you give me?'

'A kiss.'

'What else?'

'Kim, come on. I mean it. This place gives me the creeps.'

'I think it's neat.'

He made a dash for her.

Kim lurched aside. He grabbed a handful of the blanket, but she got away. Laughing, just as he'd guessed. She ran along the beach, kicking up plumes of sand, angling gradually closer to the dark shadow cast by the boardwalk. Baxter, in pursuit, couldn't rush full speed because of the blanket. He gathered it in as he chased her. Once it was wadded and pinned under his left arm, he began to catch up. But Kim was already far ahead of him.

She looked over her shoulder. In a sing-song voice, she called, 'Slow poke, slow poke, you're so slow it ain't no joke.'

Doesn't she realize?

Realize what? We're alone out here. She's having a good time. *I'm* the one with the problem. But Baxter didn't like the way she was getting closer to the boardwalk, closer to its long shadow and the dark land of pilings below the fun zone.

She glanced back at him again. 'Catch!' she called, and pulled the sweatshirt over her head and tossed it high. The wind snagged the shirt and tossed it towards the shadow. Baxter almost caught a sleeve as it tumbled away. He dodged to the left and snatched it off the sand at the edge of the darkness. He ran a few more strides, then had an idea. He stopped.

'So long, Kim. Have fun walking back to the motel.'

She slowed. She halted. She turned around and put her hands on her hips. Her chest was heaving as she tried to catch her breath. Her breasts rose and fell. The rest of her skin was dusky. Her breasts looked as if they'd been dipped in cream. And the cream had been licked off the nipples, leaving them dark.

Baxter stared at her. She stared back.

'I don't think you're going anywhere,' she said.

The beach seemed no less forbidding than before and Baxter felt as if eyes were watching from the black area under the boardwalk, but Kim was right. He no longer had the urge to escape from this place.

Kim was bare to the waist, exposed and vulnerable.

Baxter wanted her.

He wanted her right here, right now.

Hands still on her hips, Kim ambled towards him.

He glanced into the dark forest of pilings, and shivered, and knew he wouldn't run.

His fear, moments ago crying out warnings to flee, now felt like icy fingers caressing him, tickling and stroking him, the fingers of a phantom whore sick with lust and aching for the party to start.

Kim halted a few paces in front of him.

'You must be freezing,' he said.

'I'm not. Feels good.'

He supposed the running had warmed her up. He no longer felt the cold, himself. The shivers that still shook his body had little to do with the chilly wind.

'Take off the rest,' he said.

In the moonlight, he saw her smile. 'Does this mean you aren't spooked anymore?' she asked.

'Just makes it better.'

Balancing on one foot, she pulled off a shoe and sock. 'I feel so *daring*, don't you?'

Baxter nodded. He glanced into the darkness. The icy fingers of his fear probed him and squeezed.

Kim hopped, her breasts jiggling as she removed the shoe and sock from her other foot. 'You just gonna stand there?' she asked, untying the knot at her waist.

'Yes,' he said.

Her sweatpants fell. She stepped on them to free her feet from the elastic around the cuffs. Then she came to Baxter, but instead of embracing him she took the blanket. She carried it into the boardwalk's shadow. As the darkness closed over her, the fear squeezed Baxter hard, too hard suddenly, no longer a lusting slut but a cruel hag hurting him.

Kim shook the blanket open.

'Not over there,' he said. 'Let's put it here in the moonlight.'

'What if somebody comes along?' Kim asked. 'This is a lot more private.'

'I want to be able to see you.'

'Ah-hah.' She came out, and Baxter's fear eased its clutch. Kim turned her back to the ocean wind. She unfurled the blanket. Squatting, she lowered it to the sand. As she pinned down two of the corners with her shoes, Baxter caught the other end and held it down. He took his shoes off, and used them as weights.

Kim crawled onto the blanket. She lay down. She rolled onto her back and folded her hands beneath her head. 'This is really great,' she said.

'Is it too cold for the oil?' Baxter asked, his voice shaking.

'I want it,' Kim said.

He found the plastic bottle in his pocket. He tossed it onto the blanket at her feet, then took off his socks and sweatsuit. He knelt in front of her.

She lay straight, legs tight together, and where her skin was tanned it was almost the same shade as the sand alongside the dark blanket but bright compared to the shadow just beyond her head. Her hands were still pressed beneath her head, her elbows out to the sides. She squirmed slightly as if relishing the feel of the blanket, or impatient for the touch of his hands.

Baxter popped open the bottle's squirt top. He squeezed a line of oil up Kim's right leg. She flinched and arched her back when the stream crossed her groin, and seemed to relax again as it drew a silver trail down her left leg. Baxter closed the bottle and dropped it. He slid his hands up her skin, spreading the slick film. Its sweet coconut aroma reminded him of cotton candy, smelled good enough to eat, made him want to lick it off her.

Kim's shaven shins were a little bristly, but her thighs felt like silk.

She opened her legs. She moaned and writhed as he rubbed her.

Baxter, leaning forward, roamed her with slippery hands. The look and feel of her was almost too much to bear, and so was the wind. It stroked the backs of his legs, swept between his legs and licked his groin, stole the heat from the cleft of his buttocks, scurried up his back, ruffled his hair.

Hoping to calm himself before it was too late, he rested his hands on Kim's hips and lowered his head and shut his eyes.

She had said it would be neat.

What an understatement.

They'd already made love twice in the motel room before going to sleep. And countless times during the previous months. But it had never been like this.

And they were only beginning. She hadn't even touched him yet.

Should've started with her back, he thought.

He felt Kim's hands. They covered his hands and slid them down between her legs.

He lifted his head. 'Eager beaver,' he said.

She smiled and squirmed and stretched her arms out straight overhead.

He stroked her with his thumbs.

She gasped.

That couldn't have hurt her, he thought, and then she scooted away, thighs sliding under his hands and he thought, *How's she doing that?*

'BAX!' she shrieked.

He looked up.

The shadow of the boardwalk was eating her, sucking her in.

No, not the shadow.

Two vague, hunched shapes dragged Kim by her wrists.

'NO!' he yelled.

She was already gone to the waist. Her moonlit lap bucked and tossed. Her legs kicked.

Baxter caught one flailing ankle. He clutched it with both hands. In spite of the oil, he held onto it. But he didn't stop her. He was dragged along with her, his knees rucking up the blanket and pushing ruts in the sand.

'STOP!' he shouted. 'What're you . . .?'

His voice froze in his throat. Beyond the two attackers, in the darkness under the boardwalk, were others. They scurried out from behind the pilings – bent, ragged shapes – eight of them? Ten?

Baxter released Kim's foot.

The moonlight lost her.

'*Don't leave me!*' she squealed.

Baxter staggered to his feet.

He stood motionless, knowing he had time to flee, then with a growl of fierce despair he rushed into the dark. He hurled himself at the pair dragging Kim. He tore them down. On top of them, he yelled for Kim to run. Bony arms hooked around him. Fingers clawed his skin. Teeth clamped on his arm and thigh. He cried out with pain and punched and tried to push himself up, but the savage things clutched him, bit him. He gagged on their stench.

'Get up! Bax! Quick!'

'Run!' he yelled. Damn her, why hadn't she run? Didn't she see all those others?

Where are the others, he wondered. They should've been on him by now.

He pounded a fist into one of the foul shapes beneath him. This time, he did some damage. The guy wheezed and jerked and released him. He drove an elbow into the midsection of the other.

Suddenly, he was free. On hands and knees, he scurried off their twisting bodies. He looked up and saw Kim.

She had found a club of driftwood. She stood tall in the dark of the shadow, between Baxter and the hideous pack, swinging the wood as if she were Davy Crockett defending a wall of the Alamo with an empty musket. None in the pack seemed brave enough to attack and risk a blow.

Baxter stared at Kim – astonished and proud and afraid.

He struggled to his feet.

And glimpsed a smudge of motion high to his left. He turned his head in time to see a crone leap from the top of the boardwalk's railing. She sailed down, arms out like the wings of a giant bat, black rags flapping. Kim saw her. Tried to leap back. But the hag folded over her, smashed her to the sand.

The silent pack rushed in.

Baxter rushed the pack.

Chapter Eleven

Mag and Charlie shambled out from beneath the boardwalk and made their way towards the stairs.

'No fair,' Charlie said. 'No fair, no fair.'

'Clam up,' said Mag.

'Gonna *miss out*!' he whined.

Mag cuffed his arm.

He grabbed the hurt and stumbled out of reach. 'Gonna miss out!'

'We was picked,' Mag said. 'Sides, we're gonna have us some fun.' She waved the motel key at him and grinned.

'I wanna be in on it.'

'Well, you ain't.'

'No fair.'

They climbed the stairs. As they scuffed across the board-walk, Charlie heard a faint, muffled scream. He knew it came from the Funhouse. Without him. Moaning, he punched the side of his head.

'Hey.'

He scowled at Mag. She dug into a pocket of her coat, pulled out a pint bottle and offered it to him. He snatched it from her hand. A couple of hits, and he felt a little better.

Still wasn't fair, though.

He took another tug at the bottle, then reached it back towards Mag.

She waved it away. 'G'on, keep it,' she said. 'I got more.'

Whenever he saw Mag around, she seemed to be equipped with a fresh bottle. And it was usually good Scotch, not cheap wine. He didn't know what her story was, but figured maybe she got disability pay. She didn't seem crippled up, but she might've pulled a cheat on the state. That would explain her riches. Disability was a lot more than general relief, maybe three times as much. On the other hand, maybe she had some money put away. Or she might just be better at begging. He'd seen her at it, now and again, and she never outright asked for money. All she did was look her marks in the eye and say, 'God bless you,' and more often than not they'd fork over some change.

Charlie kept the bottle and worked on it, and it was good stuff. It heated him up. It gave him a buzz. By the time he finished the bottle, he was following Mag up the stairway to the motel's balcony.

She unlocked the door of room 210, and they stepped inside. Charlie shut the door. Mag flicked a wall switch, and a lamp came on beside the bed.

'Land,' she said, 'ain't this the berries, though?'

Charlie stood by the door and watched while she wandered the room. She seemed awfully chipper about being here. She found a wine bottle in the wastebasket and upended it, dribbling the last few drops into her mouth. On the dresser was a pack of Salems. She shook a cigarette out, stuck it between her lips and fired it with a match. She ran her hands over the bed. Plucking the cigarette from her mouth, she picked up a pillow and rubbed her face with it. She stopped at each of the open suitcases and inspected what was inside. Then, she went into the bathroom.

She didn't come out.

From where he stood, Charlie couldn't see what she was doing in there. Maybe she'd found something good. He hobbled forward and stopped when he spied her through the doorway.

Mag's coat was a heap on the floor. She stood behind it, unbuttoning the front of her sweater. The cigarette hung from a corner of her lips, its ribbon of smoke curling into one eye and making her squint. She got the sweater off, dropped it onto her coat, and started fumbling with the buttons of her old plaid shirt.

'What're y'doing?' Charlie asked.

'Mind yer own beezwax.'

'I wanta go.'

'Tough toenails.'

'I'm gonna miss out.'

'You already missed out. Stop your bellyaching.'

He guessed she was right. Even if they left right now, it would all be over by the time they got back. 'No fair,' he muttered.

'This here's your first clean-up,' Mag said. 'You oughta be happy you ducked it this long.'

'Poop,' Charlie said.

Mag scowled at him, and pulled her shirt off. She wore a grey sweatshirt. She started lifting that, and Charlie caught a glimpse of grey skin blotchy with sores and scabs. He turned away fast.

Mag giggled. 'Oooo, Charlie's shy.'

'Ain't neither,' he said. But he didn't look again. He crawled onto the bed and flopped. The sheet felt smooth and good against his face. It smelled nice, too. He supposed it smelled from the woman they got. Oh, she was sure something, and he was missing all the fun.

He heard water start to splash, heard the skidding clink of a shower curtain.

He closed his eyes.

'Hey! Looky here.'

He woke up, rolled over and saw Mag in front of the dresser, facing him. She wore a low-cut white nightie that he could see right through and wished he couldn't. A string of pearls hung against her bony, mottled chest. There were rings on her fingers, bracelets on her wrists, and pearl earrings on each ear. The lobes of her ears dripped blood onto her shoulders. Her lips were red and glossy. She was grinning at Charlie with brown stubs of teeth as she drew a brush through her long black hair.

'Ain't I the purty one?' she asked.

'Like a whore that's three weeks dead,' he told her.

Her eyes bugged out. She hurled the brush. It clopped Charlie over the left eye. As he dropped onto the bed, she rushed at him, squealing. He rolled away and curled up, hugging his head. The mattress rocked him as she leaped onto it.

'No-count cockless bag of shit!' she cried out.

Charlie yelped and whimpered as she pranced on the mattress, kicking and stomping him, as she sat on him and yanked his hair and rapped his head with sharp knuckles. Finally, she left him alone. But he didn't move.

When he heard her weeping, he sat up.

Mag was sprawled on the carpet, hands tight against her face.

He got up and went to her.

He kicked her in the ribs.

'Even-Steven,' he muttered.

She just stayed there sobbing while Charlie gathered up the man's clothes and toiletries and took them to the suitcase.

In a pants pocket, he found a wallet with almost three hundred dollars tucked inside the bill compartment. He didn't dare take any of the twenties. He'd be in trouble, sure, if he tried that. A few months back Edgar'd been on clean-up and the next day Nasty Nancy spied him paying for a quart of bourbon with a ten-dollar bill. When you went on clean-up, it was okay to keep clothes. But nothing else.

Edgar claimed he found his ten on the beach. Nobody bought the story, though, and they'd made him 'walk the house.'

Charlie fingered through the money again. Along with the twenties and a few tens in the man's wallet, there were eight one-dollar bills. Charlie thought he might take a chance on some of those. Who's to say he didn't get them from some generous marks?

He glanced over his shoulder at Mag. She had rolled onto her side, and her head was turned away from him.

Nobody'd ever know.

But suddenly, his last sight of Edgar filled his head and Charlie shuddered, legs going weak and shaky, scrotum shrinking tight, ice in his stomach, gooseflesh crawling up his spine.

With trembling hands, he closed the wallet and slipped it

into the pocket of the man's pants. In a front pocket, he found a key case. He kept that, and put the pants inside the suitcase.

As he shut the suitcase, Mag came up beside him. He cringed and raised his arms to protect himself, but she didn't strike.

'Let me in there,' she said. Charlie stepped back. She brushed past him and stepped to the corner near the wall. There, she opened the woman's suitcase. She peeled the nightie off. Charlie squeezed his eyes shut. 'Damn fool,' she muttered. When he opened them again, she had pink shiny panties on, and was stepping into a pair of green slacks. She fastened the slacks. Grinning at Charlie, she lifted a black bra out of the suitcase and draped it over his face. Then she lifted out a green pullover sweater. She put it on. Sighing, she rubbed it against her belly and hanging breasts. 'Nice,' she said. 'You get yourself some nice duds, Charlie.'

'I like what I got,' he told her.

'Damn fool.' She unclasped the pearl necklace and dropped it into the suitcase. She tossed in the rings. She took the earrings from her bloody lobes. Charlie saw that the earrings were for pierced ears, and hers weren't pierced. At least they hadn't been. They were, now.

She took white socks and tennis shoes from the suitcase, put them on, then went to the closet and came out wearing the woman's nylon windbreaker. She retrieved her clothes from the bathroom, and stuffed them into the suitcase. After that, she wandered around gathering the rest of the woman's things.

'You got the keys?' she asked.

Charlie held up the key case. She plucked it from his hands.

They latched the luggage, and Mag went to the door. Charlie lifted both suitcases off their stands. He followed her outside.

In the east, the sky was pale. But the sun wouldn't be up for a while, yet. From the balcony's height, he had a good view. He saw no one. The street in front of the motel was deserted. There were about ten cars in the parking lot.

Mag hurried ahead of him. He struggled along with the heavy suitcases. By the time he came to the bottom of the stairs, Mag had already found the car to match her key. It was a blue BMW. She opened the trunk while Charlie hurried across the parking lot.

He swung the suitcases into the trunk.

Mag, in the driver's seat, leaned over and unlocked the passenger door for him. He climbed inside. The car smelled new.

Its engine thundered to life. Mag backed it up, then swung it towards the exit.

'How 'bout a ride?' Mag asked, gunning it onto the street.

'I wanna get back,' Charlie said.

'Yer too late for the fun.'

Maybe not, he thought. 'I don' care,' he told her.

She muttered something that Charlie couldn't make out. But she took him towards Funland, the car weaving a little as she raced it up the middle of the street and sped through the blinking red traffic light. She stopped it with a hard lurch that flung him at the dashboard.

'You take the stuff,' she told him.

She gave him the keys. He opened the trunk and removed the suitcases. Then he stepped to her window and handed back the keys.

'What're y'gonna do?' he asked.

Mag grinned at him. 'Take her for a spin. Don't ya fret, fool, I'll leave the thing a good ways off.'

The car squealed, laying rubber, and shot away, heading north.

Charlie picked up the suitcases.

He lugged them up the stairs to the boardwalk.

He wondered how long they'd been gone. Too long, probably. The fun was sure to be over by now.

Never know, though.

Sometimes it lasted pretty long.

He quickened his pace.

Chapter Twelve

Robin crawled out of her sleeping bag. The morning was grey with fog. Shivering, she sat on the nylon bag. She searched her pack, took out fresh underwear and socks, her blue jeans and sleeveless shirt. She swept her eyes over the tops of the dunes surrounding her encampment. She saw nobody, and the sand was piled high enough to conceal her from anyone who might be near by.

Quickly, she slipped the folded money out of the front of the underpants she was wearing. She tucked the bills into the front pocket of her jeans. Then, she took off the T-shirt and panties she'd slept in, and put on the clothes from her pack.

She had used her rolled windbreaker for a pillow. She picked it up, uncovering the sheathed knife that lay on her ground cloth. Once she had the windbreaker on, her shivers subsided.

She slipped the knife into a side pocket of her pack.

Then she put on her hiking boots. The chill of them seeped through her socks, but her body heat quickly warmed them.

She stood up and climbed the sand slope. From the top, she had a clear view of the rolling, grass-tufted dunes and the flat beach stretching out to the ocean. Gulls whirled and swooped through the grey air. A man was running along the shore, his black lab trotting at his side. Far down the beach, in the area near Funland, a man was hunting for treasure with the help of a metal detector. Even farther away, surfers stood around in their wetsuits and others were on the water – some riding in on combers, but most of them either paddling out, belly down on their boards, or already way out on the rolling slate of the sea, legs dangling, roosting there as if content to sit.

Her attention strayed from the surfers as she noticed someone descending the main stairs from the boardwalk. A woman in a white sweatshirt and red shorts, a satchel swinging at her side. She was a long way off.

Those were the stairs that Robin had gone down last night, and she was amazed that she had walked so far.

The kid by the ticket booth had really spooked her. The kid, and his friends who hadn't shown up yet. They had to be trollers. Why else would they be meeting there at that hour?

Robin looked the other way.

She had put just about as much distance as possible between herself and the kid. No more than forty or fifty feet ahead, a chainlink fence marked the end of the public beach. Beyond it, set far back from the shore, stood somebody's house.

The tide was in, now, waves washing past the end of the fence. Last night, she could've stepped around that post without getting her feet wet, and taken refuge beyond the barrier. But she'd been reluctant to trespass.

Her place in the dunes, she thought, had been fine.

The kid's hadn't found her there.

She wondered if they'd tried.

'Now there's as fair a maiden as ever claimed a heart.'

Robin whirled around. The man stood on the crest of the dune behind her camp site. A bum. Fat and old and wearing soiled clothes, a knobby staff in one hand. She felt squirmy inside as she wondered how long he'd been watching her. Had he been hiding, spying on her while she dressed?

'Professor E. A. Poppinsack,' he said, doffing his hat. The hat was a faded brown bowler. Red feathers, tucked into the band on each side, stuck up like wings. He was bald, but he had a thick moustache with ends that curled up in points. He wore a dirty buckskin jacket, fringe swinging in the breeze, and plaid pants that looked more suited to a golfer roaming the links than a bum on the beach. 'Top of the morning to you, dear. Have a spot of tea?'

Robin shook her head. 'Sorry,' she told him. 'I don't have any.'

'Ah, but I have. Join me, won't you? Let us sit upon the ground and tell sad tales of the deaths of kings.' Without waiting for a reply, the man turned away and descended the slope. He held his staff high. Its tip twirled a bit when he was out of sight.

Odd bird, Robin thought. But she'd liked the merry twinkle in his eyes, and he'd seemed harmless enough. His outfit made him look, somehow, like a medicine man – the kind of fellow who might have wandered into frontier towns, hawking elixir from the back of his wagon.

Curious, she followed him over the dunes. His encampment was directly behind hers, forty or fifty feet further inland, in a depression surrounded by high drifts of sand.

'Welcome to my estate,' said Poppinsack. He gestured to his rolled sleeping bag. Robin sat down on it. The old man crouched over the pot of boiling water on his propane stove, and added water from a canteen.

'All the comforts of home,' Robin said.

'Indeed, unencumbered by the nuisances of the mortgage, tax, insurance and utilities. God provides, Poppinsack abides.' He fetched tea bags from the bulging pocket of his buckskin coat, turned off the flame beneath the pot of boiling water, and plopped in the two bags – along with their strings and paper tabs. 'Shall we allow that to steep for a bit?' he asked.

He lowered himself onto a nearby slope. 'Are you a Puck or a Pip?'

'A Robin.'

'Ah, Cock Robin. Cockless, as the case may be.'

The remark unsettled her. Maybe this man wasn't just a harmless eccentric.

'Born to be hanged, mayhap, but not hung. Words. Words are Poppinsack's passion. The music of the mind. Twenty-six letters, infinite realms.'

'I write some poetry myself,' Robin told him, relaxing somewhat. 'Songs.'

His eyes lit up. 'A bard?' He slapped his knees, and dust popped from the faded plaid of his pants. 'We're kinsmen, then. Sing me a song.'

Smiling, Robin shrugged. 'I don't have my banjo.'

'Fetch it, then, and sing for your tea.'

'Why not.' She got up and hurried off. Descending the sand bank to her camp, she was struck by the close proximity of the two sleeping places. She wondered whether Poppinsack had been aware, all night, of her presence. If so, he hadn't tried anything. She realized that she felt more comforted than troubled by knowing he'd been near by.

She hadn't been completely alone, after all.

If the trollers had found her, would Poppinsack have come blustering to her rescue, brandishing his staff?

Banjo case in hand, she returned to his 'estate'. She took out the instrument and sat on his bedroll.

'Was it you I heard yesterday?' Poppinsack asked.

'It might've been. I was playing on the boardwalk.'

'While I played words on the strand.'

'Played words?' she asked.

'Beowulf, Tennessee Williams, Mickey Spillane. Smitting Grendel, flying with the bird that never lands, plugging a dame in the guts. "It was easy." And you my dear, performed the background score. It's a pleasure to make your acquaintance. Now, sing me a song.'

'There's a new one I've been working on. I'll test it out on you.'

Smiling, Poppinsack closed his eyes, folded his hands on the lap of his buckskin coat, and leaned back against the sand.

Robin's fingers flew over the banjo strings, lifting out a quick, spangled tune. After running once through the melody, she started to sing:

> Darling, I've been here and I've been there
> And I've been next to nowhere.
> I've been upside down, and inside out,
> Topsy-turvey and tossed about.
> I've been flying high, and crashing low.
> I laugh and cry wherever I go –
> And it's all from looking for you,
> And it's all from looking for you.
>
> You ain't got a face and you ain't got a name,
> But I'm gonna find you just the same.

I'll know you by your swaggering walk
And the way I tremble when you talk.
You're the guy with the sunlight in your eyes,
With the laugh that makes my goosebumps rise –
And I'll keep looking for you,
And I'll keep looking for you.

You're the moon and stars and the sunlit sea,
And yabba-dabba doo and diddly dee,
I ain't writ more so I gots to stop.
Boppity hoppity dibbidy dop.

Nodding and grinning, Poppinsack applauded. 'Minstrel girl,' he said. 'The Robin is a bardling sure. "Laugh that makes my goosebumps rise", oh dear.'

'You think that line sucks?' she asked.

'Fetching. *You're* fetching. And I shall fetch the tea.' He pushed himself off the sand, went to his duffle bag and searched inside it. After a few moments, he came up with a glove and two plastic mugs. Wearing the glove on his hand, he poured steaming tea into one of the mugs and brought it to Robin. He smelled as if he'd doused himself with cologne, but under its sweet aroma lurked a dark, musty odour. Purple capillaries webbed his cheeks. His veiny, bulbous nose was so pitted that it reminded Robin of a huge strawberry decomposing. Trapped in the hairs of his moustache were bits of old meals.

Poppinsack, she decided, looked better at a distance.

'Care for cream?' he asked.

'You have cream?'

'Not a drop. Care for a dollop of rum?' he asked, and pulled a plastic flask from a pocket of his coat.

'Thanks, anyway.'

He filled a mug for himself, splashed some rum in, and returned to his seat on the dune's slope.

Robin inspected her tea. She was glad to find nothing afloat in it. She took a sip. 'Good,' she said.

Poppinsack drank from his mug, sighed and smacked his

lips. 'Tell me, minstrel girl, what curse has brought you to this blighted beach?'

'I'm just wandering, seeing the world.'

'Fleeing from what, and whom?'

She shook her head. 'What makes you think I'm fleeing from something?'

'Your hurt and haunted eyes.'

'You're nuts.'

'I've seen all things in the heaven and in the earth. I've seen many things in hell. How, then, am I nuts?'

'Poe, right?'

'Mercifully butchered. And what tale has your heart to tell?'

She saw no reason to keep the truth from Poppinsack. 'My father died. My mother had a fiancé more interested in me. I hit the road. End of story.'

'And how have you fared on the road?'

'I'm still kicking,' Robin said. 'What's your story?'

'To outmatch the wit of your brevity, I am a book bum.'

'Are you really a professor?'

'I have ceased to profess. 'Tis far more pleasurable indeed to horde pearls than to cast them before swine.'

'So you gave up teaching and now you read all the time?'

He nodded and drank his spiked tea.

'How long have you been here in Boleta Bay?'

'Forever and a day.'

'Aren't you afraid of the trollers?'

He gazed at Robin and lifted his thick grey eyebrows. 'Are you not afraid of the *trolls*?'

'We're trolls, aren't we? I mean, I guess the kids might think so.'

'Thar be trolls and thar be trolls,' Poppinsack said, sounding a lot like Robert Newton playing Long John Silver. 'Thar be them that's harmless, and thar be them that ain't. Poppinsack could tell such tales of madness as would turn a wench's blood cold and freeze the chambers of her heart.'

Robin wrinkled her face at him. 'You trying to scare me, or what?'

'You're a roving bard and minstrel,' he said, dropping the pirate growl. 'You're a smart dame, and long on moxey. But under it all, you're a kid and you don't know the score.'

'Maybe I know more than you think. I've been around some.'

'And have you been God's spy in the court of the damned?'

'Whatever that means,' she muttered.

'Hie thee away from here. Take a powder, hit the road, ride your thumb to Frisco or LA, hop on a bus to Palookaville.' And in a voice suddenly void of borrowed rhetoric, he said, 'Get the hell out of town, Robin. If you stick around, you might just disappear.'

She stared at him.

'Everybody knew Cock Robin. Nobody knows where she's gone.'

'You really are scaring me.'

'The robin that flies today won't be a dead duck tomorrow.'

'If it's so dangerous around here,' she asked, 'why do you stay?'

'Why, indeed? Perhaps because the mermaids sing to me.' Poppinsack finished his tea. 'Farewell,' he said.

Robin nodded. 'My cue to exit?' she asked.

'Your company has been much appreciated. Heed my warning and flee.'

'I think I will,' she told him. 'This place gives me the creeps, anyway, and you're about the fourth person to warn me so far.' She drank the last of her tea, set the mug down on the ground, and closed her banjo case. 'Thanks for the tea,' she said, standing up.

'And I thank you for the song.'

With a wave, she turned away and climbed the dune out of the Poppinsack's encampment.

In a coffee shop two blocks east of the boardwalk, Robin ate a breakfast of fried eggs, sausage links, hash browns, and toast. While she worked on the meal, her mind kept straying back to the strange old man and his warnings.

Evil trolls. Disappearances. The court of the damned.

101

Weird stuff. But he might've made it up, just wanting to scare her away. Maybe he felt that she had invaded his territory, or something. Perhaps he simply enjoyed scaring people.

But he'd seemed a little spooked, himself.

Maybe he believed what he'd told her, but none of it had any basis in reality. After all, he was a boozer.

Whether or not the stuff was true, Robin's experiences with trolls last night had been unnerving, and the kids were an actual threat.

Reason enough to blow this town.

When she finished eating, she picked up the tab. Breakfast had cost $4.80. She pulled the pack of money from her jeans pocket and folded it open.

She spread the bills.

Her mouth fell open. Her stomach sank.

She looked through the stack again and again.

Every bill was a one.

Yesterday, after leaving the downtown bank, six of them had been twenties, one a ten.

She'd been robbed?

Impossible.

She'd kept the money in her front pocket. Her jeans were tight. Nobody had ever come close enough to sneak the money out, much less remove the high denominations, replace them with ones, and slip the pack of bills back into her pocket.

She remembered paying for dinner. She remembered buying the movie ticket. She'd used the ten for the ticket, and the twenties were still there when she folded the dollars that came as change.

After leaving the movie theatre, she'd given a buck to the bum on the street. He certainly hadn't pulled the switch. Then, the money had stayed in her pocket until after she took her jeans off. She remembered sitting on her sleeping bag, shivering as she stripped and put on her T-shirt and panties. She hadn't looked at the money, then. She'd stuffed her hand into the pocket, pulled out the folded bills, and slipped them under her waist band. After that, she put her clothes in the pack and crawled into her sleeping bag. She could remember the feel of the money against her skin.

This morning, the pack of bills was where she had left it. She remembered taking it out and putting it into her jeans. Later, she'd been close to no one but Poppinsack, and he hadn't touched her. He couldn't have pulled the switch.

But someone had.

Between last night at the movie theatre and right now in the coffee shop, somebody had taken her money, substituted singles for twenties, and returned it to her.

And there was only one possible time when it could've been done.

While she slept.

I slept in the movie theatre, she thought. It might've happened then.

But she doubted it. There'd been quite a lot of people in the theatre. Who would've dared trying to rob her in front of so many witnesses? And even if someone tried, he never could've worked a hand into the pocket of her jeans while she was sitting up like that. Not without waking her. The jeans were just too tight.

No. As much as she wanted to believe the robbery had taken place in the movie theatre, she knew it hadn't.

The money was taken after she'd bedded down for the night.

In spite of the restaurant's warmth, chills crawled up Robin's back. She squeezed her legs together. She saw Poppinsack kneeling beside her in the dark, sliding open the zipper of her sleeping bag, maybe after already searching her boots and pack and guessing that whatever money she might have was kept on her body. She imagined his hands roaming over her while she slept, not just seeking the money but feeling her up, finally a hand slipping inside her panties and taking out the bills and touching her there, too.

Cockless Robin.

The dirty bastard.

And he gave me tea and I sang for him, and all the time he had my money and *he knew what he'd done to me.*

Robin's face burned. Her heart pounded. She trembled.

He robbed me and groped me while I slept, and then he pretended to be my friend.

So much for his warnings to leave town.

Hoping I'll be gone before I find out what he did.

She left her tip on the table, shouldered her pack and picked up her banjo case, and went to the front counter. After paying the cashier, she had only seven dollars.

She stepped outside.

Wouldn't dare leave town now, she thought, even if I wanted to.

Seven dollars was as good as nothing. That short, she'd be too vulnerable on the road.

Feverish with humiliation and outrage, she strode towards the boardwalk.

Funland hadn't opened yet, but workers were there getting ready for the crowd. Down on the beach, clean-up crews were dumping trash barrels and raking débris out of the sand. A few bums were also going through yesterday's litter. But not Poppinsack.

Several joggers were out, running along the shore. A man in leotards was doing a peculiar routine that looked like slow-motion ballet. A little kid was on her knees, parents watching, father snapping photos while she dug in the sand. There were no sunbathers; there was no sun. The surfers were gone. No one was in the water. The lifeguard was at her station, anyway. She wore red shorts and a white sweatshirt.

She was the one Robin had seen earlier.

Just before Poppinsack surprised her.

Robin trudged on. She left them all behind. Finally, forty or fifty feet from the chainlink fence marking the boundary of the public beach, she turned away from ocean. She climbed up and down the dunes.

In a sheltered depression, she set her banjo case on the sand and slung the pack off her back. She took her knife from the pack and slipped it into a rear pocket of her jeans.

He'll deny it, she thought. What're you going to do, cut him up?

We'll see.

Damn it, nobody messes with me!

She found the place where she had slept, where Poppinsack had crept up on her in the night and . . . *handled* her.

From there, she knew where to find him.

She rushed over the dunes. Charging up the last slope, she jerked the knife from its sheath.

And then she reached the top.

He was gone. All that remained were two sodden brown tea bags lying in the sand.

Chapter Thirteen

Jeremy climbed down the stairs to the beach. The sun had broken through, back around noon, and a lot of gals were sprawled out, sunbathing. But they held no interest for him. His eyes swung towards the lifeguard station.

She was there.

Tanya.

Even at this distance, he recognized Tanya by her size and curves, her tanned legs and golden hair.

The sight of her made him ache.

He wished he could go to her, take her in his arms, kiss her, feel her body pressed against his.

I can at least go over and say hi, he told himself. Tell her I was here last night, and how Cowboy came to let me know it was off. Yeah, I could say that. Maybe we'll chat a while.

But he didn't move. He couldn't force himself to take even one step closer.

He gritted his teeth hard.

Such a goddamn chicken.

If I only knew her better. Maybe after we've done one of these trolling things together. Then it'll be like we're buddies.

He climbed back up the stairs to the boardwalk. Cowboy had said to meet him here this afternoon, but hadn't been specific about the time. Jeremy turned in a circle, trying to spot his friend.

He suspected that Cowboy was somewhere along the south end of the boardwalk. The good rides and attractions, including Liz's dunk tank, were in that direction. But Jeremy hadn't seen much of the north end. He had all afternoon to find Cowboy, so he headed that way.

The people passing near him looked much the same as those he'd seen yesterday: many were sleazy; plenty were slobs; there were tough guys and rowdies; he saw wild groups of teenagers; there were a few, but only a few, people who looked harmless and well-groomed and nicely dressed. Those were mostly couples and families. Probably on vacation.

Yesterday, before meeting Cowboy, he'd felt intimidated by the assortment of unsavoury characters. But not today. Though he was alone, he didn't *feel* alone. He knew he had friends nearby. Not just Cowboy, but Liz in the dunk tank, Tanya out on the beach, even teenagers who were strangers to him but probably were friends of Cowboy or the others, and therefore almost like Jeremy's own friends, though they didn't know him.

He felt as if he belonged.

And then he heard the distant tinny strains of banjo music. The music came from somewhere ahead, past the pavilion.

Did it come, he wondered, from the bitch who'd snapped at him last night?

He kept walking, and the music grew strong.

Ahead, up near the end of the boardwalk, an audience was clustered around the musician. Or musicians – it sounded like more than one. Did she have friends? Where were they last night?

What if she recognizes me and sicks them on me?

I didn't do anything to her.

Her friends won't dare try anything, he told himself. There are too many people around.

Jeremy reached the outer edge of the audience. He side-stepped until he found a gap.

She was playing alone.

'Battle Hymn of the Republic'? At first, it seemed to be. Then it was turned into 'Dixie'. Then, 'When Johnny Comes Marching Home' worked its way into a tune that was a mix of all three.

The bitch was good.

And good to look at. Kind of boyish, but feminine, too. Her arms were bare. Her faded blue shirt was unbuttoned partway down, showing a narrow strip of her chest.

A final flourish, and the song ended. People clapped and yelled. Some stepped forward to toss money into her banjo case. Jeremy was ready to duck if she should look in his direction, but she kept her head down, her eyes low.

When she raised her head, he slipped behind a tall man.

'Here's a piece I composed myself,' she said. 'You might call it an anti-war song . . . or you might not.'

She started playing. Jeremy eased over and peered at her. She was gazing straight ahead, off to his right, at about the same spot where she'd kept her eyes during the last number.

She began to sing along with the quick pounding music of the banjo.

> It's the greatest weenie roast
> That the world has ever seen –
> We got fires coast to coast,
> In our hair and in our jeans.
> We got hot lemonade,
> And we sure got fries.
> Though we ain't got shade,
> We got crisp cherry pies.
> We got steamy watermelon

And marshmallows, too –
If you're willin'
There's plenty to drink and chew.

So grab yourself a weenie and join in the fun
And for Godsake don't burn your buns.

Sick, Jeremy thought. But some of the people in the audience laughed and hooted as if they thought it was funny.

Though the song went on, he had heard enough. He moved away from the crowd and hurried back down the boardwalk.

She was a bitch, all right. Making fun of nuclear war. He wished he'd stood up to her last night. Slugged her in the face and thrown her down.

Ripped her shirt open.

Not so tough now, are you, honey?

How do you like *this* weenie?

Maybe she'd write a song about how much fun it is getting the shit kicked out of you and raped.

Almost as if reading his mind – or maybe just troubled by the look on his face – a female cop fixed her eyes on Jeremy. She was coming towards him. A man was with her. They both wore white T-shirts, blue caps and shorts. Except for their gunbelts, he wouldn't have guessed they were cops.

She nodded as the guy talked to her, but she didn't take her eyes off Jeremy.

What is she, psychic?

Trying to be casual about it, he turned his head away.

She's going to stop me, he thought.

His face felt hot. His heart pounded. He felt shaky inside.

I didn't *do* anything!

She walked right past him.

He sighed.

He gave her a few seconds, then looked over his shoulder. Her face was turned towards the other cop.

Stupid bitch, he thought. Why'd she want to stare at me like that?

Good-looking, though, for a cop. He realized that she looked a lot like Tanya. The hair hanging below her cap had the same golden colour. Her back was just as broad, her legs as tanned and strong.

She could almost be Tanya's older sister. Or her mother.

Her mother. Fat chance.

Besides, the cop was too young for that.

He saw the straps of her bra through the T-shirt. Lowering his eyes, he watched the way her buttocks moved inside the blue shorts.

He wished he hadn't been so quick to look away when she'd been approaching. He'd only noticed her eyes. He would've liked to check out her front.

Someone wandered in behind her, blocking Jeremy's view.

He sidestepped, trying to see her again, but it was no use.

'Hey, amigo.'

He swung around and grinned. 'Hey, man, you're always sneaking up on me.'

'Scoping out the local fuzz?'

'She's got a nice ass,' Jeremy said, and started following Cowboy down the boardwalk.

'A nice everything, Duke.'

'You know her?'

'Officer Delaney. Seems okay. She's just been on the board-walk a couple weeks.'

'Is she actual police?' he asked. 'Or just some kind of a rent-a-cop?'

'The real McCoy. This here's a public park. Patrolled by the BBPD, not some rinky-dink private security outfit.'

'Not even a night watchman or anything?'

'Nope. Just the local fuzz. Matter of fact, makes it easy for us. All we do is post a lookout and scram if a patrol car shows up. Which ain't all that often. The cops on graveyard, seems like they spend most of their time at the doughnut shop.'

'So, they've never caught any of you?'

'Never come close,' Cowboy said. 'Hey, check it out.' He stopped walking and nodded to the right, where people were leaving the fenced area in front of the Tilt-a-Whirl. Through the gate staggered a slim girl clinging to the arm of her boyfriend as if she were too dizzy to stand on her own. Jeremy guessed they were both about twenty years old. She wore blue jeans shorts, cut off so high they had no legs at all. The side that he could see had a slit running up to her belt. Her T-shirt had been chopped off, half-way down. It was long enough to cover her breasts, but not by much, and the ragged edge hung inches away from her body.

She looked hard, though. Her hair, bleached white, stuck out in all directions. Her earrings were red feathers. Her lipstick was silver. She snapped gum.

Her boyfriend looked twice as hard. He wore motorcycle boots and faded jeans. He had a knife case on his belt. He was shirtless, tanned and muscular. A dagger wrapped by a snake was tattooed on his chest. From his earlobe dangled something that looked like a miniature set of handcuffs.

Outside the Tilt-a-Whirl's gate, those two turned around and waited for another couple.

The next guy looked wiry and mean. He had a Mohawk haircut, dyed purple. He wore a brass band around his neck, another on his upper arm, and a brass earring. He was bare to the waist and wore black leather pants. He had no tattoo that Jeremy could see, but he wore a knife case just like his friend.

The girl at his side had a shaved head. Her thin black eyebrows, curving upwards, reminded Jeremy of Ming the Merciless. He could see her nipples through her tank-top. They were big dark discs. The fabric jutted out as if being poked by fingertips. Her breasts seemed much too large for her small frame. The front of her shirt swayed and bobbed as she walked. It was tucked into a black leather mini-skirt. She wore black boots that reached nearly to her knees.

'Now there's a couple of gals I wouldn't kick outa the bunk bed,' Cowboy said, and started following the group down the boardwalk.

'I bet they bite.'

'Yeah, bite me, babes. Oooo.' Cowboy walked fast, staying close behind them. 'How about the bald one?'

Jeremy wanted to warn him to keep voice down.

'Chrome-dome.'

'They're gonna hear you.'

'Check out those butts. Swish, swish, swish.'

The group angled to the left, and Cowboy hurried after them. They stopped in front of a sideshow called Jasper's Oddities. A bony old man, standing on a platform by the entrance, swept the top hat off his head and leered down at them.

'Step right in, folks. See the amazing, astonishing wonders of Jasper's Oddities. Right this way, folks. Don't miss out. See the two-headed baby, the hairless orang-utan of Borneo, the mummy Ram Cho-tep, and other rare and mysterious wonders. Yes, sirs, step right in. Bring in the ladies. They'll quiver and shake at the sights. They'll swoon in your arms. Step right in, folks. Three tickets is all it takes. You couldn't ride the Hurricane for that. Three tickets each, cheap at any price. See the Oddities, collected by yours truly, Jasper Dunn, world explorer and renowned connoisseur of the truly bizarre. Never before on the continent of North America has such a collection been offered under one roof. Offered for your perusal and delight. Step right in, folks.'

'Bet it's a rip-off,' Mohawk said to his friends in a voice loud enough for Jasper to hear. The old man grinned. He was missing a front tooth. 'Me, I went in a freak show one time, all it had was fucking pictures of the dudes.'

'I assure you,' Jasper said, 'my exhibits are genuine. And in days gone by, when yours truly had a freak show, each and every specimen was present in the flesh, remarkable and hideous beyond your wildest fantasies. They, alas, are no more. The honourable folks of this fine town prevailed, and the freaks were cast out like the spoiled garbage of yesterday's meal. However, their memory is preserved in the Gallery of the Weird, a truly astounding collection of photographs which you may see when you enter Jasper's Oddities.'

Mohawk's head bobbed up and down. 'What'd I tell you, fucking *pictures*.'

'You are in error, young man. The only photographs are those you'll see in the Gallery of the Weird. Each and every oddity is authentic, there for you to gaze upon – and touch, if you dare.'

'Let's go for it,' said the tattooed guy. 'What'd you say?' he asked his girlfriend.

She shrugged. Her half-shirt rose with her shoulders, a frail curtain that lifted briefly and gave Jeremy a glimpse of the pale underside of her breast. 'I'm kinda hungry,' she said. Her voice sounded low and husky.

'Yeah,' said the hairless one. 'Let's get some fries.'

Jasper raised a hand. 'Did I mention that today is Ladies' Day? The young women enter for absolutely no charge, no charge whatsoever, absolutely free with the paid admission of their escorts . So step right up. See the Oddities. Right this way.' He swept his top hat towards the open door behind him.

'Yeah, I'm doing it,' said the tattooed guy. He dug some tickets out of his pocket. 'Come on, Jingles.' He grabbed the girl's arm and pulled her towards the stairs.

Mohawk took out some tickets, too.

'And how about *you*?' Jasper asked, his watery eyes turning to Jeremy and Cowboy.

'We're in,' Cowboy called.

Jeremy's stomach went cold. 'I don't know,' he muttered.

'Chicken?'

I'm not a chicken, he told himself. 'I haven't got any tickets,' he said.

'That's okay,' Cowboy said. 'I got plenty.'

He'd wanted to watch Jingles in the half-shirt climb the stairs, but she was already at the top by the time he looked. He saw only her back as she followed her boyfriend through the doorway. The girl in the leather skirt was still climbing the stairs, but Mohawk blocked the view and he missed his chance to see up her skirt.

Jeremy realized that he didn't really care. He wouldn't have enjoyed the peeks, anyway. Not now. Not knowing that he had to enter Jasper's Oddities.

Jasper gave him the creeps.

He didn't want to see the weird stuff inside.

Even though the girls wore such scanty clothes and so much showed, he didn't want to be in a confined place with those weirdos.

But he couldn't let Cowboy think he was chicken.

He went up the stairs behind Cowboy, who handed a strip of tickets to the skeletal old man.

Chapter Fourteen

Oh, just great, Jeremy thought. Bad enough, being in here with those four geeks, but Jasper had followed him through the doorway. The old fart probably wanted to make sure nobody screwed around with his collection.

The door swung shut, cutting off the light from outside.

Jeremy had expected the interior of Jasper's Oddities to resemble a small room in a museum. Instead, he found himself in a corridor. The only light came from shaded bulbs placed below each of the framed photographs that lined the walls.

The Gallery of the Weird.

Jingles and her friends had stopped in front of the first photo. From where Jeremy stood, he couldn't see what it showed.

Jingles giggled. 'He could get ya coming and going,' said the tattooed guy.

'Gimme a break,' Mohawk said. 'He ain't real. It's trick photography.'

Jeremy flinched as hands clasped his shoulders. Gooseflesh

spread up his back. 'Pardon me, young man,' Jasper said, and let go and stepped past him. Cowboy lurched out of the way. For all his bravado, he must've been nervous, too.

Jasper hurried on. He stopped at the far side of the picture. 'Behold Jim and Tim, the Siamese twins.'

'We can read,' the hairless girl said.

'Let's get to the real stuff,' Mohawk said. 'Who gives a hot fuck about a buncha stupid pictures.'

'These are photographs of the most unusual, bizarre . . .'

'Does he *have* to breathe down our necks?' Jingles blurted.

'Yeah, man. Get outa our face.'

'As you wish,' Jasper said, and slinked away down the corridor. He didn't disappear, though. He stopped at the corner and stood there waiting in the darkness.

'Good going.' Cowboy said, taking off his hat and brushing it against Mohawk's shoulder. 'That's tellin' the old sack of fart gas.'

'Screw off,' Mohawk said.

'Well, pardon my ass, Chingachgook.'

Jeremy groaned.

'You lookin' to get busted up, boy?'

Cowboy opened his mouth. Jeremy elbowed him.

The hairless gal put an arm around Mohawk and said, 'Come on, Woody. Don't fool with them scrotes.' They turned away, and Jeremy held onto Cowboy's arm.

'Let's give them some room,' he whispered,

'You hear what she called us?'

'Those guy's clean our clocks.'

'They don't scare me.'

Jeremy saw that the others had wandered further down the corridor. They weren't stopping to inspect the photos. Apparently, they felt the same way as Woody and wanted to get to the real stuff.

Jeremy stopped at the photo of Jim and Tim, the Siamese twins. The two young men were joined at the hip. They shared something that looked like a double-pouched G-string. The sight of them made Jeremy feel queasy, but he stayed in front of the picture and stared at it.

'They're getting away from us,' Cowboy said.

'I want to see this stuff,' Jeremy lied.

'Well shoot. Stay, then.' Cowboy went on ahead.

Jeremy hurried after him. He gave the photographs only quick glances as he passed by them, and was rather glad he didn't have a chance to look more closely. What he glimpsed as he rushed along wasn't pleasant: a man with an extra arm, a small, withered thing that grew out of his chest; a furry woman in a bikini who had a face with a canine snout; a man with his tongue sticking out, a tongue that looked eight or ten inches long; a legless man doing a handstand; a woman with two heads; a woman with three breasts in a row, bare except for sparkling pasties with tassels; a giant man standing beside a midget who came up to his knees; and a man with arms so long that his hands almost touched the floor.

The photograph of the long-armed man was the last in the corridor. Jasper no longer stood in the corner. He must've followed the punkers.

Jeremy took a deep breath. He felt shaky and a little nauseous. The close, stifling air didn't help. It smelled like an old house, abandoned and sealed tight for years. Lifting the front of his shirt, he wiped the sweat from his face. Then, he followed Cowboy around the corner.

They stepped past the wall. A second corridor, similar to the one they'd just left, stretched towards the front of the building. The four jerks were gathered at the first display. Jasper stood beyond them, almost invisible except for his pale face.

'Let's wait,' Jeremy whispered.

'Don't be a woos,' Cowboy told him, and walked towards the group, but not quickly.

'It winked at you,' said the tattooed guy. His hand was on Jingles's back, up under her T-shirt.

'Did not,' she said. She sounded worried, though.

'Which head?' Woody asked, and laughed.

They moved on towards the next exhibit, and Jeremy saw that they'd been looking at a human foetus in a jar. 'Far out,'

Cowboy said. He stopped in front of the platform and leaned close to the lighted bottle. Jeremy stayed beside him, but didn't bend down. He could see just fine from where he stood.

The fluid in the bottle was yellowish and murky. The skin of the suspended foetus looked yellow, too. The thing had two heads. Its eyes were open.

Jeremy wondered if the thing might've come from the two-headed woman whose photo he'd seen in the Gallery of the Weird.

Cowboy stuck his face so close to the jar that his nose nearly touched it. 'Looks just like a little old man,' he said.

Jeremy swallowed hard and turned away. The group was clustered near the next oddity. Hairless and Woody stood together, arms across each other's backs. Tattoo was standing partly behind Jingles, his hand moving slowly up and down her side.

'Check it out,' Cowboy said.

Jeremy looked at him.

He clutched the jar in both hands and gave it a quick shake. The foetus tilted, swayed, turned. Bits and flecks of something swirled in the fluid.

Jeremy gagged. He clutched his mouth. Praying he wouldn't vomit, he whirled away. He blinked tears from his eyes and saw Jasper standing motionless in the dark. The old man must've seen what Cowboy did. But he raised no protest. Apparently, he didn't care.

By the time Cowboy lost interest in the foetus, Jingles and the others had moved on. A mummy remained – brightly illuminated by a spotlight at its feet.

'That ain't Karloff,' Cowboy commented, heading for it.

It looked like no mummy Jeremy had ever seen in horror movies or museums.

It wasn't wrapped.

It was a dried-up, brown cadaver, held into a standing position by a harness of leather straps nailed to the wall.

It had no eyes. Its jaw hung open. Its right arm was gone.

'Looks like he's made out a beef jerky,' Cowboy said.

For the sake of decency, a rag had been tied around its pelvic girdle. Jeremy supposed the old man had done that.

When Cowboy crouched and lifted the rag, Jeremy shut his eyes.

'Ooooph,' Cowboy said. 'Who let the air out? Come here and check this out.'

Jeremy opened his eyes, but averted them from the mummy. There were two more exhibits in this corridor. The four geeks had apparently finished looking at both, and were turning the corner. 'The gals are getting away,' he warned.

'Well, shoot.' Cowboy stood up and hurried forward. Approaching the next display, he slowed his pace. He angled towards it, but turned his head towards the end of the corridor as if he were torn between inspecting the oddity and catching up to the girls.

The oddity won.

Jeremy had caught a glimpse of it, so he stayed as far away as he could. 'Haven't you ever been in here before?' he asked.

'Never had the urge before. Can't stand that crud, Jasper. Jesus, look at this sucker.'

This sucker was a black spider nearly three feet in height.

Jeremy took another quick look at it, and kept walking.

He supposed it must be dead, stuffed.

If it weren't, it would be in a cage, not standing there on its display platform with nothing between it and the customers.

He hurried towards three shrunken heads on pedestals. He was glad to see them. Their monkey-like faces with stitched eyelids and lips seemed almost friendly compared to the other oddities he'd seen.

From behind him came Cowboy's voice. 'Jasper's Giganticus.' He sounded as if he were reading. probably from one of the hand-lettered cards tacked up close to each exhibit. 'Discovered by Jasper Dunn in the jungles of New Zealand, April 10, 1951. Poor critter,' he added in his regular voice. 'Reckon its mother whacked it with an ugly stick.'

'Some shrunken heads over here,' Jeremy said, wishing Cowboy would come away from the damn spider.

'Yeah? Anyone we know?'

He heard Cowboy's footsteps. They came up behind him. 'Yeah. Hmm. Let's go.' Cowboy didn't stop for a close look at the heads, but kept walking.

Jeremy went after him. Before turning the corner, he glanced back at the spider. It was still on its pedestal. Of course, he told himself. What did you expect?

He stepped around the wall, and halted abruptly. He'd thought the punkers would be halfway down the corridor by now, but they were still gathered in front of the first exhibit.

This oddity *was* in a cage. More of a display case, actually. Jeremy had a good view of it through the glass or clear plastic side. It didn't seem to be alive.

Like the mummy, it was held upright by leather straps.

'That ain't no hairless orang-utan of Borneo,' Tattoo said.

'Why, you seen one before?' Jingles asked.

'I seen orang-utans at the zoo, and that ain't one.'

It didn't look like an orang-utan to Jeremy, either. More like what you'd get, he thought, if you took the Creature from the Black Lagoon and gave it claws instead of flippers and changed its lizardy skin to flesh that was white and smooth. Though it looked more than six feet tall and powerfully muscled, something about the texture of its flesh made it seem soft and a little slug-like.

It wore nothing except a G-string. The garment's black pouch was enormous.

'What is this thing, really?' Tattoo asked, turning his head towards Jasper, who was standing some distance off.

'I was requested to remain "out of your faces",' Jasper replied, 'such as they are.'

'It's nothing but a rubber suit,' Woody said. 'The worldwide explorer picked it up at a rummage sale in Hollywood.'

'Yeah,' his girlfriend agreed. 'I seen it in a flick.'

'I assure you,' Jasper said, 'the creature before you is authentic, as are all my Oddities. Less than a decade ago, it lived and breathed. It rampaged, committing murder and rape.'

'Gimme a break,' Woody muttered.

'I think it's your old man, Chingachgook.'

Jeremy's stomach dropped.

Woody whirled around. His eyes seemed to be bulging from their sockets. His mouth hung open. He was breathing hard. Except for the quick rise and fall of his chest, he didn't move.

Then, his hand moved to the knife case on his belt. He unsnapped the flap and drew out a folding knife. He started to pry the blade from the handle.

'Uh-oh,' Cowboy said. He grinned, tipped his hat, then spun around and lunged around the corner.

Jeremy raced after him.

'Let's get 'em!' he heard Woody yell.

Cowboy blasted open the door. Sunlight struck Jeremy's eyes. Squinting, he saw Cowboy vault the wooden railing and drop to the boardwalk. He did the same. His feet hit the planking. His legs folded and his knees pounded the wood. Wincing, he scurried forwards and tried to stand.

Someone landed on his back, smashing him down.

'Gonna trash you, fuckhead.' Woody's voice.

He felt his hair being grabbed. His head was yanked up, scalp burning with pain, and he *knew* Woody was about to slash his throat. Instead, the guy jerked his hair downwards, bouncing his forehead on the boardwalk.

'Hey, creepo,' Jeremy heard. 'He didn't do nothing.' Cowboy's voice.

Woody crawled off his back, making sure to dig in with his knees before leaving.

'Come 'n get it, jack-off,' Woody said.

Jeremy got to his hands and knees. Lifting his head, he saw all four of the creeps in front of him. They had Cowboy surrounded. Cowboy wasn't even trying to run away. He just stood there, turning around slowly, grinning at each of them.

Woody and Tattoo both had their knives out. They were grinning back at him.

Spectators had formed a semi-circle around the group. They looked excited, eager to see what might happen next. Did they think this was some kind of *performance*?

'Last time I saw turds like you,' Cowboy said, turning from Jingles to Woody, 'was just before I flushed.'

You idiot! Jeremy thought.

Tattoo darted in from the side. Cowboy danced out of the way, but the knife jumped at him and sliced his forearm.

'Hey now, ratface . . .'

Woody charged at him from the rear.

Jeremy threw himself forwards. Diving, he caught one of Woody's ankles. As the guy flopped flat, Jingles rushed over and stomped Jeremy's forearm. He cried out. She raised her boot to stomp again, and he pulled his arm in quickly and started to roll away from her. Jingles pranced after him. She stopped his roll when Jeremy was on his back – by ramming her boot down on his belly.

For an instant, as the foot descended, he realized he had a wonderful view right up the front of her chopped off T-shirt. He saw the round undersides of her breasts, even the bottom parts of her nipples. Just the sort of view he'd been hoping for.

Great, he thought.

Then his body seemed to explode with pain and his breath blasted out.

Chapter Fifteen

Up ahead, a bum swatted at the woman standing in front of him. The miniature cassette recorder flew from her hand. It tumbled, nearly striking a passer-by in the face. As the woman whirled away from the bum to go after the recorder, Dave got a side view and saw that she was Gloria.

'Ace reporter in action,' Joan said.

'Christ,' Dave muttered.

Joan drew her nightstick from the ring on her belt and headed for the bum. Dave strode towards Gloria. She scooped the recorder off the boardwalk and shook it near her ear as if to find out whether it had developed a rattle.

'Gloria.'

Her head snapped toward him. For an instant, she looked startled and disoriented. Then, she smiled. 'Oh, it's you.'

'Yes, it's me.' He couldn't keep the annoyance out of his voice. 'What the hell are you doing?'

'I was trying to conduct an interview, but . . .'

'No please, no please!'

'Shut up.' Joan prodded the bum closer to Gloria. His watery eyes looked terrified.

Signing, Gloria shook her head. 'Don't hurt him. Leave him alone. He didn't do anything. I . . . intruded on his territory.' She met his eyes. 'I'm awfully sorry. I didn't mean to get you in trouble.'

'Let him go,' Dave said.

'Take a hike, mister,' Joan told the bum, and slipped the nightstick into her belt.

He wandered away, muttering to himself.

'I'm sorry, you two,' Gloria said.

Joan shrugged, smiled, and said, 'No problem. Are you all right?'

'Fine. I didn't mean to cause any trouble. I've been trying to get their side of the trolling story . . . and meeting with a good deal of resistance. They just don't trust me.'

'They're all paranoid,' Joan told her.

'Why don't you find yourself a different story,' Dave said. 'You're never going to get any straight answers from . . .'

'COPS!'

Dave pivoted away from Gloria. A kid, ten or eleven years old, was racing through the crowd. He turned and pointed behind him. 'COPS!' he yelled again. 'A fight! Knives!' He slowed down as he got close to them. 'Somebody gonna get killed! Fronta the Funhouse!'

Dave yanked the radio from his belt. He thumbed the speak button, 'Officers need assistance. Funland. In front of Dunns.' For good measure, he added, 'Send ambulance.' He jammed the radio back onto his belt, and took off after Joan.

She had already sprinted past the huffing boy. Dave put on the steam, but couldn't catch up to her. He didn't like the idea of Joan being first. Not heading into a situation they knew so little about. The kid had said there were knives. Plural. At least two knives, but how many? Dave wished he'd taken a second to get more information.

Find out soon enough, he thought.

'Wait up!' he called to Joan.

She didn't wait up.

'Damn it,' he muttered.

Worried and frustrated as he felt, Dave had to admire her moves. God, she was fast! And the way she darted and dodged around the people in her way reminded him of O. J. Simpson in the old days, going for a touchdown.

Her moves were too damn good.

He had a last glimpse of her blue shorts, then the milling crowd blocked her from Dave's view.

The group of spectators Joan saw in front of Jasper's Oddities reminded her of banjo girl's audience. Except there were more here. And some were rushing away. And the rest weren't standing still, listening; instead, they jumped and shouted.

She stopped running and worked her way into the crowd, squeezing between the onlookers, snapping, 'Out of my way! Police. Move aside. Out of the way. Police. Move it!' Some refused to budge. They didn't want the show stopped. She fought her urge to knock them out of the way. She stepped around them.

People elbowed her.

Someone yanked the seat of her shorts, and she felt them slip down a bit before she batted the hand away.

Then she broke through the front of the crowd.

Like entering an arena.

'POLICE!' she shouted, rushing forward and trying to make sense of what she was seeing. 'BREAK IT UP!'

A teenaged male with a bloody face was bent over, driving a knee up into the stomach of a female. The female was naked except for cut-off jeans. The blow from the kid's knee lifted her feet off the boardwalk.

A second female, this one in a leather skirt and torn tank-top, pushed herself off the wood and charged the boy. She knocked the boy off his feet, and all three tumbled into a heap.

Drawing her nightstick, Joan turned her attention to the other group of fighters.

She wished she'd seen them first.

She rushed at them.

'POLICE!' she yelled.

The one on top, a freak with a purple Mohawk, leaped off the body and turned on Joan. He had a knife in his right hand, a severed ear in his left.

Behind him, a kid was sprawled on the boardwalk, clutching the side of his head. Another guy, under him, apparently an accomplice of the one with the Mohawk, thrust the victim aside and started to get up.

'BOTH OF YOU FREEZE!' she shouted.

She glimpsed movement out of the corner of her eyes, looked to the left and saw the two females fleeing. Joan had thought they were victims, but she quickly changed her mind. The crowd parted to make way for them. The kid stayed put, sitting on the boardwalk and wiping the blood off his face with a white T-shirt.

Joan snapped her eyes back to the pair of shirtless males. They both had knives. They glanced at each other.

'DROP YOUR WEAPONS!'

The one who'd been under the victim shook his head. The one holding the ear shook his head.

Joan considered going for her sidearm.

Right, she thought. And blow away a few spectators.

'DROP 'EM RIGHT NOW!' That was Dave's voice. It came from just behind her.

123

The grinning jerk with the Mohawk haircut popped the severed ear into his mouth. He started to chew, and Joan thought, *They could've sewn it back on, you fuckhead!*

The ear flew out of his mouth and slapped gently against Joan's right breast an instant after her shoe drove into his solar plexus. It clung to her T-shirt. She cupped her free hand over it at the same moment the toe of her shoe caught the guy under the chin. Blood and bits of broken teeth exploded from his mouth. His knife sailed into the crowd at his back. Then he slammed the boardwalk and lay motionless.

His friend spun around. One of the spectators didn't get out of his way fast enough. He jammed his knife into the man's stomach, shoved the squealing guy backward, and rushed through the quickly parting crowd.

'I've got him,' Dave said.

As Dave went after him, Joan crouched by the kid squirming on the boardwalk. 'I've got your ear,' she said. 'They'll put it back on. You'll be good as new.' She hoped so. He appeared to have several other wounds.

She heard sirens.

'An ambulance'll be here in a minute. Hang on.'

'Reckon I ain't got much choice,' the kid muttered.

She hurried forward, and knelt beside the man who'd been knifed in the torso. He was conscious, clutching his wound, whimpering and trying to dig his heels into the boardwalk.

She placed her empty hand on his hands, and gently squeezed them. 'You'll be all right. Keep that pressure on the wound. Ambulance is on the way.'

Then, she left him, deciding her best immediate course of action was to check out the wounds of the kid whose ear had been taken off, administer whatever first aid she could before the ambulance arrived.

Dave hurled himself over the railing and dropped to the beach. When his feet hit the sand, he let himself tumble forward. He rolled on his shoulder, came up facing the ocean, couldn't spot the kid running away, and pivoted in time to see the kid dashing at him from under the boardwalk.

Not in time to avoid the thrusting knife.

As the blade sped toward him, he twisted sideways. Instead of plunging into his chest, it ripped across him. He didn't feel pain, but he heard a tearing sound and felt a streak of warmth along his ribs.

He grabbed the attacker's wrist. With his other hand, he smashed the back of the elbow. He heard a pop, felt the joint go. The guy cried out and dropped the knife.

Dave threw him down on the sand. Kneeling, he yanked the broken arm up behind his back. The kid screamed, but didn't resist. In seconds, Dave had him cuffed.

Jingles sat with her back against a piling, deep in the shadows beneath the boardwalk. Her stomach ached from catching that jerk-offs knee. It seemed to help, sitting curled up this way, hugging her legs to her breasts.

'How long's it been?' Lorna asked.

'Who knows? An hour?' Maybe even longer, Jingles thought. It seemed like ages ago that she'd heard the sirens. She'd peed herself when the kid smashed her, and her damp shorts hadn't been uncomfortable at first. After a while, though, they'd started making her skin feel hot and itchy. It seemed as if she'd been living with that forever. 'Maybe a couple hours,' she added.

'I bet the cops've cleared out by now,' Lorna said.

'So what?'

'Maybe we oughta get going.'

'Oh, right. I'm sure. Case you hadn't noticed, I'm missing something. That rotten dickhead.'

'What're we gonna do?'

'I don't know.' Jingles stood up, and let go of her belly long enough to pluck the damp seat of her cut-offs away from her rump. Turning around, she peered through the dark forest of pilings. She saw segments of bright, sunlit beach. A few people were wandering by. 'How about you go out and find me a top?' she suggested.

'What, like grab a bikini off someone?'

'Or a towel.'

'Just like that, huh? Then the cops nail me and you're still under here with your tits in the breeze.'

Jingles stepped back behind the post and met Lorna's eyes. 'You got any money?'

'I left my purse in the car.'

'Yeah, me too. Shit. Those shops up there, they're loaded with stuff. How about going up and lifting me something?'

'Get real. Look at me.' She plucked at the front of her clinging tank-top. 'Where'm I gonna stash you a blouse or whatever, huh?'

Jingles shook her head. She could see right through the thin fabric of her friend's top. Nothing could be hidden under the skirt, either. It was way too short.

'You don't gotta stash it anywhere,' Jingles explained. '*Wear* it. Grab a blouse, put it on, they'll think it's yours.'

'Forget it. Look at me. You think I can waltz into some shop and get away with *anything*?'

'Guess not,' Jingles admitted. Lorna was right. Eyes would be on her the whole time because of her shaved head and clothes that revealed so much of her body. People had stared at her *before* the fight. Now, her lower lip was split and puffy. Now, a strap of her top was broken, leaving her right shoulder bare, the strap hanging down so that her breast was partly uncovered. Everybody would watch her. For one reason or another.

'One look at me,' Lorna said, 'a damn shopkeeper'd send for the cops.'

'Not if it's a guy,' Jingles said.

'No way. Forget it.'

'Then how about going to the car?' she asked.

'Woody locked it.'

'So break a window.'

'He'd kill me.'

'He ain't gonna kill nobody. He's probably behind bars. So you smash a window and get the purses and buy me . . .'

'You think I'm nuts? Break into the car in broad daylight?'

'I'd do it for you'

'Easy for you to say, since you ain't.'

'Gimme your shirt, I'll go out and grab something.'

'Yeah, no thanks. Leave me here alone? You get picked up, and I'm stuck. Huh-uh. I can just see me trying to hitch a ride back to Three Corners, my . . .' Her eyes went wary. 'Don't even think about it. I can take you.'

'Maybe, maybe not.'

'Come on, we're pals. I'm gonna stick with you. We'll figure something.'

Jingles pushed her hands down the rear of her shorts. Her buttocks felt cool and a little sticky. She scratched with her fingernails. That felt very good. She closed her eyes and kept on scratching.

Even if she could manage to get Lorna's shirt, there'd be hell to pay later on. Lorna wouldn't rest until she got even. Woody'd be in on the payback, too. He might've got away from the cops. Even if he didn't, he'd get out on bail pretty quick. Jingles didn't like the thought of having either one of them mad at her. She would end up trashed real good.

'Look,' Lorna said. 'How about we wait till dark? Then we jump whoever comes by, and get you something to wear. Good idea?'

'That's *hours*.'

'You got any better ideas?'

Jingles shook her head. 'Guess not.'

They sat and waited, several feet apart, each with her back against a piling as concealment from anyone on the beach who might pass by and look into the shadows under the boardwalk. After a while, Lorna stretched out on the sand, crossed her arms beneath her head and shut her eyes.

Jingles listened to the waves washing in against the shore, footsteps passing overhead, distant sounds of calliope music, the faint, far-off roar of the Hurricane.

There was nothing much to look at: the sand in front of her; some discarded bottles, bags and rags probably left behind by winos; pilings as thick as telephone poles; the foundations of some buildings.

Not many foundations. She supposed that most of the buildings just rested on pilings. Where there were no foundations, the area under the boardwalk stretched into almost total darkness.

We could go exploring in there to pass the time, she thought. Maybe even find a front way out.

What good would that do?

Put us closer to the parking lot.

If there's a way out, she told herself, there'd be light.

Besides, she had no desire to enter such darkness. Might be somebody there.

Jingles wished she hadn't thought of that.

Once it was in her mind, though, she couldn't get it out.

Might be winos and perverts crawling around.

So what? Long as she kept her eyes open, nobody could sneak up. There was a good stretch of dim light between her and the real black area. First sign of trouble, she'd make tracks, shirt or no shirt.

We wait for dark, she thought, and we won't be able to see nothing under here.

But the alternative was worse. Even wearing a top, she'd stand a good chance of getting busted by the cops if she poked her head out of here in daylight.

Nobody under here but us, anyhow, she told herself.

She didn't like staring into the dark area, though.

She turned her eyes to the nearby foundation. She guessed it probably belonged to the Funhouse, since it was right next to the Oddities place and it was two storeys high. That big, it probably needed a foundation.

The cinderblock wall rose all the way up to the planking of the boardwalk. The grey blocks were decorated with crude artwork, the kind of stuff Jingles had seen, and sometimes drawn, on the walls of bathroom stalls. Among the sketches of sex organs were cartoon-like drawings of skulls, spiders, snakes, mutilated bodies. Words scribbled around and over the pictures mostly referred to sex acts, but others were more disturbing. She read such phrases as, 'Suk my blood', and 'Rip her up', 'Beware!' and 'Satan Rules'.

One phrase, 'Inter my parler', was scrawled on the wall above a patch of criss-crossed boards near the middle of the foundation.

Jingles supposed that the planks covered a hole in the cinderblocks. Some of the winos had probably broken through the foundation, hoping to take shelter inside the abandoned funhouse, and the boards had been put up to keep them out.

After dark, she thought, this place is probably crawling with bums.

We'll be gone by then. Soon as the sun goes down, we're out of here.

But before the sun went down, the fog came in. The area of darkness in front of Jingles spread closer. She found that she could no longer see the artwork and slogans on the cinderblock wall – which was just as well, since much of the graffiti made her nervous. But the afternoon's heat was stolen away.

Shivering, Jingles eased away from the post. On hands and knees, she looked toward the beach. Out beyond the boardwalk, the air looked grey and misty.

A few people walked by. She could see them all right.

The fog was heavy enough to block out the sun, but not so thick that it would offer cover for their escape.

The sand seemed a lot warmer than the air, so Jingles crawled to her place behind the piling and lay down. She crossed her arms under her face for a pillow. That was better. The chilly air still crept over her back, but her front felt good, nestled in the sand.

She looked to the right. Lorna was still sprawled there, sleeping. She turned her head the other way.

She squinted through the faint light at the patch of boards on the funhouse's foundation.

If she could pry some of those boards away . . .

Probably nice and warm inside.

She gritted her teeth to stop their clicking.

Wait in there till dark. Safe and cosy.

Jingles pushed herself up. On her knees, she brushed the sand off her skin. Then she crawled over to Lorna and shook the girl awake.

Lorna rolled onto her side, curled up and hugged herself. 'God, it's freezing!'

'Come on.'

'What?'

'You'll see.'

Lorna followed Jingles to the boarded area of the foundation. 'What're we doing?'

'I think we can get in.'

'Oh, shit.'

'You rather freeze?'

Jingles dug her fingers under the end of a plank, and pulled. She expected resistance.

Figured the boards were nailed into the cinder blocks.

But the entire patch of criss-crossed wood swung toward her like a door.

It is a door!

Christ. Through the opening in front of her was total darkness. But she felt heat swelling out.

'I don't like this,' Lorna muttered.

I don't either, Jingles thought. An actual door. A secret door. She didn't like it at all.

But the heat felt wonderful.

'It's warm,' she said. 'Come on.'

Jingles stepped into the darkness. Lorna entered after her. Jingles pulled the door shut.

'Yeah,' she said. The warmth seemed to seep into her skin. Her shivering stopped. She sighed. 'This is great, huh?'

Then she felt hands all over her.

Chapter Sixteen

After taking a shower, Dave removed the sodden bandage that had been applied at the emergency room. The cut, about two inches below his right nipple and nearly four inches long, was cross-hatched with stitches so it resembled a zipper. Though the blade had sliced through his skin, it hadn't penetrated to the muscle tissue.

If he'd been a little slower turning aside . . .

The thought of the blade plunging straight into his chest made him feel queasy.

You really lucked out, he told himself.

He put together a fresh bandage of gauze and tape, and pressed it over the wound.

In his bedroom, he combed his hair and got into a robe. He went into the kitchen for a beer. As he opened the refrigerator, the doorbell rang.

He hadn't really expected Gloria to come by. He'd seen the look on her face when Joan got into the ambulance with him. She hadn't bothered to show up at the emergency room. But she must've decided to come by, after all, and offer her sympathy or congratulations – or interview him for the *Post*.

Cop breaks arm of juvenile brawler.

He just ought to tell her he's not up for an argument, and ask her to come back some other time.

Maybe she's not here for that, he thought as he approached the door. Maybe she wants to comfort me. I could go for some comforting of the right kind.

He opened the door.

'Hey there, tiger.'

He felt a smile break out. 'My own Chuck Norris.'

'I brought you some medicine,' Joan said, and lifted a bottle of champagne from the paper bag she was bracing against her chest. Dave saw the foil-wrapped top of another bottle inside the bag.

'Come on in,' he said.

She shrugged with one shoulder. 'I just wanted to drop these off for you. I'm not in the habit of barging in on people.'

'So break the habit.' He waved her inside, and shut the door. 'Sit down, make yourself comfortable. I'll put some clothes on.'

'Don't bother on my account.' Though she said it in a way that seemed light and joking, her face reddened.

'Right back,' he said. He hurried to his bedroom. There, he shed his robe and stepped into underwear and corduroy pants. He put on a plaid shirt, slipped his feet into mocassins, and rushed back into the living room.

Joan was bending over the coffee table, setting the twin bottles of champagne on top of the flattened bag. She smiled at him, straightened up, and rubbed her hands on the sides of her skirt.

The skirt was very short. It was part of a white, denim dress that had a zipper up the front. The zipper wasn't pulled to the neck. The opening showed a narrow V of skin. Joan's sleeves were rolled halfway up her forearms.

'I like your outfit,' Dave said. 'You seeing Harold later?'

'I doubt it. Threw this on figuring it might perk you up.'

'Consider me perked.'

She laughed. 'Good. Mission accomplished.'

She went with him into the kitchen.

'So, how are you feeling?' she asked. 'That was a nasty gash he gave you.'

'It's not so bad.' As if calling his bluff, the wound burnt him with pain when he reached into a high cupboard for the wine glasses. He grimaced.

Joan put a hand on his shoulder. 'You'd better take it easy, pal.'

'I wonder how the others are doing.'

'I just stopped by at the hospital.' Joan took the glasses from him, and headed for the living room. 'It was touch and go with

Willis for a while, but he's going to make it. They think they saved the kid's ear. It's a bit mangled, but it's back on his head.'

'Thanks to your lightning foot,' Dave said, not even trying to keep his admiration out of his voice. 'You *destroyed* that guy.'

Joan looked around at him. A corner of her mouth was tipped crooked. 'That's what the doctors think, too.'

'Are you kidding?'

'He still hasn't regained consciousness.'

'Is he going to?'

'They don't know.'

'Oh, Jesus.'

'Hey, it's his tough luck. Come on, let's drink. Sit down.'

Dave lowered himself carefully onto the sofa. Leaning back against its soft cushion, he watched Joan peel the foil off one of the bottles. 'The cork isn't plastic,' he said. 'Must be good stuff.'

'Safeway's best.' She removed the wire hood and dropped it onto the table. Clamping the bottle against her side, she began to twist the cork out. 'Any heirloom pottery you'd like me to target?'

'Just don't hit me.'

She pointed the cork away from him, and let fly. With a loud *pwomp*, it shot across the room and landed in a rocking chair. A wisp of white vapour curled out of the bottle's mouth, but foam didn't gush out.

'Nice job,' Dave said.

Joan filled the glasses. She handed one to Dave, took one for herself, and sat down beside him. 'Here's to quick reflexes and narrow escapes,' she toasted.

'I'll drink to that.'

They clinked the rims of their glasses, and drank. 'Real good,' Dave said.

'I nearly picked up a six-pack instead, but I figured, what the hey. Isn't every day we get a chance to subdue a pair of knife-wielding bad-ass cruds. Calls for a celebration.'

'That it does. How's my guy?'

'His arm'll be good as new by the time he leaves prison.

That's maybe ten years down the road – assuming Willis doesn't succumb.'

'He's not a juvie?'

Joan wiggled her eyebrows. 'Nineteen.'

'Great. How old's his buddy?'

Her cheery look slipped a bit. 'Same. Not that it matters much. I don't see a trial in his future.'

'He'll be all right.'

Joan shrugged, forced a smile, and took another sip of champagne. 'His name's Woodrow. Would you believe it? Woodrow Abernathy. A name like that, he's trotting around with a purple broom on his head like some kind of a freak out of *Mad Max*. Did you see him stick that kid's ear in his mouth?'

Dave nodded. He watched Joan's eyes. Her eyes usually seemed confident, somewhat amused. Now, they looked a little frantic. He saw confusion in them, and pain and fear.

'I mean, if Woodrow was hungry, he could've had a hot dog.'

'You did the right thing,' Dave said. He patted her thigh, meaning only to comfort her, but the smooth feel of her skin sent a sudden surge of heat through him. He brought his hand back quickly and rested it on his own leg. 'The creep knew what he was doing. He wanted to destroy the ear.'

'My first kick did the job.'

'He was still armed.'

'I could've taken the knife away. I didn't have to demolish him.' She finished the champagne in her glass, filled the glass again, and topped off Dave's. 'I shouldn't have done it,' she muttered.

'He'll probably be all right. If he's not, you can figure you saved somebody down the road. His next victim . . . victims.'

'Yeah. I've been telling myself that. Shit.'

'Is this the first time you've ever hurt someone?'

'Broke a guy's collar bone last year. Stopped him for speeding and he threw a punch at me. Hardly in the same category as scrambling a kid's brains.'

'Comes with the territory,' Dave said. 'I killed a guy once. Back when I was LAPD. A drug bust. The guy sprayed a Mac 10 in my direction.'

'Jesus.'

'Wonderful thing about those weapons, you have 'em on full auto and they spit themselves empty in about two seconds. The bastard really filled the air with lead, but he ran clean out of ammo about the time he'd worked the spray in my direction. While he tried to change magazines, I put four rounds in his chest.'

'Jesus,' she said again.

'It was a pretty clear case of him-or-me, don't you think?'

'I'd say so.'

'The guy was scum. He'd spent half his life behind bars . . . a few years here for assault with a deadly weapon . . . a few years there for rape . . . a few more for armed robbery. At age eighteen, he was out long enough to blow away a creep who stiffed him in a coke deal, but the search warrant didn't hold up so the charges were dropped.'

'Not a nice guy,' Joan said, looking and sounding more like her usual self.

'Not nice at all. And then he tries to mow me down with a goddam submachine gun. And I drop the hammer on him, and the guilt turns me into a basket case. I was messed up for *months*. Makes no sense at all.'

'Makes sense to me. Now.'

'That's how I ended up here. Small town, I figured it'd be *peaceful*, you know? And it generally is. It's no LA. What brought you here?'

'A family move. Mom married a poet who'd been out here for a writer's convention and couldn't wait to get back. You know how artsy this place is.'

'The town's schizophrenic,' Dave said.

'You noticed, huh? Downtown thinks it's Carmel, and south end's a Mecca for rednecks.'

'And you throw in the military for some extra colour.' He remembered the way she'd acted with the sailors yesterday. 'Were you in the navy, or something?'

'My dad was. We lost him in Vietnam. The Mekong Delta. He was a gunner on a patrol boat.' She took another drink of champagne. 'Anyway, so Mom had this thing with the poet, and she moved us out here. That was three years ago. I got started on a Master's programme in library science at the university . . .'

'You, a librarian?'

With the back of her wrist, she knocked him gently in the arm. 'You got a problem with that, tough guy?'

'Hard to picture you. How did a future librarian end up a cop?'

'Mom and her poet pulled a disappearing act. I needed a job, and I met some cops during the investigation. Beth Lanier and I hit it off pretty well. She's the one who put the idea into my head. The rest is history.'

'How come I didn't know about all this?' Dave asked.

'Never asked.' Smiling, Joan took his empty glass, set it on the table with hers, and drained the bottle into them. She started to open the second bottle.

'I was here when you joined the force,' Dave said.

'Nobody ever said anything about your mother disappearing.'

'Lone Wolf Carson? There's probably a lot of stuff you never heard about. Everybody but you musta knew.' She laughed softly. 'Known,' she corrected herself.

She aimed the cork at the rocking chair where the first had landed, and shot it. This time, foam began to gush from the bottle. 'Whoa shit!' she gasped. The white froth tumbled into the glasses, filling them both too fast, and kept rolling out so she swung the overflowing bottle up to her mouth and gulped the suds.

'Don't choke yourself,' Dave warned, laughing. He leaned forward and watched her throat work, watched champagne trickle down her chin and neck, down her wrist and forearm, watched the bottom of the bottle drip onto her leg and dress.

It was no longer erupting when she lowered it and sighed. She made a silent burp. Her face went red and she looked downward. 'Gosh, I'm sorry.'

'No sweat.'

She rubbed her wet thigh and spread her legs and peered down at the upholstery. 'Don't think I got any on your couch,' she muttered.

Dave joined her in looking, but didn't notice the upholstery. He saw only her smooth inner thighs and glimpsed her pink panties and felt a sudden swell of desire and turned his head away.

'Don't worry about the couch,' he said, his voice coming out a little shaky. 'I'll get you some paper towels.'

'Thanks. I'm sorry.'

'Don't worry.' He pushed himself up, wincing slightly as a burning sensation reminded him of his wound, then hurried into the kitchen and pulled a yard of paper towels off the roll beside the sink.

When he came back into the room, Joan was standing. She looked up at him, a self-disgusted smirk on her face. The front of her white dress was blotchy with wet spots that gave the fabric a slightly grey colouring.

She shook her head as she took the towels from him. Instead of using them on herself, she wadded them into a huge ball and picked up the champagne bottle and dried it, then got down on her knees and lifted the glasses out of the puddle and wiped their bases and moved them to a dry spot and mopped the table's surface.

Dave almost told her not to bother. It was an old table and the champagne wouldn't hurt it, anyway. But he kept his mouth shut and watched her.

This was a Joan with all her toughness gone. This was a Joan slightly sloshed, embarrassed and sad and vulnerable. Still as beautiful and strong as before, but upset. And, because of that, somehow more alluring than ever.

She stood up, the wad of towels in her hand. 'Want to point me to a waste basket?' she asked.

Dave stepped around the table and took the wet clump from her. He tossed it onto the table. He put his hands on her shoulders. He looked into her eyes.

She shook her head. 'I'd better go.'

He said nothing. He eased her forward, and Joan wrapped her arms around him. Her smooth cheek slid against the side of his face. He felt the tickle of her breath on his ear, and he whispered, 'You're *taller* than me,' and he felt her laugh – gusts of warm air on his ear, her back shaking just a bit under his hands, her belly pulsing against his, her breasts moving slightly with her laughter, rubbing his chest.

She squeezed him hard, and he winced. 'Ouch,' she gasped. 'I'm sorry.'

He pushed a hand up into her thick hair and turned her head, turned her mouth toward his, pressed his mouth to her open lips, felt their softness and wetness, felt her breath enter him.

The doorbell rang and Joan lurched back and looked at Dave, her eyes wide and questioning.

He shook his head.

Joan ran a forearm across her slick mouth.

The bell rang again.

'Gloria?' she whispered.

'I don't know.'

'You got a back door?'

'Forget it. Sit down and have a drink.'

'God, Dave.'

'I won't have you sneaking out.'

'I shouldn't be here.'

'Yes you should. Sit down, relax.'

Grimacing, she bent over the table and picked up her glass. She took it to the rocking chair. She flinched as the doorbell rang again. Quickly, she grabbed the two corks off the cushion, straightened her dress and sat down.

Dave went to the door and opened it.

He forced himself to smile.

'How are you feeling?' Gloria asked, glancing at his chest then gazing into his eyes.

'Not bad.'

She stepped into the doorway, leaned against him, wrapped her arms around his neck, and tipped her face up for a kiss.

Dave didn't want to kiss her. He didn't like the way she clung to him. She felt small and bony and tense, and she was hugging him too hard.

He wondered if Joan was watching.

Probably not, he thought. She was probably sitting in that rocker with her eyes turned in the other direction and wishing she were anywhere else.

He kissed Gloria on the mouth. Her lips were cool and stiff, but they parted and she thrust her tongue into his mouth with a nervous urgency that chilled him.

He backed away. Her eyes looked stunned, annoyed. 'What's gotten into . . .?'

'Joan's here,' he said, and watched Gloria's mouth snap shut. 'Come on in.'

'Oh. Oh?' She made a tight, curled smile and stepped past him.

Joan rose from the chair. 'I just dropped by for a minute to bring our conquering hero some medication.' A smile on her face (a smile that, to Dave, seemed sick with guilt), she raised her nearly empty glass for Gloria to see that the medication was champagne.

'That was very thoughtful of you,' Gloria said.

Dave saw that Joan had raised the zipper of her dress a few inches higher. The moist spots on the fabric hadn't quite gone away. They were faint, though.

'I'll get another glass,' Dave said.

'Are you sure I'm not interrupting?' Gloria asked.

Joan shook her head.

Dave rushed into the kitchen. He reached into the cupboard with his left hand, this time, and managed not to awaken his pain as he took down a wine glass.

When he returned to the living room, Gloria was seated on the couch. Where Joan had been sitting.

Could she feel Joan's warmth on the cushion?

So what if she can? Dave told himself.

She sat stiffly, hands folded on her lap, eyes darting from Joan to Dave.

He didn't want to think about what she must be feeling, right now.

He took the glass to the table and lifted the champagne bottle. 'Just a dab,' Gloria said. 'Besides, I see there's not much left.'

'We've been knocking it back pretty good,' Dave said, hoping to lighten the situation. Gloria arched an eyebrow. He filled her glass halfway to the top before she stopped him.

He turned towards Joan with the bottle. She shook her head. 'No more for me, thanks. I really should be getting home.'

'Oh, don't rush off on my account,' Gloria said.

'Debbie and I usually eat about now.' She stood up. 'Are you going to take tomorrow off, Dave?'

'No, I'll be in.'

'Can't keep a good man down,' Gloria said.

Dave set down the bottle and walked Joan to the door. 'Thanks for coming by,' he said. 'The medication helped.' He stepped onto the porch with her, but left the door open for Gloria's sake.

'Sorry if I made trouble for you,' Joan whispered.

'You didn't.'

'Don't bet on it.'

He wanted to hold her. He kept his hands at his sides. 'Take it easy, huh?'

'You, too.'

He watched her walk to her car. Then, with a sigh, he entered the house and closed the door.

'You two must've had quite a party,' Gloria said.

'We had a tough day. Both of us.'

'Did you enjoy consoling one another?'

He leaned over the table and filled his glass with champagne. He took it to the rocker.

'Oh, that's nice. Keep your distance.'

'You're in a lousy mood.'

'Oh, and I should be delighted to walk in and find Joan here, half smashed?'

A few choice disclaimers ran through Dave's mind: it's not what you think; nothing happened; there's no reason to be jealous.

Lies.

'What was I supposed to do?' he asked. 'Send her away?'

'And miss out on the sheer pleasure of her company? I hardly think so.'

'She doesn't come in and start giving me a hard time.'

'Oh, I suspect she gave you a very hard time. I saw that cute little dress she was wearing. I saw the guilt on her face . . . and yours. What were you doing before I put in my untimely appearance? More than drinking, I should imagine.'

'Don't push it, Gloria.'

'Oh, I touched a nerve?'

'I got stabbed today. I'm really not in any mood for one of your scenes.'

'Didn't she kiss it and make it all better?'

'What's happened to you?'

'To me?' Her eyebrows darted high.

'You've turned into a real bitch. All of a sudden, the past couple of weeks, you've been acting like your chief goal in life is to give me grief. If it isn't my eating habits, it's my politics. If it isn't that, you're giving me shit about Joan. I'm sick of it.'

'And I'm sick of her. Has that occurred to you as a possibility? It's not enough you spend eight hours a day with your golden girl, you insist upon inflicting her on me *all the time*. It's Joan did this, Joan said that. We even had her to a goddamn *barbecue* so you wouldn't be deprived of her presence on your day off.'

'Calm down.'

'Do you know how many times we've fucked since she came into the picture?'

Dave didn't answer. He took a drink of champagne.

'Not once. Not once!'

'Well . . .'

'You've been putting it to her all along, haven't you? Haven't you!'

'I think you should leave, now.'

'You and that slut have been . . .'

'Shut up!' He lurched to his feet and pointed at the door. 'Get out. I've had enough.'

Gloria sprang up, glaring at him, shaking her head. 'Oh, this is cute. This is very cute.' Back rigid, she walked towards the door. 'So long, Gloria,' she said, not looking back. Her voice was a quiet, lilting sing-song. 'Ta-ta. I had my fun with you, time to throw you away. You're no match for the golden Amazon bitch. Ta-ta. Fuck off, now, there's a good girl.'

'Wait,' Dave said.

He didn't want her to wait; he wanted her gone, but not like this. It shouldn't end this way, Gloria jabbering about being discarded like trash, sounding like a madwoman.

She opened the door.

'Gloria.'

She stopped. She turned around and raised her eyebrows. 'Did the pig speak? Is it sorry? Is it feeling guilty? And what does the pig have to say?'

Forget it, he thought. What he said was, 'Oink.'

Gloria's face blanched. She whirled and strode away, leaving the door wide open.

So much for friendly partings.

She called me a pig. One last dig. The flaming radical reformer hurling her final insult, her most scornful epithet, a tired leftover from the sixties when she was a child and hippies preached peace and burned the flag and spat on cops.

God, Dave thought, I've really hurt her.

But what can she expect from a pig?

He drank the rest of his champagne.

The hell with her, he told himself.

He felt sick inside, the way he might've felt if he'd just run over a dog.

He heard a car door slam shut. He heard an engine start. Soon, the engine sound faded.

He stepped to the front door and shut it.

Then he went to the table and filled his glass to the top. He sat down on the couch.

He sat down where Joan had been sitting. Gloria had sat there, after her. But he let his mind go back to the time before Gloria showed up.

He drank, and his mind lingered on Joan, filled itself with all she had said and done, with the look of her and the smell of her and how she had felt in his arms.

Chapter Seventeen

Instead of calling it quits at six, as she had done yesterday, Robin took a short break. She ate a hot dog, then stationed herself above the main stairs to the beach and resumed playing and singing.

It hardly seemed worth the effort.

Few people had remained at Funland after the fog rolled in, and even fewer seemed willing to stand around and listen to her music. She was cold, herself. Though the windbreaker kept her top warm, the chill moist air seemed to soak through her jeans. She couldn't play with gloves on. Between songs, she tucked her hands into the warmth under her armpits.

As she stood there in the cold, playing for two or three people and sometimes gaining a quarter for her efforts, her mind wandered to all the places she would rather be. Warm places. A cafe, the movie theatre, her sleeping bag. She even imagined herself checking into a motel and settling into a bathtub full of hot, hot water.

But she had to be here, instead. Thanks to Poppinsack.

Working for a few coins to build up her stake. So she could afford warm places, so tomorrow or the day after she could afford to hit the road out of this nest of bums, thieves and trollers.

All day, she'd been keeping a lookout for the fat old man in his buckskin jacket and feathered derby.

He must've made himself scarce, just in case she had ignored his advice to flee town.

Or maybe he just went on a buying spree.

For $120.00, he could buy a lot of books and booze.

The bastard.

He'd better not have spent it all.

But she realized that, as much as she wanted to get her money back, the money wasn't her main reason for wanting to confront Poppinsack. He'd *messed* with her while she slept. For that, she would get him.

First, she would make him confess. She knew that he was the guilty one. But she needed to hear him admit it. After all, there was a slim chance (fat chance, she thought) that somebody other than Poppinsack had crept into her encampment, pawed her and stolen the money. She had no proof against him.

While her hands were busy playing a Stephen Foster medley (though she realized she had no audience at the moment), her mind replayed the scene she had already imagined so many times. She is crouched out of sight and Poppinsack comes staggering over the crest of the moonwashed dune. He sees her and doffs his hat. 'Ah-ha, we meet again. How do you fare, Cockless Robin?' Pretending he's glad to see her. And coming down the slope.

She stands and pulls her knife on him. 'You've got something that belongs to me, you thieving rat.'

'Nonsense. Balderdash.'

'Turn your pockets out,' she snaps.

'You do me wrong, lassie. Twas't Poppinsack dipped into your dainties and snatched the treasure.' Realizing he has said too much, he swings his staff to clobber her.

Robin ducks the whooshing stick, rushes in and rams her long blade into his belly.

She wondered why the fantasy always led to her stabbing the old man.

I'm not going to stab him, she told herself.

Not unless things get really bad.

What *will* I do, give him a piece of my mind?

'Don't try it!' she suddenly shouted, clamping her hands over the banjo strings as a wino lurched in from the side, crouched beside her case and clawed out a folded dollar bill. 'Hey!' She took a step towards him, but he lurched away, spun around and ran, his long coat flapping behind him.

Robin stood there, watching him flee, wanting to go after him. If she left her things here . . .

The bum tried to run past a man coming down the board-walk. The man swung an arm up. The bum's face hit it. He flopped onto his back. The man stepped on his wrist, bent down, and took the bill. When he lifted his foot off the wrist, the bum scurried towards the side of the boardwalk, rolled under the railing, and dropped out of sight.

The man came towards her, holding up the dollar and smiling. Robin saw that he wasn't very old, maybe eighteen. He wore jeans and a plaid shirt, and his hair was short. He looked athletic and clean-cut, the kind of guy you might find wearing a varsity letter sweater in the halls of a high school.

'Here you go,' he said, and gave the dollar to her.

'Thanks.' Robin stuffed it into a pocket of her windbreaker. 'You didn't have to go to all that trouble.'

'No trouble. It's always a pleasure to clothesline a guy who'll stoop to stealing from a woman.'

'Name's Robin,' she said, and held her hand out.

'Nate,' he told her, shaking it.

His hand felt warm and strong.

'How's business?' he asked.

'Booming,' Robin said, and swept an arm towards her huge, invisible audience.

'That's how it is, usually, when the fog's in. I went ahead and closed up early.'

'You work here?'

'Sure.' He gestured behind himself with a thumb. 'Have you checked out the arcade?'

'Huh-uh.'

'Well, if you had, I'm the guy who would've given you change.'

'I'm the gal who wouldn't have needed any. I've got quarters up the . . . I get a lot of quarters.'

'The way you sing and play, you oughta be on a stage getting twenty bucks a head.'

'Well, thanks.'

'I've been listening from the arcade. Couldn't make out the lyrics too well, but you sure play a mean banjo. I've never heard anything like it.'

Robin smiled and shrugged.

'Matter of fact, it isn't right for me to enjoy it that much and not shell out.' He reached to his rear pocket and took a wallet out.

'No. Please. You nailed that bum for me . . .'

'I insist.' He took out a twenty dollar bill.

'No. Don't be ridiculous.'

'I don't want to force it on you.'

'Then put it away. Please.'

'I tell you what. Suppose you sing a song for me, and I'll throw a buck or something into your case.'

'I guess that's fair enough.'

She took a couple of steps backwards, and began to play for her audience of one. As she picked the quick, bouncy lead-in, she saw a smile spread across his face. His head bobbed with the rhythm, and Robin began to sing:

> Kelly and Katie took off one day
> For the Land of Purr where the kitty-cats play.
>
> They packed their pockets with nacho chips,
> Bubble gum, jelly, and chocolate lips,
> Then hit the road for the Land of Purr
> So fast on their skates they were just a blur.
>
> Along about noon they stopped for a snack
> Under the shade of a bamboo shack –

Where who should they meet but a cat named Clew
Who said, 'I'm Clew! So who are you?'

'We're Kelly and Katie and we're on our way
To the Land of Purr where the kitty-cats stay.'

'May I come, too?' asked the cat named Clew.
'I'm hungry here since the birdies flew –
And I have no ears, as you can see,
So I can't hear the mice when they're close to me.'

'It's been three weeks since I've munched a bird
And a mouse hasn't passed these lips, my word! –
Since the awful day that the Dog of Toff
A year ago chewed my ears right off!'

'Oh, dear! Poor Clew!' said Kate and Kelly.
'Please eat some nacho chips and jelly.
After you've cleaned it off your fur
You can come with us to the Land of purr.'

So Clew ate a snack, and when she was through
Each girl gave a skate, so Clew had two –
And they all set out. What a happy crew!
They hit the road and away they flew.

Kelly, Katie and little grey Clew
Were off for the land where the grass was blue
And the sky was green and the kitty-cats grew
Soft and beautiful and
Sometimes
Often
Uh-oh!
A little weird, too.

Smiling at Nate, she did a quick shuffling dance as she
finished the tune.

He clapped, and shook his head. 'Hey, that was great!'

'A little silly, maybe . . .'

'It's *your* song?'

'Yeah, I write a lot of them. That one's meant for kids, actually, in case you hadn't guessed. It goes on and on.'

'Really? They run into that Dog of Toff?'

'Sure do.'

'I've got to get a move on, but I'd sure like to hear the rest of it sometime.'

'I guess I'll still be around tomorrow.'

'Good. Don't rush off.' Bending over, he dropped a folded bill into the banjo case.

'Thanks,' she said.

'It was really nice meeting you, Robin. See you tomorrow, huh?'

She nodded. 'See you. And thanks for the help.'

'Any time.' He started backing away. 'So long.'

'Bye.'

He raised a hand in farewell, then turned around and strode towards the main gate.

Poppinsack peered at the clock behind the bar. 'Today,' he said, 'has tumbled into tomorrow and become yesterday. And a fine day it was, indeed.'

He hoisted his glass of Scotch towards the clock, winked, and gulped it empty.

He climbed off the barstool and tucked his half-read paperback into the duffle bag. It went in on top of his other new books and bottles. He clipped the bag shut, and hefted it. 'Ah, 'tis a weighty matter. Santa's own bag, itself, was never packed with such delights. Yuletide in summer.'

Singing 'Deck the Halls', he lumbered to the tavern door and stepped outside,

He sucked the fresh night air into his nostrils, and sighed. 'Delicious,' he proclaimed. 'The elixir of the gods, best savoured with a belly full of hooch.'

He adjusted the canvas strap of the duffle bag on his

shoulder, tipped back his hat with the knobby handle of his cane, and continued on his way.

Fog hung heavily over the street, so he couldn't see Funland. He knew it was straight ahead, though. And he knew it was already closed for the night.

He felt a little quiver of fear.

Normally, he would've been safely tucked away in the dunes long before Funland shut down.

'Poppinsack has spreed too late,' he said. 'But one must sail when the tide goes out, and spree when the purse is full. And full of gratitude is he to she who provided so generously for the night's entertainment. I thank thee, Robin red-breast. And have you flown the coop? Or do you wait in ambuscade to retrieve your filched funds? There's a hearty, foolish lass. A dame that's long on moxey and short on brains, doomed to be brained.'

He chopped the air with his cane. 'Felled, poleaxed, dropped like a sack of tomatoes. And a ripe tomato she is, my lovely songbird, minstrel, bard, my Robin red-breast of the smooth hot breasts, my cockless Robin of the saucy quiff. Shall we meet in mortal combat on the strand this night? Prepare yourself to taste my staff, and then my staff.'

But as he lumbered past the Lighthouse Bar, a man came out.

Poppinsack stopped and turned towards the door. In the few seconds before it swung shut, he saw the dim lights inside, the smoky air, the colourful array of bottles along the far wall. He heard laughter, talking, the song of a woman from the juke box, the soft click of pool balls, the tinkle of glass. He felt the warmth of the bar's air. Best of all, he *smelled* it. He sucked into his nostrils the familiar, cosy aromas of sawdust, stale smoke from cigarettes and cigars, and the heady mix of sweat, urine, and booze.

'Bless the gods,' he said. 'Poppinsack feels a fresh thirst coming on.'

With that, he entered the bar.

* * *

149

Robin sat on the soft roll of her sleeping bag, waiting for Poppinsack at the bottom of the sand slope where he had camped last night.

He's probably too smart to come back, she told herself again.

But I told him I was getting out of town. He'll think I'm long gone. And even if he knows I stuck around, he'll never think I have the guts to jump him.

What if he *doesn't* come?

How long do I wait?

Though she was huddled down, hugging her knees to her chest, the cold kept her shivering. She longed to be warm inside her sleeping bag. But what if she got into the bag, and even fell asleep, and then he showed up? She would be at his mercy.

Robin rose to her feet, as she'd done every so often since settling here, and climbed the sand slope. At the top, she scanned the area. Though she heard the surf rushing in, the fog was so thick that she couldn't see the ocean. The pale, blowing vapours only allowed her to see twenty or thirty feet in any direction, and nothing was visible except the deserted dunes.

She supposed that she might've missed Poppinsack while she was sitting at the bottom. He could've found himself a nearby place to camp. Maybe he'd even returned to his old spot, peered down and spied her, and crept off, planning to keep away from her – or sneak in after she fell asleep.

She knew she ought to scout around for him.

But the fogbound, desolate landscape made her nervous. She didn't even like to be standing up here, exposed. It didn't feel safe. She wanted to be at the bottom, hunched low and out of sight.

Come on, if you're coming, she thought.

As she looked around, she began to fear that someone *would* come wandering out of the fog. Maybe not Poppinsack. Maybe two or three mad, gibbering trolls. Right now, they were just out of sight. If she stayed up here a moment longer, they would shamble into view and spot her.

Robin whirled around, rushed to the bottom of the slope and sank onto her rolled sleeping bag.

This is ridiculous, she told herself. I'm just spooking myself. Nobody's out there.

Anyone could be out there.

And if she got into her bag and went to sleep, anyone could creep up on her.

What the hell am I doing here? she wondered.

Nothing good can come of this. If Poppinsack shows up right now, maybe I get some of my money back and maybe I don't. One of us is bound to get hurt. At best, it's him and not me. Then I'll have that on my conscience. Instead of just the guy I stabbed at the bus depot, I'll have two guys I'll wish I hadn't hurt.

Even if I get *all* my money back, it won't be worth the guilt.

With the guy at the bus station, at least I didn't have a choice. He attacked me. This would be my choice.

Forget it, she decided.

And felt, at once, as if an awful burden had been cast aside.

She strapped the sleeping bag to her pack frame, shouldered the pack, lifted her banjo case, and climbed again to the top of the dune. Though she checked around to make sure nobody was approaching, her imagination conjured no phantoms. She no longer felt so exposed and vulnerable.

She trudged northward over the mounds of sand. Soon, she came to the chain link fence marking the boundary of the public beach. She followed it towards the sound of the combers. The sand became smooth and hard-packed under her boots. The black ocean came into view.

The tide was out, so she didn't get wet when she stepped around the end of the fence.

On private property now, Robin felt as if she'd crossed into a territory that was beyond the reach of the trolls – and the trollers, though they were the least of her worries. The trollers, after all, were rational humans, not crazies.

She walked in the direction of the house, and soon it appeared through the fog. Its windows were dark.

The house stood on pilings.

Ducking down beside the porch stairs, she gazed into the black area among the posts. It looked like a cosy place to spend the night.

A real intrusion, though, to sneak in there right under someone's home. And she might be spotted, coming out in the morning.

Robin realized she didn't care.

All that mattered was finding a secluded place where she might sleep in safety.

She dropped to her knees and began crawling into the darkness, dragging her banjo beside her.

Chapter Eighteen

Jeremy stopped beneath the dim, grinning face of the clown. He saw no one ahead – only the deep darkness under the roof of Funland's entryway, the lesser darkness of the boardwalk beyond, and fog like a pale curtain suspended at the far side of the railing.

He lighted the numerals of his wristwatch. 12:58.

He was two minutes early. He supposed that Cowboy was still in the hospital. Though he felt nervous about meeting the others without Cowboy present for moral support, the urge to be with Tanya had been so strong that he'd decided to come, anyway.

Maybe they won't even meet tonight, he thought with a mixture of hope and dismay.

As he stepped past the ticket booth, a hand clamped his shoulder and spun him around. A huge guy grabbed the front of his jacket, jerked him up onto tiptoes.

'It's all right.' Tanya's voice.

The guy set him down.

A girl came in from the side, followed by a cluster of teenagers. She wore a dark sweatsuit and her face was blurred by shadow, but Jeremy knew from her size and pale hair that she was Tanya.

'I didn't think you'd show up,' she said.

'I didn't know if I should,' he told her, and wished his voice didn't sound so weak. 'But I came last night, and . . . do you know about the fight? Me and Cowboy . . .'

'We heard about it.'

'I saw him tonight,' Liz said, stepping up beside Tanya.

'Is he okay?'

'They put his ear on. He might be out of the hospital tomorrow.'

'Great.'

'He said you showed hair.'

'Yeah, good going,' said a girl he didn't recognize.

Jeremy felt himself blush. 'Well, I tried to help.'

'Wish I'd been there,' said the big guy. 'I would've killed the fuckers.'

'One of the cops damn near did.' That came from the girl he didn't know. She took a stride forward, pressing between Tanya and Liz, and offered her hand. 'Nice to meet you, Jeremy. I'm Shiner.'

'Nice to meet you,' he said, shaking her hand. She looked slim in her windbreaker and jeans. She had light coloured hair. Though he couldn't see her well in the darkness, he got the impression that she was pretty, and maybe younger than Tanya.

She stepped back, and a guy standing on the other side of Tanya extended his hand. 'I'm Nate,' he said.

'Hello.' Jeremy shook the hand. It felt strong, but it didn't try to crush him. He remembered Cowboy telling him that Nate was Tanya's boyfriend. 'Welcome aboard,' Nate said.

I don't stand a chance, he thought. The guy looked like a jock – a handsome jock, at that.

'I'm Samuel,' said the big guy who'd grabbed Jeremy from

behind the booth. He wore a letter jacket with an enormous B on its chest. A varsity letter, probably for football. Or for Sumo wrestling, Jeremy thought.

Samuel shook his hand. And squeezed it hard.

'You can call me Samson.'

'You can all call me Duke if you want,' Jeremy said, pulling his hand free and flexing the fingers. They still worked. 'Cowboy came up with that.'

A small, skinny kid wearing glasses came in from the side. 'Greetings and salutations. I'm Randy. You may call me Randy.' He smiled.

'Or Sandy,' Liz said.

'You'll have to excuse Elizabeth, Duke. She resents anyone whose IQ exceeds her own, which is roughly equal to that of an oyster.'

She swatted the back of his head.

Tanya shoved her. 'Cut it out.'

'He's such a toenail.'

'Save it for the trolls,' Tanya said.

'Let me in,' came a whiny, female voice. 'I wanta meet him, too.' She pushed her way in from behind the others. She had a pudgy face. Her dark hair enclosed her head like a football helmet. She wore a tight jumpsuit of stretchy fabric that hugged all her bulges. 'I'm Heather,' she said, pumping his hand.

'Hi,' Jeremy said.

She moved in close. Her breasts and stomach pushed against him. Her breath smelled of onions. 'Hey, you're kinda cute.'

He managed to smile and thank her.

'That's everyone except Karen,' Tanya said, and looked over her shoulder. 'Come in here and meet Duke.'

'Yeah, yeah.'

Tanya sidestepped, and a brunette moved in from the rear. A beret was tilted atop her head. Around her neck was a silken scarf, one end draping her shoulder, the other slanting downward and draping her right breast. She wore a jumpsuit similar to Heather's, but the body it hugged looked slender and compact and somehow hard.

'Hi,' Jeremy said.

'God, I can't *tell* you what a thrill it is to meet you.'

Her sarcasm gave Jeremy a sinking sensation.

'It's nothing personal,' Randy explained. 'Karen lavishes her disdain on every creature of the male gender.'

'Which includes you out,' Liz remarked.

'Another clever retort from the cretin.'

'So now you've met everyone,' Tanya said. 'I suppose Cowboy's told you what we do here?'

'Go after trolls?'

'You got any problem with that?' Karen asked.

'No. Hell, I think they're a pain in the ass.'

'What have they done to you?' Nate asked.

Jeremy shrugged. 'Nothing much, I guess.'

'Then why do you want to help us trash them?'

He knew better than to reveal the truth: that he had no special grudge against the trolls, that he simply wanted to be part of the group and close to Tanya. He didn't care what they did out here at night, so long as he could be with them.

But he couldn't say that, so he thought about his first afternoon on the boardwalk when the bum jumped in front of him and started begging. He remembered the man's wild eyes and brown teeth and sour stench. He remembered his own confusion and disgust. Most of all, he remembered his fear – the fear that had made him feel small and helpless and shameful.

He heard anger in his voice as he said, 'I hate them. They hang around and bother everybody. They bug you for money. They're dirty and they stink. They act crazy. They're creeps. I think they ought to be tossed out with the garbage. They *are* garbage. They ask me for a quarter, I want to give them a knee in the nuts.'

'My man,' Samson said, and clapped him on the shoulder.

'Right on,' Liz said.

'They're disgusting and creepy,' the girl called Shiner said, 'but it's more than that. They're *evil*. That's why we come out here, night after night. They do things. They attack people. They make people *disappear*.'

155

Some of the others nodded. Nobody disagreed.

Jeremy felt himself going shaky inside. 'They make people disappear?' he asked, trying to keep his voice steady, but not succeeding.

'We haven't, like, seen it happen,' Heather said.

'It's conjecture on our part,' Randy explained, 'that the trolls are responsible.'

'It's them, all right,' Shiner said. 'They got my sister. She went for a walk on the beach one night, and . . . just vanished. They got her.'

'We don't know that for sure,' Nate said. 'We don't know what happened to Shiner's sister, or any of the others. But people do disappear without a trace. I guess that happens everywhere, but it happens here a lot.'

'Happens to our own trolls,' Samson added. 'The ones we nail? Most of 'em, we never see again.'

'We used to think we were scaring them out of town,' Nate said. 'But we're not so sure of that, anymore.'

'They get got,' Liz said, and giggled.

'We suspect,' Nate went on, 'that other trolls come along after we've left.'

'And mop up for us,' Liz said.

'Christ,' Jeremy muttered.

Samson's head bobbed. 'If we don't handcuff 'em to something or glue 'em down or stick 'em someplace where nobody can get at 'em, they're gone with the wind. Most often, anyhow. Some get through, but most don't.'

'What . . . what do the trolls *do* with them?'

'Gobble 'em up,' Liz said, and giggled again.

'We don't know,' Nate said. Jeremy groaned.

'You don't have to get involved,' Nate told him.

'Nothing to be scared of,' Heather said. 'They've never got any of us.'

'We're the getters,' Liz added.

'But you need to know the score,' Nate said. 'This is heavy stuff we're doing. If you're with us, you'll be an accomplice in the eyes of the law. Whatever any one of us does to a troll, we're all equally guilty just by the fact of our presence. Do you understand that?'

'Sure,' Jeremy said.

'So far, we haven't been touched by the cops. But that could change. Our luck might run out. Sooner or later, some of us might get busted. Could be you.'

'If you rat on us,' Liz said, 'we get you.'

'I wouldn't rat.'

'You still want to join up?' Nate said.

'Yeah, sure I do.'

'Okay,' Tanya said. 'Let's get on with the initiation.'

Initiation? The word conjured images of being tormented by the others, of suffering through a test in which he would be the victim of their scorn and cruelty. But if he passed the test, he would be accepted. No longer an outsider. One of them.

Jeremy's heart was beating fast and he felt as if cold hands were squeezing his bowels.

'Tonight,' Tanya told him, 'you're the bait. We wait here, and you wander up and down the boardwalk till a troll hits on you.' She dug into the pouch-like pocket at the belly of her sweatshirt, and drew out a card. She handed it to Jeremy. 'Give him this.'

'Or her,' Randy added, 'in the event that the troll is of the female gender.'

Jeremy held the card close to his eyes. The hand-printed message was large and dark enough for him to read it. 'DEAR TROLL, GREETINGS FROM GREAT BIG BILLY GOAT GRUFF.'

In spite of his uneasiness, he felt a grin stretch his mouth. 'Neat,' he said.

'It's our calling card,' Tanya told him.

'Most of them maggots can't read,' Samson said. 'We think it's a cool touch anyhow.'

'Yeah. I like it.' He slipped the card into a pocket of his jacket. 'So, I give it to the troll, and then what?'

'You signal us.' Tanya drew a shiny whistle from inside her sweatshirt, slipped its chain over her head, and passed it to Jeremy. 'Just give it a short blow.'

He closed his hand around the whistle. It felt warm. It held the warmth of Tanya. It had been under her sweatshirt, resting against her skin, and now it was in his hand. He imagined the whistle down there, swaying on its chain as she walked, brushing the sides of her smooth, bare breasts.

'Then all you do,' Tanya said, 'is keep the troll from getting away until we show up.'

He nodded, hearing her but paying little attention as he dropped the chain over his head and tucked the whistle inside his shirt. Now, it was against *his* bare skin.

'Any questions?'

'Huh?'

'Are you ready?'

'Which way do I go?'

'Take your pick.'

He turned towards the south end of Funland since that was the area he knew best. A hand clapped his shoulder. A hand patted his rump (and he liked that and wondered who had done it, but he didn't look back). A few voices quietly wished him good luck.

Then he was striding down the boardwalk alone.

He raised a hand to the front of his jacket and pressed the whistle against his chest. He thought again about where it had been. Then he realized that it had touched more than her breasts. She not only wore the whistle, but she had *used* it – maybe today on lifeguard duty, maybe a few nights ago to summon the trollers. It had been in her mouth, clamped between her lips, filled by her warm breath, wetted by her spittle, touched by her tongue.

Jeremy lifted the whistle out of his shirt. He put it into his mouth. Could he taste her? The whistle seemed to have no more taste than an empty spoon. Still, to know that it had been against her skin and in her mouth . . .

The low, forlorn moan of a foghorn rolled through the night, intruding like the blare of an alarm clock stunning him out of a sweet dream. The magic of the whistle vanished. He was suddenly aware that he was alone on the boardwalk, bait for a troll.

He went cold inside. He felt his scrotum shrivel up tight, his penis lose its stiffness and pull itself in as if to hide.

Looking over his shoulder, he saw only a few yards of dark boardwalk, the iron railing on one side, a game booth on the other side. The booth was a faint, indistinct shape through the fog. There was no sign of the group.

He stopped walking for a moment, and listened. The night seemed strangely quiet, as if the fog not only blinded him, but muffled sound.

He wished he could hear them talking, back there.

They have to be quiet, he thought, so trolls don't hear them.

Maybe he had just walked out of hearing range.

Maybe they left.

They wouldn't do that, he told himself.

But what if that's part of the initiation? They send me out by myself and a troll comes and I blow the whistle and – guess what? Surprise! You're on your own.

That'd be an initiation, all right.

Would they do that to me?

Sure. Why not? That's what initiations are all about. Trick the new guy. Shaft him. See if he can take it.

I can take it.

I'll show them.

He started walking again. He squinted, straining to see more deeply into the fog. The planks of the boardwalk looked wet. To the right was a bench. Empty, thank God. Beyond it, he saw the ghostly, hooded cars of the Tilt-a-Whirl.

He wondered if *those* were empty.

The whistle felt glued to his lips. He peeled it off, let it hang against his jacket, and licked his lips.

He quickened his pace.

He tried to stay in the middle of the boardwalk. The places off to the sides were where the trolls might lurk – in among the rides or booths. If he stayed in the middle, he wasn't so likely to be taken by surprise.

Then he saw, off to his left, the wooden stairway and platform and entrance of Jasper's Oddities.

Right here is where we had the fight, he thought. He *liked* thinking about the fight. In his mind, he had relived it over and over again. The pounding he took had been worth it. He'd helped Cowboy ('You showed hair'), and he'd trounced those girls and felt them up and even ripped the shirt off one and got a good look at her tits. Whenever he remembered it, he felt excited and proud and got a hard-on.

Now, he tried to call up those feelings, but couldn't.

His mind refused to replay the fight.

Instead, it focused on the displays inside Jasper's Oddities. The Gallery of the Weird with its grotesque photographs. Worse, the *real* stuff. The eyeless mummy hanging by straps, an old rag hiding its groin. The giant spider. The hairless orang-utan of Borneo – or whatever it *actually* was. The disgusting, yellow, two-headed foetus in its jar of murky fluid.

All that stuff was just inside the building, there. Just beyond its closed door.

Jeremy felt sick and frightened, knowing he was so close to such a collection of horrors.

He walked faster.

The way the Oddities building was joined to the Funhouse forced him to remember the photo of Jim and Tim, the Siamese twins connected at the hip.

At least the Funhouse had been closed down. He was glad of that, glad that he'd had no opportunity to try *it* out.

He wished he'd stayed away from the Oddities.

I'll be lucky if I don't get nightmares from that shit, he thought.

But if he hadn't gone into Jasper's Oddities, the fight wouldn't have happened.

You've got to pay for the good stuff.

Pay with the bad stuff. Like this right now. This is the cost of joining up with the trollers and getting to be with Tanya. Just like looking at the damn oddities was the cost of the neat fight.

Why doesn't a troll just *come* so I can get it over with?

Suppose one doesn't come? he wondered. Do I have to wander back and forth all night?

Do I pass the initiation if I don't get one?

His heart gave a sickening thump as he heard footsteps rushing towards him. From behind? He whirled around. Eyes searching the fog, he jammed the whistle between his dry lips. His other hand slapped the pocket of his corduroys and felt the lump of his folding knife. He wondered if he should dig it out. Then he remembered the card in his jacket.

He reached for it.

A dim shape, darker than the fog, came running at him. Suddenly, it stopped. It was still obscure, as if standing behind pale gauzy veils.

'Is that you, Jeremy?' a voice asked.

A girl's voice.

'Yeah. Who's that?'

'Shiner,' she said.

She stepped towards him. He saw her blowing hair, the blur of her face, her dark windbreaker and jeans. He took a deep breath, and let it out slowly.

She squeezed his arm. 'Come on back,' she told him. 'One's coming in the front way.'

'A troll?'

'Yeah. Quick. We're going to nail him.'

Chapter Nineteen

They stopped running, and Jeremy let Shiner lead him by the hand. They pressed their backs against the wall of a shop. As he tried to catch his breath, he saw Samson crouching behind the ticket booth. Heather stood at his rear. Nate and Liz were against the wall at the other side of the entryway.

Where were the others?

Where was Tanya?

A movement caught his eye, and he realized someone was waiting on the flat roof of the ticket booth. All he could see was a faint curve of back, but he figured it must be Tanya. The others were in sight except for Randy and that bitchy girl, Karen. It had to be Tanya. The booth was seven or eight feet high. Samson, he guessed, must've helped her get up there.

As he gazed at her, he heard a man's low slurred voice.

The troll?

From the sound of it, he must be nearby.

'Who killed Cock Robin?' he intoned. 'Who laid her low? "'Twas me," says I, "whom you shall know by the name of . . . Poppinsack, me." Bug-fuck. In this kingdom by the sea. And all the clouds did lower o'er her tomb.'

Shiner, still holding Jeremy's hand, inched sideways along the wall. Jeremy stayed with her. Leaning forward, he looked past her and saw the man staggering towards the darkness beneath the archway.

A fat old guy in a weird, feathered hat and a jacket with blowing fringe. He carried a walking stick in one hand, a duffle bag on his back.

'To pee, to piss, perchance to take a whizz,' the man proclaimed, turning to the wall.

He sounded to Jeremy like a drunken actor, one with a rich voice like Richard Burton in the *Hamlet* movie he'd seen in English class last year.

Jeremy heard a splashing sound.

The guy was taking a leak right there in the entrance, no more than three yards from where Nate and Liz stood, waiting.

At least the dirty old fart's back is toward us, Jeremy thought. But he could feel himself blushing. He wished Shiner weren't here to witness this.

'And in that whizz, perchance to flood the very marrow of the land and soak the roots of Satan's beard. 'Tis a fine thing. 'Tis meet that we should meet, this night, in the warm bosom of . . . 'Tis meat, indeed.' He chuckled. 'And shall the cockless Robin meet this meat? This staff of life?'

The splashing stopped.

Shiner turned her head. She smiled at Jeremy. He made a disgusted face, but wasn't sure how well she could see it.

The old troll turned away from the wall.

Jeremy was glad to see nothing hanging out.

He wasn't so glad to see the troll start staggering at an angle across the entryway – a route that was bringing him towards the place where he stood with Shiner.

'What ho! What ho! 'Tis a brave night to be abroad. A broad, a chick, a dame, a quiff. A rose by any other name. Arise, my rose, or be forever fallen!'

He weaved, flung up a hand, and caught himself against the side of the ticket booth.

'Steady as she goes! I am an ancient mariner. Not a cross but an albatross. I plugged it with my gat. It falls on me to tell my tale to every tail will hear it. And every piece that hears my piece will have no call to fear it. And every . . .'

Tanya leaped from the roof of the ticket booth.

She dropped. Feet first. Crouching slightly. Arms out. Sweatsuit flapping. Pale hair swept up by the wind of her descent.

Jeremy heard the quiet slap of her soles striking the leather shoulders of the troll's jacket. He heard a grunt of pain and surprise.

The old man's knees folded and he crumpled forward. Tanya hopped off his shoulders as if he were a diving board. She cleared his back. She landed on her feet and stumbled away for a few steps before finding her balance. By the time she turned around, the troll was sprawled face-down.

'Let's get him,' Shiner whispered. She tugged Jeremy's hand, pulling him away from the wall. Staying beside her, he rushed toward the fallen bum.

Shiner got two kicks in. Jeremy went ahead and gave him a good one in the side. Then the others arrived. Samson hurled the duffle bag out of the way, and they rolled him over. He seemed too stunned to struggle. Hands grabbed his arms and ankles, stretched him out. Heather stomped on his belly. Randy, who'd found the troll's walking stick, whacked him across the chest with it, barely missing Liz's head.

Wheezing, he jerked a hand free of Shiner's grasp. His closed fist struck her in the chest and she tumbled backwards off her knees. Jeremy caught the troll's wrist. The hand flew open. He clutched the middle finger and yanked it back until it snapped and the troll yelped in agony.

Liz drove an elbow into his chest, just below the throat.

Karen kicked him in the groin.

His head jerked up. Samson pounded him between the eyes and his head shot down and bounced off the wood.

He went limp.

'Okay,' Tanya said. 'That's enough. Let's get him up.'

Jeremy helped. The old man seemed to weigh a ton. But when they raised him off the boardwalk, Samson drove a shoulder into his midsection and hefted him.

'You got him all right?' Nate asked.

'No sweat,' Samson answered, but his voice sounded squeezed as if the load was almost too much for him. 'Where do we want him?'

'Follow me,' Tanya said.

Nate lifted the duffle bag. 'What's he got in here, bricks?'

Tanya led the way, Nate on one side, Karen on the other. Samson strode along behind her, the fat troll folded over his shoulder, limp arms swinging against his back. Jeremy saw that the broken finger was sticking out at a right angle from the rest of the hand.

Shiner came up beside him. 'Are you okay?' he asked.

'Fine.'

'He sure clobbered you. But I busted his finger for him.'

'Good going.'

They turned left, and headed down the boardwalk.

Randy hurried to the front, holding the knobby cane high, the feathered derby perched on top.

Like a severed head on a pike, Jeremy thought, though he wasn't sure where the image came from. A movie? A drawing in a history book?

Somebody patted his rump. He looked back, and saw Heather behind him. 'How you like it so far?' she asked.

He shrugged. He didn't know what to say. He felt a little frightened and guilty, but also very excited. His heart was pounding, his mouth was dry, and his throat felt tight. All he said was, 'Neat.'

'A blast,' Heather said. 'But it's gonna get better.'

A blast, all right, he thought. Not as great as his fight with the girls, but almost.

He wondered if this counted as his initiation. Whether it did or not, he *felt* as if he now belonged, He'd joined in, he'd hurt the troll, and Shiner and Heather were acting as if he was one of them.

'What happens next?' he asked.

'It's up to Tanya,' Shiner said.

Heather added, 'You can bet it'll be cool,' and put an arm around his back. He felt her big, soft breasts against his upper arm, and wanted to pull away.

Of all the girls here, why did *she* have to be the one snuggling up to him?

Tanya was too much to hope for, of course, but he liked Shiner and she didn't seem to have a boyfriend here. Even though the darkness had made it impossible, so far, to get a good look at her face, she seemed pretty. She certainly wasn't a fat slob with stinky breath.

Just what I need, he thought. This one hanging all over me.

Shiner, walking on the other side of Jeremy, quickened her pace and moved ahead, leaving him with Heather.

Who slid a hand into the rear pocket of his corduroys and rubbed his rump. 'Good and warm,' she said.

'Too bad Cowboy's missing out on the fun,' he told her.

'He's an asshole.'

The word, coming from her, sounded especially gross.

'He's my best friend,' Jeremy said.

He hoped she might back off, hearing that. Instead, she gave his butt a playful squeeze and kissed his ear.

Jeremy turned his head away.

And saw Jasper's Oddities through the fog. An image filled his mind of Heather inside – an exhibit – her bloated, naked body suspended in a harness of leather straps. She looked as if she were made of white bread dough that hadn't gone into the oven yet. The straps sank into her flab so far they were almost out of sight. Her tongue lolled out. Her dead eyes were rolled upward so he could only see their whites. The picture made him go hot with shame.

She's just being nice to me, he told himself. She's probably lonely. It's not a crime.

The troll suddenly began to struggle. With his good hand, he pounded Samson's back.

Samson bent at the waist and hurled him down. The troll crashed against the boardwalk. Before he could move, he was surrounded.

Jeremy, free of Heather, sighed with relief and stepped on the man's wrist.

'Don't hurt him,' Tanya ordered. 'Just bring him along.'

'I've got him,' Samson said. He grabbed one side of the troll's thick, handlebar moustache and started pulling.

With lots of gasps and whimpers and groans, the old guy got to his feet.

Samson walked beside him, leading him by the moustache.

'Over here.' Tanya hurried on ahead, Randy rushing after her with the derby wobbling high above him. They both melted into the fog. Then Karen and Nate vanished, too.

Jeremy heard the squeak of a gate swinging open.

'Where'd you go?' Samson called.

'The Ferris wheel,' Tanya answered.

'Oh, wow.' That came from Heather. Close behind him.

Jeremy hurried forward and caught up with Shiner. 'What's going on?' he asked.

'We're about to find out,' she said.

Samson and the troll, with Liz walking close behind the troll as if to grab him if he should somehow free himself, angled across the boardwalk towards one of the low fences that enclosed each of the rides. They passed through the open gate.

The Ferris wheel stood beyond the gate, mostly hidden by the fog. Jeremy could see only the front of it: a few of the gondolas, some distinct and others vague in the greyness; the curves of the wheels connecting them; spokes running inward towards the axle, but fading, and vanishing entirely before they reached it.

More came into view as he walked with Shiner through the gate. He saw the elevated platform. The lowest gondola was there, where it had been stopped at the end of the last ride of the night to let its passengers out. Dim shapes stood near it. He saw Samson leading the troll up the few stairs, Liz hurrying after them.

'Ooo, this is gonna be good,' Heather said. Instead of latching onto Jeremy again, she hurried past him and bounded to the top of the stairs.

Shiner stayed at Jeremy's side while they climbed the platform.

'Everybody here?' Tanya asked.

'Anyone who's not here,' Randy said, 'speak up.'

'You're as funny as crotch rot,' Liz told him.

'Okay,' Tanya said. 'Let's air this bastard out.'

Samson, standing in front of the troll, kept him on tiptoes by dragging upward on his moustache. Liz, Janet, Heather and Shiner began to undress him. He danced and whimpered a little as they did it, but offered no real resistance. Tanya watched like a foreman, arms folded across her chest, nodding with approval.

Soon, they had the troll down to his longjohns.

Jeremy was surprised. He'd thought nobody wore longjohns – just actors in cowboy movies. But this old fart wore them, all right.

Heather and Liz peeled them off him.

Jeremy couldn't believe it. He felt shocked, and his skin burned with his embarrassment.

The guy was as hairy as an ape. The mound of his sagging belly was in the way, so Jeremy couldn't see his privates and was glad to be spared the sight. But Liz and Heather were on

167

their knees, having drawn the longjohns down his legs, and they stayed there, inspecting him, whispering to each other, giggling. The guy obviously wanted to cover himself, but Janet and Shiner had his arms. So he just whimpered.

Heather reached up.

The troll's eyes widened and his mouth dropped open.

'What're you, desperate?' Liz muttered.

'I just wanta see if . . .'

'That's enough,' Nate snapped.

'Let's get on with it,' Tanya said. 'We didn't post a guard, so we'd better finish up and get out of here.' She reached out towards Randy. He dug into a pocket, took out something that clicked and rattled, and gave it to her.

Jeremy saw that it was a pair of handcuffs.

'I'll get the thing going,' Nate said, and ducked away.

The troll was guided to the Ferris wheel and forced down. The gondola started to swing backward when his rump hit the footrest, but the platform stopped it.

As if he suddenly realized that the pain of the beating and the humiliation of being stripped were mere preliminaries to the main event, the troll shrieked and went wild. He kicked, squirmed, flung his arms at the kids trying to hold him down.

Tanya kicked him in the belly. His breath blasted out and he slumped against the front edge of the gondola's seat, whinnying as he struggled for air.

She swung the metal safety bar down and clamped it.

A motor rumbled to life. Jeremy felt the platform begin to vibrate under his shoes.

Astonished, he muttered, 'It'll *go*?'

'Nate's folks own the thing,' Liz said.

Tanya finished with the troll, and stepped aside. He was still sitting on the footrest, sprawled backward against the seat, fat hairy legs sticking out.

His hands hung beneath the safety bar, suspended there by the chain of the cuffs.

'Watch it,' Tanya warned. Jeremy and the others stepped out of the way. 'Okay, Nate,' she said.

Nate, over at the side, worked a lever forward.

The Ferris wheel lurched, and slowly started to turn. As the gondola moved backward, rising, it rocked away beneath the weight of the troll. He slipped off the footrest and cried out as the bracelets tugged at his wrists.

'No!' he yelled. 'Please!'

A second later, he was hanging straight down – all his weight borne by the handcuffs, by the connecting links, by the safety bar.

The Ferris wheel lifted him higher, then squeaked, and stopped with a slight jerk that made him yelp. He swayed up there, six or eight feet above the ground.

'Take him higher,' Tanya said.

'That's high enough,' Nate told her. 'He's an awfully big guy. Something could give out.'

'Let me down. Please? I'll get out of town. I'll do anything. PLEASE!'

'Give him one spin over the top,' Tanya said.

'Christ, yeah!' Heather blurted.

'Make him *ride* it!' Liz said.

'I don't think we . . .'

'Shit!' Tanya snapped. 'Give it to him! He's a fucking *troll*!'

Nate shook his head.

He kept shaking it as Tanya strode towards him. '*I'll* do it, then – shit.'

'Tanya,' he said. But he didn't try to stop her.

She rammed the long lever forward. With a quick lurch that dragged a shriek out of the troll, the wheel started turning.

The naked, kicking troll flew upward as if being sucked into the fog. He screamed all the way up. He kept on screaming after Jeremy couldn't see him anymore.

Tanya tugged the lever backward.

The Ferris wheel stopped.

The screams of the troll came down through the fog.

'God,' Shiner muttered, 'he must be right near the top.'

'A good place for him to spend the night,' Tanya said.

'Let's bring him down,' Nate told her. 'I'll take care of it.'

'Fine,' Tanya said. 'In the morning. Go ahead and shut it off.'

'We can't . . .'

The troll had never stopped screaming, but the pitch suddenly jagged high. It made Jeremy's teeth ache. Goosebumps prickled his skin.

He heard a thump.

The screaming stopped.

Another thump.

'Oh Jesus,' Nate murmured.

And down through the fog came the troll, striking spokes and braces, bouncing off them, cartwheeling, flipping, tumbling like a mad acrobat.

Chapter Twenty

The platform shook when he crashed against it.

Nobody said a word. There was silence except for the rumble of the Ferris wheel's motor.

Jeremy stared at the body. It lay only a couple of yards from him, face up on the floor between two of the gondolas. The shadows weren't dark enough to shroud it. The face looked black with what was surely blood. The nose was mashed flat. One leg stuck out sideways as if it had been wrenched from its socket. The other stood straight up from the knee. The hands, still cuffed, rested on the hill of the troll's belly. A spike of bone protruded from the left forearm.

Jeremy turned his eyes away from the corpse and looked around the group. Everyone was motionless, gazing at it.

Liz raised a hand to her mouth. He wondered if she was about to vomit. *He* felt a little like throwing up. But she began to make strange, muffled noises, and he realized she was giggling. A moment later, she said, 'Woops.'

Shiner said, 'Oh, God. Now we've done it.'

'He fall down go boom,' Heather said.

Nate broke away from the group and shut down the motor.

'Everybody stay cool,' Tanya said.

'What *happened*?' Randy muttered.

'Obviously,' Tanya said, 'the safety bar wasn't strong enough to support him.'

'We killed him,' Randy said.

'Brilliant deduction, dickhead.' From Liz.

'Look,' Tanya said, 'the main thing now is not to panic. We've got to get rid of him and clean up. Nobody ever has to know this happened. Liz, Karen, Heather, I want you to clean up the blood. Go get a bucket and mop. Jeremy, get the guy's stuff together and throw it under the boardwalk. Shiner, help him. Samson, you give me a hand with the body. Nate, go get your surfboard. We'll float him out and dump him.'

'What about me?' Randy asked.

'Do us a favour and stick your head up your ass,' Liz said.

'You can stay with me,' Tanya told him. She pushed the sleeves of her sweatshirt up her forearms, ducked beneath the outer rim of the Ferris wheel, and crouched by the body. Samson followed.

Nobody else moved.

Tanya lifted the sideways leg by its ankle and swung it inwards. As she lowered the other leg – the one bent upwards from the knee – Randy spun around, gagging. He threw himself against the platform's railing and vomited.

'Good going,' Liz said. 'I'm not cleaning *that* up.'

Somebody squeezed Jeremy's arm. He looked, and saw that it was Shiner. 'Let's take care of his junk,' she said.

He turned away from the grisly sight of Tanya and Samson struggling with the body, and started to pick up the troll's clothes.

Nate brushed past him, and hurried down the stairs. Then Liz, Karen and Heather left.

'I'll help you guys,' Randy said. He still had the came in one hand, the derby hanging on its top. The derby fell off when he bent down to pick up the longjohns. It rolled under the Ferris wheel, and he scrambled to retrieve it.

Jeremy saw that Tanya and Samson had the body out from under the wheel. Tanya was holding the legs up while Samson dragged the body by its arms. They were moving it towards the rear of the platform.

'I never thought something like this would happen,' Shiner whispered.

'It's pretty gross,' Jeremy told her.

'God.'

He picked up the shoes and socks. And looked up in time to see Samson and Tanya lift the troll over the railing behind the Ferris wheel. They dropped him towards the beach.

On the way back, Samson grabbed the duffle bag. He lifted it and followed Tanya down the stairs.

'I guess we've got it all,' Shiner said.

With Randy in the lead – but no longer holding the derby high on the staff like a trophy – they climbed down from the platform. They walked through the open gate. Tanya and Samson were off to the left, climbing over the boardwalk's railing. Samson must've already tossed the duffle bag down. He and Tanya jumped, and vanished from sight.

When Jeremy reached the railing, he saw them striding across the beach. They took only a few steps before the fog devoured them.

The duffle bag lay in the sand straight below him. He emptied his arms over the railing. The troll's shoes dropped fast, but the socks and pants fluttered down. So did the shirt released by Shiner. It sailed down, bellowing, sleeves out. The wadded leather jacket plummeted, and hit the sand before the shirt. Randy hurled the cane. It stabbed the sand and stood upright like a spear. He kept the derby in his hand while he ducked between the bars of the railing.

Standing there, he hesitated. With the stiff brim of the derby, he nudged his glasses more firmly against his face.

'You don't have to jump,' Shiner told him.

'I'm not afraid.'

'Liz isn't here to razz you.'

'Tanya jumped, I can jump.' And he did. His feet hit the sand, his knees folded, and he seemed to dive forward. After getting up, he watched Shiner and Jeremy climb over the railing.

Hanging onto the outside of the bars, Jeremy could see why the smaller kid had been reluctant to leap from such a height. But the others had done it. He didn't want to look like a chicken by turning around and trying to lower himself off the boardwalk so the drop wouldn't be as great.

Shiner leaped.

As she fell, Jeremy stepped into space. He didn't want to think about the troll, but suddenly he imagined himself as the old man plummeting from the top of the Ferris wheel, knowing he was as good as dead. For just an instant, terror seized him.

Then his feet struck the sand. The impact collapsed his knees. His rump was pounded, and a knee clipped him on the chin, jarring his teeth together. He flopped onto his back. As he sat up, Shiner reached down to give him a hand. He took hold of it. She pulled, helping him to rise.

'Are you okay?' she asked.

Nodding, he ran his tongue across the edges of his teeth. He half expected to find some chipped, but they seemed all right.

'You should've rolled,' she told him.

'Yeah, I guess so.'

'If you don't require my assistance,' Randy said, 'I'll catch up with Tanya.'

'Sure,' Shiner said. The boy rushed off into the fog.

Jeremy and Shiner wandered around, bending over and gathering the troll's scattered clothes.

'I kind of feel sorry for Randy,' she said. 'He's a pretty sensitive kid. This was rough tonight.'

'That's for sure.'

'He's not . . . into this like some of us. He's only here because he's got some kind of crush on Tanya.'

173

'Really?'

Shiner stepped up close to a piling and tossed the troll's jacket and pants into the darkness.

'Shouldn't we take the stuff in under there? Maybe like scatter it around some?'

'No. Just throw it. There's probably trolls.'

'Jesus.'

'Yeah. We'd better not hang around too long.'

Jeremy hurled the shoes, socks and shirt, then backed away. 'You think anybody saw what happened?'

'You mean trolls? Some might've. They're always hidden around. I bet they know everything that goes on.' She picked up the longjohns, pulled the cane out of the sand, and retrieved the feathered derby.

Jeremy lifted the duffle bag. It was awfully heavy. 'Will they tell?' he asked.

'Not a chance.'

They stopped just under the edge of the boardwalk, and Shiner threw the troll's things into the darkness.

'I'd better carry this in a little ways,' Jeremy said.

'No, don't. Just toss it under. It'll be picked clean by morning, anyway.'

'I wonder what he's got in here.'

'Look and see.'

He realized he didn't really want to know. Holding the canvas bag by its strap, he swung it forwards and let go. It vanished. A second later, it landed with a soft thump and a clinking of glass as if bottles were knocking together.

'Some trolls'll be glad to find that,' he said.

'Tha's a fack.' The dry, withered voice came out of the blackness in front of him.

He flinched rigid. Shiner grabbed his arm. He wanted to spin around and run, but she held onto him and walked slowly backwards. He heard her breathing hard.

'Aren't you glad you didn't go under there?' she asked after several strides.

'God.'

'Like I told you, they're hiding all over the place.'

'The bastards.'

'I have all kinds of nightmares about getting caught by them. That's about the worst thing I can imagine, you know?'

'I've got a knife,' Jeremy said.

'Me, too. And a whistle.'

He realized that he still had Tanya's whistle hanging from his neck.

'You'd better get a whistle for yourself,' she said. 'And blow it like crazy if you ever get in trouble. Just never come out here without the rest of us.'

'Not a chance.'

'I guess we're okay.' She let go of his arm and turned around.

Jeremy turned around, too. Then, he looked back over his shoulder. The black space beneath the boardwalk was a vague blur through the fog. He tried to spot the Ferris wheel, but it was out of sight.

'I bet you never thought you'd get into anything like this,' Shiner said.

'That guy biting it.' He shook his head.

'Bad. Real bad. Makes me feel kind of sick, you know? I mean, he was a troll, but still . . .' She leaned against his side, and Jeremy put an arm across her back. 'It was pretty terrible, anyway.'

'Yeah.'

They kept walking. He could see nothing in front of him except sand and the fog.

'I hope he doesn't wash in sometime,' Shiner said. 'That'd be awful if people are on the beach and he comes in, you know?'

From the sound of the surf, Jeremy guessed they must be getting close to the shore. But he still couldn't see the water or Tanya and the others.

'Nate's going to take him out on a surfboard?' he asked.

'I guess so.'

'Does he have to go all the way home to get it?'

'No. Shouldn't take him very long. He keeps it in a

storeroom in the arcade. He surfs in the morning sometimes before the place opens.'

'He's Tanya's boyfriend, huh?'

'Yeah.'

Jeremy noticed that his feet no longer pushed into the sand. The beach felt solid. It slanted downwards slightly. Here and there, it was littered with dark clumps of kelp that looked less like seaweed than like strange, tentacled creatures dead on the shore.

A ragged fringe of white foam spread towards him. Shiner stopped walking. A couple of yards before reaching their feet, the foam settled and faded away. Jeremy heard the water receding, a fresh wave washing in.

'The others must be over there,' he said, nodding to the left.

Shiner turned her head that way. Then she looked forwards again. Her hand tightened against his side, so Jeremy pressed her a little bit closer.

'I guess we should go over there,' she said.

'Yeah.'

But she didn't move, so neither did Jeremy. He realized his heart was beating more rapidly than before.

He wondered what she would do if he tried to kiss her.

That made his heart race so fast he felt a little dizzy. He imagined the soft warmth of her lips, her arms going around his back, the feel of her body pressing against him.

But he thought, Who are you kidding? You wouldn't dare.

Once he'd abandoned the idea, his heart started slowing down.

This is fine just standing here, he told himself.

He wondered what she was thinking about.

Maybe she's *wishing* I'll kiss her.

Oh yeah, sure.

But what if she *is*, and I don't, and she thinks I'm just not interested?

I'm so damn gutless.

Then it occurred to Jeremy that this was very weird – to be in an agony about kissing a girl when, not many minutes ago, he'd watched the troll crash to his death. He ought to be feeling sick with guilt.

I didn't kill him, he told himself.

The whole thing was Tanya's idea, and she's the one who cuffed him to the Ferris wheel and made it go up. It didn't have anything to do with me. I was just there.

'You'd think we could hear them,' Shiner said.

'Should we try to find them?'

'Do you want to?' she asked.

He shrugged. He wanted to stay right here. And *that* was weird, too. Tanya was the one he was crazy about, not Shiner. He could be with Tanya right now – looking at her, hearing her voice.

But I wouldn't be holding her like this, he thought. She's Nate's girl. I don't stand a chance with her.

What makes you think you stand a chance with Shiner?

She likes me. I know she does.

Maybe she has a boyfriend. Maybe she's only hanging onto me because she's cold, and it doesn't mean anything.

'I think I might quit trolling,' she said.

'Really?'

'I don't know. Killing a guy like that. I hate the trolls, but killing them . . .'

'If you quit, when'll I see you?' The words were out before he had a chance to think about them and back off.

She turned her face towards Jeremy.

'Why don't you give me your number?' she said.

His heart felt like a drumming fist.

'I . . . we just got our phone. I don't know the number. If you give me yours . . .'

'I can't,' she said. 'I'd like to, but I'm not allowed to get calls from boys.'

'Huh?'

'My mother, she's . . . a little peculiar. She thinks I'm too young to have a boyfriend.'

'How old are you?'

'Sixteen.'

'Same here.'

'Maybe we could meet somewhere,' she suggested.

'Sure.' He felt as if he could barely breathe. 'Yeah. That'd be great.'

'How about here at the beach tomorrow afternoon? The fog'll probably burn off by noon. How about one o'clock? We could meet over by the lifeguard station.'

'Great.'

Shiner squeezed him against her side and he thought, *Now! Kiss her now*. He felt as if he might explode if he didn't sweep her into his arms, right now, and mash his mouth against hers – but he froze. He just couldn't force himself to do it.

She wants you to!

All he could do was stand there.

Then someone came striding along the beach in front of them and they both flinched.

Nate. Barefoot and wearing a wetsuit. Carrying a surfboard under one arm.

He turned and came towards them. A few strides away, he stopped. His head swivelled from side to side. 'Where are the rest of them?' he asked.

'Over there someplace,' Shiner said. She raised her left arm and pointed.

He started away. 'You coming?' he asked.

'Yeah, I guess.'

Shiner let go of Jeremy, and they both started walking along behind Nate. Jeremy's side felt cold where she had been pressed against it.

'Tanya?' Nate called.

'Over here.' Tanya's voice seemed to come from far away, but straight ahead.

Shiner took hold of Jeremy's hand. Her warmth seemed to flow up his arm and fill him. He found himself thinking about tomorrow. It would be like having a real date with her. He hoped she was as pretty in the sunlight as she seemed in the darkness. She would probably be wearing a swimsuit – maybe some kind of a bikini. And they'd be meeting near the lifeguard station, so Tanya would be there. He could look at both of them.

It'll be great, he thought.

Then, he saw three faint, dark figures standing in the fog ahead of Nate. The naked body of the troll lay at their feet. The cuffs had been removed.

Shiner didn't let go of his hand when they joined the group. Jeremy was glad. In away, it seemed as if she were showing him off, saying, 'Look what I've got.'

He felt as if the two of them had suddenly become a 'couple'.

'Anybody see you?' Tanya asked Nate as he set his surfboard down beside the corpse.

'Nope. Maybe some trolls, but I didn't spot any.'

'This is one troll they won't be getting their hands on,' Samson said.

He and Nate crouched at the other side of the body. They rolled it over onto the surfboard. Jeremy's stomach clutched a little when he saw the broken legs flop loosely. But he was relieved that the troll was face down, now, penis out of sight. There was a dark splotch on one of the buttocks. A birthmark?

'He's going to slide right off there if we don't strap him down,' Nate said. 'I couldn't find any rope. Any of you wearing belts?'

'Yeah,' Samson said. 'Won't go around him and the board, though.'

'We'll need a couple, at least.'

'I've got one,' Jeremy said.

Shiner said, 'Me, too.'

'Sorry,' said Randy, and lifted his jacket as if he felt he needed to prove he had no belt.

While Jeremy removed his belt, he watched Shiner raise her windbreaker above her waist, open her belt and slide it through the loops of her jeans. She wore a plaid shirt. The side of it was untucked and bunched up. A small, pale patch of skin showed near her hip. Once the belt was off, she tugged the windbreaker down again.

'Are you going to bring them back?' she asked Nate as she gave it to him.

'I'll sure try.'

'It was a present from my sister,' she added.

Her sister. The one who vanished. The one the trolls got. When Jeremy had heard about it earlier, Shiner had been a stranger. Now, she was special to him and he felt a tug of sorrow for her loss.

Nate buckled Jeremy's belt to Samson's. While Samson held an end of the surfboard off the sand, he slipped the joined belts underneath it. Samson lowered the board. Nate straddled the body, brought up the ends of the belts, and fastened them in the middle of the troll's back. He used Shiner's belt to strap the troll's ankles against the surfboard's tail.

'Okay,' he said. 'All set.'

'Not quite,' Tanya said. She stepped around the body and approached Jeremy. 'Let me have the card,' she told him.

He was confused. What card? Didn't she mean the whistle? Then he remembered. He dug into his pocket, found the Billy Goat Gruff calling card, and handed it to her.

She smiled at him.

'Here,' he said. 'You can have your whistle back.' He took it off and dropped it into her hand.

'I guess you didn't need it,' she said, and slipped the chain over her head. A finger of the hand that held the card hooked the neck of her sweatshirt out, and she dropped the whistle down her front. 'Let's just say you got initiated,' she told him.

'We *all* got initiated,' Nate said.

Tanya stepped to the front of the surfboard and squatted down. Reaching between her knees, she turned the troll's face toward her. She pulled the chin. The mouth opened. She stuffed the card inside, then clapped the mouth shut.

'I'm not sure that's such a good idea,' Nate said.

She left it there, and stood up. 'The guy's fish bait,' she said.

'Besides, nobody'll be able to read it, anyway, by the time he's been in the water a few minutes.'

Nate shrugged. He muttered, 'What the hell.'

Then he and Samson lifted the surfboard off the sand. They carried it like a stretcher down the beach.

The others followed. Jeremy saw the thin, foamy edge of the water sliding towards him, but he kept going. Cold wetness soaked through his shoes and socks.

He saw the ocean. Black waves, crested with white, rolled towards him out of the fog.

He imagined the troll sinking out there, all alone in the cold dark water, and felt himself go frozen inside. It's not like the guy's alive, he told himself. He's dead. He won't feel a thing. He won't *know*.

But the awful, frigid feeling stayed.

They all halted except Samson and Nate. Randy moved over close to Tanya. Shiner curled her fingers around Jeremy's hand.

The two boys waded out with their cargo. They set the surfboard down in knee-deep water. As Samson hurried back, Nate pushed the board further out.

A wave broke over the head and back of the dead man.

After it washed by, Jeremy saw Nate behind the surfboard, pushing it in front of him.

Shiner turned Jeremy towards her and held him tightly against her body and pressed her face to the side of his neck.

When he looked again towards the ocean, he saw only the surf and the fog.

Chapter Twenty-one

After roll call, Dave sat at his desk to prepare his report on yesterday's incident at Funland. He relived it all in his mind as he pecked the typewriter keys. When he wrote of Joan's decisive moves against the knife-wielding perpetrator, his thoughts drifted away to the other, vulnerable Joan in her anguish over demolishing the kid. He lingered on the way she'd felt in his arms, and how it had been, kissing her.

Joan's desk was off to the side. He looked at her. She was leaning back in her swivel chair, phone at her ear, legs stretched out. Like Dave, she wore her bright blue BBPD jacket over her beach uniform. The jacket wasn't fastened. It hung open in a way that showed her right breast stretching the fabric of her T-shirt.

As he stared at her, she sat forward and cradled the phone. She swivelled towards him. She raised her eyebrows. 'Woodrow Abernathy regained consciousness two hours ago,' she said.

'Glad to hear it.' He was glad for Joan, not for Woodrow. Other people would probably suffer in years to come because the creep had pulled through, but Joan wouldn't have to live with the guilt of knowing she'd destroyed him.

Smiling slightly, she shook her head. She took a huge breath that swelled her chest, let it out, and slumped forwards as if the air in her lungs had been all that was holding her up. Her forearms dropped against her thighs. Then, she just sat there, hunched over and gazing at the floor.

Dave typed more of his report, but his eyes kept straying over to Joan. He wished he could go to her. They weren't alone, though.

Finally, she sat up straight. She met his eyes. Her head tipped a bit to one side. She smiled, and slapped her open hands against her knees. 'About ready to go, partner?'

'I'm almost done here.'

'I'll hit the john and meet you in the car.'

He watched Joan stride away. Without the distraction of her presence, he quickly finished the report, signed it, and took it to the chief's in-basket.

By the time he reached the patrol unit, Joan was already sitting behind the steering wheel. He climbed in. She drove out of the parking lot and headed for Funland.

'You must be pretty relieved,' he said.

She nodded. 'How are you doing? How's the chest?'

'A little stiff and tender. Not bad. Thanks for the medication.'

Joan grimaced. 'I'm really sorry about all that.'

'About what?'

'Guh . . . what could I *possibly* be sorry about? All I did was make a goddamn spectacle of myself, get soused, spill the goddamn champagne, throw myself at you, mess you up with Gloria. Shit. Nothing much.'

'It was a disgusting display,' Dave said.

She didn't look at him. He saw her lips press together in a tight line. Her head nodded once in sharp agreement.

'The worst damn part of the whole thing,' Dave continued, 'was when we kissed.'

Her head jerked towards him. For a moment, her eyes were wide with shock. Then they narrowed. A corner of her mouth tilted upward. 'Liar,' she said.

'Ah, you caught me.'

'I thought I'd made that kid into a vegetable. And you'd been stabbed. But it was like some kind of a victory, too – we'd stomped those scrotes. So I just thought it'd be nice to *be* with you, you know? We're partners. It seemed like the right thing to do, commiserate and hoist a few . . .'

'There was nothing wrong with it.'

She glanced at him. 'I'm your partner, but I'm not a guy. That's what screwed it up. Would've been the right thing, except for that little detail.'

Dave reached over and patted her shoulder. 'Don't fret. I *think of you* as a guy.'

'Yeah. Right.'

'A guy who's *taller* than me,' he added, hoping she would remember he'd first made that observation yesterday while he was embracing her.

The way her face softened, he knew she remembered.

'My only regret about yesterday,' he said, 'is that Gloria showed up and I had to stop kissing you.'

Joan swung the patrol car into Funland's parking lot. She stopped it, shut off the engine, and looked into Dave's eyes. Her hand curled over his thigh.

'What about Gloria?' she asked.

'She's out of it, now.'

'Aw, geez.' Joan lowered her eyes. She seemed to be staring at her hand as it began to move slowly up and down his leg.

'Don't worry about her,' Dave said.

'No, of course not. All I did was steal her guy out from under her.'

'I was never really hers.'

Joan's hand stopped moving. She peered into his eyes, frowning. 'Maybe you'll say the same thing about me, someday. "Don't worry about Joan. I was never really hers."'

'I've been yours since our first patrol together,' Dave said. 'You just didn't notice.'

Her eyebrows darted up. Her lips curled into a wiseguy smirk. She slapped his leg and said, 'Bullshit.'

'What about you and Harold?'

'I was never really his.'

Dave grinned. 'You were head-over-heels for me since our first patrol?'

'Don't flatter yourself.'

He tried to look shocked. 'You mean you weren't?'

'I just knew I liked your legs.'

Robin saw a few familiar faces in her audience. Not Nate's though. Where was Nate?

He'd said he would see her today.

She'd been watching for him all morning. It was nearly noon, now.

She wondered if she should take a break and visit his arcade. That might seem pushy, though.

He'll show up, she told herself.

He has to.

It worried her, though. She'd half expected to find him waiting when she came back from breakfast and took up her usual position at the north end of the boardwalk.

Maybe he's just too busy at the arcade to get away.

He'll show up.

As she played and wondered about Nate, she noticed that Dave and the female cop had joined her audience. They had been stopping briefly each time their foot patrol brought them to this end of the boardwalk. Dave hadn't given her a talk since the first day, but he always nodded and smiled when he showed up.

Yesterday, she'd been tempted to tell him about Poppinsack. Each time she saw him listening to her music, she'd thought about it. He seemed like a good guy. He'd probably go out of his way to help her. But he would have to ask how the theft happened. That would be just too embarrassing. Besides, yesterday she'd still hoped to confront Poppinsack, herself, and if the old creep ended up stabbed or something, she didn't want any cops knowing she had a problem with him.

She could tell Dave now, since she no longer planned to nail the guy. But that still left the problem of telling him that the money had been stolen out of her panties.

I might tell his partner, she thought. It wouldn't be so bad, talking to a woman about something like that. Robin liked her, even though they'd never spoken. She had a terrific smile, and her eyes looked friendly.

Robin considered it while she played. She wondered if there was any point. By now, Poppinsack had probably spent most of the money. Besides, he was nowhere around.

When she finished the number, Dave came up, nodded to her, and tossed a folded bill into her banjo case. She thanked him. He smiled, gave her a little wave, then headed away with the woman.

'Let's hear "Weenie Roast",' called a heavy-set guy who'd been in her audience several times during the past three days.

'You got it,' she said, and started in on the song.

As usual, people shook their heads, laughed or groaned.

She was just finishing when she spotted Nate at the rear of the small group. A quick rush of excitement made her forget the lyrics for a moment. She got back on the track, and ended with a flourish.

She waited for the clapping and hoots to die down, then announced that she would be taking a short break. People moved forward to drop money into her case, and wandered off.

Nate stayed.

He stepped up closer to her. Over his T-shirt, he wore a money apron with bulging pockets that jangled as he moved. His arms looked muscular. He had a deep tan that she hadn't noticed last night.

A real hunk, she thought, and smiled at herself. A stupid term, hunk. But appropriate.

'That's a nasty little song,' he said.

'I'm a nasty little woman.'

He shook his head and smiled. The smile seemed a little strained.

'Hey,' she said. 'About last night. You went ahead and gave me the twenty. You weren't supposed to do that, you know.'

'I had nothing better to do with it.'

'Well, you've got to let me buy you lunch.'

'I have to get back to the arcade,' he said. 'I left Hector in charge, and he's a doufuss.'

It sounded to Robin like an excuse.

'That's okay,' she said, and shrugged and hoped he couldn't see her disappointment.

'I just wanted to come by and say hi, see how you're doing.'

She tried to smile. 'I thought maybe you wanted to hear more of "The Land of Purr".'

'Some other time, maybe,' he said.

'Whenever.'

'I've gotta get back.'

He just stood there, looking at her. He seemed so different from the energetic, cheerful guy Robin had met last night. Weary, *deflated*.

Concern for him pushed aside her disappointment. 'Are you all right?' she asked.

'Sure.'

'Maybe you're coming down with something.' She took a step forward and pressed an open hand against his forehead. The skin of his brow felt smooth, moist, and hot. 'I think you've got a little fever,' Robin said, lowering her hand.

He made a tired smile. 'What are you, a nurse?'

'Just a gal.' *Cockless Robin*. Damn you, Poppinsack. 'We've all got built-in thermometers on our hands. You'd better go home, take a couple of aspirin and get plenty of rest.'

His smile perked up slightly. 'I guess I could use the rest, anyway. I didn't get much sleep last night.'

'Neither did I,' Robin said, remembering her restless hours under the beach house.

'Where did you sleep?' Nate asked.

'On the beach.'

Frowning, he shook his head. 'You shouldn't do that.'

'I know. The trolls, the trollers.'

His frown deepened. 'It isn't safe.'

'I've noticed.'

'Has someone bothered you?'

'I was robbed in my sleep, two nights ago. And, of course, you know about that creep last night. Thanks again.'

'You oughta stay off the beach, Robin.'

'I like the fresh air.'

'That twenty I gave you, you could've stayed in a motel.'

She shrugged. 'I'm saving up for a BMW.'

'It's nothing to joke about.'

'I can eat good breakfasts for a week on twenty bucks. I'd rather have that than a roof over my head.'

'I don't want you getting hurt.'

'I can take care of myself.'

'That's a stupid-fuck thing to say.'

Robin flinched.

Nate shook his head, squeezing his eyes shut. 'I'm sorry. Jesus.' He rubbed his face. 'I shouldn't have . . . I'm sorry.'

'It's all right.'

'I've gotta go. See you around.' He hurried away.

Robin watched him until he disappeared in the crowd. She wondered what was wrong with him, really. Though his brow had felt slightly feverish, she didn't think he was sick – he seemed depressed or upset, not ill.

Could it have anything to do with her?

That didn't seem likely.

But he'd sure been in a hurry to get away.

Robin thought that they'd made some kind of connection last night, that he was eager to see her again. She'd tried not to read too much into it, but he had been on her mind a lot ever since their meeting. Especially once she had given up the idea of trying to jump Poppinsack.

Lying in the dark space beneath the house last night, she'd slept fitfully. She'd flinched awake, time and again, certain that someone was crawling towards her or that she'd been discovered by those who lived in the house. Huddled there, feeling small and frightened, she had comforted herself with thoughts of Nate.

It all seemed a little stupid, now.

He was just being nice, last night, and you blew it all out of proportion.

A feeling of sadness hollowed her out. She had been on the road a long, long time – drifting, savouring the freedom, not minding much that she was alone, and looking forward to each new day. It had started with running away, but it had soon become an adventure, a quest.

It had led her here.

And she realized, now, that she had allowed herself to hope that it was over.

Nate could've been what she'd been looking for.

Could've been.

But wasn't.

She stood there with a loneliness inside that felt as vast and cold as the ocean.

'I'm getting a case of the hungries,' Joan said.

'What do you feel like?'

During her two weeks of patrolling the boardwalk with Dave, she'd sampled food from most of the shops. She ran the list of possibilities through her mind: hamburgers, cheeseburgers, hot dogs, chili dogs, submarines, fish and chips, fried clams, Mexican food and Chinese and Greek. 'What were those gizmos in the pitta bread with the lamb stuff and sour cream?' she asked.

'Gyros?'

'Yeah. Does that sound good to you?'

'They're kind of messy,' Dave said. 'I wouldn't want you to embarrass yourself by slobbing.'

'Screw you,' she said, and bumped into him.

'Any time.'

'Don't hold your breath, partner.' She saw that they were passing the main entrance. 'Why don't I ditch our jackets?' she suggested. 'You can go ahead and order, I'll meet you there.'

'What do you want to drink?'

'Beer, but I'll settle for Coke or Pepsi.'

'You want onions?' he asked, taking off his jacket.

'Just ice.'

He handed the jacket to her. 'I am having onions on my gyro,' he said, speaking with slow precision. 'Would you care for onions on your gyro?'

'I promise I'll care for them,' she said, smiling as she watched Dave roll his eyes upward. 'I'll feed them, take them for walks, clean up after them.'

'I'll take that as a yes.'

'I wouldn't want you to be the only one with stinky breath.'

'Won't matter,' he said. 'I'll be holding it.'

Smiling, Joan turned away from him. She pulled her jacket off as she walked past the ticket booth. She glanced back and saw that he was watching her. Nice.

189

It had been a terrific morning once their talk in the car was out of the way and she knew where they both stood. She still felt a little guilty about Gloria, but she figured she could live with that burden. Gloria hadn't been right for him, anyway.

And I am? she asked herself as she trotted down the stairs. Damn straight I am.

It felt so good.

Joan arrived at the patrol car. She tossed their jackets into the trunk, slammed the trunk shut, and hurried back through the parking lot.

She breathed deeply, savouring the fresh smell of the ocean. The sun warmed her, and the breeze caressed her. She felt light and compact and strong and vibrant. She liked how the breeze ruffled her T-shirt and shorts against her skin. She liked the weight of the utility belt around her hips, and the way the leather creaked. She liked the feel of her muscles sliding under her skin. She even liked the hungry feeling in her stomach.

Then, she saw two bums sitting on the concrete stairs. Two female bums. And she stopped feeling good.

Her breath snagged. Her heart raced. Her stomach felt cold and numb. The muscles of her legs seemed to go soft and shaky.

One of the bums was Gloria.

My God, she thought. Losing Dave might've hit the woman hard, but to disintegrate this much so fast . . .

She suddenly realized it was a disguise.

The shock started to wear off.

Gloria hadn't fallen apart, after all. She'd done that piece about trolling a couple of days ago, and yesterday she'd been trying to interview bums on the boardwalk. Now, she had taken it one step further – one major step – and made herself up to look like one.

She'd done a good job of it, too. Her hair, normally black and well groomed, was a tangled mop streaked with grey. Her face looked dirty. She wore a dingy grey sweatshirt that gaped with holes – probably made by scissors, Joan thought. An

190

undershirt showed through the holes. Her faded skirt, a purple thing with a flower pattern, looked like a reject from a thrift shop. She wore red tights under the skirt. One knee of the tights was slit open. Instead of shoes, or over her shoes, she wore brown paper grocery sacks tied at the ankles with twine. On the stair beside her rested a grocery bag intended to represent the receptacle for all her worldly goods.

Either that, Joan thought, or it's a spare shoe.

So far, Gloria hadn't noticed Joan. Her head was turned towards the subject of her interview – a fat, older woman wearing a knitted cap and overcoat. The woman's pasty white knees were bare below the edge of the coat. Her calves looked as if they were being choked by the bands of her brown, knee-high nylons. She wore big, scuffed army boots.

As she talked, she waved her hands around, scrunched up her face and rolled her eyes. Gloria nodded. The way she nodded in response to the woman's babbling was enough to blow her cover, Joan thought. It showed she was alert, focused. Not that the troll was likely to pick up on such a clue.

Joan took a step towards the women.

Then turned away and trotted up the stairs.

I'm not going to interfere, she told herself. The hell with it. Gloria's a big girl.

But she knew she would have to tell Dave.

Chapter Twenty-two

Jeremy left the bathroom and rushed into the kitchen. His mother was on her knees, applying contact paper to the bottom of a cupboard. He looked at the clock. Ten minutes till one. He should've been on his way by now.

Mom pulled her head out of the cupboard and frowned at him. 'Are you all right, honey? You've been running to the toilet every five minutes.'

That was an exaggeration, but he *had* gone three times during the past hour. 'Must be something I ate,' he said.

'If you've been eating junk at Funland . . .'

Cramps hit him again. Gritting his teeth, he hurried back to the bathroom. He tugged his swimsuit down and dropped onto the toilet seat just in time.

Jeez, he thought, now I'm really going to be late.

He was sure his problem had nothing to do with what he'd been eating. He suspected it had to do with a dead troll, or maybe it had to do with Shiner. As if his bowels wanted to stop him from returning to the scene of the death, or prevent his date with the girl. Or both.

He finished, and rushed back into the kitchen. The clock now showed two minutes till one.

'Would it be okay if I take the car?' he asked.

'I have a hair appointment at two,' Mom said. 'I'll drive you to the beach, if you'd like. But I'm not sure you should be going anywhere in your condition.'

'I have to. I'm meeting someone. I'm going to be late if I have to take my bike.'

'All right. Go on out to the car. I'll be along in a minute.'

'Thanks,' he said.

He waited in the car. As he sat in the passenger seat, the tightness came back. Goosebumps scurried over his skin.

It's just nerves, he told himself. I *can't* have to go again. It'll stop once I'm there.

Mom arrived and climbed in behind the wheel. She backed the car out of the driveway. 'Are you sure you're okay?' she asked.

'Yeah.' He wondered if she could see the goosebumps on his face.

'Maybe it isn't something you ate,' she said. 'It might very well be that you're upset about going back there after what happened yesterday.'

He knew she was referring to the fight with the four creeps, and nothing else.

'I guess I am a little nervous about that,' he said.

'You have to be more careful, honey. There seem to be a lot of unsavoury characters who hang around that area. As you found out.'

'Yeah.'

'And I'm not so sure that Cowboy is a good influence.'

'You've never even met him.'

'Do you think the fight would've happened if you'd been alone?'

'Probably,' he lied. 'Anyway, I'm not seeing Cowboy today. I think he's still in the hospital.'

'Then who are you meeting?'

'A girl.'

Mom turned her head toward him. She smiled and raised her eyebrows, looking both pleased and surprised. 'I wasn't aware you'd met any girls.'

'She's a friend of Cowboy's. She's really nice,' he added quickly, wondering if he'd made a mistake in linking her to Cowboy. 'You'd like her.'

'What's her name?'

'Shiner.'

'Doesn't she have a real name?'

'I only met her yesterday.' He realized that his cramps had subsided. Explaining things to Mom was a distraction that must help.

'Is she your age?'

'Yeah, I think so.'

They reached the boulevard at the foot of the hill, and Mom stopped for a traffic light. 'Is she pretty?'

He almost said that he'd only seen her in the dark, but caught himself. 'Yeah, kind of.'

'Well, I think that's grand. It's about time you met a nice girl. I'd like to meet her sometime. Maybe you should ask her over for dinner one of these nights.'

'Mom, I hardly even know her yet.'

The light went green. She drove forward and turned left toward Funland.

'There's something you're not telling me, Jeremy.'

That's sure an understatement, he thought.

'Is there something about this Shiner that isn't . . . right?'

'No.'

'She isn't a beach bum or a delinquent . . .?'

'I told you, you'd like her.'

'Then why are you so reluctant to invite her over?'

'I'm not reluctant. I already told you, we just met. I can't all of a sudden ask her over. It'd be weird.'

'If you're afraid I might not approve of her . . .'

'It isn't that. *Jeez!*'

She gave him a sharp glance. 'If you're so ashamed of this girl that you won't let your own mother meet her, then something is very definitely wrong and you'd better think twice before you get involved with her. We've only been in this town a few days, and you've already managed to get into trouble. I'm not at all sure your new friends are the sort of people you should be associating with.'

'They're just normal kids.'

'With odd nicknames. You're not involved with some kind of a gang, are you?'

'No. That's ridiculous.'

'I'd like to meet this Shiner.'

'Okay, okay. I'll see if she wants to come over some time.'

'I'd like to meet her today.' The car slowed as it approached the parking lot entrance.

'You can just drop me off in front,' Jeremy said.

'I think I'll go with you and meet this girl.'

'You mean *now*?'

Nodding, she swung the car into the parking lot and took a ticket from the man beside the booth.

'Mom, no! Jesus! You'll ruin everything!'

'You're only sixteen years old. I won't have you getting involved with some kind of tramp or criminal . . .'

'She's not! Damn it, Mom!'

'Don't use that language with me, young man. I'm your mother, not one of your hoodlum friends.' She jolted the car to a stop in a parking space. 'Let's go.'

Jeremy shook his head. 'You can't come with me.'

'Don't tell me what I can't do.'

'Then I'm not getting out of the car.'

'That's fine with me. I'll drive you home.'

'Mom, please!'

She stared at him. The hardness seemed to melt out of her face. 'I only want what's best for you, honey.'

'There's nothing wrong with Shiner,' he said, his voice shaking. He felt as if he might start to cry. 'She's nice. She's not a tramp or anything.'

'I'd like to meet her and see for myself. I've been a teacher so long I can tell a good kid from a rotten one in about a second.'

'I'll ask her to come over. Okay? But you can't go out on the beach with me. Please. It'd ruin everything. These kids here, they like me. They don't think I'm a wimp or a fag or a momma's boy. If you walk me out there like I'm a four-year-old, I'd never live it down. I'd be screwed in this town, just like I was in Bakersfield. I might as well stick my head in the oven.'

'Don't you ever say that.'

'I'm sorry,' he muttered. 'But I hated it, the way things were before. I've got a chance, here. Don't mess it up for me.'

He saw tears in his mother's eyes. Her lips were pressed tightly together. Nodding, she reached out and stroked his cheek. 'I just want to make sure you don't get hurt.'

'I know. Trust me, though, okay?'

'Have a good time. Ask the girl to have dinner with us tonight.'

'I will. Thanks, Mom.' He leaned across the seat and kissed her.

Then he climbed from the car. He walked around its rear. Mom looked at him through the driver's window. Her eyes were still red, but she smiled. He waved. She drove away.

God, he thought, she'd nearly blown everything.

He never should've mentioned Shiner. He never should've asked Mom for a ride. He should've just taken his bike.

Well, you learned a lesson. From now on, keep your mouth shut.

He saw a couple of trolls sitting on the steps. They were busy talking to each other. He rushed towards the top, taking the stairs two at a time, hoping to get out of range before either of the trolls decided to hit him up for money.

In front of Jeremy stood the main ticket booth. He remembered Tanya leaping from the top of it. And how he and Shiner had rushed to the felled troll and kicked him, and how Shiner got slugged in the chest and how Jeremy snapped the old guy's finger.

Dead now, under the waves.

Jeremy felt as if he couldn't get enough air.

At least the cramps are gone, he thought as he gasped, trying to fill his lungs.

When he crossed the boardwalk, he glanced to the left and saw the distant, towering structure of the Ferris wheel. It looked so *high*. He saw the old man falling through the fog.

He rushed the rest of the way across the boardwalk and trotted down the stairs to the beach. He headed for the lifeguard station. It was too far away for him to recognize Shiner among those sprawled on the sand around it.

Would he recognize her, he wondered, if he could see her?

Only a portion of the platform in front of the lifeguard shack was visible from this angle, and no one seemed to be there.

Though he kept walking, his head swung around and he gazed back at the Ferris wheel. He didn't want to look at it, but couldn't help himself. The gondolas of the spinning wheel were bright red against the pale sky.

Again, he saw the old troll falling.

He saw the broken body on the platform under the wheel. He saw Tanya pushing down the leg that was sticking up the wrong way from its broken knee.

He felt cold and tight in his stomach.

It wasn't my fault, he told himself.

He wondered if Funland was ruined forever, now. What if he could never come here again without being tormented by the memories of last night?

Some of it was good, though. Being part of the group – the first time in his life he wasn't an outsider. The way he'd felt when Tanya gave him the whistle. And afterwards on the beach with Shiner. Holding her.

It was like you thought before, he reminded himself. You've got to go through it all. The bad stuff's part of the good stuff. It's all mixed together and one thing leads to another and you wouldn't be meeting Shiner here today, probably, if the old coot hadn't fallen. That's what brought you together.

'It's worth it.'

It has to be worth it.

As if those thoughts had released him from the need for further punishment, he found that he was able to look away from the Ferris wheel.

He was a lot closer to the lifeguard station, now.

He spotted someone on its platform. Not Tanya. A male in red swimming trunks.

Disappointment tugged at Jeremy.

I didn't come here to see Tanya, he told himself.

But he realized that wasn't true. He'd come here to be with Shiner, but he'd expected Tanya to be at her post. Even if he didn't go to her, he would've been able to watch her. Gaze at her standing there golden in the sunlight, her hair and T-shirt and red shorts fluttering in the breeze, her legs long and powerful and bare.

He remembered hurling the remains of his waffle cone at her, day before yesterday.

What a dumb-ass thing to do. What a great thing to do. That's what proved I'm not a wimp. If I hadn't done that, maybe she wouldn't have let me meet the trollers.

He thought about how she had forced him to clean the ice cream off her leg. His mind lingered on that, savouring the memory of the slickness and the way she'd made him go up inside the leg hole of her shorts.

Shiner might be nice and even pretty, Jeremy told himself, but she's no Tanya. She's a girl; Tanya's a . . . a what? Something more. A force? A . . .

'Jeremy?' The call came from a girl kneeling on a blanket, waving an arm at him. Her blanket was spread out several yards this side of the lifeguard station.

Would've had a good view of Tanya, he thought as he raised a hand in greeting and walked closer. He was surprised to realize that he suddenly felt no more than a mild sense of regret over Tanya's absence.

Shiner bore only a vague resemblance to the girl last night. In the dark, he hadn't been able to see the shine of her yellow hair. Maybe that's where she got the nickname, he thought. The dark had also hidden the deep blue of her eyes, the soft tan of her skin. Her teeth had been grey; now they were brilliant white. The features of her face had been smudged with shadows; now he could see the shapes of her eyes and nose, her lips, her delicate chin.

She was beautiful. But cute, too. The cuteness came from her smile. It was a wide stretch of a smile that seemed too big for her face. It creased her cheeks. It crinkled the skin around her eyes. It *filled* her eyes with a look of happiness and maybe a touch of mischief.

It's the smile, he thought. The smile is why she's Shiner. The smile slipped sideways a trifle. 'What's wrong?' she asked.

He realized that he had stopped walking. He was standing there, gazing at her like a dope from seven or eight feet away. Embarrassed, he shook his head and stepped to the edge of her blanket.

'Sit down and stay a while,' she said.

He dropped to his knees. His heart was slamming. He could hardly believe that this was the girl from last night – the same girl who'd been at this side when they threw the troll's junk under the boardwalk, who'd leaned against him as they walked the beach, who'd held him tightly there at the end as the body was being floated out. If he'd known she looked like this . . . Good thing you didn't, he thought. You would've been a wreck.

'What's *wrong*?' she demanded, her smile gone and worry in her eyes.

'You're . . . so beautiful.'

The smile returned, this time sheepish, as her face went red.

'I'm not so hot,' she said. 'But thanks.' She patted the blanket in front of her. 'Come on, sit down.' She moved backward on her knees to make more room for him, then sat and crossed her legs.

Jeremy sat down facing her.

'I thought you weren't going to show up,' she said.

'I'm sorry. I had trouble getting away from home.'

'No problem. I've only been here a few minutes, myself.' A corner of her lip lifted slightly. 'It wasn't easy, coming back after what happened.'

'I know what you mean.'

'Aren't you awfully warm in that shirt?' she asked.

'Yeah.' He took his sunglasses from a pocket and put them on. Then, he took off his shirt. He rolled it into a bundle, being careful not to let his wallet and keys fall out, and dropped it onto the blanket. 'That's better,' he said.

With the sunglasses on, he allowed himself to look at the rest of Shiner.

'Does it bother you?' she asked.

She wore a one-piece suit, not a bikini.

'What?'

It wasn't low cut. Its neck was as high as the top of a T-shirt, and straps went over her shoulders.

'The guy.'

But it was black and the thin, glossy fabric was skintight.

'Yeah,' he said. 'It bothers me a lot.'

It hugged her breasts, which were somewhat cone-shaped and pointed.

'Me, too. I keep seeing him . . . everything.'

It clung to her ribcage and slanted down against her flat belly.

'It's like a nightmare,' she continued. 'But it really happened, didn't it.'

It swept inwards, leaving her hips bare, and was very narrow where it passed between her legs.

'Nothing we can do will change it,' Jeremy said.

The way she sat, he could see the bare hollows where her legs joined her groin. He didn't see any pubic hair.

'I guess,' he added, 'it'll get easier as time goes by.'

The inner sides of her thighs, turned upward, glimmered with suntan oil.

'I sure hope so.'

Jeremy raised his eyes to her face. 'I'm sorry the guy got killed,' he said, 'but I'm awfully glad I met you.'

A corner of her mouth lifted. 'I'm glad we met, too.' Leaning forward, she reached out and put a hand on his knee. It rested there for a moment, then rubbed him, then patted him and went back to her own knee. 'You want some of my suntan oil?' she asked.

'Yeah, okay.'

She uncrossed her legs, swung them away from Jeremy, and stretched out on her side. Bracing herself up on one elbow, she reached into the side pocket of a denim bag. She pulled out a plastic bottle of oil and gave it to him.

Head resting on her hand, she watched him spread the oil over his skin. He was glad he'd spent some time in the sun so he wasn't white. He knew his body wasn't great, but he'd worked out enough to develop his muscles so he no longer looked so much like a skinny weakling.

When he finished, he gave the bottle back to Shiner. He rubbed his slick hands on his swimsuit. Then he lay down on his side, facing her.

'Do you need the sunglasses?' she asked. 'I like it better when I can see your eyes.'

Jeremy felt a flutter of alarm. Had she noticed the way he'd inspected her?

He took the glasses off.

She smiled. 'You've got neat eyes.'

'Thanks. So do you.'

For along time, they stared into each other's eyes. Hers

were so blue that even their whites seemed to be tinted with the colour. Her face was so close to him that apparently she couldn't focus on both his eyes at once. Her gaze flicked slightly from side to side. He supposed that his did, too.

It felt very strange to be staring at each other this way. It felt good, but strange. Nothing like this had ever happened to Jeremy before. It made him feel shaky inside.

It was as if she were looking into him.

And I'm looking into her, he thought.

He found it hard to believe that this was the same girl who had kicked the troll, last night. The toughness didn't seem to be there, now. He saw only softness, and a bewildering mixture of joy and sorrow, knowledge and curiosity and hope.

He wished he knew what she was thinking.

Maybe she's wondering what *I'm* thinking.

Maybe she's waiting for me to kiss her.

He wondered how it would be, kissing her. He knew he wouldn't do it – not now, not here on the beach. But he also knew that they would kiss, sometime. It was almost a sure thing. They'd nearly kissed, last night. Now, there was a lot more between them. A lot more.

'I wish all these people weren't around,' Shiner said.

Chapter Twenty-three

'Yeah,' Jeremy said. 'Me, too.'

'Why?' Shiner asked.

He smiled. 'Hey, that's not fair. You're the one who said you wished we were alone.'

'But you agreed.'

'Well, sure.'

'What would you do if nobody else was around?'

'What would *you* do?'

Shiner reached out and stroked the side of his face. 'I think I might want to kiss you,' she said. 'Is that what you were thinking, too?'

'Yeah.'

She twisted onto her stomach, held herself up on her elbows, and looked around at him. 'Not with other people around, though. That's why I wished we were alone. It's supposed to be a private thing, you know? Don't you think so?'

'Yeah.'

'I think it's disgusting when I see people making out on the beach in broad daylight in front of everyone. It just shows they don't have any self-control.'

'Or self-respect,' Jeremy added, staring at Shiner's back. Which was bare except for two straps that crossed between her shoulder blades, and a triangle of shiny black fabric that started just below her waist and looked as if it were glued to her buttocks.

He wondered if she would ask him to put suntan oil on her back.

'Where did you move here from?' she asked.

'Bakersfield.'

'Did you have a girlfriend?'

'Not exactly.'

'What does that mean, not exactly?'

'There was nobody I actually went out with. Just some girls in school who were okay.'

'They don't have any boys in my school.'

'Really?'

'I go to St Anne's. It's all girls.'

'So you haven't had any boyfriends?'

She smiled and shrugged one shoulder a little. 'I've had some. Nobody I really cared much about, though. And I never got to see much of them, not with my mother the way she is. She has a way of scaring them off.'

'Sounds like my mother.'

Shiner rolled over and folded her hands under her head. There went my chance to oil her back, Jeremy thought.

'They're so protective,' she said, one eye shut against the sun, the other squinting at him.

'Yeah, that's for sure. I got the third degree when I told my Mom I was meeting a girl here.'

'Probably shouldn't have told.'

'I know. What a goof. Now, she wants to meet you.'

'She does, huh? She afraid I'll corrupt you?'

'Yeah.'

Shiner raised a hand to shield her eyes from the sunlight, and stared at Jeremy. 'Maybe she's right.'

'I hope so.'

She laughed. 'If you want to get corrupted, you'll have better luck with someone else. Like Heather.'

'Give me a break.'

She put the hand down again and shut her eyes. Her elbow was near Jeremy's eye. The underside of her arm, though turned upwards, had almost no tan at all. The hollow of her armpit looked smooth and white and soft.

'I'll meet your mother if you want me to,' she said, keeping her eyes shut.

'You don't have to.'

'No, it's all right. If it'll make things easier for you.'

'Okay. I'll meet yours, too.'

'When hell freezes over. Forget about mine. That'd be the last I'd ever see of you.'

'She can't be that bad.'

'Believe it.' Shiner rolled onto her side. 'How about tonight?'

'Hey, you really don't . . .'

'We're getting together at Tanya's house at eight. You're invited.'

'No kidding?'

'This is her day off. She asked me to tell you about it. All of us are supposed to be there. Trollers only.'

'Like a meeting, or something?'

'I don't know. This is a first. It must have something to do with what happened last night.'

'Man.'

'Should be interesting, huh?'

'Yeah, I'll say.'

'Anyway, I'll be driving myself over, so why don't I give you a ride? That way, I can meet your mother when I come to pick you up. Put her mind at ease.'

'That'd be great!'

'You think she'll let you come?'

'Sure. Once she's met you, she'll . . . She'll like you. Hell, she'll be overjoyed. But what about your mom?'

'No sweat. I'll make up a story, tell her a friend from school's having a party. She'll buy it. She believes whatever I tell her. She's so strict it drives me crazy, but she trusts me. I can get away with just about anything.'

Shiner went silent. Jeremy lay down beside her. He folded his hands under his head. His elbow brushed against her elbow. She didn't move it out of the way. He kept his elbow there, touching hers, and shut his eyes.

The heat of the sun pressed down on him. He felt the mild breeze roaming over his skin.

Everything's going so great, he thought.

She would kiss me if nobody was around. Tonight, we'll be alone in her car.

He wondered what would happen at Tanya's house. It made him excited and nervous to think about that.

But he felt even more excited, more nervous, about being in the car with Shiner. Maybe she wouldn't take him straight home after the meeting. Maybe she would park someplace dark and deserted. Maybe they would do more than kiss.

Robin couldn't shake the cold, hollow feeling that had settled into her after Nate left. She played her banjo and she sang, but she ached inside.

It felt like homesickness.

It'll pass, she told herself.

She'd gone through a heavy period of *real* homesickness after running away, two years ago. It hadn't come at once. In the beginning, there had only been rage against Paul, anger against her mother for taking up with him, fear that she would be caught and sent back to them, and fear for her own safety on the road. The homesickness didn't hit until she'd been gone for more than a week. When it came, it was crushing.

She'd been walking through a small town just after dark. It was October. A chilly wind tumbled leaves past her. She smelled wood smoke from chimneys. On both sides of the street, warm light glowed from the windows of homes.

It hit her then. The loss. The sudden understanding that she was outside, alone, unloved, with no hope of ever returning to the home that had once been so cozy and safe and full of happiness.

She fell apart, but she kept on walking, striding into a wind that filled her gaping mouth and blew her tears across her cheeks.

She hadn't been able to stop crying until sometime later that night when she decided to return home. She would find a way to deal with Paul. Maybe even go to the police.

The next morning, she'd started hitching her way back.

A man named George picked her up. He was about forty, cheerful and talkative. It went fine for a while. Then, he stopped the car on a deserted stretch of road with nothing but cornfields all around. He turned to Robin. She saw the look in his eyes, and she knew what was coming.

It was the same dazed, feverish look she'd seen so many times in Paul's eyes.

'Don't try it,' she said.

'Aw now, don't be that way. I've been nice enough to give you a lift.'

She wanted to leap from the car. But her pack and banjo were in the backseat. She couldn't escape from George without risking the loss of them.

Her knife was in the side pocket of her pack.

She unfastened her safety harness and faced him. 'Just let me get my things and leave, okay?'

He unfastened the top button of her shirt.

Voice shaking, she said, 'You don't want to do this. I've got syphilis.'

He smiled and opened more buttons. 'Imagine that. So do I.' With both hands, he spread her shirt open.

Her fist crashed into his nose. Blood gushed from his nostrils. Hurling herself at him, Robin clutched his throat and slammed his head against the driver's window. His eyes rolled in their sockets. She shook him by the neck, bouncing his head off the window until he sagged. Then, she tore the key from the ignition. Hanging onto it, she left him behind the wheel, hurried from the car and unloaded her pack and banjo.

She tossed the key case onto the floor between his feet, gathered her things from the roadside and ran into the cornfield. Hiding there, she got out her knife.

She waited for George to come looking.

While she waited, she thought about how foolish she'd been, wanting to go home. She had no home. Paul was there, and Paul was worse than George.

Before long, she heard the car drive away. She waited a few more minutes, then walked out to the road. It stretched straight in both directions. George's car was out of sight. She turned west, and started walking.

That was the end of her homesickness.

But this felt like homesickness – this empty, longing ache that Nate had brought to her.

She took a break. After her audience had scattered, she gathered the money out of her banjo case, latched her banjo inside, and carried her case and backpack to a nearby bench.

She piled all her money onto her lap, and counted.

She had a total of $63.75.

She took a cotton sock from her pack, and filled it with loose change. She folded the paper money and tucked it into a pocket of her jeans.

Though she didn't have a wristwatch, she suspected that she still had time to reach one of the banks in town and exchange her coins for bills. From there, she could go to the bus terminal and buy a ticket out of this place.

No reason to stay, she told herself. She had enough money to hold her for a while, even if she spent half of it for a bus ticket. Nate was certainly no reason to stay. And it would be good to get away from this nest of bums and thieves and trollers before she ran into real trouble.

Leaning forward, she stuffed the sock full of change into the side pocket of her pack.

Someone sat down on the bench. Robin looked up to see who it was.

Nate.

He smiled at her. He didn't look haggard or troubled anymore. 'How's it going?' he asked.

'Okay.'

'Sorry about before. I shouldn't have talked to you that way.'

'It's all right,' Robin said. Her heart was pounding hard.

'I was worried about you. That's why I blew up. See, I know what can happen to people around this place. I don't want you getting hurt. And sleeping on the beach . . . you're just asking for it.'

You don't have to worry anymore, she thought. I'll be out of Boleta Bay by dark. Gone forever.

And I'll never see you again.

Frowning, he stared into her eyes. He pressed his lips into a tight line and shook his head. 'I don't want you to get the wrong idea,' he said.

'About what?'

'I want you to take this.' He dug into a front pocket of his pants and brought out a key attached to a big oval of green plastic. He put it into Robin's hand.

She turned the tab over. In raised white-painted letters were the words Wayfarer's Inn and an address. The key had a room number on it.

'No argument,' Nate said. 'The room's already paid for. I knew it wouldn't do any good just to give you the money and

207

ask you to use it on a motel.' He shrugged. 'You'd just save the money for your breakfasts.'

Robin's throat felt tight. Her heart felt like a fist punching inside her chest.

'You don't have to worry,' he told her. 'I'm not going to show up there and try to put moves on you. Hell, I don't even know the room number. I just want you to stay safe.'

She took hold of his hand and squeezed it. 'That's . . . awfully nice of you,' she said. Her voice was shaking. 'You shouldn't have done it, but . . .'

'You will use it, won't you? The room?'

'Okay. But let me pay you for it.'

'No way.'

'Really. I've got some money to spare, now.' She heard herself laugh. Her eyes were suddenly wet. 'I was going to buy a bus ticket this afternoon, but now I guess I'll stay.'

'You were going to leave?' He looked stunned, and she felt his hand tighten.

'Well, yeah, but . . . Can't leave now, can I? Not with a motel room waiting.'

'You were just going to go away? I thought you'd be sticking around here.'

She sniffed. She shrugged.

'I have to get back to the arcade,' Nate said. 'But you promise you'll use the room?'

'I promise.'

'Great.'

'But you've got to let me pay for it. You can't be spending so much money on me. Geez, you're busting your hump working for peanuts at that arcade . . .'

'My family owns it,' he said, smiling. 'The arcade, the Hurricane, the Ferris wheel and the Tilt-a-Whirl. We're pretty well off. In fact, we're filthy rich. I drive a Trans Am, for Godsake, and live in a twelve-room house with a swimming pool and tennis court. So I can afford a motel room for you, don't worry.'

'You convinced me,' Robin said, staring down at the key. 'I accept the gift. Thank you.'

'My pleasure.' He pulled his hand away, and rose from the bench. 'So I'll see you tomorrow, okay?'

'If not sooner?'

'This isn't some kind of a trick, Robin. I told you, I didn't even look at the room number.'

'I believe you.'

'Hope you enjoy it,' he said, and turned away.

'It's 240,' she called. 'Room 240.'

Nate looked over his shoulder. He gazed at her with wide eyes. His mouth hung open slightly.

'Just in case you want to check up on me,' Robin said, 'see if I'm really there.'

'I don't know. I don't know.' Shaking his head, he hurried away.

'You'd better wake up and turn over, or you'll burn.'

Jeremy opened his eyes. Shiner was on her elbow, smiling down at him.

'I can't believe I fell asleep,' he said. He felt hot and heavy as if weighted down by the sun.

'You were zonked. Didn't you get any sleep last night?'

'Loads,' he said.

Shiner laughed. 'Roll over,' she said. 'I'll put stuff on your back.'

When he heard that, the weight seemed to vanish. He quickly turned onto his stomach and rested his chin on his crossed arms.

'What time did you get home?' she asked.

'About three.'

'Me, too.'

He squirmed as a warm stream of oil zigzagged his back. Then, he felt Shiner's hands. They slid over his skin, spreading the fluid.

There was nothing *romantic* about the way she touched him. She swept the oil around as if this was an ordinary task, and Jeremy wondered if maybe she was trying hard not to let it seem like anything more. But the smooth rubbing felt wonderful to him.

'How long do you suppose Nate was out there?' she asked.
'I don't know.'

'I was starting to think he'd drowned, or something. God, it was so spooky, waiting for him.'

'That's for sure.' Jeremy remembered being so spooked that when he finally saw Nate coming back, he'd thought for a moment that it was the troll surfing towards him through the fog.

Shiner's hands glided down his sides.

'I'm sure glad you were there,' she said. 'I would've really freaked out, I think. It almost made it okay, hugging you like that.'

'That part was nice,' Jeremy said.

He felt oil dribble onto the backs of his legs. When her hands began sliding, he squirmed and turned slightly to ease the pressure on his penis. She rubbed the tops of his legs, and the outer sides. She rubbed the inner sides of his calves. Higher up, though – above his knees – she left the inner sides untouched. The very fact that she stayed away from that area confirmed Jeremy's suspicion that she knew this was a sex thing and didn't want it to seem that way.

Her hands went away. 'All through,' she said. 'Would you mind doing my back?'

'No. Sure.'

She lay down and Jeremy knelt beside her, bending at the waist in an attempt to hide his bulge.

She unfastened the straps at her shoulders, and flipped them out of the way.

Something like a striptease, but innocent, too. She wasn't *really* stripping, just getting the straps out of the way so they wouldn't leave pale marks on her tan. Girls almost always did that when they sunbathed. It meant nothing.

But Jeremy knew that she knew what she was doing.

She stroked her hair, parting it away from the nape of her neck. She was smooth and bare all the way down to the glossy seat of her swimsuit.

Jeremy squirted curly trails of oil onto her back, stood the bottle between his knees, and began to spread the oil with both hands. Her skin was warm and slippery.

I've gotta not think about it, he warned himself, horribly aware of his aroused condition.

This was a lot like wiping the ice cream off Tanya.

Don't think about that!

He quickly finished her back, leaving her sides unoiled because – God! – that'd be getting awfully close to her breasts and that might be too much to stand. He wondered if he dared to do her legs. But he couldn't not do them.

'Did you walk home alone?' he asked, trying to take his mind off the situation as he moved sideways past her rump and knelt by her legs.

'Yeah,' she said. 'It's not very far.'

He squirted the fluid onto the backs of her legs. It started to trickle down between them. He thought, Oh no! and quickly rubbed away the dribbles, trying not to think about where his hands were. 'I wish you would've let me walk you home,' he said, his voice shaking.

'Then, you'd know where I live.'

'What's wrong with that?' He quickly spread the oil down her calves.

'I don't let any of the trollers know where I live,' Shiner said. 'Or my real name, for that matter.'

Jeremy stopped.

Done. Thank God.

He capped the bottle. He flopped onto his back and brought his knees up. 'Why don't you want anyone to know?' he asked.

'It's in case something goes wrong. One of us might get caught by the cops. It hasn't happened yet, but it could. I don't care what anyone says about promising not to talk. Maybe some of them wouldn't, but it'd only take one. The cops or DA or somebody would promise a lighter sentence for naming names, and that'd be pretty tempting. Next thing you know, they've rounded up everyone. Except me.'

'So none of the trollers know who you really are?'

'Or where I live. So I can't get fingered. I tell you what, too

– after what happened last night, I'm really glad I've kept it that way.'

'Yeah,' Jeremy said. He felt a little let down that she didn't trust *him*, but he could see the wisdom of keeping her identity a secret. 'I wish I'd done the same thing,' he said.

'Does anyone know who you are?'

'I told Cowboy my last name. Where I live, too.'

'Well, don't worry about it. It wouldn't have worked for you. The only reason I can get away with it is because I go to a different school. None of the other trollers go to St Anne's. They all attend the public school, and that's where you'll be going in September, isn't it?'

'Yeah.'

'So they'd find out who you are when school starts. You couldn't have stayed anonymous no matter what.'

'Man, that's the pits.'

'You shouldn't lose any sleep over it. Nobody's been caught, so far, and I have a feeling that the trolling is over.'

'Really?'

'I'll bet that's what the meeting tonight is all about. I mean, nobody ever counted on someone getting killed. That changes everything. I think Nate has probably talked Tanya into breaking up the group.'

Jeremy felt a sudden sense of loss, as if he'd just been told that all his friends were moving out of town.

'I know I'm finished with it,' Shiner said.

'But we'll still see each other, won't we?'

'I hope so. I don't know any reason why not, do you?'

'No. Jeez, I'd like to see you all the time.' Speaking those words, he felt a warm rush of guilt. As if he were betraying someone. But who? Tanya? Cowboy? The whole group of trollers? Or Shiner herself?

Chapter Twenty-four

Straddling the padded bench of her weight machine, Joan adjusted her grip on the bar handles. The pulley squeaked as she drew the bar down to her chin and let it up, lifting and lowering the 110 pounds on the cable behind her back.

Maybe she would give Dave a call as soon as she finished her workout, and see how things went with Gloria. It was after seven, now. He ought to be done.

She pulled the bar down again.

How many was that, six?

Her heart was pounding with quick solid thumps, she was breathing hard and her sweatshirt felt sticky inside.

Six more, she thought, and you're through.

She had already spent half an hour working out. After some simple warmup exercises, she'd started to run through her karate moves. The karate depressed her, though. She kept seeing her foot smash into Woodrow Abernathy's chin. She'd been feeling great until those memories started up, so she knocked off the karate and moved on to the weight machine. She'd worked on each muscle group until she ached, and this was the last.

She drew the bar down one more time, let it up, and released the grips. She fluttered the shirt. Air buffeted her hot, moist skin. Then she lifted the shirt and wiped her dripping face.

She felt fine except for a touch of guilt about skipping the karate. Strength was all well and good, but the karate kept her quick, and kept her balance and agility finely tuned. Still, she was reluctant to try it again.

An idea came that cheered her up a lot. She went to the old stereo in the corner of her exercise room, selected an album from the cabinet, and placed the record on the turntable. She carefully lowered the arm onto the band she remembered so well, then stepped to the corner of the mat.

John Denver's high, clear voice began singing 'Calypso'. She danced onto the mat in time with the music and did three handsprings to the opposite corner. Her timing was off just slightly. She staggered off the mat. There goes your ten, she thought. But she whirled around and continued her routine, dancing, kicking, leaping, spinning, doing cartwheels and somersaults, and finishing with a triple back flip that used to bring down the house but tonight landed Joan on her butt.

Clapping came from the doorway.

She saw Debbie standing there, a smirk on her face. 'How'd a Klutz like you ever make the state finals?'

'I wasn't five-eleven, then.'

'I'd show you how it's supposed to be done, but I've got to get going.'

'Don't let me stop you.'

'Do I look all right?'

She wore white jeans. The blue of her shiny blouse brought out the blue in her eyes. Her face had a faint, reddish glow from her afternoon at the beach. Her blond hair curled softly around her face.

'You look great,' Joan said. 'You'll knock the fellows dead.'

'If any are there.' Debbie wrinkled her nose. 'You know Jessica. She's such a goody-two-shoes, I'll be lucky if there's a guy within miles.'

'Well, have fun anyway. And be home by twelve.'

'If it's too much of a drag, I might be home a lot earlier. You going to see Dave tonight?'

'I don't know.'

'Maybe you could have him over and show him your floor exercise. I'm sure he'd go ape – especially the way you nearly lose your sweatshirt on the cartwheels.'

'Aren't you going to be late or something?'

Debbie laughed. 'When do I get to meet him?'

'What do you want? *I* haven't even gone out with him yet.'

'I'd like to see what he looks like.'

'If you're all that eager, come over to the boardwalk while we're on duty tomorrow.'

214

'Yeah. Thanks, but no thanks.'

'What've you suddenly got against Funland? You used to go there all the time.'

'That was before Big Sister started walking the beat.'

Joan grinned. 'I cramp your style?'

'Might, if I went there and tried to have fun.'

'Well, sorry about that. But a job's a job.'

'When'll you get reassigned?'

'Who knows? But don't worry, I won't be there forever.'

'Just all summer, my luck.'

'If you miss the place so much, go on my days off. Or some night, as long as you go with friends.'

'Anyway,' Debbie said, 'I'd better get out of here or I'll be late. So long. Don't do anything I wouldn't.'

'Haw, haw.'

Debbie raised a hand in farewell, then stepped out of the doorway.

Joan sat on the floor and did some stretching exercises until she heard the car drive away. Then, she went to her bedroom. Her stomach fluttered as she sat on the edge of her bed and lifted the telephone onto her lap.

Silly to be jumpy about calling Dave, she told herself.

She gazed at the phone.

Christ, I'm not a damn teenager.

She took a deep breath, lifted the handset, and dialled.

His telephone rang eight times before she hung up.

Okay. So he's not home. Big deal.

That doesn't mean he's still at Gloria's. And even if he is, so what? Afraid they'll make up?

No chance.

What makes you so sure? Hell, they were going together hot and heavy till a few days ago. And he obviously still cares about her, or he wouldn't have been so upset when I told him about the bitch playing dress-up.

He was upset for the same reason as me – because he felt responsible.

Joan wished they'd skipped lunch and rushed right over to

find her. But Dave hadn't wanted to. 'The hell if I'm going to ruin my meal chasing after her. She wants to pull a dumb stunt like that, it's her problem.'

Lunch was ruined, anyway. Joan had been too upset about Gloria to enjoy the gyro, and she suspected that Dave's appetite had also suffered a trouncing. Worry and anger had a way of turning food tasteless.

When they finished eating, they headed for the Funland entrance. Joan waited by the ticket booth while Dave went down the steps. But he came back in about a minute and explained that Gloria was no longer there. They resumed their patrol, expecting to run into her along the boardwalk. During the afternoon, they spotted eight or ten derelicts. No Gloria, though.

At the end of their tour, Dave had said he would drop by Gloria's house and try to warn her off. He hadn't seemed eager about it, but they'd both known it was something that needed to be done.

She'd been jilted and gone off the deep end.

It was their fault.

It would be their fault if her stupid 'undercover work' got her pounded or raped or worse.

Somebody had to talk some sense into her, and Dave was it.

Joan gazed at the phone, wondering if she should try calling again. Maybe Dave had been in the shower.

Maybe *I'll* take a shower, and try him when I'm done.

She wished she'd gone along with him. But Dave didn't ask, and she didn't offer. The less Gloria saw of her, the better.

That was obvious.

She lifted the telephone onto the nightstand, stood up, and went down the hallway to the bathroom. She shut the door and locked it.

Big tough cop locking the door, she thought.

She *always* locked it before taking a shower or bath. Always, when she was alone in the house.

Something creepy about it. Something to do with being cut off from the rest of the house and water running so you couldn't hear what might be going on out there. Something to do with a movie called *Psycho*.

The air felt humid from Debbie's bath. And the aroma of her cologne was almost overpowering. What had she done, spilled the stuff?

Joan slid the window open a few inches. She pulled off her shoes and socks, hung her sweatsuit on the knob, and stepped to the tub. The bathmat still showed Debbie's footprints. It felt soggy where the girl had stood.

Leaning over the edge of the tub, Joan reached for the hot water faucet and flinched when the doorbell rang. Gooseflesh swarmed up her body.

The bell rang again, a faint chiming sound.

She grimaced and straightened up.

Great timing, she thought. Here I am, bareass.

She felt annoyed at being startled, vulnerable in her nakedness, and reluctant to get back into her sweaty clothes.

Just stick it out, and whoever it is will go away.

The doorbell rang again.

Debbie? she wondered. Maybe there was car trouble, or . . . Brilliant, Sherlock. She has a house key.

Maybe it's Dave.

He didn't answer his phone because he was on his way over here?

Wishful thinking.

But it might be Dave.

Might be a goddamn door-to-door soliciter or Jehovah's Witnesses.

If it *is* Dave . . .

She rushed to the bathroom door, leaped into her sweatpants (which were just as moist and clammy as she'd feared), hooked her sweatshirt off the knob, and pulled it down over her head as she hurried to the front door.

She peered through the peephole.

Harold.

Shit!

She considered pretending she wasn't home. But she hadn't

exactly tiptoed to the door. It would be horribly cruel not to open up if Harold knew she was in.

Should've gone ahead and taken the shower.

She opened the door and twisted her face into a smile.

He glanced at her face for an instant before lowering his eyes in typical Harold fashion. 'I'm sorry,' he said. 'Did I catch you at a bad time?'

'No. Huh-uh. I'd just finished my workout. Come on in.' She stepped aside.

He entered and shut the door. 'I suppose I should've phoned first, but . . .' He shrugged.

'That's okay. Could I get you a drink or something?'

'Some white wine would be nice, if you have any.'

'Sure. Come on.' She headed for the kitchen, Harold following. Her heart was beating fast. She felt a little tight and sick inside.

He wasn't supposed to show up. Didn't he get the message? Hadn't she made it clear enough the other night?

Obviously not.

She'd been about as clear as possible without coming right out and saying she didn't want to go with him any more.

Squatting down; she took a bottle of white Zinfandel from the cupboard. 'I'm afraid it isn't chilled,' she said. 'You want ice cubes?'

'Just one. Don't want to water it down too much,' he added, and gave out a tiny coughlike chuckle that sounded miserably nervous.

Oh, he got the message, all right.

But he's here anyway.

Joan gave the bottle to him. He went to the drawer where she kept the corkscrew. He'd been here for dinner three times, so he knew right where to find it.

Good old Debbie. Sharp kid. After the *first* dinner, she'd said, 'Harold's a dingus. Why are you wasting your time with him?'

'He's nice,' Joan had said.

'So's popcorn. That doesn't mean you'd go on a date with it.'

'If you were going to the Summer Film Festival, you might.'

'I'm serious. Dump him and find a *guy*. You're a cop, you must know *guys*.'

Joan set a pair of wine glasses onto the counter. She dropped an ice cube into one, and left the other empty. Harold was having trouble with the cork. Bending over, he clamped the bottle between his legs, gripped its neck, and tugged the handle of the corkscrew.

As Joan watched, she remembered popping open the champagne at Dave's house yesterday.

If only I were there right now, she thought.

He isn't there.

He's dealing with Gloria, and I've got to deal with Harold. We each have our own messes keeping us apart.

Harold popped the cork. He filled the glasses, and handed the one without ice to Joan.

'I hope you don't mind me dropping by like this,' he said as they walked into the living room.

'No, that's fine. I'm kind of a mess, is all.'

'You look terrific. As always.'

'Thanks,' she muttered.

Harold sat on the sofa. Joan sat down beside him.

No reason *not* to sit with him, she told herself. On the nights when he'd had dinner here, they'd spent plenty of time on the sofa sipping brandy and talking, and twice Debbie'd gone to the movies, they'd been alone just as they were now, and the most he'd ever done was hold her hand.

That's not how it's gonna go down this time, she thought. Bet on it.

'I was planning to call you,' she said.

Harold nodded. He took a sip of wine, then gazed at his glass. 'I understand that. And I can well imagine what you would've had to say. I wasn't especially eager to hear it. Each time the phone rang, I thought it was you and . . . This is not at all easy for me, Joan. To come here like this. I've felt . . . physically ill . . . all day.'

'I'm sorry,' she murmured.

He held up one hand as if to ward off her apology. 'It's not your fault. It's me. You were absolutely correct in what you said about me the other night. I *am* a coward. I always have been. I've always avoided every possible risk – physical, emotional.'

He looked at her, smiled bleakly, and returned his gaze to the glass. 'I was actually twenty-five before I had my first sexual encounter. And that was a case of the girl seducing me. I had no interest in her. She was . . . not attractive. In fact, she was distinctly unappealing. As was every female I've ever dared to approach.'

'Thanks a heap,' Joan said, hoping to cheer him up.

'If you remember correctly, you approached me.'

She remembered. She'd been in the student bookstore. It had the best stock in town. Harold was standing in the aisle of the poetry section, and she'd mistakenly thought he worked there and asked if they had Shel Silverstein's *Where the Sidewalk Ends*. 'I've got *A Light in the Attic*, and it really cracks me up.'

'They're children's books, you know,' he'd said.

'Really? Well, Sylvia Plath gives me a headache.'

He'd laughed at that.

After they found the book and she bought it, they walked out of the store together and she said, 'Why don't you come over to the student union with me? I'll buy you some coffee and lecture you on the merits of Silverstein and Dr Seuss.'

There, she'd learned that this was his first year at the university. She explained that she used to work at the library, and they grew more comfortable together as they discussed the motley assortment of characters who comprised the staffs of the library and English department.

'I was . . . instantly smitten,' Harold said. 'I could hardly believe that I was in the company of a woman who was not only exceedingly attractive, but intelligent and well read and witty. That sort of thing had never happened to me before. I found it incomprehensible that you would even speak to me, much less . . .'

'I like you, Harold. I really do. I've enjoyed our times together.'

'Enjoy.' He made a small huff through his nose. 'Such a pallid word. To me, the times we spent together were . . . like glimpses of paradise. Which is why I never dared to risk it all, why I never . . .' He shook his head.

'Put moves on me?'

'I wanted to,' he admitted, frowning at his wine glass. 'You've no idea how much I've wanted to kiss you, embrace you. I've dreamed of . . .'

The jangle of the telephone stopped his voice.

Joan's heart lurched.

Dave? It had to be Dave.

The phone rang again, again.

'Aren't you going to answer it?' Harold asked.

'No,' she said, and rested a hand gently on his knee. The phone rang seven more times.

The silence when it stopped felt heavy and dark. Harold began to weep. He reached out and set the wine glass onto the table, then turned his face away from Joan. She rubbed his back. She could feel it hitching under her hand as he struggled to stifle his sobs.

'I know it's over,' he said in a choked voice. 'You were looking for a . . . a Rhet Butler, and I'm . . . not even an Ashley. A Prufrock, that's what I am, nothing but a Prufrock.'

'Hey, come on. Everything's going to be okay.'

'No. No, I don't think so.'

'We'll still see each other, Harold. We'll still be friends. And really, it was never more than that. Maybe we both wanted it to be more, but it never was. So we'll leave it that way, and stop trying to make it something else.'

He sniffed. He shook his head. He wiped his eyes.

'We'll go to the movies next week.'

'No. I couldn't. God, I don't want your pity.'

'Well then, the hell with you.'

His head jerked around. His eyes were wet and red. His cheeks were shiny with tears. He looked at her eyes. He looked at her smirk. And a laugh sputtered out of him.

'Take my pity or take a leap, Gonzo.'

He laughed again.

The telephone began to ring. 'This time, I'm going to get it. Take the opportunity to pull yourself together.'

He stayed on the sofa. Joan rushed into the kitchen and grabbed the telephone. 'Hello?'

'Hi there. It's me.'

'Hiya, Me,' she said, and felt a warmth come into her. 'How'd it go?'

'It didn't. I went over to her place and she wasn't home. In fact, I went over twice. Once before supper, once after.'

'You think she's still out playing games?'

'Wouldn't surprise me. I'm going to drive down to the boardwalk and search around, but that'll take a while. I just wanted to talk to you first, let you know what's going on.'

'I was starting to get worried. Hey, how about letting me go with you?'

'I think it'd just make matters worse if we're together, and . . .'

'I know. I know that. Shit.'

'Are you all right?'

'Yeah. It's just that I miss you.'

'You miss me?'

'No, I'm sick of your face. Of course I miss you. I thought we might see each other tonight. I called you a while ago.'

'I called you, too.'

'Yeah, I thought it was you. I couldn't answer it. If you really think Gloria will freak out or something if we're together . . .'

'Aah, let her. I'll come by and get you. How about ten minutes?'

'How about half an hour? I need to take a shower.'

'Can't it wait till I get there?'

'Haw haw. In your ear, Davey boy.'

'I'll have to think about that.'

'See you later.' She hung up and went back to the living room. She stopped at the edge of the table. Harold was sitting up straight. He was no longer crying. 'You all right?' she asked.

'As well as can be expected, I suppose.'

'You'll pick me up for the film next week?'

He made a limp smile. 'Ah, my cue to evacuate the premises.'

'Afraid so. I have to get cleaned up and leave. That was Dave. We've got a little bit of an emergency we need to take care of.'

Nodding, Harold drank the last of his wine.

He stood up. Joan took hold of his hand, and they walked towards the door. 'The film?' she asked.

'I don't know.'

'Let's give it a try and see how it goes. Unless, of course, you dump me between now and then for someone even more beautiful and charming than *moi*.'

'The dumping, my dear, has already been done. Not by me, of course.'

The words wrenched her. She'd thought she had healed his wound. All she'd done, she realised, was slap a bandage across it. The gash was too big for such a flimsy patch. She could almost see the tide of blood.

Harold opened the door.

Joan clutched his arm to stop him from leaving. She turned him to face her. He didn't look tormented, now. He looked resigned, defeated, a little dazed and hollow in the eyes.

'I wish I could make it all right,' she said.

'You get an E for Effort.' He eased his arm out of her grip, and walked out into the dusk.

Joan closed the door. She leaned back against it. She let out a deep sigh.

She felt awful. She was glad that he was gone. She was glad that it was over.

It *was* over. He'd lost, and he wasn't about to accept the consolation prize of friendship.

And she was *glad*.

And it was not too different from kicking Woodrow Abernathy in the chin. A feeling of relief and joy because she'd taken care of business, finished the matter, brought a bad situation to a quick end. But guilt that was like grey rain in her soul.

Chapter Twenty-five

'It was very nice to meet you, Mrs Wayne.'

'Well, it was nice to meet you, too, Shiner.'

'I have to be home before midnight, so I'll get Jeremy back here around eleven-thirty. Is that all right?'

'Fine, fine. Have a good time, kids.'

Jeremy opened the door for Shiner. As she walked out, he smiled at his mother. She made a face at him – eyebrows rising, eyes rolling upward, lips pursing – a face that said, 'I can't believe it. How did you possibly manage to latch onto a girl like *this*?'

Once the door was shut, he took hold of Shiner's hand. 'You wowed her!'

'But of course.'

'She was all set to hate your guts.'

'She's nice. I like her.'

They reached the kerb. Shiner unlocked the passenger door for Jeremy, then walked around the front of the car.

'You sure look nice tonight,' he said as she slipped in behind the steering wheel.

'Thanks. You, too.'

He wished she were wearing a dress, but she looked awfully good in the white jeans. And he liked the way her blouse seemed so light and clingy. If he held her, it would feel slick and he would be able to slide it on her skin.

She had an aroma that made him think of the way the air might smell in a forest after a spring rain.

She started the car and pulled away from the kerb. 'I've been thinking,' she said, 'and there's no law says we *have* to go to this thing at Tanya's. It's going to be a bummer, you know. A lot of talk about that guy who kicked it. We could do something else. Go to the movies, or fool around at Funland or something.'

'Don't you *want* to go?' Jeremy asked.

'If you do. I'm just saying we don't have to.'

The idea of going to a movie or to Funland with Shiner excited him. On the other hand, he hated to miss Tanya's party.

'I'm pretty curious about it,' he said.

'Okay. We'll go, then. No problem.'

'Are you sure?'

'It was just a thought. And, I mean, we *should* go. Tanya wants everyone to be there. I've just got cold feet, I guess.'

'You're scared?'

'No, not scared. A little nervous, maybe. I don't know, I have this feeling I'm going to wish we'd stayed away.'

'Maybe we'd better not go, then,' he said, being gallant and self-sacrificing and feeling dismal about it.

'No. Hey, you don't want to miss the thing. And I'm not sure whether I do or not. Maybe it'll be terrific.'

'Let's just go for a while,' Jeremy suggested. 'Just put in an appearance and see what's going on. Then, if we feel like it, we'll split.'

'Sounds good to me,' Shiner said.

He settled back into the car's bucket seat.

The rest of the trip was wonderful. Jeremy felt nervous, but excited, too. He was alone in the car with Shiner, his girlfriend, his actual girlfriend who wasn't a dog, who was – as Letterman would put it – 'a fabulous babe'. She was beautiful and his. And they were on their way to a party. At Tanya's. Where anything might happen but where one thing would happen for sure: he would be in Tanya's presence. And she wasn't a fabulous babe, she was a Force of Nature.

It's really happening, he assured himself. Right now. To me.

When Jeremy came out of his reverie, he saw that they were on a residential street that he'd never seen before. 'Where are we?' he asked.

'You might call it "the other side of the tracks".'

'Huh?'

'We're heading into the north end. Where the rich folk live.'

'Tanya lives over here?'

'Sure. She's loaded. Her father's a chiropractor and her stepmother's a lawyer.'

'If they're so rich, why does she have to work?'

Shiner steered the car into a narrow lane that slanted up a wooded hillside. 'Well, she obviously doesn't have to. She likes it. Look what she does. She's a lifeguard. Stands around on the beach all day, looking fabulous, the centre of attention for every guy within eyeball distance – and now and again she gets to play hero.'

Shiner sounded a little amused, and maybe as if she were above such things, herself.

'You kind of sound like you don't like her,' Jeremy said.

'No, I like her fine. I just don't *adore* her, the way everyone else does.'

Is she including me? Jeremy wondered. Does she know? How could she?

Shiner stopped at a Y in the road. She took a sheet of paper from the blouse pocket over her left breast and unfolded it. In the faint, bluish light of dusk, Jeremy saw that it was a rough map drawn with a ballpoint. Shiner frowned at it for a while. Then swung to the left, and drove slowly up the road.

Jeremy could see no houses. Just woods and sometimes a driveway entrance with a mailbox beside it. The houses, he guessed, were hidden in the trees far above the winding road and far below it.

'How did you meet Tanya?' he asked, wanting to get away from the subject of adoration. 'You don't go to the same school, and she lives . . . do you live up here, too?'

'Hell, no. I'm over on . . . in your neighbourhood. I met her by hunting out the trollers. Everybody in town was talking about them – and Great Big Billy Goat Gruff. I started sneaking out late at night, and pretty soon I found them. I just explained that I wanted to join up, and why . . .'

'Because of your sister?'

'Right. And they put me through the initiation. I've been with them ever since.'

'Was it always the same kids?'

She nodded.

'Mostly. A couple of them moved away, and Randy wasn't with them yet. He got involved after Tanya pulled him out of the drink. She did mouth-to-mouth, and he woke up and figured he'd died and gone to heaven. He's been one of her worshippers ever since.'

Shiner stopped. She peered through the windshield at the road sign, then checked the map again. 'Okay, that's Avion,' she said, nodding to the right. 'Her place should be the third driveway.' She drove forward.

The third driveway was on the left side of the road, and slanted upward with a steep grade. Shiner shifted to first gear, turned onto the driveway, and started to climb it slowly, the engine racing. Jeremy wasn't sure what he expected to find at the top. A cabin or cottage would've seemed about right. But when the road levelled off and the forest opened, he saw something that looked very much like a Southern plantation house – complete with a veranda and white columns. He supposed it was smaller than the real thing, but it seemed awfully big to be sitting up here above Boleta Bay.

The whole top of the hill must've been lopped off to make room for the house, its three-car garage, and grounds. The driveway looped around the front lawn and led to a broad, paved area to the right of the garage. There, five other cars were already parked.

Shiner parked beside a Jeep that had a Confederate flag on its radio antenna.

She took hold of Jeremy's hand as they walked toward the veranda. Her hand felt moist.

She really *is* nervous about this, Jeremy realized. Why? What does she think might happen?

At the top of the stairs, they stopped in front of twin oak doors. Jeremy pushed the doorbell button. From inside came the sound of chimes playing a few bars of *My Old Kentucky Home*.

'Are they Southerners?' Jeremy asked.

'Who knows? Tanya isn't. She grew up here.'

The door on the right swung open.

'Howdy there, Duke, Shiner.' Cowboy clapped him on the shoulder. 'Long time no see, pardner.' The whole right side of his head looked like one huge bandage with a big hump where his ear must be. He wore his old, battered Stetson. There were a few bandages on his arms, and Jeremy could see others through the thin white fabric of his T-shirt.

'Come on in, folks. Join the party.' As they followed him across the foyer, he said, 'I hear you aced a troll last night. Fuckin'-A, and I missed it.'

'How are you feeling?' Shiner asked him.

'Like the old lady that bit the hatchet.'

He led them down a staircase into a huge, carpeted room with furniture along the panelled walls, a pool table, and a bar at the far end. All the trollers were there.

Jeremy's eyes sought out Tanya. He spotted her bending over the pool table, lining up a shot. She was barefoot, wearing white shorts and an oversized shirt with tails so long that they almost covered the shorts. The shirt was a plaid of bright blue and yellow. The way she was bent over, its loose front probably didn't even touch her body.

Karen, standing beside Nate at the other side of the table, looked as if she might be trying for peeks.

Tanya banked the eight-ball into a corner pocket and punched her fist into the air. Nate shook his head. Apparently, the shot had just won the game for Tanya.

Randy, at a corner of the table, waved a greeting towards Jeremy and Shiner.

Tanya set her cue stick on the table, turned around and smiled. 'Glad you made it,' she said, coming forward. Jeremy saw the way her shirt moved, and quickly raised his eyes to her face.

Someone patted his rump. He looked over his shoulder and tried to keep his smile as he met Heather's tiny, pig-like eyes.

'How's it hanging, Duke?' she asked.

He shrugged.

Samson, behind her, winked and hoisted a glass full of red liquid.

Liz, off to the side, held a glass with the same stuff in it.

The three of them – Heather, Samson and Liz – had all been at the bar a minute ago when Jeremy first scanned the room.

Heather bumped soft bulges against Jeremy's side. 'Why don't you get some punch and join the party?' she said.

'So what's the occasion?' Shiner asked, slipping an arm around Jeremy's back as if to let Heather know he wasn't available.

'Let's just call it a wake,' Tanya said. 'A tribute to the "good troll".'

'Only good troll's a dead one,' Cowboy added. 'Shit, I should've been there.'

'And I thought *I* was good at the high-dive,' Liz said, hooting out a laugh. 'That guy did the best damn triple back-somersault . . .'

'He lost points on his entry, though,' Samson said.

'Yeah. I'd only give him an eight.'

Some of them laughed. Shiner didn't. Neither did Nate.

'I propose we all get drinks,' Tanya said, 'and hoist one to the memory of the good troll.'

She led the way to the bar, stepped behind it, and uncapped a litre bottle of rum.

'Yo ho ho,' Heather said.

Tanya dumped half the bottle's contents into the cut-glass punch bowl. The liquor slurped into the red juice with soft plopping sounds. Setting the bottle aside, she stirred with a glass dipper.

When everyone held a glass full of the spiked punch, she raised her own glass. 'To the one who took the big dive,' she toasted, 'and shall be known henceforth as Fish Food.'

'I'm not going to drink to that,' Nate muttered.

'Lighten up, would you?' Tanya said. 'He was a fucking *troll*.'

'He was a human being, and we killed him.'

'We didn't kill him. It was an accident.'

'A lucky accident,' Liz added.

229

'And I missed it,' Cowboy said.

'We murdered him,' Nate said.

Tanya stared at him. She looked annoyed, frustrated. 'It was an accident. He would've been okay if he hadn't been a fat slob. He would've been okay if *your* Ferris wheel had safety bars worth a shit.'

Nate's face went slack. 'You think I don't know that?' he asked, his voice little more than a whisper.

'Okay,' Tanya said. 'We went out to nail a troll and we nailed one. He happened to die. All the moaning and whining in the world isn't going to bring him back to life . . .'

'Who'd *want* to?' Liz said.

'So let's just have a good time, huh? I didn't ask everybody over here to bellyache about it. The whole idea's to loosen up, have some drinks, fool around, and put the whole thing behind us. We all know what happened out there. None of us is happy about it.'

'Speak for yourself,' Liz said. 'Me, I think it's great. One less troll in our face. We oughta do it to all of 'em.'

Grinning, Cowboy rubbed her hair. She smiled and put an arm around him.

'I'm with Liz,' Samson said. 'Fuck em all. The deader the bedder.'

Nate gave him a betrayed look, then turned his eyes to Tanya. 'It has to stop. We should've stopped it a long time ago. It's just been getting more and more out of hand. Something like this was bound to happen . . .'

'You sound like that shit-editorial in the paper.'

'That shit-editorial was right! We proved it right last night, didn't we? And don't give me this crap about not being happy about it. You were *delighted* that the old guy fell. You've been itching to . . . you tried to set the one on fire Tuesday night!'

'Could've had us a weenie roast,' Cowboy said.

'Are you all crazy?'

'It's war, man,' Samson said.

'What'd they ever do to you?'

'They piss me off.'

'Oh, isn't that wonderful. They piss you off, so you kill them?'

'You dumb fuck, that was an accident and you know it.'

'You're in this because of me,' Nate said. 'Same with you, Cowboy. Remember? I wanted you to help me kick ass because of what they did to Tanya. You never had anything much against the trolls. I talked you into it. And it's time to stop. We kicked ass. We paid them back a hundred times over. For Tanya and for Shiner's sister.'

Nate's fierce eyes moved across the faces of the trollers and stopped on Randy. 'What've you got against them? Nothing, that's what. You just have this thing about Tanya. Is it worth killing for? Same with you, Karen.'

Smirking, Karen gave him the finger.

'What'd they do to you, Heather? You're just in it for the company. And great company we are! Lose some weight and join the world.'

Heather pressed her lips together and blinked at him.

Nate's eyes met Jeremy's. 'I don't know what your story is. Do you hate the trolls? Do you want to kill them? Or is this just some kind of a social club like it is for Heather?'

Jeremy, face hot, didn't dare speak.

'Some goddamn war,' Nate said, glancing at Samson.

'You've had your say,' Tanya told him. Her voice sounded calm, but hard. 'Now, get out of my house.'

'Call it off,' he said. 'You're the only one who can. You tell them it's over, and it's over.'

'All that's over is you and me.'

'You're right about that.'

For just a moment, she looked stunned. As if she'd expected him to be staggered, maybe to relent or ask for forgiveness. Jeremy got the feeling that she didn't want to lose him. Her upper lip made a tiny twitch. 'Go on,' she said. 'Get the fuck out of here.'

'You're obsessed, Tanya. Don't drag them all down with you.'

'GET OUT!'

231

He set his glass on the bar counter. 'I'm leaving. Anybody else? Samson? Cowboy?'

'Not me,' Samson said. 'Sorry, pal. I'm with Tanya on this one. We gotta clean the place up. I'll quit my trolling when I can walk around all day without some slime-bag asking me for two bits.'

'Same here,' Cowboy said. 'Far as I can see, nothing's changed. I hate to lose you for a friend, and I hope it don't come to that, but we got us a job to do, here.'

Nate kept shaking his head while he listened to Samson and Cowboy. When they finished, he glanced around at everyone. 'You're all making a big mistake,' he said. 'She's turning you into a gang of thugs.'

Alone, he walked towards the stairs.

'Don't even think about going to the cops,' Tanya warned.

He stopped and looked back. 'I'm not trolling anymore,' he said. 'But that doesn't make me an asshole who'd snitch on his friends.' Then he started up the stairs and disappeared.

'Chicken-shit bastard,' Tanya muttered. 'Who needs him, anyway.' With a trembling hand, she lifted her glass high. 'No trolls,' she toasted.

'No quarter,' said Cowboy.

They all gathered in close around Tanya and clinked their glasses together.

Chapter Twenty-six

Robin sat on the bed in the motel room, propped up with two pillows behind her back, and stared at the television while she waited for Nate.

There was a chance, she knew, that he might not come at

all. Giving her the key, Nate had assured her that he wouldn't make a visit. She had believed him, too. But telling him the room number had been a clear invitation.

He'd seemed surprised and confused.

For all Robin knew, he might have a regular girl. Maybe he was with her, right now. Or maybe he was still working at the arcade.

He owns it, she reminded herself. He could get someone else to run the place, or he could even shut down early. He shut it early, last night.

Come *on*, Nate. Where are you?

From the time Robin arrived at the motel, she'd been expecting him to show up at any moment. While she waited, she took the opportunity to use the laundry room downstairs. Wearing a T-shirt and gym shorts, she stuffed all her dirty clothes into the washer, started it up, then hurried back to her room for a shower. She wanted to be clean for him. But she took the shower fast, fearing that Nate might knock and she would miss it.

Maybe that's just what happened, she thought now as she waited on the bed. Maybe he came, knocked, and left. If that's how it went, he'll come back and try again. Won't he?

Except for the time in the shower, she couldn't have missed him.

She'd waited in the room while her clothes were drying. When she went to dinner, the balcony in front of her room was always in sight. She'd taken a booth at the window of the cafe across the street, and watched for him.

Back in her room after dinner, she ached for a long, hot bath. While the tub filled, she stayed out of the bathroom so the noise of the rushing water wouldn't prevent her from hearing Nate's arrival. She arranged clothes on the bed so she could get into them fast: panties, a bra, and a pale blue dress she'd bought at a souvenir shop that afternoon before leaving the boardwalk.

With the water off and the bathroom door open, she didn't need to worry about missing him. She settled down, sighing as the hot water wrapped her body. A bath was a rare luxury.

Most of the time, she kept herself clean by washing in restrooms. Coffee shops and gas stations often had doors that locked, so she could strip down and do a good quick job of it. Occasionally, she used shower rooms at public swimming pools and YMCAs. Many beaches had outside showers for getting the sand and saltwater off before heading home, and she took advantage of them when she could, though she had to keep her swimsuit on. Often, she bathed in streams and lakes, which were always cold.

Only when she checked into motels did she get to take a hot bath in a tub. Usually once a month. If she could afford it.

Then, she would take marathon baths. Often fall asleep in the tub. Wake up with the water cool and her skin pruned. And take another the next morning before checkout time.

Tonight, she didn't fall asleep. Though the caressing heat seemed to steal away all her strength, she wouldn't allow herself to drift off. If she slept, she might not hear Nate's knocking.

When the drowsiness threatened to overpower her, she left the tub. She dried herself with a threadbare towel. It was a tiny thing. She wrapped it around her waist. Though the corners met, there wasn't enough for a tuck. She hung the towel on a bar and left the bathroom. She returned with her toothpaste and brush. She cleaned her teeth.

She took a fresh towel from its clamp on the wall. Sitting on the bed, she rubbed her hair dry. Her skin was hot and moist from the bath. A breeze came in through the open window, lifting the curtain, cooling her. When she felt dry enough so her clothes wouldn't stick, she put them on.

Then, she brushed her hair in front of the big mirror over the bureau.

She was pleased with the way the dress looked. It was a short-sleeved pullover. It hung almost to her knees.

A dark blue emblem above her left breast showed a silhouette of the Ferris wheel with the Hurricane roller coaster in the background. Both owned by Nate's family, she thought, smiling. It read FUNLAND above the illustration, BOLETA BAY, CALIFORNIA below it.

The dress was soft and clingy. In the shop, she'd been concerned that it might be a nightshirt until she noticed that one of the clerks wore an identical garment.

It does look like a nightshirt, she thought as she studied her reflection. She went to her pack and took out her freshly laundered belt. The belt was woven of bright reds and blues to match her banjo strap. She tied it loosely around her hips, its ends hanging down the side of her left leg. Now, the dress looked like a dress.

She put on her necklace of white shells. The V neck of the dress was wide and low enough to let the necklace show. In the mirror, the shells resting against her tanned skin looked as white as her teeth.

Slowly, she turned around, watching her reflection.

She looked like Robin the tourist or Robin the co-ed. Certainly not like Robin the street musician.

Cockless Robin.

Poppinsack.

Her skin went hot.

The bastard.

Don't ruin it thinking about him.

Hope you rot, you . . .

Forget him.

Nate, where *are* you?

Robin saw that a new programme was starting on the television, and realized a full hour had passed since she'd finished dressing. She climbed from the bed. At the window, she parted the curtains and looked outside. Night had fallen. Must be nine, she thought.

She considered walking to Funland. She saw herself entering the arcade, stepping up to Nate and asking for some change. At first, he didn't recognize her. Then, he said, 'I don't believe it. Is that really you?'

But he might not be happy to see her. Maybe she'd read him wrong, and he really wasn't interested.

Instead of smiling, he might frown and say, 'What are you doing here?'

He'll come, she told herself.

And no more than a yard away, he walked past the window and did a double-take when he saw her and Robin wondered if her mind were playing tricks. Nate stepped up close to the screen. A smile tugged a corner of his mouth. 'I guess you're here, all right.'

'I guess so.' She hurried over to the door and opened it.

He stood on the balcony, staring in at her. 'You look . . . very nice.'

'Thanks. Come on in.'

His eyes shifted and he glanced into the room behind her. 'Maybe we should . . . would you rather take a little walk? It's nice out tonight.'

She felt an odd mixture of disappointment and relief. 'Okay. Sure. Just a minute.'

He waited while she put on white socks and tennis shoes. 'How's the room?' he asked.

'Great. I love it. Especially the bath tub.'

She snatched the motel key off the dresser, stepped onto the balcony, pulled the door shut, and tested the knob. Then, she turned to him. 'I don't have a pocket,' she said.

Nodding, he took the key from her and slipped it into a pocket of the chamois shirt he wore like a jacket over his T-shirt.

'Now, don't lose it.'

He smiled. 'I'll try not to.'

They began walking side by side along the balcony. There was no fog, but the night was cool and breezy. Nate probably felt just right in his heavy, long-sleeved shirt and jeans. Robin, in her thin dress, shivered.

She thought about going back to the room for something warm to wear. But she didn't want to ruin the way she looked by putting on her windbreaker or sweatshirt. The chill wasn't that bad.

They trotted down the stairs and crossed the motel's parking lot.

'Where are we going?' she asked.

'Anyplace but Funland,' Nate said.

'Good choice.'

At the sidewalk, they turned their backs to the distant amusement park. The street was brightly lighted and noisy with passing cars. People were all around, entering and leaving stores, walking by.

'Did you close the arcade early?' Robin asked.

'No. My brother-in-law's working it. Where would you like to go? Are you hungry?'

'Not right now.'

'How about a movie?'

'It's fine with me if we just walk. Maybe we could get off the main drag, though, and find someplace a little more peaceful.'

'Good thinking.'

They were in the middle of a block when a troll staggered around the corner. He started toward them, shambling along with short, unsteady steps, scowling and shaking his fists, blurting jibberish in an angry voice.

'Why don't we cross here,' Nate said.

'Good thinking.'

He smiled and took Robin's hand. They waited for a break in the traffic, then hurried to the other side of the road. When they got there, he didn't let go of her hand.

'I'm getting a little tired of those people,' Robin said.

'Everyone's tired of them.'

'Maybe the trollers have the right idea.'

Nate said nothing. At the corner, he led her to the right. The street ahead sloped upward, but it didn't look steep. A lone car was approaching. All the other cars in sight were parked at the curbs, or in driveways. The houses were small and close together. The only person in sight was a woman walking her dog.

'This is a lot better,' Robin said.

'It's a nice town. Mostly. It has a lot going for it.'

'The downtown section is pretty ritzy.'

'A lot of artists and poets and things. And people with money who like the atmosphere.' He looked at Robin. 'You're a poet.'

'Not *that* kind.'

'Yeah, your stuff makes sense. At least from what I've heard. But this is still a good place for . . . creative people. A lot of bookstores, and the university. Coffee shops where you can sit all day and write. I think Funland is great. I see too much of it, but I get a kick out of the place. It's wild and picturesque and trashy.'

'You like trashy, do you?'

'In its place. But there are a lot of different sides to Boleta Bay. You can't judge it all by a couple of bad experiences on the boardwalk.'

'You with the Chamber of Commerce?'

'It's just that Funland is its own thing. The whole town isn't . . . seedy. It has a lot that's nice about it.'

'Are you saying I shouldn't be in such a hurry to leave?'

'Yeah.'

Robin felt a quick spread of warmth in the pit of her stomach. She squeezed his hand.

'Are you going anywhere?' he asked. 'I mean, are you on your way to Hollywood or something?' She laughed.

'Hardly. I'm just a roving minstrel girl.'

Cockless Robin.

The echo of Poppinsack's voice, this time, seemed faint. Being with Nate, she supposed, had robbed it of the power to upset her.

'If you don't have any real destination,' he said, 'why don't you stay around for a while?'

'I guess I could.'

They crossed a deserted road. Nate led her onto a walk-way that traversed a park. The park was dark except for a few lamps along the walk. In the spray of glow beneath each lamp was a bench.

From here, she could see several of the benches.

Each was empty.

'Where are all the trolls?' she asked.

'There's a neighbourhood patrol. They've discouraged the riff-raff.'

'Sort of like a grown-up version of the trollers?'

'Not much. They're good citizens. From what I've heard, the trollers aren't much better than thugs. That's why I don't want you sleeping down near the shore. That's where they hunt. The boardwalk, the beach. I know you're not a troll . . .'

'Well, thanks.'

Nate halted and faced her. He took her other hand in his. Holding both, he stared into her eyes. He was frowning. 'It's nothing to joke about. They *hurt* people, and they might hurt you if they catch you around there at night.'

'What am I supposed to do?' Robin asked. She wished her heart would slow down. But it kept racing. Because she knew what was going on here. Nate planned to fix it so she could stay. Because he wanted her to be with him.

Jesus!

Trying to keep her voice steady, she said, 'You're asking me not to leave town. At the same time, you're saying I might get attacked by the trollers if I stay. And I already know the bums are dangerous. So I'm risking my butt if I sleep on the beach. You can't put me up in a motel every night.'

'We'll find you a place to stay.'

'That would take money. I'm in short supply of it. And I'm not going to let you pay.'

'I'll give you a job. We'll put you on the payroll.'

'I don't know, Nate. I . . . my music's important to me. It's *me*, you know? If I had a real job . . .'

'A job doing what you do now. But not down at the end of the boardwalk. In front of my family's concessions. The arcade, sometimes.' He smiled. 'So I can hear you. And see you. But mostly over by the Hurricane and Ferris wheel. The lines can get awfully long for those rides. You'd be entertainment for the people while they wait. We'll pay you an hourly rate. Start you off, say, at seven bucks an hour. You still go ahead and collect from them – wouldn't want to cheat your audience out of the joy of showing their appreciation.'

'And I'd keep the tips?' she asked.

Smiling, he said, 'What do you think this is, a charity?'

'I hope not. I can't see paying someone just to help your customers pass the time of day.'

'At quitting time, you turn over a percentage of your take. Forty percent. And you keep sixty, over and above whatever we pay you.'

'It's awfully generous, Nate.'

'Hell, it's good PR. Once word gets around, I wouldn't be at all surprised if people don't start coming to Funland *just* to hear you.'

'I'm not that good.'

'Don't bet on it. We'll see how it goes. Maybe down the line, we'll even set up some actual concerts.'

Grinning, Robin shook her head. 'You've got some pretty big ideas, fella.'

'You just don't know how good you are. And it isn't just your music. Your music's great, but it's more than that. It's you. I've watched your audiences. Those people . . . they fall in love with you.'

His words excited her. Robin knew she had magic. She'd noticed that many of those who watched her play seemed enthralled, that often the same people appeared in her audiences day after day. But to hear Nate speak of it was thrilling and a little embarrassing.

They fall in love with you.

She suddenly wondered if Nate meant that *he* had fallen in love with her.

'Is it a deal?' he asked.

Though she hadn't felt cold since about the time they rushed across the street to avoid the troll, she was shivering again. 'Couldn't hurt to give it a try,' she said.

He squeezed her hands and shook them up and down. 'Great,' he said. 'Great.'

'Don't break my hands off, kiss me.'

A familiar look of surprise and confusion came to his face. It was the same expression Robin had seen that afternoon when she told him the room number.

He let go of her hands. He raised his arms. She stepped into them and pressed herself against him. He felt warm and solid. He felt like a home.

Don't count your chickens, Robin started to warn herself.

Then his mouth was there and she seemed to be melting into him.

Chapter Twenty-seven

'There it is,' Dave said when he spotted Gloria's Volkswagen.

Driving up and down the lanes of the parking lot, they'd passed at least twelve other VW bugs. But this one was hers. Dave recognized the licence plate. And he recognized the bumper stickers: 'No Vietnam in Nicaragua' and 'One Nuclear Bomb Can Ruin Your Whole Day'.

'Guess she's here, all right.' Joan said.

Dave found an empty space nearby, and parked. Before leaving the car, he took his flashlight out from under the seat.

'Do we start with the boardwalk?' Joan asked.

'I suppose. Great way to spend our time off.'

'I could think of better things to do, if I really put my mind to it.'

'Do they include me?'

'Might.'

Dave slipped an arm beneath the back of her open jacket. As they walked towards the front of the lot, he moved his hand slowly up and down her side. He felt her warmth and smoothness through the blouse. Each time his hand drifted down close to her hip, his knuckles brushed the walnut grip of the off-duty .38 clipped to her belt.

'What do we tell Jim and Beth?' she asked.

'Ohhh boy.'

'We're bound to run into them, you know. Beth's no problem. But Jim isn't likely to let it alone. If he gets the idea we're going together, it'll be all over the department. The brass gets wind of it, and one of us'll be reassigned.'

'We'll just have to play innocent.'

Smiling, Joan patted his rump. 'Think you can keep your hands to yourself?'

'Sure. No sweat.'

She peeled his hand off her side. 'Better start practising.'

They crossed to the walkway. Dave looked both ways, scanning the pavement and the grassy slope in front of Funland. A few other couples were nearby, heading for the entrance. And he spotted someone lying on the grass near the wall of the old pavilion at the far north end. From this distance, the person looked like a pile of clothes. The heap next to the form was probably a pack.

'Over there,' Dave said.

Joan nodded. 'Let's check it out.'

As they approached the sprawled figure, Dave saw that the face was bearded.

Joan must've noticed it, too. 'Unless Gloria's hormones flipped out,' she said, 'that ain't her.'

'Let's go around this end anyway. If we go back to the main entrance, we'll have to waste time doubling back.'

'I hope he's asleep.'

He wasn't. He got up and stumbled down the slope in time to block their way. The nearby lamp provided plenty of light for Dave to see the glare in the man's eyes – a wild, mad look that reminded him of Charles Manson. 'Help a fella down on his luck.' It wasn't a plea. It was a demand.

Dave said, 'We're looking for . . .'

Joan grabbed his arm and tugged him off the kerb.

'Lookin' for *God*?' the man blurted. 'Tha's me! Gimme a buck.'

'Get lost!' Joan called over her shoulder as she dragged Dave along beside her.

'Ge' fucked, cunt! Huh? Wha'sa matter witcha, cunt?'

Dave jerked his arm free. He whirled toward the man. '*I'll* give you something, you filthy . . .!'

'Gimme a buck! Gimme a buck 'r I'll put the cursa squirmy death on ya!'

'Dave!'

His left arm was suddenly grabbed from behind. He realized it was cocked back, ready to swing. In the hand was his sixteen inch, metal flashlight.

'Dave!' Joan snapped again. 'Don't! Come on! Let's go!'

He let Joan guide him backward off the kerb. As she pulled him along, he sidestepped, keeping his eyes on the derelict.

In a leaping frenzy, the guy yelled, 'Fuck ya!' He jammed the middle fingers of both hands together in front of his snarling mouth and blurted, 'Cursa squirmy death, cursa squirmy death! Whammy whammy presto fuck ya!'

He kept on leaping, waving his arms and shouting. Once they rounded the corner of the pavilion, they couldn't hear him any more.

Joan leaned back against the wall. She seemed to sag against it. She shook her head.

'Are you okay?' Dave asked.

'Me? You were gonna *brain* him.'

'Yeah. I lost it for a second there.'

'That's for sure. Jeez.' She pushed herself off the wall. She rested her wrists on his shoulders and caressed the back of his head. 'I appreciate the gallantry, pal, but you don't have to defend my honour. I don't give a rat's ass what a troll calls me.'

'I do.'

'Macho pig.'

'That's me.'

The way she massaged his scalp and neck soothed his tension, made him feel a little drowsy.

'Now you got us whammied with the curse of squirmy death.'

'Bummer,' he murmured. 'Should I go back and pay him a buck to take it off?'

243

'Give him five. Can't be too careful.'

Dave started to move back, but she clamped his neck.

'Where do you think you're going?'

'Oh.' He realized she'd been joking about the five. Of course. Pay the guy to remove some ridiculous curse? But it *had* seemed like a good idea, there for a second.

Joan's grip on his neck relaxed, and she started massaging him again. He let his head droop. He let his eyes shut.

'From now on,' she said in a smooth, soft voice, 'let's just keep our distance from any trolls we happen to run into. I don't think we want to be asking them about Gloria. Wouldn't find out anything anyway, not from those people. And we might just blow her cover.'

'Okay. That makes sense.'

'Besides, they scare me shitless.'

That remark was like a rock plopping into the still pond of his lethargy. He lifted his head and smiled, amused by her language but touched by her confession of fear. He put his hands on her sides. 'Maybe I'd *better* get that curse removed.'

'A *superstitious* macho pig.'

'Can't be too careful. We're talking "squirmy death" here.'

She drew Dave's head toward her and kissed him lightly on the mouth. Dave felt her breasts push against him. He wrapped his arms around her, underneath her jacket, and slid his hands up and down her back. She turned her head, taking away the soft moist warmth of her mouth.

'We'd better find Gloria,' she whispered, her breath tickling his ear.

'Why don't we just forget about her? Let's get out of this place and . . .'

'That'd be nice.'

'It's her game. She wants to play Ace Reporter, who're we to stop her?'

'Keep talking. Maybe you'll convince yourself.'

'Damn it.'

'Let's just give it an hour or so.' Joan said. 'Then we'll go back to my place. Whether we find her or not. We don't have to stop her. We don't even have to warn her. All we have to do is *try*. Give it a fair try.'

'She knows the dangers,' Dave said.

'But that won't do our consciences a whole lot of good if she gets hurt.'

'Okay. We'll give it an hour.' He eased himself away from Joan and checked his wristwatch. 'It's nine-forty, now.'

'Funland closes at eleven. Let's give it till then.'

'What time does Debbie's party get over?'

'She's supposed to be home by midnight.'

'This is the pits.'

Joan stared into his eyes. 'I know. But it's only one night. Then we'll be done with Gloria.'

'Yeah. It'll be worth it, I guess, just so we won't have to feel guilty for *not* doing it.'

They climbed a flight of concrete stairs at the corner of the pavilion. This end of the boardwalk wasn't crowded. During the past few days, a small crowd had been gathered here for the banjo girl. Dave tried to remember her name. A bird name. Dove? No, Robin. A cute gal. He wondered where she was. This was no place, at night, for a lone girl. Not with crazies around like that bastard they'd just run into. Not with trollers on the prowl, some nights, looking for indigents to torment. He hoped she'd taken his advice to stay in motels.

'Should we check in there?' Joan asked, nodding towards the pavilion's doorway.

Dave didn't see any trolls on the boardwalk between this door and the one at the pavilion's far end. 'Just a quick walkthrough,' he said.

They went inside. The big auditorium was brightly lighted and warm. Calliope music accompanied the spinning merry-go-round in the centre of the floor. Along the walls were booths where people could buy specialities such as fudge, salt-water taffy, soft pretzels, churros, nachos, straps of beef jerky, or ice cream. At one end was a snack counter for burgers, hot dogs, fries and pop. There were booths that sold Funland souvenirs: ash trays, plates, tomtoms, rubber knives, shot glasses, coffee mugs and pennants. Others offered assortments of sea shells. Others sold Funland T-shirts, sweatshirts, caps, and plastic visors.

Dave had often seen the place jammed with people. Tonight, it wasn't especially crowded. Quite a few people were wandering around, some sampling food, some browsing for keepsakes, a few snapping photos of their kids on the carousel.

He didn't see any bums.

He didn't see Gloria.

'Hungry?' he asked.

'No. You go ahead and get something, though.'

He shook his head.

'We can have a snack when we get to my place.'

'Okay.' He appreciated the reminder that they would get to Joan's place later.

We could be there right now.

Thanks a heap, Gloria.

They exited at the next door. Stepped out onto the boardwalk right into the path of Jim and Beth.

Beth's head drew back, doubling her chin. Her eyes opened so wide she looked as if her lids might get stuck up there. One side of Jim's face curled up, giving him a cross between a smirk and a snarl.

Thirty seconds, Dave thought. Thirty damn seconds, and we would've missed them.

'Well, I'll be screwed, chewed, and tattooed,' Jim said. 'Hello, young lovers, wherever you are.'

'Don't jump to conclusions,' Dave said. He decided that sounded stupid.

'We're looking for Gloria Weston,' Joan told them.

'Planning a ménage à trois?'

Jim knew that Dave had been going with Gloria. Hell, *everyone* knew. It had been a source of constant ribbing from most of his fellow officers – the cop and the nosy pinko reporter.

'How about waiting till we're off duty?' Jim suggested. 'We'll have a fivesome.'

'Try to pull your head out of your butt for a minute,' Joan said, 'and listen up. Weston's gone undercover to get a lice-eye view of the life of a troll.'

'Figures. What's the big deal?'

'It isn't healthy,' Dave said.

'Have you seen her?' Joan asked.

'I don't *look* at those maggots. They put me off my feed.'

'Would we recognize her?' Beth said. 'Has she altered her appearance?'

'Mussed up her hair,' Joan said, addressing Beth. 'She's wearing a grey sweatshirt, purple skirt, and red tights. They're all pretty filthy and ragged. And she's got grocery bags. Two on her feet, and she's probably carrying the third.'

'She's wearing *bags* on her feet?' Beth asked.

'The latest fashion in troll footwear,' Joan said.

'She really got into this, didn't she?'

'You haven't seen her?'

'I doubt it. I think I would've noticed the bags. What do you want us to do if we find her?'

'We're not trying hauling her in,' Jim said, 'she'll scream bloody murder – all over the pages of that rag she works for.'

'Just keep an eye on her,' Dave told him. 'We'll be looking around, ourselves. We'll check with you before closing time. The thing is, I wouldn't be at all surprised if she isn't planning to spend the night out here someplace. She doesn't do things halfway. She wants to find out what it's like to be a troll. She's going to stick it out.'

'You ask me,' Jim said, 'it's none of our business.'

'She could get hurt,' Beth said.

'And wouldn't *that* be a pity?' He met Dave's eyes. 'Sorry, man. I understand you got something going with her. But whistling Jesus, she crucifies us every time she plants her ass in front of the typewriter. You read that trash on the trollers?'

'I didn't like it any more than you did.'

'So she wants to cosy up to those runny sores on the rump of humanity, let her. Spends some time with 'em, she'll change her tune. That's for damn sure. She might start calling for mass executions.'

'That's not very likely,' Dave said.

'Yeah. "They were children once, who stayed up all night waiting for Santa." Last time I saw that kinda shit, it was floating in the toilet bowl.'

'You're making me sick,' Beth said.

Jim scowled at her. 'I know what *you* think of that . . . lady.'

Beth looked pretty sheepish all of a sudden. She shrugged and met Dave's eyes. 'I still wouldn't want anything to happen to her.'

'Gloria doesn't know what she's getting into,' Joan said. 'We just want to warn her off.'

'We'll keep an eye out for her,' Beth said.

'Thanks.'

'Yeah,' Dave said. 'We appreciate it.'

As he stepped past Jim, the man winked and whispered, 'Lucky fuck. My advice, lose Weston.'

Dave shook his head and kept walking.

'That wasn't so bad,' Joan said.

'We'll see.' Just ahead were the stairs leading down to the beach. Dave was suddenly glad they'd run into Jim and Beth. 'Maybe we can speed things up some by skipping the rest of the boardwalk. They'll spot Gloria if she's up here.'

'Beth might, anyway. I think Jim would like to see her move in with the trolls.'

'I can see his point,' Dave admitted. 'But how about it? We leave the boardwalk to them?'

'Sure.'

They trotted down the concrete stairs. Joan stopped when she reached the sand. 'Where do we start?'

'I don't know.' Dave scanned the beach. It was pale with moonlight. There were dark patches, here and there, that appeared to be people on blankets. Most of the people were in pairs. Some were sitting, but many were lying down, embracing.

Dave saw a lone man running along the shore. A dog trotted ahead of him to check out a group of three people coming from the opposite direction. The dog wagged its tail. One of the three, a woman with a pony tail, squatted down to ruffle its fur. Off to the right, a couple was strolling past the front of the life guard station.

'Wonder if anyone's getting it on,' Joan said.

Obviously, she was intrigued by the people on the blankets. 'Kind of nippy for that,' Dave said.

'Love breeds desperate measures.'

'Want to check them out?'

'I'd rather find Gloria.'

'That's what I meant.'

'I'd be awfully surprised to find her out in the open,' Joan said. 'She's into the lifestyles of the down and dirty. She'll be where she's most likely to meet trolls.'

'Around here, that doesn't narrow the field by much.'

Joan swept an arm back, thumb pointing behind her as if she were trying to hitch a ride.

'I know,' Dave said.

'I know you know.'

'You don't want to go under there, do you?'

'Do we have any choice?'

'Sure we do.'

'Are you looking for Gloria, or just pretending?'

'You and Jiminy Cricket.'

Joan took his hand. 'Let's check it out before I lose my nerve.'

They turned around, walked past the stairs, and entered the darkness beneath the boardwalk. Dave switched on his flash-light. Its strong beam thrust out a shaft of brightness. Shadows from the pilings lurched and swayed as the light swept by.

A yelp of alarm made him flinch, and Joan almost crushed his hand. Someone scuttled from behind a post, was lost in the black, then found again by the flashlight beam. Dave couldn't tell whether it was a man or woman. But it wore dirty brown pants and an overcoat, so he knew it wasn't Gloria. It scurried towards the rear, whining. Dave turned the light away.

'Holy jumping Judas,' Joan muttered.

'You sure you're up to this?'

'I can take it if you can.'

'I'm not sure about my hand.'

'Sorry.' Joan eased her grip.

They stood motionless while Dave played the flashlight over the area ahead. 'Looks okay,' he whispered.

'Most of them are probably farther back.'

He aimed the beam to his left. Saw a woman with a dirty face peering at him from beside a distant post. Saw a few huddled shapes far behind her.

Goosebumps scurried up his back.

He swung the light away fast.

Joan muttered, 'Shit.'

'Should we check them out?'

'No.'

'What happened to Jiminy Cricket?'

'There're limits.'

'Glad to hear it.'

'Try calling out.'

'Gloria?' he shouted. 'Gloria? You there?'

Voices, five or six of them, some low and gravely, others high-pitched, called, 'Gloria? Yoo-hoo, Gloria? Glorrrria?'

Dave moaned. He hurried forward, holding on tightly to Joan's hand, dodging the posts that blocked the way. The voices kept asking for Gloria. They sounded *amused*.

To the left, a heap of dark blankets broke open and a gaunt man bolted up. Joan lurched aside, crashed into a piling and gasped and staggered back against Dave.

'Saaay,' the troll piped. 'How's about two bits for an old soldier down on his luck?'

Throwing an arm around Joan, Dave rushed her out from under the boardwalk. The moonlight found them. They didn't stop until they were far out onto the beach.

Joan hugged him in a fierce clutch. She was panting, chest rising and falling against him, breath hot on his ear.

'Are you okay?' he asked.

250

Her cheek rubbed his face as she nodded.

'Did you hurt yourself?'

'Not much. My shoulder a little.'

'We shouldn't have gone under there.'

'God, those *people*.'

'Trolls.'

'What if Gloria's there?'

'That's her problem.'

'Damn it.'

'We're not going back in there,' Dave said. 'I don't care what you say.'

'Let's go.'

'No.'

'To my place.'

'Are you sure?'

'I want to get out of here. Right now.'

But she kept herself clenched to Dave, and didn't move.

'Couple of real chickens, aren't we?' she said after a while.

'Kentucky fried.'

'It's not as if they could've hurt us, or anything. I mean, were armed.'

'And you're Kung Fu city.'

'Could've choppy-sockied them all over the place.'

'On the other hand, who's to say they don't have weapons of their own?'

'That's a pleasant thought.'

'Did you mean it about leaving?' Dave asked.

'I meant it. Let's go.'

Chapter Twenty-eight

'I'd just as soon get going,' Shiner said.

'It's early, it's still early.' Jeremy's voice sounded slightly muffled to him, as if his ears were plugged. Can booze do that to you? he wondered.

Shiner squeezed his arm and shook him gently. 'Come on. Everybody's polluted. Including you.'

'I'm fine,' Jeremy said. 'Can't we stay a little longer?'

'If you really want to. But just a few more minutes, okay?'

He looked down at the glass in his hand and saw that it was empty. He decided against getting a refill just now. Shiner wouldn't like it. She really didn't seem to be enjoying herself much. She should've been drinking like the rest of them. After her first glass of spiked punch, right after Nate left, she'd switched to Pepsi.

'Wanna dance?' Jeremy asked.

'Not much. I'm all danced out. And they keep playing that crap. I hate that crap.'

'It's the Beastie Boys.'

'Whoopie.'

Only Karen was still dancing. A few minutes ago, she'd stripped down to her bra and panties. She was writhing and shaking, her hair flying, her breasts bobbing wildly as if the bra wasn't even there. Her skin was glossy with moisture. Her eyes were fixed on Tanya.

Tanya didn't seem interested. She was staring at her drink and paying no attention to Karen. She'd been dancing, herself, a little earlier. But she'd kept her clothes on, and kept a glass of punch in one hand. Now, she slumped on the sofa with her bare feet resting top of the table in front of her. Randy was stretched out, his head on her lap, one arm hanging down towards the floor. He appeared to be asleep.

Passed out is more like it, Jeremy thought.

Randy'd been guzzling the punch. He'd acted pretty funny for a while, giggling and doing his 'famous impressions of dead Presidents' such as Chester A. Arthur and Thomas Jefferson, and giggling a lot and wearing his glasses upside down. Then, he'd collapsed onto the sofa.

Jeremy wished *he* could be the one on the sofa with Tanya.

Only not zonked out. Wide awake.

He imagined himself with her, but not lying there the way Randy was. Sitting up. Tanya straddling his lap the way Liz was on Cowboy in the recliner across the room. They'd been like that for a long time. Jeremy suspected that Cowboy's hands were up inside her sweater.

'Are you ready to go yet?' Shiner asked.

'What time is it?'

'Ten-fifteen. But you said we could leave early. Nothing's going on, anyway.'

'Couple a minutes?'

'What're you waiting for? Think Karen's going to take off the rest?'

'I don't even like her,' Jeremy protested.

'You sure like looking at her. Personally, I happen to find it repulsive. You do know what she's doing, don't you?'

'Dancing.'

'Trying to get Tanya turned on.'

'Tanya's no lesbo.'

'Oh, you're an expert?'

'She was Nate's girl.'

'Yeah, and Nate's out of the picture and she's *really* depressed. Maybe Karen'll get lucky.'

'Nah.'

'Maybe one of the *guys'll* get lucky.' Shiner looked at Jeremy and raised an eyebrow. 'Maybe you. Is that what you're hoping for?'

He felt heat rush to his face. 'No!'

'Yeah. Sure.'

'Honest.'

Her eyes narrowed slightly. 'Then prove it. Let's leave right now.'

Oh God, Jeremy thought. What'll I do? What if I say no? This could be my big chance.

'Okay,' he said. 'We can leave.'

Shiner's lips formed a narrow line. She gazed into his eyes and nodded. 'Good,' she said. Her hand found his, and she squeezed it gently.

'I gotta use the john, though.'

'Hardly surprising,' she said. She smiled. 'You'll have to wait for Heather to get out. That'll give you a while longer to ogle Karen.'

He pushed himself away from the panelled wall. The bath-room door was shut, all right. Determined not to ogle Karen, he turned his eyes to Shiner.

She really *is* beautiful, he thought.

He wondered what would happen in the car. It was still early. She didn't have to be home until midnight, so they'd have a long time if they parked somewhere.

Heather stepped out of the bathroom. She looked saggy. Her bloated face was pale.

'Did you find him?' Samson asked her.

Heather looked confused. 'Huh? Who? Find who?'

'Ralph. I heard you calling for him, "Ralph! Ralph!"'

'Hardy har har har. You're as funny as a pregnant polevaulter.'

Samson, a wide dazed smile on his face, staggered to the bathroom, hugged the doorframe and peered inside. 'Ralph? Ralph, you in here?'

Jeremy slumped against the wall and wrinkled his nose at Shiner. 'I think she barfed in there.'

'I do believe you're right.'

'It's gonna stink.'

'There's probably a john upstairs.'

'I'll ask.' He pushed himself off the wall again, and headed for Tanya. Tanya would know. Aware that Shiner was probably watching him, he walked very carefully. And he didn't look at

254

Karen. He stepped between the edge of the table and the sofa. He bumped Randy's arm, but the boy didn't wake up.

Tanya raised her head and smiled at him. 'Hey, Duke. How's it going?'

'Great,' he said. 'I was just . . .'

'Get over here, sit down.' She took her feet off the table and set her glass on it. Taking Jeremy's hand, she towed him past her knees and pulled him onto the sofa beside her. 'You having a good time?' she asked.

'Yeah. Terrific.'

'Good, good.' She wrapped an arm across his shoulders. 'You're a good fella, Duke. You're a real good fella. Know what I like about you?'

He shook his head. The motion of it made him dizzy.

'You got loyalty. Loyalty and guts.' She rubbed his shoulder. Staring into his eyes, she nodded agreement with herself. 'I didn't wanta see that guy die. You wanta see that guy die?'

'No.'

'Course not. But I don't hear you whining about it and bugging out. No sir. You got loyalty and guts.'

'Thanks,' he said.

'You're a true friend. We're *all* true friends. We're family, you know?'

'Yeah.'

'We're gonna wipe out those fuckin' trolls. Were gonna lay 'em waste.'

'Damn right.'

She turned toward him. Her leg pressed his leg. She pulled him against her chest and kissed him.

Tanya's kissing me, he told himself.

He couldn't believe it.

He wondered if Shiner was watching.

He didn't care.

He'd dreamed of this since the first time he saw her, and now it was happening, really happening.

Her full lips were soft and warm and moist. And open. Her breath was going into his mouth. Her breasts were pushing against his chest. Her hands were rubbing his neck. He put his arms around her and hugged her tight. Her tongue thrust into his mouth.

Then, her face eased away from him.

It can't be over yet, he told himself. He felt cheated, as if he'd just awakened from a dream – the best dream ever, one that had just started. The loss of it made him ache. At the same time, he felt an intense joy. How could he feel so horrible and so wonderful at the same moment?

Her lips and the skin around them looked wet.

That's my saliva, Jeremy thought. Mine. God.

Looking into his eyes, she squeezed his leg. 'Come with me,' she said.

Stunned, he rose from the sofa. Tanya scooted over, easing Randy's head onto the cushion, and got up. She led the way to the stairs.

Shiner was no longer standing by the wall. Jeremy looked around. She was gone.

Had she actually left?

Doesn't matter, he thought. Oh God, where are we going? Away from the others. Someplace where we can be alone. What's going on?

We gonna *do it*?

His mouth was dry, his heart thumping as he climbed the stairs behind Tanya.

I don't even know *how*! What if I mess up and she laughs at me?

At the top of the stairs, she took hold of his hand.

'Where're we going?' he asked, his voice coming out hushed and ragged.

'My room,' she said.

Her words seemed to suck out the last of Jeremy's breath. He gasped for air as he walked with her.

'I've got something for you.'

His legs trembled as he climbed the broad, carpeted stairs to the second floor of the house.

He wondered where her parents were. Shiner'd said they

might be upstairs, staying out of the way. But this was Friday, so maybe they'd gone out.

What if they come back and catch us?

Jeremy walked with Tanya down a hallway and entered a room. Tanya flicked a wall switch, and lamps went on. She shut the door.

Jeremy was standing inside the biggest bedroom he'd ever seen. It had an enormous bed with lamps on either side, a bureau, a dressing table with a mirror, a roll-top desk, a television with a VCR, a Compact Disc player, a recliner, a sofa, and shelves that were crowded with animal dolls, trophies, framed photographs, and books. It had its own bathroom. From where he stood, he could see the sink.

The bedroom's thick carpet was pale blue; the bedspread and curtains were pink. There was a faint, sweet aroma that reminded him of the smell of suntan oil.

Tanya's room.

Where she sleeps. Where she changes clothes. Even where she goes to the toilet, showers and takes her baths.

And I'm here.

And we're going to do it. *Right there on her bed.*

'You better sit down before you keel over,' Tanya said. She guided him to the side of the bed. He sank onto it, and clutched his knees to hold himself steady.

She went to the rolltop desk. She removed something from a drawer, and kept it hidden behind her back as she walked towards Jeremy.

A rubber?

She stopped in front of him. 'Put out your hand,' she said.

He held his hand out. His fingers were fluttering.

Into his palm she dropped a double-edged razor blade.

Confusion and icy prickles of fear moved in with his breathless excitement.

'Just hold it for now,' Tanya said. She knelt on the floor and placed her hands on his thighs. The feel of her hands, so close to his groin, sent waves of heat rushing through him.

'Tell me why you joined up with us.'

'To . . . to hunt trolls.'

'Why?'

'Cowboy. He invited me.'

'Is that all?'

Jeremy shrugged. 'I guess it was partly to make friends. Specially you,' he added, and felt a drop of sweat trickle down his side.

'Especially me. I know. Everybody's in it because of me.'

Except Shiner, he thought. But Shiner's out of it, now.

'The trolls hurt me bad,' she said. 'We're after them because of that. That's why it started. We go after them for revenge. Last night, you joined in the revenge. You joined for my sake.'

Jeremy nodded.

She stood up and began to unbutton her big, loose shirt.

This can't be happening, Jeremy thought. I don't believe it.

He watched her hands move slowly down the front of bright blue and yellow plaid, unfastening each button along the way. When the last was open, she spread the shirt.

The sight seared Jeremy's mind, slammed his heart, sank his stomach, jammed his penis erect though his scrotum and anus went cold and tight.

'They did this to me,' Tanya said as the shirt dropped to the floor behind her.

She stood before him, wearing only her white shorts. Her skin had a soft tan. Even her breasts. They were big, firm, wonderful. In the glow of the lamplight, they looked polished. As if they'd been buffed to a glossy sheen. Their dark nipples jutted out.

The scar began as a slick pink curve alongside her left nipple. It swept across the underside of the breast and streaked downward. It was as wide as a fingertip, pale pink, shiny, a little puffy. It passed the edge of her navel and vanished at the waistband of her shorts.

Tanya opened her shorts. She pushed them down around her thighs.

She was smooth and hairless.

The stark rip skidded over her mound, and under it, and

seemed to miss the soft, open flesh below by a fraction of an inch.

'A broken wine bottle,' Tanya said.

Jeremy nodded. Her words seemed to come from a great distance. He couldn't take his eyes off her. He felt dizzy and sick, stunned by her nakedness, pained by the ugly scar, astonished that she was showing herself to him.

'Three of 'em got me in the lifeguard shack,' she said. 'Trolls. They'd spent the night there. I tried to kick 'em out, and they jumped me. One of 'em broke a wine bottle on my head. Then they stripped me.'

'God,' Jeremy murmured.

'One of 'em did this.' Her fingertip touched the scar tissue at her groin, and slid slowly higher, tracing the tear up her belly and ribcage and breast. 'He slobbered on me while he did it. The other two held me down. Then, he raped me. Grunting and slobbering. He smelled like stale wine and sweat and garbage. When he finished, the other two had me. One fucked me in the ass. One came in my mouth. Before they left, they pissed on me. All over me. On my face . . .'

She stepped out of her shorts. With one foot, she flicked them aside. On her knees, she reached beneath the bed. She dragged out a heap of brown bath towels. She spread two of them on the carpet at Jeremy's feet, and left the others wadded nearby. Stepping onto the double thickness of towels, she said, 'Cut your hand.'

Jeremy nodded. He felt as if his mind had collapsed while he'd listened to her story.

He switched the razor blade to the trembling fingers of his left hand. He pressed its edge into the palm of his right. Blood welled up, and he cupped his hand to hold it.

Tanya took the razor from him. She slid it against the skin of her mound, and a crimson thread appeared alongside the scar. She lifted Jeremy's bleeding hand. She pressed it tightly against her cut. Blood squeezed, spilling around the sides of his hand, trickling down her legs, dripping onto the towel under her spread feet.

She felt hot through the blood. Beneath her skin, there seemed to be a curving ridge of bone. Jeremy kept his hand bent back as far back as possible, not daring to touch what was below the ridge. But Tanya pressed his fingers upwards. Into slippery folds of flesh.

'Your blood is in me,' she whispered. She was breathing hard. She was moving just slightly, rubbing herself against his hand. 'My blood's in you. You're my . . . lover in blood. Say it.'

Jeremy heard himself repeat the words.

She guided his hand upward, keeping it pressed to the scar. The scar felt like a narrow, puffy ribbon. His hand left a red smear as it slid up her belly, up her ribcage to her breast. Her breast was pushed upward and sideways by his moving hand. The nipple bent like springy rubber as his thumb passed over it. She slid his hand higher, and Jeremy rose to his feet. His hard penis felt trapped inside his pants, squeezed and bent.

She lifted his hand to her mouth. She kissed its cut palm. She licked the blood from it. Gazing into his eyes, she took his thumb into her mouth. She sucked and licked it clean, then did the same with each of his fingers.

'Your blood and mine,' she whispered. Her lips and chin and cheeks were dappled with it. She lowered his hand. She placed the razor blade in his palm. 'Keep this with you to remember.'

'I'll never forget.'

'I know.'

Jeremy took a handkerchief from his pocket, wrapped the blade and closed his fingers around it, pressing the cloth to his wound.

'Go on home, now,' Tanya said in a gentle voice. 'I'll see you tomorrow.'

His throat tightened.

He was supposed to leave?

He was so *turned on*! So was she!

It can't stop now!

He suddenly blurted, 'But aren't we gonna . . .?' She touched a finger to his lips. 'You'll have to prove yourself, first.'

260

'How?'

'With time. And loyalty. And courage.'

'Not tonight?'

'Not tonight. But soon, maybe.'

At the bedroom doorway, he stopped and looked back at Tanya. She stood on the towels, facing him, naked and smeared with blood. 'I love you,' he said.

'And I love you, Jeremy.'

He left her there.

When he reached the bottom of the stairs, he heard faint sounds of music and voices and laughter from the trollers below. He wondered if he should go down and rejoin the party.

He didn't want to.

And Tanya had told him to go home. She hadn't told him to go downstairs with the other trollers.

One of them might give him a ride, though.

I can walk, he told himself.

He trotted down the veranda stairs, stepped off the kerb, and began to stride along the driveway.

The air smelled of pine trees. The night was not especially cold, but Jeremy shivered as he walked. His throat was tight. He squeezed his arms across his chest. The handkerchief and razor were still in his hand.

He felt so *strange*.

Dazed, confused, disappointed, empty and weak.

Wrecked.

But, at the same time, elated.

He felt like leaping and shouting with joy. He felt like weeping. And somewhere in Jeremy was an odd desire to get home and hide under the covers of his bed and stay away from Funland and the beach and Tanya and all the trollers forever.

Chapter Twenty-nine

Gloria woke up in the back seat of her Volkswagen. She had no idea how long she'd been asleep. When she looked out the window, however, she saw that the parking lot was deserted except for three or four other cars.

So Funland was closed for the night.

With a tremor in her stomach that felt like a mixture of excitement and fear, she lifted her grocery bag. She pushed the seatback forward, opened the door, and climbed out. She locked the door. Then, she headed for the main entrance of Funland.

Her day hadn't gone as well as she'd hoped. She'd approached numerous derelicts, but most of them had chased her off, muttering curses or shouting like lunatics. Some seemed angry, others frightened. Whatever the reason, and in spite of her costume, they wanted no part of her. Others simply appeared to be dwelling inside peculiar, dangerous worlds of their own invention – worlds that excluded Gloria.

All day, she had succeeded in carrying out interviews, of sorts, with only three subjects: Mosby, Dink and a woman who refused to reveal her name. She'd taped the conversations on the Sony micro-cassette recorder under her sweatshirt. Maybe she'd got something she could use, but she doubted it.

She wanted pathos. She wanted heart-wrenching stories of noble people whose lives has been smashed to ruins by cruel blows of fate. She wanted tales of such woe that tears would spring to the eyes of her readers. She wanted them not only to weep for these people, but to be stirred to action. To demand aid for the homeless outcasts of society, food and shelter, and most of all to cry out against the ruthless gang of teenagers who preyed upon them,

Mosby, Dink and the other one hadn't given her much to work with.

They were truly ruined people, but incapable of telling their tales.

Gloria must've spent an hour talking with Mosby on the steps in front of Funland, and heard about nothing except dogs. Dogs were the reincarnations of dead Nazis, and carrying out a plot to destroy mankind by dumping radioactive faeces in populated areas. Mosby, a crusader, fought the peril at every turn by treating dogs to meals of broken glass concealed in hamburger.

Dink, a scruffy, bearded man in his early twenties, claimed to be a researcher from a planet called Zanthion. The population of Zanthion was entirely male. Faced with certain extinction, they'd sent Dink to investigate the reproductive system of the female Earthling. The 'travel gate' would be closing in two hours, so he had almost run out of time. If he failed to learn the mysteries of the 'secret source', his species was doomed. Gloria was his only hope. She'd asked how she could help. 'You gotta let me probe yer source wit' my 'vestigation rod.' At that, Gloria told him to stick his 'vestigation rod up his 'testinal terminus. Then, she hurried away.

Gloria had met the third indigent in an alley after dark. This woman seemed rational, though she refused to tell her name. 'Don' tell nobody my name,' she'd said. 'They know yer name, they can tag ya.' Gloria decided not to press the issue. Instead, she walked with her, listening to a lecture on how people 'throw out perfeckly good stuff', while the woman stopped her shopping cart at each trash bin and dug for treasures. Mostly, she collected newspapers, cans and bottles to redeem for cash at the recycling centre. But she also collected scraps of food – the litter of half-eaten meals – and stuffed them into her mouth with grunting relish. Frequently, Gloria gagged and turned away.

So far, things hadn't gone at all the way she'd hoped. But she was sure to find some fresh subjects on the boardwalk this time of night. Or on the beach. A homeless person with *appeal*, please. Someone who would capture the hearts of her readers.

At this hour, she might even run into trailers. She had a stun gun in her grocery bag in case they tried to get rough. But once she identified herself, they might be eager to give their side of the story. That'd certainly be a scoop.

You've got to come up with something, she told herself as she trotted up the stairs to Funland's main entrance. You write it the way it's gone so far today, and you'll sound like a propagandist for Great Big Billy Goat Gruff.

And wouldn't Dave like *that*?

Rotten, two-timing bastard.

What did I ever see in him, anyway? Should've known better than to get involved with a macho, reactionary pig.

The familiar, cold feeling of loss clutched Gloria.

Fuck him, she told herself.

She wished she'd had the courage to show herself to Dave. All day, she'd toyed with the idea of going onto the boardwalk and confronting him. He would've been shocked. 'Have you lost your mind? Don't you know how dangerous this is?' She would've smirked and said, 'I'm sure you care. You've got your golden Amazon bitch pig.'

But the golden Amazon bitch pig would've been there with him. Gloria knew it would've hurt too much, seeing them together. So she'd stayed away.

They're probably rutting right now, she thought. She pictured the two of them in bed, sweaty and grunting. But then it wasn't Joan under Dave. Gloria could feel him on top of her, feel him inside her. Squeezing her eyes shut, she dropped onto a bench and shook her head sharply from side to side, trying to dislodge the images.

It's over, she told herself. Stop thinking about him.

He was so gentle, sometimes. And so funny. And so caring. And in bed . . .

The hell with him.

He never had it so good, and he threw it away for that golden-haired slut.

He'll regret it, someday. He'll be sorry.

'I give him two weeks,' she muttered. 'Two weeks, and he'll

come to a rude awakening. He'll see just how good he had it, and he'll come begging. And I'll laugh in his face.'

Bullshit. I'll throw my arms around him and . . .

'Where're the goddamn trolls?' she asked, raising her head and looking both ways. The boardwalk, moonwashed and splashed with black shadows, looked deserted.

'Let's have some action here!' she yelled. 'Bring on the bums! Bring on Great Big Billy Goat Gruff! Bring on *something*, God damn it! Let's stop wasting my fucking time, here!'

A huge patch of blackness broke away from the shadows across the boardwalk.

And ran at her.

Jesus! she thought. *I didn't mean it!*

She sprang to her feet, grocery bag flying from her lap. Her blanket spilled out of it. So did the stun gun. It clattered and skittered across the planking, and she knew she couldn't get to it in time.

The blackness had a white face, a big flapping coat. Its arms were stretched towards her like the arms of some kind of horror movie geek.

'Leave me alone!' Gloria shrieked. She flung herself to the right, out of its path, and ran as hard as she could. Footfalls pounded behind her.

At once, she regretted bolting in this direction. She should've leapt the railing and dropped to the beach. Or gone to the left, tried to dodge the troll and make it out to the street. But now she was racing south on the boardwalk, deeper into the abandoned fun zone. No way out on her left. No way out on her right without climbing fences that surrounded the rides.

Chance it? she wondered.

The thudding footfalls of the troll didn't seem to be getting closer. She risked a glance over her shoulder. He was about twenty feet back, farther away than he'd been when she bolted from the bench.

He looked like a giant.

But he wasn't *fast*.

He won't win any track races, Gloria thought. But her terror didn't subside at all. Not a bit of it. She heard high whiny noises squeaking out of her as she tried to quicken her pace.

If he gets me, he'll rip me up.

That's absurd, she told herself. I'm not a kid. He's not a homicidal giant. This isn't a fairy tale. This isn't a nightmare.

What's the worst that can happen, really?

He rapes and kills me.

A nasty corner of her mind whispered, *That isn't the worst.*

She glanced back again. Now, the troll was even farther behind.

I'm going to make it! If I don't trip. If he doesn't corner me. If there aren't *others* waiting in the dark places up ahead.

God, she wished the trollers were here!

Where *are* you, Billy Goat Gruff?

Maybe *he's* Billy Goat Gruff.

He's a troll. He's a troll. A kid's worst nightmare of what's lurking under the bridge. Jesus!

Just ahead, on the right, was the Tilt-a-Whirl. Gloria wondered if she should try for it. What if she had trouble getting over the fence? Once she stopped running, the troll would be on her in seconds. If she snagged her skirt, or . . .

No. She didn't dare.

Keep running, she told herself. Widen your lead. *Then* go for a fence.

Once you're on the beach . . .

Light suddenly spilled out of a doorway on the right. It wasn't at boardwalk level, but at the top of a raised platform.

Dunn's place, she realized.

His Oddities place.

Jasper Dunn's tall, cadaverous figure appeared in the lighted doorway. He was wearing his top hat and tails. He raised his cane high and twirled it. 'Over here!' he called to her. 'Quickly!'

Gloria raced for him.

She never thought she would be glad to see Jasper Dunn.

Better him than what's behind me, she thought.

Breathless, she bounded up the wooden stairs.

'Quickly, quickly,' Jasper urged her. 'You'll be safe here.'

He stepped out of the way. Gloria flung herself through the doorway.

When she shrieked and whirled round to flee, he rammed the tip of his cane into her belly. She folded and dropped to her knees.

Behind her, trolls whispered and giggled.

'Shall we have her walk the house?' Jasper asked.

Trolls cheered and clapped and whooped.

The worst that can happen . . .?

Gloria suddenly knew she was about to find out.

Chapter Thirty

Dave shut off the alarm and blinked at the clock, confused for a moment until he remembered why he'd set the alarm to wake him half an hour early; he'd wanted time to check on Gloria before heading in to work.

Pain in the ass.

Not half the pain of last night, though – going out to search for her. Putting Joan through that. The business under the boardwalk had really frightened her. And hurt her. Back at her place afterwards, she'd opened her blouse enough to slip it off her shoulder, and they'd both taken a look. Her upper arm had a nasty bruise from the collision with the post.

Dave remembered that he'd only glanced at the bruise before turning his eyes to the smooth, unblemished areas, savouring the mellow hue of her tanned skin against the stark white of her bra strap and the way her blouse was pulled crooked and taut over the rise of her breast.

He lay back on the bed, closed his eyes, and let his mind linger on the memories.

The hollow of her throat. The hollow above the curve of her collar bone. The way her head was twisted sideways as she strained to study her injury. 'Scarred for life,' she'd said.

'You'll just have to keep your shirt on.'

'Pity.' Raising her arm, she made the blouse fall back onto her shoulder. She didn't bother with the buttons. She placed her hands on Dave's sides and gazed into his eyes. 'So,' she said. 'Here we are.'

'Alone at last.'

'Not a minute too soon.'

He kissed her smile and felt it vanish, and Joan clutched him hard against her – so hard that her ribs pressed his wound and he flinched. She whispered 'Sorry' into his mouth. She relaxed her hold on him, but kissed him with even greater urgency.

Urgency. Hunger. She acted as if she'd been unleashed, and Dave felt the same way. They'd been kept apart too long.

Dave yanked the blouse tails out of her jeans. He swept his hands up her back. Squirming against him, she sucked his tongue into her mouth. He undid the catches of her bra. All her back, waist to shoulders, was silken and warm under his hands.

Then came the soft thud of a car door bumping shut. Joan pulled her mouth away. She stared into his eyes. She stood rigid. 'It's Debbie,' she whispered.

Moments later a doorknob rattled. A key ratcheted into a lock.

In the time it took for Debbie to enter the kitchen door and reach the living room, Dave and Joan broke apart and sat down at opposite ends of the sofa. Joan had time to wipe her mouth dry. Dave had time to pick up the *TV Guide*.

When the girl walked in, he looked up at her. He was stunned. Though Debbie wasn't identical to Joan, she bore an amazing resemblance. Her body, not so developed, was definitely feminine but had a boyish look about it. Her face still had the look of a girl in early adolescence, a freshness and innocence that would soon be left behind and lost forever. Dave felt a small tug of sorrow. This was much the way Joan must've looked at sixteen, and he regretted that he hadn't known her then.

He rose to his feet as she approached. 'You're home early,' Joan said.

'The party was a drag.' Her mouth twisted as if it didn't know what to do with itself – whether to smile or sneer or grimace. She pressed her lips into a tight line. She shrugged. She looked at Dave, and held out her hand.

'I'm Dave,' he said, shaking it.

'Yeah, I figured. Nice to meet you.'

'In case you haven't guessed,' Joan said, 'that's my sister Debbie.'

'Hi, Debbie.'

'So, did I interrupt something here?'

'Just having a friendly chat,' Joan said.

'Oh, I'll bet.'

'It turned out that there *weren't* any boys at the party, huh?'

Something happened to Debbie's face. It looked for a moment as if she were about to smirk and make a quip. Then her eyebrows puckered downwards, her eyes filled with tears, her mouth stretched crooked and her chin trembled.

Joan looked stricken. 'Debbie! My God, what's . . .?'

Shaking her head fiercely, the girl rushed out of the room.

Joan leapt to her feet. She met Dave's eyes. 'I'm sorry. Damn it. I'd better see what's wrong.'

'I'll make myself scarce.'

'You don't have to leave.'

'Yeah. I should. Take care of Debbie. I'll see you in the morning.'

'Damn.'

'Yeah.' He pulled her against him, gave her a quick kiss, and released her. She hurried towards the hallway. Her shirt tail was draping the seat of her pants.

Dave glanced at the clock on the nightstand.

You're going to waste your whole half-hour, he thought. No, not a waste. Not at all.

He rolled out of bed, gritted his teeth when the morning air wrapped his body, and hurried to put on his robe. He knotted its belt as he headed for the bathroom.

He wondered if Joan had fastened her bra on the way to Debbie's room.

The girl had sure picked a lousy time to come home.

Poor kid, though. She'd been awfully upset. Must've had a rough time at that party.

Whatever the problem, Joan had probably made it better. Wouldn't be easy to stay upset with her comforting you.

Half an hour later, his hair still damp from the shower, Dave hurried out to his car. He tossed his jacket onto the passenger seat – always good to have it along in case the fog should roll in – and backed out of the driveway.

He felt wonderful. Soon, he would be with Joan again.

Maybe they could get together tonight and not be interrupted. Ask her over to *his* place, maybe.

And tomorrow was their day off.

Have to think of something . . .

He turned the corner, making a left toward Gloria's house, and a shadow blew in across his good mood.

Just let her be there, he thought.

The last thing he needed was to spend another day worrying about her.

She'll be there, he told himself.

Please. I want it over.

He swung around the next corner, peered up the block, and saw Gloria's Volkswagen in the driveway of her house.

He muttered, 'Dumb bitch.'

He thought, Thank God.

Torn between relief that she'd made it home and anger that she'd caused such trouble with her stunt, he pulled in behind her car. He leapt out, and rushed to her door. He jabbed the doorbell button, heard the ringing inside the house, waited.

Come on, damn it! Move your tail.

He listened for her footsteps. And remembered other times

he'd stood here, times when he'd been eager to hear Gloria approaching the door. Those times were not very long ago.

How could everything change so quickly?

A hot wave of guilt spread through him.

She brought it on herself by being such a . . .

Bullshit. *I* did it. Joan came into the picture and I saw what I was missing. Gloria never stood a chance.

I'll be nice to her, he thought. I won't yell. I'll just explain, as gently as possible, that going undercover as a troll is a stupid, dangerous . . .

Where is she?

Dave pounded on the door, shaking it in its frame.

'Gloria,' he called. 'Come on, open up. We need to talk.'

She didn't open up.

Her house key was in Dave's hand, still clipped to his key case. He fumbled it away from the others, unlocked and opened the door partway. He put his head into the gap. The living room looked deserted. There was a stillness to the house.

She's not here, he thought.

But he called out, anyway. 'Gloria? I'm letting myself in.'

He swung the door wide and entered.

'Gloria!' he called again.

She was a very sound sleeper and always locked her bedroom door before retiring for the night, so Dave supposed he might've failed to wake her. He strode down the hallway. The bathroom door stood open. She wasn't inside. He continued on to her bedroom.

Its door wasn't shut. The bed wasn't made. Obviously, Gloria had spent the night here.

He felt reluctant to step through the doorway. He'd spent so many hours in this bedroom. It was nearly as familiar as his own. He knew every inch of it. He knew the feel of the bed, and which floorboards creaked if they were walked on. He knew the patterns of shadow and light on the ceiling in the dead of night. But now, the room seemed out of bounds. As if the house had been sold furnished to a stranger, and he was an unwelcome intruder.

He took four steps into the bedroom. Though eager to retreat, he scanned the room.

The chair beside her closet door was piled with clothes.

On top of the heap was a dirty grey sweatshirt. From where he stood, Dave could see ragged holes in it. A corner of purple fabric drooped off the chair's seat. The legs of red tights hung to the floor. The tights, like the sweatshirt, gaped here and there with holes.

These were the clothes that Joan had described to him, yesterday at lunch. *Must've been up half the night snipping away at them.*

Dave walked to the chair. How many times had he thrown his own clothes onto it? Gloria rarely used it for that, herself. She must've been really beat when she came in last night, too tired to bother putting them away or tossing them in the hamper.

Maybe left them heaped up, on purpose, to improve their rumpled appearance.

Dave picked up the sweatshirt. He wondered how she'd made it so dirty. Probably took it out back and rubbed it in the garden soil. He flung it onto the bed. He lifted the next garment off the chair seat. A grimy white T-shirt. She hadn't been at this with scissors.

He wrinkled his nose at the faint, stale odour of sweat, and tossed the shirt aside.

She's sure got into the spirit of her masquerade. Even down to the small detail of going without anti-perspirant.

He picked up the skirt. Joan was right about it. Gloria hadn't owned a frumpy thing like this; she must've picked it up at the Salvation Army store, or someplace else that sold cast-off rags.

It was the kind of skirt that fastened at the side with a button and zipper.

The button was gone.

Not only was the button missing, but so was a small patch of fabric where it must've been sewn to the waistband.

As if Gloria had ripped the skirt open.

Gloria, or someone else.

Dave frowned. He felt a tightness in his chest.

Maybe the skirt came this way, he told himself. Maybe she'd used a safety pin, or something, to keep it fastened.

He inspected the fabric closely, looking for the telltale, tiny holes that would've been left by a pin. He didn't find any. After flinging the skirt onto the bed, he got down on his hands and knees and searched the carpet. He found no button.

That doesn't mean it's not around here someplace.

He looked for the button on Gloria's nightstand, and on top of the bureau.

This is crazy, he thought. Upset about a stupid button. It could be anywhere.

Could be on the boardwalk. On the beach. Where someone yanked her skirt open.

Christ, don't jump to conclusions.

Dave's hands were trembling as he picked up the red tights. They were dirty and torn, but Gloria had undoubtedly made them that way on purpose.

A pair of black panties remained on the chair. He picked them up. He had seen her wearing them, or similar ones. There was little to them other than a thin elastic waistband and flimsy, sheer fabric a few inches wide at the top that tapered down to almost nothing where it would pass between her legs.

Dave scowled at the panties. For some reason, he found them as disturbing as the lost button.

Why? They weren't torn.

They were the style she usually wore, even under business suits. Said they kept her feeling sexy.

Not the kind of underwear you'd likely find on a troll, but she probably wouldn't have carried the disguise *that* far.

Dressed like a bag lady till you get to her sexy undies.

Then, gangbusters.

Nobody would know except Gloria. She'd like that. So what's wrong here? Dave wondered.

He dropped the panties onto the chair, stared at them, and knew.

What the hell were they doing at the bottom of the pile? Underneath the tights that had to come off first. They should've been *on top* of the tights, probably on top of the skirt, as well.

For that matter, they should've been on top of the entire heap. She nearly always took her panties off last. Often left them on, and nothing else, while she paraded around the house doing last-minute chores before bed; hanging up clothes, brushing her teeth, turning off lights.

Why were her panties at the bottom of the pile?

Dave could think of only one explanation; her clothes had been removed elsewhere, then carried to the chair. Hold it, he told himself. Hold it just a second here. Don't get crazy. Gloria probably took them off in the bathroom, had a shower, and brought them in herself.

He hurried to the bathroom and searched for the button. He didn't find it.

Doesn't mean I'm wrong.

Makes a lot more sense than thinking someone else was involved.

He opened the medicine cabinet. Gloria's toothbrush stood upright in a mug. He rubbed the bristles. They felt dry. She hadn't brushed her teeth this morning.

He stepped to the bathtub. The bottom of the tub looked dry. Gloria's washcloth, draped over the shower curtain rail, wasn't even slightly damp. It would probably still be moist if she'd used it after coming back last night.

Too many things wrong.

She *had* to come back last night. Her car's in the driveway.

Dave left the bathroom. His heart was pounding. He felt tight and sick inside.

He walked the, entire house, searching for Gloria.

For her body? No. Come on, you're making too much out of this.

But he looked in every room, in every closet, behind and under furniture where there were spaces large enough to conceal a person.

Along the way – partly, he suspected, to protect himself from the knowledge of what he was *really* looking for – he kept an eye out for any detail that might prove she had returned alive and well last night.

He found Gloria's keys and purse on the dining room table. The eighty dollars in the billfold convinced him that robbery wasn't a factor. But the presence of the purse told him nothing more. She probably hadn't taken it with her, yesterday. Joan said she'd been carrying a grocery bag.

The only grocery bags he found were neatly folded and clipped to a plastic holder on the back of the utility room door, or being used as liners for her wastebaskets. None of the wastebaskets contained wadded sacks. The one she'd been seen carrying and the two she'd worn on her feet were missing.

She might've discarded the makeshift bootees before heading home. But what about the other? Could've left it in the car.

I'll check the car.

He wondered if it was locked.

And suddenly realized he'd seen her keys on the dining-room table.

Her keys are here. Gloria isn't. And the house was locked.

Okay, so maybe she walked somewhere and took along a spare house key.

Too damn much is wrong.

He took the key case with him, and hurried outside. He peered into the side windows of the Volkswagen. A grocery bag, stuffed full, was on the floor behind the passenger seat. He opened the driver's door, sat down, swung the seatback forward and lifted the bag onto his lap.

It contained nothing except the old blanket that Gloria usually kept in the car's trunk.

Where's her cassette recorder? She never went anywhere without that.

He checked inside the glove compartment. No recorder.

Maybe it's in the house, and I missed it.

But something *else* was wrong.

Dave reached out and gripped the steering wheel. He stretched his legs until his feet touched the floor pedals.

275

The wheel and pedals were the right distance away for him. Too far away for Gloria.

Someone had adjusted the seat's position to give himself leg room.

Someone Dave's height had been the last person to drive Gloria's car last night.

He squeezed his eyes shut, slumped in the seat, and heard himself groan.

Chapter Thirty-one

The telephone jangled, startling Robin awake. She saw the ceiling above her, realized that she was in a bed instead of her sleeping bag, and knew where she was. She also knew who was calling. She rolled onto her stomach. Propping herself up on an elbow, she reached to the nightstand and brought the telephone's handset to her ear. 'Hello?'

'This is your wake-up call.'

'Hi, boss.' Her raised position allowed cool air to come in, so she shoved the pillow under her chest and sank onto it.

As she reached back to cover her bare shoulders, Nate said, 'Did you get a good night's sleep?'

'Not very. And it's all your fault.'

'My fault?' He sounded perplexed, amused. 'How could that be? Bad choice of motels? Was it too noisy? Was the bed lumpy? What? I got you back early. I left right away.'

'That's the thing. You stayed.'

'Huh?'

Robin shifted the body a little, just to feel the caress of the warm pillow and sheets. 'I couldn't get rid of you. You kept me awake half the night.'

'Wish I'd been there to enjoy it.'

'So do I.'

The earpiece went silent except for the empty, distant sound of white noise.

'You still there?' Robin asked.

'Sorry. I was busy punching myself.'

'Aw, don't do that.'

'Boy, do I feel like a dope.'

'You're not a dope. You're a sweetheart.'

'Yeah?'

'Yeah.'

'I wish I'd known how you felt.'

'You knew. Didn't you?'

'Yeah. I guess so. But I just didn't want you thinking the whole idea was so I could . . . stay. I mean, that's how it would've looked. Right? Getting you the room. *Hiring* you. I didn't want it to look like I was just pulling cheap tricks to get you in bed.'

'Whereas we understand, of course, that that's precisely the case.'

The soft whuff of a laugh came through the phone. Robin could almost feel the breath of it against her ear.

'You're something else,' Nate said.

'You, too.'

'Are we still on for breakfast?' he asked.

'Sure. I'm ready when you are. How fast can you get here?'

'Ten minutes, if I push it.'

'So push it.'

Robin hung up and scurried out of bed. The chill morning air gave her goosebumps. She shivered as she hurried into the bathroom, used the toilet and brushed her teeth. A bath would feel wonderful. She didn't have enough time. She knew she could've asked Nate to wait a while, but the bath didn't matter. All that mattered was being with him again as soon as possible.

When he left last night, Robin felt as if he'd taken part of her with him. It was peculiar, not to feel quite whole. But it didn't hurt much, because she knew the missing piece would be restored to her when he showed up again.

The missing piece is Nate, she thought as she washed at the sink. Or maybe it's my heart. How about both?

She wondered if there might be a song in the concept of the missing piece.

He borrowed my heart and he walked away, but he'll bring it back when he comes to stay . . . Bring it back on a silver tray? Screw the tray, sounds like John the Baptist,

With my heart in his pocket, he walked off that night. I reckon he'll return it in the morning light. If his dog don't eat it, I'll be all right.

Robin grinned at her wet face in the mirror, then grabbed a towel and dried herself. She left the bathroom. Wanting to look her best for Nate, she decided to wear her new dress. The dress with its Funland emblem would, she thought, also be more appropriate for her new job as an actual employee.

She had just finished knotting the sash at her hip when she heard footsteps on the balcony. There was a knock at the door. 'Hold on a minute,' she called. Stepping in front of the mirror, she brushed her hair. Then she rushed to the door and opened it.

Nate stepped into the room. And into Robin's arms. She squeezed herself hard against him. Their mouths joined. The part wasn't missing, anymore.

She was all together again.

Easing herself backwards, she looked up into his eyes and whispered, 'I missed you.'

'I missed you more.'

'No you didn't.'

'Yes I did.'

'Yes you did.'

He laughed. She felt his breath on her lips.

His hands moved gently down Robin's back. They didn't stop at her sash. They curved over her rump, then pressed it, bringing her tight to his body.

Wanting to look at him but reluctant to break the contact, she bent backward from the waist. 'I haven't packed my stuff, yet.'

'You've got plenty of time. Checkout's eleven, and it's only eight, now. You might want to relax here for a while after breakfast.'

'Ah-ha!'

She saw a bath in her future, after all.

'What time do I have to start earning my keep?'

'When you're ready. Just come to the arcade. I've got a back room where you can leave your things.'

'Sounds good.'

'Yeah. So. Ready for breakfast?'

'Starving.'

'Good.'

She kissed him again, then left him for a moment while she got her handbag and room key.

Holding hands, they walked along the balcony. The day was clear, but a cool breeze made Robin shiver until they left the shadows of the motel and started across the parking lot. There, the warmth of the sun took the chill away.

Nate led her to the passenger side of a red Trans Am.

'I guess you weren't kidding when you said you're loaded.'

'Nope.' He opened the door for her.

'There's a really good place right across the street, you know.'

Smiling, Nate threw the door shut. 'You're the breakfast expert.'

They crossed the street and entered the coffee shop. They sat facing each other at a window booth. A waitress filled their mugs. Robin took a sip of coffee, gazing over the mug's rim at Nate. Steam drifted upwards, hot against her nose and eyes.

'I don't know when I've ever felt this good,' she said.

'You should stay in motels more often.'

'It's not just the motel. It's everything. Most of all, it's you.'

Nate blushed. 'I'm not all that wonderful.'

'You beat up old ladies?'

Though he smiled as he said, 'Worse than that,' Robin saw a grim look come into his eyes.

'Are you all right?'

'Just hungry.' He picked up one of the menus and studied its back.

Robin looked at her menu.

'What do you recommend?' he asked. 'Being the breakfast expert that you are.'

'Number one. The two eggs, country sausage and hash browns.'

'I should've known. And I bet you like your eggs sunny-side-up.'

'Right.'

The waitress came, and they ordered. When she was gone, Nate stared out the window.

'It's a beautiful day,' Robin said.

'Yeah.' He looked at her. 'Too bad we have to waste it working.'

'It's all right with me.'

'We can quit at five. I've got Hector coming in.'

'Hector the doufuss? I thought you didn't trust him to run things?'

'Well, in an emergency . . .'

'What's the emergency?'

'I have to be alone with you. I'm gonna go crazy.'

Robin felt a warm, swelling sensation inside. Her throat tightened. She reached across the table and held Nate's hand.

'I thought we might go over to my house,' he said. 'I'll barbecue a couple of steaks. We can swim in the pool.'

'I think I might be able to live with that.'

'Great. Great.'

'You mentioned something about being alone with me. Where are your parents while all this is going on?'

'Where they are right now. San Francisco. They won't be back till next Wednesday.'

'Wednesday?' Robin's heart suddenly began to pound very hard.

'You can stay till then. If you want to. We'd have the run of the place.'

She murmured, 'God.' She was trembling. Along with the terrible excitement and hope, she felt nervous.

It's happening so fast.

'You don't have to,' Nate said. 'I mean, I don't want to push you into anything. We have a couple of guest rooms. Or if you'd rather stay in a motel until we can find you a place . . .?'

'I'm just a little overwhelmed, is all. Jeez.'

'Well, don't try to decide right now. About staying over. But you'll come for the steaks, won't you? Then . . . whatever you want. See how you feel when the time comes.'

When the time comes.

'Okay. You can count on me for dinner. And . . . we'll see about the rest.'

The waitress came with the food. Robin stared at her plate.

'What's wrong?' Nate asked.

'I'm not sure I can eat.'

'I'm sorry. Look, if it bothers you about tonight . . .' He shook his head, frowning. 'I didn't mean to upset you. I'll go back when we're done eating, and register you for a couple more nights. I've got tomorrow off. We can spend the day apartment hunting. Okay? You're still planning to stay, aren't you? I haven't . . . scared you off? Me and my damn mouth. I *knew* I shouldn't have tried to get you to . . . shit, I really blew it this time. It's not like I wanted you to shack up with me. I know that's how it must look, but . . .' He stopped. He looked perplexed. 'What's so funny?'

'You.'

'Me?'

'All rambling and flustered.'

'I don't know what I'm doing anymore.'

'If you ask me, you're doing fine.'

A corner of his mouth turned up. 'Yeah?'

'Yeah.'

'I just don't want you to think I'm trying to . . .'

Smiling, Robin raised her hand. 'Hush,' she said. 'Eat.'

He shrugged, looked as if he might start to speak again, but stopped himself and began to work on his breakfast.

Robin, too, began to eat. Her heart was slamming. She could hardly swallow, but she washed down the food with water and coffee, and kept shovelling more into her mouth, determined not to let Nate notice her turmoil.

He looked pleased. 'You got your appetite back?'

'So it would seem. I think your speech cured me.'

'Now that you don't have tonight hanging over your head.'

'Guess so.'

'Well, I never should've . . .'

'Eat, okay?'

'Was this motel all right?' he asked, nodding at it through the window, 'We could check you into a different one, if . . .'

'This one's just fine.'

Nate finished his breakfast in silence. He kept looking at Robin and trying to smile. She could see that he was not only disappointed, but embarrassed.

Robin walked behind him to the front counter. He paid. He held the glass door open for Robin.

Outside, she took his hand. 'Come on, cheer up,' she said. 'It's not the end of the world.'

'I know. I'm sorry.'

At the kerb, they waited for a break in traffic. Then, they rushed across the street.

'There'll be other times,' she said.

'Yeah.'

'I don't want to spend all day wondering what's going to happen tonight. Can you understand that?'

'Sure.'

'I'd get my fingers tangled in my banjo strings and forget how to sing.'

They stopped in the parking lot. 'I'll go ahead to the office and . . .'

'Come on up for a minute. I want to give you something.'

'Okay.'

They climbed the stairs. They walked along the balcony. Robin took the room key from her purse. The point of the key clicked and skidded around the lock hole.

'You're a nervous wreck,' Nate said.

'And it's all your fault.' Finally, the key went in. She turned it, and opened the door. Nate followed her into the room. He didn't see Robin hang the Do Not Disturb sign on the outside knob before shutting the door.

He turned around. From the look on his face, Robin could see that he didn't suspect. He was still fighting his disappointment about tonight. But being very brave about it.

Robin wrapped her arms around him. She gazed into his eyes. And saw confusion.

'Those other times?' she said, her voice shaking. 'Well, this is the first of them.'

'Huh?'

'I'd be wrecked all day, waiting for tonight.'

Nate looked shocked. 'You're kidding,' he whispered.

'Think so?'

His moan seemed more agonized than happy. He pulled Robin hard against him and she found his lips with her mouth.

Chapter Thirty-two

'He didn't go for it?' Joan asked when Dave returned from the chief's office.

'He agreed it was peculiar, but thought we'd be jumping the gun to launch an investigation. If Gloria hasn't turned up by tomorrow . . .'

'The old twenty-four-hour crap,' Joan said. 'Same thing I got when my mother disappeared.'

'You didn't come up with anything?'

Shaking her head, Joan took her jacket off the back of her desk chair and slung it over one shoulder. 'I made the calls. The people at the paper haven't heard from her since yesterday morning. Nobody fitting her description turned up at the hospital. Or the morgue.'

'That's something, anyway.'

They walked out to the patrol car. Joan tossed her jacket into the trunk, then slid into the passenger seat. The car was warm. She rolled her window down. Dave got in behind the wheel and drove out of the parking lot.

'It had to be someone who didn't want suspicion directed at Funland or the beach area,' Joan said. 'If there really was foul play, that's the only thing that makes sense. Otherwise, why bother?'

Dave nodded. 'They went to a lot of trouble to make it look like she came home last night.'

'That was no easy trick.'

'Not too hard. The lot's nearly empty after closing time and they could tell she had a VW by the key. The registration in the glove compartment has her address.'

'Had to be somebody pretty sharp,' Joan said. 'And someone who knows the town. I can't see a bum pulling a gimmick like that. Their heads are too messed up.'

'Maybe not all of them.'

'All of them *I've* seen. This is way out of their league. It almost had to be the trollers.'

'Or a third party we're not even aware of. Could be she ran into a serial killer, something like that. We're about due. Haven't had one here since Gunderson, back in '82.'

'Possible,' Joan said. 'But I'd put my money on Great Big Billy Goat Gruff and the gang. They probably jumped her, thinking they had themselves a troll.'

'She would've corrected that impression pretty quick, I think.'

'Told them who she is? She's not stupid. If they knew they had Gloria Weston, it'd get pretty nasty.'

'It'd get nasty enough if they thought she was a troll. If they figured out she wasn't . . .' Dave shook his head. 'Suddenly, they're confronted by a lucid victim. Someone capable of fingering them, testifying against them.'

'Kill her? Dave, that's a mighty big step for a bunch of kids who've never really done worse than beat up some bums and . . . leave them in compromising positions.'

'If it's that or getting busted.'

'Yeah. Jesus. I know.'

'They wouldn't have fooled around taking her car and clothes home unless they'd known she wasn't going to be turning up. Ever.'

'This is getting awfully damn grim.'

'She knew better,' Dave said.

'Real consolation.'

'Yeah.'

Dave slowed the car and swung into the Funland parking lot. 'Look,' Joan said, 'this is just "worst case scenario" stuff. Gloria might be fine. There are other explanations. She could've met someone last night. A guy. Maybe an old friend. Maybe they had a few, somewhere, and he drove her home in the bug. She changed clothes, and went off with him.'

'Leaving her keys and purse in the house?'

'You said she'd got a spare house key.'

'It's a nice theory,' Dave said. 'I hope you're right. But it's got too many holes in it.'

'There could be simple explanations for the holes, too.'

Dave swung into a parking space and killed the engine. He looked at Joan.

'I know,' she muttered.

'Damn it, we tried to warn her.'

'Yeah. We did. But we should've tried harder.'

'We didn't know something like this would happen.'

'I just wish we had it to do over again. We could've stopped her. *I* could've stopped her. I could've gone over to her when I saw her sitting there on the steps in that ridiculous troll costume.'

'She just would've told you to go to Hell.'

'She'd still be alive, Dave. I would've *seen* to it. Shit, I would've kept her handcuffed inside her house last night, if that's what it took.'

'We didn't know. We can't blame ourselves. We knew it was dangerous, but . . . life is dangerous. I could get shot on duty today . . .'

Joan felt something shrivel inside her. 'Hey, don't say that.'

'The point is, I'm taking the risk every time I put my uniform on. Would you blame yourself and think you should've kept me handcuffed at home?'

'I'd blame myself for not blowing away the bastard first.'

Dave smiled. 'That's different. I might blame you for that, myself. The thing is, we didn't know her damn stunt would get her dead. *If* she's dead. We don't even know that, for sure. Come on, we'd better get over to the boardwalk.'

They left the car. Joan met him behind it. She wished they were alone, so she could hold him.

'We'll get whoever did it, Dave. We'll nail him – or them. We'll find out what they did to her.'

'Really? How do we do that?'

'Come back tonight. After closing time. I'll dress up.'

'Use you as bait? No way.'

'It's something we have to do. And you know it.'

Jeremy sat hunched over the kitchen table, slicing apart his fried eggs, bacon and toast, and forking mixes of them into his mouth.

'You certainly have yourself an appetite for someone at death's door,' his mother said.

He nodded and scooped more food into his mouth. He'd never had a hangover before. He'd always heard that people in his condition were repulsed by the mere thought of food, but he felt ravenous.

Of course, he'd barfed on the way home last night. That could account for the maddening hunger.

'I really ought to ground you, you know.'

He looked up at her. The movement of his eyes was like a rheostat turning up the pain in his head from dim to bright. 'I told you I'm sorry. Geez, what do you want? It wasn't my fault Shiner had a flat.'

'And whose fault was it that you came home drunk?'

'I didn't know the punch was spiked.'

'I'm sure.'

286

'I didn't. Besides, everyone else was drinking it.'

'If everyone else jumped off a . . .'

'I know, I know. God, I said I was sorry. You don't have to crucify me.'

'Don't talk that way.'

He leaned back in the chair and closed his eyes. They felt hot and dry under his lids. And too big. As if they'd swollen to twice their size with some kind of terrible, throbbing pressure. 'I learned my lesson,' he muttered. 'I feel like . . . horrible. I promise, I'll never drink again. Just don't ground me. Please? I'm supposed to meet Shiner at the beach.'

'That's another thing. Shiner. She certainly had me fooled. I thought she was a perfectly nice young lady.'

Jeremy opened his eyes and frowned. 'She is.'

'I don't call it nice to go to a party and get drunk. Not when she has the responsibility of driving you home afterward. There's no excuse for that. And you should've known better than to get into the car with someone who . . .'

'Mom, she didn't drink. All she had was Pepsi.'

'I'm supposed to believe that?'

'It's the truth. She didn't have any booze.'

'So *she* knew the punch was spiked?'

'No. She just doesn't like punch.' In spite of the pain pulsing through his head, he came up with an idea. 'I remember now. She said she's diabetic. That's why she didn't have any punch. She was drinking sugarless Pepsi.'

'Hmmm.'

He didn't know whether his mother bought that or not. Then, he wondered why he was trying so hard to defend Shiner. Hell, she'd gone off and left him.

With good reason.

Maybe they could make up, though. If he ever saw her again.

But the main thing – Shiner was his excuse for going to the beach this morning. He had to convince Mom of her innocence, or she might keep him home.

'If he couldn't go to the beach and see Tanya . . .'

287

'She figured out the punch was spiked,' he said, 'and warned me. That's when I stopped drinking the stuff.'

'Well, I might have been a bit hasty in my assessment of her.'

'She liked *you*. She told me she wished her mother was more like you.'

'Really?' Mom raised her eyebrows, looking surprised and pleased.

'Yeah, she thought you were neat.'

'Well, that's all very well and good, but I still think you'd better just stay in the house. I can't condone last night's behaviour.'

'Shiner's *expecting* me. She'll be waiting. She'll think I stood her up.'

'Alexander Graham Bell invented a convenient device . . .'

'I don't know her number, Mom. And she isn't listed. They were getting all these crank calls last year, and . . . please. It's not fair to Shiner. She was going to take a picnic lunch, she'll have gone to all that trouble, and she'll be waiting there not knowing what happened to me. It just isn't fair.'

'You should've thought of that last night.'

'Right!' Jeremy snapped. 'Fine.' He flung his knife and fork down. They crashed against the plate, and his mother flinched as if she'd been slapped. Tears glimmered in her eyes. 'I'll stay home. I'll stay home *forever*. Ruin my life, why don't you? The first time in my damn life I make a friend, and all you want to do is wreck it. If you hate me so much, why don't you just shoot me and get it over with!'

He shoved his chair back and raced from the kitchen.

'Jeremy!' she cried out after him.

'The hell with it! The hell with everything!'

He ran to his room and threw himself onto the bed. His head roared with pain. It felt as if daggers were being plunged into his brain. He clamped the pillow down over his ears and lay there, sobbing in agony.

A few minutes passed before he heard the footsteps he expected. The mattress tipped slightly as his mother sat down on the edge of the bed. Her hand stroked his back.

288

'If it's that important to you,' she said. Her voice was muffled, but Jeremy could hear it trembling. He loosened his grip on the pillow but kept it over his head. 'I don't want to stop you from having a picnic with a pretty girl. I was your age once, myself, you know. I understand these things.'

'I'm sorry,' he said. 'I shouldn't have . . . yelled and gone crazy.'

'That's right, you shouldn't have. But I suppose I was being a little harsh. You do need to be punished, though. I'll dock your allowance for two weeks – and you wash the dinner dishes.'

'For how long?' he muttered.

'The same. Two weeks.'

'That's pretty stiff.'

He heard her laugh. She gave his rump a gentle swat, and he felt the mattress rise.

He rolled over and sat up as she walked towards the door. She looked back at him. Her eyes were red, her face wet.

'Thanks, Mom,' Jeremy said.

'Even if we have our little problems, honey, I still love you. Don't ever think I don't.'

'I know. I love you, too.'

'You'd better get a move on, now. You don't want to keep Shiner waiting.'

He kissed Robin gently on the mouth. 'I wish I could stay,' he whispered.

'Me, too. But I don't want to make you late.'

'We'll have tonight. And tomorrow, and the next day.'

'You'll get tired of me.'

'I'll never get tired of you.' Nate kissed her mouth again and eased himself backward, kissing her chin, the side of her neck. His penis slid out of her. The loss of it gave Robin an empty ache, but she still held the feel of it like an after-image. He kissed each of her nipples, her sternum, her belly. Then, he was kneeling above her, looking down with wonder and sadness in his eyes.

Robin folded her hands beneath her head. She raised her knees, and pressed them gently against his sides.

'I've never . . . felt this way about a girl before,' he said. He ran his hands slowly down her thighs. 'What is it about you, anyway?'

'I'm easy?'

'Are you?'

'No. Just for you.'

'I think I'm in love with you. It's not because of . . . what we just did. I was in love with you before.'

'I was in love with you before, too. I still am, only more.'

'Same here.' He rested his hands on her knees. 'God, I wish I didn't have to go.'

'I'll go with you.'

'No. Stay and take that bath.' He smiled. 'Now, you *really* need it.' He patted her knees, then climbed off the bed.

Robin rolled onto her side. She watched him bend down and pick up his underwear. His body was sleek and muscular, his skin deeply tanned but white where shorts had kept the sun away.

As he stepped into his jeans and fastened them, Robin rose from the bed. She sat on its edge, feet on the carpet, and watched Nate get into his T-shirt, socks and tennis shoes.

It felt strange, being naked while he was dressed.

It felt just fine.

She stood up, and he came to her. He put his hands on her hips. He gazed into her eyes. 'Guess I'll see you in an hour or so,' he said. 'Just come to the arcade whenever you're ready.'

'I'll make it quick. I already miss you.' She wrapped her arms around him, hugged him tight, and kissed him.

Jeremy rode his bike close to the kerb, going slowly and coasting because the exertion when he had to pedal fuelled the pain in his head. He was feeling a lot better, now. The clean, fresh breeze seemed to help.

So did the prospect of eating a waffle cone when he reached Funland. Though he'd never had a hangover, he somehow knew that ice cream would smother the flames in his stomach.

He remembered hurling the remains of his waffle cone at

Tanya, wiping the mess from her leg, going up inside her shorts, and then his thoughts slipped to last night in her bedroom and the memories of that set his heart racing, pounding hot pain into his head.

Don't think about it, he told himself.

But now that his mind had entered the room, he couldn't tear it away.

The images whirled and tumbled, took Jeremy's breath away, made his heart slam until he thought his head might explode. He squeezed his eyes shut. Felt the bike lurch sideways. Snapped his eyes open and saw that he'd swerved out into the middle of the lane. A car horn blared. Without looking back, he twisted the handlebars to the right. The car sped by. Someone yelled, 'Asshole!' Jeremy's front tyre rubbed the kerb, and he put his foot on the pavement to hold himself up.

He shut his eyes tight and clutched his head. The images of Tanya kept staggering through his mind, jumbled and twisted. Instead of erotic, they seemed nightmarish and sickening. But he couldn't get rid of them. For a long while, he thought he might vomit or pass out.

The beach, he told himself. I've got to get to the beach.

He saw himself flopping onto the hot sand.

That would be good. Just lie there and not move and not think.

Imagining himself sprawled on the beach, he felt the pain begin to subside. He thought about the peaceful sounds of the surf and seagulls.

Finally, no longer crushed by the pain, he took a bottle of aspirin out of his shirt pocket. He popped the cap off, and dry-swallowed three tablets.

They seemed to get stuck somewhere in the middle of his chest.

A drink. Need something to drink.

He looked around and saw a soft drink vending machine beside the office of the motel just ahead. He climbed slowly off his bike. He lifted it onto the sidewalk and rolled it toward the office.

Movement on the second storey balcony caught his eye.

Just a guy leaving one of the rooms.

Something familiar . . .

The guy's back was turned. He was lingering in the doorway, apparently speaking to someone inside. He raised a hand in farewell, pulled the door shut, and started walking along the balcony.

With the side view, Jeremy recognized him.

Nate.

Forgetting his need for a drink, Jeremy turned his bike around and rolled it towards the corner. He walked it across the street. At the other side, he glanced back and saw Nate climb into a red sports car. He walked a little farther, listening. He heard the engine thunder to life. When the sound began to fade, he looked again and saw the car moving away.

He pushed his bike back to the corner.

He peered at the closed door of the motel room.

What the hell had Nate been doing in there?

A motel room. Ten o'clock on a Saturday morning.

He must've been with a girl. Jeremy could think of no other explanation.

Tanya? Was Tanya in there?

It didn't make sense.

He spotted a coffee shop directly across the street from the motel. If he got a window seat, he would be able to watch the door and see who came out.

And he could get himself a drink to wash down the aspirin that seemed to be burning a hole in his chest.

Keeping an eye on the door, he walked his bike to the coffee shop.

Chapter Thirty-three

The Pepsi made the aspirin ache fade, though not quite vanish entirely.

Nobody had come out of the motel room by the time Jeremy finished his drink.

He was beginning to feel pretty good. The soda helped his stomach, and he supposed the aspirin was working on the pain in his head. It also helped, just sitting there.

For a while, he sipped the water of the melting ice cubes up through his straw.

The coffee shop had plenty of vacant tables and stools at the counter, but he felt guilty about lingering with his glass empty. He caught the eye of the waitress, and asked for a hot fudge sundae.

He'd planned on a waffle cone at Funland. He supposed he could still buy one, later on, if he felt like it. But for now, he needed something in front of him so he wouldn't look as if he were loitering.

The sundae came, and he ate so slowly that the ice cream was soupy by the time he spooned the last of it into his mouth.

Still, nobody had come out of the motel room.

Nate *couldn't* have been alone in there. He'd stood in the doorway for a few moments before leaving, obviously talking to someone.

It had to be a girl, didn't it?

A girl, but not Tanya. It couldn't be Tanya. They'd both been so angry at each other last night when Nate left the party.

What if they made up?

Jeremy was tired of wondering about such things. The same thoughts must've gone through his mind at least once every five minutes.

The girl *might* be Tanya. But he didn't believe it, wouldn't believe it. If they'd made up and gone to a motel, it ruined everything. Tanya had to stay mad at Nate. She had to. Otherwise, Jeremy wouldn't stand a chance.

Who's in there, damn it?

What if she doesn't come out? I can't sit here all day.

Jeremy wondered if he should order something else. Maybe another pepsi. He looked for his waitress. She was clearing a table near the door, her back to him.

He glanced out the window again.

The door of the motel room swung open. A girl stepped onto the balcony. A slim girl wearing a powder blue dress that looked like a jersey. Her bright blonde hair was nearly as short as his own. Though she was too far away for Jeremy to make out the features of her face, the hair gave her away. So did the slender build. And the backpack and instrument case.

The banjo girl!

The bitch who had snapped at him Wednesday night on the boardwalk, just before Cowboy showed up. The bitch he'd found the next day singing that sick nuclear war song about a weenie roast. The bitch he'd imagined himself taking on, wrestling, pinning down.

He watched her stride along the balcony. There was a bounce in her stride as if she were awfully happy about something.

Yeah, he thought. Happy. She got screwed by Nate.

Wait till Tanya hears about this!

He stared at her slender, tanned legs, at the way the dress clung to her small rump. The backpack bounced as she trotted down the stairs.

Jeremy dug out his wallet. He slapped a dollar onto the table for a tip, snatched up his bill and hurried to the counter. Nobody was there. Fidgeting, he looked back and saw her enter the motel office. Probably to drop off the room key, or register herself for another night.

At last, his waitress stepped behind the cash register. He paid, and rushed out the door. Unchaining his bike, he saw the girl leave the office. She started walking in the direction of Funland. Of course.

He waited for a break in the traffic, then walked his bike across the street. When he reached the other side, the girl was half a block ahead of him. He mounted his bike, and followed.

Incredible, he thought. Tanya's going to blow her stack. She'll *never* make up with Nate, not after she hears about this. Nate screwing the banjo girl. Man, the bitch was only one step away from being a goddamn *troll*.

Explains why Nate turned against everyone at the party. Not because he felt guilty about the fat old guy taking a header off the Ferris wheel. Just wanted us to think that was why. The real reason, he'd fallen for one of the enemy. No wonder he wanted the trolling to stop.

No wonder he sounded off and split.

He had someplace to go.

The motel.

So he could screw his troll.

'Wow,' Jeremy said. 'Holy shit.'

Staying half a block behind the girl, he followed her to Funland. While she hurried up the main stairs, he chained his bike to the rack. He lost sight of her when she passed through the entryway.

On the boardwalk, he scanned the milling crowd. This was Saturday. He'd never seen the place this packed. He wandered through the jam of people, searching for her. Then, he gave up.

It didn't matter.

He was sure he would be able to find her later, if he wanted to. Before long, she would probably start playing her banjo. He could simply follow the sound of the music.

The main thing was to tell Tanya what he'd seen.

Blow Nate out of the water.

And score points with Tanya. *You'll have to prove yourself*, she'd said. *With loyalty*. Well, this sure ought to show his loyalty.

Maybe this would be enough.

He went down the steps to the sand.

Stopped.

His head turned to the left as if pulled by a magnet. Kept turning until his neck would allow it to move no farther.

He stared at the Ferris wheel.

Brightly spinning. Then dark, shrouded by fog. He heard the old man's scream rake the night, heard the ringing thuds as he pounded the struts, saw him tumbling down.

Jeremy grinned.

One down, a hundred to go.

They've *all* gotta pay.

Me and Tanya, we'll wipe them out.

Still grinning, he turned away from the Ferris wheel and began to walk across the sand.

Like the boardwalk, the beach was overflowing with people. He made his way carefully around their blankets, towels, canvas chairs, and even passed a few umbrellas. Wet kids were running by, their laughter and shouts mixing with the manic voices of DJs and rock from radios that seemed to be everywhere. People read, slept, ate and drank, talked to friends or lovers, rubbed suntan lotion on skin that was white or pink or richly tanned.

Jeremy didn't pay much attention to the men.

But he studied the women as he walked past them.

Soon, he was dry-mouthed and breathless, hard, achy. His throbbing heartbeat pounded blood into his head, awakening the pain that had nearly disappeared.

He tried to stop looking at the sprawled, exposed bodies.

Then, he saw a blonde girl in a black, backless suit. Shiner? His heart bucked. His head roared.

What'll I do?

Talk to her. Apologize. Maybe it's not too late.

Her head lifted and he saw her face. Tiny eyes, a sharp nose, thin lips, a sunken chin. Not Shiner, after all.

Thank God, he thought.

He felt spared. He felt disappointed.

You didn't *want* it to be Shiner, he told himself.

I'll have Tanya, soon. Tanya's almost mine.

He looked up and squinted toward the lifeguard station. On the platform stood a man in red trunks.

'Shit!'

Jeremy pounded fists against the sides of his legs.

She'd had yesterday off. She must have today off, too.

I've gotta tell her about Nate!

Head spinning with pain, he dropped to his knees. He took off his shirt, spread it in front of him, and lay down. He folded his arms under his face.

I'll go home, he thought. I'll go home and phone her.

Wait. No. There are pay phones on the boardwalk.

He thought about getting up, but he didn't want to move. The hot sand felt good beneath him. The sun's heat weighed him down. A mild breeze ruffled his hair and caressed his back.

Later. I'll do it later.

'Well, durn me if it ain't the Duker.'

The voice seemed to come from far away.

Something soft whupped against Jeremy's back. Moaning, he rolled onto his side and looked up at Cowboy. 'Hi,' he said. Though he felt groggy and leaden, his headache was gone.

He wondered how long he'd been asleep.

Cowboy spread a towel on the sand, and sat down cross-legged, facing Jeremy. He wore his old Stetson, and a tight, bikini style swimsuit. He looked as if he had an earmuff taped to the side of his head. Otherwise, he wasn't bandaged. Jeremy didn't count, but he guessed there were six or eight cuts on his arms, chest and belly. Some had stitches. All the wounds looked brown and gooey, and a little red around the edges.

'Don't you believe in bandages?'

'Sun'll do 'em good. How you doing, old hoss?'

'Okay, I guess.'

'Me, I'm as hungover as a dead whore on a fence post.'

'Me, too. It's getting better, though.'

'How come you didn't stick around last night?'

'It was Shiner,' he said, wondering if anyone knew she had left without him. 'She had to get home early.'

'You didn't tell her about the treatment, did you?'

Jeremy felt heat rush to his face. 'The treatment?'

'Your blood pact.'

Cowboy *knew* about that? Trying not to sound shocked, he said, 'No. I didn't tell Shiner.'

'Good thing. It's only between Tanya and the guys. And Karen, since she's a lezzie. The rest of the gals, they ain't in on it.'

'She's done that with *all* the guys?' Jeremy asked.

'Sure. And Karen, like I said.'

He nodded slowly. He felt cheated, robbed. He thought Tanya had done the ritual because she considered him special. He thought he'd been singled out. Maybe there's some mistake, he told himself. Maybe Cowboy's talking about something different.

'You had the blood pact,' he said. 'How'd it go?'

'Man, freaked the needles right offa my cactus.'

'I mean, what did she do?'

Cowboy blew through his pursed lips. 'It was *weird*, man. You aren't gonna believe this.'

'I'll believe it.'

'I'm home alone, right? This is a Saturday night last summer, and my folks are off at a party, and I haven't met up with Liz yet, which accounts for my being alone. I was down in the den watching *Evil Dead II* on the VCR. You ever seen that?'

'Yeah. It's cool.'

'How about when that guy's hand gets possessed and he starts bashing himself over the head . . .?'

'What about Tanya?' Jeremy asked.

'Okay, I'm all by myself and watching this sucker in the dark, so I'm pretty spooked, anyway. This is only like a month after Tanya got out of the hospital. We'd been sneaking out and trying to find the actual shits that done the job on her. It was just her, Nate, me and Samson. We knew some bums had laid her open with a busted bottle. That was no big secret. Was even in the papers. But we didn't know *everything* they'd done to her. Maybe Nate did, but he never let on. Anyway, we ran into plenty of bums, but not the right ones. We pounded a few of 'em, anyway, and took 'em on rides outa town. Then, we quit.'

'You quit?' Jeremy sat up. The skin of his back felt very hot and stiff. He knew he had probably burned. He picked up his shirt, shook the sand off it, and draped it across his shoulders.

'Quitting was Nate's idea. He didn't see much point in going on with it, seeing as how we couldn't find the creeps that slashed Tanya. We all figured they must've hustled their sorry butts outa town.'

Jeremy nodded. 'So you were watching *Evil Dead*, and then what happened?'

'Well, I had to take a leak so I stopped the movie and went into the John. We've got one downstairs, you know, just outside the den. It's got a shower. No bathtub, just a shower stall. So I'm standing there with my back to it, and I finish up and tuck ol' Sneaky Pete back inside my pyjamas and I'm reaching out to flush and all of a sudden I hear the shower curtain whip open. Screaming Judas, woulda scared the piss outa me, only I'd just gone. I spin around, and there's Tanya. Man, she's standing there in the shower stall, buck naked and holding a butcher knife.'

'A butter knife?'

'Fuck, man. I figured this is it. Figured she'd flipped out and I was gonna be a carved goose.'

'Christ,' Jeremy muttered.

'Only she doesn't come at me. She doesn't say shit. Just looks me in the eyes and starts sliding the point of that knife down her scar.' Cowboy shook his head slowly from side to side. His eyes were fixed on Jeremy, but they looked as if they were seeing Tanya, instead. 'Just touching it, you know? Not hard enough to cut herself. And real slow. All the way from her tit down to her pussy. Goddamn. Weirdest thing I ever saw. And that bod.' His eyes seemed to come into focus. 'How'd you like that bod, Duke? You ever seen anything like it?'

'No.'

'Tanned all over, and . . .'

'Well, what happened? Come on.'

'Yeah, okay, so she done this thing with the knife. And finally she says, "This is what they did to me, Cowboy. But they did worse." Then, she tells me the whole story. All the stuff they did to her.'

'Yeah, she told me.'

'Then she says, "They have to pay. Will you help me make them pay?" I start to remind her how we couldn't find the guys, and she puts the knife to her mouth to shush me. "Trolls are all the same," she says. "If it hadn't been those three, it would've been three others. It could've been any of them. They're all evil. They have to pay."'

'I guess it made some sense. I don't know. I was pretty shook up. Bet you were, too.'

Jeremy nodded.

'So I told her I'd go hunting trolls with her from now till Doomsday, if that's what she wanted. When I said that, she took holda my hand and got me into the shower stall with her. I figured ol' Sneaky Pete was about to have the time of his life, but what she does is take the butcher knife to my hand.' Raising his right hand, he pointed out a small, pale scar on his palm.

Jeremy raised his own hand so Cowboy could see the tiny mark left by the razor blade.

'Not much of a cut,' Cowboy remarked. 'Can't hardly see it.'

'Sure bled, though.'

'Mine, too. So then, she cut herself.'

'Down there?'

'Fuckin' A right, down there.'

'And made you hold it.'

'You betcha. Held my hand right against her twat and she says, "Your blood's in me, my blood's in you. We're blood lovers." Not blood brothers, like that Injun thing you hear about, blood lovers.'

'Said the same thing to me. Pretty much. So, then what? Did you make it with her?'

Cowboy's eyes widened. 'Did you?'

'No.'

He looked relieved. 'Me neither. But she kinda hinted

it might go that way if I stuck with her and kept on going after trolls. Don't know if she really meant it. Hasn't happened yet.'

'You don't think it was just a lie, do you?'

'Who knows? I keep waiting. Maybe I just haven't proved myself enough.'

'Has she done it with any of the other guys?'

'Nate. But I guess they were doing it before, so it didn't have nothing to do with the pact. If she's put out for any of the other guys, I haven't heard about it. But I know she did the "blood lover" thing with 'em.'

'Maybe she wouldn't do it because of Nate.'

Cowboy grinned. 'Now, that's a dandy thought. Hope you're right. Maybe our turn's coming up.'

'Now that Nate's out of the way.'

'Guy must have rocks in his head, dumping her like that. We're all itching to put it to her, and he's got it made, and he throws it all away. Just 'cause he's got his shorts in a knot over killing a damn troll.'

'Yeah,' Jeremy said.

He thought, That's not why, at all. But hell if I'm going to spill it.

The truth was his secret, his edge, and his alone.

Nobody gets to tell Tanya about the banjo girl but me.

'Are we meeting tonight?' he asked.

'Yup. Sure as shootin', Duke. Same time, same place.'

That's too long to wait, he thought. Much too long. I have to tell her *now*.

Chapter Thirty-four

'Look who we've got here,' Joan said. She didn't sound very happy to see the boys.

Dave stayed at her side as they crossed the boardwalk towards the pair. Both kids had corn dogs, and were munching and talking while they strolled along. Joan stepped in front of them. They looked startled, at first, then came up with nervous smiles.

'How are you fellows doing?' she asked.

'Reckon I'm all in one piece,' said the kid in the cowboy hat. The side of his head was bandaged. He wore a skimpy swimsuit and no shirt, as if he were showing off the wounds on his torso. The cuts looked a little raw, and a lot like the one Dave had seen that morning in the mirror. 'I sure want to thank you,' the kid told Joan. He glanced at Dave. 'You, too. I was about two steps short of the ol' stew pot.'

'Glad we could help,' Joan said.

'How's the ear?' Dave asked, trying to remember the guy's name.

'Well, he's stitched on good and tight.'

'You really took care of that guy,' the other kid said. Wayne. Something Wayne. He looked in pretty good shape except for the faint shadow of a bruise on his forehead. 'No kidding. The way you got him in the chin, looked like you were going for a field goal.'

Joan's face went red. Dave knew it wasn't a glow of embarrassed pride. 'I'm just glad things worked out,' she said.

'So, what's the story on Chingachgook and his pal?' asked the one whose ear had been taken off. 'They cooling their heels in the hoosegow?'

'They're both in custody,' Dave said. 'One's still in the hospital.'

'Hope it's the one tried to gobble my ear.'

'It is,' Dave said.

'Man, I just bet,' Wayne said, looking at Joan with awe in his eyes. 'I thought he was a gonner, the way you nailed him. That was *really* cool.'

'There was nothing cool about it.' She turned to the other kid and glared at him. 'I'm glad you weren't hurt any worse than you were, but you were asking for trouble and you got it. And you got a lot of people hurt, including an innocent bystander and my partner. So you'd better watch your step, buddy. You cause any more trouble around here, I'll be on you like wet on rain.'

'Yes, ma'am,' he said, looking stunned and guilty. Dave suspected that the look was a sham. 'I'm sorry.'

She glanced at Dave. 'Let's go.'

He stayed beside her as she hurried away.

'Couple of shitheads,' she muttered.

'Well, they got hurt pretty good for their trouble.'

'I think the Wayne kid enjoyed it. He stripped the shirt right off that one gal. Probably got in some feelies.'

'Two against one, and they were both bigger than him.'

Joan smiled. 'You on his side?'

'He had to defend himself. Even if they were girls. Some are tough.'

'Yeah? Think so?'

'I know of one, for sure.'

'She's bigger than you, too. But you've got prettier legs.'

Dave looked down to compare. 'I'd say it's even.'

She patted his rump.

'Watch it, partner. None of that.'

'Forgot myself.'

'Not that I don't appreciate it. When you get to my place, you can do it to your heart's desire.'

'What time do you want me?'

'How's six?'

'How about seven? I'll need some time to take a bath and get my costume together.'

The costume. They hadn't discussed her plan since early

303

morning. Dave had been hoping the whole idea might just evaporate, but he supposed he knew, all along, there wasn't much chance of that. Once Joan has made her mind up about something . . .

You wouldn't want it any other way, he told himself. Suppose she was happy to wash her hands of Gloria? Said the bitch got what she deserved, it's none of our business, forget about her and let's have a ball? You'd think she was a heartless jerk.

It's her heart making her do this.

Making her take such a risk.

She sure doesn't *want* to come back here after the place closes. She's probably more scared than me. But she isn't going to back out.

Heart *and* guts.

'Let's wear vests,' he said.

Joan gave him an amused frown. 'Who's going to be shooting at us?'

'I'm serious.'

'So am I. Those things cramp my style, and we've got no reason to think the trollers go around with guns.'

'I'd wager they carry knives, at least. I'd rather catch the next blade in Kevlar.'

She met his eyes. And nodded. 'I'd rather you did, too. Okay, we'll go with the vests.'

'How about the rest of your ensemble?' he asked.

'Violins, a clarinet . . .'

'No brass,' he added. 'You've got too much of that already. But have you decided what you'll wear?'

'In addition to the vest? I don't know.'

'You haven't got a closet full of filthy rags?'

'Maybe we could roll a bag lady.'

'I could stop by Gloria's and pick up her stuff for you.'

The cheerful, mischievous look vanished from her face. 'Wouldn't fit.'

'The tights might be a little snug . . .'

'God, I'm not gonna wear Gloria's tights. Or anything else.

They're hers. And they've been pawed by the creep who . . . took them off her.'

Joan's words jammed images into Dave's head of Gloria on her back, struggling and screaming as rough hands ripped at the clothes.

'Besides,' Joan said, 'if I wore her stuff, it might destroy evidence.'

'Yeah.'

Evidence. The hairs of a stranger. Maybe blood. Maybe semen. Dave hadn't noticed anything like that, but the crime scene guys were experts. The smallest trace . . .

'Are you all right?'

'Thinking about evidence.'

'I'm sorry. I shouldn't have mentioned it.'

'No, you're right. I made a mistake touching her stuff in the first place.'

'That's how you figured out . . .'

'Yeah. That, too. Exactly. Just like I said, a mistake. If I'd kept my hands off her things, we wouldn't be any the wiser. We wouldn't be doing this, tonight.'

'Shame I can't get her in stereo,' Cowboy said, cupping a hand behind his bandaged ear.

'She's pretty good, isn't she?'

The banjo girl was standing near the long line in front of the Hurricane, tapping her foot as she pounded out 'The Rock-Island Line'. Wearing what she was, she didn't look like a bum any more. Jeremy liked her dress. It was short, showing off her slender legs, and the weight of the banjo pulled it tight against her breasts.

She's still no Tanya, Jeremy thought.

How could a guy like Nate go with her, when he already had Tanya? It didn't make sense.

Unless it might be something about the way she seemed kind of innocent and mysterious.

Innocent. Sure. Jeremy remembered how she'd snapped at him, Wednesday night. She's a bitch, he thought. And tough as nails. Probably about as innocent as a whore.

I've gotta tell Tanya about her!

Why did Cowboy have to show up and get in the way?

Jeremy felt as if time were running out, as if his chance would be lost forever if he didn't get in touch with Tanya soon.

The banjo went silent. Cowboy clapped, as did several people waiting in the line for the roller coaster, and others who had stopped on the boardwalk to listen.

'Reckon I wouldn't mind plucking *her* strings.'

You'd have to stand in line behind Nate, Jeremy thought. 'I wouldn't kick her out of bed, either,' he said.

She strummed a lively tune on the banjo, and started to sing.

I had me a guy and he lived in the bog
With an old .44 and a one-eyed dog.
The dog was mean, and so was he,
But they weren't near half as mean as me.

Jeremy felt a hand clutch his shoulder. 'Hang on, buddy,' Cowboy said. 'I've gotta take me a whiz.'

'See you later.'

He watched Cowboy push slowly through the crowd. Then, he hurried in the opposite direction.

Finally!

By the time he reached the payphone near the main entrance, he figured Cowboy had probably finished in the john.

Won't know where to find me, though. Might not even bother to look.

Trembling, he swung the directory toward him on its chain. He flicked through the pages. Ashland. Only three Ashlands. Two were Ronald Ashland, DC. He remembered that Shiner had said Tanya's father was a chiropractor. One entry was for the father's office on Grove, but the other showed a street address on Avion.

Muttering the phone number that went with the Avion listing, Jeremy picked up the handset, dropped a quarter into the slot, and dialled.

The ringing sounded faint, muffled by the noises of the crowd and rides and calliope music. He pressed the phone hard against his right ear, and jammed a finger into his other.

That helped.

He heard the ringing more clearly.

God, he thought, I'm actually calling Tanya. The beat of his heart quickened, and he could feel it awakening his headache. The plastic handset felt wet and slippery.

Maybe she's not home.

He almost hoped she wasn't.

What am I doing?

Lovers in blood. Loyalty. You've gotta prove yourself. You want her, don't you?

YES!

'Hello?' A female voice.

'Hi. Tanya?'

'Just a moment, I'll call her to the phone.'

Must've been her mother. Went to get her. She's home! Jeremy looked around and scanned the crowd. So far, no Cowboy.

Come on, Tanya. Come on!

'She'll be right along,' said the mother's voice.

'I've got it, Mom.' Tanya's voice. Jeremy heard the other phone click down.

'Hi,' he said. His heart pounded. His head pulsed with pain. 'It's Jeremy. Duke.'

'How are you doing? Have you heard we'll be meeting tonight?'

'Yeah. Cowboy told me.'

'You'll be there, won't you?'

'Sure! The thing is, I've gotta tell you something. It's about Nate.'

'Rotten bastard.'

'Yeah, he sure is. But the thing is, I saw him this morning. He was at a motel. With a girl.'

Tanya said nothing.

307

'I'm sorry,' Jeremy said after a few moments of listening to the silence. 'I just thought I oughta tell you.'

Tanya mumbled something.

'What? I didn't hear that.'

'Who was she?'

'I don't know her name. She's that girl who's been playing banjo on the boardwalk. Maybe you've seen her. She's sort of skinny. Real short blonde hair like a guy's. She's eighteen or twenty, I guess. She plays for money. People toss it into her banjo case. She's here right now, over by the Hurricane.'

'I've seen her around.'

'Well, Nate was in a motel room with her. I don't know if they spent the night, but he came out at around ten this morning. I just happened to be walking by when I saw him. He didn't see me, though. So anyway, I waited around in a restaurant for about an hour and kept my eye on the room to find out who he'd been with. I mean, after last night, I didn't think it was you, you know? And it was that girl who plays the banjo. She finally came out and I followed her over here to Funland. So anyway, maybe she's why he . . . you know, acted weird and split, last night.'

'Had her stashed in a motel.'

'Yeah.'

'The dirty prick.'

'He sure is,' Jeremy said. 'Man, he must be crazy, dumping you for a goddamn troll. She's not even close to being as pretty as you. Nobody is.'

'Thanks. You're a good guy.'

His heart seemed to swell. In spite of his raging headache, he felt a glow of pride and hope. 'I just thought you oughta know about it. I mean, after last night . . . we're lovers in blood.'

'That's right. And you did the right thing, telling me about this. I owe you.' She went silent again.

She owes me. Does this mean I proved myself? Yeah. Probably. God!

'Is Cowboy with you?' she asked.

'Not right now. I got away from him to call you.'

'Does he know about any of this?'

'No. I kept it quiet. I didn't tell anyone. I figured nobody oughta know except you. I mean, it's sort of a personal thing, and . . .'

'That's good. Don't tell anyone. This is our secret, just you and me. You said she's still there on the boardwalk?'

'Yeah. Singing a bunch of stupid songs.'

'Okay. Will you do me a favour?'

'Sure. Anything.'

'Keep an eye on her. Follow her if you can. I want to know where we can get our hands on her tonight.'

'I don't have a car.'

'That's okay. Just do the best you can. And give me a call when you find something out.'

'I will.'

'Good. Good man. We'll get together later. Just you and me.'

Chapter Thirty-five

It was a very long afternoon. Robin tried to lose herself in the music, and often went for several minutes without thinking of Nate. The tunes with lyrics were the best for that; she had to focus on the words. But between numbers and when she played those that didn't require singing, her mind lingered on him.

She felt comfortable and full and glowing. And excited and a little nervous when she wondered what would happen next.

There's no reason to worry, she told herself again and again. The Big Thing was already taken care of. It wouldn't be hanging over their heads, making them nervous and awkward. They'd be free to enjoy themselves . . .

If five o'clock ever arrives.

Sometimes, she ached to be with him. When the ache got very bad, she took breaks and went into the arcade and just the sight of Nate was enough to soothe the longing. They talked and she followed him around, enjoying his friendly manner with the customers. Most of the kids treated him a like an old pal. He passed out coins, showed newcomers the basics of some of the games, and insisted that Robin play Space Invaders and Jet Assault and Super Mario Brothers. But she never stayed long, for she didn't want him to think she was taking advantage of the situation.

The best time had been their lunch break. They picked up pizza slices and Pepsis at one of the stands, and ate in the back room. 'My home away from home,' he'd called it, and Robin had commented that it looked more like a sporting goods store. A desk cluttered with paperwork stood in the centre of the small room, but in the corners were volley balls, running shoes, and a Frisbee. Several swimming suits, towels, a face mask and snorkel, a sweatshirt and wetsuit hung from hooks. Propped against one wall was a surfboard.

'Will you teach me to surf sometime?' she'd asked.

For just a moment, his eyes looked bleak. Robin wondered if he'd had a bad experience surfing. Maybe a friend had drowned, or something. But the look passed quickly. He nodded while he chewed his pizza. 'Sure thing. I'll turn you into a California girl.'

'Like, rad, man.'

And when they finished eating, he leaned back against the door to prevent anyone from barging in. Robin leaned against him. They held each other and kissed for a long time.

She wished she were in his arms right now.

It must be almost five, she thought as she played her Beach Boys medley. The last time she'd asked someone the time, it

310

had been four thirty-five. That *seemed* like an hour ago.

Time may fly when you're having a good time, but it creeps when you're waiting.

She segued from 'Surfin' USA' into 'California Girls'. And smiled at the reaction. Whenever she went into that one, her audience went wild, cheering and clapping. It had been that way since her arrival at Funland. She picked and strummed, thumb plucking the drone string, and saw Nate behind a couple of teenaged girls who were mouthing the words, waving their arms and gyrating.

She finished to cheers and applause. People wandered in from the crowd in front of her, from the Ferris wheel line behind her, tossing money into the banjo case at her feet, several stopping for a moment to offer compliments. She thanked them all, then announced, 'That's it for now folks.' She heard some moans and protests. Then came more applause, and more people stepped forward with kind words and money.

'You were a hit,' Nate said.

'Went pretty well,' she admitted, crouching down to gather the money. 'Didn't think five o'clock would ever get here, though.'

'Yeah. Same here.'

She passed coins and bills to Nate, then latched her banjo inside the case. They walked to the arcade. In the back room, they counted the money. It came to $48.50. 'Not a bad haul,' Nate said. They split it sixty-forty. He gave Robin her portion, then handed a cheque to her. 'What's this?'

'A week's advance on your wages.'

'You don't have to do that.'

'If you don't want it . . .'

'Well, I didn't say that, exactly.'

He laughed and kissed her. 'Ready to go?'

'I've been ready for a while. Like maybe just eons.'

Nate held her backpack while she slipped her arms into the straps. He carried her banjo case, and they walked through the noisy arcade.

* * *

Jeremy whirled around, grabbed the railing and stared out at the beach the instant they stepped out of the arcade. He waited a few seconds, then looked around. He couldn't spot them at first, and felt a quick flicker of panic. Then a group of bikers strutted out of the way. He saw Nate and the girl walking along the far side of the crowded boardwalk. Their backs were towards him.

He followed, picking up his pace and closing the gap, afraid he might lose them.

If he lost them after all this . . .

He couldn't believe how long he'd been forced to wait. Hours and hours. After the call to Tanya, he'd returned to the girl's audience. Cowboy should've been there, but wasn't. Maybe he'd gone off, looking for Jeremy. But time passed, and he didn't return. Jeremy felt a little miffed at him. What kind of friend goes off and deserts you? He was relieved, though. Keeping an eye on the girl would've been difficult if Cowboy had kept hanging around.

Once he realized that Cowboy wasn't likely to come back, he got away from the girl's audience. As long as he could hear her, he was doing his job. He spent some time sitting on a bench and watching the people go by. He visited nearby game booths and watched people try to win prizes: tossing basketballs at hoops that looked too small for the balls; hammering little contraptions to send rubber frogs flopping head-over-heels towards a pool where you won if they happened to land on one of the circling lily pads; shooting squirtguns into the open mouths of plastic clown faces in hopes of being the first to fill and explode the balloons on their hats.

Occasionally, he wandered over to food stands. He bought drinks, and swallowed aspirin. He ate nacho chips smothered with melted cheese. Later, an ice cream sandwich. Later still, a corndog on a stick.

About once an hour, the girl took a break. Each time, she packed up her banjo and headed straight for the arcade. She hung around with Nate, sometimes played games, then returned to the boardwalk but not to the same place. She seemed to have three different locations: in front of the arcade, near the line for the Hurricane, and at the Ferris wheel.

She was playing for the Ferris wheel crowd when Nate showed up. Jeremy watched her from a distance, and thought, This is it. Somehow, he knew that this was not just another break. Maybe because Nate had come to her. Maybe it was the fact that she handed the money to him. Or it might've been a subtle change in the girl – an eagerness about the way she gathered up the money and packed her banjo and walked away with him.

He followed them to the arcade. Entering, he saw them disappear into a back room. Then, he took his position at the far side of the boardwalk, near the railing, and waited. They came out less than ten minutes later, Nate carrying the banjo case, the girl wearing her backpack.

This *is* it, he thought.

Just don't lose them now, he told himself, hurrying to narrow their lead.

He followed them past the main ticket booth. From the top of the stairs, he watched them step off the sidewalk, cross the road, and angle across the parking lot. He watched them climb into Nate's red sports car. The car drove slowly out of the lot, and headed east.

Jeremy rushed to the pay phone. He dialled Tanya's number. The phone at her end rang only once. 'Hello?'

'Tanya, it's me. Jeremy.'

'I've been waiting. What's going on?'

'They just left. In Nate's car. A red sports car?'

'The bitch was with him?'

'Yeah. I don't know where they're going, but . . .'

'I think I know. I'll make sure, though. You did really good, Duke. Really good. Are you going to be home later?'

'Yeah, sure, I think so.'

'I'll call you around nine. We'll get together tonight. Just you and me. Before the trolling.'

'Okay. Great!'

Tanya hung up.

Jeremy hung up. He stared at the phone. His mouth felt as dry as paper, his heart drummed and he panted for breath.

I did it, he thought. Oh man, oh man! *Just you and me*.

Even before they started up the narrow road into the hills, the houses looked big and expensive. Robin knew that higher up – where Nate was taking her – the homes must be fabulous. She didn't find the notion comforting.

Her family hadn't been poor. With both her parents working, they'd got by just fine. Then there was the life insurance money. But they'd never been rich. Not even close to rich.

'Something the matter?' Nate asked.

'I'm feeling . . . a little bit out of my league.'

'I don't get it.'

'You live up here in a huge house. You drive a car that must've cost more than my Dad made in a whole year.'

'What's that got to do with anything?'

Robin shrugged. 'I don't know. Shouldn't you be going with a débutante, or something?'

He laughed. 'Well, you'll do until a deb comes along.'

'What happens if your parents find out about you and me?'

'What do you mean, if?'

'What do *you* mean?'

'They'll find out Wednesday,' he said. 'No if. I'll introduce you.'

'Great. They should be delighted to find out you've taken up with a street musician.'

'We'll tell them you're a débutante.'

'Right.'

'You'll knock them dead, Robin.'

'Yeah. I'm sure I will. Cardiac arrest. Their son and the bum.'

'You're not a bum. You're an employee. And you weren't a bum before you were an employee. You're an artist, a poet, a musician. They'll love you.'

'That I doubt.'

Nate swung the car to the side of the road and stopped it.

The road was deserted, shadowed by overhanging trees. Ahead on the left was a mailbox and the gated entrance of a driveway, but no homes were in sight.

He switched off the engine and set the emergency brake. He turned to Robin. Reaching out, he curled a hand behind her neck. His hand rubbed her gently while he stared into her eyes.

'Just because my family has money,' he said, 'it doesn't mean we're bad people.'

'I know that, but . . .'

'Nobody's going to dump on you. Especially not my parents. All they'll care about is whether you're a decent person, and you are. They'll love you. Same as I do. Well, not *exactly* the same.'

'I should hope not.'

'We won't announce that you've been staying over. That'd be pushing it. I mean, they're terrific but they are my parents. They'd bounce off the ceilings if they found out about that. Even then, I'd be the one to catch hell and they'd figure you were my innocent victim.'

'Yeah?' She smiled. 'You know that from experience?'

'Oh, I've been caught a couple of times doing what I shouldn't.'

'Caught with girls in the house?'

'Once or twice. None that ever stayed over, though. You'll be the first. You're the first in a lot of ways.'

'How?'

'You're my first banjo-picker.'

'Creep.'

'You're the first I've ever fallen in love with.'

Robin's throat tightened. 'Really?'

'Really.' He drew her towards him by the hand on her neck. She turned on the seat and leaned closer. As they kissed, his hand moved up the back of her head. She felt his fingers slide into her hair. His other hand closed gently over her breast. She moaned into his mouth.

'I love you so much,' she whispered.

'Would you love me more if I were poor?'

'Probably.'

'Now who's the creep?'

'I wish we'd met a long time ago,' she said, and squirmed as he rubbed her breast.

'Me, too. God, I do wish that. It would've made. . . such a difference.'

'But I almost feel as if I've always known you. Does that make sense?'

'No.'

She laughed into his mouth, and kissed him again. 'Yes, it does,' she said.

'If you say so. You're the breakfast expert.'

'What does breakfast have to do with anything?'

'Makes sense to me.'

'Are you making fun of me?' she asked.

'Yeah.' He kissed the tip of her nose. As he stroked her hair, his other hand slipped away from her breast. 'Ready to go?'

'Let's went.'

He started the car and steered it back onto the road. Shortly after they rounded a bend, the road split into a Y. The lane sloping down from the left had a stop sign. A white Triumph was waiting there. The girl in its driver's seat was a blonde wearing sunglasses. Nate glanced towards the car and suddenly flinched as if he'd been poked in the back. He gunned the engine, swung the wheel, and they sped up the road's right-hand branch.

'Uh-oh,' Robin said.

Nate grimaced at her, and shook his head. He checked the rearview mirror.

'Who was that, your girlfriend?'

'Former.'

'Does she know that?'

'Yeah. We broke up. It's all over.' He looked again at the rearview.

Robin twisted around and peered out the back window. The road behind them was empty. 'It's over but it isn't, huh?'

'What do you mean?'

'If you're afraid she might come after us . . .'

'You never know with her. She does crazy things, sometimes.'

'A jilted woman with tendencies towards craziness. Great. I should've ducked.'

'Don't worry.'

'Why not? You're worried.'

Nate glanced at the rearview mirror again, then swept the car across the downhill lane and gunned it up a driveway. He downshifted. The engine thundered as the car climbed the steep slope. The narrow, curving driveway was bordered by trees that kept out all but spots and patches of sunlight. Robin couldn't see any house.

'Did you dump her because of me?' she asked.

'There were other things, but . . . yeah, I guess you entered into it.'

'Does she know that?'

'She does now, I suppose.'

'Wonderful.'

They roared over the crest of the slope. Straight ahead, beyond a lawn shadowed by several trees, stood a dark wood house that reminded Robin of ski lodges she'd seen during her travels. Not quite as huge as a ski lodge, but big, with steeply slanted roofs, a covered porch, and high balconies.

'Neat,' she said. 'Makes me want to yodel.'

'Feel free.'

'I don't want to ruin your ears for you.'

The driveway turned, and they followed it alongside the lawn. Nate fumbled with a remote device clipped to the sun visor. Ahead of them, a garage door began to rise. It was one of three, and nearest to the adjoining house. The engine noise swelled as the car entered the garage. Then it sputtered to silence.

Nate pulled the key from the ignition and faced Robin. 'Here we are,' he said in a hushed voice. He managed a smile, but it looked awfully nervous.

Robin realized she was suddenly trembling. Her heart was thumping hard, and her chest felt tight.

'Guess we might as well go in,' Nate said.

'Guess so.' She climbed out. Her legs felt weak and shaky. She closed her door and stared over the roof of the car. Nate gave her that nervous smile again, then ducked out of sight to retrieve her banjo and pack. Robin stepped around the rear of the car. 'Do you feel right about this?' she asked.

'You mean, coming here?' He backed away from the door with his hands full, and kneed it shut. 'I'm a little jittery, I guess.'

'About your girlfriend seeing us?'

'Former girlfriend. And no, it isn't really that.' He set down the banjo case and pushed a button on the wall. As the garage door rumbled shut, he unlocked and opened a door into the house.

Robin picked up the banjo. She followed him inside, and saw that they had entered a large kitchen. He shut the door. He set her pack on the red tile floor. She put down her banjo beside it.

She slipped her arms around him. Head back, she gazed into his eyes.

'You're trembling,' he said.

'You, too. So what have you got to be so jittery about?'

'It's just being here with you, I guess.'

'Afraid we'll get caught?'

'No. It's you.'

'I make you nervous?' Robin asked.

'Yeah.'

'Good. You make me nervous, too. That doesn't make sense, does it? I mean, after the motel . . .'

'Maybe we're both afraid of blowing it.'

'I think you may be right.'

'I care so much about you, Robin. It's like . . . there's so much at stake. If I screw up, somehow, and lose you . . .'

'I love you. If you screw up, I'll still love you. Unless you burn the steaks.'

Chapter Thirty-six

'What do you think?' Joan asked.

Debbie, sitting at the kitchen table, looked up from the half-eaten pizza that Joan had brought home for her supper. She stopped chewing. Her eyes widened.

Joan stepped closer, paused and turned, posing like a model walking the ramp at a fashion show.

She'd spent the past half-hour in her bedroom, preparing the attire: dingy sneakers with holes in the toes that she only kept around for working in the garden; baggy, faded blue sweatpants; a loose grey sweatshirt; and an old green stocking cap that she'd last worn a year ago when she went deep-sea fishing on a charter boat.

Even before checking herself in the bedroom mirror, she'd known the clothes didn't look scruffy enough. The mirror confirmed it. So she used scissors to start a hole just above the left knee of her sweatpants, dug her fingers into the hole and stretched it wide, ripping the fabric until it gaped like a slack mouth. She made a similar tear in the sweatshirt a few inches below her right breast. Then, she touched up the outfit with brown shoe polish, lightly brushing the polish here and there, creating a nice illusion of mottled filth. For no good reason other than that she liked the idea, she knotted a red bandana around her right knee. Finally, she wrapped herself in the tattered brown blanket that used to go along on family outings when she was a kid. She swept a side of it over her head, held it there like a hood, and once again inspected herself in the mirror. Her face was all wrong – too clean and smooth, the eyes too sharp. No wens or whiskers, she thought, and made a grim smile. But the costume itself looked just fine, so she went into the kitchen to show Debbie.

'What's going on?' Debbie asked, her voice muffled by pizza. 'Somebody having a masquerade party?'

'Am I fetching?'

'Fetching barf. You look like a *troll*.'

'Thank you.'

'You're not seriously going *out* looking like that?'

'Don't you think Dave will find me alluring?'

'Gimme a break. What're you doing?'

'Going trolling.' She draped the blanket over the back of a kitchen chair, plucked off the stocking cap, and went to the cupboard where she kept her liquor. 'I'll be playing the role of bait.'

'Are you nuts? What do you mean?' Debbie sounded upset.

Joan crouched and opened the cupboard door. She took out a bottle of bourbon. 'It's all right,' she said. 'Dave will be with me. We'll be heading over to the boardwalk after Funland closes.'

'Why?'

'We're going to bust some trollers. We hope.' She unscrewed the bottle cap, poured bourbon into her cupped hand, and splashed it onto the front of her sweatshirt. Adding more, she said, 'Do you know who Gloria Weston is?'

'No.'

'She wrote for the *Post*. She did that piece on the trollers a few days ago.' Joan took a sip of the bourbon, then capped the bottle, put it away and stood up. 'Gloria went undercover as a troll last night to get herself a scoop, and she disappeared.'

'Oh, Christ.' Debbie looked shocked and sick, as if she'd just spotted half a worm on the pizza slice poised near her mouth.

'We think the trollers got her.'

'So you're going out to . . .'

'To see if they'll try for me.'

'Joany, you can't!'

Joany. Debbie hadn't called her that in years.

'Hey, it'll be all right.' Joan went to her. She stroked the back of Debbie's head. The girl gazed up at her, face red and anguished. 'Nothing will happen to me, honey. I promise.'

'Sure, you promise. I bet Mom didn't think anything would happen to her, either.'

Joan sighed. She shouldn't have told Debbie of her plans.

'Dave will be there. If we can't take care of a handful of teenaged hoodlums . . .'

'What about the *trolls*?' she blurted. 'What if it wasn't the kids that did something to that reporter? What if it was the trolls, and they come after you? That place is *crawling* with them. What if they get you, and . . .?'

'First, I don't think trolls are the problem.'

'They got Mom!'

'You just think they did. We don't *know* what happened to Mom. We'll probably never know. But no trolls are going to get their hands on me. I wouldn't let one get close enough.'

'Yeah, sure.'

'Dave and I will both be armed. I don't care who – kids, trolls – nobody gets funny with a gun in his face.'

'What if you don't have enough bullets?'

'You worry too much.' She mussed Debbie's hair. 'Hey, we run out of ammo, it's choppy socky time. I'm deadly weapons from head to toe.'

'It's not funny.'

Debbie began to cry.

Joan crouched down and caressed her sister's cheek. 'Hey, come on, no tears.'

'You're all I have.'

'I'll be very careful. I can't promise nothing will go wrong. Hell, an airplane could crash into the house right now and wipe us both out. You can't control everything. You just be as careful as you can, but you do what has to be done. I have to go out there tonight.'

'Why?'

'It's my fault that Gloria Weston disappeared. She was Dave's girlfriend. She played dress-up and got nailed because of us, because she was upset and wasn't thinking straight.'

Debbie sniffed and blinked. 'Because Dave dumped her?'

'That's right. So we owe her. Do you understand?'

'No. If she did something dumb, it's her problem.'

'It's our problem, too. Now, I'd better go take my bath and get ready, or I'll be late to Dave's.'

'How would you like it if *I* went to Funland in the middle of the night?'

'I wouldn't, honey. Of course not. And I don't expect you to like it that I'm going. But I'm not in the habit of keeping secrets from you. You wouldn't want that, would you?'

'No, I guess not.'

'You just have to be brave about this kind of thing. My job gets dangerous sometimes, but I'm a pretty dangerous gal myself.' Smiling, she ruffled Debbie's hair. 'You'd better finish your pizza before it gets cold.' She stood up, took her cap and blanket off the chair, and headed for her room.

From the living-room window, Dave saw Joan's car stop at the kerb. He hurried to the front door and opened it. Joan came up the walkway, a grocery bag in her arms. The last time she'd come to his house, she had also been carrying a grocery bag. Champagne in that bag. He guessed, however, that this one held her troll costume.

He wished it didn't.

The stuffed bag was a sharp reminder of what lay ahead.

Always something bad ahead of us, he thought. Won't we ever get a chance to be together without a sword hanging over our heads?

We've got hours before we have to go, he told himself. Just try not to think about later on. It doesn't have to ruin things.

Coming up the walkway, she saw him and smiled.

What if this is it? What if this is our last time with each other?

The thought shook him. He told himself it was ridiculous, but realized he was taking a mental picture of her. To store this moment in his memory.

She looked wonderful. Her hair was golden and glossy in the evening sunlight, and blowing slightly. She wore her short white dress – the one she'd worn Thursday when she came with her 'medication' to perk him up. The sleeves were rolled up her forearms. Her bare legs looked tawny and sleek and strong.

'How's my guy?' she asked, climbing the front stoop.

'Okay, I guess.'

'You don't sound very sure.'

He stepped backward through the doorway. She entered, and he shut the door. She set the bag down. She put her arms around him. They kissed.

Dave held her tightly. He felt her warmth and her strength and her softness. The pressure made his chest wound sting, but he didn't ease his hold.

I won't lose her, he told himself. No way.

She patted his rump, and took her mouth away and he felt the smoothness of her cheek against the side of his face. Her hair smelled clean and fresh. 'Are you all right?' she asked.

'Yeah.' He relaxed his arms and held her gently. 'I'm just not overjoyed about our little mission.'

'That's not for a long time.'

'That's what I keep telling myself.'

'Five hours. Five whole hours.'

'And maybe there'll be a call from the governor.'

'You *are* in bad shape.' She looked him in the eyes. 'Did you get the vests?'

'Yeah.'

'Then we're protected. Barring, of course, the fulfilment of the cursa squirmy death.'

'Very funny.'

'Very hungry.'

'Is that a hint?'

'I had to watch Debbie eat pizza. You got any pizza? Huh? Do ya, do ya?'

'How about shish kebabs?'

'Even better.'

'And beer,' he said.

'I like beer.'

'Does it make you a jolly good fella?'

'If it makes me a fella,' she said, 'we're both in for a big letdown.'

Her mouth went to his again. As they kissed, her hands slid up and down his sides. He caressed her back, curled his hands over the firm mounds of her buttocks, slipped her dress a little higher. Her panties felt skimpy and silken. He smoothed the fabric against her rump, then moved his hands above the thin elastic band and stroked the sleek bare curves of her lower back, her sides.

Her stomach growled. She laughed softly into his mouth.

'Is that another hint?' he whispered.

'Are you barbecuing the shish kebabs?'

'Uh-huh.'

'Is the fire going yet?'

'Not yet.'

She kissed him briefly. 'You'd better start that one, too.'

Joan eased away from him. Looking into his eyes, she rubbed her wet lips with the back of a hand. She straightened her dress. 'We can probably get back to this other thing later,' she said. 'Do you think you can remember your place?'

'I don't know.'

'I'll remind you. I've got a memory like an elephant.'

'And an appetite to match.'

They went into the kitchen. Dave took cans of beer from the refrigerator, popped them open, and gave one to Joan. She followed him outside through the sliding glass door. She sat on a padded lounge and sipped her beer while he dumped charcoal briquettes into the grill, piled them neatly with tongs, squirted fuel over them and lit the fire.

'It'll be a while,' he said.

'Do you need help with anything?'

'Nope. We just have to wait for the fire. Would you like something to nibble on?'

She shook her head. 'I've got to start watching my figure.'

'Something wrong with it?' he asked, turning a lawn chair towards her and sitting down.

'So far, so good,' she said. 'But you know how it goes. We

start letting ourselves go to pot the minute we hook the right guy.'

He felt a glow spread through him. 'I'm the right guy?'

'Oh, I think there's a good chance of it.'

'And you've hooked me?'

'Oh, I think so.' She gave him a snug smile. There was a glimmer of mischief in her eyes. 'What do you think?'

'Good chance of it.'

She lifted her beer, shutting her eyes as sunlight caught the top of the can. The reflection lit her face briefly with a bright disk. Dave watched her throat move as she swallowed. She set the can on a tray beside the lounge. She stretched, and her raising arms drew the front of the dress upward, moulding it against the undersides of her breasts. She folded her hands behind her head. She straightened out her legs.

'This is very nice,' she murmured.

'What is?'

'Just lying here. The sunlight, the beer, the smell of the fire. You. And knowing that nobody will barge in and ruin things.'

'We've had a run of bad luck that way.'

'I'm glad you had a chance to meet Debbie, though.'

'She's a beautiful young lady.'

'She likes you.'

'We barely met.'

'She's a quick study. And super-critical about the guys I go with. You seem to be the first to pass inspection.'

'Good taste on her part.'

'She's got a keen eye for losers. Not me. I'm more like our mother. She always fell for weak guys with sad eyes. She must've been a basset hound in a previous life.' Joan opened her eyes and frowned at Dave. 'I guess it's an overdeveloped mothering instinct. It can screw you up, get you involved with guys who are . . . I don't know, more like children than men. That's no good, and I know it. I saw what it did to my mother. She wanted a knight in shining armour, but when it came right down to it, she always wound up with a lackey. I don't want that happening to me. But it *was* happening to me. Time after time. It seems like I'm always getting attracted to guys who can't stand on their own two feet. In my previous life, I guess I was a crutch.'

'I wouldn't mind leaning on you,' Dave said. He meant it. From the look in Joan's eyes, he could see that she knew he meant it.

'Any time,' she said. 'Shining armour, that's heavy stuff.'

'So you think I'm a knight, do you?'

She smiled. 'Close enough.'

'Are you a damsel in distress?'

'Frequently.'

'You're pretty tough for a damsel.'

'I'm not so tough,' she said, and a soft, pleading look filled her eyes. It was the look he'd seen when Joan spoke of destroying Woodrow Abernathy with a kick. It was the look of a little girl who needed to be hugged and assured that everything would be all right.

Dave rose from his chair. He straddled the lounge, and Joan scooted towards him, wrapped her legs around him, pressed herself against him. 'It's all right to be tough,' he whispered, brushing her lips with his mouth. 'I like you when you're tough. But I like you when you're not, too. I like everything about you. Almost everything.'

She drew her head back. The vulnerable look was gone from her eyes. Their mischief was back. 'Uh-oh. You mean I'm not perfect?'

'Well, there's one little thing . . .'

'I know, I'm taller than you. I'll always wear flats. I'll buy you lift shoes.'

'Don't bother. I like it that you're tall. Your body is perfect just the way it is. Every inch of you . . .'

'You haven't seen every inch.'

'I will.'

'That all depends. What's wrong with me?'

'You won't get mad, will you?'

'I might get even.' He saw a shadow of worry in her eyes. 'What is it, Dave?'

'I wouldn't want you to be a coward. But . . . sometimes . . . Like the way you went climbing up the damn Hurricane to help the guy they put up there. Like the way you went rushing off ahead of me to break up the fight. Like the way you're so determined to go out on the boardwalk tonight. I don't want to lose you. I don't want to ever lose you.'

'You're saying I've got more guts than brains?'

'I don't want to knock your brains. But less guts might be an improvement.'

'That's sweet,' she said.

'I couldn't stand it if something happened to you. I love you.'

'You love me?' she asked.

'Yeah.'

'I love you, too.'

'Heroes don't last long, Joan. And I want you to last. I want you to be with me till we're old and doddering.'

'So we can lean on each other,' she whispered.

'Right.'

'I'd like that.'

Chapter Thirty-seven

When the telephone rang, Jeremy leapt from the sofa, saying, 'I'll get it.'

His mother looked up from her book only long enough to nod, then resumed reading.

He knew it was early for Tanya's call. Without even looking at his wristwatch, he knew. He'd been horribly aware of the slow passage of time all afternoon, all evening. The minutes had crept by while he waited on the boardwalk for the banjo girl to join Nate. After his second call to Tanya and her promise to phone him at nine – and *meet* him later – *just you and me* – time had crawled at an even slower pace.

The call was half an hour early.

But it saved him an endless half-hour of agony.

He snatched up the handset of the wall phone in the kitchen. Though he was sure that his mother could hear nothing over the sounds of the television in the living room, he spoke softly. 'Hi. Tanya?'

'Terrific.'

It wasn't Tanya's voice.

'Shiner?'

'Sorry to disappoint you.'

'No, that's okay.' His face felt burning. 'It's just ... Tanya said she'd phone me about tonight. You know, the trolling.'

Shiner was silent for a few moments. 'Is it on for tonight?'

'Well, I don't know. That's what she'll be calling about.'

'I suppose you're planning to go.'

'I haven't decided yet.' He realized that it hurt somewhere deep inside, lying to her.

'Really?'

'What about you?' he asked.

'No way. I told you, I'm done with it. And I think you should quit, too.'

'I've thought about it.'

'It's going to hit the fan. It really is. Nate was right to quit when he did. I think we all should, but nobody's going to listen to me. Except you, maybe. Do you still care about me, Jeremy?'

'Sure. Of course I do.'

'Honest?'

'Yeah.'

And that, he knew, was not a lie.

'What about Tanya?' she asked. He heard the pain in her voice.

'There's nothing going on.'

'I saw her kiss you.'

'Well, she was drunk. So was I. It didn't mean anything. She was kissing *everybody* last night after you left. I guess she was just grateful that we hadn't quit on her, like Nate.'

'Don't tell me you didn't like it.'

'I wish it had been you.'

More silence. Then she said, 'I'm sure.'

'I mean it. She's not . . . my type. You know? She's weird.'

'I could've told you that.'

'I wanted to be with *you* after the party.'

'I wanted to be with you, too. Until you kissed her.'

'She kissed *me*. It wasn't my fault.'

'It really hurt. It hurt a lot. I mean, I know she's gorgeous and she's got every guy in the world drooling over her – not to mention Karen, for godsake. But I thought . . . I thought you and I had something going, you know?'

'We did. We do. I really like you. When I figured out you'd left the party, it really messed me up. I left right away, myself. It took all the fun out. I couldn't stay without you there. I felt so out of place. And like lonely all of a sudden.'

'I'm sorry,' she murmured.

'No, I'm the one who's sorry. I messed up so bad.'

'How did you get home?'

'I walked.'

'Oh, no. You walked? That's miles. I figured somebody'd give you a lift.'

'After you left, I didn't want anything to do with the rest of them.'

'It must've taken you all night.'

'Just a couple of hours.'

'God, I'm so sorry. I knew I shouldn't have gone off that way. I felt rotten about it. But I had to, you know? I was awfully upset.'

'Can we see each other again, sometime?'

'Why do you think I called you, doufuss?'

He could almost see her smile when she said that. Her beaming Shiner smile.

'My mom's out on a date,' she said. 'I'm all alone here. She won't be back for hours. I thought maybe you'd like to come over.'

'That'd be great!'

Tanya.

Tanya would be calling soon.

He'd forgotten. He couldn't believe that he'd forgotten. The promise of her call, of their later meeting, had been his sole focus, his obsession, all evening.

'Great,' Shiner said. 'I'll give you the address. Do you have a pencil and . . .'

'Wait. I can't. I can't come over. It'd be great, but my mom's here and there's no way I can sneak out.'

'You don't have to sneak out. Just tell her you're going for a bike ride, or something. It's not all that late. I'd really like to see you.'

Jeremy sighed. She's alone, he thought. Jeez. We could do stuff, make out. She wants to make out, or she wouldn't be asking me over with her mother gone. She wouldn't risk it. She must really want me bad.

But Tanya.

'I just can't,' he said. 'Mom won't let me out of the house. She grounded me because of last night. I got in late, and also she knew I'd been drinking. I really caught it. So she isn't about to let me leave.'

'You won't come over here, but you'll go trolling.'

'Mom'll be asleep by then. Besides, I only said I might go trolling, I didn't say I would.'

'Did they go out last night after the party?' Shiner asked.

'I don't think so. I went right home. Why?'

'Nothing,' she muttered. She was silent for a moment. 'Look, if you can sneak out later for the trolling, you could come here instead. I'm sure my mom's going to be gone most of the night. We'd have lots of time together. How about it?'

Shit! He could miss the trolling. He wouldn't mind that. But the meeting with Tanya beforehand . . .

How do I get out of this? he wondered.

'Think up a good one,' Shiner said.

'Hey, come on.'

'If you'd rather be with Tanya, why don't you just admit it?'

'It isn't that.'

'No. I'm sure.'

'I'll look like a chicken if I don't show up.'

'I'm not going to beg, Jeremy. It's your choice. Who is it going to be, me or Tanya?'

'That's not fair!'

'Okay. Well, I guess that pretty much answers it. Goodbye.'

'Shiner!'

She hung up.

'Shit!' Jeremy jammed the phone down. He hurried into the bathroom, locked the door and leaned against it. Baring his teeth, he pounded his fists against his legs. He slid down the door until the floor stopped him. He hugged his knees.

The bitch! he thought. Damn her! It wasn't fair!

Fuck her anyway, she wants to be like that.

He clamped his teeth on his knee and bit hard enough to feel pain. The taste of his corduroy trouser leg was dry in his mouth.

I could've gone to her house, he thought.

He pictured himself on a sofa with Shiner in a dimly lighted room. He could feel her in his arms, feel her mouth against his. She was all soft and smooth, and she smelled of suntan oil.

His teeth loosened their grip. He closed his mouth and pressed his lips against the moist corduroy.

It would've been so wonderful.

So right.

It's not too late, he thought. If I call her back . . .

Then, I'd miss out on Tanya.

He saw himself in Tanya's room last night, saw her standing before him naked and glossy, felt her skin under the slick layer of blood. Heat spread through the pit of his stomach. He felt the stirrings of arousal. He began to tremble, aching for her but afraid of her.

She's *bad*, he thought. She's probably crazy. I shouldn't want her. I should stay away from her. What's wrong with me? God!

So call Shiner. Go to her tonight. When Tanya phones, just say . . .

Jeremy heard footsteps in the hallway. Then came a knocking on the door.

'Honey? There's a call for you.'

His heart lurched.

He crawled away from the door before answering. 'I'll be right out.'

He scurried the rest of the way to the toilet, flushed it, then got to his feet and hurried back to the door. He opened it. His mother looked at him, frowning slightly. 'Is everything all right?'

'Yeah. Fine. Who's on the phone. Shiner?'

'She didn't say.'

'Must be. She told me she'd call back.'

As he hurried away, Mom said, 'Now, don't make any plans without checking with me first. You're still in trouble around here, young man.'

'Yeah, I know.' Before entering the kitchen, he glanced back and saw her step into the living room. He picked up the phone.

Let it be Shiner, he thought. Please.

'Hello?'

'It's me.'

Tanya.

He felt a quick pull of disappointment and loss. Then heat rushed into the empty place. His heart quickened. 'Just a second,' he said.

'Have you got it?' His mother's voice on the extension.

'Yeah. Thanks.'

She hung up.

'Okay,' he said. 'She's off.'

'Can you get away later?' Tanya asked. 'Around midnight?'

'Midnight?'

'It'll be just you and me. We'll meet the others later.' He felt as if his breath had been sucked out. He managed to say, 'Yeah.'

'We'll take my car. I'll park across the street from your house.'

'Okay.'

'Are you all right? You sound funny.'

'Just excited,' he said.

'So am I. I can hardly wait. Midnight.'

'Yeah.'

'See you then, Duke.'

'See you.' He hung up the phone, turned around and stared at the wall clock. Ten till nine. Three hours and ten minutes to go. Forever.

Not forever.

Midnight would get here. He knew that. And somehow he suspected that it might arrive too soon.

He was hot and sweaty, but shivering anyway. He clenched his teeth to hold his jaw still. He wrapped his arms tightly around his chest.

Felt like his *lungs* were shaking.

I'll take a shower, he thought. A hot shower. It'll make the shivers stop. And it'll help pass the time. Besides, I want to be clean for her.

He walked unsteadily towards the bathroom, images twisting through his mind of Tanya's scar, her bare breasts, Shiner's smile, the razor blade sliding on Tanya's flesh, the comfortable, exciting feel of Shiner's hand in his, the suck of Tanya's mouth taking the blood off his fingers. Spreading suntan oil on Shiner's back. Spreading blood up Tanya's belly and breast.

Chapter Thirty-eight

Robin sat cross-legged on the sofa, a folded towel beneath her to protect the upholstery from the dampness of her bikini pants. She played her banjo and sang for Nate.

He sat on the floor in front of Robin, a dreamy far-away look on his face as he gazed at her. His hair was mussed from the swimming. It shimmered golden in the light from the fireplace at his back. The fluttering light burnished his bare shoulders and thighs. The wine in the glass that rested on his knee gleamed like a ruby. He didn't sip the wine while she sang.

Ending a piece, Robin said, 'It's getting a little warm in here.'

'I could turn the fireplace off.'

'No, don't. It's lovely.'

'It makes you glow,' he said.

She drew a forearm across her wet face, and looked down at herself. Her chest gleamed in the ruddy firelight as if it were slicked with oil. Her bikini top was no longer damp from the pool, but its edges were darkened with moisture. 'That's sweat,' she proclaimed.

'Your sweat's beautiful.'

Beads of it dribbled down her sides. She lowered her arms and smeared them to stop the tickling. 'Beautiful or not,' she said, 'I'm gonna warp my banjo.' She lifted it away from her belly, slipped the strap off her head, and used a loose corner of her towel to dry its back. She lay the banjo on the sofa beside her.

'That's all?' Nate asked.

'I don't want to bore you.'

'I could listen to you forever.'

'Maybe I'll write a song just for you.'

'I'd like that. What would it say?'

'Oh, I don't know.' She reached to the table, picked up her wine glass and took a sip. 'A lot of stuff rhymes with Nate. Great, first-rate . . . fate.'

'Mate,' he added.

'Yeah. Mate. That's a loaded one, isn't it?'

'Says a lot.'

'Nautical, too. Nautical's good on the banjo.' She picked up the instrument again, played a few bars of 'Blow the Man Down', and began to sing:

I've got a first-mate
And his name it is Nate.

Yo-ho, I think he's just great!

He's sweet and he's sexy
From his toes to his pate –

And oh how I love to mate with my Nate!

Laughing, he shook his head, set his wine glass on the carpet and clapped. 'Fantastic. What's a pate?'

'That's the top of your head.'

He put a hand up there and ruffled his hair. 'Sexy, huh? And my toes, too?' He wiggled them.

'You making fun of my song?'

'I love your song.'

'I know it's sort of silly,' she said. 'Most of my stuff is. The banjo's not meant for serious stuff. It's bright and plucky.'

'Like you.'

'Is that how you see me?' she asked.

'Only part of the time. I see you a lot of different ways. Serious, sad, innocent, full of hope, afraid . . . but brave, too. You must be damn brave, going on the road the way you did.'

'That was just plain desperation.'

'I feel like there's so much I don't know about you, Robin. I want to know everything.'

'I'm just a simple gal who likes the banjo, big breakfasts and hot baths.'

'Hot baths, huh?' Smiling, he finished his wine. 'I bet you'd love the spa.'

'Hey, that'd be terrific.'

'It'll take a while for the water to heat up,' he said, getting to his feet. 'You want to wait here while I turn it on?'

'I could use some fresh air.'

He picked up the wine bottle and watched as Robin stood, took her towel off the sofa and mopped the sweat from her face and body. She draped the towel over her shoulders. Then she picked up her wine glass and followed him to the sliding door. His back was shiny in the firelight. The seat of his tight blue swimsuit gleamed. The fabric was dark in the centre, dampened by sweat in a narrowing triangle between his buttocks.

She put a hand low on his back and rubbed the slippery wetness of his skin as he tugged the door.

He smiled over his shoulder at her.

'Yo-ho,' she said.

Then the chilly air got her. 'Yo-*yikes*!' she blurted, suddenly shuddering.

'Get in the pool quick! Save yourself!' He reached for the wine glass, and Robin gave it to him.

Hunched over and hugging herself, she abandoned Nate and trotted over the concrete towards the deep end of the pool. She tossed the towel behind her. She leaped, hit the water and felt it rush up her body, cool but warmer than the night air. Her feet touched the bottom. She rose slowly to the surface and swam until she again found the pool's floor. Though it slanted down steeply behind her, it was just right. Standing on tiptoes, she was covered to her chin.

She saw Nate in the darkness near the fence, bending over a unit of boxy equipment and pipes, turning knobs.

'How can you stand it?' she called in a shaky voice.

'Will power.'

'Get your will power into the pool before it freezes and breaks off.'

He finished and walked slowly towards the pool's shallow end.

'What a he-man,' Robin said.

He curled his arms up like a body builder showing off his biceps.

'Mr Universe,' Robin said.

'Want me to turn on the pool lights?' he asked.

'Yeah. All the better to see your magnificent body.'

He wandered off again, and flicked a switch near the door.

The patio remained dark, but the pool suddenly filled with light. He came back to the edge. Pale blue reflections shimmered on his skin as he crouched and dived. He darted out low over the water, knifed in with barely a splash, and glided straight and smooth to the far wall. There, he stood and turned to Robin. He waded towards her, standing tall though he must've been freezing from the chest up. Below the surface, his body wavered and rippled.

'You look like something in a funhouse mirror,' Robin said. Her chin shook as she spoke.

'The kind that makes you ten feet tall?'

'The kind that make you wobbly.'

The water rose around him. When it almost reached his shoulders, he was near enough. Robin drew herself against him.

'You're shivering,' he said.

'How come you're not?'

'Man of iron. Are you nervous, or just cold?'

'Just freezing. I'm over being nervous. That was a life ago.'

'We didn't blow it,' he said.

'You didn't burn the steaks.'

'Lucky me.'

Where their bodies were pressed together, a warmth grew. The warmth spread through Robin, calming her tremors but not making them vanish entirely. Where she wasn't tight against Nate, the water rubbed her like an October breeze.

'We could've waited in the house,' he said.

'I'm all right now. Sort of.'

'Just think of all that hot water pumping into the spa.'

'How long will it take?'

'It's probably a little warmer right now.'

'Then what the hell are we doing in the pool?'

'Kissing.'

'No we're not.'

'Yes we are.' He pressed his open mouth against Robin's. His wet lips were chilly at first. But his tongue was warm. His arms tightened their hold, and he began to step backwards.

Robin hugged him with her arms and thighs. She felt the water slipping over her, sliding down, baring her to the cold air.

Finally, he turned and lifted her onto the tile wall of the spa. 'Thanks for the ride,' she said.

'I'll go turn the bubbles on.'

He stepped away from Robin, breaking the warm bond. The cold stole her breath away, but only for a moment while she swivelled around. Then she sank into the mild, soothing water of the spa. It wasn't hot. It wasn't even warm. But it wasn't chilly, either. It was wonderful. Sighing, she settled onto a smooth, bench-like ledge, and the water covered her to the shoulders. She stretched out her legs, let them drift upward. Something that felt like a summer wind blew against the side of her left thigh. She put her hand there, moved it against the pressure, and found a hole low down in the wall – a hole that gushed hot water. She went to it and sat in front of it. The heat pushed against the small of her back and spread out against her. She moaned with pleasure.

Suddenly a rushing sound filled her ears. All the water in the spa began to froth and bubble. It seemed to throb, pulsing against her skin.

Nate came out of the darkness. He had the wine glasses, the bottle and towels. He set them near the edge of the spa, filled the glasses, then climbed down. He handed a glass to Robin. She took a drink. The wine was cool in her mouth, but once swallowed it seemed to glow inside her, radiating warmth.

Nate sat across from her, only his head and glass-bearing hand above the surface. His body, reddish in the murky crimson light from the bottom of the spa, was visible but blurred through the boiling water. His face was smudged with shadows. Distorted and unfamiliar.

'You look like the boogy-man,' she said.

'Thanks a bunch. You look kind of like an evil queen, yourself.'

She cackled. 'Who's the fairest of them all, ducky?'

One of his feet stroked her shin. 'The fairest is Robin. Cock Robin.'

Cockless Robin.

Poppinsack.

'A bum called me that,' she said. The water was very warm, now. Cozy. Steam drifted off the churning surface, a pink mist that was shredded and scattered by the breeze. She drank more wine. 'Cock Robin,' she said. 'He also called me Cockless Robin.'

'Bastard,' Nate muttered.

'He was a funny guy. I actually liked him, at first. Poppinsack. He really had a way with words. He reminded me of those medicine show guys you see in old cowboy movies. Hawking a cure-all from the back of a wagon. You should've seen him, all decked out in a buckskin jacket with fringe, feathers in his derby hat.' Nate's foot dropped away from her shin. 'A real character. I liked the guy, and then he robbed me.'

'Robbed you?'

'Yeah. While I was sleeping on the beach. Before I even met him and he acted so friendly and gave me tea. All the time he was being nice to me, he knew what he'd done.'

Nate shook his head slowly from side to side.

The theft had been buried inside Robin like a secret shame. Sharing it with Nate felt good and right. She needed to tell him the rest.

'My money? I kept it in my underwear.' She expected a hot rush of embarrassment, but it didn't come. 'I was asleep and he stole it out of my underwear. Got knows what else he did . . . his hands in there. Then he goes and calls me "Cockless Robin".'

Nate muttered something that was lost in the gurgling sounds of the water.

'What?'

'Nothing.'

'I wanted to kill the creep.'

'I did.'

'What?' Robin asked, certain that she hadn't heard him correctly.

'I killed him.'

She gazed at Nate, stunned. She set her wine glass down, and went to him. She knelt between his legs in the swirling hot water, and put her hands on his thighs.

'An old guy with a walrus moustache,' he said.

'Yeah.'

'I killed him Thursday night.'

'I don't believe it,' Robin said. But she *did* believe it. Nate was too grim to be joking. 'How?' she asked.

'You know about the trollers.'

'You're a troller?'

'I was. Not anymore. After what happened to the old man . . . I lost my stomach for it. It was awful. And it was my fault. They couldn't have started the Ferris wheel without me. I had the key. We didn't know he'd fall, but . . .'

'How did it happen?'

'We cuffed him to the safety bar of one of the gondolas, and took him up. The bar wouldn't hold him. He fell. He fell from the top, screaming. Then, I took his body out on my surfboard. I took him way out, belted to it, and dumped him.'

'God,' she muttered.

'It was the night I met you.'

She remembered waiting for Poppinsack that night. Waiting in the fog with her knife, then getting spooked and hurrying away to find safety under the house beyond the public beach. 'I was going to take him,' she said. 'I was going to get my money back. I was waiting for him in the dunes.'

'Well, we killed him.'

'I might've, if he'd shown up. I had my knife out. I wanted to hurt him. I wanted to make him pay.'

'At least . . . it helps some, knowing what he did to you. Maybe he deserved it. Still makes me sick to think about it, though.'

'I know,' Robin murmured. 'I'm sorry.'

'So how do you like it? You've been making love with a murderer.'

She gently rubbed his legs. Her throat was tight with sorrow for him. 'It sounds like it was an accident.'

'Well, it *was* an accident. He was too heavy for the safety bar. But we set it up, you know? He was up there because of us. Everybody wants to say it was an accident, but we did it to the guy. He was a troll, and we nailed him. Most of the others seemed pretty happy that he fell. I'm sure Tanya was overjoyed. She's been out for their blood ever since we got into this Billy Goat Gruff thing. And she's been getting a lot worse, lately.'

'The girl at the stop sign?' Robin asked.

'Yeah. She's been losing it, you know? I can't really blame her. Some trolls messed her up really bad – cut her up, raped her, all kinds of stuff. So, you know, it's not surprising that she hates trolls. I do, too, for what they did to her. She used to be . . . innocent, happy. She was never mean to anyone.'

'You loved her, didn't you?' Robin asked.

He hesitated. He put his hands on her shoulders. 'I used to love Tanya. Before the trolls got her. They killed the part of Tanya that I loved.'

'I'm sorry,' Robin whispered.

'Now, she's just full of hate. All she cares about is nailing trolls.' He shook his head. 'We got so *much* revenge for her. She's had a feast of it, but she keeps wanting more. Her appetite's been getting worse and worse. Now that she's actually killed one . . . I hate to think what they'll do to the next troll they catch. But at least I won't be part of it. I only wish I'd quit sooner. Before it came to killing. But I didn't. Now, I'm a murderer.' His hands moved up and gently caressed the sides of Robin's head. 'I have to live with it,' he said. 'And I guess I had to tell you. Better to lose you now than later.'

'You haven't lost me,' she said.

'Weren't you listening? I'm . . .'

'I killed a man once.'

'No.' Nate's fingers tightened on the sides of her head.

'Yes. I think I did, anyway. I try to tell myself he might've lived. Every day, I try to tell myself that. But I don't really believe it. My knife's big, and I shoved it right into the middle of his chest. Maybe he didn't die. He probably did, though.'

Groaning, Nate drew her forward. Robin climbed onto him and straddled his lap. He slipped his arms around her and held her tightly. 'Aw, Jesus,' he murmured close to her ear. 'Robin, Robin.'

'He attacked me,' she said. Voice cracking, she added, 'Doesn't make it any better, though.'

'Aw . . . aw. God, I'm sorry. I'm so sorry.'

'We're a hell of a pair, huh?'

His body began to shake against her. He was crying. Holding her tight and jerking with sobs, his breath hitching. Robin cried, too.

Caressed by the hot throbbing water, they hugged one another and wept.

Chapter Thirty-nine

At eleven o'clock, his mother set her book aside and started to watch the television news.

'I guess I'll go on to bed,' Jeremy said.

She looked surprised. 'What about *Saturday Night Live*?'

'Not on,' he reminded her. 'And its summer replacement stinks. Besides, I'm really tired.'

She arched an eyebrow. 'I can't imagine why, getting in at one o'clock last night.'

'Yeah.' He kissed her, told her goodnight, and went to his bedroom. With his door shut, he gathered the clothes he would wear later. He slipped his Swiss Army knife into a front pocket of his corduroy pants. From the bottom drawer of his desk, he took Tanya's razor blade. *Keep this with you to remember*, she'd said. It was still wrapped in his handkerchief. The white cloth was smeared and blotched with dried, brown blood.

He unwrapped the blade and looked at it. Memories of last night rushed in, seizing him with fear and desire.

Who needs the razor as a reminder? he thought. Who's going to forget *that*?

But Tanya had asked him to keep the razor with him.

He wound the handkerchief around the blade and tucked it into a pocket of his cords.

Then, he rolled up his clothes and pushed the bundle under his bed. He tossed his robe over the back of a chair. He turned off the light, and got into bed.

The glowing face of the clock on his nightstand showed eleven-fifteen. Half an hour before time to get dressed and sneak out.

The minutes crawled by.

His mind seethed with fevered images. Tanya and Shiner. Their faces, their bodies, their smells, their voices. Shiner and Tanya. And detours into memories of the troll falling from the Ferris wheel, Tanya straightening his broken legs, Jeremy earlier snapping the guy's finger to pay him back for striking Shiner. Detours into Jasper's Oddities, Cowboy shaking the jar of the foetus, the huge awful spider, the leathery remains of the mummy, Cowboy's wisecracks, the chase and the fight and jerking the shirt off the wild girl and feeling her breasts. A detour to Karen dancing at the party, sweaty in her transparent bra and panties. A detour to the dry, amused voice of the troll calling *Tha's a fack* from the darkness under the boardwalk. Every detour led him back, soon, to Tanya. To Shiner. The thoughts of Shiner hurt him with guilt and loss. The thoughts of Tanya strained him with hard desire. He wanted her, he ached for her. He felt dirty for choosing her instead of Shiner. And afraid.

The sound of footfalls in the hallway released Jeremy from the dark turmoil of his thoughts. He heard a door close, running water, the flush of the toilet, and finally his mother's footsteps passing his door as she went to her bedroom.

Eleven thirty-five.

He waited for the minutes to pass, his mind occupied now with thoughts of sneaking out but sometimes slipping into fearful wonder about what might happen in his rendezvous with Tanya.

At a quarter to twelve, he rolled silently out of bed. He stuffed his pyjamas and robe under the covers. Naked and shaking, he knelt beside the bed and reached beneath it for his clothes. He sat on the carpet and put them on.

Then, he crept to his door. He eased it open. The hallway was dark, even in front of his mother's room. But he suspected she hadn't yet fallen asleep. Holding his breath, pulse pounding in his head, he trailed his fingertips along the wall to help guide him, and made his way forward, the rubber soles of his shoes silent on the floor.

At the front door, he slipped the guard chain off its runner and lowered it gently. He turned the latch. The tongue of the dead bolt made a quiet thump. He turned the knob, swung the door slowly open, stepped onto the porch, and closed the door behind him.

Beyond the porch screens, the street was bright with lamplight. A few cars were parked along the kerbs. One of them might be Tanya's. He knew he was early, though. Maybe she hadn't arrived yet.

Maybe she won't come.

The thought filled him with hope, ripped him with agony.

He shut the screen door carefully, and stepped down the stairs.

If she doesn't come, he told himself, I could walk over to Shiner's.

Look, I changed my mind. Can I come in?

Hell, I don't even know the address.

Across the street, the headlights of a parked car shot bright beams and then went dark.

Jeremy's heart jumped.

He quickened his pace. At the sidewalk, he glanced back at his house half hoping to see lights bloom in the windows, the door fly open, his mother rush out yelling, *And just what do you think you're doing, young man*?

The house was dark. He'd made a clean escape.

He stepped into the street. An arm waved to him from the open driver's window of the car that had flashed its lights. He returned the wave. He rushed around the car's front, noting that it was an old Ford LTD. The passenger door swung open as he approached it, but the interior remained dark. The dome light was either out of order or Tanya had disconnected it on purpose.

Stopping beside the door, he crouched and peered in. Tanya was shrouded in shadow, her features masked and blurred, but familiar enough to wrench Jeremy's breath away. He dropped onto the passenger seat. He tugged the door shut.

'Here,' Tanya said.

He scooted towards her. The engine was running, but not smoothly. He could feel the car vibrating under him. Though the windows were rolled down, unpleasant odours of gasoline and stale cigarette smoke lingered in the air. And there was another scent, musky and humid, strange to him but somehow making him think of jungle nights and savages. It came from Tanya.

She turned to face him. She wore a dark sweatshirt and sweatpants. She took hold of Jeremy's hand – the one he had cut with the razor – and pressed it to her lips. With her other hand, she pulled the loose front of her sweatshirt away from her body. She guided Jeremy's hand under the shirt, up her hot bare skin to her breast. Leaving it there, she put her arms around him and leaned towards him and kissed him. Her mouth seemed to engulf him. She moaned as he fondled her breast. It was so incredibly smooth, its nipple big and jutting and springy. He rubbed his hand all over it while her tongue swirled inside his mouth. He squeezed it. He fingered the slick scar below the nipple and traced it downward, stopping only when he reached the drawstring of her pants, wanting to follow the scar lower but not daring. He glided his hand up again, felt the whistle tumble beneath it, and swept his hand toward her other breast. Suddenly, he didn't dare touch it. He clutched the whistle.

Tanya's mouth went away.

'We have to get going,' she whispered. 'Later. We'll have time later. For everything.'

Jeremy nodded. He took his hand out of her sweatshirt.

She kissed him gently, her lips slick against him. Then she took something out of the pouchlike pocket at her belly. 'These are for you,' she said.

Jeremy held the flimsy packet up to the windshield.

'Surgical gloves,' Tanya explained. 'We don't want to leave fingerprints.' She took another packet out of her pouch, opened it and put the gloves on.

'We have to wear them now?' Jeremy asked. He didn't want his hands covered. He wanted them bare and feeling Tanya.

'The car's hot,' she said.

'Oh,' he muttered. His stomach seemed to tighten. He could feel his penis start to shrink. 'You mean you stole it?' he asked.

'Of course.'

He squinted at the ignition. There was no key in it, but the car was running.

'Jeez,' he said.

She turned to the front, released the emergency brake, tugged down the shift lever, and swung the car away from the kerb. 'We'll be leaving it at Funland,' she said. 'Don't worry, the owners will get it back. But we can't take a car they might trace to me.'

'What're we going to do?' Jeremy asked.

'Get us a troll,' she said. 'I know right where to find the perfect troll for tonight.'

'Really? Where?'

'Nate's house.'

Robin, braced up with an elbow against the mattress, gazed at Nate. He looked as peaceful as a child. His arms and legs were spread out, just as they'd been when he fell asleep beneath her awhile ago. His chest rose and fell slowly with long breaths. Robin rested a hand on his chest. Though his skin looked golden and warm in the wavering candlelight, it was cool to the touch.

She rolled cautiously away from him, and left the bed. At the foot of it, she picked up the sheet and covers that had been kicked to the floor while they made love. She spread them over him. He didn't move.

Robin smiled.

The poor guy is wiped out, she thought.

Who isn't?

She felt weak all over, herself. Her muscles were warm and shaky, as if they'd been turned into pudding. The area around her mouth felt puffy and tingling from the ceaseless kissing. Her cheeks burned slightly from the chafe of his whiskers. So did her shoulders, and the sides of her neck, and her breasts. Her nipples were tender and achy. She felt mushy and a little raw inside.

Maybe we overdid it just a bit, she thought, and smiled again.

She walked towards the dresser, watching her slow progress in the mirror. The way she held herself and hobbled, she looked as if she expected any quick movement to jostle something loose. When she reached the dresser, she bent over and puffed out each of the candles. Then she made her way to the nightstand on Nate's side of the bed and blew out that candle. She was tempted to crawl over him, but she didn't want to disturb his sleep. So she forced her weary, aching body to circle the bed. Before snuffing the last candle, she bent over and carefully eased Nate's arm down against his side.

At last, she blew out the candle and slipped under the covers. She rolled towards Nate in the darkness, squirmed closer until she felt the heat of his skin, and rested her arm gently on his chest. She listened to his breathing. She kissed his shoulder.

He made a quiet whimpery sound.

Dreaming a bad dream.

Robin rubbed his chest, hoping to distract him from whatever bad images had seized his sleeping mind. The sound of his breathing didn't change. He still slept. Robin listened, ready to wake him if he should whimper again.

Was he dreaming of Poppinsack's fall?

She wished she could make it go away from him. Kiss him and make him well.

If love could only cure him . . .

But he was doomed to live with the guilt. He had his burden, and Robin had hers.

Thank God we told each other, she thought.

She had loved him before, but the sharing of their awful secrets had been like a fire that fused their souls to one another.

She remembered herself in the spa with him, clutching his wracked body tight against her while she sobbed, their tears mingling, and how she felt as if they were one person and how they kept crying while they kissed.

As her mind lingered on the memories, she slipped into sleep.

Tanya shut off the headlights. Darkness collapsed over the road ahead. She swung onto a narrow driveway that rose in front of the car like a dim, grey path through the woods. She shifted to a lower gear, but didn't accelerate, apparently to prevent a swell of engine noise that might warn of their approach.

'Are you sure they're here?' Jeremy whispered.

'They're here,' Tanya said. 'It was supposed to be me.'

'Huh?'

'We had it all planned. His folks are gone till Wednesday. I was going to stay with him.'

'Gosh.'

'The rotten shit.'

'He must be crazy dumping you for that girl.'

'Bad mistake. He's gonna find out how bad.'

They came to the top of the slope. The house beyond the clearing was a vague shape of steep roofs. All its lights were out. Moonlight gleamed on some of the windows. It looked gloomy and abandoned.

Jeremy hoped it *was* abandoned.

He felt sick with dread.

He had to stand by Tanya, no matter what, but it would be wonderful if they got into the house and nobody was there.

He rubbed his sweaty hands on the legs of his corduroys, but they were encased in the gloves and stayed wet.

It'll be all right, he told himself.

She'd said she would take care of Nate. Jeremy only had to worry about the girl. That shouldn't be a problem. He'd taken on two of them in front of the Oddities – and loved it. Here was his chance to fight the banjo girl.

So strange. After his first encounter with her on the boardwalk, he'd imagined how it would be.

Tanya seemed to be breathing life into his wildest dreams, making them real with her dark magic.

I don't want to fight that girl, he thought. I don't want it real.

He trembled with fear, trembled with a sharp ache of desire. *Please, let nobody be home.*

The car glided to a stop in front of the house's porch. Tanya shifted to park and set the emergency brake. The engine rumbled quietly as she opened her door and climbed out. Jeremy almost reminded her to turn it off, but realized she had no key.

He got out. He moved on shaky legs to the front of the car while Tanya removed something from the back seat. She came towards him carrying a paper sack at her side.

'What's in that?' he whispered.

'Stuff,' she said. 'You'll see.'

He followed her up the porch stairs to the front door. With a key from her sweatshirt pocket, she unlocked it.

At least we don't have to break in, Jeremy thought.

Tanya swung the door open. Inside was darkness.

They entered the foyer, and she shut the door without making a sound.

Jeremy heard only the drumming of his heart. It pounded so hard he thought he could feel the blood surging through his vessels.

Tanya squatted down. She set the bag on the floor. When she reached into it, there came a quiet metallic rattle. Jeremy recognized the sound and thought of the old bum. In the faint light from the windows, he saw Tanya's arm come out and lift towards him. He saw the dangling bracelet of a handcuff. She gave the cuffs to him, and slipped a second pair into her sweatshirt pouch.

She pulled a hammer out of the bag and handed it to Jeremy.

He felt his breath squeeze out. His stomach knotted. Icy fingers seemed to clench his scrotum.

She took out a hatchet for herself and stood up, leaving the bag on the floor.

Jeremy whispered in a choked voice, 'We aren't going to kill them, are we?'

'What's the fun of that?'

'What're we gonna do?'

'The girl comes with us. Nate doesn't. Come on.'

Shivering and weak, he followed Tanya to a stairway. They climbed slowly towards the second floor. Each time a stair creaked, Jeremy flinched. Somehow, the mad thud of his heart was causing a dry clicking noise in his throat. He swallowed hard, and the sound stopped.

The stairway seemed endless.

I could've been at Shiner's right now, Jeremy thought. God, why didn't I go there instead?

Handcuffs. A hammer. A hatchet.

It was worse than he could've imagined.

He pictured himself whirling around and racing down the stairs – running from the house and from Tanya and from whatever form of madness waited for him in the minutes ahead.

Then, he remembered his hand inside her sweatshirt.

We'll have time later. For everything.

She was three stairs above him, barely visible in the darkness. He knew that she was naked under the sweatclothes.

He knew that he wouldn't run.

She waited for him at the top of the stairway. 'Don't do anything till I say so,' she whispered.

Jeremy nodded. He pushed the handcuffs into a pocket of his jacket.

Side by side, they walked down the hall. Tanya stopped at

the open door of a bedroom. She peered inside. For a long time, she didn't move. Then, she pressed the head of the hatchet against Jeremy's back and nudged him forward. He entered the room. In the dim moonlight from the windows, he saw a bed. The covers were mounded.

It's them.

Tanya was right. They're here.

What if she lied about killing them?

What am I doing here?

She closed the door. She nudged Jeremy's left forearm with the hatchet, then put it into his hand. Why wasn't she keeping it for herself?

She wants both hands free, Jeremy realized as he watched her sneak across the room, not towards the bed but towards a dresser by the wall. At the end of the dresser was a straight-backed chair. She picked it up, and started to return.

If I don't let her have the hatchet . . .

She set the chair down silently on the carpet in front of the door, tipped it backward, and eased its backpiece under the knob.

The chair would prevent anyone from entering the room, but Jeremy knew it had a different purpose. It was there to stop a quick escape.

She took hold of the hatchet. Jeremy made no attempt to keep it from her. She switched it to her left hand, gripped his wrist and guided him to the foot of the bed. From here, he could hear the breathing of the people beneath the covers.

Tanya glided along the left side of the bed. She bent low over the sleeping form. Her right hand took the hatchet.

Jeremy saw the hatchet rise.

Chop down.

NO!

The thud flashed pain through his own head. He cringed and felt his legs go rubbery, but he heard a harsh gasp and the covers on the other side of the bed suddenly flew up. 'Get her!' Tanya snapped.

The girl was naked and dusky against the white sheets, one hand thrusting the blankets aside as she squirmed to free her legs and sit up.

He dived onto her, smashing her down. The mattress bounced her against him. She twisted and writhed. He pinned one hand, but the other was free and he couldn't catch it because of the hammer. Her nails ripped streaks of fire down his cheek. He let the hammer fall. As it pounded the floor, he grabbed her wrist.

Now I've got you!

She bucked, hurling him sideways. He fell. His back slammed the carpeted floor. The hammer jabbed his shoulder blade. She came down on top of him, whimpering and snarling. She bit his chin and he cried out, released her wrists, and punched her in the face. The blow ripped her teeth from his flesh. In a frenzy of pain, Jeremy grabbed the short hair over her ears and twisted her head, rolling with her as he forced her sprawling onto the floor beside him.

She drove a knee into his stomach. His breath blasted out. He doubled up, hugging his belly.

'What the fuck's going on!' Tanya's voice.

Sucking for air, Jeremy saw the girl push herself up and get to her feet.

The room filled with light.

The girl seemed to freeze in position, hunched over and ready to run, head turned, looking over her shoulder towards the other side of the bed.

'Don't move a muscle,' Tanya warned.

Jeremy struggled to sit up. Panting and clutching his chin, he saw Tanya glaring at the girl. She was bent over Nate's motionless body, the hatchet poised for another strike. In the light from the lamp beside her, he saw that Nate's face was bathed with blood that spilled out of a gash on his forehead. No huge, gaping wound, though. Tanya hadn't chopped him with the hatchet's sharp edge. But it was the sharp edge, now, that hovered above him.

'Get her clothes for her, Duke. She's gotta look right.'

Nodding, he picked up his hammer and stood. He stepped closer to the girl. She hadn't moved since Tanya turned the lamp on. She didn't look back at Jeremy.

'Put your hands on your head,' he gasped.

Her body straightened. She raised her arms and interlaced her fingers on top of her head.

Jeremy stared at her back, her smooth tanned skin, the pale mounds of her buttocks, her slender legs.

He took his hand away from his chin. The rubber glove was slick with blood.

He raked the claws of the hammer down the middle of the girl's back. She made a hissing sound, and flinched rigid as the claws gouged twin furrows in her skin. Blood began to well from the rips.

He glanced at Tanya.

Tanya nodded. She wore a tight smile.

Jeremy stepped to the front of the girl. Her eyes fixed on him. They looked frightened and hurt, but they were filled with loathing as if she longed to destroy him.

He smeared his blood onto her chin and cheeks. He slapped her face, rocking her head sideways. But she faced him again. She bared her teeth and kept glaring at him, but didn't resist as his hand moved over her, caressing, squeezing, pinching. When he rammed the hammer head into her belly, she folded and dropped to her knees, wheezing for air. His knee crashed her mouth shut, snapped her head backward, and she tumbled sprawling onto the floor.

'That's enough,' Tanya said. 'We're running low on time.'

While he searched for the girl's clothes, Tanya cuffed one of Nate's hands to the bedframe. Jeremy found the backpack inside the closet. He took jeans and a faded blue work shirt from the pack. He tossed them onto the girl and watched her slow, pained struggle to put them on. Before she could button the shirt, he snatched her by the hair, hauled her up, and cuffed her hands behind her back.

He took off his belt, slipped one end through the buckle, and dropped the loop over the girl's head. Tanya grabbed Nate's keys off the top of the dresser. She stuffed them into her pouch, then turned off the light.

'Okay,' she said. 'When we get outside, I'll bust a window to make it look like a break-in. Don't let me forget.'

'Right,' Jeremy said.

Pulling his belt like a leash, he led the girl into the dark hallway.

Chapter Forty

The bed wobbled slightly, stirring Dave from sleep. Through his closed eyelids, he saw light. Is it morning? he wondered. Joan had made him set the alarm clock for midnight, but maybe he'd turned it off in his sleep, or something. He hoped so. He hoped it was morning.

A bare bottom sat down on him. He squirmed under the pleasant weight and opened his eyes. With a tug of disappointment and fear, he saw that the light came from the bedside lamp. Joan was straddling him, hands against the mattress near his shoulders. She smiled gently and lowered herself. Her nipples touched his chest, and she rocked herself to make them move, stroking him. Then he felt the solid warm heaviness of her breasts. They pushed against him. Her mouth covered his. He ran his hands slowly up and down her back.

She lifted her mouth away from him. 'Time to shine, honey.'

'Time to *rise* and shine,' he said.

He saw the familiar mischief in her eyes.

'Oh,' he said. 'I get it.'

She kissed him again, then said, 'We have to go.'

'I was afraid of that. What time is it?'

'Twelve-thirty.'

'What happened to the alarm?'

'I shut it off. I was awake, anyway.'

'Couldn't sleep?' Dave asked.

'Didn't want to. It seemed like such a waste of time. It was so much nicer, staying awake and looking at you.'

'Voyeur.'

'You got it, pal.'

'You should've woken me up.'

'Didn't want to. You've had a hard night. You needed your sleep. That's why I didn't wake you up sooner, too.' She kissed him once more. 'Okay, now, at 'em.'

She climbed off Dave, taking away her weight and smoothness and heat. He sat up and pulled the blanket to his waist. He watched Joan step into her panties, watched her pull a T-shirt down over her head. When her face reappeared, she said, 'Show's over. You can get dressed, now.'

Dave scooted to the edge of the bed. He lowered his feet to the floor, but didn't stand up.

Instead, he watched Joan slip into one of the dark blue vests he had picked up at the station that afternoon. She fastened it shut around her torso with Velcro straps. 'You look like you're ready to go water skiing,' he said.

'Wishful thinking.' Squatting beside the grocery bag, she took out a shoulder harness. She slipped into it, and tucked her S & W .38 into the holster below her left armpit. A smaller holster went around her right ankle. She filled it with a chrome plated semi-auto. Still another harness came out of her sack. Dave shook his head as she got into it. She straightened the leather sheath against the right side of her ribcage, and slid a long, double-edged knife into it.

'God Almighty,' Dave said. 'Where do you get your stuff, from *Soldier of Fortune* magazine?'

'How'd you guess?'

'Anything else? Have you got an Uzi in there?'

'This about does it.' When she reached into the sack again, she came out with a pair of grey sweatpants that looked as if they'd been dabbed with shoe polish.

355

Richard Laymon

Dave got up from the bed. He took fresh underwear and socks from his dresser, and put them on while Joan covered the top part of her arsenal with a baggy sweatshirt. The shirt had rips in it that showed the blue of her Kevlar vest. The tears in her pants showed bare leg.

'My sexy Rambo,' Dave said. Like Joan, he put on a T-shirt to keep the vest away from his skin. Then he got into his jeans and vest, and running shoes. He went to the closet for his own weapons: a snub-nosed .380 with a clip-on holster that he fastened to his belt on the right, and a 9 mm Beretta with a shoulder harness.

'You don't travel exactly light yourself,' Joan said, nodding at the Beretta.

'We oughta be able to take on an army,' Dave said.

'Debbie thinks we may have to.'

'You told her, huh?' Dave slipped into a heavy plaid shirt and watched Joan knot a red bandana around her thigh. 'What's that for?'

'Style. Yeah, I told her. Probably should've kept it to myself, but I don't like to do that. She was not pleased, to say the least. She's afraid I won't come back.'

Joan's words made a cold knot in Dave's belly. 'I don't blame her,' he said.

'She's more worried about trolls than the teenagers. Still thinks they had something to do with Mom.' Joan carried her socks and a ratty old pair of running shoes to the bed, sat on its edge, and tried to hunch over to put them on. 'Damn,' she muttered, having trouble because of her vest and harnesses.

'Allow me,' Dave said.

'My knight. So chivalrous.'

Kneeling in front of her, he started to put the socks on her feet. 'You're pretty good at this,' she said, ruffling his hair. 'You can be the official sock-putter-onner for our kids.'

He smiled up at her. 'Our kids?'

'Or don't you want any?'

'Of course I do.'

'How many?'

'As many as you want,' he said, and suddenly wished she hadn't mentioned kids, hadn't touched him with dreams of the future. A future that might not be there. The night ahead loomed in front of Dave like a black wall, and he feared there might be nothing beyond it.

That's ridiculous, he told himself.

But they got Gloria.

Gloria was alone. She wasn't armed. This is a whole different ballgame.

He finished tying the shoes, and rubbed Joan's thighs through the soft fabric of the sweatpants. He slipped a hand inside one of the rips. 'Maybe we should check Gloria's place on the way over,' he said.

'What's the point? She won't be there, we both know that.'

'Couldn't hurt to check one more time. It'll only take a few minutes.'

Her eyes darkened. 'I don't want to go in there again.'

'You can wait in the car,' Dave said. They'd driven over after dinner. Joan had gone in with him, and the experience had obviously upset her. She'd walked stiffly through the house, clutching Dave's hand, a grim look on her face. He couldn't blame her. It was the home of his former lover, a woman who had probably been murdered last night, whose ruined body had likely been discarded in some lonely place where the killers hoped she would never be found.

When Dave started showing Gloria's cast-off clothes to her, she'd shaken her head sharply, blurted, 'I don't want to see that stuff,' and nearly dragged him out of the house. It was no wonder she didn't want to go there again.

'I'll make a phone call, instead,' Dave told her.

'If you want.'

He went to the telephone on the nightstand and dialled Gloria's number. After three rings, the line opened. 'Hello. This is Gloria.'

Dave's heart jumped.

'Gloria?' he asked. He saw Joan's head snap towards him, stunned surprise on her face.

'I'm not home right now, but if you'd like to leave a message . . .'

'Shit,' he muttered. 'It's her answering machine.' He'd probably left messages on the damn thing a hundred times. How could he have let it fool him, lift his hopes? Joan's face was slack with disappointment.

' . . I'll be back to you as soon as possible.'

Right, he thought. Sure you will.

Dead. She's dead, and talking to me just as if nothing is wrong.

Her machine beeped, signalling him to leave his message.

He remembered how she used to complain about hangups.

He remembered how she often talked to him, home after all, once he'd identified himself.

'It's Dave,' he said.

Joan's lips curled. She looked sick.

'If you're there, for godsake pick up the phone.'

He listened to distant, empty sounds.

'Gloria? It's Dave. Are you there?'

I'm talking to a dead woman.

He hung up.

Joan came to him and put her arms around him.

'We might as well get it over with,' he muttered. He hugged her tightly, feeling her stiff vest, the gun and knife, but also feeling the warmth of her legs, the softness of her cheek. He kissed her. 'If I lose you because of this . . .'

'We owe God a death,' she said.

'Just what I wanted to hear.'

''Tis not due yet.' She gently swatted his rump, and stepped away from him.

He watched her reach into the paper bag, pull out a stocking cap and drag it down over her head until only a fringe of blonde hair showed around its edges.

She raised her eyebrows. 'Am I devastating yet?'

'Gorgeous.'

She picked up the bag, which still had something in it.

'You *do* have an Uzi.'

'Just an old blanket,' she said.

'What's that for?'

'More style.'

In the living room, Dave waited while she opened her purse. She took her badge out of its leather case. 'Can't forget this,' she said. 'Have you got yours?'

He patted his wallet.

Joan lifted her sweatshirt and pinned the shield to a strap of her shoulder harness. Then she picked up her bag again, and they left the house.

Dave locked the door with his house key, found the ignition key, and walked beside Joan towards the driveway where his car waited.

Waited on flat tyres.

'What the hell?' he muttered.

He walked around the car. All four tyres were mashed against the pavement by the weight of the car. Joan, he saw, was heading for the street.

She looked back at him. 'Mine, too,' she said.

'You're kidding.' He caught up with her. Joan's car, parked at the kerb, rested on four flat tyres. 'I'll be damned.'

'Looks like somebody decided to sabotage our mission,' she said.

'That's crazy. It was probably just some kids . . .'

'One kid in particular. My sister.'

'Debbie? You think she did this?'

'She must've. It can't be just some weird coincidence. God, she must be a lot more upset than I thought.'

'Does she know where I live?'

'You're in the book, partner. She just looked you up, hiked over here and had at 'em.'

'Well, good for her!'

'The little beast. Wait'll I get my hands on her.'

Dave tried to force the smile off his face, but didn't succeed. 'She's a spunky kid. Must run in the family.'

'I'm gonna strangle her.'

'She just did it because she loves you.'

'Yeah, I know. I'm gonna draw and quarter her, the rat.'
Dave laughed.

'Yeah, yuck it up. Right.' Turning away from him, she crouched beside the front tyre.

'It isn't slashed, I hope.'

'Debbie wouldn't go that far. I'm sure she just let the air out.' Joan rubbed her hands on the side of the tyre. Standing up, she rubbed her face.

'Good grief,' Dave said.

She lowered her hands. Her brow, cheeks and chin were smudged with grime that looked grey and smoky in the street-lights.

'I know. Style. Does this mean we're still planning to go?'

'I am.'

'Great,' he muttered. 'Should I go in and call a cab?'

'Let's just walk. It's not that far.'

'All right. Hang on a minute, though. I want to get my flashlight.' He walked towards his car, feeling strangely cheerful. Nothing was about to stop Joan, but the flat tyres would certainly slow her down. A hike to the beach should take the better part of half an hour.

A reprieve.

Thank you, Debbie. Thank you very much. I owe you for this.

I'll buy her an ice cream cone, he thought, and grinned.

He unlocked his car, took the flashlight out from under the driver's seat, then ambled back towards Joan. 'Let's take it slow and easy,' he said. 'God forbid one of us should turn an ankle.'

Chapter Forty-one

'How's it going back there?' Tanya asked, glancing over her shoulder.

'Fine,' Jeremy said. His own voice sounded strange to him – a little whiney, but mean. 'Just fine.'

The girl was stretched across the back seat, pinned down by his weight on her belly. He bounced on her, and heard a gush of breath that pleased him.

They passed a street lamp. Its light swept briefly across the girl's bare chest. He took off his gloves. He pinched her again, and felt her flinch.

It made him feel good to hurt her, but it didn't turn him on. He felt cheated.

Could've been great, back here sitting on the bitch. Her hands were cuffed behind her back. Her shirt was open. She was *at his fucking mercy*.

She might as well have been a guy, for all the lust he felt.

He slapped her. She winced. He slapped her again. 'You ruined me, you cunt!'

'Hope so,' she muttered.

He made her cry out.

'Take it easy,' Tanya said.

'What'm I gonna do?' he asked. 'You see what she did to me? How'm I gonna go home with my face like this? What'm I gonna tell my mom?'

'Don't worry about it.'

'God, I can't go home.' Gingerly, he fingered the torn flesh of his chin. Touching the wound brought fresh tears to his eyes.

'We'll think of something,' Tanya told him.

'Everybody's gonna know I was in on this. All they gotta do is look at me.'

'I'll take care of you,' Tanya said. 'There's nothing to worry about.'

'Easy for you to say. It's not your face.'

'It's my ass. We're in this together, Duke. It's all right. I'll take you home in the morning and tell your mother that a dog attacked you on the beach. I'm a lifeguard. She'll believe me.'

Yeah! That might work. He felt a little better. He'd have to come up with a story to explain why he'd left the house without telling her, but that shouldn't be too hard.

'What about Nate?' he asked.

'He's deader than shit.'

A horrible keening noise burst from the girl. She began to writhe and buck under Jeremy. He rammed his fist down, smashing her just below the ribcage. The blow made her sit halfway up as her breath exploded out. Then, she slumped down again, wheezing loudly.

'She won't be in any shape to talk, either,' Tanya said. 'We'll make sure of that.'

'*I'll* make sure of that.' Jeremy twisted sideways and worked on her. She flopped and jerked, shuddering with pain, and he knew she'd be screaming if she had any air.

'Not yet, for godsake. Everybody gets a crack at her. We don't want to cheat the others out of their fun.'

'I'm not killing her.' He glared down at the girl. Her head was flying from side to side, lips peeled back as if stretched by fingers trying to rip her mouth wider. 'Am I killing you?' he asked her. 'Huh? Naw. Maybe just hurting you a little bit. Maybe just a little bit. How's this *feel*, huh? And this?'

He felt the car stop.

'Okay,' Tanya said. 'We're here.'

She climbed out, and opened the passenger door beyond the girl's head. Reaching in, she grabbed her under the armpits. Jeremy lifted himself up, and watched Tanya drag her from the car. He crawled out after her.

He shut the door quietly. The girl was on her back, Tanya straddling her and fastening the buttons of her shirt. 'Get her legs,' Tanya said.

The girl thrashed, trying to kick him, but he got her legs apart and hugged them tightly against his sides. Tanya raised her shoulders. Together, they lifted her and carried her up the stairs. They passed beneath the moonlit, grinning face of the clown. In the entryway, shadows closed over them.

Something pale stepped out from behind the ticket booth.

Jeremy sucked a quick breath and froze. He felt the girl's legs pull in his grip as Tanya took one more step. Then, Tanya halted, too.

'It's just me.'

No!

Guilt rushed through him, hot and sickening.

Shiner, standing in the darkness, wore white clothes that almost seemed to glow. Her arms were folded across her chest. The ocean breeze stirred her hair.

She doesn't know what I've done, Jeremy told himself. But her presence was like a brilliant light, and he saw his deeds in that light as sordid and horrible.

What have I done?

Oh God, what have I done?

'The others here yet?' Tanya asked.

Shiner shook her head.

'We've already got ourselves the troll for tonight's festivities,' Tanya said.

'So I see. Jeremy, let go of her and come with me.'

'What's this shit?' Tanya snapped.

'Stay out of it,' Shiner said. She came towards Jeremy. 'You're going to get in real trouble if you stay.'

'If you don't like it,' Tanya said, 'get out of here.'

'Shut up. Jeremy.' She put a hand on his shoulder. It suddenly tightened. 'What happened to your face?'

'We had some trouble with this one,' he muttered.

'Jesus.'

He released the girl's legs. She started to thrash. Tanya wrestled her away, flung her facedown onto the floor of the boardwalk, and planted a foot on her back to keep her still.

'Does it hurt?' Shiner asked.

'Yeah. A lot.'

'I'm sorry. But it wouldn't have happened if you'd come to

363

me tonight. I know I'm not as . . . exciting as Tanya. I know you want her. Hell, you're a guy. Who wouldn't? The thing is, she's going to ruin you. Look what happened to you.'

'Tell her to get the fuck out of here,' Tanya said.

'She's right,' Jeremy said. 'Go away.'

'I'm not going anywhere. Not unless you come with me.'

'I'm not leaving,' he said.

'Yo!' Cowboy called. 'All set to kick some troll ass?'

'Got one here,' Tanya said.

Cowboy and Liz walked over to her. 'Hey, hot damn!'

'A trollette,' Liz said.

'We've also got a traitor.'

'Yeah?'

'Shiner.'

'Naw. What gives, Shiner babes? You're not quitting on us, are you?'

'Turned chicken?' Liz asked.

Cowboy came closer. Shiner let go of Jeremy's shoulder and faced him.

My pal, Jeremy thought. He felt a wonderful sense of relief and gratitude. It was like the time that Cowboy had chased the begging troll away from him.

'Tell me it ain't so,' he said, sounding concerned.

'I'm done with trolling,' she told him.

'You're joshing me, right? These're the low-life scum-suckers that did your sister.'

'Greetings, gang.' Randy. 'Hey, you got one already?'

'Shiner wants to bail out,' Liz said, disgust in her voice.

'Really?'

'What's that car doing in front?' Samson had arrived.

'Duke and I brought the troll in it,' Tanya said.

'You left it running.'

'Doesn't matter.'

'Say, what we got here? A gal? All *right*!'

'We'll get to her in a minute. Duke has to *make the goddamn traitor go away*.'

'She ain't no traitor,' Cowboy said. 'She's just riled up.' To

Shiner, he said, 'What's the story? You upset 'cause of the one that bit the dust?'

'That's one thing. It's all gotten out of hand, Cowboy. Look what this one did to Jeremy.'

Cowboy peered at him. 'Holy heffer shit. That bitch do this?'

'She bit me,' Jeremy said, his voice shaking. 'And scratched me.'

'Well, she's durn sure gonna wish she hadn't.'

Liz and Randy came over to look at him. Samson didn't. He was kneeling beside the girl, turning her over.

Randy pushed his glasses higher on his nose, squinted at Jeremy's face, and muttered, 'Gosh.'

Liz said, 'She's gonna die.'

Their sympathy for his injuries made Jeremy's throat tighten. These are my friends, he thought.

I didn't do anything to the girl that they wouldn't have done.

They're on my side, even if Shiner isn't.

The hell with Shiner, anyway. Who needs her? Heather was suddenly there, nudging Randy aside. Her pale, bloated face came very close, and Jeremy smelled her onion breath. 'Poor Dukey,' she said. She put her arms around him. Her breasts and belly felt like swollen bags of jelly. She pushed her hands into the back pockets of his corduroys and rubbed his rump.

Shiner pulled her away.

'We're leaving,' she said. 'Come on, Jeremy.'

'No.' His voice came out strong. His friends were here, now. So many friends. They were on his side. 'I'm not going. If you don't like it, lump it.'

She tugged the shoulder of his jacket.

Then, someone hooked an arm around Shiner's throat and yanked her backward. Her arm flew up. She clutched the head of her attacker, twisted and ducked. The body flew up behind her, legs kicking, and slammed the boards at Shiner's feet. She lurched backward a few steps and raised her open hands, ready to defend herself.

Nobody else went for her.

Karen, gasping, lay sprawled on the boardwalk where Shiner had thrown her.

'Everybody just stand still and listen to me,' Shiner said. 'Nate was right. It's gone too far. But I'm not here to stop you from going after trolls. I hate them as much as any of you. I still do. They took my mother from me.'

'Sister,' Cowboy corrected her.

'No, my mother. I don't have a mother, thanks to the trolls. But I have a sister, and some of you know her. My real name is Deborah Delaney. My sister is Joan Delaney, the cop who's been patrolling Funland the past few weeks.'

Cowboy lifted a hand to the bandaged side of his head.

'Yeah,' Shiner said. 'She's the one who saved your ear for you.'

'I'll be hog-tied.'

'Your sister's a *cop*?' Tanya blurted.

'I knew you wouldn't let me troll, if I told you about her. But I'm not trolling anymore. I came here to warn you. Joan's coming here tonight, dressed like a bum. She and her partner. They'll be coming to bust you guys. I let the air out of their tyres, but I don't think that'll stop them. For all I know, they might get here any second. You're my friends. You especially, Jeremy, but the rest of you, too. I don't want Joan to arrest any of you. And I don't want her getting hurt, trying. So, please, call it off. At least for tonight. Call it off and get out of here, before it's too late.'

She stood there, breathing heavily, her head turning slowly as she looked at each of them.

Tanya stepped towards her.

Shiner stiffened. She raised her hands again.

Karen, on her knees, muttered, 'Nail her.'

'Shut up,' Tanya said. She held out a hand to Shiner. 'Thanks for the warning, Debbie. You're all right. Even if your sister *is* a cop.'

Shiner took the offered hand. Tanya drew the girl closer, released her hand, and put her arms around her.

They hugged each other.

Jeremy couldn't believe his eyes.

He half expected Tanya to knee her in the guts.

They parted, and Tanya turned to Jeremy. 'Go with her if you want. Nobody'll hold it against you – against either of you.'

'I can't,' he said.

Not after what we've done, he thought. Not with my face like this. It's way too late.

'I'll stick with you,' he told Tanya.

'Good man. All right, trollers! You heard what Debbie said. Cops are on the way. We've gotta make it quick. Randy, you stand watch. You see anyone coming, blow your whistle like crazy and run for it. Let's do it!'

She squeezed Shiner's arm, then hurried towards the cuffed girl. The others went to join in.

Shiner stepped up to Jeremy.

'I'm sorry,' he said.

'Me, too. What the hell, I guess I'd be after Tanya, too, if I was a guy. Still friends?'

'Sure. If you want me for a friend,' he added in a trembling voice.

'I do.'

'Great. And thanks for . . . warning us.'

'Hey, what're friends for?'

He wanted to embrace her, but he kept his arms at his sides. He knew that he could never hold her again.

He had removed himself from the part of the world where teenaged boys and girls dated, hugged and kissed, made out in innocent, questing passion. That was the world where he and Shiner might have dwelled. But it was lost, now, forever.

'Go for it, hoss!'

Some others cheered.

Jeremy looked away from Shiner and watched Samson lift the handcuffed girl. He hoisted her off the boardwalk by the front of her shirt and the crotch of her jeans, swung her up, and raised her over his head as if she were a living barbell. He led the way. The others followed, except for Randy.

'I guess you don't want to miss out,' Shiner said.

Jeremy shook his head.

'Let's go, then.'

'Aren't you leaving?'

'I told you before. I'm not leaving without you. You stay, I stay. Somebody's got to look out for you.'

They hurried to catch up with the group.

The procession moved quickly down the moonlit board, walk. Tanya, taking the lead, rushed to the gate of the fence that surrounded the Ferris wheel. She opened it for Samson, and climbed the wooden platform.

At the top, Samson lowered the girl. He held her standing while Tanya stepped behind her. Jeremy heard a quiet click and realized that Tanya was unlocking one of the cuffs.

'How're you gonna get the thing running?' Samson asked.

'I've got Nate's key.'

'Hot damn,' Cowboy said.

'Let go of her.' Samson released his grip on the girl's shirt front. As she sagged backwards, Tanya braced her up, reached around her, ripped open the shirt and yanked it off.

'All *rights*,' Samson said.

'Get her pants.'

Samson tugged the jeans down her legs. Tanya, arms around the girl's chest, hoisted her up. Samson pulled the jeans off her feet and tossed them aside.

'Who wants some fun?'

'What about the cops?' Samson asked.

'Forget the cops. Who wants to fuck her?'

'I don't know,' Samson said. He caressed the girl's breasts. 'I wouldn't mind, but she's a troll, you know? Wouldn't want to catch something.'

'Well, I reckon . . .'

Liz jabbed Cowboy's arm.

'Reckon not,' he muttered.

'Jeremy?'

His heart pounded.

Not with Shiner watching.

He just couldn't.

Besides, Tanya had promised about later.

'Not me,' he said.

'Bunch of candy asses.' She drove a knee up. The girl jerked as it smashed against her rump. The blow lifted her feet off the boards. Tanya hurled her down. The platform shook as she slammed against it. Dropping to her knees, Tanya pinned the girl's hands. 'Come on, somebody!'

Karen scurried forward and crawled over the girl, moaning as she delved, caressed, squeezed, licked and sucked.

'You don't want to be in on this,' Shiner whispered.

I want to be *doing* it, Jeremy thought, feeling guilty and hating Shiner for being here to shame him.

The girl bit the top of Karen's head.

Yelping, she clutched her scalp. Then, she battered the girl's face with her fists until Samson pulled her off.

'Let's run her up there and haul on out,' he said. 'Those cops are gonna show up.'

'Yeah, yeah, okay.'

Tanya and Samson dragged the girl to the bottom gondola. Tanya propped her against the seat, rump on the footrest, She swung the safety bar down, hooked the connecting chain of the handcuffs over it, and closed the empty bracelet around the girl's wrist.

'If she falls, too . . .' Shiner muttered,

'One more good troll,' Liz said. 'Give her a ride!'

'Hang her high!' from Cowboy.

Tanya pulled a calling card from the pocket of her sweatshirt. 'Greetings from Great Big Billy Goat Gruff,' she said. She took a small plastic case from her pocket, opened it, and held up a straight pin for everyone to see. She poked the pin through the middle of the card. The girl winced and her legs flinched as Tanya stuck it into her, just above the left breast.

'God,' Shiner muttered.

Liz laughed. 'Looks like a name tag. at a nudist convention.'

Tanya hurried over to the machinery. Moments later, the motor rumbled, sending vibrations through the platform. The wheel began to move, dragging the girl's bare heels over the boards as she was swept backwards.

The gondola tipped out from under her. She let out a sharp gasp as her weight was borne by her cuffed wrists.

The wheel picked up speed, carrying the moonlit girl quickly to the top. Just as she swept over the crest, Tanya stopped the wheel. The girl snapped rigid. She shrieked. She looked as if she might be torn loose. Jeremy half expected her arms to be wrenched from her sockets, and he pictured her naked, armless torso falling through the night. But nothing gave. After the harsh tug, she seemed to be flung upwards. She dropped straight again and dangled there, her pale body suspended in front of the swinging gondola.

All the trollers on the platform stared up at her.

'Holy jumping Judas,' Cowboy muttered.

'Well shit,' Liz said. 'Isn't she gonna fall?'

The motor went silent.

Jeremy, suddenly alarmed, hurried over to Tanya. 'She's alive,' he whispered. 'We can't leave her alive. Christ, she'll tell . . .'

'Don't worry, huh? The cuffs are loose. Real loose. I'm surprised she hasn't already fallen. That stop should've done it. She must be keeping her hands fisted.'

'What if she *doesn't* fall?'

'She will. I don't give her ten minutes.'

'You sure?'

'I told you, it's my ass, too. She'll be taking a big dive.' Tanya stepped past Jeremy. He followed her, and they joined the others. All their heads were tilted back. The gondola had stopped rocking. The girl dangled straight down, her rump against the edge of the footrest. She looked limp.

Is she passed out? Jeremy wondered. If she's out cold, why hasn't she fallen yet? Maybe the cuffs aren't as loose as Tanya thought.

'Okay,' Tanya said. 'Let's get out of here.'

They hurried down the stairs, and out the gate. Standing in the middle of the boardwalk, Jeremy again looked up. From here, he had a very good view of the girl. She was incredibly high. A fall would kill her for sure. She wasn't moving at all. Her head hung. But he couldn't see whether or not her fists were clenched to keep the cuffs on.

A brilliant burst of light suddenly hit his eyes.

Heather blurted, 'Shit!'

Jeremy snapped his head around. No more than thirty feet away stood a giant troll with a camera at his face. Its flash blinked again.

'Get him!' Tanya yelled.

They charged the troll. He whirled away, camera swinging at his side by its strap, and vaulted the railing. He dropped towards the beach and vanished.

'Get him!' Tanya shouted again. She was first to reach the railing. She hurled herself over it. Samson rolled over the top bar, turned around and leaped. Cowboy cleared the railing and held onto his hat as he plummeted. Karen and Liz climbed the railing while Heather squirmed under it. Jeremy started to climb. Shiner grabbed the back of his jacket.

'Don't,' she said.

'The guy *took a picture*!'

'They'll take care of him.'

He knocked her hand away and straddled the bar.

'Please. Damn it, please!'

He shook his head, climbed down onto the edge of the boardwalk, and jumped. The beach pounded his feet. His legs folded, and he rolled over the sand. As he pushed himself up, Shiner landed beside him.

'Leave me alone!' he snapped.

'I'm coming with you.'

'I don't *need* you.'

But she stayed at his side as he rushed after the others into the darkness beneath the boardwalk.

'Where is he?' Tanya's voice.

'Oh, God, we can't lose him.' Karen.

'We'll get him.' Cowboy. 'We'll nail his sorry ass.'

'Dance on his face.' Liz.

'Christ, it's dark down here.' Samson.

'Everybody shut up,' Tanya said. 'Maybe we can hear him.'

Off to the left, a patch of ruddy, shimmering light appeared in the blackness.

'There! There!'

'Judas priest, a fucking door.'

The huge form of the troll was silhouetted against it as he crouched and entered. Then he was gone, but the light remained.

They rushed towards it, dodging the thick pilings that supported the boardwalk.

The next shape Jeremy saw silhouetted against the light was Tanya. She didn't hesitate for an instant. She lunged inside. The others followed.

As Jeremy stepped through the opening, he heard the faint, distant shrill of a whistle.

'That was Randy,' Shiner whispered behind him. 'Joan's here.'

Jeremy thought she would rush off to join her sister. But she put a hand on his back, and entered.

'The cops are here,' Jeremy announced. 'Randy just blew his whistle.'

'They won't find us,' Tanya said. 'Close the door.'

Shiner pulled it shut.

They were crowded into a small room lighted by candles on wall holders. The door at their backs was tight against a concrete wall. Another door on the left. Ahead of them was a staircase.

Cowboy tried the second door. 'Locked,' he said.

'Where the hell are we?' Heather asked, her voice low and whiny.

'Looks like a basement,' Samson said.

'Brilliant deduction,' Liz muttered.

'Tha's a fack,' came a dry, ancient voice from above. 'Welcome t' Jasper's Funhouse.'

Tanya pulled a folding knife out of the pouch of her sweatshirt. She pried its blade out.

Jeremy dug into a pocket for his Swiss Army knife.

He saw Samson, Karen and Cowboy produce knives of their own.

'Everybody ready?' Tanya whispered. She scanned the group, her eyes glinting and fierce in the candlelight, then turned around and began to climb the stairs.

Chapter Forty-two

Robin's eyes were squeezed shut in pain and fear, but she opened them just a crack when she heard sudden shouts. The shapes of the trollers, far below, started running up the board-walk.

Her stomach seemed to take a sudden drop.

God, she was so *high*!

A blink of light flicked a quick white glare over the tiny figures. It came from a big man ahead of them, who suddenly ran to the railing, leaped over it, and rushed out of sight under the boardwalk.

The kids, in pursuit, started throwing themselves over the railing.

Are they leaving me up here? she wondered.

Are they done hurting me?

No. No, they aren't done. They'll come back. They have to kill me. I'm a witness.

Oh God, Nate.

Deader than shit.

They murdered him. Tanya did.

But why did she cuff him to the bed? Maybe she lied to that kid. Duke, she'd called him Duke. She wouldn't have cuffed Nate if he was dead, would she?

Maybe.

Maybe he's alive.

I can get help for him, if I get down from here.

If I don't get down, they'll come back and kill me. Tanya or Duke will. Maybe they won't do it in front of the others, though.

All they had to do was start the wheel going again, make it stop once more, and she'd probably go flying.

The last stop had almost torn her loose.

It was like being yanked downward by a mighty giant. The steel edges of the bracelets tore at her, and she'd thought her hands might rip off. Her fists had been clenched all the way up and over the top. If they hadn't been, she was sure she would've been jerked out of the cuffs.

The end of Robin.

Even now, her fists were all that kept her from falling.

Open your hands, she thought, and it's all over.

Out of your misery.

Just one big pain, and that's it. All the pain gone.

I don't want to fall!

A numbness was starting to replace the pain in her hands. She felt blood trickling down her arms and sides. The breeze off the ocean turned the blood cold. It also chilled the long, raw wounds on her back, but those didn't seem to be bleeding now.

The hands get numb enough, she thought, or you lose enough blood to pass out, and it's all over.

She knew that her nose and lips had bled, but that had stopped. So there was just her wrists and hands, and a single dribble of blood working its way down her left breast from the damn pin hole.

Like to pull the pin out and stick it in Tanya's fucking eye!

Robin tucked her head down, thinking it might be possible to pluck out the pin with her teeth. But she couldn't quite reach it. Her chin was in the way.

Worried about a pin.

Gonna fall to my death any second, and I'm worried about a goddamn pin.

Her chin brushed a corner of the card. She winced as its slight movement jostled the pin under her skin.

Then she saw, far below her, three dim figures shambling over the boardwalk. They came from three different directions as if each, on its own, had spied the morsel suspended from the Ferris wheel.

One halted directly below her. His bald pate gleamed in the moonlight. When he looked up, Robin saw that one eye was covered by a patch. His mouth drooped open.

Gooseflesh rushed up her skin. She pressed her legs together.

While the one-eyed troll gazed at her, another shuffled through the gate. The third followed him into the fenced area beneath the wheel.

Robin heard a quiet whimper escape from her throat. She heard the rush of the surf. And she heard the far-off blast of a whistle.

'What was that?' Dave asked.

'Sounded like a police whistle,' Joan said.

'Did it come from the boardwalk?'

Joan shook her head. 'I don't know. It seemed to come from that direction.'

'Maybe whoever belongs to that car . . .'

She frowned at him. 'Somebody might be in trouble,' she said, and started to run.

Dave broke into a sprint and caught up with her.

They raced up the sidewalk alongside the Funland parking lot.

If someone *is* in trouble, he thought, it might be over before we get there.

He suddenly regretted that their cars had been disabled, and wished he hadn't taken such delight in their brief reprieve.

Jeremy stepped onto the landing. We must be at the ground floor, he thought. A door was there. Tanya tried to turn its knob, shook her head, and started up the next flight of stairs. Samson climbed them at her side. Karen went next, followed by Cowboy and Liz.

'I don't like this,' Heather whispered. She was behind Jeremy, holding onto the bottom of his jacket.

'I think we were *supposed* to come in after that guy,' Shiner said.

Jeremy's grimace made the wounds on his face stretch and sting. He wished Shiner hadn't said that. It was bad enough, being inside the funhouse, without having to worry about the possibility that they'd been *lured* into it. He thought about how gloomy the old, boarded place looked from the boardwalk. And it was right beside Jasper's Oddities. His mind lingered on what he'd seen in there – the Gallery of the Weird and those monstrous displays. The Oddities was part of the same damned building. It might even open into here.

At the next landing, the stairway ended. Those ahead of Jeremy halted. He climbed the final step. Looking past them, he saw a dark hallway.

'Wish we had some flashlights,' Samson whispered.

Tanya stepped to the wall and lifted the single candle out of its wrought-iron holder. She started slowly forward, and the others followed. Shiner, clutching Jeremy's left arm, pressed herself against his side and matched his small strides.

Tanya gasped, 'Jesus!' and lurched away from the wall as a hand darted out at her.

'Two bits, ducky?'

From the other wall, a hand snatched the hat off Cowboy's head. Blurting 'Shit!', he grabbed it back and stumbled against Liz.

'Oh Jeez!' Liz cried out. 'Jeez!'

Jeremy felt his guts shrivel. In front of him, trolls were *inside the walls*, faces pressed to barred openings, arms stretched out, hands grabbing for the kids as they hurried along. The trolls laughed, jeered, squealed with delight and yelled.

'Two bits! Gimme two bits!'
'Suck me, sweets!'
'How's about a buck!'
'Fun 'n games, fun 'n games!'
'Ours now!'

'Whee, yes!'

'Fuck me, fuck me!'

'Dead meat! You're all dead meat!'

Heather shrieked. Jeremy whirled around. A toothless crone, both arms outside the bars, had Heather by the sleeve of her jumpsuit. Jeremy slashed one of the hands. The old woman yelped and let go. Heather, still screaming, stumbled away and ran for the stairs. She bounded down the stairway and out of sight.

'Let's go with her!' Shiner shouted close to his ear.

'No!' he gasped. 'You go if you want. I'm sticking with Tanya.'

'Idiot!'

He went after the others. In the glow of Tanya's candle, he saw them hurrying single-file down the middle of the hallway, troll arms straining to reach them through the bars. A hand grabbed his shoulder, and he sucked a harsh breath before he realized it was only Shiner.

The hallway went dark.

Tanya's candle had gone out.

'A door!' he heard her yell over the frenzied voices of the trolls.

Reaching into the black, Jeremy touched cloth. Cowboy's denim jacket? He blurted, 'It's me,' and held on.

'Everybody in!' Tanya called. 'Quick, quick!'

'Jumping Judas!'

Jeremy lost his grip on Cowboy's jacket. His shoulder bumped something. A door frame? He stepped forward. His feet sank into a soft, springy substance.

'What is this?' Samson's voice.

'Foam rubber floor,' Liz said. 'It's a funhouse thing.'

'Some fun.'

'I want to get out of here!' Karen whined.

'Last one in, shut the door!' Tanya ordered.

He felt Shiner's hand release him. 'I've got it,' she said. He heard a door thump shut and latch, and the wild voices of the trolls faded to a dull murmur.

Richard Laymon

'Okay.' From Tanya. 'Everyone here?'

'Heather ran off,' Jeremy said.

'Reckon she's the smart one,' Cowboy said.

'Let's get out of here,' Karen pleaded.

'It's like they were waiting for us,' Samson said. 'I say we scram.'

'Yeah,' Liz agreed.

'We have to get the camera from that guy.'

'What for?' Samson asked. 'So he's got pictures. Kids on the boardwalk. Big deal. They don't prove nothing. This is bad shit, here.'

'Ain't worth it,' Cowboy said.

There was silence for a moment. Jeremy heard only his heartbeat, and the breathing of himself and others all around him.

All around him.

Shiner was at his side, and he thought the rest of them were ahead of him. But quiet sounds of breathing seemed to come from everywhere. The hot, stuffy air smelled foul.

'Okay,' Tanya said. 'We'll go back the way we came and get the hell out of here.'

Shiner held onto Jeremy's arm and stepped behind his back. He heard a harsh metallic rattle. Her fingers tightened their grip. 'The door's locked,' she whispered.

'Oh shit.'

'I don't think we're alone,' Liz said, the pitch of her voice climbing with panic.

Something soft and wet lapped the back of Jeremy's hand. His right hand. The one that held the knife flat against his leg.

Something licking it like a dog.

'Yaaah!' He jerked his hand up.

The black room erupted with gasps of alarm, yelps and shrieks and curses.

Shiner's hand flew away from his arm.

He wheeled around to find her. His leg was clutched, hugged tight to a body. He staggered, trying to stay up, but his feet sank into the deep rubber and he fell.

The assailant scurried up his legs. A stench of rotten garbage filled his nostrils. His shirt was torn open. Hair tickled his belly. A face pushed against him, and he felt its nose and whiskers, its dry lips, its quick wet tongue. He grabbed a handful of greasy hair, tugged the face away from him, and rammed his knife down. The blade punched in deep – somewhere near the middle of the back, Jeremy thought. The attacker cried out, jerked rigid and twisted away, rolling off Jeremy but wrenching the knife from his grasp.

He sat up fast and stared at the blackness in front of him. He blinked to make sure his eyes were open.

All around him were sounds of struggle.

Off the floor, he thought. It's the worst place to be.

He got to his knees. Someone tumbled against his back, knocking him forward. He scrambled, kicking at the body, freeing his legs. Gasped as his face met skin. He lurched backwards. A hand clamped his raw chin and tried to shove him away. As pain streaked from his wound, a voice in front of him said, 'Jeremy?'

The hand flew from his chin to his shoulder and pulled him closer. Shiner flung her arms around him.

Holding each other, they struggled to their feet. They took a few staggering steps, and bumped the rubber of a wall.

Off to the side, a vertical band of light appeared. Faint-yellowish light. Suddenly, the band spread wide.

'A door!' Shiner whispered.

Beyond it, a hallway glowed with candlelight.

Someone lurched through the doorway, escaping.

'Let's go!' Jeremy gasped.

Hanging onto each other, they rushed for the door. The way ahead of them was cluttered with the faint silhouettes of bodies struggling on the floor, others kneeling, some up and staggering. They dodged, leaped. Hands grabbed at them, and they kicked and twisted their way free. Someone lunged in from Shiner's side. Her elbow sent the troll hurling backward.

A dark shape blocked the doorway.

Jeremy threw himself at it.

Hands clutched his jacket, yanked him forward, and flung him into the lighted corridor. Tanya caught him. Turning away from her, he saw Samson tug Shiner out of the black room.

Cowboy was leaning against a wall, Liz sobbing against his chest.

The door slammed shut.

Samson tried the knob, then hit the door with his shoulder. It didn't give. He rammed it again.

'For godsake, don't!' Tanya blurted.

'Karen's not out.' He shot his foot forward, smashing it against the door just beside the knob. Still, the door stayed shut.

Samson turned around and leaned against the door frame, shaking his head. His face was twisted with an expression of horror.

Shiner put a hand over her mouth. She stared at Jeremy. Her eyes looked wide and dazed. She was breathing hard. Her white blouse was open to her belly, twisted and hanging off her left shoulder. Her shoulder was streaked with scratches. She had a bloody handprint on the white cup of her bra.

Jeremy went to her. Gently, he lifted the blouse onto her shoulder and drew the front shut. He put his arms around her. She was panting for air, trembling.

'It's all right,' he said. 'It's all right.'

Vaguely, he wondered why he had gone to Shiner instead of Tanya.

It felt good, though.

'Poor Karen,' she whispered.

'Let's worry about us,' Tanya said from somewhere behind Jeremy.

Shiner squeezed herself tightly against him.

Then, they separated. Shiner took hold of his hand.

Cowboy and Liz were still embracing. He had lost his hat. He still had his knife, though. It was a folding Buck knife with a wicked-looking blade. The blade was slick with blood. So was the hand that held it flat against the small of Liz's back while his other hand stroked her hair.

A rear pocket of her jeans hung like a flap below her rump. She had lost one of her sneakers.

Except for his mussed hair, Samson looked as if he hadn't been touched. But his arms were wrapped tightly around his chest, and Jeremy could see that he was shaking. If he still had his knife, it didn't show.

Tanya's knife was at her side, clenched in her right hand. The sleeve of her sweatshirt was drenched in blood to her elbow. The front of her sweatshirt, dark and sodden, clung to her breasts and belly. Her pants, too, looked drenched in blood from her waist to her knees.

A corner of her mouth turned up. 'Don't worry, Duke. It's not mine. Just this,' she added, and touched a knuckle to a torn crescent of skin over her left cheekbone. That side of her face was sheathed with blood. Trickles spilled off her jaw and ran down her neck.

He went to her, pulling the wadded handkerchief out of his pocket. He took the razor blade from it, dropped the blade into his shirt pocket, and gave the handkerchief to her.

'Thanks,' she muttered, pressing it to her wound. 'Guess what, Duke? Now you've got a good excuse for your face. You can tell your mom the trolls nailed you.'

'If I ever see her again,' he said.

'Don't worry, you will.' Looking towards the others, Tanya said, 'We'll all get out of here. Right?'

Only Samson answered. He said, 'Yeah, sure.'

'Let's get to it.' Tanya waited while the others gathered in close to her. Shiner took Jeremy's hand again. Her mouth twitched as she tried to smile. There was dread in her eyes.

Tanya took the lead.

This section of hallway had no barred openings in its walls. There was no sign of trolls.

Not until Jeremy's shoes scraped a metal grating on the floor and he looked down and saw the blur of a face. He sprang off the grille. 'They're under us!' he blurted.

Samson, standing on a similar panel just ahead of him, leaped forward.

Jeremy looked back. Cowboy swooped Liz up. Cradling her in his arms, he stepped onto the grate. He danced on it, stomping it with his boots.

Jeremy and Shiner continued through the hallway. Beneath the next grille were two faces. The trolls watched in silence as they took long strides and cleared the grate without stepping on it.

Jeremy heard Cowboy, still back there, prancing on the first grate. 'I'll be durned if I'm not starting to . . .'

A deafening clap pounded Jeremy's ears. Even as he whirled around, he knew he would see Cowboy dropping through the floor, Liz in his arms.

But he was wrong.

Cowboy still stood on the grate. Liz was falling. He was bringing up his knife as something swept down at him.

A man. A naked, burly man with a hairy back and a bald head. Swinging down head-first like a live pendulum from the trap door in the ceiling. Ropes around his ankles. A meat cleaver in each hand.

He yelled, 'Wheeeee!' as he flew towards Cowboy.

Cowboy hopped backwards. The cleavers flashed, trying for Liz. But she was flat on the floor. The blades chopped the air above her, missing by inches. The man began his upward arc, going for Cowboy with the cleavers.

Cowboy lunged at him and leaped backwards again. The body jerked, twisted on its ropes like a swing knocked crooked, and crashed against the wall. One of the cleavers sank into the wall. The other dropped to the floor.

Cowboy snatched that one up as the man swung downwards. Swung over Liz, showering her. Swung towards Jeremy and Shiner, spinning. The handle of Cowboy's knife jutted from his throat. He spouted blood and urine.

Cowboy jumped over Liz and threw himself against the man. Slammed him against the wall. Went at him with the cleaver. Shiner twisted her head away as Cowboy hacked him. The blow split him down the middle. Intestines slopped out like coils of wet snakes.

Jeremy doubled over, retching.

His vomit cascaded onto the grate at his feet.

Someone below him gasped, 'Ugh!'

When he finished and straightened up, Cowboy was helping Liz to her feet. The body hung in the middle of the hallway, swaying and turning. Jeremy didn't let himself focus on it. Instead, he watched Cowboy and Liz step past it.

Cowboy had a cleaver in one hand, his knife in the other. Liz held the second cleaver.

As she stepped past the body, she gave it a whack in the chest. The blow severed a small section of hanging guts, which fell past the man's face and hit the floor with a soft wet smack.

Jeremy gagged and covered his mouth. This time, he didn't throw up.

Cowboy grinned. His eyes and teeth were white. The rest of him was red. He looked as if a tub of gore had been dumped over his head. Jeremy could *smell* it. 'Weak stomach, Duke?'

'You sure creamed him.'

'Massacred the son of a whore, huh? No quarter.'

'Thought you were goners,' Samson said.

'Are you both all right?' Tanya asked. Her voice came from close behind Jeremy.

'I reckon I could use a bath,' Cowboy said.

Liz laughed and slapped his chest. Blood flew off his shirt like red dust.

'Okay,' Tanya said. 'Let's keep going. Everybody look sharp. God knows what we're gonna run into next.'

They started to walk. Jeremy stepped on gratings without any hesitation. They all stepped on the grates. As if the weird attack and Cowboy's slaughter of the swinging man had numbed them to such matters as trolls lurking below their feet.

They watched the ceiling. They watched the walls.

They came to the end of the hall.

On the right was a closed door. On the left was a dark opening.

Tanya pulled a candle from its holder, knelt in front of the opening, and leaned forward. The candle and her head vanished for a moment. Then she stood up. 'I don't know,' she said.

'What is it?'

'A slide.'

'A slide?' Samson asked.

'This is a fucking *funhouse*,' Liz reminded him.

'Where does it go?'

'It goes down,' Tanya said. 'I couldn't see much of it. But it should take us down to the ground floor.'

'Yeah,' Samson said. 'And whatever's waiting for us there.'

'Better than being up here.'

'Why don't we try that door?' Shiner asked.

'Good thought,' Liz said. '*You* try it.'

'No, don't,' Jeremy warned.

'I'll try the slide,' Tanya said.

'Don't,' Jeremy told her.

'What're we supposed to do, stay here? Let me borrow that chopper of yours, Cowboy.'

He held it out. Samson took it from him. 'I'll go down first,' he said. 'You guys wait up here till you hear from me.'

Tanya kissed his mouth.

Jeremy expected to feel a pang of jealousy, but he didn't. The guy deserves a kiss, he thought. Better him than me.

'Good man,' Tanya said. 'This is one I owe you.'

He made a sick-looking smile. Turning away, he sat on the floor. He scooted into the opening. Tanya gave him the candle. 'It'll probably blow out, anyway,' he said, but he kept it. He clutched the cleaver against his chest, hunched forward, and dropped out of sight.

Tanya knelt and peered in after him.

'Get ready to go fast,' she said. 'He'll need us.'

Suddenly, a shriek welled out of the opening. Not a shriek of fright, but a high ragged cry of agony.

'Samson!' Tanya yelled.

'Oh sweet Jesus!' Samson wailed. 'Oh, mother of . . . Ahhhh! Ahhhh!'

'What is it?' Tanya called.

'I'm . . . I'm . . . God, IT HURTS!'

'Should we come down?'

'NO! NO! For Godsake!'

'Maybe the door,' Shiner said. She squeezed Jeremy's arm, then rushed across the hallway.

'Wait!' he yelled.

She yanked the door open and lurched back fast. She whirled around, gasping, as the troll sprang out. A gawky, grey-faced man with a wild black beard. He grabbed the back of Shiner's blouse and yanked her off her feet. Jeremy leaped to save her. She was falling backwards, eyes bulging, hands reaching out for him. A cleaver, apparently thrown by Liz, flipped end over end and flashed past the man's head, just missing him, and vanished into the dark room at the back. Jeremy's fingers grazed Shiner's fingers. They flew away from him. He cried out, 'NO!' as she was hurled into the room. The door struck his upper arm, knocking him sideways, and slammed shut.

An instant before he threw himself against the door, Jeremy heard the clack of a sliding bolt. He clutched the knob, twisted it, tugged at it, crying 'NO! LET HER OUT! LET HER OUT, YOU BASTARD!'

He pounded the door, smashed at it with his shoulder, kicked at it.

The door stayed shut.

He sank to his knees, weeping.

Chapter Forty-three

Seconds after hearing the faint sound of the whistle, Robin saw a kid run out onto the boardwalk. He was the one, she guessed, who'd been left behind by the others to stand watch for the cops.

That's what the whistle meant.

The cops are coming.

I just have to last, she thought. They'll get me down.

If they know I'm here.

The kid was *so far* away.

He stopped in the middle of the boardwalk. There, he turned around in circles, probably wondering where his friends had gone. He looked like a little kid lost in a supermarket, trying to find his mom.

If he was calling, Robin couldn't hear him.

His head swung around as he glanced over his shoulder towards the Funland entrance. Then he ran straight ahead. Robin saw him start down the beach stairs. After that, her left arm blocked her view.

She looked down again.

No sign of the three trolls. But she knew where they had to be. Behind her. Probably on the Ferris wheel's platform. Probably trying to start the thing going.

She wished she could see what was happening back there.

A handcuff suddenly slipped up her left hand, scraping over the knuckle of her thumb. Her stomach seemed to drop out from under her. Gasping, she willed her fist to clench.

Her fingers tingled with the effort.

The cuff slipped up her hand.

CHRIST!

Her fingers hooked the curved rim of the bracelet, and she held on, heart suddenly thundering, feet kicking.

NOW! her mind shouted. NOW OR NEVER! CHRIST!

Right hand balled in a tight fist, left hand clinging to the cuff, she bent her arms at the elbows and drew herself upward. Higher, higher. The edge of the footrest rubbed against her rump, then against the backs of her thighs. Her muscles ached. The cuffs felt like knife blades pressing into her fingers and fist. She whimpered and groaned, pumped her legs as if trying to climb the rungs of a ladder that wasn't there. The gondola rocked, its footrest nudging her forward and easing away, swinging her.

Slowly, she rose until her bleeding left wrist was in front of her eyes. Then she came to her fingers squeezed tight over the curved steel of the bracelet, her other hand pinched inside the right cuff. She forced herself higher. Her eyes were inches from the connecting chain. Higher. Up to the safety bar. Higher until the bar was even with her chin.

Now what? she wondered.

Her arm muscles burned. She gritted her teeth. Sweat stung her eyes. Sweat or blood trickled down her sides and was turned cold by the ocean breeze.

GO FOR IT!

Robin gripped the safety bar with her right hand, released the cuff and grabbed hold with her left hand. She thrust her head forward, catching the bar under her chin.

Her sudden motions set the gondola rocking. Its footrest shoved at the backs of her knees.

Swinging by the bar, she jerked her legs up. When the footrest swept forward again, it brushed the bottoms of her feet. She flung herself away from the bar, thrusting her body backwards, and tumbled onto the seat. The gondola pitched madly as if it wanted to toss her out. She spread-eagled herself, jamming her heels against the metal lip of its floor, shoving herself hard against the seatback, grabbing the sides.

Soon, the gondola slowed to a gentle sway.

Robin brought her arms down, slid her legs together. She sat there for a few moments, shuddering and gasping for breath.

I made it, she thought.

My God, I made it!

With the thumb and forefinger of her right hand, she pinched the head of the pin and gave it a quick pull. The pin slid out of her chest. The breeze lifted the card free and sent it tumbling away into the night. Robin tossed the pin after it. The hole felt sore and itchy. In a way, it seemed more irritating than her other wounds. They were serious hurts, but this one was pesky. She rubbed it with the heel of her hand.

When it felt better, she lowered the hand onto her lap and pulled the cuff off. She dropped the cuffs onto the seat. She flexed her hands. Though they still felt a little numb, blood was beginning to circulate better. Her fingers tingled as if they'd been asleep.

A chilly gust buffeted her. Gritting her teeth, she folded her arms across her chest, cupped a breast in the warmth of each hand, and squeezed her legs together.

Now all I've got to worry about, she thought, is dying of exposure.

She suddenly remembered the three trolls somewhere below. Icy fear spread through the pit of her stomach.

They can't get me, she told herself.

If they could start the wheel going, they would've done it before now.

Maybe they're just lying low until the cops . . .

The cops!

Robin leaned slowly forward and gripped the safety bar. She peered past the side of the gondola. The area near Funland's main entrance was deserted. She scanned the entire length of the boardwalk. The moonwashed planking looked grey as driftwood. The shadows were black smudges.

Maybe the kid's whistle had been a false alarm.

Maybe he saw cops, but they were on the way to some other destination.

Give them time, she told herself.

Though it seemed like forever since the kid blew his whistle, it was probably no more than two or three minutes ago.

They might still show up.

The thought no sooner passed through her mind than a dark figure stepped out of the entryway's shadows. Robin caught her breath. Then let it out, sighing with frustration.

This wasn't a cop, it was a goddamn troll. She shuffled along, hunched over like an old witch, wrapped in a blanket that covered her head.

Wait!

That girl who'd warned the others – she'd said her sister the cop would be coming dressed as a troll.

That's her!

Robin scooted across the seat, leaned as far as she dared over the safety bar, thrust an arm out, waved and shouted.

In the middle of the boardwalk, Joan slowly turned around.

No one.

Where the hell are they? she wondered.

Somebody *had* to be here. There'd been the whistle. There was the car parked in front, its engine running.

Shouldn't have wasted time at the car, she thought. That had eaten up a minute or two.

The car might be all we'll get, she told herself. It had been hot-wired, obviously stolen. Maybe by the same people who nailed Gloria.

But where are they now?

And where's their victim?

Somebody in the back seat had bled.

They must be around here.

At least they won't be driving off on us, she thought.

While Dave was copying the licence plate number, Joan had cut the ignition wires with her knife, then rolled up the windows and locked the doors.

They aren't going anywhere. Not in that car.

She turned around and shook her head. 'The place looks deserted,' she said.

A silhouette, backlighted by the glow from the parking lot, appeared in the darkness beside the ticket booth. 'What do you want to do?' Dave asked.

'They've gotta be somewhere.'

'Do you want me out there with you?'

'It'd blow the cover.'

'If they've already got someone, they might not try for you anyway.'

That was true enough. And the whistle might've been blown by a sentry, warning his friends that intruders were on the way. They might have fled up the beach, or scattered and hidden themselves somewhere among the rides or buildings of Funland.

'Just stay close enough to keep an eye on me,' Joan said. 'I'll head on down the boardwalk, see if I can draw them . . .'

'Behind you!'

She whirled around. Two pale figures rushing up the stairs from the beach.

Their hands were empty.

A boy and a girl.

No threat from these two, Joan thought.

The guy had a slight build, and wore glasses that gleamed in the moonlight. A chrome whistle hung from a chain around his neck. The huffing girl beside him had a face as round as a bowling ball. She was dressed in a jumpsuit that bulged over bouncing piles of fat.

Could these be trollers?

A wimp and a blimp.

But they might have friends nearby, watching, waiting to pounce.

Joan released the grips of her .38 and took her hand out from under her sweatshirt. She held the hand towards them, palm up.

Might as well play it to the hilt, she thought.

Hope they didn't hear Dave.

Still a few strides away from her, the two kids halted. They glanced at each other. They were both out of breath.

'How's about a couple of bits?' Joan croaked. 'Ain't had me a bit t'eat in . . .'

'I think we need help, officer,' the boy said.

Officer?

'Something awful's happening,' the girl suddenly blurted. 'I got away. I got out and I don't know what's going on, but I think it's awfully bad. The trolls. Trolls in the walls. You gotta come.'

'Dave!' Joan called over her shoulder.

He hurried forward. He had his Beretta out, barrel raised beside his head.

'They've made me. They say there's some kind of trouble.'

'Pat 'em down,' Dave said. 'Hands on your heads, kids, and interlace your fingers.'

'We haven't done anything,' the boy protested, but he followed instructions. So did the girl.

'What're you doing out here?'

'Nothing.'

'We'd better let them talk,' Joan said. Flinging her blanket off, she stepped behind the boy and started to frisk him. 'Something's going down.'

'The others . . .' the girl said. 'We went in a . . . a basement . . . and . . .'

'Let's hear about last night,' Dave said. 'Tell us about the troll you got last night.'

Joan felt a long, hard bulge in the boy's right front pocket. 'Got something here.'

'We didn't do anything last night,' the boy said. 'If you waste time giving us the third degree about some stupid . . .!'

Joan stuffed her hand into his pocket.

'Hey! You don't have a search warrant. I've got my rights!'

'You've got the right to shut up,' Joan said.

'Please!' the girl whined. 'Our friends!'

'Your friends are trollers,' Dave said. 'If they've gotten into a mess, too damn bad. Let's go back to last night.'

Joan pulled a knife from the boy's pocket. She thumbed a button on its handle. The blade sprang out and locked. 'Switchblade,' she said. She closed it, and tossed it underhand to Dave. He glanced at it. He pushed it into a pocket of his jeans.

'You kids are in deep shit,' he said. 'Now, I want to hear everything you know about a woman you and your friends nailed here last night.'

Done frisking the boy, Joan stepped behind the girl and started to pat her down. Her flesh felt loose and soft under the velours jumpsuit.

'We weren't here last night,' the boy said. 'I don't know what you're talking about.'

The girl began to sob. 'They're gonna be killed! They're *all* gonna be killed! I just know it!'

'She's clean,' Joan said.

'Okay. Well, we've got this one on a weapons charge.'

Joan stepped in front of them. 'Where are the others?' she asked.

'They want to *bust* me. Don't tell them.'

'I have to! It was so bad! You weren't there, you don't know how bad it was.'

The boy's face twisted with indecision.

'They aren't gonna bust you, Randy. They can't. If they bust you, they've gotta bust her sister, and . . .'

Joan's heart lurched. 'Whose sister?'

'Yours,' the boy said.

'Shiner,' the girl said. 'Betty.'

'Debbie,' the boy corrected her.

Joan went cold and rigid.

'Jesus Christ,' Dave muttered.

Debbie. A troller. No, that was impossible.

Trolls in the walls.

They're gonna be killed! They're all gonna be killed!

'Show us where they are,' Joan said.

'No.' The kid grabbed the girl's sleeve and glared at Joan. 'First you have to promise you won't . . .'

Joan's open hand hit his face. His head snapped sideways. His glasses flew off and skidded across the boards.

'Move it!' she yelled in the girl's face.

The girl swung around and trotted towards the stairs, Joan close behind her.

'It'll be all right,' Dave said.

'NO!' Robin shouted. 'COME BACK!'

But they didn't hear her. They'd heard none of her yells. They'd never even glanced in her direction.

She was just too far away, too great a distance down the boardwalk and too high up for her voice to reach them through the sounds of the wind and surf.

Clinging to the side of the gondola, she watched the fat girl rush down the stairs to the beach, followed by the woman and man. The kid bent down. He picked up his glasses and put them on, stood there for a few moments as if he didn't know what to do, then ran to catch up with the others.

All four of them disappeared beneath the boardwalk.

Robin groaned.

She leaned further out over the side of the gondola, and peered down.

The platform beside the Ferris wheel was deserted.

Where had the trolls gone?

Twisting her head around, she saw them.

On the wheel. Climbing its struts and spokes. Coming for her.

Chapter Forty-four

'You won't do Shiner any good crying about it,' Tanya said. She pulled Jeremy to his feet. Through his tears, he saw Cowboy step to the door, jerk its knob, shake his head. 'We've gotta keep going,' Tanya said. Her open hands rubbed his chest.

'She was just here 'cause of me.'

'She was a troller like the rest of us. She took her chances, month after month, before you even came along.'

'Can't we do something?'

'She's likely dead as monkey shit by now,' Cowboy said.

'You've gotta be brave,' Tanya said. 'For me. You're my soldier. You're my lover.' She pulled him gently toward her. She lifted the bloody front of her sweatshirt. Though Cowboy and Liz were right there, probably watching, neither of them said a word. Tanya rubbed her breasts against him. They felt a little sticky from the blood that had soaked through her sweatshirt, but they were smooth and soft.

This is wrong, Jeremy thought. Wrong for her to do this ... everything that's happened ... Shiner ... Shiner's gone ... I couldn't save her ... Shouldn't be doing this to me ...

Even as tears rolled down his cheeks and his breath hitched with sobs, he felt heat spreading low inside him.

'You're my brave lover,' Tanya said.

Jeremy took one of her breasts in his hand and caressed it. 'Yes,' she said. 'Yes, feel me. I'm alive. I'm yours.' She squeezed him gently through the front of his pants. 'When we're out of here, you'll have me.'

He sniffed and nodded.

'That's in case savin' your own hide ain't incentive enough,' Cowboy said.

Tanya backed away from Jeremy. She pulled her sweatshirt down and turned to the opening low in the wall. She squatted. 'Samson?'

No answer.

Jeremy hadn't noticed any sounds from Samson since the moment Shiner opened the door and ...

He saw it all again in his mind – the horrible troll, the stunned, pleading look on Shiner's face, the cleaver flying by, the door slamming. To be locked in a room with that monster ... Oh, God!

She'd told him once that her greatest fear was to be caught by trolls. Now, it had happened.

Jeremy hoped she *was* dead. Hoped that she had died quickly. So much better than to be alive while that hideous troll *did things* to her.

I'm sorry, he thought. God, Shiner, I'm so sorry. It's my fault. If only I'd gone to your house tonight ...

'Samson must've bit it,' Cowboy said.

'This is our only way out,' Tanya said.

'I'll go down,' Jeremy said. He sniffed and wiped his eyes. 'I'll go first.'

Tanya nodded. 'Okay. Good man.'

'Let's try to lower him down,' Liz said. 'You know, hang onto him.'

'Good,' Tanya said. 'Go down headfirst, I'll hang onto your feet and go down after you. Liz, you take my feet.'

'I'll be the anchor,' Cowboy said.

Tanya gave her knife to Jeremy. She took a candle off the wall, and gave it to him.

Holding the knife and candle out ahead of him, Jeremy lay on the floor and squirmed forward, thrusting himself along with his elbows and knees. The metal sheet of the slide below his face shimmered golden in the candle light. There were wooden walls on both sides, a wooden ceiling about three feet above the ramp. Not far down the slide, darkness swallowed the meagre light. He squinted, but saw nothing in that darkness.

'Can you see him?' Tanya asked.

'No. I can't see much.' He scooted forward, bending at the waist. First his elbows and chest, then his belly met the cool slick surface. He felt Tanya's hands wrap around his ankles. They held him, pushed him, and in seconds the entire length of his body was stretched flat against the slide.

For a few moments, he didn't move. Then he started downward again. He pictured Tanya above him, being lowered as he'd been.

'See anything?' Tanya asked.

'Not yet.'

'Here I come,' Liz said.

Jeremy slid lower, lower. At the dim border of his candle's glow, he saw the head and shoulders of Samson. 'I see him! Samson? Samson?' The boy neither answered nor moved. 'It's like he's stopped here.'

'Is he dead?' Tanya asked.

'I don't know. I guess so.'

'Can you tell what happened to him?'

'Huh-uh.'

He stretched his arms out. His fists pushed against the tops of Samson's shoulders. He shoved at the body. It shook slightly, but didn't slide away. 'He's stuck,' Jeremy said.

'Can you get past him?'

'I don't know. Maybe you'd better let go of my feet,' He felt

Tanya release him. He raised his head. Samson's eyes and mouth were wide open. The arms were raised from the elbows, fingers hooked down as if he had died clawing at the darkness.

'Do something,' Tanya said.

'Yeah. Okay.' He lifted his fists and slid until his throat pushed against the top of Samson's head and his elbows met the dead boy's shoulders.

There, with the candle high, he gazed down the length of the body. He saw no wounds. But Samson's legs were spread, and below them the slide gleamed with blood.

Not far beyond Samson's feet was the end of the slide.

'I see the bottom,' Jeremy announced.

'What happened with Samson?'

'I think there must be knives or something under him. I think they're in the slide.'

'Jesus,' Tanya muttered.

'Okay, I'm going over him.'

Jeremy pushed himself up, clamped Tanya's knife in his teeth to free his right hand, and began to move forward, squirming, lifting himself onto the body. The head turned sideways under his chest. He felt the tickle of Samson's hair, the bristle of his whiskers. He had a sudden fear of the clawed hands, so he pushed Samson's arms down before squirming further. The body wobbled under him. It slipped a few inches, and he heard wet ripping sounds as he rode it. When the body halted, Jeremy studied the bloody slide to make sure there were no blades waiting for him, then scurried over the rest of Samson, wanting off him fast no matter what might be in the darkness below. He felt the head press against his groin. He felt the cool damp of Samson's jeans against his chest, then the slippery metal of the slide. He grabbed the boy's leg as if it were a banister, using it to ease him along, to slow his descent and prevent the candle from blowing out.

Holding onto Samson's shoe, he glided to the lip of the slide. He listened. He heard nothing except his thudding heart, his gasping breath, and sounds of movement on the slide behind him.

If trolls were waiting for him, they were being very quiet. Candle in front of him, he dragged himself forward. The floor was a yard below his face. He raised his head and swung it from side to side. In the light of the candle, he saw a section of hallway.

He saw no trolls.

He scurried off the slide and stood up. He scanned the darkness beyond the candle's glow. Then he turned to the slide. 'I'm down,' he called, his voice rasping and shaky. 'I don't see anyone. It looks okay.'

'I'm on my way,' Tanya said.

'Hurry.'

'There,' the girl said. She pointed. Dave swept his flashlight past a piling. It lit the concrete wall of a building's foundation. The wall was scribbled with grafitti. 'More to the right,' the girl said. He moved the light. The pale disk of its beam found a patch of boards. 'It's a door. It opens up. They went in there. It's the funhouse. We were chasing some guy.'

Dave stepped past Joan and rushed to the wall. He clamped the flashlight under his arm, and pulled at the edge of the boards. They swung outwards. He leaned into the opening. A small enclosure. Lighted candles on the walls. A staircase leading upwards. He looked over his shoulder, but couldn't see anyone back there. 'They went up the stairs?' he asked.

'Yeah,' came the girl's voice. 'We all did. But I chickened out and ran. All those trolls.'

'All right,' Joan said. 'You two get out of here. Go home.'

'Aren't you arresting me?' the boy asked.

'No. Go home.'

'Jeez. Thanks.'

'Sorry I hit you, kid. Now go!'

Seconds later, Dave saw the dim shape of Joan rushing towards him. She came into the faint light from the candles, reached under her sweatshirt and pulled out her revolver. Her face, smeared with grime from the tyre of her car, was intended to make her resemble a troll. Instead, she looked like a

397

commando camouflaged for a night raid. Dave saw fear in her eyes. And outrage.

'We'll get her,' he said.

'Bet your ass we will,' Joan said, and rushed past him.

'Hold it!' he snapped.

She stopped and looked around.

'I go first. Stay with me. Stay *glued* to me, damn it.'

Joan nodded.

Flashlight in one hand, pistol in the other, Dave bounded up the stairs, taking them three at a time. At the first landing, he covered Joan while she tried the door. It was locked. They raced up the stairway to the second floor.

In front of Dave was a dark hallway. He swept it with his flashlight. Nobody ahead. But his blood seemed to freeze when he saw barred, window-like openings along the walls.

Trolls in the walls.

He saw no trolls, though.

He flinched as something nudged him. Just Joan. Pressing against his back.

'Don't stop,' she whispered.

He started forward, shining his light from wall to wall. Faces rose behind the bars. The dirty, leering faces of men and women. A small whimper came from Joan.

All along the corridor ahead, arms reached out, flopping and waving like the tentacles of a beast that lived in the walls.

Dave rushed forward, Joan at his back.

The trolls in the walls laughed and jeered, begged for coins, tittered, snapped obscenities and threats. Fingertips brushed Dave's arms, plucked at his sleeves. Someone yelped, but it was the outcry of an injured man, and Dave guessed that Joan had struck one of the reaching hands.

At least she's not blowing the bastards away, he thought.

He was tempted, himself, but he kept his finger off the trigger.

He batted a hand away with the barrel of his flashlight.

As the beam of his flashlight skittered through the dark, it lit a door in front of him.

* * *

Robin knelt on the seat of the gondola, clutching its back. She gazed down through the maze of wires, unlighted bulbs, struts and spokes at the three trolls who were slowly climbing the Ferris wheel.

'Pritty pritty,' called the nearest one. He was about twenty feet away, climbing a spoke that would lead him to the highest gondola. Once there, he would be able to come at her along the outer wheel, which had only a gradual slant before it met the side of Robin's carriage.

He was lean, grey-faced, bald except for a fringe of hair around his ears. He wore a dark suitcoat and slacks that looked as if they'd been made to fit a much larger man. The wind fluttered his clothes, and he was near enough for Robin to hear their quiet flapping. 'Gonna getcha!' he squealed.

'Yessir. Don' go nowhere, pritty!' He wheezed out a laugh as if he thought that was a great joke.

'I get her first, you piece of shit,' snapped the man below him. The one with the patch on his eye.

His voice was strong. He didn't sound crazy or loaded.

The third troll was lower than the other two, apparently climbing with more caution. He seemed like a distant threat.

These creeps will get to me long before he does, Robin thought.

The one in the oversized suit grabbed the side of the uppermost gondola. He turned his face to her and grinned. 'Ooooo, yer all mi . . .'

He shrieked as the one-eyed troll tugged a cuff of his trousers, yanking him downward. He kicked and squirmed for a moment, then lost his hold and tumbled away. Robin caught her own breath as she watched him fall, twisting through the moonlight. He landed head-first on the platform. The Ferris wheel shook with his impact.

The one-eyed troll climbed to the side of the upper gondola. Instead of getting into it, he pulled himself onto the narrow steel beam of the outer wheel. Straddling the beam, he began to work his way towards Robin.

* * *

On the floor at the foot of the slide, Jeremy found another candle. He supposed Samson had dropped it. He used his candle to ignite its wick. The light seemed to double around him. He spotted the meat cleaver. It must've flown off the end of the slide, for it lay in the middle of the hallway.

Holding both candles in his left hand, he squatted and snatched up the cleaver and hurried back to the slide.

He watched Tanya crawl out. She pulled herself forward, walking her hands over the floor. Her sweatpants hung around her knees. Her bare rump and the backs of her legs looked wonderful in the soft glow of the candles.

She dropped onto the floor, rolled onto her back, and lay there gasping.

Jeremy felt as if his breath were being sucked out.

'Look there,' someone whispered.

'Yummy, yum yum yum.'

'Poke her, young fella,' urged the raspy voice of a woman.

Jeremy's stomach clenched. Tanya gasped, jerked the sweatpants to her waist and bolted up.

'Awww.'

'Havin' fun yet, kiddies?'

Raising his candles high, Jeremy looked up. Grates on the ceiling. Faces pressed to the strips of metal.

'Fucking trolls!' Tanya snapped.

A string of drool spilled onto her forehead. She wiped it off with a bloody sleeve, grabbed Jeremy's arm and pulled him close to the wall so they no longer stood beneath any of the grates.

'I'd like to kill 'em all,' he whispered.

His remark brought laughter and jeers down from the ceiling.

As they waited, he handed Tanya's knife back, and gave her one of the candles.

Liz crawled out of the opening, stood up and joined them.

'Another girlie.'

'More the merrier.'

'Hurry it up, Cowboy!' Liz called.

'Cowboy?' A troll giggled. 'They got 'em a cowboy.'

'Strip down, gals. Gimme a peek. C'mon, be nice.'

'Eat shit,' Liz snapped.

'Lemme eat you!'

Finally, Cowboy came out. But not headfirst, like the others. His boots appeared. He crawled backwards, dragging Samson after him. The huge body tumbled off the slide, smashing Cowboy to the floor.

The back of Samson's jeans were ripped and bloody. A slab of flesh from his inner thigh hung out. One blade had done that. A second had split his inseam. The sight made a cold ache in Jeremy's groin.

Cowboy crawled clear, and Tanya crouched beside Samson. 'Two big knife blades sticking up right outa the slide,' Cowboy said. He spoke loudly to be heard over the laughter, squeals of delight and remarks from the trolls in the ceiling. 'Fuckin'-A. All I could do to get him off the things. One of 'em got him right in the nuts.'

'One must've clipped his femoral,' Tanya said. 'That's why he died so fast. You don't last a minute when that gets hit.'

'Must've been one bad sucker of a minute,' Cowboy said.

Tanya patted Samson's back. Then, she stood up. 'Okay, let's get going.'

'I ain't gonna leave him here,' Cowboy said.

'That's crazy,' Liz said.

'He's too big for us to carry,' Tanya said. 'We'll be lucky to get out of this hell-hole ourselves, we sure can't make it hauling around a stiff.'

'No way I'm leaving Samuel here. He was my friend. What do you suppose these fuckin' trolls'll do to him when we're gone?'

'He's dead,' Liz said. 'He isn't gonna care.'

'Well, I reckon I care.'

He rolled the body over, took hold of its hand, and pulled it to a sitting position. Jeremy crouched at Samson's back, and lifted. Then Tanya joined in.

They raised Samson off the floor. Cowboy ducked and hoisted the body in a fireman's carry.

Just the way Samson carried that fat old troll to the Ferris wheel, Jeremy thought. Only Cowboy was a lot smaller than Samson.

'You got him okay?' Tanya asked.

'Yeah.'

Liz stayed at his side, and Jeremy walked with Tanya.

He kept the cleaver in his right hand and held the candle ahead of him, squinting, trying to see beyond its glow as they made their slow way through the corridor. The trolls went silent behind them. There didn't seem to be any openings in the floor, walls or ceiling along this section of the hall. That was a relief, but Jeremy half expected an attack at any moment, and he knew it might come from anywhere.

It's up to me, he thought.

With Samson dead and Cowboy burdened under the big guy, Jeremy felt as if he had become the group's main protector.

I'll take care of them, he told himself. Me. Duke. I'm the main man, now.

He felt a small flicker of pride.

Just ahead of him, the hallway suddenly looked *round*.

'I'll check it out,' he whispered, and took quick strides past Tanya.

He stopped at the edge of a contraption that looked like an enormous barrel lying on its side. A wooden barrel. Its inside walls bristled with spikes that gleamed in the light of his candle.

He nudged the rim with his foot.

His touch started the barrel into a slow spin.

Tanya brushed against his side. 'Real cute,' she muttered.

'We can't go this way,' Jeremy said.

Liz appeared at his other side, and peered at the turning cylinder. 'Shit. They sure rigged this damn place. How're we gonna get through there? It'll tear us to pieces.'

'We'll get through,' Tanya said. 'Cowboy, haul Samuel on over here.'

Chapter Forty-five

Dave swung the door open. He probed the room with his flashlight, and what he saw made him want to run from the funhouse. But he knew they couldn't leave without Debbie. He stepped inside. 'Police officers!' he snapped. 'Drop your weapons! Up against the wall!'

Joan entered. 'Oh dear God,' she muttered. The door bumped shut.

Shoulder to shoulder, they swept their handguns back and forth as the powerful beam of Dave's flashlight moved through the darkness.

The trolls climbed off each other. They climbed off sprawled, motionless bodies. They shambled to the right side of the room, a couple of them tossing knives to the soft rubber floor, and pressed their backs against the wall. About a dozen of them. Most wore little or nothing. All were drenched with blood.

Four bodies remained on the floor.

Two males, two females.

Naked and mauled. Dave saw caved-in faces, eyeless sockets, slashed throats, a severed arm, a man whose chest had been stripped of skin. He saw worse, and jerked his flashlight away from the carnage. He stared at the trolls lined up against the walls.

'What *are* you?' he whispered.

A wizened old crone cackled, raised a hand from her side and said, 'What're you? What're you?' As she spoke, her hand worked, moving the 'mouth' of the bloody sock it wore. Dave aimed his pistol at her face.

'Bullet in the bean,' her sock puppet chanted. 'Slug in the noodle. Bad for the brain-pan, that.'

'Shut up!'

Joan stepped forward. She stood over one of the female corpses. Dave lit it for her.

It was young and slender. The legs stuck straight out to the sides as if a couple of trolls had played tug-o-war with them. Not much was left of the breasts. Nothing was left of the face.

'It's not Debbie,' Joan muttered.

How could she tell?

Dave couldn't bring himself to ask.

He saw for himself that the other mutilated female wasn't Joan's sister. This corpse was fat.

Joan stepped over the body. Turning around, she walked backward toward the door at the other end of the room. 'Let's go,' she said.

Dave swept his light over the trolls at the wall. 'What about these . . . things?'

'I don't care. Let's just leave 'em.'

'After what they've done?'

'I don't care. I want Debbie.'

Dave started across the room, shining his light on the bodies, stepping around them, his shoes sinking into the soft rubber mat, sliding on the blood. He aimed the beam forward to light Joan's way. He shone it on the trolls along the wall.

Joan waited until he was close to her, then opened the door.

'Anybody comes out after us is dead,' he warned. Then he followed Joan through the doorway. He pulled the door shut and tried its knob. The door was locked. But just from this side, probably.

He backed away from it, pistol ready in case it should fly open, half hoping the trolls would make a try for them.

* * *

Jeremy, crouching, put his cleaver on the floor and gripped one of the steel spikes to hold the barrel as steady as possible while Tanya crawled through. In the light from her candle, he could see Liz and Cowboy at the other end, also gripping spikes. Their efforts weren't enough to keep the barrel from rocking slightly from side to side while Tanya made her way over Samson.

It sickened him to think they were using the boy this way. But none of them could've got through alive if they hadn't dropped the body across the bottom of the barrel. Samson was tall enough to stretch most of the way from one end to the other, and thick enough to absorb the full length of the four-inch spikes.

Must have twenty or thirty in him, Jeremy thought.

Samson can't feel them.

If he knew what was going on, he might even be happy about it. He was like a bridge that might get his friends out of here. And he would probably like the idea of Tanya squirming over him like that.

Tanya was almost out, now. She stopped, sank down against Samson, kissed his lips and whispered, 'Thank you, Samuel.'

They're all calling him Samuel now, Jeremy realized. As if it weren't right to use his nickname anymore.

Tanya raised herself. Kneeling on Samson's chest, high up near his shoulders, she reached out. Jeremy set his candle on the floor. He grabbed her wrists and pulled as she sprang forward.

They stumbled together away from the barrel.

When they crouched down to hold it for Liz, it was rocking slowly, lifting Samson's body from one side to the other. In spite of the motion, he didn't slip or slide at all. He might have been glued to the thing. But he wasn't.

Robin pressed her shuddering body tight against the back of the seat and watched the troll scoot slowly along the Ferris wheel's rim.

He was almost near enough to reach her.

She prayed that he would fall.

Though he moved cautiously, he didn't seem afraid of that. His legs were hugging the narrow beam, his hands sliding forward, gripping it, pulling himself closer to her. He never looked down at his hands. His single eye stayed on Robin.

She had thought about trying to get away. She had even turned from him, for just a few moments, peered over the front of the gondola, and weighed her chances of reaching the safety of the next car down.

It was about eight to ten feet below her, but farther out. Too far out to attempt a leap into its seat. More than likely, she would miss and fall behind it. She might be able to shinny down one of the outer wheels which slanted down from the side of her gondola, but even that seemed like too great a risk.

Face it, she'd thought, you're a chicken.

She'd spent too long out there, dangling in mid air.

Besides, getting to a lower gondola would be no more than a temporary solution.

It would put her closer to the other troll, who was still a good distance below.

Unless she was ready to try climbing all the way down . . .

No way.

I'll make my stand right here, thank you.

Now, with the one-eyed troll no more than an arm's length away, she wondered if she had made the right choice.

'Don't come any closer,' she said. 'I'll knock you down, damn it!'

A grin slid up his face.

Robin reached down to the seat. The cuffs lay there beside her right knee. She curled her fingers inside one of the bracelets.

'I'm warning you,' she said.

'I'm trembling.'

Hanging onto the seatback, she thrust herself away as the troll's left hand dropped onto its edge. He leaned towards her, the gondola rocking under his weight. Before he could lurch forward and pounce in beside her, she grabbed his wrist. She tore his fingers from the seat, shot her other hand up from beside her leg, and swung at him. The loose cuff, flying at the end of its short chain, lashed his cheek. The impact knocked his head sideways. His mouth jerked open in pain. Robin twisted on her knees, yanking his clutched wrist across her body, tearing him off the beam and letting go.

The troll yelped with alarm.

His right hand caught the back of the gondola. His left hand batted the air. Before it could find a hold – while he hung only by his right hand, twisting and kicking – Robin clawed his fingers off the edge.

He dropped straight down, yelling, 'NOOOOOO!'

Joan had felt stunned and disgusted by the carnage in the dark room, nearly numb with worry about Debbie, but only a little frightened.

This spooked her.

A man hanging by his feet in the middle of the hallway. Waiting for them.

She felt as if an icy snake were squirming through her bowels. A chill climbed her back. Goosebumps swept up her legs and arms, prickled her face and the nape of her neck. Her nipples went achy and hard. Under her tight stocking cap, her scalp seemed to crawl.

She halted and stared at the man.

What's he doing there!

He didn't move.

Just waited, hanging in shadows, not quite reached by the light of the few candles glowing along the walls of the corridor. Something about his indistinct shape made Joan suspect he was naked. And something about his shape was wrong.

She raised her revolver, aimed at him, and started walking closer.

'How does it look ahead?' Dave asked.

She glanced around at him. He was still walking backwards, keeping his eyes on the door of the dark room. 'See for yourself,' she said.

He turned. 'Jesus!'

He swung his flashlight forward. Its beam found the hanging man.

He groaned.

Joan felt an odd mixture of revulsion and relief. The guy looked sickening, his guts drooping out like that, but this wasn't any worse than what she had seen in the room. She was glad to know that he was dead. He wasn't so scary anymore.

Dave turned the flashlight away from him.

Joan waited for Dave to come up beside her, then quickened her pace. When they neared the body, he hurried ahead. He kept his flashlight off it. He turned sideways, back to the wall, and stepped past it. Joan did the same.

Then she ran behind him. A couple of times, she heard metal gratings ring under her shoes.

She recalled the stories of how Jasper Dunn used to lurk in his funhouse and peer up skirts. This must be where he'd done it, she thought.

The next time she came to one, she glanced down and saw the faint, pale blur of a face. She gasped.

Dave's head snapped round.

'Nothing,' she said. 'Keep going.'

She saw more faces beneath the slatted panels.

A goddamn audience.

Dave halted. He had come to the end of the hallway. On the right was a closed door. On the left was an opening low in the wall.

He went to the opening, knelt down, and shined his light inside. 'Christ,' he muttered.

'What?'

'It's a slide.'

Joan crouched behind him and looked over his shoulder. The slide gleamed like silver. Three-quarters of the way down, twin blades stood upright as if hunting knives had been plunged in through the back of the metal ramp. The blades and the lower portion of the slide were smeared with blood.

'Somebody went down it,' Dave whispered.

Joan squeezed his shoulders.

Not Debbie, she thought. *It wasn't Debbie. Please.*

'The others must've gone a different way,' she said. 'I don't know. After the first kid, the rest of them might've got past the knives okay.'

'Crawling over him?' *Or her*.

'Yeah.'

'God.'

'Let's see about that door,' Dave said.

He gave the flashlight to Joan. She stood in the centre of the hallway, left hand at her hip, shining the light on the door, right arm extended, aiming, finger ready on the trigger of her Smith & Wesson. She knew by the door's hinges that it would swing outward when it opened.

Dave positioned himself to the right of the door, his weapon raised, its muzzle close to the frame. Reaching across his body with his left hand, he turned the knob and tugged.

The door stayed shut.

He looked at Joan and shook his head.

'Why don't we shoot it open?' she said.

'If it's locked, the kids didn't go this way.'

'Maybe it locked behind them.'

'I think they took the slide.'

'Well, we can't.'

A bolt snicked.

Dave flinched. Joan's heart lurched.

He threw the door wide.

'Freeze!' Joan snapped.

The bloody thing on its knees in the doorway smiled. 'Don't shoot, Joanie.'

'We couldn't get him out of there if we wanted to,' Tanya said.

'And we don't want to,' Liz added.

'I sure hate to just leave him for the trolls,' Cowboy said.

'We left Shiner,' Jeremy reminded him.

'And Karen,' Tanya added. 'Don't worry, we'll figure a way to get them out. We'll put in a call to the cops, or something. But first we've got to get ourselves out of here in one piece.'

'Yeah, I reckon.'

'You want this back?' Jeremy asked, offering the cleaver.

'You go on and keep it. I've got my toad-sticker.' He turned around and said, 'Adios, there, Samuel.'

They started walking down the hallway, Tanya and Jeremy in the lead, Cowboy and Liz close behind them.

They stopped at a set of double doors.

Jeremy's stomach knotted.

Tanya muttered, 'Shit.'

Jeremy kicked one of the doors. It flew open, and he lurched backwards as he glimpsed someone in the candlelit room ahead of him – a skinny kid, red with blood, holding a candle. As the door swept back at him, he realized that the kid was himself.

He pushed the door wide and held it open.

Saw himself holding it open.

The room, about three times the width of the hallway, was panelled with mirrors. The candles standing upright on its floor reminded Jeremy of the spikes in the barrel. The surrounding mirrors multiplied their number, and filled the room with tongues of brilliant fire.

No mirrors on the ceiling. Up there were grates. For the spectators.

The mirrors in front of Jeremy showed only him and candles – no waiting trolls. He stepped through the door.

As the others came in, he wandered beneath the nearest grate and saw a dirty, bearded face above him. 'Hiya, kid. How come y'ain't dead yet?'

'Fuck you,' he said.

'Scrappy little pisser, ain't ya?'

Jeremy raised his candle high, stretching upward, rising on tiptoes. Its flame licked up between the metal slats. The troll cried out as his beard caught fire.

'Ha!' Jeremy blurted.

'Good going, Duke!'

Jeremy watched the screaming troll shove himself up. Kneeling in the crawlspace above the ceiling, he slapped at his fiery beard, but the flames swept up his face, caught his wild tangle of hair. In seconds, his head was a ball of fire.

'How you like it, bitch!' Cowboy yelled.

Jeremy lowered his gaze to the mirrors in front of him. Cowboy, Liz and Tanya all held candles high, were reaching towards other grates, jumping, shoving fire at the faces of the trolls above them. Liz laughed as she did it. Cowboy snapped curses, let out wild Rebel yells, called out, 'Remember the

Alamo!' and 'Remember Sam!' Tanya did it in silence, rushing about the floor, dancing among the upright candles, stabbing her flame into the grates. Her sweatshirt flew up as she leapt, baring her tawny, scarred belly.

Trolls gasped and shouted. At least a few of them, caught by surprise, squealed as fire found them.

'It's all right, now.' She was on her knees, hugging her sister, crying. Debbie clung to her and wept.

Dave's throat was tight, and he had tears in his own eyes as he watched their reunion.

We did it, he thought. We got to her in time. Though God knows what she'd gone through.

Dave stepped to the other side of Joan, crouched and picked up the flashlight. Slipping behind Debbie's back, he entered the room. It was the size of a large closet. It seemed to have no way out except for the single door.

A dead man lay sprawled in the middle of the floor. Beside his leg was the sodden red rag of Debbie's blouse. Her bra was clutched in his right hand.

Dave shone his light on the man's face.

Though the bushy beard and hair were matted with blood, Dave recognized him.

The troll who'd put the curse of squirmy death on them.

The troll with Charlie Manson eyes.

Now, he had no eyes at all – just empty, wet sockets.

His lower lip, probably torn by Debbie's teeth, hung by one corner. It looked like a slug lying dead on his bearded chin.

His head was resting against his right shoulder. The left side of his neck gaped open, split wide by the blade of a meat cleaver that stood upright in the wound.

His overcoat and shirt were spread open. The shiny red skin of his chest was furrowed with rows of scratches.

Dave turned around. Joan's face was pressed to the girl's cheek, her eyes shut. He wondered if she'd seen the carnage yet.

Debbie's back and buttocks had been raked by fingernails.

Her underpants, one side torn away, hung at her knees. Her jeans were down, gathered around her ankles.

Dave stepped past the two hugging, weeping women. He leaned against a wall and shut his eyes.

God, the savagery of the fight that must've gone on inside that dark, locked room! It seemed incredible that Debbie had prevailed.

Maybe not so incredible, he thought. Hell, she's Joan's sister. What a kid!

She must've gone at the guy hand to hand before she was able to finish him off with the cleaver.

'We . . . we've gotta help the others,' Debbie said.

'The hell with the others.'

'They're my friends.'

Dave looked at them. Joan was helping the girl up. He turned his eyes away when Debbie bent down and tore at the remains of her underwear. He heard the ripping cloth.

'Where did he hurt you?' Joan asked.

'Doesn't matter.'

'Did he . . .?'

'He didn't screw me.' She sniffed. 'Can't believe I'm alive.'

'Neither can I,' Joan said.

'When I heard you guys talking . . .' Her voice cracked.

'It's all right,' Joan told her.

'Dave, is that guy dead in there?'

'You didn't see him?' he asked, looking at her. She was pulling her sweatshirt off.

'He's dead,' Debbie gasped through her sobs. 'He better be.' She wiped the tears from her eyes with bloody hands. She had pulled her jeans up and fastened them. Parts of the jeans were still white.

Though her torso was smeared with blood, Dave saw no wounds.

Joan removed her shoulder holster and the knife rig. She took off her bullet-proof vest.

Her T-shirt looked glued to her skin. It was white. Its whiteness struck Dave as strange and comforting. He'd seen so much blood in the past few minutes that he'd begun to feel as if scarlet was the natural colour of things.

Joan put the vest on her sister, and fastened its Velcro straps. She gave her sweatshirt to Debbie. The girl wiped her face with it, then pulled it down over her head while Joan quickly slipped into the harnesses again.

Bending down, Joan removed the small semi-auto from her ankle holster. She gave it to Debbie.

Debbie stepped past her, heading for the slide.

'Wait!'

'I know. Something wrong with it.'

As Dave stepped close to Joan, she took hold of his left wrist and swung it sideways, aiming his flashlight into the room. 'Jesus Christ,' she muttered.

They both flinched as someone cried out in agony and alarm. In seconds, the air was full of shouts, laughter and screams, some faint, others loud. They seemed to come from somewhere down the hallway. Dave snapped his head in that direction. He saw smoke drift up through one of the floor gratings. Smoke, and the shimmery light of fire.

'What the hell's going on?' Joan said.

'We'd better get out of here fast,' Dave said.

Debbie took hold of Joan's hand.

Dave rushed past them, dropped to his knees, and shone his light down the slide.

'Let's go back the way we came,' Joan said.

'We can't!' Debbie blurted. 'My friends are down there! We've gotta save them!'

'I think we can make it down the slide,' Dave said.

Chapter Forty-six

'That oughta show 'em,' Tanya gasped.

'Hope the place burns to the ground,' Liz said.

'Not till we get our tails outa here,' Cowboy said. Candle in one hand, knife in the other, he started into the mirror maze. Liz rushed after him.

Jeremy, staying close to Tanya's side, headed for the opening in the wall of mirrors. Someone above the ceiling was still screaming. He heard others whimpering and sobbing up there.

We hurt them, he thought. Maybe even killed one or two.

Like to kill them all.

Like to burn the fucking place to the ground, barbecue every damn one of the trolls.

But he doubted that setting some hair on fire had been enough to do the job.

Just as well. The idea of burning up Shiner appalled him. Samson and Karen would be cremated, too. They deserved better than to have their bodies go up in smoke with the trolls who had murdered them.

He saw Liz vanish among the mirrors. But she reappeared, along with Cowboy, when Jeremy entered a gap in the front panels. They were over to the left. He thought. It was hard to tell exactly where they were. With mirrors on both sides and in front of them, reflections were everywhere. A multitude of bloody kids with candles, knives and meat cleavers. Images within images, receding and diminishing. Jeremy couldn't tell the real Cowboy and Liz from their glass doubles. Then they disappeared, and Jeremy was surrounded by images of only himself and Tanya. He probed ahead with the cleaver. Walked toward himself and Tanya, duplicates matching them on both sides. A corner of the heavy blade tapped glass. He reached to the right and met no resistance, so he turned that way just in time to see Cowboy and Liz – or their reflections – vanish around a corner.

'Hold up,' Tanya said. 'Let's not lose each other.'

Jeremy hurried forward, keeping his shoulder against Tanya, rubbing the knuckles of his left hand along the glass to guide him.

'Well, I'll be hogtied.'

His knuckles lost the glass. He stepped forward, reached sideways and nudged Liz's back.

'Hey, watch it with the candle,' she warned, flinching away from him.

'Sorry.'

'Look what I've found,' Cowboy said.

Jeremy stepped sideways to see past Liz's head. Cowboy was in front of him – or somewhere – bending down. He stood up and turned around. His knife was clenched in his teeth. His candle was in one hand. In the other was a camera with a flash attachment.

'Fantastic.' Tanya said.

'She's a beaut, too,' he said around the knife. 'A Minolta.'

'Who gives a shit?' Liz said. 'Take the film out.'

'I'm just gonna keep the whole thing.' He slung the strap over his head, wincing slightly as his hand brushed against his bandaged ear.

'Keep it if you want,' Tanya told him. 'But get the film out of it right now. We can't take a chance on losing it.'

'Okay, you say so.' He lowered his head and squinted at the camera, trying to figure it out. 'I'm not real sure . . .'

'BEHIND YOU!' Tanya shouted.

Liz screamed.

Cowboy jumped with surprise and whirled around, snatching the knife from his mouth as a giant of a troll loomed out of the mirrors and swung an axe down. Ten giants. Fifty of them. Countless monstrous trolls chopping, splitting Cowboy's head down the middle. Gore sprayed the air. The halves of his head dropped toward his shoulders. His legs shot forward. His rump pounded the floor. The troll ripped his axe free and started to raise it.

415

Liz, still screaming, lurched towards Cowboy. She crouched at his back, slipped her hands under the sides of his head and lifted them as if she thought she could put him back together.

'NO!' Tanya yelled.

The troll took one long stride toward Liz.

Jeremy hurled his cleaver. It flashed in the candle light as it flipped end over end. Its blade thudded into the troll's chest. He bellowed. But he didn't go down. The cleaver stayed buried in him as he swung his axe sideways.

Jeremy heard a wet smack.

Liz's head flew from her neck, tumbling, streaming hair and blood. The axe didn't stop. It swept past her and smashed the mirror on her right. Liz's head hit the mirror, bounced to the floor and rolled.

Her headless body was still crouched behind Cowboy. Blood spouted from the stump of her neck like water from a thick hose. Beyond the bodies, the troll was turned sideways. He twisted, swinging his axe away from the smashed mirror. As he raised it towards his shoulder, Tanya dashed to Liz's back and leaped through the geyser of blood. She slammed against him. It must've been like hitting a tree. The troll didn't budge. She bounced off his chest and was thrown backward onto the bodies. The cleaver, knocked crooked by Tanya's impact, stayed in the troll's chest for a moment, then fell and hit the floor with a clatter.

He stood above her, axe raised over his shoulder. Jeremy saw the handle of Tanya's knife protruding from his throat.

He stood tall and motionless, then toppled backwards. The head of the axe shattered the mirror behind him. He fell through the disintegrating glass, his back breaking through the bottom of the panel as shards rained down on him.

All the candles were out except Jeremy's.

But its single tongue of flame was multiplied by the mirrors, filling the scene with a fluttery orange glow.

He watched Tanya climb off the bodies of Cowboy and Liz.

She crawled onto the felled troll, reached beyond his head, then scurried off him, dragging the axe.

Standing astride his hips, she raised the axe. Jeremy saw it swing down, heard the wet thud as it struck.

Bending over, Tanya pulled her knife from the troll's throat. Then she stepped off the body. 'Come here and get the axe,' she said, her voice husky and breathless. 'We can use it.'

Jeremy nodded. He moved forward, glanced at Liz and Cowboy, turned his eyes away from them and looked at the dead troll. Tanya had left the axe in his face.

Good, Jeremy thought.

And slipped on the blood-slick floor. Yelping, he flapped his arms.

Shook his candle out.

Darkness dropped like a black cloak over his eyes.

He fell onto the bodies of his dead friends.

At the top of the slide, Dave wrapped his kevlar vest around his shoes. 'Here goes,' he muttered.

Joan squeezed his shoulder.

He pushed off and sped down the slide, sitting upright, legs tight together in front of him, flashlight aimed at the twin, upright blades. His feet struck the blades, stopping him with a jolt. Through the vest and soles of his shoes, the edges felt no sharper than a couple of steel rods.

He clamped the flashlight between his thighs, pointing its beam at his shrouded feet. He lay back, stretched his arms overhead, and called out, 'All set.'

Debbie came down on her belly, hands first. Dave caught them, halting her glide. He drew her down to his face. 'Take the flashlight with you,' he said. 'Be careful going over the knives. And have your pistol ready when you get to the bottom.'

Straddling him, she squirmed down his body. She took the flashlight, scooted lower, and rose to her hands and knees to crawl over his upright feet and the blades. 'Made it,' she whispered.

She hunkered at the end of the slide, shining the light around. Then, she climbed off.

'Okay, Joan.'

Joan came down. As she struggled onto him, the side of one breast rubbed his cheek. Dave felt its softness through the thin, damp fabric of her T-shirt. Its touch was like a memory of the real world.

There is a real world out there, he thought.

He lifted his hands. He caressed her back as she worked her way down his body. He caressed her buttocks, the backs of her legs.

'You pick odd times to get fresh,' she whispered.

He laughed softly.

'There's a real world out there,' he told her. 'Believe it or not.'

'I'm glad you reminded me.' She squeezed his knee. 'We're doing okay so far, huh?'

'Doing just fine.'

Then she crawled over his feet, skidded to the end of the slide, and Debbie helped her off. She took the flashlight and aimed it at his feet.

Dave sat up. He bent his knees until he could reach the vest with his hands. Pressing it against the blades, he freed his feet and stretched his legs down until he was astride the covered knives.

'Seemed like a good idea at the time,' he muttered.

Joan passed the light to Debbie, then climbed onto the end of the slide. She shoved her knees against the bottoms of his feet, and reached up.

'Ah-ha,' Dave said.

'Ah-ha,' she repeated.

As she clutched his wrists, Dave leaned forward. She tugged. His rump lifted off the slide. The inner sides of his thighs rubbed the padded blades. The back of his head scraped along the top of the enclosure. Joan suddenly gave him such a pull that he nearly folded in half. His knees buckled. He hit the ramp, and tumbled with Joan until the slide was no longer under them. They hit the floor.

After untangling himself, he retrieved the vest. He held it towards Joan. She shook her head. 'It's yours. Put it on.'

'I want you to wear it,' Dave said.

'Well, *I* want *you* to wear it.'

'I don't want you wearin' nuffin',' came a voice from the ceiling. 'C'mon, sweet stuff, lemme see . . .'

'Bastard!' Debbie snapped. She shoved her arm straight up, aimed her pistol at the grate, but didn't fire. Shaking her head, she lowered the pistol.

'Hey, sweet stuff,' the troll said.

'Babes, babes, babes,' said another.

'Tasty bits.'

'Where are the others?' Debbie yelled at the ceiling. 'Where are my friends?'

Trolls laughed.

'Oh, they been by, they been by.'

'Bound fer Hell.'

'Let's go,' Joan said. She swept the walls with the flashlight, probed the darkness of the hallway to the left, and jogged in that direction.

'Bye-bye, sweets.'

'Say hi to Webster!'

Dave nudged Debbie's back, and she started to run.

He hurried after her. He slipped his arms into the vest as he ran. Though he wanted Joan to wear it, he saw no point in wasting time with an argument.

Joan and Debbie crouched at the edge of the barrel that filled the hallway. Dave stepped up behind them as Debbie muttered, 'Oh jeez, no.'

A dead kid was stretched out inside the barrel. All around him, the wooden staves bristled with spikes.

'One of your friends?' Joan asked.

'Samson.'

'Looks like they used him for a bridge,' Dave said.

'I guess we do, too,' Joan said.

Debbie curled her left hand against the side of her mouth and shouted through the barrel. 'HELLO! JEREMY! HEY, YOU GUYS, IT'S SHINER! CAN YOU HEAR ME?'

No answer came.

'JEREMY? TANYA? COWBOY? LIZ? IT'S SHINER. WE'VE GOT GUNS! WAIT UP! OR COME BACK! YOU'LL BE ALL RIGHT! WE'VE GOT GUNS!'

Still, no answer.

'Damn it,' she muttered.

'I'll go first,' Dave said. He stepped around them. He swept the edge of his shoe against one of the spikes. The barrel rocked from side to side. 'Christ,' he said.

Joan and Debbie grabbed the spikes near the rim of the barrel to hold it steady.

Dave knelt on the dead boy's shins. They felt steady under him. Of course they do, he thought. They're nailed down.

Leaning forwards, he gripped the boy's thighs and started to crawl.

Robin, kneeling on the seat and clutching its back, watched the troll climb onto the beam that led straight to her gondola.

The same route the other had used.

Well, she'd taken care of that one.

Two down, one to go.

This guy was bigger than the last troll. He had a round face, hardly any neck at all, and shoulders the size of hams. His eyes were small and close together. Pig eyes, Robin thought. A squat, upturned nose. A tiny slit of a mouth, lips tight.

He really looks like a pig, she thought.

But he also looked, somehow, like a little boy in a body that had bloated out of control.

He wore a ballcap with its peak turned up. The skin around its sides was hairless.

'Go back,' she said. 'I don't want to kill you.'

As she spoke those words, she saw herself in the steaming spa with Nate, holding him tightly, both of them weeping for the deaths they had caused.

She saw Nate sprawled on the sheet. His bloody head.

She felt her throat tighten.

Oh God, Nate.

Had he deserved it? she wondered. Was all this some kind of rough justice at work?

'I really don't want to kill you,' she pleaded, her voice sliding to a higher pitch. 'I don't want to kill anyone.'

The troll straddled the beam and stared at her.

'Just go away,' she begged. 'Please.'

The troll lowered his head. Looking down at the dead ones? He hunched himself over and hugged the beam.

He's afraid, Robin thought. He doesn't want to fall.

'If I knock you off here,' she said, 'you'll be broken to pieces.'

He began to make soft whimpery sounds.

Oh no, Jeremy thought. We forgot the camera.

It was back there somewhere, hanging around Cowboy's neck, the incriminating film still in it.

He decided not to tell Tanya.

She might insist they return for it. They'd come a long distance, winding their way through the total darkness, bumping into mirrors, often backtracking when they found themselves at dead-ends. To go back now . . .

To be in the same place with those bodies again . . .

Jeremy shivered as he remembered falling onto Liz and Cowboy. Trying to get up, he'd pushed a hand into something sodden and mushy.

Besides, he told himself, the film doesn't matter. Most of the kids in the pictures were already dead.

There're just the two of us. And Heather. Lucky Heather. She'd fled down the stairs before it got bad.

We should've gone, too.

If only I'd listened to Shiner.

I got Shiner killed.

It seemed like ages ago, and the pain and guilt of it seemed muffled by all that had happened since.

It was probably fifteen minutes ago, he thought.

The head of his axe bumped glass. He swung it slowly to the left, met no resistance, and turned in that direction. Tanya followed, her hand tight on his shoulder.

If we had a candle, he thought, we'd be out of this thing by now.

We could've smashed straight through with the axe, fuck the maze.

But doing that without light would've been disastrous.

They'd discussed it, and both agreed that they'd be cut to pieces if they tried.

This was taking forever, but at least they might get through with their skin intact. If they didn't get jumped by more trolls.

Jeremy turned, and turned again.

And saw a glimmer of light.

'All *right*,' Tanya whispered.

The faint glow ahead of them turned out to be a reflection. The axe thudded the mirror. Jeremy turned, and the light was stronger.

Instead of a mirror, there was suddenly a hallway to his left. Candles on the walls. He stumbled free of the maze, and took a deep breath.

'Made it,' Tanya whispered. She hugged herself against his back, then stepped around beside him.

Along the left side of the hallway were barred windows like those they'd passed in the corridor above. Jeremy saw no trolls behind the bars.

'So where the hell's our audience?' Tanya said.

'Maybe they all cleared out. Maybe the fire scared them off.'

'I wouldn't bet on it.'

Midway down the hall, on the right, was a door. Another door waited at the end. 'What'll we do?' Jeremy asked.

Tanya said nothing. She looked from one door to the other. She frowned.

'The one at the end,' Jeremy said, nodding towards the far door. 'It might be the one at the stairway.'

'If it is, you can bet they've got a nasty surprise waiting for us.'

'Yeah. They aren't gonna let us just walk away from this.'

'Fuck the doors,' Tanya said. 'Let's chop our way out.'

'Yeah!'

'No more playing by their rules. We've got the axe, we can play the game our own way.' She took a few strides forwards, turned to the right, and tapped the wall with the point of her knife. 'There's probably some kind of room through there. All we've gotta do is bust in, then we can knock a hole in the wall and maybe step right out onto the boardwalk.'

'Sure hope so.'

Tanya moved aside. Jeremy raised the axe overhead and swung with all his strength. Its heavy blade bit into the wall. As he tore it loose, a thick splinter of wood split away and dropped to the floor. He put his eye to the narrow gap.

Darkness on the other side.

Stepping back, he chopped again. The entire head of the axe broke through the wall.

'It's going to work!' he blurted.

'Damn right!'

As he struggled to free the trapped axehead, a sudden sharp tug yanked the haft from his hands.

In the instant it took him to realize what was happening, the entire length of the handle vanished into the hole.

'Oh Jesus,' he gasped.

'We'd better get . . .'

They both jumped as a chunk of the wall flew at them. Jeremy glimpsed an inch of the axe blade before it withdrew.

Now they've got it. And they're coming for us.

Jeremy heard maniacal laughter.

It came from him.

Tanya tugged his arm, and they ran down the hallway.

Ran until the floor dropped out from under their feet.

Then, side by side, they dropped into the black chasm of the funhouse basement.

Chapter Forty-seven

Whirling away from the three corpses in the mirror maze, Debbie hunched over and vomited. Joan rubbed her back while she heaved.

The poor kid had been through hell. And it's not over yet.

The worst is over, Joan told herself. The worst had to be in that closet upstairs, alone and fighting for her life. She was damn lucky to survive. With her mind in one piece, too. A lot of people might have flipped out, having to deal with something like that.

She's holding up pretty well.

Losing her dinner, it's probably a good sign. Shows she's still in touch with reality.

'This one must've come down a goddamn beanstalk,' Dave said. His trembling voice sounded astonished and disgusted.

Debbie finished. She straightened up, sobbing, and wiped her mouth with the front of her sweatshirt.

'Two of them are kids,' Dave said. 'One's a girl. The other's the guy from the fight.'

'Our fight?' Joan asked.

'The one with the ear.'

'Oh, no.'

She'd saved his ear for this. So he could get his head split open in this mad perversion of a funhouse.

Debbie turned around. She sniffed and rubbed her eyes. 'That's Cowboy,' she said. 'And Liz. God!' She slapped a hand to her mouth and squeezed her eyes shut.

'Is anybody left?' Joan asked her.

She nodded. 'Jeremy,' she said through her hand. 'And Tanya. Only them.' She took her hand away, pressed her face to Joan's shoulder and hugged her tightly. 'Jeremy's my friend, Joanie. I tried to stop him. I don't want him to die.'

'Okay,' Dave said. 'We're going through this thing the fast

way.' He drew his pistol. He shouted, 'ANYBODY CAN HEAR ME, BETTER HIT THE DECK! HIT THE FLOOR! BULLETS ARE COMING!'

Standing at the feet of the giant, dead troll, he clamped the flashlight between his legs, aimed at the mirror in front of him, and fired.

Debbie jumped as the shot blasted the silence. She stuck her fingers into her ears.

Joan covered her own ears.

Dave kept firing, the Beretta roaring, jerking his hand, walls of mirrors exploding in front of him as the .380 calibre slugs smashed through them. Disintegrating glass flashed in the beam of his flashlight. He swept the muzzle just a bit from side to side, blasting a corridor straight through the maze.

Some forty feet ahead, a glow of candle light appeared. The size of the lighted area grew as Dave kept firing, knocking apart more mirrors.

After thirteen shots, he dropped the magazine into his palm. He shoved a fresh magazine up the pistol's handle and jacked a cartridge into the chamber.

Joan and Debbie stepped carefully around the bodies. They stopped beside Dave. Looking past him, Joan saw the dark rubble of shattered glass, then a lighted hallway.

And bodies sprawled on its floor.

Dave rubbed a trembling hand across his mouth. 'God,' he muttered. 'I warned 'em to duck.'

'Then they should've ducked,' Joan said.

'Maybe they couldn't hear me.'

'Let's go.' She pulled the flashlight from between Dave's legs, ducked under jagged teeth of glass, and started walking through the litter of demolished mirrors. The glass crunched under her shoes. 'Be careful back there,' she said.

She proceeded slowly.

Sometimes, before stepping through a panel, she knocked hanging shards out of the way with the barrel of her revolver. She heard Debbie and Dave close behind her, glass tinkling and popping under their shoes.

425

Ahead, some of the people in the hallway began to move.

Roll over, crawl, stand up.

At least three bodies stayed down.

Those Joan saw rising were not kids.

Nor did they look like trolls.

She felt a chill squirm through her. Her skin began to crawl.

She remembered that Jasper Dunn used to be the proprietor of a freak show. He'd been forced to close it down after some of his freaks got loose and attacked people in the funhouse.

He'd closed the show.

Obviously, he'd kept his freaks.

Made a home for them in his funhouse.

Behind Joan, Dave groaned.

A hand clawed at the back of her T-shirt, peeled the wet cloth away from her skin, tried to pull her backward. In a low, shaky voice, Debbie said, 'I wanta go back. Please, Joanie. Can't we just go back?'

As Jeremy dropped into darkness, he expected his descent to be stopped with a bone-jarring crash. Instead, he landed on something springy. A net? It sank under his back, then lifted him. The taut lines quivered as he tried to untangle his arms and legs from them.

They felt gluey.

They stuck to him.

He heard Tanya gasping. To his right, and not far away. Her struggles shook the netting.

'You okay?' he whispered.

'What *is* this shit?'

In front of Jeremy and off to his left, a door opened.

That's the other door, Jeremy realized. The one at the foot of the stairway.

The way out is right there.

Someone entered, carrying a kerosene lantern. Jeremy squinted as the harsh glare from the lamp's twin mantles stabbed his eyes.

He saw that the tall, cadaverous man wore a top hat and tails. Jasper Dunn.

Trolls poured through the doorway behind Dunn, crowding the small balcony on which he stood. They were oddly silent.

As Jeremy's eyes adjusted to the light, he saw more.

He saw too much.

He felt as if he were collapsing inside, shrivelling into a black ruin.

The sticky cords that held him trapped were the strands of a web spread across the funhouse basement. A spider web. Hanging in it, suspended several feet above the sand, were the crushed husks of people wrapped in grey, transparent silk.

Tanya shrieked.

He twisted his head towards her.

Saw her writhing and bucking.

Saw *the spider* scurrying over the top of the web, rushing in from a corner of the basement.

A spider like the one he'd seen in Jasper's Oddities.

But bigger, much bigger.

Jasper's Giganticus. Jeremy heard Cowboy's voice deep inside the abyss of his mind. *Discovered in the jungles of New Zealand.*

The one in the display might've been this spider's baby.

'NO!' Tanya yelled. 'NO!'

The web swayed and bounced under the weight of the rushing black beast.

Its eyes were yellow. Its mouth looked like a huge, open sore. Its fangs dripped.

The black, bloated thing *danced* over the web.

And onto Tanya.

Her shriek ripped his ears.

The spider's mouth muffled her scream. Jeremy saw its fangs sink into her face.

Her tangled body flinched rigid, jerked with spasms.

Jeremy twisted sideways, freeing his right arm from the trapped sleeve of his jacket. He reached to his shirt pocket. For the razor blade he'd put there after giving the handkerchief to Tanya.

A quick slash across the throat.

Maybe he could die before the spider came for him.

The pocket of his shirt was empty.

He'd lost the razor. Maybe while going down the slide. When didn't matter.

It was gone.

Jeremy heard gunfire as the legs of the spider wrapped around Tanya, squeezing her like a monstrous lover.

Robin heard the faint, hard claps of gunshots. She looked over her shoulder. Saw nothing except the deserted, moonlit boardwalk. The muffled tone of the shots made her wonder if they came from under the boardwalk, or maybe from inside one of Funland's buildings.

After a few seconds, they stopped. The only sounds she heard were her heartbeat, the rushing wind, the wash of a comber hurtling itself at the beach, and the troll whimpering quietly behind her.

She turned her head forwards again.

The troll was still four or five feet away, hugging the steel beam.

He'd frozen there.

He'd come this close, and lost his nerve.

Obviously, the height had suddenly got to him.

Robin remembered her own experiences with climbing. Shinnying up trees when she was a kid, once in a while working her way up bluffs and mountainsides during her travels. You could go along just fine for a while. Then, sometimes, it just hit you. Stark, paralysing fear. You knew you were going to die. All you could do was hang on, waiting to fall.

Until something broke the spell.

Killed the curse.

And you were suddenly able to function.

This guy, she thought, will either fall or come to his senses.

If he comes to his senses, I'll be fair game again.

But she didn't want him to fall.

The troll raised his head when Robin began to sing.

I climbed a mountain peak last night
To see what I could see,
To take a peek at the moon so bright
And the stars in the midnight sea.

He sat up and stared at her.

On his way through the broken mirrors, Dave saw enough of those in the hallway ahead to know they were remnants of Jasper Dunn's freak show.

He'd heard stories about them, seen their photographs a number of times in the Gallery of the Weird.

Supposedly, they had scattered and left town after the show was shut down.

Six years ago. Shortly before he arrived from Los Angeles. All that time, they'd been living here in the funhouse?

Those who hadn't been hit by his bullets were standing in the hallway only a few yards beyond the last shattered mirror. Standing motionless, watching.

Dave didn't want Joan to be first out of the maze.

First to face this crowd of deformities.

He hurried past her.

Without Joan's back blocking the way, he had a clear view.

On the floor, her throat torn open by a slug, lay Donna the Dog Woman. Sprawled beside her, writhing in pain, was a shirtless man with a withered brown arm in the middle of his chest. Julian, the Three-Armed Man. His little brown hand was clutching the bullet wound near his left shoulder. Wonderful Wilma lay near him, naked except for leopard-skin bikini pants. One hand was clamped to her bleeding thigh. Her other arm pressed in modesty across her two normal breasts, the third mound uncovered, pale and sweaty below her wrist.

Only Donna dead, Dave thought. Could've been worse.

But God, he wished he hadn't hit any of them.

Stepping through the last shattered mirror, he aimed his pistol at Snake-Tongue Antonio. 'Drop the axe,' he said.

The man's tongue slid out of his mouth. As he glared at

Dave, the pink slab of tongue slithered from one side of his face to the other, licking tears from under his eyes.

'I don't want to shoot you,' Dave said.

'Drop it,' Joan snapped, coming up beside him, also taking aim at Antonio.

The two-headed woman, who had a name for each head which Dave couldn't recall, turned both faces towards the man. She reached out a hand and patted his shoulder. He glanced at her, retracted his tongue, and made grunting sounds.

One head nodded at him. The other's face smiled gently.

He dropped the axe to the floor.

'I'm sorry,' Dave said. 'I'm sorry about the shooting. I didn't mean for anyone to get hit.'

'We didn't know you were here,' Joan said. She holstered her revolver and gave the flashlight to Dave. Bending down, she started to untie the red bandana knotted around her leg.

Dave lowered his pistol, but kept it in his hand. He doubted that these people would try anything. They seemed wary, confused, sad. And he saw something like hope in the eyes of a few.

'We're trying to find my friends,' Debbie said. 'Did you see them? Do you know where . . .' Her voice faltered. 'Their throats,' she whispered.

Some of the people nodded. Others grunted. Jim or Tim, one of the Siamese twins, touched a finger to the scar on his throat and mouthed a breathy, voiceless noise. 'Haaaspaaa.'

'Jasper?' Dave asked. 'Jasper Dunn?' Nods, more grunts.

'He *cut your vocal cords*?' Joan blurted.

'Hyesss, hyesss, Haaaspaaa.'

'Jesus,' Debbie muttered.

'He was keeping you prisoners here?' Dave asked.

The two-headed woman pointed at a door-size opening someone had chopped into the corridor wall.

'We're gonna get you out of here,' Joan said. Dropping to her knees, she wrapped the bandana around Wilma's leg wound and knotted it tight.

'What about Jeremy?' Debbie asked, her voice high and pleading. 'We have to find him!'

'We will, don't worry.' Joan looked at the others. 'Two kids,' she said. 'A boy and a girl. Did you see them? Do you know where they are?'

The crowd parted, turned. A few hands pointed down the hallway.

Dave saw a door on the right, another at the far end.

But between here and the hallway's end was a square of darkness where the floor should have been.

A trap door?

Debbie bolted. She leaped the body of Donna the Dog Woman and dashed through the break in the group.

'NO!' Joan shouted.

Dave rushed after her.

Debbie was nearly clear of Jasper's freaks when a hand darted out and grabbed her ankle. She yelped, crashed to the floor and skidded.

Dave pounced and gripped the back of her neck, holding her down as she struggled to rise.

He looked back. A bald man lifted his head and made a grim smile. He had no legs. But he had two muscular arms, and the hand of one was wrapped tightly around Debbie's ankle. Andy the Amazing Torso Man.

'Thanks,' Dave said.

He winked.

Joan patted his shoulder, stepped over him, and crouched on the other side of Debbie. 'Dumb kid,' she muttered. 'Just stick with us and don't . . .'

Debbie gasped and flinched rigid.

Squeals and grunts erupted behind them.

Dave snapped his head around. Jasper's freaks were going wild, some pointing down the hallway, others rushing towards the ragged hole in the wall, some racing for the ruins of the mirror maze.

'Dave.'

Joan's voice. A mere whisper.

431

'Dave?'

He looked at her.

Joan's wide, stunned eyes met his for an instant, then looked away.

Toward the other end of the hallway.

Dave followed their lead.

And saw black, insectile legs waving in the candle light. They hooked over the edge of the floor. Claws clicking and scraping on the wood, a huge spider clambered up from the darkness below the trap door.

On its back rode Jasper Dunn, top hat perched rakishly a top his head, a revolver in each hand.

Can't be.

Dave felt as if he had been clubbed in the belly.

He gasped at the spectacle – the monstrous spider scurrying towards him, Jasper mounted up there like a crazed cowpoke brandishing six-shooters.

Can't be happening.

Dave rose on numb, shaky legs, pulling Debbie up with him by the back of her neck. 'Go,' he said. His voice sounded far away. 'Run.'

She stood beside him, frozen.

Joan rose to her feet, going for her .38 in slow motion as Dave raised his Beretta and Jasper brought down both barrels in their direction. Gunfire roared through the hallway. Bullets snapped past Dave's face. The hat sailed off Jasper's head. Debbie, hit, flew backward. An eye of the beast exploded in a red mist. A slug smashed through Jasper's right wrist and his revolver tumbled away. At the same moment, one caught him in the face. It snapped his head sideways and tore off half his chin. But he stayed on the spider, blasting at them with his remaining gun. The beast was less than six feet away. It would be on them in seconds.

Dave concentrated his firepower on it. A bullet slashed the side of his arm, but he stood steady, squeezing the trigger. One of the spider's front legs broke. As his bullets pounded holes in its squat, bristly head, he saw Joan rush forward.

'NO!' he yelled.

The spider seemed to stumble. Its abdomen dragged the floor, but it still scuttled closer, palps coming at Dave like pincers.

The last shot from his Beretta exploded another of its eyes.

Reaching for his .38, he saw Joan, knife in hand, jump over two of the spider's thrashing legs. She no longer had her revolver. Must've emptied it.

Jasper aimed at her face. He wouldn't miss. A pointblank shot.

Dave drew his .38.

But raising it seemed to take so long . . . so long.

He heard Jasper's hammer snap down.

A quick hard clack.

No blast.

It had fallen on a spent cartridge!

Now Dave's gun was up, levelled at Jasper, but he held fire. Afraid of hitting Joan as she hurled herself against the bloated side of the spider, just behind Jasper. She vaulted onto the beast. Jasper, twisting, rammed an elbow into her. She hooked an arm beneath his ruined chin, jerked him backward, and her right arm swept in around him and plunged the knife into his chest. She pulled the knife out, rammed it in again, then flung him sideways. He toppled from his mount, sliding, falling head first among the spider's legs.

As its pincers caught Dave.

They clamped him just below the knees.

How could it still be alive?

He fired, jerking the trigger fast, pumping round after round into its head as the beast squeezed his legs together and he toppled backward. He was hammering at spent shells when he heard Joan screaming. His back slammed the floor.

What's she screaming about? Dave wondered.

Shoving himself up with his elbows, he saw Joan still on top of the spider. Screaming like a banshee as she thrust her knife into the hump of its back.

She's screaming about me.

As he twisted and tried to kick free, the pincers began to pull him. He slid over the floor towards the spider.

It raised its head.

What was left of its head. A hideous, oblong thing shattered by bullets, caved in, cracked and split, red and yellow fluids gushing from its wounds.

The fucking thing's dead in its tracks! Dave's mind screamed. *Why's it doing this to me?*

It dragged him.

Squealing, he rammed his right foot against its single, dripping fang. He shoved at it, trying to keep himself back.

Antonio leapt past him, swung his axe down with both hands, and split the spider's head in half. The pincers loosened their grip. Dave tore his legs free and scrambled backwards as the man chopped again.

He rolled onto his side.

Face to face with Debbie.

As they stared into each other's eyes, the wet crunching sounds of the chopping went on.

She scooted closer to Dave.

He put an arm around her back, pulling her against him, and felt the girl's face press the side of his neck.

'The bullet hit your vest?' he whispered.

He felt her nod.

Robin kept singing as the troll inched closer. Then she stopped, and reached out to him. He gripped her hand. She held it tightly as he climbed onto the seat.

Gasping and shuddering from the ordeal, he sat down beside her. With one hand, he clutched the side of the gondola. The other held Robin's hand against his leg.

She pressed her legs together, wondering if she'd been crazy to let this troll in with her. She used her free arm to cover her breasts. 'It's okay,' she said. 'You're safe now.'

He flinched as gunfire erupted again.

Robin looked away from him. The shots sounded as if they might be coming from inside Jasper's Oddities or the funhouse, which were on the far side of the boardwalk about halfway between the Ferris wheel and the main entrance. The last time, the shots had sounded like rapid fire from a single gun. Now, it seemed that several weapons of different calibres were firing at once.

The troll released her hand. He slid an arm across her shoulders and drew Robin against the side of his quaking body.

It's all right, she told herself. He's just scared.

She realized that the gunfire had stopped. Then came a quick series of blasts, and the shooting ended again.

Slowly, the troll relaxed. She could feel his shudders fade. He began to caress her arm from shoulder to elbow. His touch made her skin crawl.

She faced him. 'That was the police,' she said. 'They'll be coming out soon.'

I hope, she thought.

God, what if the cops had *lost* that shootout?

'When they come out,' she said, 'they'll get us down from here. So you'd better not try anything, you understand?'

He turned towards her, a knee pushing against the side of her leg. Though his eyes were hooded with shadow, she could feel their gaze roaming her body. 'Denny likes you,' he said. His voice wasn't high and childish, as Robin had expected from this man who looked like an overgrown boy. It was low, raspy.

Holding her shoulder, he slid the other hand up her thigh. 'Soft,' he said.

Robin grabbed his wrist. 'Don't,' she whispered. 'Please.'

'Denny likes you,' he said again.

'Then don't.'

He took his hand off her leg, and she released it. His other hand left her shoulder. He fumbled with the buttons of his filthy, ragged trench coat.

'Denny, no.'

He opened the coat. He wore a sleeveless undershirt and baggy trousers. The tight shirt bulged over massive muscles.

I won't stand a chance.

He'll only hurt me worse if I struggle.

435

Damn it, I'm not gonna let him rape me!
This is what I get for helping him.

Denny pulled the coat off his arms and tugged its tail out from under his rump.

He draped it over Robin's shoulders.

Her throat tightened. As she slipped her arms into the sleeves, the man cupped a hand gently over her right breast. 'Soft,' he said. Then he took his hand away, drew the coat shut and began to button it.

When he finished, Robin leaned against him.

'Thank you, Denny,' she said. 'Robin likes you.'

He put an arm across her shoulders.

'Sing?' he asked.

'Sure.'

Chapter Forty-eight

She was singing 'Amazing Grace', Denny holding her and slowly rocking their perch high above the boardwalk. The song took Robin back to her father's funeral. Her dad's old buddy, Charlie MacFerson, had played the bagpipes at her side while she stood by the grave with her banjo, strumming the tune and singing the melancholy words.

This time the song was for Nate.

Her voice trembled. Tears streamed down her cheeks.

Denny looked at her and cocked his head. Then he pulled off his ballcap. He put it on Robin. It was way too big for her. It slipped down, covering her eyes. She kept singing as he slid it back on her head and turned it sideways.

Over the tremor of her voice, Robin heard a quiet thud. A chunking sound. A chopping sound.

She went silent.

Off to the left, a slat of wood flew off the front wall of Jasper's Funhouse and clapped the boardwalk. The pale beam of a flashlight probed through the narrow gap.

The chopping went on. Wood flew and clattered down.

Soon, the opening was the size of a doorway.

People began to emerge from the funhouse.

Denny pointed. He began to laugh.

Robin could hardly believe what she saw. A woman down there seemed to have *two* heads. A man clutching his shoulder had a growth on his chest that looked like a small arm. A man – one of the cops she'd seen earlier – stepped through the break in the wall, carrying a man who had no legs.

Denny slapped his leg and pointed as a tall, lean man helped a woman through the opening. The woman, clad only in bikini pants, seemed to have three breasts.

A man, or two men, sidestepped through the gap. They looked as if their hips were glued together.

A girl with a flashlight came out, turned to the opening and shined her light on it while a woman ducked through, carrying a limp body.

Robin's stomach clenched as she gazed at the boy who was cradled in the woman's arms. She was too far away to make out the features of his face, but she knew him. She knew him by his size and dark hair and clothes, by the raw wound on his chin – made by her teeth.

That bastard Duke.

Dead?

Where's Tanya? she wondered. Where are all the others?

Did they get away?

The woman crouched. She set Duke's body down on the boardwalk in front of the funhouse. As she started to rise the kid suddenly grabbed the front of her T-shirt and tried to pull himself up. The woman fell to her knees. Duke screamed in her face.

Denny yelped with alarm and flinched.

Robin, patting his leg to soothe him, watched the woman

twist Duke's hands from her shirt and pin them to the board-walk. Still screaming, he writhed and bucked and thrashed his legs.

The girl gave her flashlight to the male cop, squatted, caught Duke's kicking feet and helped hold him down.

Robin took off the ballcap. She put it on Denny's head and tipped the bill up the way he liked it. 'Time we let them know we're here,' she said.

'Denny likes it here.'

'I guess there are worse places to be,' she told him.

The gondola rocked back as she leaned forward and gripped the safety bar.

It tipped wildly when Denny did the same.

She shouted, 'Help! Up here!'

Denny shouted, 'Help! Up here!' He grinned at her.

Down on the boardwalk, heads turned.

Chapter Forty-nine

'Are you ready for the big finale?' called Maxwell the Somewhat Magnificent.

The crowd in the stands yelled and cheered.

'I'll require a courageous and beautiful volunteer from the audience. No men need apply.' Even as arms went up, he pointed at someone in the third row. 'You. I think you'll do just fine.'

As the young woman rose from her seat and started making her way forward, men in the audience whooped and whistled their approval.

Joan said, 'Oh my God.'

'It's Debs!' Kerry blurted, and bounced on Dave's lap. 'What's she going to do?'

'Watch and find out,' Dave told her.

'Doesn't Steve get to go up, too?'

'Boyfriends probably get in Maxwell's way,' Dave said.

'But he's all alone.'

'They wanted to sit by themselves,' Joan explained to the four-year-old.

'Can't imagine why,' Dave said.

''Cause you're old farts,' Kerry said.

Dave gently cuffed the side of her head. 'Watch your language, young lady.'

She laughed.

Then laughter erupted from the crowd as Maxwell the Somewhat Magnificent tried to mount his unicycle, clinging to Debbie, pretending to lose his balance as the wheel rolled and twisted under him. He fell against her, hugging her, squeezing her rump through the seat of her white jeans. Finally, perched unsteadily on the high seat, he lurched away. He careened around the stage, spinning and jerking as if out of control.

At last, he seemed to find a semblance of balance. He mopped his brow with a red bandana.

Debbie turned to leave, but he said, 'Wait, wait! You don't get off that easy!'

Maxwell's assistant appeared with three flaming torches. He gave one of them to Debbie.

'Dear thing,' Maxwell said, 'she's carrying a torch for me.'

He kept up the banter, telling Debbie, 'You really light my fire,' making nervous queries about her throwing arm, then instructing her to toss the torch to him. '*To* me, not *at* me. I'm gentle, but I'm not tinder.'

The audience didn't respond to the pun, so he swept an open hand above his hair. Dave knew what the gesture meant – that the joke had gone over the heads of the crowd. He'd seen a lot of performers make the same sign during the years he'd been bringing his family to the Funland Amphitheater. He always found it annoying.

It didn't go over our heads, he wanted to yell. It just wasn't funny.

439

Debbie tossed each of the three torches to Maxwell the Somewhat Magnificent. The third went high. Maxwell swept backward on his unicycle and made a catch that Dave considered Truly Magnificent.

While he juggled the torches, he thanked Debbie and suggested that she meet him after the show to help him 'put the fires out.'

Her long blonde hair flew from side to side as she shook her head. Still shaking her head, she turned around and waved to the cheering audience. Then she rushed down the stairs as if eager to escape Maxwell's further remarks.

Kerry leaned sideways and tugged the sleeve of Joan's sweatshirt. 'Mommy, why don't *you* go up?'

'No thanks, honey.'

'Come on, it'd be fun.'

'I don't think Maxwell needs another dupe just now,' Joan told her.

'What's a dupe?'

'Somebody to poke fun at.'

'Besides,' Dave said, 'Mommy's already done it. She went on stage once with Fred the Magician. So did you, kiddo.'

'Me?'

'You were in Mommy's tummy.'

'God, don't remind me,' Joan said. 'The worst experience of my life.'

'Were you a dope?'

'I sure felt like one, honey.'

'You've gotta admit,' Dave said, 'the guy had an amazing assortment of bun jokes,' Dave said.

'He was pregnant with quips,' Joan added.

Maxwell finished his routine, leaped from his unicycle and bowed. Then, he did an encore. Blindfolded by his assistant, he juggled the torches. He ended by dropping onto one knee, reaching under his leg and catching the last torch before it hit the floor of the stage.

Putting his arms around Kerry, Dave clapped in front of her stomach. She grabbed his wrists and helped.

Maxwell the Somewhat Magnificent left the stage after many elaborate bows.

The lights went out. The audience fell silent. Dave heard the faint sounds of calliope music, voices and laughter from the boardwalk. He heard the distant roar of the Hurricane.

'Is it time for Robin?' Kerry whispered.

'I imagine so,' Dave said.

'Is she going to sing "The Land of Purr"?'

'She promised you she would.'

'Hope she doesn't forget.'

In the darkness, a voice boomed over the loudspeaker. 'Ladies and gentlemen, the Funland Amphitheatre is proud to present a very special attraction. Our next performer has just returned from her most recent engagement at the Grand Ol' Oprey.'

Dave heard eager murmurs from the audience.

'You may have heard her songs on the radio. You may have seen her on the Dolly Parton special last month.'

Let's get *on* with it, Dave thought.

'OUR OWN BOLETA BAY SONGBIRD, FUNLAND'S BANJO QUEEN, *MISS ROBIN TRAVIS*!'

The audience went wild. Joan's shoulder pressed against Dave. Her breath tickled his ear as she said, 'Nate sure laid it on pretty thick.'

'What do you expect?'

The crowd roared as brilliant lights hit the stage. Robin stood motionless in front of her band, smiling.

She wore an outfit that Dave hadn't seen before: a buckskin jacket with fringe swaying in the breeze; a shiny white blouse; and a short leather skirt that left her slim legs bare to the tops of her white boots.

She glanced back at her band. Drums began to pound through the noise of the cheering crowd. Robin faced forward. Her right boot tapped the stage in time with the drum. With the first notes of her banjo, a hush descended on the audience. A quick, twangy tune filled the night. A roar came up again as those in the stands recognized the intro to 'Gypsy Girl'.

I am the gypsy banjo girl.
I've wandered far and near.
I am the gypsy banjo girl
With a song for you to hear.

It's a mountain song,
It's a desert song,
It's a song of the windblown sea.
It's a prairie song
And a woodland song –
It belongs to you and me.

Kerry bounced on Dave's lap, and he heard her soft voice as she sang along. Joan leaned against him and slipped a warm arm around his back.

'My next number is very special to me,' Robin announced midway through the show. 'I sang it for a fellow named Nate the night we met. He must've liked it, 'cause he married me. So this one's for you, Nate, and for another special friend, Kerry Carson, the daughter of my two favourite cops.'
Then, she began to sing.

Kelly and Kerry went off one day
For the Land of Purr where the kitty-cats play.

They packed their pockets with nacho chips,
Bubble gum, jelly, and chocolate lips . . .

Kerry twisted round on Dave's lap. 'It's *me*!' she blurted. '*I'm* in it!'

After Robin's final song and the standing ovation, she played and sang three encore numbers. Then the stage went dark. Seconds later, when the amphitheatre lights came on, she and the band were gone.
Dave, Kerry and Joan waited. When the crowd had

diminished, Joan folded the old brown blanket she'd used to cover the bleacher seats. Dave took hold of Kerry's hand, and they started down.

Debbie and Steve met them just outside the amphitheatre's entrance. The rides and attractions had already closed for the night. The bright carnival lights were dark, but lamps near the boardwalk railing still glowed to illuminate the way for the departing concert-goers. Funland seemed strangely quiet.

'You going to let me have your autograph?' Debbie asked Kerry.

'Huh?'

'Well, you're a big celebrity now, you know.'

'Both of you,' Joan said.

'God, don't remind me. I've never been so embarrassed in my life. I wanted to curl up and die when he was grabbing me that way.'

'He never could've gotten onto the unicycle without your valuable assistance,' Dave told her.

Debbie bared her teeth and punched his shoulder.

'Now now, children,' Joan said.

Debbie took hold of Steve's hand. 'Anyway, we'll see you guys later, okay?'

'Where are you off to?' Joan asked.

'Pete's Pizza. Since Steve has to go home tomorrow, and everything, we thought we'd . . . you know, make the most of it.'

'Can I go, too?' Kerry asked.

'No you may not,' Joan told her.

'Whyyy?'

'Because it's late, young lady. You should've been home in bed hours ago.'

'I'm not sleepy.'

'You'd cramp their style, kid,' Dave explained.

'No, I won't.'

'It's fine with me if she wants to come along,' Steve said.

'Sure,' Debbie said, rubbing the girl's hair. 'This is a big night for her. Wouldn't want to spoil it, now.'

Dave and Joan looked at each other. Joan shrugged. 'It's okay with me. If you're sure.'

'We'll have her home in an hour or so,' Steve said.

'Maybe we should *all* go to Pete's,' Dave suggested.

Kerry looked up at him and shook her head. 'You'd crump our style.'

'Besides,' Joan said, 'I want to take a stroll on the beach.'

Dave caught the look in her eyes. 'Me, too.'

They stood together and watched their daughter walk away with Debbie and Steve.

'Two lovebirds and a duck,' Joan said.

'She'll have fun.'

'They sure won't get much smooching done with her around. Speaking of which.'

She faced Dave.

He looked up and down the boardwalk. It appeared deserted.

He put his arms around her, pulled her close, and kissed her mouth. While they embraced, the lamps went dark.

'Let's go down to the beach,' she whispered against his lips.

They strolled along the boardwalk, Joan cuddling against his side. At the bottom of the stairs, they stopped while Joan shook open her blanket. The beach was pale with moonlight. Beyond it, the ocean looked black except for the white froth of combers rolling towards shore.

'Want to share?' she asked.

'You bet.'

They draped the blanket over their shoulders and pulled it closed in front. 'Nice and snuggly,' Joan said.

'And private,' Dave added, slipping a hand under her sweatshirt. He caressed the sleek skin of her back.

'Privacy from whom?'

'You never know.'

Joan looked over her shoulder. Towards the darkness under the boardwalk. Dave felt her back stiffen.

He snapped his head around.

He saw no one.

'Now you've got us both spooked,' Joan said. Smiling, she

slipped a hand into the seat pocket of his corduroys. 'Creep.'
She gave his rump a squeeze.

'Come on.' He led her forwards, anxious to put some
distance between themselves and the black area that stretched
under Funland.

Probably *are* some derelicts under there, Dave thought.
Boleta Bay still had its share of them. Not many, though. Not
nearly as many there'd been before that night so long ago.

Trolls had fled from the funhouse even before the police
swept through it in the early morning hours. By noon, there
was not a troll to be found near the boardwalk or beach. Many
were spotted on roads leading out of town.

Some who didn't flee fell victim to outraged citizens. They
were beaten, taken for rides to the city limits, even murdered.
In the weeks that followed, the bodies of fourteen trolls were
discovered: in alleys, dumpsters, under the boardwalk, in the
woods outside town. All but three of the corpses had been left
with hand-printed cards or signs that read, 'Greetings from
Great Big Billy Goat Gruff and Friends.'

The killers were never apprehended.

Soon, not a troll could be found within miles of Boleta Bay.

Jasper's Funhouse and Oddities were demolished that winter.
The first event to take place in the amphitheatre erected in
their place was the June wedding of Nate and Robin.

To Dave, the wedding had seemed like an exorcism – a holy
ceremony that banished all remnants of evil from the place
where so much horror had been.

That summer, a few drifters and beggars began to appear.
They met no harm at the hands of the townspeople. Indeed,
they seemed different from those who had haunted the area in
the days of Jasper's Funhouse. Somehow, they seemed less
threatening.

Less threatening, but the sight of one never failed to remind
Dave of the night in the funhouse, never failed to send chills
crawling over his skin. Joan, he knew, had the same reaction.

When they reached the shore, she glanced back again as if
to make certain they hadn't been followed.

'Is the coast clear?' Dave asked.

'Looks okay.'

She opened her side of the blanket as Dave eased against her. He lifted her sweatshirt above her breasts. He caressed them. Her skin was pebbled with goose bumps, her nipples standing erect. She moaned softly. 'Let's find a place to spread the blanket,' she whispered.

'Right out here in the open?'

She looked up and down the beach, then pointed at the life guard station a hundred yards or so to the north. 'It's dark under there,' she said.

Dave kissed her breasts, then drew the sweatshirt down. With the blanket wrapped around themselves, they walked over the hard-packed sand towards the patch of black shadow.

'It's going to be cold,' Dave said.

'It's your job to keep me hot, fella.'

'Well, I'll sure try.'

'And I'll return the fav . . .'

A dark shape rose like a hump on the deck in front of the elevated life guard shack. Joan pressed herself hard against Dave's side. Her hand tightened on his hip.

The moonlit form dropped to the sand, stumbled, went down on its knees, then stood and began to shamble toward them.

'Oh shit,' Joan muttered.

It was a man. A troll. His wild tangle of hair and beard shone like snow under the pale moon. He wore a dark overcoat that looked many sizes too large for his skinny frame. The cuffs of his baggy trousers were rolled up. His white ankles were bare. One of his ragged sneakers had no laces, and flopped under his foot as he staggered closer.

He held out a hand.

'Let's get out of here,' Dave said.

'Gimme a quarter?' The voice was harsh and whiney. It sounded too young to be coming from a white-haired troll. 'Jes' a quarter? How 'bout it, folks?'

'Give him something, Dave.'

Dave's hand trembled as he took out his wallet. He felt sick, frightened, and angry that this damn intruder had ruined things. But he felt sorry for the guy, too. He took out a five-dollar bill and gave it to the troll, being careful not to let the scrawny hand touch him.

'God bless ya! God bless bote aya!'

He whirled away and scampered up the wooden stairs of the life guard station.

Dave and Joan hurried over the sand towards the distant stairway to the boardwalk. He could feel her shaking against him. 'It would've been nice,' he said.

'*Will* be nice. In our own bed.'

'We can spread this old blanket on it and pretend we're on the beach.'

'Leave the windows open.'

'Let's take some sand along and make it authentic.'

'Let's not.'

Five whole bucks. Five smackaroonies.

God bless 'em.

He wondered who they were. They'd looked a little familiar. Maybe he'd seen them around, someplace.

Could be, the gal'd been one of his nurses at the funny farm. He tried to picture her dressed in white, smiling and giving him pills.

Maybe that was it.

He shoved the bill into his shirt pocket. Dropping to his knees, he squinted at the boards of the platform.

He knew the spiders were there. He just couldn't see them. Too dark, even with the moonlight.

From a deep pocket of his coat, he took the can of insect spray. The white mist hissed from its nozzle. He crawled along, sweeping it back and forth, trying not to miss an inch of the deck.

'That'll getcha,' he muttered. 'Yeah! No way y'gonna get ol' Duke.'

When he was sure it was safe, he slipped the can into his

447

pocket. He took out a bottle of red wine. Holding it up to the moon, he shook it.

Still a few good swallows in there.

He popped the cork and began to drink.

The Stake

This book is dedicated to
Frank, Kathy & Leah De Laratta
great friends
fellow explorers
&
ghost town busters

Prologue

He had stalked the demon to her lair. Now, he waited. Waited for dawn, when she would be most vulnerable.

The waiting was the worst part. Knowing what was to come. The legends, he'd learned, were not to be trusted. The legends were wrong in so many ways.

Vampires slept in beds, not coffins – a clever ruse to fool the unknowing. And although daylight sapped their powers, it did not render them helpless. Even after dawn, they could wake from their sleep of the dead. They could fight him, hurt him.

He rubbed his cheek. His fingers trembled along crusty ridges of scab. She'd had sharp fingernails, the one in Urbana.

He shuddered with the memory.

He'd been lucky to save himself.

Maybe he'd used up his luck on that one. Maybe, this time, it wouldn't be fingernails ripping his cheek. Maybe, this time, teeth would find his throat.

Ducking down against the steering wheel, he reached under the driver's seat and pulled out a bottle of bourbon. He twisted off its cap. He drank. The liquor was lukewarm going down, but it spread soothing heat through his stomach. He wanted to drink more.

Later, he promised himself. No more until the task is done.

You must keep your wits about you, he thought. It was the liquor that almost got you killed last week.

Again, he rubbed his scratched cheek.

He took one more drink, then forced himself to cap the

451

bottle. He slid it under the seat. As he straightened up, a car turned the corner ahead. Its headlights were on, but the morning sky was light enough to show the rack on top. A patrol car.

He threw himself down across the passenger seat.

His mouth felt dry. His heart thundered.

It's not right, he thought. I shouldn't have to live like a fugitive. I'm as much a servant as those police out there.

He held his breath as the patrol car cruised by. It passed so close that he could hear crackles, squawks and a garbled voice from its radio. He regretted his decision to leave the windows down. They might find that suspicious. But his car would've been stifling if he'd kept it closed up.

He breathed again as the sounds faded.

He stayed low, counting slowly to one hundred. Then he sat up and peered out the rear window. The red tail-lights were mere specks.

Opening his door, he leaned out and studied the sky. It was still gray beyond the peeked roof of the vampire's dwelling. He placed a foot on the curb, straightened up and peered over the roof of his car. To the east, the sky was pale blue.

From long experience, he knew that the sun would soon appear above the horizon.

It would be up by the time he was in position.

He sank back into the car. His silver crucifix hung against his chest. He fingered its chain and pulled the cross out from under his shirt. Then, he lifted a leather briefcase off the floor in front of the passenger seat. Reaching into the case, he pulled out a necklace of garlic cloves. He looped it over his head.

Briefcase in hand, he stepped out of the car.

The overgrown lawn was surrounded by a picket fence. He swung the gate wide, kicking its bottom past tufts of weed that were high enough to hold it open. Coming put this way, he would be carrying the body. He didn't want the gate slowing him down.

The porch stairs creaked under his weight. The screen door

groaned. Inside the porch, he used a wicker chair to prop the door open.

Twisting the knob, he found that the front door wasn't locked. That made it easy. He wouldn't need his pry bar. He crept silently into the house, and didn't shut the door.

He knew where to find her room. Shortly after she'd entered, last night, lights had appeared in the front windows to the right of the porch. She'd stepped up to each of the windows, and lowered the shades.

The house was silent. The faint light that found its way into the living room cast a gray shroud over the old sofa, the rocking chair, the lamps and piano. The wallpaper looked faded and stained. Above the piano hung an oil painting of a forest clearing with a peaceful, running brook. In the gloom, it looked dim and somber as if dawn hadn't yet come to the forest scene.

At the far corner of the room was a wood-framed entrance to a hallway.

He crept to the hallway and followed it to the open door of the vampire's bedroom.

His mouth went dry and his heart pounded as he gazed in at her. She lay on a bed between the two windows, curled on her side, facing away from him. The first rays of the morning sun glowed against the blinds, filling the room with an amber hue. She was covered only by a sheet. Her dark hair was spread against the pillow.

Crouching, he set his briefcase on the floor. He spread its top, reached in, and lifted out the hammer.

A sledge with a heavy steel head and a foot-long haft.

With his other hand, he took out a pointed stake of ash wood.

He clamped the stake in his teeth.

He stood up. Staring at the vampire, he willed her to roll over. Face up or down, it didn't matter. He could pound the stake through her back as easily as her chest. But she had to be lying flat, not on her side.

Somehow, he'd known this would be a difficult kill.

Should he wait? Eventually, she was bound to turn over.

The longer he waited, the more danger of being seen when he carried the body out. And he *had* to do that. Take it far away in the trunk of his car and hide it where it would never be found.

People vanished all the time, and for many reasons. But to be discovered here with a stake in her heart . . .

The police would mistake it as the work of a homicidal maniac. The news would spread. The populace would panic. Worst of all, a legion of vampires would suddenly be put on guard that a hunter was in their midst.

And this morning's efforts would be in vain, for the police or coroner were certain to pull the stake from her heart. She would live again to prowl the night.

No. She had to disappear.

A floorboard creaked as he stepped to the side of the bed. She moaned. squirmed a little beneath the sheet, but didn't turn over.

The stake still held in his teeth, he reached out with his left hand. He pinched the sheet where its edge curled over her shoulder. As he eased it down, she continued to take long, slow breaths. But his own breathing quickened.

The sliding sheet revealed her naked back, the smooth curves of her buttocks, her sleek legs.

She was a vampire, a vile, murdering demon. But her body was that of a slender young woman, and he felt a stir of heat in his groin as he studied her. He trembled with the familiar mingling of lust and terror – a sensation close to ecstasy that always came upon him at such moments. He used to feel ashamed of his desire. Finally, however, he'd come to consider it a reward for his sacrifices. A payment, of sorts, bestowed upon him to balance out the risks.

Without it, he would have lost the will, long ago, to continue his crusade. He knew this to be true. Confronting vampires of the male gender, he felt no such arousal. Only revulsion. As a result, he had ceased to seek them out. He considered this to be his greatest failing, but often told himself that he was doing his share. He was one man against a horde. He couldn't dispatch them all. He had to be selective. So he selected the women. Horrid as they were, they excited him.

Her left arm lay against her side, bent at the elbow, the rest out of sight. Its skin was pebbled with tiny bumps from the cool, morning air. Leaning forward, he peered over her upper arm at the swell of her breast. It had goose flesh, like her arm. Her nipple stood erect. From this position, he couldn't see her other breast.

As he stared, saliva began to spill over his lip. He tried to shut his mouth, but the stake was in the way. He jerked his left hand up to catch the drool, but not in time.

A string of spit dribbled onto the vampire's arm.

Mumbling, she slid a hand out from under her pillow, brushed the wetness, rolled on to her back, and frowned as if perplexed. Still, her eyes were shut. She took the hand away. It fell onto the mattress beside her hip. It rubbed the sheet, then rose and came to rest on her thigh, the end of her thumb sinking into the thick nest of hair at her groin.

As he watched, full of dread that she might awaken, yet trembling with a fever of desire, he took the stake from his teeth. He knew he should wait no longer.

But he hesitated. His eyes roamed her sleeping form.

Though she might be centuries old, her face and body were those of a teenaged girl. She looked no older than seventeen or eighteen. She looked lovely, innocent, delicious.

If only she were human, and not a foul, loathsome creature of the night.

He ached to kiss those lips which had sucked so much innocent blood. He ached to caress those breasts, to savor their velvety smoothness, to feel the soft rub of those nipples against his palms. He ached to spread those legs and slide deep into her heat.

If only she weren't a vampire.

Such a shame. Such a waste.

Get it over with, he told himself.

He leaned farther forward, knees pressing against the side of the mattress, and raised his hammer high. His other hand twitched and fluttered as he lowered the tapered shaft toward her chest. The shaking point passed over her left breast, moved slightly higher, hovered half an inch above her skin.

There.

One strong blow, and . . .

Her eyes leaped open. She gasped. She clutched his wrist, twisted it with all the might of her demonic powers. Crying out, he watched in horror as the stake dropped from his numb fingers and fell, blunt end first, toward her other breast.

A feeling of utter desolation swept through him like an icy flood.

Without the stake . . .

As it bounced off her breast, he strained against her grip, praying to retrieve it. But her fierce hold was too powerful. The stake slid out of sight beyond her ribcage.

He knew, then, that all was lost.

Still, he swung the hammer down at her face. Snarling, she yanked his trapped wrist. She flung up her other arm, blocking the blow as he fell toward her.

He sprawled across her chest. An arm clamped tight against his back and she bucked beneath him, squirming and turning, tumbling him over her body. He no sooner hit the mattress than she scurried on to him and smashed a knee into his groin.

His breath blasted out. Stunned with agony, he saw the wooden shaft in her hand. Watched her raise it above his face. He tried to ward off the blow, but his stricken muscles failed to obey.

He had just enough breath to choke out a scream as the stake's point punched through his eye.

Explorers

Chapter One

'How about a little detour on the way home?' Pete asked. He started his van moving. Its tires crunched over the gravel of the parking lot.

A detour. Sounded good to Larry. But he said nothing. He knew that Pete's suggestion had been directed to those in the seats behind them. If the wives didn't go for it, the matter was closed.

'You aren't gonna get us lost again, are you?' Barbara asked.

'Who, me?'

'He gets us on those back roads, no telling where we'll end up.'

'I always get us home, don't I?'

'Eventually.'

Pete glanced at Larry. A corner of his mouth turned up, lifting that side of his mustache. 'Why do I put up with this? I ask you.'

Before Larry could come up with an answer, Barbara leaned forward and hooked a tawny forearm across her husband's throat. 'Because you love me, right?' she asked. She nipped the ridge of his ear.

'Hey, hey, calm down. You want to run me off the road?'

She wore a sleeveless blouse. A sprinkling of freckles showed on her deeply tanned shoulder. Though the air conditioner was blowing cool air into the van, the skin above her lip gleamed with moisture under a fine, curly down. Larry didn't want to be caught staring, so he looked away. Just ahead, an old-timer dressed like a prospector was leading a burro along the road's dusty shoulder.

Larry wondered if the guy was for real. Silver Junction, the town they were leaving behind, was full of characters in old west getups. Some seemed like the real article, but he had no doubt that most were simply playing the role for the benefit of the tourists.

'So how about it?' Pete asked as Barbara released him. 'Want to do some exploring?'

'I think it'd be fun,' Jean said. 'Are you in a hurry to get home, Larry?'

'Me? No.'

'He always hates to lose a day,' she explained. 'I have an awful time trying to drag him out of the house.'

'The day's already shot,' he said.

'Same to you, fella,' Barbara said.

'Woops. Didn't mean it that way. It's been great.' It *had* been a nice change from his usual seven-day work schedule. Fun being out with Pete and Barbara, wandering the old town, watching the gunfight on Main Street, having a burger and a couple of beers in the picturesque saloon. 'I need to get out more, anyway, or I'd run dry.'

'Everything we do ends up in his books,' Jean explained, 'but he still hates to be dragged away from his almighty word processor.'

'That's what keeps a roof over our heads.'

Pete tipped his head back as if to carom his voice off the top of the windshield, the better for Barbara to hear. 'Let's take him to that ghost town.'

A ghost town.

A warm, pleasant tightness came to Larry's chest and throat.

'You think you can find it?' Barbara asked.

'No sweat.' He turned to Larry, grinning. 'You'll love it. Just your kind of place.'

'It's pretty spooky, all right,' Barbara said.

'He'll be in hog heaven.'

'I bet you get a book out of it,' Pete told him. 'Call it *The Horror of Sagebrush Flat*. Maybe have some weirdos lurking around, chopping up everyone.'

Larry could feel himself blushing a little with the stir of pride that came whenever people started referring to his grisly novels. 'If I did,' he said, 'you wouldn't read it.'

'*I* will,' Barbara assured him.

'I know you will. You're my best fan.'

'I'll wait for the movie,' Pete announced.

'You'll have a long wait.'

'You're gonna make it,' he said, nodding at Larry and narrowing one eye.

Barbara gave the back of his head a gentle whack. 'He's *already* made it, dickhead.'

'Hey, hey, watch it with the hands.' He smoothed his mussed hair. The thick black hair was threaded with strands of gray. His mustache, with a lot more gray in it, looked as if it belonged on an older face.

'You'll be a wizened, silver-haired old coot,' Larry said, 'before they ever make a movie of one of my books.'

'Aah, bull. You'll make it, mark my words.' He tilted his head. '*The Beast of Sagebrush Flat*. I can see it now. I've gotta be one of the characters, right?'

'Of course. You're the guy driving.'

'Who's gonna play me? Has to be someone suitably handsome and dashing.'

'Peewee Herman,' Barbara suggested.

'You about ready to die, honey?'

'De Niro,' Larry said. 'He'd be perfect.'

Pete raised an eyebrow and stroked his mustache. 'Think so? He's kind of old.'

'You're no spring chicken,' Barbara said.

'Hey. Thirty-nine. Hardly counts as one foot in the grave.'

'Before you start losing your eyesight, you'd better watch for the turnoff.'

'I know just where it is. Never fear. I've got a natural instinct for these things. De Niro, huh? Yeah, I like that.'

'You'd better slow down,' Barbara told him.

'Don't get your shorts in a knot, huh? I know exactly where we're going.'

The van swept around a curve of the two-lane blacktop and shot past a road that led off to the left.

'That was it, smart guy.'

He leaned against his door and watched the road recede in the side mirror. 'Naw.'

'Oh yes it was.'

'They never listen to us,' Jean said.

'That wasn't it,' Pete muttered, stepping on the brake. The van slowed. He pulled onto the gravel shoulder, stopped, cranked his window down and stared back. 'You really think that's it, honey?'

'If you don't believe me, keep going.'

'Shit.'

'Maybe we *won't* be visiting a ghost town today,' Jean said, sounding amused.

Larry turned in his seat and looked at her. Smiling, she rolled her eyes upward. That expression was as good as words. *What've we gotten ourselves into?* Like Larry, she always got a kick out of the good-natured bickering that went on between Pete and Barbara. But they'd seen the arguments turn nasty, and had occasionally overheard quarrels that sounded truly vicious coming from the couple's next-door house.

'Why don't we give that road a try?' Larry suggested.

'It's not the one.'

'Prince Henry the Navigator,' Barbara muttered.

'Maybe we should flip a coin,' Jean said.

'Do you have a map?' Larry asked.

'Pete doesn't believe in them,' Barbara told him, her voice pleasant. Amazing how she reserved the sarcasm for her husband. 'It's up to you, Peter. I've offered my opinion. Feel free to ignore it.'

'Oh, hell,' he muttered. He started to turn the van around, and Larry saw the look of relief on Jean's face.

'If it's the wrong road,' Larry told Barbara, 'we hold you personally responsible.'

She bared her teeth at him, then laughed softly.

'That's tellin' her, pal.' Pete turned the van onto the sideroad and stepped on the gas. He drove up the middle, ignoring the faded white line. There wasn't enough left of the speed limit sign to read its numbers. The metal had been riddled with bullets. Some of the holes looked fresh, but many were fringed with rust. Pete pointed at the sign. 'There's some local color for you. Ol' Barb's *really* gonna be in trouble if we not only take the wrong road but get shot in the bargain.'

'We'll duck if we see any bargain hunters,' Larry said.

'Ha! Good one! I hate to tell you, they're in the back seat.'

'Can't miss at this range,' Jean said.

'We're dead meat.'

'You've got nothing to worry about, Petey. You're no bargain.'

'I know. I'm priceless. I'm also smart enough to know this isn't the road to Sagebrush Flat. But here we are, anyway.'

'It was a good decision,' Larry assured him. 'In my vast experience, I've found it always wiser to go along with female advice.'

'That's because it's usually right,' Jean said.

'Either way,' he told Pete, 'you can't lose. First, you make them happy by doing what they tell you. That's the main thing. Let them think they're in control. They love it. Then, if it turns out they were right, everything's cool. If it turns out they were wrong . . .'

'Which is usually the case,' Pete added.

'Do they know what thin ice they're on?' Jean asked.

'If they're wrong,' Larry went on, 'then you have the pleasure of basking in the glow of superiority.'

Pete grinned and nodded. 'Hey, you oughta put that in one of your books.'

'It *was* in one of his books,' Barbara said. 'If I'm not mistaken, a redneck cop spoke pretty much those very words in *Dead of Night*.'

'Yeah?'

'No kidding?' Larry asked, amazed that she had remembered such a thing.

'Don't you remember?'

He'd quoted one of his own characters without even realizing it? Odd, he thought. And a little disturbing. 'I don't know,' he admitted. 'If you say so, I guess it's there.'

'The philosophy at work,' Pete said.

'No, I mean it. I write so much . . . That book was a long time ago.'

'I have the advantage,' Barbara said. 'I just read it last month.'

'Hey, maybe you're becoming that guy. Turning into your redneck cop. There's an idea for a story, huh? A writer starts turning into this character he made up.'

'Has possibilities.'

'Well, if you use it, remember where you got the idea.'

'Ah-ha!' Barbara said. 'Over on the left.'

Looking across the road, Larry saw the ruins of an old structure. It no longer had a roof. The door and window panes, if it ever had them, were gone. The upper portions of the walls had crumbled away, and some of the rocks that might once have formed the square enclosure now lay in rubble around it – returning to the desert from which they'd been taken.

'Well,' Pete said, 'I guess this *is* the right road.'

'Prince Henry.'

'Doesn't look like much of a ghost town,' Jean remarked.

'That isn't it,' Barbara told her. 'But we stopped and had a look around before we got to Sagebrush Flat.'

'Nothing much there,' Pete said. 'Wanta take a quick look?'

'I'd rather get onto the main attraction.'

In spite of Jean's earlier comments about her difficulties in getting him out of the house, they'd taken several day trips during the past year to explore the region. Sometimes with Pete and Barbara, a few times by themselves or with Lane – when they could drag their seventeen-year-old daughter away from home. On those outings, Larry had seen plenty of ruins similar to the one they were leaving behind. But not a real ghost town.

'Don't you always wonder who lived in places like that?' Jean asked.

'Prospectors, I should think,' Pete said.

' "Dead guys," ' Larry quoted.

'Leave it to you. The morbid touch.'

'Actually, that was Lane's comment. "Dead guys." Remember, hon?'

'She went back to the car and waited for us, that time. She wanted nothing to do with it.'

'I know the feeling,' Barbara said. 'I think this stuff's interesting, but you gotta know that whoever lived there's been pushing up daisies for a while.'

'Cactus,' Pete said.

'Whatever. Anyway, dead. Makes it kind of spooky.'

'All the better for Larry here.'

'Doesn't bother me,' Jean said. 'I just think it's neat to see where they used to live, and, you know, imagine what it must've been like. It's history.'

'Speaking of history,' Larry said, 'what do you know about this ghost town of yours?'

'Not much,' Pete told him.

'*He* doesn't even know where it is.'

'It must be in some of those guide books,' Jean said.

'Nope. We checked.'

'I guess it's nothing all that special,' Pete said. 'Maybe it's not an official ghost town, or whatever it takes to get noticed – just a wide spot in the road that got deserted.' He suddenly grinned at Larry. 'Hey, suppose it's just there for us? You know? Like a figment of our imaginations.'

'A *ghost* ghost town.'

'Yeah! How about that? Another idea for you. You're gonna have to start paying me a consultant's fee.'

'You'd do better if you wrote the books yourself.'

'Hey, maybe I oughta give it a try. How long does it take you to knock out one of those things?'

'Six months, maybe, to write one. About twenty-five years to learn how.'

'You'd better just stick to repairing televisions,' Barbara said.

'We coming up on the turnoff?' he asked.

'I'll let you know.'

'We didn't get any chance to explore the place, last time,'

Pete said. 'Spent too much time screwing around back at that pile of rocks.'

'Watch it, buster.'

'Anyway, we had to get home for some party you were having, so we just drove right on through Sagebrush.'

God, Larry thought, he'd meant it literally. Otherwise Barbara wouldn't have reacted that way. They'd actually screwed in that old ruin. Inside those tumble-down walls. No door. No roof. Right out in the open, almost.

For just a moment, he was there. On top of Barbara. Her eyes were half shut, her lips peeled back, her naked body writhing under him as he thrust.

He banished the image, ashamed of his minor betrayal and the desire it stirred. No harm in daydreaming, he told himself. He had such fantasies often, and not just about Barbara. But he'd never cheated on Jean. He planned to keep it that way.

'You're coming up on it,' Barbara said.

Pete slowed nearly to a full stop by the time he made the right hand turn. The road ahead looked as if it had gone ignored by a generation of repair crews. Only a few faint traces remained of its center line. The gray, sun-baked asphalt was cracked, crumbling, pocked with holes.

The van pitched and bounced, swerved to miss the worst of the potholes. Larry found himself hanging onto the arm rest.

'You want to slow down?' Barbara suggested.

'You want to get there, don't you?'

'In one piece, if that's feasible.'

A bump rammed the seat against Larry's rump. His teeth clashed.

'Goddamn it!' Barbara snapped.

'Okay, okay. Didn't see that one coming.'

After he eased off the gas, the ride was still rough, but not punishing. Larry relaxed his grip on the arm rest. Looking out his side window, he saw the rusted hulk of an overturned car. Its roof was mashed in, and it had no wheels. It was well beyond the embankment bordering the road, surrounded by the desert's litter of broken rock, by cactus and scrub brush. He couldn't imagine how it had come to be belly-up. He considered mentioning the wreck, but decided to keep silent. The thing would probably inspire another story concept from Pete.

No doubt a perfectly mundane explanation for how it got there. Maybe it broke down, and was abandoned by the roadside. People had come along later, pushed it out there for the hell of it, and flipped it over. Had nothing better to do. If someone wanted to salvage the tires, rolling the thing probably seemed more sensible than jacking it up, one corner at a time.

Not just someone.

Larry felt a quick rush of joy.

A roving band of desert scavengers. A primitive, bloodthirsty pack.

Maybe they don't just wait for breakdowns. Maybe they block the road or booby-trap it, then ambush the unlucky travelers. They slaughter the men. They take the women back to their lair – maybe an abandoned mine – for fun and games.

Not bad. Worth toying around with later to see if he could make it work. He needed a new idea. And soon.

'Just around the bend,' Barbara said.

Larry peered out the windshield, but the view ahead was blocked by low, rocky slopes. The road curved through a gap between the desolate rises.

Maybe I can work the ghost town into the scavenger idea, he thought as they entered the narrow pass.

'Thar she blows!' Pete announced.

Chapter Two

Along the road leading into Sagebrush Flat were the remains of shacks that had been picked apart by the desert winds. Houses of stone, adobe and brick had fared better, but even those looked battered, their doors hanging open or gone, their windows smashed. Here and there, boards lay scattered on the ground near doorways and windows. Larry supposed that the lumber had once been used to seal the dwellings.

The weathered walls of the old houses were pocked with bullet holes, scribbled with sketches and messages in spray paint. Contributions from visitors to this dead town, making a playground of its carcass.

Many of the yards were bordered by broken-down fences. Along with cactus and brush, Larry saw pieces of old furniture in front of some houses: a sofa, a couple of cane chairs, an aluminum lawn-chair with its frame twisted crooked. One house had a bathtub off to the side. Another had an overturned bathroom toilet that looked as if it had been the subject of target practice. The rusted hood of a car was leaning against a porch. Nearby lay a couple of tires, and Larry recalled the abandoned, tireless car he'd seen a few minutes ago.

'Isn't exactly Beverly Hills, huh?' Pete remarked.

'Love it,' Larry said.

'Gee, and we forgot our spray cans,' Jean said. 'How can we properly deface the place without our paint?'

'We could shoot it up some.' Pete reached beneath his seat and came up with a revolver. It was sheathed in a beltless holster. Larry recognized it as the .357 Smith & Wesson that he'd fired a few times when they'd gone shooting last month. A beauty.

'Put that away,' Barbara said. 'For godsake.'

'Just kidding around. Don't get your balls in an uproar.'

As he concealed the handgun under his seat, Barbara said, 'Men and their toys.'

Pete swung the van off the road and stopped beside a pair of gasoline pumps. He beeped the horn a couple of times as if signaling for service.

'God,' Barbara muttered.

'Hey, wouldn't it be something if a guy *showed up*?'

Larry gazed past the pumps. The porch stairs led up to a country store with a screen door hanging by a single hinge. A faded wooden sign above the doorway identified the place as Holman's. A row of windows faced the road. Not a single pane was still intact. The window openings looked like mouths with sharp glass teeth.

'Might as well start here,' Pete said.

'Great,' Larry said. He thought it might be interesting to go through some of the houses they'd passed on the way in, but those could wait for another day. He was more eager to explore the downtown area.

He climbed out of the van. The wind and heat hit him. Jean grimaced when she stepped down. The wind blew her hair back, made her blouse and skirt cling to the front of her slim body as if they were wet.

'Better lock up,' Pete called.

'There's nobody around to steal anything,' Barbara said.

'Would you rather I take the magnum along?'

'Okay, okay, we'll lock the doors.'

Larry took care of their side. They met Pete and Barbara in front of the van.

'I would feel better if we took the gun with us,' Pete said.

'Well, I wouldn't.'

'You never know about a place like this.'

'If you think it's dangerous, we shouldn't be here.' Barbara tossed her head to clear her face of blowing blond hair. The wind parted her untucked blouse below the last button, and Larry glimpsed a triangle of tanned belly.

'Might be rattlers,' Pete said.

'We'll watch our step,' Jean told him. Like Larry, she was

469

no doubt eager to end the gun debate before it could escalate into a quarrel.

'Yeah,' Larry said. 'And if we run into any bad guys, we'll send you back here for the artillery.'

'Oh, thanks. While you guys hide.'

'You wouldn't mind, would you, honey?'

He answered by clamping a hand on Barbara's rump. The way she flinched and jumped away, he must've done it hard. She whirled toward him. 'Just watch it, huh?'

'Let's see what's in Holman's,' Jean said, and hurried toward the stairs.

Larry went after her. 'Careful,' he said. The boards, bleached pale, were warped and threaded with splits. The one before the top was broken in the middle, half gone and half hanging down by rusty nails.

Jean held the railing, stepped over the demolished stair, and made it safely across the porch. While she dragged the screen door open, Larry climbed the stairs. They creaked under his weight, but held him.

'You better not try it,' Pete warned Barbara, looking back at her as he trotted up the old planks. 'You'll snap 'em like matchsticks.'

'Give it a rest,' she said.

Larry admired her restraint. It seemed so damn stupid of Pete to poke fun at his wife's size. She was big, probably a shade over six feet tall. Though not a bean-pole like many tall women, she certainly wasn't overweight. Larry had seen her in all kinds of attire, including swimsuits and nightgowns, and considered her body terrific. He knew that Pete was proud of her appearance. But sometimes, the guy let his envy creep in. Pete was compact and powerful, but lifting all the weights in the world wouldn't give him the six inches of height he would need to meet Barbara eye to eye.

Instead of calling him 'short stuff' or 'pip-squeak', she'd simply told him to give it a break. Admirable.

She climbed the stairs without bursting any of them.

Inside, Holman's smelled of dry, ancient wood. Larry

expected the place to be stifling, but the shade and the breeze from the broken windows kept it bearable. A thin layer of sand coated the hardwood floor. It had blown into small drifts against the walls, the foot of the L-shaped lunch counter, and the metal bases of the swivel stools along the counter.

The eating area occupied about a third of the room. There had probably once been tables between the counter and wall, but they were long gone.

'Bet they served great cheeseburgers,' Jean said. She was very fond of diners with character. To Jean, dumpy old places that many people would disparage as 'greasy spoons' promised delights unattainable in clean and modern fast-food chains.

'Shakes,' Barbara said. 'I could go for one about now.'

'I could go for a beer,' Pete said.

'I think I saw a saloon up the road,' Jean told him.

'But they only serve Ghost-Lite,' Larry said.

'Let's break a few out of the van before we move on.'

'You've got beer?' Larry could *taste* it.

'Surely you jest. The desert's one dry mother. You think I'd brave her without my survival stash?'

'All *right!*'

Pete headed for the door.

'Aren't you going to look around?' Barbara asked.

'What's to see?' He hurried outside.

'I guess he's right,' Jean said, scanning the room.

'The rest of it must've been a general store,' Larry said. 'I bet they carried everything.'

Nothing remained, not even shelves. Except for the lunch counter and stools, the room was bare. Behind the counter was a serving window. Farther down, Larry saw a closed door that probably connected with the kitchen. Past the end of the counter was an alcove. 'That's probably where the restrooms were.'

'I think I'll check out the lady's,' Barbara said.

'Lotsa luck,' Jean told her.

'Can't hurt to have a look.'

She walked into the alcove, opened a door, and whirled away clutching her mouth.

'Apparently,' Larry said, 'it did hurt to take a look.'

Barbara scrunched up her face.

'You're a little green around the gills,' Jean told her.

She lowered her hand and took a deep breath. 'Guess I'll find a place around back.'

They left Holman's. She followed the porch, jumped off, and disappeared around a corner of the building.

Larry and Jean went to the van. When Pete came out, he had four bottles of beer clutched to his chest. 'Where's Barb?'

'Went behind the building.'

'Answering a call of nature,' Jean said.

He scowled. 'She shouldn't have gone off by herself.'

'She may not want an audience,' Jean explained.

'Damn it. Barb!' he yelled.

No answer. He called again, and Larry saw a trace of worry in his eyes.

'She probably can't hear you,' Larry said. 'The wind and everything.'

'Take these, okay? I've gotta make sure she's okay.'

Jean and Larry each took two bottles from his arms. 'She's only been gone a couple of minutes.'

'Yeah, well . . .' He hurried away, jogging toward the far end of Holman's.

'Hope he doesn't tear her head off,' Jean said.

'At least he's worried about her. That's something anyway.'

'I sure wish they'd quit bickering.'

'They must enjoy it.'

Jean wandered toward the road, and Larry stayed at her side. The bottles of beer felt cold and wet in his hands. He took a drink from the one in his right.

'You'll be having to go, yourself, if you don't watch it.'

'Don't let Pete come to my rescue,' he said, and turned his attention to the town.

The central road had broad, gravel shoulders for parking. The sidewalks were concrete, not the elevated planking common to such old west towns as Silver Junction where they'd spent the morning. The citizens had made some modern improvements before leaving Sagebrush Flat to the desert.

'I wonder why they left,' Larry said.

'Wouldn't you?'

'I wouldn't live anywhere that doesn't have movie theaters.'

'Well, I don't see any.'

Neither did Larry. From his position in the middle of the road, he could see the entire town. Not one of the buildings had a movie marquee jutting over the sidewalk. He saw a barber pole in front of one small shop; a place on the left with a faded sign that proclaimed it to be Sam's Saloon; about a dozen other enterprises, altogether. He guessed that they'd once been hardware stores, cafes, possibly a bakery, clothing stores, maybe a pharmacy and a five-and-ten, a dentist's and doctor's office, (and how about an optimistic realtor?), and certainly a sporting goods store. Not even the smallest back-country town in California was without a place to buy guns and ammo. Way at the far end of town, on the left, stood an adobe building with a pair of bay doors and service islands in front. Babe's Garage.

The centerpiece of town appeared to be the three-story, woodframe structure of the Sagebrush Flat Hotel, right next door to Sam's Saloon.

'That's the place I'd like to explore,' Larry said.

'Sam's?'

'That, too. But the hotel. It looks like it's been around for a while.'

'We'd better go there next, then. No telling how long this little expedition's going to last, those two start fighting.'

'We'll have to come back by ourselves, sometime, and really check the place out.'

'I don't know.' She drank some beer. 'I'm not sure I'd want to come here without some company.'

'Hey, what am I, chopped liver?'

'You know what I mean.'

He knew. Though he and Jean shared a desire for adventure,

473

they were limited by a certain timidity. The presence of another couple seemed to erase that weakness.

They needed back-up.

Back-up like Pete and Barbara. In spite of the bickering, each was endowed with self-confidence and force. Led by that pair, Larry and Jean were willing to venture where they wouldn't go on their own.

Even if we'd known about this place, Larry thought, we wouldn't have dared to explore it by ourselves. The chance of a return trip, at least in the near future, was slim.

Jean turned around and looked toward the corner of Holman's. 'I wonder what's keeping them.'

'Should we go find out?'

'I don't think so.'

Larry took a swig of cold beer.

'Why don't we get out of the sun?' Jean suggested.

They wandered back past the van, climbed the rickety stairs to Holman's shaded porch, and sat down. They rested the two extra beers on the wood between them. Jean crossed her legs. She rubbed her bare thighs with the base of her bottle. The wetness left slicks on her skin. She lifted the bottle to her face and slid it over her cheeks and forehead.

Larry imagined Jean opening her blouse, rolling the chilled, dripping bottle against her bare breasts. She wasn't the kind of woman who would ever do that, though. Hell, she wouldn't even step out of the house unless she had a bra on.

Too bad life can't be more like fiction, he told himself, and drank some more beer. A gal in one of his books would have that wet bottle sliding over her chest in about two shakes. Then, of course, the guy would get in on the action.

That'd be a scene worth writing.

You'll never get a chance to *live* it, not in this life-time, but . . .

'Larry, I'm starting to get worried.'

'They'll be along.'

'Something must be wrong.'

'Maybe she has a problem.'

'Like the trots?'

'Who knows?'

'They'd be back by now if *something* hadn't happened,' Jean said.

'Maybe Pete got lucky.'

'They wouldn't do that.'

'Obviously, they did it back at that old ruin we passed.'

'Sounded like it. But they were alone. They wouldn't do that here with us waiting.'

'If you're so sure, why don't we go around back and look for them?'

'Go right on ahead.' She gave him an annoyed glance.

'Nah.' He put a hand on her back. Her blouse was damp. He untucked it and slipped his hand beneath it. She sat up straight, and sighed as he caressed her.

When he fingered the catches of her bra, she said, 'Don't get carried away. They could show up any second.'

'On the other hand, maybe they won't show up at all.'

'Don't kid around like that, okay?'

'I'm not entirely kidding.'

'Maybe they *are* screwing around.'

'You said they wouldn't.'

'Well, I don't know, damn it.'

'Maybe we'd better go see.'

Jean wrinkled her nose.

'If they did run into trouble,' Larry said, 'we aren't making matters any better by procrastinating. They might need help.'

'Yeah, okay.'

'Besides, their beers are getting warm.'

He picked up the bottle for Pete, stood, and waited for Jean. Then, they walked to the end of the porch. Larry peered around the corner. The area alongside the building was clear, so he leaped down. Jean covered the mouth of Barbara's bottle with her thumb, and jumped.

'I don't know about this,' she said.

'They can't expect us to wait forever.'

Larry led the way, wanting to be a few strides ahead of Jean in case there really was trouble.

At times like this, he wished his imagination would take a holiday. But it never left him alone. It was always busy churning up possibilities – most of them grim.

He pictured Pete and Barbara dead, of course. Slaughtered by the same pack of desert scavengers he'd dreamed up when he saw the overturned car.

Maybe Pete had been killed, Barbara abducted.

We'd have to go looking for her. Run back to the van first, and get Pete's gun.

Maybe they both got killed by a criminal using the old town as a hideout.

Or by an old lunatic on the lookout for claim jumpers.

Maybe they'll just be gone. Vanished without a trace.

Pete has the keys to the van. We'd have to walk out of here. He supposed the nearest town was Silver Junction.

God, it'd take hours to get there. And maybe someone would be after them, hunting them down.

'Better warn 'em we're coming,' Jean said.

He stopped near the corner of the building, looked back at her, and shook his head. 'If they ran into someone . . .'

'Don't even think it, okay?'

From the look on Jean's face, he could see that she'd already considered the possibility.

'Just go ahead and call out,' she said. 'We don't want to barge in on something.'

Speak for yourself, he thought. If Pete was having at her, he wouldn't mind a glimpse of it. Not at all. But he kept the thoughts to himself.

Without looking around the corner, he yelled, 'Pete! Barbara! You all right?'

No answer came.

A second ago, he'd pictured them rutting. Now, he saw them sprawled dead, murderous savages hunched over their bodies, heads turning at the sound of his voice.

He gestured for Jean to wait, and stepped past the end of the building.

Chapter Three

'Where are they?' Jean whispered, pressing herself against his side.

Larry shook his head. He couldn't believe the two of them were actually gone. 'They probably just wandered off somewhere,' he said. The idea that he would catch them fooling around had been the product of wishful thinking, and he knew that his worries about murder had been farfetched. But so had his worries that they'd disappeared.

'We'd better find them,' Jean said.

'Good plan.'

But all he saw were the back sides of the other buildings, and the desert stretching away toward a ridge of mountains to the south.

'Maybe they're playing some kind of a trick on us,' Jean suggested.

'I don't know. Pete was awfully eager for his beer.'

'People don't go for a leak and vanish off the face of the earth.'

'Only on occasion.'

'It's not funny.' Her voice was trembling.

'Look, they've got to be around.'

'Maybe we'd better go and get the gun.'

'It's locked in the van. I don't imagine Pete would be very happy about a broken window.'

'PETE!' she suddenly shrieked. 'BARB!'

A distant voice called, 'Yo!'

Jean's eyebrows flew up. Her head snapped sideways, and she squinted out at the desert.

Some fifty yards off, Pete's head and shoulders rose out of the wasteland. 'Hey, y'gotta see this!' he shouted, and waved for them to approach.

Jean glanced at Larry, rolled her eyes, and sagged as if her air had been let out.

He grinned.

'I think I may kill them myself,' Jean said.

'I'll go get the gun.'

'Break *all* the windows, while you're at it.' Her voice sounded shaky.

'Come on, let's see what they found.'

'It better be good.'

They walked over the hard, baked earth, moving carefully as they stepped on broken rocks, avoided clumps of cactus and greasewood. Near the place where Pete waited was an old smoke tree. Larry guessed that Barbara had wandered farther and farther away from Holman's looking for a suitably large bush or rock cluster, and had finally decided upon the tree. Its trunk was thick enough to afford privacy, and there was shade beneath its drooping branches.

Pete was standing some distance from the tree. At his back, the ground dropped away.

'What'd you find?' Larry asked. 'The Grand Canyon?'

'Hey, glad you brought the suds.' He lifted the front of his knit shirt and wiped his face. 'It's *nasty* out here.'

Larry handed the full bottle to him.

The depression behind Pete was a dry creek bed some fifteen or twenty feet lower than the surrounding flatlands. Barbara, sitting on a rock at the bottom, looked up and waved.

'Did you forget about us?' Jean asked Pete.

He finished taking a swig of beer, then shook his head. 'I was just on my way to get you. Figured you might want to see this.' He started down the steep embankment, and they followed.

'We were getting a little worried,' Larry said, watching his feet as he descended the rocky slope. 'Thought you might've fallen victim to a roving band of desert marauders.'

'Yeah? That's a good one. Make a good story, huh?'

Barbara stood up and brushed off the seat of her white shorts. 'God, it's hot as a huncher down here,' she said as they approached. Her blouse was unbuttoned, its front tied, leaving her midriff bare. The knot was loose enough to leave a gap.

Her bra was black. Larry saw the pale sides of her breasts through its lace. 'No breeze at all,' she added.

'What's the big discovery?' Jean asked, handing a beer to her.

'It's no big deal if you ask me.' She tipped the bottle up. Larry saw a bead of sweat drop from her jaw, roll off her collar bone, and slide down her chest until it melted into the edge of her bra.

'Over here,' Pete said. 'Come on.'

He led the way to a cut eroded into the wall of the embankment. There, lying in shadows and partly hidden by tangles of brush, was the demolished carcass of a juke box. 'Must've come from that cafe,' he said, nudging its side with his shoe.

'How'd it get all the way out here?' Jean asked.

'Who knows?'

'The thing's no good, anyway,' Barbara said.

'It's seen better days,' Larry said, feeling a touch of nostalgia as he pictured it standing fresh and bright near the lunch counter in Holman's. He guessed that someone had dragged it out and used it for target practice. It would've made a tempting target, all decorated with bright chrome and plastic – if the shooter happened to be an asshole who took pleasure from destroying things of such beauty. After the box was blasted to smithereens, it had probably been shoved off the edge of the slope for the fun of watching it tumble and crash.

Larry crouched beside its shattered plastic top. The rows of record slots were empty. The tone arm dangled from its mount by a couple of wires.

'Probably worth a few grand,' Pete said.

'Forget it,' Barbara told him. 'He thinks we should take it with us.'

'She's sure a beaut,' Pete said. 'A Wurlitzer.'

'Think you could get it working?' Jean asked.

'Sure.'

He probably could, Larry thought. The guy's house was a museum of resurrected junk: televisions, stereo components, a toaster oven, lamps, a dish washer and vacuum cleaner, all once discarded as useless, picked up by Pete and restored to working order.

'You might get it playing again,' he said, 'but it's too messed up to ever look like anything.' Its chrome trim was dented and rusty, one side of the cabinet was smashed in, the speaker grills looked as if they'd been hit by shotgun blasts, and bullets had torn away at least half the square plastic buttons used for selecting tunes. 'You probably can't even get replacement parts for a lot of this stuff,' he added.

'Sure would be neat, though.'

'Yeah.' Turning his head sideways, Larry blew dust and sand from its chart of selections. Bullets and shot-gun pellets had ripped away some of the labels. Those that remained were faint, washed out by rainfall and years of pounding sunlight. Still, he could make out the names of many titles and artists. Jean crouched and peered over his shoulder.

'There's "Hound Dog",' he said. ' "I Fall to Pieces", "Stand by Your Man".'

'God, I used to love that one,' Jean said.

'Sounds like it's mostly shit-kicker stuff,' Pete said.

'Well, here's the Beatles. "Hard Day's Night". The Mamas and the Papas.'

'Oh, they were good,' Barbara said.

'This one's "California Dreaming".' Larry told her.

'Always makes me sad when I think about Mama Cass.'

'All right!' Larry grinned. ' "The Battle of New Orleans". Johnny Horton. Man, I must've been in junior high. I knew that sucker by heart.'

'There's Haley Mills,' Jean said, her breath stirring the hair above Larry's ear. ' "Let's Get Together". And look, "Soldier Boy".'

'Here's the Beach Boys, "Surfin' USA".'

'Now we're talking,' Pete said.

'Dennis Wilson, too,' Barbara said. 'So many of those people are dead. Mama Cass, Elvis, Lennon. Jesus, this is getting depressing.'

'Patsy Klein's dead, too,' Jean told her.

'And Johnny Horton, I think,' Larry said.

'What do you guys expect?' Pete said. 'This stuff's all at least twenty, thirty years old.'

Barbara took a few steps backward, stumbled when her sneaker came down on a rock, but managed to stay up. Sweaty face grimacing, she said, 'Why don't we get out of this hell hole and look around town? That's what we came here for, isn't it?'

'Might as well.' Jean pushed against Larry's shoulder and rose from her squat.

'Let's see if we can lift this thing,' Pete muttered.

'Oh no you don't!' Barbara snapped. 'No way! You're not carting that piece of trash home with us. Huh-uh.'

'Well, shit.'

'If you want an old juke box so bad, go out and buy one for godsake. Jesus, it's probably got scorpions in it.'

'I think you'd better forget it,' Larry said, rising to his feet. 'The thing's beyond saving.'

'Yeah, I guess. Shit.' He gave his wife a sour look.

'Thanks a heap, Barbara dear.'

She ignored his remark and started climbing the slope. Below her rucked-up blouse, her back looked tawny and slick. The rear of her shorts was smudged with yellow dust from the rock where she'd sat. The fabric hugged her buttocks, and Larry could see the outline of her panties – a narrow band inches lower than the belt of her shorts, a skimpy triangle curving down from it. Jean, climbing behind her, was hunched over slightly. Her blouse was still untucked. It clung to her back, and the loose tail draped her rump.

Pete was watching, too.

'Couple of good-looking chicks,' he said.

'Not bad.'

'You ever get the feeling they run our fucking lives for us?'

'Only about ninety-nine percent of the time.'

'Shit.'

'It's for our own good.'

Pete choked out a laugh, slapped Larry's arm, and took a long drink of beer. 'Guess we'd better be good little boys and go with them.' He glanced back at the juke box. He sighed. He shrugged. 'Adios. No more music for you, old pal.'

'So much for that,' Larry said when he saw the pad-locked hasp across the double doors of the Sagebrush Flat Hotel.

Pete fingered the lock. 'Doesn't look very old.'

'Maybe someone's living here,' Barbara said.

'Hey, Sherlock, it's locked from the outside. What does that tell you?'

'Tells me we'd be trespassing.'

'Yeah,' Jean said. 'The doors are locked, the windows are boarded. Somebody's trying to keep people out.'

'Kind of sparks my curiosity. What about you, Lar?'

'Sparks mine, too. But I don't know about breaking in.'

'Who's gonna find out?' Pete turned away from the doors. He stepped off the sidewalk, bent over and swept his head slowly from side to side in a broad pantomime of scanning the town's only road. 'I don't see anyone. Do you see anyone?'

'We get the point,' Barbara told him.

'I'll just mosey on over to the van.' He started across the pavement, walking at an angle toward Holman's.

'What's he got in mind?' Jean asked.

'God knows. Maybe he's planning to ram the doors open.'

'That'd be rather drastic,' Larry said.

'It's a matter of pride, at this point. A challenge. Pete wouldn't be Pete if he let a little thing like a lock keep him out.'

Jean rolled her eyes upward. 'I guess this means we're going to explore the hotel whether we want to or not.'

'Just consider it an adventure,' Larry suggested.

'Yeah, right. Jail would be an adventure, too.'

Pete climbed into the rear of the van. A few seconds later, he jumped down, swung the door shut, and waved a lug wrench overhead. It had a pry bar at one end. In his other hand was a flashlight.

He's really going to break in, Larry thought. Good Christ.

Barbara waited until he was closer, then called, 'We've been having some second thoughts about this, Pete.'

'Hey, what's life if you don't take a little chance now and then. Right, Lar?'

'Right,' he answered, trying to sound game.

'You're a lot of help,' Jean muttered.

Pete bounded on to the sidewalk, grinning and brandishing his tire iron. 'Got my skeleton key right here,' he announced. 'Fits any lock.'

'Anybody want to wait in the van?' Barbara asked.

'Aah, pussy.'

'Well, I guess I'd like to have a look around,' Larry said.

'Good man.'

Pete gave the flashlight to Larry. Then, he rammed the wedge end of the bar behind the metal strap of the hasp. He yanked with both hands, throwing his weight backward. Wood groaned and split. With a sound like a small explosion, the staple burst out of the door, bolts and all. 'Well, that was a cinch.'

He shoved the bar under his belt, turned the knob on the right, and pulled the door open.

'I suppose we could always say we found it like this,' Barbara muttered.

'You won't have to *say* anything. Half an hour or so, we'll be long gone.'

'If we don't get shot for trespassing.'

Ignoring her remark, Pete leaned into the doorway and called, 'Yoo-hoo. Anybody home?'

Larry winced.

'Here we come, ready or not!'

'Cut it out,' Barbara whispered, slapping the back of his shoulder.

'Nobody home but us ghosts,' he said in a low, scratchy voice, and turned around grinning.

'Real cute.'

'So who's coming in?'

'I think we should all go in or none of us,' Larry said,

483

hoping Pete wouldn't figure him for a pussy. 'I don't think we should split up. I'd be worried the whole time that something might happen to the gals while we're in there looking around.'

'Good man,' Barbara said, and patted his back.

'Guess you're right,' Pete admitted. 'If they got themselves raped and murdered while we were in there, boy would we feel like a couple of heels.'

'Exactly.'

'Real cute,' Jean said, borrowing not only Barbara's phrase but also her disdainful tone.

'What do you say?' Barbara asked her.

'They'll hold it against us forever if they can't go in on our account.'

'Admit it,' Pete said. 'You're dying to come with us.'

'Let's get it over with,' Barbara said.

Larry gave the flashlight back to Pete, and followed him into the hotel. In spite of the closed doors and boarded windows, sand had found its way into the lobby. It made soft scraping sounds under their shoes.

'We probably shouldn't leave the door open,' Jean said. There was a tremor in her hushed voice. 'In case someone comes by.' Without waiting for a reply, she closed the door, shutting out most of the daylight.

Light still came in around the doors, spilled through cracks and knotholes in the planks across the windows – pale, dusty streamers that slanted down to the floor. Pete turned his flashlight on. Its beam pushed a tunnel of brightness into the gloom. He swept it from side to side.

'Boy, there's a lot to see in here,' Barbara whispered. 'What a find!'

The lobby was bare except for a registration counter. On the wall behind the counter were cubbyholes for mail or messages. Over to the left, a wooden staircase rose steeply toward the upper floors.

'Should we check in before we have a look around?' Pete asked.

'Probably no vacancies,' Larry whispered.

'A couple of real comedians,' Jean muttered.

Pete led the way to the counter, pounded its top and said in a loud voice, 'How does a guy get some service around here?'

'Creep. You want to hold it down?'

'What's everybody whispering for?' He vaulted the counter, dropped into the space behind it, and ducked out of sight. He reappeared, rising slowly, the flashlight at his chin to cast weird shadows up his face. Where the beam touched him, his skin gleamed with sweat.

Goofing off like a kid, Larry thought. But he sometimes pulled the same gag, especially around Halloween, more to amuse himself than to frighten Jean or Lane. They had come to expect such antics. The old flashlight-on-the-face routine hadn't scared Lane since she was about two.

It did make Pete look strange and menacing. Larry knew that if he let his mind go with it, he *would* get a shiver. 'Mmmyes?' Pete asked, pitching his voice high. 'May I help zee veary travelers?'

'Yeah, you can help,' Barbara said. 'Take a flying leap at a doughnut hole.'

'Vee have no doughnuts, ma'am.'

'God, it's hot in here,' Jean whispered.

'A damn oven,' Barbara said.

'Anything back there?' Larry asked, carefully avoiding his friend's face.

'Only me and zee spirit of zee night clerk, who hung himself many years ago.'

'If we're going to look around,' Jean said, 'why don't we, and get out of here?'

'I'd like to have a look upstairs,' Larry said.

'Vait. Let me ring for zee bell captain.'

'Oh, the hell with him,' Barbara muttered. 'Come on.' She turned around and headed for the stairs. Jean went after her, and Larry followed. Barbara's legs and the bare part of her back were nearly invisible in the darkness. Her white shorts and blouse, pale blurs, seemed to float above the floor on their own. Jean, in darker clothes, was a faint smudge in front of Larry.

He heard Pete strike the floor and stride up behind him, sand crunching under his shoes. The flashlight beam flicked across the backs of the women, swung over to the staircase, and swept upward, skimming past balusters, tossing their long shadows against the wall. Midway up was a small landing. The remaining stairs rose to the narrow opening of the second floor corridor.

'You don't want to go first, do you?' Pete asked in his normal voice as Barbara started to climb.

'If I wait for you, we'll be here all day.'

The light moved downward, gliding just above the stair treads, and something touched by the low edge of its aura winked like gold. A small, questioning breath of surprise came from Pete. The light skittered backward and down. Its bright center came to rest on a crucifix. 'Christ,' he whispered.

'That's right,' Larry said.

The crucifix, directly below the landing, was attached to wood paneling that closed off the space beneath the staircase.

'What is it?' Barbara asked, leaning over the banister near the bottom of the stairs.

'Somebody left a crucifix on the wall,' Larry told her.

'Is that all?' She leaned farther out, then shook her head. 'Big deal,' she said.

Jean stepped around the side of the staircase for a closer look.

'Anybody want a souvenir?' Pete asked. He strode toward the crucifix.

'No, don't,' Larry warned.

'Hey, somebody just forgot it here. Finders keepers.'

'Leave it alone,' Barbara said from her perch on the stairs. 'For Godsake, you don't go around stealing crosses. That's sick.'

'We can put it in our bedroom. It'll keep the vampires away.'

'I mean it, Pete.'

The cross was made of wood. The suspended figure of Jesus looked as if it might be gold-plated. Pete reached for it.

'Please don't,' Jean said.

He looked at her. 'Oh,' he said. 'Oh, yeah.' Apparently, he had just remembered that Jean was Catholic. He lowered his hand. 'Sorry. I was just kidding around.'

'Reason prevails,' Barbara muttered. She pushed herself away from the banister and resumed climbing.

She got as far as the landing.

The wood creaked under her weight, then burst with a hard flat crack like a gunshot.

Barbara sucked in her breath. She flung her arms up as if trying to find a handhold in the dark air as she dropped straight down.

Chapter Four

'My God!' Pete shouted.

Jean, racing up the stairs, called out, 'Hang on!'

'I'm slipping! Hurry!'

Larry dashed toward the foot of the stairs. He didn't hear Pete coming. 'Where *are* you, man?'

'Get up there and grab her!' Pete snapped.

'Oh shit,' Barbara groaned.

Larry swung himself around the newel post. As he rushed up behind Jean, he saw the hazy glow of Pete's flashlight ahead and to the right of the stairs. Hadn't the guy moved? Was he still down there in front of the crucifix?

Jean sank to her knees at the edge of the landing.

Barbara, her back to the lower stairs, looked like someone being swallowed by quicksand. She was hunched forward, pressing her chest against the remaining boards, bracing herself up with her elbows.

Jean crawled aside to make a space for Larry, then hooked an arm under Barbara's left armpit. 'Gotcha,' she gasped. 'I gotcha. You're not gonna fall.'

'Are you okay?' Pete called up.

'No, damn it!'

Larry dropped against the landing and stairs. Looked down into a six-inch gap between the broken planks and the white of Barbara's blouse. Blackness.

A bottomless pit, he thought. An abyss.

Ridiculous, he told himself. Probably no more than a six or seven foot drop, all told, from the landing to the lobby floor. She was already about halfway there.

What if the floor doesn't extend under the staircase?

Or she breaks through that, too?

Even if she had only a four foot fall, she would end up trapped under the staircase. And the broken boards might scrape her up pretty good on the way down.

He squirmed forward until his face met the hair on the back of Barbara's head. He wrapped his arms around her. They squeezed her breasts. Muttering, 'Sorry,' he worked them lower and hugged her rib cage.

'Pete!' he yelled.

'You got her?' Pete's voice still came from below.

'Just barely. If you'd give us a goddamn hand!'

He heard a crack of splitting wood. For a moment, he thought that more of the landing was giving out. Nothing happened, though.

'Yah!' Barbara yelped, jerking in Larry's embrace. 'Something's *got me*!'

'It's just me, hon.'

For an instant, a pale tongue of light licked the darkness beside Larry's right shoulder. It had risen through the broken boards.

Pete's under us, he realized.

'How'd you get down there?' Jean asked. She sounded amazed, relieved.

'Tire tool magic,' Pete said. 'Okay, I've got you, hon. Let's lower her gently.'

'No no no, don't! I'll fall.'

'We gotta get you down outa there.'

'Well, boost me up, okay?' Her voice was controlled, but tight with pain or fear. 'If I try to go down, I'll get wracked up even more.'

'All right. We'll give it a try. You guys ready up there? On the count of three.'

'You gonna push her up by her legs?' Jean asked.

'That's the idea. One. Two.'

'Take it easy,' Barbara urged him, 'or I'll end up with a bunch of wood in me.'

'Okay. One. Two. Three.'

Barbara came up slowly through the break as if she were standing on an elevator. Still hugging her chest, Larry struggled to his knees. She swayed back against him. He slid a hand down the slick, bare skin of her belly. She gasped and flinched. Then he grabbed her belt buckle, yanked upward, pulled her hard against him, and she came to rest sitting at the brink of the gap.

'Okay,' she gasped. 'I'm okay. Give me a second to catch my breath.'

Larry and Jean held onto her arms.

'All right up there?' Pete asked. The beam of his flashlight swept back and forth through the break in front of Barbara's knees.

Barbara didn't answer.

'She's safe,' Jean called down.

The beam slid away, and only a faint glow drifted out of the opening.

'I want to go home,' Barbara muttered. Larry and Jean held her steady while she leaned back and drew her legs up. She planted her shoes against the rim of splintered wood at the gap's far side.

'*Jesus!*' Startled, scared.

Barbara went rigid. 'Pete! What's wrong!'

'Holy jumpin' . . . Oh, man.' Not quite so scared, now. Amazed. 'Hey, you're not gonna believe this. Honest to motherin' God. Larry, get down here.'

489

'What?'

Barbara leaned forward and peered between her spread legs. 'What is it?'

'You don't want to know.'

'This is no time for games, Peter.'

'You're just damn lucky you didn't wind up down here.'

For a moment, no one said anything.

Then Pete's voice came up through the crevice. 'You would've had company.'

Shivers ran up Larry's back.

'There's an old stiff in here.'

He's kidding, Larry thought. But his body knew that Pete was telling the truth. His cheeks suddenly felt numb. He had trouble getting enough breath. His bowels went shaky. His scrotum shriveled up tight as if someone had just grabbed it with a handful of ice.

'Oh jeez,' Barbara muttered. Jean and Larry got out of her way as she twisted around, grabbed the banister, and struggled to her feet. They followed her down the stairs. She held the railing and moved slowly, hunched over just a bit. Her blouse now hung all the way down her back.

'I knew I didn't like this place,' Jean whispered.

Barbara went straight to the hotel door and threw it open. Daylight flooded in. She stopped in the doorway and turned sideways. She was squinting. Her teeth were bared. Though Larry was several feet away, he could see her trembling. Her hands shook as she pinched the edges of her blouse and spread its front wide. She gazed down at the raw band of skin across her belly.

Her breasts looked very white through the open patterns of her bra. Larry glimpsed the darker skin of her nipples. She was too hurt and dazed for modesty, and Larry felt like a cheap voyeur taking advantage of her carelessness. In spite of the guilt, he didn't want to look away. There was a dead body under the stairs. Somehow, the sight of Barbara's skin through the black lace bra eased his sick dread.

But he forced his eyes lower. The right leg of her shorts was rucked up higher than the left. Both thighs were scraped, her shins bleeding. The right was worse than the left, but both legs had been abraded in the fall.

Jean went to her. 'You really *did* get wracked up.'

'You're telling me.'

'Where is everyone?' Pete called. His voice sounded muffled.

'Barbara's really banged up,' Larry answered. 'Come on out of there and let's go home.'

'You've gotta see this! It'll just take a minute.'

I don't want to see it.

'Man, your wife is hurt.'

'What's one more minute or two? We've got a *dead body* here. You're a writer, for godsake. A *horror* writer. I'm telling you, this isn't something you want to miss. Come on.'

'Go ahead if you want,' Jean told him. 'We'll start on over for the van.'

Larry wrinkled his nose.

Barbara nodded, still grimacing and shaking. Her face and chest were shiny with sweat. Larry found himself looking again at her breasts. 'Go on,' she said. 'It'll make him happy.'

'You gals don't want to see it?'

'You've got to be kidding,' Jean said.

'Just make it quick,' Barbara told him.

He turned away from the door. He walked slowly across the lobby floor. Glancing back, he saw Jean and Barbara step outside.

He felt abandoned.

I don't have to be here, he thought. I could be out there with them.

He did not want to see a damn corpse.

But his weak legs kept moving him away from the sunlight.

Alongside the staircase, a wide section of paneling had been ripped loose and gaped open a couple of feet. The glow of Pete's flashlight showed through the space. Larry turned sideways, and stepped into the enclosure.

'Thought you were going to chicken out on me,' Pete said. 'Can't miss a chance like this.'

He found Pete standing on a couple of boards that had fallen from the landing. He looked frozen there, back rigid, his right arm straight out, aiming the flashlight almost as if it were a pistol. Aiming it at the coffin that was jammed headfirst against the underside of a low stair.

Keeping the body covered.

The body was already covered, at least to the neck, by an old brown blanket. The blanket was rumpled as if it had been tossed into the coffin by someone who didn't care to straighten it.

The corpse had long, yellow hair. The skin of its face looked tight and leathery. Larry saw sunken eye-lids, hollow cheeks, lips that were stretched back in a mad grin that exposed teeth and gums.

'You believe this?' Pete whispered.

Larry shook his head. 'Maybe it isn't real.'

'My ass. I know a stiff when I see one.'

'Looks almost mummified.'

'Yeah. Guess we oughta check it out, huh?'

Shoulder to shoulder, they moved slowly forward. Pete kept his light on the corpse.

Hideous, Larry thought. He'd never seen such a thing. His experience with bodies was limited to three open-casket funerals. Those people had looked almost good enough to sit up and shake hands with you.

This one looked as if it might want to sit up and take a bite out of you.

Don't think that stuff, Larry told himself.

The underside of the stairway slanted down in front of them. They had to duck as they stepped to the foot of the coffin. Pete sank into a squat and waddled in farther. Larry started in, crouching. But after one step, a sense of suffocation stopped him. The stairs seemed to be pressing down on him, wanting to shove him lower, to rub his face in the corpse. He dropped to his knees and reached out, ready to brace himself on the wooden edge of the coffin. Just before he touched it, he realized what he was about to do. He jerked his hands back and clutched his thighs.

The blanket piled on top of the corpse didn't cover its ankles and feet. They were bare, the color of stained wood, and bones showed through the tight skin. The nails were so long that they curled over the tops of the toes. Larry recalled that hair and nails supposedly continued to grow after death. But he'd heard that that was just a myth; they only *appeared* to grow because the skin sank in around them.

'Bet it's been here a long time,' Pete whispered. He reached over the side of the coffin. With his index finger, he brushed the corpse's forehead.

Larry moaned.

'What's wrong?'

'How can you *touch* it?'

'No big deal. Try it. Feels like shoe leather.' He drew his finger across a blond eyebrow.

Larry imagined Pete's finger sliding down the ridge of the eye socket, touching the lid, denting it, sinking in to the second knuckle.

'Go on and touch it,' Pete urged him. 'How you going to write about this stuff if you don't experience it?'

'Thanks, anyway. I'll rely on my imagi . . .'

'We changed our minds.'

He flinched at the sound of Barbara's voice. So did Pete. Pete's head slammed the underside of a stair. He cried, 'Ah!', ducked down close to the face of the corpse and grabbed the back of his head. 'Shit! Damn it, Barb!'

'Sorry.'

Larry looked over his shoulder at the women, and smiled. Though his startled heart was drumming, he was *glad* they were here.

He felt as if some of the real world had come back.

'Guess you weren't kidding,' Barbara whispered. 'Jesus, look at that thing.'

'Yuck,' was all Jean said.

Barbara crouched over the end of the coffin, Jean stayed behind her and peered over her head.

'Didn't want us to have all the fun?' Larry asked.

'That's about the size of it,' Jean said, her voice hushed.

'Curiosity got the best of us,' Barbara added. Then she reached into the coffin and touched the foot of the corpse.

She's just like Pete, Larry thought. Whatever their differences, they're sure a set.

'I think I'm bleeding,' Pete muttered.

'That makes two of us,' Barbara said, still rubbing the deadfoot. 'It's like the skin on a salami.'

'Salami's oily,' Pete told her. 'This is more like leather.'

'Okay, we've seen it,' Jean said. 'Everyone ready to go?'

'Yeah, just about.' Pete stopped rubbing his head, reached one arm down over the covered torso, and snatched off the blanket. Larry lurched backward on his knees, wishing to God he'd known this was coming. He'd already seen too much.

Now, the corpse was stretched in front of his face.

It was naked.

It was female.

It had a wooden stake in its chest.

'Holy shit,' Barbara whispered.

'Let's get out of here!' Jean gasped in a high, tight voice. She didn't wait for a consensus. She bolted.

Pete threw the blanket down. It landed in a pile, covering the blunt top of the stake, the corpse's flat breasts and the slats of its ribs. Barbara leaned forward, grabbed a bit of the blanket, and jerked it down to cover the groin.

Blond pubic hair.

Larry groaned.

Then he was scurrying after Barbara. The white seat of her shorts was still smudged with yellow from the rock where she'd rested in the creek bed.

Seemed like a century ago.

Why did we do this?

Larry followed her through the open section of paneling.

Jean was still in the lobby. Her fists were clenched at her sides, and she was prancing as if she had to pee. 'Let's go, let's go!' she gasped.

Larry waited for Pete.

Together, they pushed the slab of wood into place.

Shutting the door of the tomb.

Pete backed away as if afraid to take his eyes off it.

In the beam of his flashlight, the crucified body of Jesus gleamed.

Chapter Five

Pete floored it out of Sagebrush Flat, and Barbara didn't say a word about the speed.

Nobody said a word about anything.

Larry slouched in the passenger seat, feeling dazed and exhausted. Though he stared out the windshield at the sun-bright road and desert, he kept seeing the corpse. And the stake in its chest. And the crucifix.

It's behind us now, he told himself. We got away. We're all right.

His body felt leaden. There was a shaky tightness in his chest and throat that seemed like a peculiar mix of terror – subsiding terror – and elation. He remembered experiencing similar sensations a few years earlier. On a flight to New York, the 747 had hit an air pocket and dropped straight down for a couple of seconds. Some of the passengers struck the ceiling. He and Jean and Lane, strapped in their seats, had been unharmed. But he'd felt this way afterward.

Probably shock, he thought. Shock, combined with great relief.

He sensed that, if he didn't keep tight control of himself, he might start weeping or giggling.

This must be where they get the expression, 'scared silly.'

'How's everybody doing?' Pete asked, breaking the long silence.

'I want a drink,' Barbara said.

'There's more beer in the ice chest.'

'Not beer, a *drink*.'

'Yeah, I could go for one myself. Or three or four. We should be home in less than an hour.' He glanced at Larry. 'You *believe* that back there? That was like right out of one of your books.'

'He hasn't written any vampire books,' Barbara said. 'You'd know that, if you ever read them.'

'Bet you will, now, right?'

'I think I'd rather forget about it.'

'Same here,' Jean said. 'God.'

'That babe had a *stake* in her heart.'

'We all saw it,' Barbara reminded him.

'And how about that crucifix? I'll bet they put it there to keep her from getting out.' He nodded, squinting at the road. 'You know? In case the stake fell out, or something. To keep her from breaking through the wall.'

'How would the damn stake fall out?' Barbara asked, sounding a little bit annoyed by his musings.

'Well, you know, a rat could get in there. A rat might pull it loose. Something like that.'

'Give me a break.'

'There's no such thing as vampires,' Jean said. 'Tell them, Larry.'

'I don't know,' he said.

'What do you mean, you don't know?'

'Well, there's plenty of legend about them. It goes way back. Back in the Middle Ages, a lot of poor jerks wound up buried at crossroads with their heads cut off and garlic stuffed in their mouths.'

'Guess ours got off lucky, huh?' Pete grinned at him. 'All she got was the ol' stake-in-the heart routine.'

'She's not any vampire,' Jean insisted.

'Somebody sure wasted her, though,' Barbara said.

'That's right,' Jean said. 'Has it occurred to anyone that we found a dead body?'

Pete raised his hand like a school kid. 'Me,' he said. 'I caught that right off the bat.' He chuckled. 'No pun intended.'

'No, I mean shouldn't we tell the police?'

'She's got a point,' Barbara admitted.

'So does our babe under the stairs,' Pete said, laughing some more. 'A point right in her chest.'

'Give it a rest, would you? This is serious business. We can't just find a body and pretend it never happened.'

'Right. We'll just tell the cops we broke into a locked hotel.'

'*You* broke into a locked hotel.'

'Hey, you want to be married to a jailbird?'

'We could make an anonymous call,' Jean suggested. 'Just explain where the body is, so they can go out and get it. Really. I mean, whoever she is, she deserves a decent burial.'

'I wouldn't want it on my conscience,' Pete said.

'What do you mean?'

'They won't bury her with that stake in her chest. Some poor slob'll pluck it right out. Next thing you know, he's a vampire cocktail.'

'That's ridiculous,' Jean muttered.

'Is it?' Making an evil laugh, he grinned over his shoulder at her.

'Watch where you're driving,' Barbara said.

'I don't think we should call the cops,' Larry said. 'Even if we do it anonymously, there's still a chance we might get dragged into the situation.'

'I don't see how,' Jean told him.

'How do we know we weren't seen? Somebody might've driven through town and spotted the van while we were admiring the juke box.'

'Or the vampire,' Pete added.

'And might've noticed the license plate number.'

'Oh, there's a pleasant thought,' Barbara muttered.

'You just never know. That's all I'm saying.'

'Hey, somebody could've even been watching us from a window or something.'

'Thanks, Peter. I really needed to hear that.'

'Even if nobody did see us,' Larry went on, 'we undoubtedly left physical evidence behind. Fingerprints, footprints, tire tread marks where the van drove over dirt. The police would probably treat the whole area as a crime scene. There's no telling what they might find. Next thing you know, they could be knocking on the door.'

'We didn't kill her.'

'Have you got an alibi,' Pete asked, 'for the night of September 3, 1901?'

'A pretty good one. I wasn't born yet. My *parents* weren't born yet.'

'You think she's been dead that long?' Barbara asked.

'Sure looked old to me.'

'I have no idea when she might've been killed,' Larry said, 'but I bet she hasn't been under the stairs there for much more than twenty years or so. I imagine she was put there *after* the hotel closed down.'

'Why's that?' Pete asked.

'The guests would've smelled her.'

'Gross,' Jean muttered.

'Well, it's true. Assuming she was put in there right after she was killed, people would've noticed the stink. She doesn't smell now, but . . .'

'You're making me sick, Larry.'

'Why do you say twenty years?' Barbara asked.

'The juke box.'

'Ah-ha. The oldies-but-goodies.'

'I don't think any of the songs I noticed were much later than the mid-sixties. That's probably when Holman's went out of business. I figure the hotel might've closed its doors around the same time as Holman's.'

'Makes sense,' Barbara said. 'So you think the body was put under the stairs sometime after, say, sixty-five?'

'It's just a guess. Of course, she could've been dead fifty years before somebody put her under the stairs. If that's the way it went, there's no telling how long she's been there.'

'Yeah,' Pete said. 'You eliminate the stink factor by having her someplace else while she's ripe, you could stick her under the stairs and nobody'd be the wiser.'

'I don't see how it matters,' Jean said. 'The thing is, she's dead. Who *cares* how long she's been under the stairs?'

Pete again raised his hand. 'I myself find it to be of more than passing interest.'

'So would the cops,' Larry added. 'I think it'd make a big difference in the way they look at the situation. If she's been dead half a century – and they have ways of figuring that stuff out – she's almost like an historical artifact. If she was only killed twenty years ago, they might very well start an active homicide investigation.'

'That's right,' Barbara said. 'Whoever put the stake in her could still be alive and kicking.'

'Speaking of which,' Pete said. He glanced at Larry, arched an eyebrow and stroked his chin. 'Wait'll you hear this one.'

'We know,' Barbara said. '*You* did it.'

'Hey, I'm being serious here.'

'That's a switch.'

'Anybody happen to notice anything odd about the front doors of the hotel?'

'Aside from the fact that we were the first to break in?' Barbara asked.

'Very good, hon. That's one thing. The place was still sealed when we got there. Just about every other joint in town was wide open. People'd busted in and done some exploring. But not the hotel. What else?'

'Are we playing Twenty Questions? Is it bigger than a bread box?'

'Here's a clue. Bright and shiny and brand new.'

'The padlock,' Larry said. 'The hasp.'

'Right! The way those suckers looked, I'll bet they were sitting on the shelf of a hardware store a month ago.'

'So?' Jean asked.

'Who put them on the doors? Who wanted to keep intruders out of the hotel?'

'Could've been anyone,' Larry answered.

'Right. And it could've been someone who hid a vampire under the stairs. Someone who's still around and trying to make sure nobody stumbles onto his little secret.'

'The same person who put the crucifix on the wall,' Larry added.

'Right.'

'Sort of a guardian, a keeper of the vampire.'

'It's more likely,' Barbara said, 'that whoever put the lock on the doors doesn't know a thing about it.'

'More interesting if he does,' Pete told her.

'Maybe for you.'

'Any chance we might stop talking about it?' Jean suggested. 'I wish we'd never stepped foot in that damn hotel.'

'You and me both,' Barbara said. 'Screw the vampire, I haven't been so wracked up since I wiped out on my bike about ten years ago. Even then, I didn't tear up my *stomach*. I'm gonna be *fetching* in my bikini.'

'Not that I didn't warn you about climbing stairs,' Pete reminded her.

'Those were pretty creaky, but I sure didn't expect them to break.'

'Maybe the vampire *willed* you to fall through. Planned to have you pull the stake for it.' Doing a Lugosi impression, he added, 'It vanted to suck your blood.'

'Oh, sure.'

'Pretty good,' Larry told him. '*You* ought to be the writer.'

'It's not a vampire,' Jean persisted.

'You know,' Pete said, ignoring her remark, 'we *should've* pulled the stake. You know what I mean? Just to see what happens.'

'Nothing would've happened,' Jean said.

'Who knows?' He leered at Larry. 'Hey, want to turn around and go back and do it?'

'No way.'

'Aren't you curious?'

'Not that curious.'

'Just try turning the van around,' Barbara warned, 'and *I'll* bite your neck.'

'Pussy.'

'Don't push it, buster. It was your big idea that got me messed up like this.'

'You could've stayed outside. Nobody was holding a gun to your head.'

'Just shut up, okay?'

He cast a glance at Larry. His expression was somewhat amused. 'Guess I'd better shut up before I get her riled, huh?'

'I would if I were you.'

'What ever happened to freedom of speech?' Though the words were spoken quietly to Larry, they were aimed at Barbara.

'That freedom ends where my ears begin,' she said.

Pete grinned at Larry, but said no more. He drove in silence.

Larry looked out at the desert. He still felt a little light-headed and nervous, but much better than before. He guessed that the discussion had helped. Putting words to it. Sharing their concerns. Especially the playful way Pete had turned the whole godawful experience into a vampire story. And the bickering between Pete and Barbara. Their nice, normal, everyday quarreling. It all helped a lot. Leached the horror out of their encounter with the corpse. Like throwing sunlight on to a nightmare.

But his anxiety started to grow when they came to Mulehead Bend. Not even the familiar sights along Shoreline Drive were enough to dispel the dread that seemed to be swelling inside him.

Pete drove slowly through the traffic – a few auto-mobiles surrounded by the usual mix of off-road vehicles, campers, vans, pickup trucks, and motorcycles. The road was bordered by motels, service stations, banks, shopping centers, restaurants, bars and fast-food joints. Larry saw the bakery where he'd bought a dozen doughnuts early that morning. He saw the supermarket where Jean did her grocery shopping, the computer store where he regularly bought floppy disks, paper and printer ribbons for his word processor, the movie theater where they had attended a horror double-feature Wednesday afternoon.

Every now and then, he caught glimpses of the Colorado River just east of the business district. A few people were still out, water skiing. He saw a house-boat. A shuttle boat was carrying passengers toward the casinos on the Nevada side of the river.

All so familiar, so normal. Larry thought he ought to feel some relief in returning to home turf, leaving behind the strangeness and desolation of the back roads.

But he didn't.

It's splitting up with Pete and Barbara, he realized. He didn't want to part with them. He was *afraid*. Like a kid who'd been telling spooky stories with his friends, and now had to walk home alone in the dark.

I'm not a kid, he told himself. It's not dark. We just live next door. And I won't be going home alone, Jean will be with me and Lane's probably back by now.

'Why don't you guys stick around for a while?' Barbara suggested. 'We'll have some cocktails, get the dust out of our throats.'

'Great!' Larry told her, wondering if she, too, was reluctant for the group to break up.

'I'll make my famous margaritas,' Pete said.

'Sounds good to me,' Jean said.

Larry felt blessed.

Pete left the traffic of Shoreline Drive behind, and steered up the curving road to Palm Court. When he turned onto Palm, their houses came into view.

It *was* good to be getting home. Now. Now that they would be having drinks with Pete and Barbara.

Lane appeared from beside the porch. She wore cut-off blue jeans and her white bikini top, and carried a plastic bucket. Apparently, she was preparing to wash the Mustang.

Pete beeped the horn as they approached. Lane turned to them and waved.

'Let's not say anything to her about the you-know-what,' Jean said.

'Mum's the word,' Pete said. He pulled into his driveway and stopped. Climbing from the van, he called to Lane, 'Feel free to do this one when you get through over there.'

'Hardy-har.'

'Have fun shopping?' Jean asked her.

'Yeah, it was okay.' She beamed at Larry as he stepped past the front of the van. 'I spent *all kinds* of your money, Dad. You're gonna have to stay home and write like a dog.'

'Thanks a lot, sweetheart.'

'Consider me a motivating force. So, how was the excursion?'

'Had a good time,' Jean told her. 'We'll be over here for a while.'

'Join us if you'd like,' Barbara said, appearing behind the van with the ice chest in her hand.

'Jeez!' Lane blurted. 'What happened to you?'

'Had a little accident.'

'Are you okay?' she asked, frowning.

'Just some scrapes and bruises. I'll live.'

'Wow.'

'Come on over, if you'd like. We'll be having some drinks and snacks.'

'Thanks anyway. I want to wash the car.'

'Well, if you change your mind . . .'

'Sure. Thanks.'

They entered the house. The air conditioning felt cool and good after the brief walk through the heat. Larry sat in his usual chair at the kitchen table. Jean sat across from him. Pete began to gather bottles from the liquor cupboard.

It was all very familiar, very comforting.

'I'm going to get cleaned up a bit,' Barbara said. 'Back in a minute, then I'll dig up some goodies.'

Pete sang a few lines of 'Margaritaville', as he dumped tequilla and Triple Sec into his blender. The blender was one of his finds. Someone had put it out for the trashmen, he'd spotted it while driving to work, picked it up and restored it to working order.

It reminded Larry of the juke box down in the creek bed. He saw himself crouching over it, and then he was on his knees beside the coffin, staring in at the withered brown corpse.

He felt himself start to shrink inside.

It's history, he told himself. We're home. It's all over. That damn thing is fifty, sixty miles away.

'Sure is good to be here,' he said.

'Better than a sharp stick in the eye. Or in the heart, as the case may be.'

Jean grimaced.

Pete split open a couple of limes and squeezed them into the blender, then tossed in some ice cubes. He took long-stemmed margarita glasses down from the cupboard. He rubbed their rims with lime, then dipped them into a plastic tub of salt. 'Okay, baby, do your stuff,' he told the blender as he capped it and pressed a button. After a few noisy seconds, the machine went silent. Pete filled the glasses with his frothy concoction, and carried them to the table.

As he sat down, Barbara returned.

'Are you okay?' Jean asked.

'Feeling a lot better.'

She looked a lot better, too.

She was barefoot, wearing red gym shorts and a loose gray T-shirt that was chopped off just below her breasts. Larry guessed that she had taken a washcloth to her legs and belly. The filth and blood were gone, leaving her skin ruddy around the abrasions. The wood had scratched her like an angry cat, and there were broad scuffs that looked as if she'd been given swipes with some heavy-duty sandpaper.

Larry watched as she put together a tray of cheese and crackers.

The back of her looked fine. Tanned, smooth, unblemished.

She brought the snacks to the table and sat down. Pushing out her lower lip, she huffed a breath that stirred the hair on her forehead. 'At last,' she said.

Pete raised his glass. 'May the vampire rest in peace and never come looking for our necks.'

'I'm gonna brain you,' Barbara said.

'I'll help,' Jean said.

Pete grinned at Larry. 'These gals, they've got no sense of humor.'

Chapter Six

Larry woke up shivering. The covers were off him, twisted around Jean as she thrashed and whimpered. He shook her gently by the shoulder. She flinched. Gasped, 'What's ... what's?'

'You were having a nightmare,' Larry whispered.

'Huh? Oh. Okay.' She rolled onto her back. She was still panting for air. 'Smothering,' she muttered, and struggled to free herself from the blankets. She shoved and kicked them down to the foot of the bed.

'I'm going to need some of that,' Larry said, sitting up.

'Huh? Oh. Sorry.'

'No problem. I'll put some light on the subject,' he warned, and gave Jean a moment to shield her eyes before he reached to the nightstand and turned on the lamp.

'Wait. I'll do it. You'll mess it up.'

'Fine,' he said, and smiled. Seconds ago, Jean had been in

the grips of a terrible nightmare. Now, she was concerned that he might foul up the job of arranging the sheet and blankets. He leaned back, bracing him-self up with locked arms, and watched her climb off the bed.

She looked as if she'd just taken a shower with her nightgown on. Her short hair was matted down, wet ringlets clinging around her ears and the nape of her neck. The sleek white fabric of her nightie was glued to her back and rump.

'You're drenched,' Larry said. 'Must've been a real corker of a nightmare.'

'Probably. I don't remember.' She bent over her side of the bed and pulled the top sheet out of the tangle. Her breasts swayed slightly inside the low-cut, lace bodice.

'You think it was about today?'

'Wouldn't be surprised.' She swept the sheet high. As it fluttered down, Larry leaned forward and caught the edge. He drew it over his naked body and eased backward onto the mattress. The sheet was enough to block out the chill of the soft night breeze. But the light-weight blanket felt even better as Jean covered him with it. She smoothed it carefully over her side of the bed, then came around to his side. Bending over him, she straightened the blanket. He slipped his arm out and stroked her rump. The night-gown felt silken and damp. Her skin was smooth beneath it, and very warm. She glanced at him, eyebrows rising. He moved his hand down the back of her leg and slipped it under the hem of her nightgown.

Standing up straight, Jean reached out and turned off the lamp. Her gown, pale in the faint light from the windows, climbed her body and fell away. Larry swept aside the sheet and blanket that she had just finished arranging so neatly. But she didn't protest.

She crawled onto the bed, straddled his legs, and eased down on top of him. As they kissed, he caressed her back and her small, firm buttocks. She lifted her legs onto his. She pressed his growing penis between her thighs and squirmed against him. Her breasts were warm, slick cushions rubbing his chest, and though the feel of her writhing body made him ache with need, her hip bones felt as if they were grinding into him.

He rolled, tumbling her onto the mattress, covering her with his body. He pushed himself up with elbows and knees to keep his weight off her. She squirmed as he kissed the side of her neck, moaned as he moved lower and kissed one nipple, then the other.

He pushed himself back. Kneeling between her open legs, he whispered, 'Just a second.'

Jean's fingers curled lightly around him, slid the length of his shaft. 'I don't think you'll need one tonight.'

'You sure?'

'Yeah.'

'Great. I hate those damn rubbers.'

'I know.' She smiled.

Bright teeth in a faint blur of face. Patches of darkness where her eyes should be.

Larry was suddenly under the stairway again, kneeling over the corpse. He felt himself go cold and tight.

Don't think about it!

He realized that Jean was about the same size as the horrible, dried up thing.

Stop it!

'What's wrong, honey?'

'Nothing,' he said.

Her shadowed skin was dark, but not *that* dark. Her breasts were mounds, not slabs. But even in the dim light, he could see the contours of her ribs. Below the ribcage, she seemed shrunken in. Her hip bones jutted.

'Honey?'

Her hand felt leathery around his small, soft penis.

Its hand.

He pictured himself knocking it away.

But he knew that this was Jean. She hadn't turned into the corpse. He wasn't hallucinating, either. This was just Jean, and his damned imagination was simply messing with him.

Not going to let it win, he promised himself.

He scooted backward on the mattress. Her hand went away from him. He kissed her belly. Warm, soft, slick with sweat. Not dry and leathery.

Stop comparing!

But when his face rubbed Jean's moist curls, he remembered the thing's blond thicket of pubic hair. A shudder passed through him.

Jean thrust fingers into his hair.

He went lower. She writhed and moaned, thrusting herself against him, clenching his hair, and he lost all thought of the corpse.

Soon, she was whimpering.

But not from any nightmare, Larry thought as she tugged his hair and he scurried up the mattress. He clamped his wet mouth to her mouth. He ran the hard length of his penis into her heat. She seemed to suck him in as if she were hungry to be filled.

'I should have ... nightmares more often,' she told him later.

'Yeah.'

She was panting beneath him, lightly stroking his back. Then, she turned her face away, worked her lips strangely, and raised a hand to her mouth. With her thumb and index finger, she pinched something and pulled it out.

'What's that?'

'A hair.'

'Where'd that come from?'

'Your mouth,' she said, shaking under him as she chuckled. She rubbed her hand on the sheet, then wrapped her arms around Larry and gave him a powerful squeeze. It was as if the hug used up the last of her strength. After a moment, she released him and sprawled out limp. She pursed her lips. He kissed them. Then he eased away, sliding out of her.

He pulled the sheet and blanket up, and scooted closer to Jean. He rested a hand on the warm curve of her thigh. Under his fingertips was a smear of sticki-ness. 'Ooo, yuck,' he said.

She laughed softly. 'Don't complain, buster. *I've* got the wet spot.'

'Want to trade places?'

'It's my wifely duty to sleep on the wet spot.' Her hand covered his, caressed it, fooled with his fingers.

In the silence, he began to worry that Jean might ask about his problem. He doubted that she would, though. Their sex life was something they rarely discussed. Besides, he'd made a rather spectacular recovery.

'Well,' he said, 'I'd better go to sleep or I won't be worth a damn tomorrow.'

'You'll have to write like a dog to pay for Lane's new wardrobe.'

'Bought out the store,' he muttered, rolling away from Jean and curling up on his side.

She laughed, then surprised Larry by snuggling against him. Normally, they slept at opposite sides of the bed.

But it felt good. Her breath warm on the nape of his neck. Her breasts and belly pressing his back. Her lap against his rump. The soft tickle of her pubic hair. Her thighs smooth against the backs of his legs. An arm came down over his side and fingers curled tenderly around his penis.

'You still horny?' he asked.

She kissed his back. 'Wiseguy. I just want to be close to you.'

'Well, I guess that's all right.'

'Thanks.'

'Are you okay?'

'I don't know,' she whispered. 'I guess so. How about you?'

'I wish we hadn't gone there today.'

'Me, too. I've never seen anything so horrible.' She pressed herself more tightly against him. 'On the other hand, you're always looking for material.'

'I could do without *that* sort of material.'

'The real thing's too much for you, huh?' she teased.

'Darn right it is.'

'Your fans would be appalled, you know, if they ever found

509

out how squeamish you really are. Nasty Lawrence Dunbar, master of gore, pussy.'

'Pussy, huh? You've been around Pete too much.'

She laughed again. 'Go to sleep, tough guy.'

Going For It

Chapter Seven

Happy trails to you,' Dad said, and swatted her butt as she stepped out the door.

She smirked back at him.

'Say hi to Roy and Dale,' he added.

'You should look so good,' Lane said, then turned away and hurried toward the car. The red Mustang gleamed in the early morning sunlight. She stepped around to the driver's side, feeling fresh and eager in her new clothes: the mottled pink and blue T-shirt; the tie-dyed blue denim jumper with its white lace trim and pink flower-bud decorations on the bib, straps and hem; and the white, fringed boots.

Dad was always poking fun at her clothes. She supposed this outfit *did* make her look like a cowgirl.

One hot, radical cowgirl, she thought, and grinned as she climbed into the car.

At least he hadn't made any remarks about the length of the skirt. Sitting down, she could feel the seat upholstery high on the backs of her legs. As she waited for the engine to warm up, she leaned close to the steering wheel and looked down. The skirt was short, all right. Any shorter might be embarrassing.

This was just right.

Sexy, but not outrageous.

She especially liked the lace around the hem of the skirt, the way its long points lay like frilly spearheads against her thighs.

I'm going to drive Jim nuts when he sees me in this.

As if he needs any help along those lines.

Laughing softly, trembling just a little with the anticipation of being at school on such a fine day in such a grand outfit, Lane backed out of the driveway. She turned the car radio to 'eighty-six point two a.m., all the best in Country twenty-four hours a day!' Randy Travis was on. She turned the volume

513

high, and poked her elbow into the warm stream of air rushing past her window.

God, she felt great.

Seemed almost criminal to feel this great.

She leaned her shoulder against the door, tipped her head and felt the wind caress her face, tug at her hair.

To think that she'd put up such a fuss about leaving Los Angeles. She must've been crazy, wanting to stay in that lousy apartment in the city full of filthy air and creeps. But she'd grown up there. She was used to it. She'd known she would miss her friends and the beaches and Disneyland. This was so much better, though. She'd made new friends, she loved the river, and the clean, open spaces gave her a constant sense of freedom that made each day seem rich with promise.

Best of all, she supposed, was the release from fear. In LA, you had to be so careful. The place was crawling with rapists and killers. Not a day went by when the TV news didn't broadcast stories of such horror and brutality that you dreaded stepping outside. Kids missing. Their bodies usually found days later, nude and mutilated and sexually abused. Not only kids, either. The same thing happened to teenagers, and even adults. If you weren't kidnapped and tortured, you might be gunned down at a restaurant or movie theater or shopping mall. And hiding at home was no guarantee of safety, either. There were plenty of nuts who simply drove around town, shooting into the windows of houses and apartment buildings.

Nowhere was safe.

Lane's joy slipped away as she suddenly remembered the chopping crashes of gunfire in the night. They were home in their ground level apartment, sitting close together on the sofa, watching *Dallas* on the TV. Lane had a tub of popcorn on her lap. Mom sat on one side, Dad on the other. All three were reaching in, hands sometimes colliding. The first blast made her jump so hard that the tub flew up, flinging popcorn everywhere. Then the night exploded as if someone on the street had opened up with a machinegun. Mom screamed. Dad shouted, 'GET DOWN!' but didn't give Lane even an instant to respond before he grabbed the back of her neck and nearly broke her in half as he rammed her forward. The edge of the coffee table skinned the top of her head. She wept and held her head and shuddered as the roar pounded her ears. Then, all she heard was a ringing. The gunfire had stopped. Dad still clutched her neck. 'Jean?' he asked in a high, strange voice. Mom didn't answer. 'JEAN!' True panic. Then Mom said, 'Is it over?'

They stayed on the floor.

Then came sirens and the loud whap-whap-whap of a police helicopter low overhead. The front draperies were bright with flashes of red and blue. Dad crawled to the window and looked out. 'Holy Jesus,' he said, 'there must be twenty cop cars out there.'

It turned out that the shots had been fired at a black family in a duplex across the street. Both parents, and three children, had been killed by automatic fire from an Uzi. Only an infant had survived the shooting.

Lane hadn't known the family. That was another thing about LA, even most of your neighbors were strangers. But the fact that they'd been gunned down, right across the street, was shocking.

Just too damn close.

Dad had reminded them about a family gunned down by mistake a few years earlier. It was a drug hit. The killers had gone to the wrong house, the one next door to the residence of their intended victims.

'We're getting out of here,' Dad said, even while the street outside was still jammed with police cars.

Two weeks later, they were on the way to Mulehead Bend.

They knew the town from having vacationed there just a month before the shooting. They'd spent a night in a motel, followed by a week in a houseboat on the river. They'd all enjoyed the area, it was fresh in their minds, and it seemed like a good place to find sanctuary from the mad, crowded hunting ground of Los Angeles.

Sometimes, the wind and heat were enough to drive you crazy. You had to watch out for scorpions and black widow spiders and several varieties of poisonous snakes. But the chances of catching a bullet in the head or getting abducted by a pervert were mighty slim.

Lane looked upon LA as a prison from which she and her family had escaped. The freedom was glorious.

She swung her car onto the dust and gravel in front of Betty's place, and beeped the horn once. Betty lived in a mobile home, as did the majority of Mulehead Bend's population. It was firmly planted on a foundation. A porch and an extra room had been added on. It looked pretty much like a normal house from the outside, though the interior always seemed rather narrow and cramped when Lane visited.

Betty trudged down the porch stair as if laboring under the burden of her weight – which was considerable. She managed to raise her head and nod a greeting.

Leaning across the passenger seat, Lane opened the door for her. Betty swung her book bag into the back seat. The fabric of her tan shirt was already dark under the armpit. The car rocked slightly as she climbed in. She shut the door so hard that Lane winced.

'Well, look at you,' Betty said, her voice as slow and somber as always. 'What'd you do, mug Dolly Parton?'

'Who'd *you* mug, Indiana Jones?'

'Yucka yucka,' she muttered.

Lane steered onto the road. 'We picking up Henry?'

'Only if you want to.'

'Well, is he expecting us?'

'I suppose.'

'You two aren't fighting again, are you?'

'Just the usual grief about my culinary preferences. I told him he's no prize himself, and if he thinks he can do better, he should go ahead and try, and good riddance.'

'True love,' Lane said.

She swung around a bend, and accelerated up the road to Henry's house. He was out in front, sitting on a small, white-painted boulder next to the driveway, reading a paperback. When he saw them coming, he slipped the book into his leather briefcase. He stood up, ran a hand over the top of his crew cut, and stuck out his thumb as if hoping to hitch a ride with strangers.

'What a dork,' Betty muttered.

'Oh, he's cute,' Lane said.

'He's a nerd.'

That was a fact, Lane supposed. In his running shoes, old blue jeans, plaid shirt and sunglasses, he could almost pass for a regular guy. But the briefcase gave him away. So did the rather dopey, cheerful look on his lean face. And the way his head proceeded the rest of his body made him look, to Lane, like an adventurous turtle.

He was a nerd, no doubt about it. But Lane liked him.

'Good morning, sports fans!'

'Yo!' Lane greeted him.

Betty climbed out, shoved the seatback forward, and ducked into the car. Henry got in after her. Hanging over the seat, he managed to pull the door shut. Then, his head swiveled toward Lane. 'Foxy outfit there, lady.'

'Thanks.'

' "She had a body like a mountain road," ' he said. ' "Full of curves and places you'd like to stop for a picnic." '

'Mike Hammer?' Lane asked.

'Mack Donovan, *Dead Low Tide*.' He dropped backward, or was yanked by Betty.

'You never talk to me that way,' the girl grumbled.

He whispered something that Lane couldn't hear over Ronnie Milsap. She turned the radio down, and heard a giggly squeal from Betty. Making a U-turn, she headed down the hill.

'So, you have a big weekend?' Henry asked after a while.

'Okay,' Lane said. 'Nothing special. I went shopping yesterday.'

'No dream-date with Jim Dandy, King of the Studs?'

'He had to go out of town with his parents.'

'*Too* bad. And I bet he didn't even have the courtesy to leave you his biceps.'

517

'Nope, I had to go without.'

'Rotten luck. Should've come to the drive-in with us. Saw a couple of dynamite films. *Trashed* and *Attack of the S.S. Zombie Queens*.'

'Sorry I missed them.'

'Sorry *I* saw them,' Betty said.

'Well, you didn't see much of them, that's for sure. Between your forays to the snack bar and the john . . .'

'Hush up.'

'We think she got a bad hot dog,' he explained.

'Henry!' she whined.

'On the other hand, could've been a bad burrito or cheeseburger.'

'Lane doesn't want to hear all the gruesome details.'

'What's going on with your dad?' Henry asked, leaning forward and folding his arms over the seatback. 'Have they started filming *The Beast*?'

'Not yet. They just renewed the option, though.'

'Terrific. Man, I can't wait to see that one. I've got rubber bands holding that book together. Read it five, six times. It's a classic.'

'I would've liked it better,' Lane said, 'if it hadn't been written by my father.'

'Ah, he's cool.'

'And apparently somewhat demented,' Lane added.

Henry laughed.

At the bottom of the hill, Lane turned onto Shoreline Drive. Most of the shops along the road weren't open yet, and the traffic was light. The station wagon ahead of her was filled with children on their way to the elementary school, which was across the road from Buford High at the south end of town. Quite a few older kids were on the sidewalks, hiking in that direction.

Henry, still resting on the seatback, swung his arm toward the passenger window. 'Isn't that Jessica?'

Lane spotted the girl on the sidewalk ahead. Jessica, all right. Even from behind, there was no mistaking her. The spiked hair, dyed bright orange, was enough to give her away.

Her left arm was in a cast.

'Wonder what happened,' Lane muttered. 'Anyone mind if I offer her a lift?'

'Yeah, do it,' Henry said.

'Terrific,' Betty muttered.

Lane swung the car to the curb, not far behind the swaggering girl, and leaned across the passenger seat. 'How about a ride?' she called.

Jessica turned around.

Lane winced at the sight of her.

'God,' Henry muttered.

Jessica was generally considered the foxiest gal in the junior class, maybe in the entire high school.

Not so foxy now, Lane thought.

From the looks of her now, she might've gone ten rounds over the weekend with the heavyweight champ.

The left side of her face was swollen and purple. Her cracked lips bulged like sausages. She had a fleshcolored bandage on her chin, another over her left eyebrow. Lane guessed that the pink-framed sunglasses concealed shiners. The girl usually wore huge, dangling rings in her pierced ears. Today, the lobes of both ears were bandaged. The low neckline of her tank top revealed bruises on her chest. Others showed around her shoulder straps. Even her thighs were smudged with purple bruises below the frayed edges of her cut-off jeans.

'How about it?' Lane called to her.

She shrugged, and Lane heard a quiet intake of breath from Henry – likely at the way the gesture made Jessica's breast move under the tight, thin fabric of her top. Only one showed. The other was discretely hidden under the cloth sling that supported her broken arm. The visible one jiggled as she stepped toward the car.

Maybe she got herself gang-banged.

Nice, Lane. Real nice.

Would've been her own damn fault.

Cut it out.

Leaning across the passenger seat, she unlatched the door and swung it open.

'Thanks,' Jessica said.

Henry dropped away from the seatback – no doubt with Betty's help – and lost his chance to watch the girl climb in. Too bad, Lane thought. He would've enjoyed seeing Jessica's leg come out through the slit side of her jeans. The bruises might've dampened his enthusiasm, but not by much.

She pulled the door shut. Lane checked the side mirror, waited for a Volkswagen to pass, then swung out.

'Are you sure you want to be going to school?' she asked.

'Shit. Would you, ib you looked like this?'

'I guess I'd probably call in sick.'

'Yeah. Well, better than habbing by old lady in by face all day. She's such a bain.'

Lane rubbed her lips together, licked them. Listening to Jessica was almost enough to make them ache.

From the backseat came Betty's voice. 'So, you going to let us in on it, or do we have to guess?'

Scowling, Jessica peered over her shoulder.

'It's none of our business,' Lane said.

'Yeah. Well, I got trashed.'

'Who did it to you?' Henry asked.

'Who the buck knows? A couple guys. Real asswibes. Beat the shit outa be and stole by burse.'

'Where'd it happen?'

'Ober backa the Quik Stob.'

'Behind the Quick Stop?' Betty asked. 'What were you doing there?'

'They dragged me there. Saturday night. I went in bor cigarettes, and they got be when I cabe out.'

'Bad news,' Henry muttered.

'Yeah, I'll say.' With one hand, she opened a canvas satchel and took out a pack of Camels. She shook it, raised the pack to her mouth, and caught a cigarette between her fat, scabby lips. She lit it with a Bic, inhaled deeply, and sighed.

'Did they catch the guys who did it?' Lane asked.

Jessica shook her head.

'I didn't think stuff like that happened around here.'

'It habbens, all right.'

Lane pulled into the student parking lot, found an empty space, and shut off the car.

'Thanks a lot bor the ride,' Jessica said.

'Glad to help. I'm awfully sorry you got messed up.'

'Be too. So long.' She climbed out, and headed away.

'Wouldn't you just die to know what *really* happened?' Betty said.

'You think she lied?' Lane asked.

'Lets put it this way. Yes.'

Henry shoved the seatback forward. 'Why would she lie about a thing like that?'

'Why wouldn't she?'

Chapter Eight

Larry drank coffee and read a new Shaun Hutson paperback for an hour after Lane went off to school. Then he set the book aside, said, 'I'd better get to it,' and rose from his recliner.

'Have fun,' Jean told him, glancing up from the newspaper as he strode past her.

He shut his office door, and sat down in front of the word processor.

He had already decided not to work on *Night Stranger* today. The book was going well. Two more weeks should take care of it.

Then what?

Ah, he thought, there's the rub.

Normally, by the time he was this close to finishing a novel, the next was pretty well set in his mind. He would already have pages of notes in which he had explored the plot and characters, and have several of the major scenes worked out.

Not this time.

Gotta get cooking, he told himself.

When the day came to write The End on *Night Stranger*, he wanted to slip a fresh floppy disk into his computer and begin Chapter One. Of whatever.

Two weeks to go.

That should be plenty of time.

You'll come up with something.

You'd better.

Eighty, ninety pages to go. Then, he would find himself facing an empty disk, a void, a taunting blank that would push him to the edge of despair.

It had happened a few times before. He dreaded going through a period like that again.

I won't, he told himself.

He formatted a new disk, and brought up its directory: 321,536 bytes to play with.

Let's just use up a couple thousand today, he thought.

A page or two, that's all it'll take. Maybe.

He punched the 'enter' key, and the screen went blank. A few seconds later, he had eliminated the right margin justification, which would've left odd spaces between the words, spaces that drove him nuts when he tried to read the hard copy. He punched a few more keys. 'Novel Notes – Monday, October 3,' appeared in amber light at the upper left-hand corner of the screen.

Then, he sat there.

He stared at the keyboard. Several of the keys were grimy. The filthy ones were those he used least often: the numbers, the space bar except for a clean area in the shape of his right thumb, some keys at the far sides that could apparently be used to give commands for a variety of mysterious functions. He didn't know what the hell half of them did. Sometimes, he hit one by mistake. The consequences could be alarming.

He spent a while cleaning the keyboard, scratching paths through the gray smudges with a fingernail.

Stop screwing around, he told himself.

He scraped Saturday's ashes out of a pipe, filled it with fresh tobacco, and lit it. The matchbook came from the Sir Francis Drake on Union Square. They'd had lunch there during a vacation along the California coast two summers ago. The vacation he thought of as the 'wharf tour.'

He set the matchbook down, puffed on his pipe, and stared at the screen.

'Novel Notes – Monday, October 3.'

Okay.

His fingertips tapped at the keys.

'Come up with something hot. Original and big. Try for at least 500 pages, more if possible.'

Right. That accomplished a lot.

He typed in, 'How about a vampire book?' Ha ha ha. Forget it. Vampires are done to death.

'Need something original. Some kind of a NEW threat.'

Good luck, he thought.

How about a sequel? he wondered.

'Maybe a sequel. *The Beast II*, or something. Worth considering, if you can't turn up anything better.'

Come on, something new.

Or a new variation on an old theme.

'Nobody but Brandner's done anything decent with werewolves. Come up with a fresh werewolf gimmick? Forget it. That TV show's got the whole thing covered. But that's not a book.'

Larry scowled at the screen.

'Forget werewolves.

'What else is there?'

His pipe slurped. He twisted the stem off, blew a fine spray into the wastebasket beside his chair, put the pipe back together, and lit it again.

A few minutes later, he had a list:

werewolves
ghosts (boring)
zombies
aliens
misc. beasts
demonic possession (shit)
homicidal maniac (done to death)
curses
wishes granted ('Monkey's Paw')
possessed machinery (King's realm)
crazed animals (see above, and BIRDS)
haunted house (possibilities)

'How ABOUT a haunted house book?' he wrote.

He'd always wanted to do one, and always reached the same stumbling block. By and large, he didn't consider ghosts sufficiently scary. Something else had to be in the house. But what?

That question took him back to the list.

He stared at it for a long time.

'Something horrible inside the house,' he wrote. 'But what?'

How about a vampire under the staircase?

Right. Just thinking about it made his insides crawl.

He was on his knees beside the coffin again, staring at the withered corpse. Feeling fear and disgust.

He wanted to forget he ever saw the thing, not spend the next few months dwelling on it.

Would make a good story, though.

'A blonde corpse under the hotel stairs,' he wrote. 'A stake in its chest. Found by some people exploring a ghost town. Could tell it just the way it happened. Fun and games.'

He wrinkled his nose.

'But they don't run off, scared shitless, like we did. Maybe some of them do. But one is fascinated. Is this a vampire, or isn't it? A character like Pete, but a little crazier. He *has* to know. So he pulls the stake. Right in front of his eyes, the thing comes back to life. Changes from a hideous brown cadaver (use Barbara's line about looking like salami?), into a gorgeous young woman. A gorgeous, naked young woman. Pete character is enthralled. And turned on. He wants her. But she has a different idea, and bites his neck.

'They don't come out, and don't come out. The others get worried, go back into the hotel to see what's keeping the guy. Nobody under the stairs. The coffin is empty.

'Little problem, bud. Vampires don't screw around in the daytime. So how come our merry band is exploring a ghost town after dark?

'Easy. They're driving through town, on the way home from an outing in the desert, and the van breaks down. Flat tire, or something.'

Ah, he thought, the old car-breaking-down-in-just-the-worst-possible-place gag.

It could work, though.

And it had a nice bonus: that wasn't the way things happened yesterday.

'Make it different enough from the truth,' he typed, 'and maybe you can handle it.

'How about taking One Big Step, and changing what's under the stairs? Not a dead gal with a stake in her chest, but a . . . a what? (A crate with a monster in it? Been done.) Could be anything. The body of a creature from outer space? A troll? Have open spaces between the stairs, and it reaches through and drags people in by the feet. Gobbles 'em up. He he he.

'Chicken.

'What's wrong with the way it really was?

'Yuck. Horror's supposed to be fun.

'But there's a real story there. Who is she? Who put the stake in her chest? Was the lock (brand new) put on the hotel doors by the same person who hid her under the stairs? Best of all, what happens if you pull the stake?

'Lies there. Dead meat.

'But what if life flows into her? Her dry, crusty skin becomes smooth and youthful. Her flat breasts swell into gorgeous mounds. Her sunken face fills out. She is beautiful beyond your wildest imagination. She is breathtaking. (And blood-taking.)

'She doesn't bite your neck, after all.

'That's because she's grateful to you for freeing her to live again. Feels so indebted that she'll do anything for you. You're her master, and she will do your bidding. In effect, you have this gorgeous thing as your slave.

'Real possibilities.'

Chapter Nine

Lane shoved her books onto the locker shelf, took out her lunch bag, and shut the metal door. As she gave the combination lock a twirl, an arm slipped around her stomach, a mouth pressed the side of her neck. She cringed as chills scurried up her skin.

'Stop it,' she said, whirling around.

'Couldn't help myself,' Jim said.

Lane looked past him. The hallway was crowded. Kids were wandering by, talking and laughing. Those who weren't with friends all seemed to be in a great hurry. Lockers slammed. Teachers stood near their classroom doorways, on the lookout for trouble. Nobody seemed to be paying any attention to Lane and Jim.

'Did you miss me?' Jim asked.

'I survived.'

'Uh-oh. Am I in trouble?'

'I don't much care to be grabbed in public. How many times do I have to tell you that?'

'Ooo, touchy. Are we on the rag?'

Lane felt heat rush to her face. 'Real nice,' she muttered. 'Who died and made you king of the jerks?'

He smiled, but there was no humor in his eyes. 'I was just kidding. Can't you take a joke?'

'Obviously not.'

He dropped the smile. 'I don't need this.'

'Good. Adios.'

Scowling, he muttered something Lane couldn't hear, turned away and joined the flow of the hallway crowd. He walked about twenty feet, then glanced over his shoulder as if he expected Lane to come rushing after him.

She gave him a glare.

He smirked as if to say, 'Your loss, bitch,' then continued down the hall.

Creep, she thought.

On the rag. What a shitty thing to say.

She leaned back against her locker and took a deep breath, trying to calm herself. She felt hot with embarrassment and anger. Her heart thudded. She was trembling.

Who needs him, anyhow? she told herself.

I *was* pretty rough on him, she thought as she started down the hallway. It wasn't as if he did anything all that awful. Just kissed my neck, really. No big crime. But he shouldn't have done it right in front of everyone. He knows how I feel about that kind of thing.

Even if I did give him a hard time, it was no reason to make a crude remark like that.

She *had* missed him. She'd looked forward, all weekend, to seeing him again.

She suddenly felt cheated and sad. Her new outfit made it worse. Like getting all dressed up for a party and being left at home.

Why did he have to act like that?

He can be such a jerk sometimes.

Whenever he didn't get his way, Lane got to see his snotty side. Afterwards, though, he was usually quick to apologize and he could be so sweet that she found it difficult to hold onto her anger.

527

She supposed the same thing would happen this time.

One of these days, she told herself, he'll go too far and that'll be the end of it.

Maybe he just did.

But the thought of breaking up with Jim made her feel empty and alone. He was the only real boyfriend she'd had since starting at Buford High – ever, for that matter. They'd shared so much. He might act like a creep sometimes, but nobody's perfect.

You're just too chicken to dump him, she thought.

In no time at all, everyone in school would know they had split up. When that happened, she would be fair game. She'd either have to become a hermit, or risk going out with virtual strangers – and some of them were bound to be creeps.

At least you know you can handle Jim.

True love, she thought. I must be out of my gourd. You don't keep going with a guy forever just because he's okay and you're afraid you might do worse.

When he tries to make up this time, I should just tell him to take a flying leap.

On the rag. A, I'm not. B, screw him anyway.

In the cafeteria, she spotted Jim at one of the long lunch tables, surrounded by his jock friends. Betty and Henry were at a corner table, sitting across from each other at its far end, several empty chairs between them and the rowdy clique of girls occupying the other end.

After buying a Pepsi at the 'drinks only' window, she went to join them. 'Mind if I sit here?' she asked.

'Okay with me,' Henry said. 'Just don't embarrass us by sticking a straw up your nostril.'

'The hell with that. How'll I drink my pop?'

'Take a load off,' Betty said.

She pulled out the metal folding-chair, and sat down beside Henry.

'So how come you're not eating with Jim Dandy?' he asked. 'Did your taste buds finally rebel at the prospect?'

'Something like that. We had a little problem.'

Betty, about to take a bite, frowned and set her sandwich down. 'Are you all right?'

Lane realized she suddenly had a lump in her throat. She didn't trust herself to speak, so she nodded.

'The dirt bag,' Betty said.

'Want me to kick his butt?' Henry asked.

'You'd need the Seventh Cavalry,' Betty told him. 'And they already bought it at the Little Big Horn.'

'Very funny.'

'I don't know why you put up with him,' she said. Her cheeks wobbled as she shook her head. 'Good Lord, girl, you know darn well you could have any guy in the school. Except for Henry, of course. I'd be forced to kill him if he made a play for you.'

'You ladies could *share* me,' he suggested.

'But I mean it, though. Seriously. Jim's always giving you grief about one thing or another. Why do you stand for it?'

'I don't know.'

'Because he's so cute,' Henry said.

'Stick it in your ear. This is serious.'

'Maybe I will dump him,' Lane said. 'It's just getting worse all the time.'

Grinning, Henry leaned sideways and slipped an arm around her back. 'Saturday night. You and me. We'll make beautiful music together.'

Lane saw a quick look of alarm on Betty's face. Then the girl narrowed her eyes and said, 'Prepare to meet your maker, Henrietta.'

'Sorry,' Lane told him. 'I'd hold myself responsible for your demise. I can't have that on my conscience.'

'I'd die happy.'

Betty's face went red. She pressed her lips together.

'That's enough, Henry,' Lane said.

He tried to hang on to his silly grin, but it fell off. He pulled his arm in. 'Just kidding,' he said.

Just kidding. That's what Jim had said. What was it? The standard excuse when a guy makes an ass of himself?

Lane opened her bag and took out the sandwich. It was wrapped in cellophane. She saw egg salad bulging out between the bread.

'Just trying to make you jealous, sweet stuff,' he said to Betty.

'You'd stand as much chance with Lane as an ice cube in a hot skillet.'

Tears suddenly burned Lane's eyes. She slapped her sandwich down hard on the table. 'I'm sorry!' she blurted. 'Goddamn it! Don't do this! You're my friends!'

They both gaped at her.

'I'm sorry. Okay?'

'Gee,' Henry said.

'It's all right,' Betty murmured. 'You okay?'

Lane shook her head.

'I know just the thing to make you feel better.'

'What?' Lane asked.

'Let me eat that sandwich for you.'

She gasped out a laugh. 'Not a chance.'

'Grab it off her, Hen, and I'll forgive you.'

He reached for it. Lane caught his wrist and pinned it to the table. 'Try it again,' she warned, 'and you'll be picking your nose left-handed.'

'He's such a klutz, he'd put out his eye.'

Lane let go. When she finished unwrapping her sandwich, she tore it down the middle and offered half to Betty. The girl leered at it, but shook her head. 'Go on,' Lane told her. 'I don't have much of an appetite, anyway.'

'If you're sure . . .' She took it.

They ate their lunches and chatted, and everything seemed normal again. But Lane knew that damage had been done. Obviously, Betty had seen through Henry's joking around – realized he would dump her in an eyeblink if he thought he stood a chance with Lane.

Break up with Jim, and sooner or later Henry probably *will* ask you out. Then, you'll be minus your two best friends.

* * *

Jessica's assigned seat in Mr Kramer's sixth-period English class was at the front of the room, just to the left of Lane's desk. Today, Riley Benson swaggered down the aisle and sat there. He slumped against the backrest, stretched out his legs, and crossed his motorcycle boots. He looked at Lane. His face, with half-shut, sullen eyes, never failed to remind her of television news photos that showed men who put bullets into people for the fun of it.

Twisting around, she saw Jessica in Riley's usual seat at the rear corner.

'We traded,' he said. 'You got a problem?'

'None of my business.'

She turned to the front. The final bell hadn't clamored yet, and Mr Kramer rarely entered the classroom before the bell. She hoped he would show up soon. Riley had a reputation for starting trouble, and she was pretty sure that she'd already been chosen as today's target.

Thanks a heap, Jessica.

The trade had to be Jessica's idea. Lane could understand that. Battered the way she was, the girl probably wanted to be as inconspicuous as possible.

It crossed her mind that Riley might be the guy who'd beaten up Jessica. She knew they'd been going together, and he sure seemed capable of such things. Maybe Jessica gave him some lip. She could've made up the mugging story.

Lane looked over at him. His fingers were rapping out a rhythm on the edge of the desk. He had dirty knuckles, but they weren't bruised or scraped. He might've been wearing gloves, though. Or done the damage with a blunt instrument of some kind.

'You got a problem?' he asked.

'No. Huh-uh.' She turned her eyes to the front.

'Bitch.'

This is really my day.

She stared at Mr Kramer's empty desk. Her back felt rigid. Her heart was thumping hard, and her face was hot.

Come on, teacher. Where are you?

'Fuckin' twat.'

Her head snapped toward him. 'Blow it out your ass, Benson.'

The bell blared and she flinched.

Riley's lip curled up. 'See ya after class. Count on it.'

'Oh, I'm so scared. I'm trembling.'

'Ya oughta be.'

In fact, she was. Now I've done it, she thought. Why didn't I keep my mouth shut?

It was little consolation when Mr Kramer entered the room. If only he'd shown up a couple of minutes ago.

Roll book in hand, he settled down against the front edge of his desk and fixed his eyes on Riley. 'I believe you're in the wrong seat, Mr Benson.'

'You got a problem with that?'

'As a matter of fact, yes, I do.'

Lane felt a grin spreading across her face.

Give it to him, Kramer.

'Please return to your assigned seat. Now.'

From the back of the room came Jessica's voice. 'I asked Riley to trade with be,' she said.

'Neverthe . . .' For an instant, he looked surprised. Then, concern furrowed his brow. 'My God, what happened to you?'

'I got wracked ub. Okay? Can I just stay here?'

'Did somebody do that to you?'

'No, I fell down the stairs.'

Maybe she had a different story for everyone.

'I'm very sorry to hear that, Jessica. But I'm afraid I'll have to insist that you both resume your proper seats.'

Riley mumbled something, gathered his books, and headed for the back of the classroom.

Good show! Lane thought.

No wonder Kramer was one of the most popular teachers at Buford High. Not only young, handsome and clever, but he had the guts to keep discipline. Plenty of other teachers would've backed off and let Riley stay.

Lane suddenly remembered Riley's threat. She felt herself go hot and shaky again.

Jessica slid into her seat. She sat up straight, facing Kramer. 'Thanks a lot, teach,' she muttered.

'You're not outside, now. Take off those sunglasses.'

That's going a little too far, Lane thought.

Jessica dropped her sunglasses on to the desk top. Lane could only see her right eye. It was swollen nearly shut. Her upper lid, shiny and purple, bulged as if someone had jammed half a golf ball underneath it.

Kramer pursed his lips. He shook his head. 'You may put the glasses back on,' he said.

'Thanks a heab.'

'Okay, we've wasted enough time. Take out your texts and turn to page fifty-eight.'

Lane watched the clock. This was the last class of the day. It had forty-five minutes to go.

He won't try anything, she told herself. He wouldn't dare.

I'll be okay if I can just get to my car.

Thirty minutes to go.

Ten.

In spite of the air-conditioning, Lane was bathed with sweat. Her T-shirt felt sodden against her armpits. Cool dribbles trickled down between her breasts. Her panties were glued to her rump.

With one minute to go, she piled her books on top of her binder, ready to bolt for the door.

The bell rang.

She pressed the books to her chest, slid out of the seat and stood up.

Kramer met her eyes. 'Miss Dunbar, I'd like to speak with you for a minute.'

No!

'Yes sir,' she said.

She sank back onto her seat and put the books down.

Why was he doing this to her? Was he annoyed because she'd seemed in such a rush to get out?

I'm doomed, she thought.

Mr Kramer stepped behind his desk and stuffed books into

his briefcase. The kids hurried out. The room had doors at the front and rear. Riley didn't leave by the front. He'd probably used the other door, but Lane forced herself not to look.

Maybe he forgot about me.

Fat chance.

Mr Kramer came around his desk and sat on its edge, facing her. He held some typed sheets in his hand.

He wants to discuss one of my themes?

But Lane could see that it wasn't hers. It looked like erasable paper. The stuff always felt sticky, and the ink had a tendency to smear if you rubbed it, but she'd used it anyway until her father had told her to 'throw away that junk and use some decent bond.' He'd gone on to say that only amateurs fooled with erasable paper, and editors hated it with a passion.

'That isn't mine,' she said.

Mr Kramer smiled. 'I'm aware of that. What I have here is a book report that I found very interesting. It was written by Henry Peidmont. Is he a friend of yours?'

'Yes.'

Henry, she knew, had Kramer for second period.

'He's quite a good student, but he does have a peculiar taste in literature. He seems to relish the macabre.'

'Yeah, I've noticed.'

Kramer fluttered the pages a bit. 'This particular report deals with a book called *Night Watcher* by Lawrence Dunbar.' He tipped his head sideways and smiled at Lane.

So that's it, she thought.

I'm not in trouble, after all.

Just in trouble with Riley.

'He's my dad,' she admitted, feeling a mix of pride and embarrassment.

'Henry mentions that in his report.'

Thanks, Hen.

'We don't have many real authors living here in Mulehead Bend. In fact, your father is the only one I'm aware of. Do you suppose he might be willing to come in, sometime, and talk to the class?'

'He might. He's kind of busy, but . . .'

'I'm sure he is. We wouldn't want to impose on him, but I think that the class might enjoy hearing what he has to say. I've never read any of his books myself. They're not exactly my cup of tea.'

'A lot of people feel that way,' Lane said.

'I've seen his books on the stands, though. And I've seen any number of students with them.'

'They need more parental supervision.'

Kramer laughed softly.

He may be a teacher, Lane thought, but he's sure a neat guy.

'I understand that the novels are pretty nasty.'

'You were misinformed. They're *extremely* nasty. I'm under strict orders not to read any until I'm thirty-five.'

'I'll bet you've disobeyed, though, haven't you?'

Lane grinned. 'I've read 'em all.'

'Under the bedcovers, I presume.'

'Some of the time.'

'Well, I'd really appreciate it if you would talk to him. If he could find the time to come in, I think the kids would get quite a charge out of it. He might want to tell them about how he became a writer, why he chose to specialize in "extremely nasty" novels, that kind of thing.'

'I'll check with him about it.'

'Fine. I won't keep you any longer, now. But let me know, okay?'

'Sure.' She picked up her books. As she scooted off the seat, she saw him glance at her legs and look away quickly.

At least somebody appreciates the dress, she thought.

Too bad he has to be a teacher.

Heading toward the door, she was hit again by the knowledge that Riley might be waiting for her.

What if I ask Mr Kramer to walk me out to the parking lot?

No way, she told herself. He might get the wrong idea. Unless I explain about Riley. And that might get Riley in hot water, and then I'd *really* be in trouble.

'See you tomorrow,' she called over her shoulder.

'Have a nice evening, Lane.'

She stepped into the hallway. Leaning against the lockers on the other side was Jim. He lifted a hand in greeting.

'I wouldn't blame you if you told me to get lost,' he said, coming toward her. 'I don't know what got into me this morning. I'm really sorry.'

'You should be.'

'You can wash my mouth out with soap, if that'd help any.'

'That's an idea.' She took hold of his hand. 'Next time, I just might.'

'Am I forgiven, then?'

'I guess so. This time.'

Together, they walked down the hall.

So much for dumping him, she thought. Guess I wasn't ready for it, after all.

Though she felt a little disappointed in herself, she mostly felt relieved.

'I was afraid I'd really blown it,' Jim said. 'All day, I kept thinking about it, and how much I'd miss you. I really love you, Lane. I don't know what I would've done if . . . well, anyway. We're okay again, right?'

'Yeah. We're okay.'

He squeezed her hand.

In the parking lot, Lane spotted Riley Benson sitting on the hood of her Mustang. They were still some distance away, and Jim hadn't noticed him yet.

But Riley saw him, scurried down, and swaggered off.

Chapter Ten

She was water skiing on the river at night. She didn't want to be there. She was frightened.

She wanted to stop but didn't dare. The thing in the water would get her before the boat had time to swing around and pick her up.

She didn't know what it was in the water. But something. Something awful.

The boat sped faster and faster as if it wanted to help her escape. She skimmed over the smooth black surface, clinging to the handle of the tow line, whimpering with terror.

Somehow, she knew that the boat wasn't quick enough. The thing in the water was gaining on her.

If they were closer to shore! If the boat took her near enough to a dock, she might let go of the line and her speed might take her gliding to safety.

But she couldn't see the shore.

On both sides, there was only darkness.

That's impossible, she thought. The river's no more than a quarter mile wide.

Where are we?

Sick with dread, she thought: We're not on the Colorado any more.

Clutching the wooden handle with her right hand, she raised her left and waved for the boat to head ashore.

Wherever that might be.

It kept its straight course.

Look at me! her mind shrieked. Damn it, pay attention!

She suddenly realized that she didn't know who was steering the boat.

Then, she saw that it was drawing away from her.

As if the tow line were stretching.

Slowly, the running lights faded with distance until they

vanished entirely. Even the sound of the out-boards died away.

There was silence except for the hiss of her skis.

The tow rope led into darkness.

She was alone.

Except for the thing under the river.

Oh God, what am I going to . . .

Cold hands grabbed her ankles, tugged her straight down. She was still on her skis, still speeding at the end of the tow line, but under the surface. The water pushed at her. It filled her open mouth, muffling her scream as the hands scurried up her legs.

She felt the thing's icy flesh against her back. It was standing on the skis behind her, riding them, reaching around her front, grabbing her hands, trying to rip them from the wooden bar. She held on with all her might.

If I let go, he'll have me!

He snapped her left arm. Broke it off at the elbow. Her hand still clutched the bar for a moment, trailing its severed forearm. Then the rushing current took them away.

A hand clamped over her mouth. It pinched her nostrils shut.

She fought to suck in air.

Somehow, she'd been able to breathe in spite of the water gushing down her throat, but the hand was different. It was solid. Her lungs burned.

She grabbed the hand and woke up and the hand was still there, mashing her bruised mouth, pinching her nostrils shut.

'Don't make a sound, Jessica.'

Frantic for a breath, she nodded. The hand lifted. She sucked air into her starved lungs.

'Had a little nightmare?' he whispered.

He was on the bed, sitting on her, leaning forward and holding her by the shoulders. Jessica was no longer covered by her sheet. In the glow of moonlight from the windows, she saw that Kramer was shirtless. From the hot feel of his skin where he sat on her, she knew that he'd removed all his clothes before climbing onto her. He had slipped her nightshirt up, too. Her left forearm rested against her chest, its cast heavy and cool.

'You bastard.'

'Shhh. If you wake up your parents, I'll have to kill them. And you. I'll have to kill everyone. You wouldn't want that to happen, would you?'

'No,' she whispered.

'I didn't imagine you would.'

'What do you want?' she asked. The stupid question of the year. What he wanted was obvious. But she'd thought it was over.

Saturday night, she'd told him it was over, told him that he could find another girl, threatened to get him fired if he didn't stop. That had been the stupid threat of the year. But after finishing his little 'lesson,' he'd said, 'I'm sick of you anyway, you disgusting slut.'

'I've been thinking,' he whispered. 'I've been worrying.'

'I'b not going to tell.'

'How do I know that?'

'Don't hurt be. Blease.'

'I didn't come here to hurt you, Jessica. I'm here for only one reason. Well, maybe two.' He laughed softly. She squirmed as a hand slid down from her shoulder and squeezed her breast. 'I'm here to teach you a lesson. A lesson about safety. For you, there is no safety. Do you understand?'

She nodded.

'If you should ever happen to tell someone about me, I'll come into your home just as I did tonight. There will be one difference. I'll have a straight razor in my hand. I'll begin by slashing the throats of your parents while they sleep. And then I'll come to you.' A fingernail circled her nipple. 'I'll cut you very badly. Everywhere. It may take all night. And just before dawn, I'll open your throat from ear to ear. Do you understand?'

'Yes.'

'Very good.' The pale blur of his face drifted down. He kissed her sore lips. 'Very good,' he whispered again.

539

Chapter Eleven

Except for the struggle on Monday morning to come up with a new story, Larry had spent the entire week on *Night Stranger*. That book was coming along fine.

But what about the next?

He didn't feel like racking his mind for a new idea. So much easier to stick with the familiar territory of *Night Stranger*. He knew where that book was going, and enjoyed the excitement of guiding it there.

This was Friday.

He couldn't keep avoiding the problem forever.

Think how much better you'll feel, he told himself, once you've come up with a great plan for the next book.

A great plan that does not include a stiff under the stairs with a stake in its heart.

He found the disk from Monday, put it into his word processor and tapped out commands until 'Novel Notes – Monday, October 3' appeared at the corner of the screen. As he cleaned a pipe and loaded it with fresh tobacco, he skimmed the amber lines. About three pages worth of material. And nothing.

A lot of crap about their vampire.

'In effect,' he read, 'you have this gorgeous thing as your slave.

'Real possibilities.'

Sure.

Better luck today.

Larry lit his pipe. Below 'Real possibilities,' he typed, 'Notes – Friday, October 7.'

'How about a tribe of desert scavengers?' he wrote, recalling the idea he'd toyed around with shortly before the van reached Sagebrush Flat. 'They arrange "accidents" on the back roads, then fall upon the unlucky travelers.

'Too much like THE HILLS HAVE EYES. Besides, I already did something along those lines in SAVAGE TIMBER.'

Larry scowled at the screen. He wished he hadn't reminded himself of *Savage Timber*. That damn novel, his second, had nearly destroyed his career. A major release, and all it did was sit in the stores, thanks to that damn green-foil artsy-fart cover.

Don't think about it, he told himself.

Come on, a new idea.

'How about a guy who finds the remains of an old juke box? He restores it to working order, and . . .'

And what?

'It doesn't have any records in it. He puts in his own. But it doesn't play the new ones. All it will play are the oldies-but-goodies that used to be in it. Back before it was shot to pieces by . . . Hey, maybe it wants revenge on the vandals who used it for target practice.

'Great. A pissed-off juke box. What does it do, scoot around and electrocute people?

'Could be like a time machine. The guy gets it working, and it shoves him into the past. So he finds himself stranded in Holman's – or a dive of some kind – back in the mid-60s.

'Has possibilities.

'Maybe the box wants him there to have a show-down with the jerks who plugged it. A motorcycle gang, or something. A real nasty bunch.

'The poor guy doesn't know what's in store for him. But he's plenty upset. It's Twilight Zone time. One minute, he's with his wife and kids, has a nice house and a good job. Suddenly, bam, he finds himself in a diner in a dying town 25 years in the past. Freaks him out. All he wants to do is get home.

'Until he finds himself falling for a beautiful young waitress. At that point, he begins to appreciate his situation.

'Things start to get ugly when a gang of biker thugs thunders into town.

'Suppose the real reason the juke box took him there was to save the waitress? Neat. The juke box LIKES her. Sometimes, alone at night after the diner closes, she has it play her favorite tunes, and she dances alone in the dark.

'The way things went down, first time around, the bikers raped and murdered her. The juke box has brought our hero back to the diner to alter the course of history – to save her.

'Which, of course, he does.

'Mission accomplished, the box lets him go home again. But he misses the beautiful waitress. (Okay, he didn't have a wonderful wife and kids. He was divorced, or something.) He goes looking for the gal. Finds her.

'She's his mother. He's his own father. He got her pregnant during their brief time together back in '65, and he was the baby she had.

'He'd have to be about 30 years old in the present. She could be about 25 when he met her in the diner.

'She had to give up the baby (our hero) for some reason. He was adopted, and always curious about the identity of his parents.

'If she is his mother, we could give him back his wife and kids.

'Neater if he finds the waitress in the present and they resume as lovers. But how would that work with their ages? Say he's 30 in the present. How could the gal be anywhere near his age when he finds her again? If she's 30 now, she would've been 5 when he saved her from the bikers.

'What if the waitress he fell in love with was her mother? That would make the daughter just his age in the present. And she is the spitting image of her mother, the gal he loved.

'Not bad. Might work.'

Larry's pipe had gone out. He could tell by the easy draw that nothing remained in the bowl but ash. He set the pipe into its holder, and returned his fingers to the keyboard.

'Our main guy resurrects the juke box. It seems evil at first, but turns out to be a force for good. And a matchmaker. He falls for the waitress, who happens to have a really cute little girl at the time. Plenty of thrills and spills and nasty crap with the bikers (make them total degenerates, monsters). By facing them down (he's scared, but comes through, proving to himself that he's a man), he ends up saving the kid who will later become his true love.

'Why not?'

Larry grinned at the screen.

All right! You've got it. Spend the next couple of days working out the details, and . . .

The next couple of days.

He muttered a curse.

The weekend was shot. As soon as Lane got home from school today, they would be hitting the road for Los Angeles to visit with Jean's folks.

Just what he wanted to do.

Especially now, with the new idea sizzling in his mind.

Can't get out of it, though. You'll just have to put the idea on hold till Monday.

It would give him something to think about while he drove. He might be able to work out a few of the main scenes, maybe even come up with some nifty new angles. But he knew very well that daydreaming about the story while he steered down the freeway would accomplish very little compared to working at the word processor. The act of typing out his thoughts seemed to give them a focus that wasn't there when he simply let his mind wander. Daydreams seemed to meander and drift. But sentences were solid, and one led to another.

Not this weekend, they won't.

This weekend's down the toilet.

Well, he tried to console himself, Jean's folks are okay. And it *is* their anniversary. I'll probably end up having a good time, even though I'd rather be . . .

He heard the doorbell ring.

Jean would take care of it.

He wondered whether he should get back to *Night Stranger*, or spend the rest of the day fleshing out his juke box story.

Call it, *The Box*, he suddenly thought.

And grinned.

'THE BOX,' he typed. 'Great title. Has a mysterious ring

to it. And Box not only refers to the juke box that sends him back in time, but also the "box," or trap he finds himself stuck in. He's boxed in by circumstances. No apparent way out. Also, the sex thing. Have one of the bikers refer to the main gal as a box. "Foxy box." And maybe the main guy is a former boxer (killed an opponent in the ring, and swore off fighting?). No, that'd be pushing it. Trite, too. But maybe there are some other "box" angles. Fool around with it.'

He heard Jean's footsteps approaching. She might come in and look over his shoulder, so he scrolled down until 'foxy box' climbed out of sight at the top of the screen.

She rapped on the office door, and pushed it open. In her hand was an Overnight Mail bag that looked large enough to hold a manuscript. 'This just came for you,' she said. 'It's from Chandler House.'

Larry's publisher.

Jean watched while he tore open the bag. Inside, he found a fat manuscript held together by rubber bands. And a type-written note from his editor:

Larry
   Here is the copyedited manuscript of MADHOUSE. The corrections are light, so I'm sure you'll be pleased.
   We would like you to make whatever changes you consider appropriate, and return it to us if possible by October 13.
   Best,
   Susan

Larry grimaced.

'What?' Jean asked.

'It's *Madhouse*. The copyedited version. I'm supposed to send it back by the 13th.' He glanced at his calendar. 'Christ, that's next Thursday.'

'They didn't give you much time.'

'That's for sure,' he muttered. 'They've had it for about a year and a half and now I get . . . six days.'

'Have fun,' Jean said. She left the room, closing the door again to keep his pipe smoke from contaminating the rest of the house.

Larry pushed his chair back, crossed a leg, rested the thick manuscript on his thigh and rolled the rubber bands off. He tossed Susan's note and the title page onto the cluttered TV tray beside his chair.

Then, he groaned.

For 'light' corrections, page one seemed to have an awful lot of changes.

Halfway down the page, his paragraph used to read, 'She tugged at the door. Locked. God, no! She whirled around and choked out a whimper. He was already off the autopsy table, staggering toward her, his head bobbing and swaying on its broken neck. In his hand was the scalpel.'

Larry struggled to decipher the changes. Words had been crossed out, others added. The paragraph was a map of lines and arrows. At last, he figured it out.

'Tugging at the door, she found it to be locked. No! Snapping her head around, she whimpered in despair, for she saw that the corpse was staggering toward her with a scalpel in his hand. His head was swinging from side to side atop its snapped neck.'

'Jesus H. Christ on a crutch,' Larry muttered.

He found Jean in their bedroom, gathering clothes from an open drawer of her bureau and taking them to her suitcase. Both suitcases lay open on the bed.

He sat down at the end of the mattress. 'We've got a problem.'

'The manuscript?'

'I just looked through the whole thing. It's been wrecked.'

'Not again.'

'Yeah.' *Madhouse* was his twelfth novel, and the third to be demolished by a copyeditor.

'What're you going to do?' Jean asked.

'I have to fix it. I don't have any choice.' He scowled at the carpet. 'Maybe I could get them to take my name off and publish it under the name of the copyeditor.'

'It's that bad?'

'And then some.'

'Why do they let it happen?'

'God, I don't know. It's the luck of the draw, I guess. This time, they happened to send my book to some idiot who thinks she's a writer.'

'Or he,' Jean said, standing up for her gender.

'Or it.'

'Couldn't you just write a letter to Susan, or something, and explain the situation? Maybe they could send a fresh copy to someone else.'

He shook his head. 'I don't think she'd appreciate that. It'd be like calling them jerks for sending it to some illiterate butcher. Besides, they already paid to have it done. And they're on a tight time schedule, by now, or they wouldn't want the damn thing back in six days.'

'Maybe you should phone Susan.'

'The last thing I need is to get a reputation as a trouble-maker.'

'So you're just going to take it lying down?'

'I'm going to take it sitting on my butt with a red pen in one hand and a copy of my British edition in the other. If the people in London didn't fix it, it didn't need fixing.' He hung his head and sighed.

Jean stepped in front of him. She rubbed his shoulders. 'I'm sorry, honey.'

'Fortunes of war. The thing is . . . it'll have to be mailed Wednesday for next-day delivery. If I go to your folks' place, that only gives me about three days to go through the whole damn thing and try to . . . save it.'

'You could take it along.'

'I wouldn't be fit to live with, anyway. Maybe you and Lane should just go ahead without me.' As he spoke the words, he realized that he didn't want to be left behind. Not for this. But he couldn't go. 'If I spend the whole weekend working on it, maybe I'll be feeling human again by the time you get back.'

'I suppose we could call it off,' she said, stroking his hair. 'Go up next weekend, instead.'

'No, don't do that. It's their anniversary. Besides, you've been looking forward to it. No need for all of us to suffer because of this crap.'

'If you're sure,' she muttered.

'I don't see any choice.'

Larry went back to his office. His throat felt tight.

You didn't want to go in the first place, he reminded himself.

But that was before he found out he would have to be laboring over *Madhouse*.

He stared at his computer screen.

Maybe there are some other 'box' angles. Fool around with it. Right. Sure thing. Maybe sometime next week.

No more working out the details for *The Box*. No more plunging toward the conclusion of *Night Stranger*.

The next few days belonged to *Madhouse*, a book that he'd finished eighteen months ago. A book that had already been published in England – and about all they had changed over there was 'windshield' to 'windscreen' and added u's to words like color.

'So who said life is fair?' he muttered, and shut his computer off.

Chapter Twelve

'I have a special announcement to make,' Mr Kramer said with two minutes remaining before the bell. 'As I've mentioned before, the drama department at city college is putting on *Hamlet* next week. I'm sure the production will be well worth seeing for all of you, and I urge every one of you to attend if you can. Now, here's the thing. I've obtained four free tickets to the Saturday night performance. Only four of you will be able to participate, but for those lucky students, I'll provide tickets and transportation.' He smiled. 'That way, you won't have to bug your parents to borrow a car.' A few of the kids laughed. 'If any of you would like to take advantage of the opportunity, just stay in your seats after the bell rings.'

Lane gnawed her lower lip. Should she stay? Jim might ask her out for that night.

We can always go out Friday night instead, she told herself.

It *would* be neat to see the play, especially with Mr Kramer. Couldn't hurt, either, in the brownie points department.

The bell rang. Lane remained in her seat.

As Jessica stepped by, she glanced at Lane and shook her head.

Probably thinks I'm an idiot, wanting to give up a Saturday night to see Shakespeare.

Maybe I am. If it turns out that Jim's busy Friday night, I'm going to kick myself. He was gone last weekend, I'll be gone this weekend. That'll make three weeks in a row if I go to the play and he can't make it on Friday.

This Saturday night was when she'd wanted to go out with him. All week, he'd been especially nice. Trying to make up, Lane supposed, for being such a creep Monday morning.

She turned on her seat. Five other kids had remained in the room.

There're six of us, and he can only take four. If I'm not picked, that'll solve the problem right there.

'I see I've got more Shakespeare fans than tickets,' Mr Kramer said. 'That's certainly gratifying, but it does present a little difficulty. We want to be fair about this.' He dug a hand into a pocket of his slacks and pulled out a quarter. 'I'll flip a coin. The first two of you to lose will have to bow out. Does that sound okay to everyone?'

Nobody objected.

'Okay, Lane, you first. Call it in the air.' He rested the coin on his thumb nail, and flicked it high.

'Heads,' Lane said.

It landed in the palm of his right hand. He slapped it onto the back of his left, kept it covered and smiled at her. 'Want to change your mind?'

'Nope. I'll stick with heads.'

He looked. 'Heads it is,' he said, tipping his hand and letting the coin drop into the other.

He didn't let anyone see it, Lane realized.

What the heck, they're his tickets.

'Okay, George, your turn.'

George won. So did Aaron and Sandra.

Jerry and Heidi, the losers, called the coin again to determine who would be first choice as an alternate in case one of the chosen was unable to attend. Heidi won.

'Okay,' Mr Kramer said, 'I'll fill you in on the details later. In the meantime, have a good weekend. Don't do anything I wouldn't.'

That comment brought a few chuckles.

Lane gathered her books and stood up. 'I'm glad you're one of the lucky four,' he said. 'Maybe I'll get a chance to meet your father when I pick you up for the play.'

'I'm sure he'll be glad to meet you.'

'I'll have to pick up one of his books and get an autograph.'

'That'll make his day.'

'And maybe we can firm up the date he'll be coming in.'

'Yeah. He said any time after the first.'

'Well, maybe we can make it more definite.'

Lane nodded. 'Have a nice weekend, Mr Kramer.'

'You, too. Try to stay out of trouble.' He winked.

'What would be the fun of that?' she said, blushing.

As he laughed, Lane waved goodbye and left the room.

The hallway was crowded with kids, noisy with slamming lockers, shouts and laughter. She leaned against a wall and waited for Jim. A few minutes later, he came along.

'I have to drop some stuff off at my locker,' Lane said. They started up the hall together.

'When are you leaving for Los Angeles?' he asked.

'As soon as I get home.'

'What a drag.'

'There's always next weekend. Next Friday, anyway. I have to go to a play Saturday night with Mr Kramer.'

'Yeah?' He glanced at her, lifting an eyebrow. 'Isn't he a little old for you?'

'Get real. It's a school function. He's taking four of us from his sixth period class.'

'Great.'

'Oh now, don't start pouting. I've got nothing on Friday night.'

'Nothing on, huh? I'd like to see that.'

'I just bet you would.' She felt a hand slide over the seat of her skirt. 'Quit it.'

'Sorry. Just trying to refresh my memory. It's been two whole weeks, you know, and now it'll be another.'

'I'm not overjoyed about it, myself. Nothing I can do, though.' She arrived at her locker and started spinning the combination dial.

'Maybe you could pretend to be sick,' he suggested. 'What if you did that, and they let you stay home by yourself? I could come over to your house tomorrow night, and . . .'

'Dream on, Macduff.'

She opened the locker and switched books, taking out those she would need for homework. Then, she shut the metal door. 'Even if I did stay home, boys aren't allowed in the house when my parents are gone.'

'Who would ever know?'

'I would. Anyway, you might as well forget it. Ain't gonna happen.' They started down the hallway. 'If you promise to behave,' Lane said, 'I'll give you a ride home.'

'What about your goofball friends, Fat and Ugly.'

Lane frowned at him. 'I don't know who you mean.'

'You know, all right. Betty and Henry.'

'Why don't you refer to them that way, okay? They are my friends.'

'God knows why.'

'Are you trying to start something?'

'No, no. Just kidding. They're wonderful people, the salt of the earth.'

'You could stand to be a little more like Henry.'

'Uh, duh.' He put a dopey smile on his face and started bobbing his head.

'Very funny,' she said, but couldn't hold back a smile. 'Stop it. That's not nice.'

'Duh, okay.'

'Anyway, Betty's mom was picking them up after school and taking them to violin lessons.'

'So it'll just be you and me, huh?'

'If you can fit your big head into the car.'

'I can try.'

At the end of the hallway, Jim held the door open for her. She stepped out and looked toward the student parking lot. She spotted her red Mustang.

No sign of Riley Benson.

After Monday, she'd expected each afternoon to find him perched on the hood. So far, he hadn't tried it again. Though they crossed paths several times a day, he'd done no more than give her tough-guy looks.

He must've given up on his big plan for revenge, she decided.

Maybe Jessica had talked him out of it.

Pays to be nice to people, she thought. Especially if they're buddy-buddy with someone who wants to wipe up the floor with you.

When Lane opened the car door, hot air poured out. They cranked down all the windows. She took a beach towel from the trunk and spread it over the driver's seat so she wouldn't burn her legs on the upholstery.

'You don't have one for me?' Jim asked.

'You're not wearing a skirt.'

'You sure are,' he said, and bent forward as if trying for a glimpse of her panties when she climbed in. 'Pink,' he announced.

'Wrong.'

She started the engine. She twisted around to look out the

rear window as she backed out of the space. She could feel her blouse pull tight against her breasts. Jim, of course, was staring at them.

'If they match your bra, they're white,' he said.

'Don't you ever think about anything but sex?' she asked, grinning at him.

'Sure. Instead sometimes I think about sex.'

She shook her head, faced forward again, and steered for the parking lot exit.

'Must be hot, wearing a bra all the time.'

'What makes you think I wear one *all* the time?'

'Every time I've seen you.'

'Are you sure?'

'Are you kidding? I can tell a mile away if a babe's got one on.'

'That's impressive.'

'How long is your car going to be out of commission?' Lane asked, hoping to change the subject.

'I'll have it off the blocks tomorrow. I wanted it ready so we could go out tomorrow night.'

'Sorry about that.'

'Maybe I'll give Candi a call.'

'I know, just kidding.'

Jim said nothing. Lane got a tight, sickish feeling deep inside. She kept her eyes on the road.

'You wouldn't mind, would you?'

'Be my guest.'

She knew that Jim was teasing. He had no intention of taking out Candi. He'd dumped her in order to start going out with Lane. The threat of taking up with her again was nothing more than a form of punishment.

'You know what they say about a bird in the hand,' Jim said.

'A good way to get a dirty hand.'

'Also, she's a lot more cooperative than some people I might mention.'

'And probably has the diseases to prove it.'

'Oooo. Mean.'

'But feel free to take her out. It's your life.'

He reached over and put a hand on Lane's leg. 'You know I wouldn't do that.'

'I only know what you tell me.'

'I miss you, that's all.'

'I miss you, too. But there's nothing I can do about this weekend.'

'Yeah, I know.' He squeezed her knee, and his hand moved slowly up her bare leg to the hem of her skirt. He caressed her thigh. It felt good.

'Just don't go throwing Candi at me every time you get upset.'

'Jealous?'

'Suppose I was always threatening to dump you for Cliff Ryker?'

'That shithead?'

'You think you'd enjoy it?'

'You wouldn't. Not if you went ahead with it.'

'He's cute.'

'Not as cute as me.' Jim's hand crept under her skirt. She pushed it away. 'He's no gentleman, either.'

'And you are?'

'I'm not like Cliff. He isn't the kind of guy who takes "no" for an answer. First time out with him, and he'd bang you till you couldn't see straight. If that's what you want, I'll be glad to take care of it for you.'

'You go out with Candi, and you'll never get the chance.'

'Hmmmm. I like the sound of that. You mean, if I don't, I do?'

'Where there's life, there's hope.'

She pulled the Mustang over to the curb in front of Jim's house. Checking the windows and rear-view mirror, she saw nobody nearby. She turned to Jim. She slipped a hand around the back of his neck. 'No funny stuff,' she said. 'Just a quick kiss.'

'How about coming in for a Pepsi, or something?'

She shook her head. 'I have to get home. My folks are waiting.'

'Ten minutes? That won't throw off your trip by much. Tell them you had to stay after class.'

I *did* have to stay after class, she thought. It wouldn't be a lie.

'Is your mother home?'

Jim answered by swinging a thumb over his shoulder, pointing out the Mazda in the driveway.

'Okay,' Lane said. 'Ten minutes. No longer, though.'

She took her hand away from his neck, and climbed out. Jim stayed in the lead as she walked up the flagstones to the front stoop. He unlocked the door, and held it open for her.

The air was cool.

The house was silent except for the hum of the air-conditioning system.

Jim didn't call out to announce that he was home.

'Are you sure she's here?' Lane asked.

'Might be sleeping. Or taking a bath. Who knows?'

They entered the kitchen. Lane leaned against a counter while Jim took a couple of cans from the refrigerator. The air smelled fresh. It was almost too cold on her skin. It chilled the damp back of her blouse.

Jim found glasses, dropped ice cubes into them, and filled them with soda.

A glass in each hand, he stepped in front of Lane. She reached for her drink. Instead of giving it to her, he stretched both arms past her sides and set the glasses on the counter. His arms closed around her, pulled her gently forward until their bodies met.

'What if your mother walks in?' Lane whispered close to his mouth.

'I don't think she will.' He tugged the tail of her blouse out of her skirt, and slid his hands underneath.

Lane let herself sink against him. She kissed him.

Shouldn't be doing this, she thought.

But she'd intended to kiss him goodbye, anyway. And his hands felt good roaming the bare skin of her back. And she liked the feel of his chest tight against her breasts. She could feel his breathing and his heartbeat.

He started to fumble with the catches of her bra.

She pulled her mouth away. 'Oh, no you don't.'

'It's all right.'

'No, it isn't.'

He unfastened the bra, anyway. She felt it go loose.

She grabbed Jim's arms and pushed them down to his sides. 'I said, "No," and I meant it.'

'Come on, what's the harm?'

'For one thing, your mother.'

'She might be in town at the beauty parlor,' he said, smiling as if he expected Lane to appreciate the news.

'The car . . .'

'She usually goes with Mary from next door. Right about three on Fridays.'

'You *knew* she wasn't here?'

Still smiling, Jim shrugged.

'You lied to me.'

'Just a little fib.'

'Terrific,' she muttered, reaching up under the back of her blouse to fasten the bra.

'Come on, don't do that.' He lifted his hands to her breasts.

'Cut it out.'

'Come on, you like it.'

'I told you . . .' She got one of the hooks fastened. He was squeezing, rubbing. She *did* like it. 'Damn it, Jim.' Not bothering with the other hook, she swung her hands around and pushed him away. 'I have to leave.'

'No you don't. Hey, come on.'

'This is what I get for trusting you, huh?'

'Look, I'm sorry I lied about Mom being here. Okay?' He looked into her eyes and gently held her shoulders. 'I just figured you wouldn't come in, and . . . we haven't been together for weeks. I get crazy wanting to be with you. Sometimes, all I can think about is kissing you and how it feels to hold you. Especially after last time.'

'That was nice,' Lane said, remembering.

She had been under orders to be home by eleven, so they'd

skipped the second feature at the movies and parked in the desert outside town. She'd refused Jim's suggestion to get into the back seat. Staying in the front, they twisted themselves awkwardly to embrace and kiss. But it was wonderful. She felt daring and romantic and sexy in the moonlit car. Her blouse came off early. She managed to keep her bra on, though. In spite of Jim's begging and his attempts to remove it. In spite of her own desire to rid herself of the garment and feel his touch without a stiff layer of cloth in the way. Finally, she'd told him, 'It's almost time to leave.' He didn't protest, simply nodded and murmured, 'I guess so.' Reaching behind her back, Lane unhooked her bra. She took it off. His mouth fell open and he stared for a long time before touching. When he did touch her breasts, his hands were trembling.

Softened by the memories of that night, she stepped forward and put her arms around Jim. She kissed him gently on the mouth. 'Apology accepted,' she whispered. 'But I really do have to leave now.'

His hands slid down her back and caressed her rump. 'What about your Pepsi?'

'Time's all up. You can walk me to the car, though.'

He squeezed her against him and kissed her hard, then stepped away. 'Guess I'll just have to wait for next Friday, huh?'

'It'll get here.'

'Not soon enough.'

'I'll miss you,' she said.

'I'll miss you more.'

'No you won't.'

'Yes I will.'

'Wanta fight about it?'

'Yeah,' he said. 'Let's wrestle.'

'Oh, you'd like that.'

'So would you.'

'Maybe.'

Holding hands, they walked to the door.

Chapter Thirteen

Larry stood at the end of the driveway, waving good-bye to Jean and Lane as the car headed off down the road. It seemed strange, being left behind.

He knew he would miss them. Hell, he *already* missed them.

On the other hand, he rather liked the prospect of being on his own for the weekend. He could do whatever he pleased, and not have to answer to anyone.

Freedom.

He felt like a kid being left home without parents or babysitter.

The car vanished around the corner. Larry turned toward the house, then raised a hand in greeting as Barbara trotted down the steps next door. A handbag swung at her hip. Larry supposed she was leaving on an errand.

'So, they took off without you.'

'Sure did.'

'Jean told me about that manuscript.' She stopped beside her car in the driveway. 'Sounds like the pits to me.'

'Gives me a good excuse to stay behind,' he said, smiling.

'If you're not too busy, why don't you come over for dinner? We'll throw some steaks on the barbeque.'

'Sounds great.'

'Good. Drop in around five, then, all right?'

'I'll be there.'

She climbed into her car, and Larry headed for the house.

Things are perking up already, he thought.

In his office, he glanced at the savaged manuscript and realized he was in no mood to struggle with it. He'd already fought his way through more than a hundred pages today, scratching out the copyeditor's misguided corrections and replacing them with scribbles to match the printed lines as they'd originally been written. That was plenty for one day's work.

He settled down in the living room with a beer and the Shaun Hutson novel he'd started reading that morning. Though his eyes traveled over the words, his mind kept slipping out of the story. He found himself imagining what Jean's folks might say when they realized he'd stayed home, wondering what he should wear over to Pete and Barbara's, thinking about how much he would like to spend all day tomorrow working on ideas for *The Box*.

Then, he was speculating about the juke box in the ditch. He wondered how much it weighed. Could two men lift it? In his book, they would have to carry it to the van. Would that be possible?

Have the women lend a hand with it. My main guy isn't married. Might have a girlfriend with him, though.

Still occupied with his thoughts, Larry set the book aside. He drained the last of his beer, wandered into the bedroom and took off his clothes.

Have one of the gals fall while they're lugging the juke box up the slope. Good. Foreshadowing that the box is going to cause trouble.

In the bathroom, he turned on the shower and stepped under its beating spray.

She tumbles down the embankment, he thought as he began to soap himself. Gets banged up pretty much like Barbara did in the hotel.

He remembered the way Barbara had looked, standing in the doorway afterward. How her legs and belly were scraped. How her blouse hung open.

The images stirred a pleasant heat in his groin.

Which turned cold when he suddenly saw himself kneeling under the staircase, gazing at the shriveled corpse.

God, he wished he'd never seen that thing!

It always seemed to be with him. Waiting. Like some kind of spook lurking in a dark closet of his mind, every now and then throwing open the door to give him another look.

558

So damn grisly and repulsive.

But fascinating, too.

As Larry washed his hair, his mind ran through the familiar questions. Who was she? Who drove the stake into her chest? Was her presence under the stairway known to the person who put the brand-new lock on the hotel doors? Could she really be a vampire? What might happen if someone pulled out the stake?

He had no answers.

He told himself, as always, that he didn't *want* to know the answers. He only wanted to forget about the thing.

Which wasn't about to happen.

Maybe we should've reported it, he thought. He'd been against that at the time. Now, however, he saw how it might've been for the best. A call to cops would've relieved them of responsibility. Like passing the baton.

We did our part, now it's your turn.

Part of the problem, he realized, was carrying the burden of knowledge.

We're the only ones who know it's there.

But we didn't do anything about it.

So the damn corpse is more than just a grisly memory, it's unfinished business.

According to the shrinks, that's what messes up your head more than anything – unfinished business.

Maybe we need to deal with it, Larry told himself. Take some kind of action to get the thing out of our systems.

'Let's drive out and get it,' Pete said.

Larry felt as if his breath had been knocked out. 'You're kidding,' he said.

'You're out of your gourd,' Barbara said.

'Hey, if he's going to write a book about that juke box, he ought to *have* it. Or better yet, *I* ought to have it. Larry can keep track of my progress repairing the thing so he gets the details right. You know? There's nothing like first-hand experience to give a book . . .'

'Verisimilitude,' Larry put in.

'Yeah, that's it.'

'I don't know,' Larry said.

He took a sip of his vodka tonic, and shook his head. He wished he hadn't mentioned *The Box*. Normally, he didn't discuss story ideas with anyone. But Pete and Barbara were part of this one. They'd discovered the juke box. Pete's desire to take it home had really been the inspiration. So the story had rolled out.

Should've kept my mouth shut.

The last thing I want to do is go driving out to Sagebrush Flat.

Pete got up from his lawn chair and checked the barbeque. The flames had died away, but Larry could tell from where he sat that the briquettes were burning. The air over the grill shimmered with heat waves. 'Be another ten, fifteen minutes,' Pete said. He turned to Barbara, arched a dark eyebrow. 'Don't you need to go inside and do something?'

'Trying to get rid of me?'

'Just trying to be helpful. We're going to have those sauteed mushrooms, we'll want them *with* our steaks.'

'They only take a few minutes,' she said. 'I'll do them up when you put the meat on.'

Good, Larry thought. He wasn't eager for her to leave. Not only was she the best defense against Pete's crazy urge to fetch the juke box, but it felt good to look at her.

She sat on a lounge in front of him, bare legs stretched out on its cushion. Her long, slim legs looked wonderful in spite of the scabbed areas. She wore red shorts and a plain white T-shirt. The shorts were very short. The T-shirt lay softly against her flat belly and the rises of her breasts. Its fabric was thin enough to show a faint pink hue of the skin underneath, the dark crust of the scabs above Barbara's waist, the white of her bra.

He watched the way her muscles moved as she sat up straight to take a drink of her cocktail and settled back again and rested the glass on the moist disk it had left just below the hip of her shorts.

'You don't want to go back there, do you?' she asked Larry.

'Not a whole lot.'

'I didn't think so.'

'It's probably too heavy for the two of us to carry, anyway,' he told Pete.

'Barbara will come along and lend a hand. Won't you, hon?'

'Not on your life.'

'She's just scared of the vampire.'

'You know it. Besides, we don't need that piece of junk cluttering up the garage.'

'It'd be great for Larry's book. He can come over and check it out whenever he needs some inspiration.' Looking at Larry, he added, 'And we can take pictures of it. You know? A photo of the actual juke box, all shot up the way it is, that'll be terrific on your cover.'

'That would be pretty neat,' he admitted.

'Jeez, don't encourage him.'

Larry smiled at her. 'I have no intention of going back to that place.'

'You're scared of the vampire, too, huh' Pete said. 'Hey, it can't hurt you. Not as long as it's got that stake in its heart.'

'I'm not worried about any "vampire",' Larry told him. 'I don't think it *is* a vampire. But stiffs give me the creeps.'

'That's a good one, coming from you.'

'I'm scared of my own shadow, man. That's what makes me good at writing those books. And I tell you, Sagebrush Flat is a lot scarier to me than my shadow. My shadow pales by comparison.'

Barbara chuckled at his pun.

'Even if there *were* no corpse under the stairway, I'd still want to stay away from that town. Just the fact that it's deserted is enough to spook me. There's something basically frightening about a place where people are supposed to be, but aren't. An abandoned town, an office building at night . . .'

'That's really true, you know,' Barbara said. 'Like a hotel really late at night when everyone's asleep.'

'Or a school,' Larry added. 'Or a church.'

'Yeah.' Her eyes widened. 'Churches are *really* spooky when nobody's there. I used to go for choir practice when I was in high school. We'd meet on Wednesday nights at eight.' She leaned forward and gazed at Larry. 'One night . . . God, I'm getting goosebumps just thinking about it.' Hunching up her shoulders, she squeezed her arms tight against her sides. 'One night, practice had been called off and I didn't know about it. I think we'd been out of town. Anyway, the choir director was sick, and everybody knew it but me. So my dad dropped me off in the parking lot and I went in.'

'You taking notes, Lar? Maybe you can use this.'

'Sounds promising so far.' He could feel himself shivering slightly as if Barbara's fear were contagious.

'There was a light on in the narthex. But the stairway to the choir loft was dark. I went up there, anyway. I figured I was just the first to arrive. The choir loft was dark, too.'

'Why didn't you turn on some lights?' Pete asked.

'I don't know. I guess I thought I shouldn't mess with anything like light switches. But also, I was afraid somebody might . . . turning on lights, you know, that'd be like giving away that I was there.' Her mouth stretched, baring her teeth.

'That's the thing,' Larry said. 'When a place seems deserted, you're afraid you aren't *really* alone.'

'That's it. Exactly. Because you can't see what's out there. God, I started thinking someone was roaming around, sneaking up on me. I even thought I heard someone creeping up the stairs.' Her right hand still held the glass on her lap. Her other hand crossed over to that arm and rubbed it as if she wanted to smooth away the goosebumps. Larry saw that her thighs were pebbled. Though she wore a bra, it was apparently of a light, stretchy fabric. Her nipples made small points against her T-shirt.

I'll have to remember that, Larry thought. A woman has gooseflesh, the nipples get erect.

Fear makes them hard.

Or is she turned on?

Turned on by the fear?

Barbara kept frowning, rubbing her arm. She seemed lost in her memory of that night.

'So what happened?' Pete asked.

She shook her head. 'Nothing.'

'Oh, that's a great story.'

'I waited around for about fifteen minutes. I was almost too scared to move. I kept staring down at the nave and pulpit and everything, and thought someone was down there in the dark. You know, *aware* of me. Watching me.'

'Coming for you,' Pete added.

'Damn right.'

'They're *coming* for you,' he said, mimicking the voice of the jerky brother in the graveyard scene of *The Night of the Living Dead*. 'They're *coming* for . . .'

'Knock it off, would you?'

'Nobody ever showed up?' Larry asked.

She shook her head. 'I finally beat it. I was never so glad to get out of a place in my life.'

'Not even the hole in the landing of the Sagebrush Flat Hotel?' Pete asked.

'That was different. I was in pain. That's not the same as being scared half to death.'

'So you finally just bolted out of the church?' Larry asked.

'Sure did. I didn't even stop to use the phone and call home. I waited in the parking lot, and Dad finally came along at the usual time to pick me up.'

'That's it, huh?' Pete asked.

'It was enough. I quit the choir, after that. Nothing was ever going to get me back into the church after dark.'

'Pretty drastic, considering that nothing happened.'

'It wasn't exactly is if nothing happened,' Larry pointed out.

'That's right. All these years have passed, and it still gives me the creeps if I think about it.'

'Still isn't much of a story,' Pete said.

'A good set-up for one,' Larry told him.

'Think you might use it?' Pete asked.

'I can just see it,' Barbara said, smiling. 'You'd probably have a homicidal maniac chasing me through the pews.'

'Something like that. Maybe Jesus gets down off the cross and stalks the gal through the church.'

'Oh, sick.'

Pete laughed. 'Hey, goes after her with a nail in each hand.'

'You guys.'

'That's good,' Larry said. 'Next morning, the preacher shows up and *she's* the one on the cross.'

'God's gonna get you for that,' Barbara warned.

'More than likely.'

'I'd better put the steaks on,' Pete said. 'Feed him quick before a lightning bolt comes down and knocks him out of his shoes.'

After dinner, Pete presented his surprise – a plastic bag containing three video tapes. 'Thought we'd have a movie marathon, unless you're in a big hurry to get home.'

With three vodka tonics under his belt, and the two beers he'd had with dinner, Larry knew he was in no condition to write, make corrections on his copyedited manuscript, or even read the Hutson novel.

Nor was he eager to be alone in his empty house.

'Sounds good to me,' he said. 'Let's see what you've got.' He inspected the tapes through their clear plastic boxes: *Cameron's Closet*, *Blood Frenzy* and *Floater*.

'Barb phoned me at the shop,' Pete explained. 'So I picked these up on the way home.' He looked quite pleased with himself.

'Oh, this'll be neat,' Larry said.

'These should put you in a great mood,' Barbara said, 'for when it's time to go home.'

'They freak you out, you can spend the night here.'

'I imagine I'll be all right.'

They started with *Blood Frenzy*. Pete watched from a recliner beside the sofa. Larry sat at one end of the sofa, Barbara at the other. After a while, she tossed a cushion onto the coffee table and propped her feet up.

When the movie ended, Pete made popcorn. Barbara disappeared for a few minutes. She came back wearing a kneelength blue robe. She filled glasses with Pepsi for everyone. Pete separated the popcorn into three bowls.

Before returning to her place on the sofa, Barbara turned off all the lights.

They munched popcorn, drank their sodas, and watched *Cameron's Closet* in a room that was dark except for the glow from the television screen.

Every now and then, Larry glanced at Barbara. She was slumped against the back of the sofa, popcorn bowl on her lap, her legs stretched out, feet resting on the cushion she had earlier placed on the coffee table. When she twisted sideways to set her empty bowl on the lamp table, the robe slipped off her left leg. She wore a pink, diaphanous nightgown. It was shorter than the robe. It didn't reach down much farther than her hip. With a quiet moan of annoyance, she flung the fallen section of the robe back on top of her thigh.

This is sure better than being home, Larry thought.

A few minutes later, she took the cushion out from under her feet. She tilted it against the armrest, swiveled herself around and swung her legs onto the sofa. She lay down on her side, head propped on the cushion. 'Let me know if I kick you,' she said.

'Maybe I should get out of your way.'

'No, that's fine.'

Pete looked over. 'Oh, here we go. For godsake, Barb, sit up. You won't last five minutes.'

'I'm wide awake.'

'You won't be. I'm warning you, I'm not gonna rewind. You drift off, it's your hard luck.'

'I'm not going to drift off.'

'Famous last words,' Pete said. 'Lar, you catch her dropping off, pinch her.'

'Don't you dare.' She tucked the robe in between the backs of her legs as if to prevent Larry from reaching up inside it for the pinch.

It was the sort of thing that Jean might do.

The casual warning and precaution hinted at an intimacy that was both comforting and exciting.

Pete used the remote to rewind the few seconds of the movie that he'd missed while complaining to Barbara.

She lasted more than five minutes. But not more than ten. Larry realized she was asleep when her legs straightened and one of her bare feet pushed against the side of his thigh. Her touch made warmth flow through him.

He waited for a while, enjoying the sensation. But it made him feel guilty. 'Pete,' he finally said. 'She's zonked.'

'Barrrr-bra.'

She flinched, lifted her face off the cushion. 'No, I'm fine.'

'You dozed off.'

'No, I didn't. I'm fine.' Her head settled down again. Her eyes drifted shut.

'Forget it,' Pete said. 'She can watch it in the morning if she wants to.'

'I'm watching,' she mumbled.

Larry tried to watch the movie. Her right foot made it difficult. So did the way the top of her robe hung open, revealing most of her right breast through the flimsy pink nightgown. The show on the TV screen was good, but the stolen glimpses were better. Sometimes, the foot rubbed him.

Near the end of the movie, she stretched out her left leg. Its foot pushed across the top of his thigh and rested on his lap. The pressure there made him squirm. He wrapped his hand around Barbara's ankle and guided her foot down beside the other.

'Huh?' she moaned. 'Sorry. Kicking you?'

'It's all right,' he said.

Pete looked around, frowning. 'Christ, Barb, you're screwing up the movie. Why don't you just go to bed.'

'Yeah, maybe I better.'

Shit, Larry thought.

She pushed herself up and staggered to her feet. 'Night, guys. Sorry I pooped out on you, Larry.'

'No problem. Thanks for the dinner and everything.'

'Glad you could make it. See ya.' She made her way around the coffee table. Larry could see through her robe when she stepped in front of him. Her breasts swayed a little as she bent over and kissed Pete goodnight.

Then, she was gone.

The room seemed empty without her.

During the final moments of *Cameron's Closet*, Larry heard a toilet flush.

Pete removed the tape from the VCR. He grinned over his shoulder. 'Free at last, free at last,' he said. 'Thank God Almighty, free at last.'

'If you want to turn in . . .'

'Are you kidding?' He pushed the tape of *Floater* into the machine and started it playing. 'Back in a second.' He hurried away.

He came back while the screen still showed its warning against unauthorized use of the video tape. He had a bottle of Irish whiskey in one hand and two glasses in the other. He sat next to Larry on the sofa. He filled the two glasses. 'Party time,' he said.

'I'm gonna be wasted tomorrow.'

'The cats are away. Gotta live it up.'

They watched the movie until their glasses were empty. Pete refilled them both, then pressed the Stop button on his remote. The horror film was replaced by a black and white John Wayne movie. Larry recognized it immediately as *The Sands of Iwo Jima*.

'Why'd you turn it off?' he asked.

A grin stretched the corners of Pete's mouth.

Chapter Fourteen

'How about a little excursion?' Pete said.

'What do you mean?'

'Sagebrush Flat.'

'You're kidding,' Larry said.

'Who's gonna stop us?'

'I don't want to go out there.'

Pete clapped a hand down on Larry's knee. His eyes gleamed with mischief, but he wasn't smiling. He looked like a kid, a kid with a mustache and some gray in his hair and with big plans to pull off a caper. 'We take the van. We drive out there, pick up the juke box, and we'll be back in two, three hours. Barb's zonked. She'll never know.'

'She'll know when she finds the thing in your garage.'

'Okay, so we'll leave it over at your place. What do you say, Lar?'

'I think it's crazy.'

'Hey, man, an adventure. It'll be great. You can use it in your book. You know, tell all about how the two guys sneak off in the middle of the night to bring the thing back. You can write it the way it happens, you know? Won't have to tax the ol' imagination.'

'It's crazy.'

'Don't you want the box?'

'Not that badly.'

'What about a photo for the cover of your book?'

'Well, that'd be neat, but . . .'

'So we'll take my camera. Maybe we won't bring the thing back, you know? Maybe we can't even lift it. But at least we'll have some pictures.'

'We could do that during the day.'

'You know the kind of heat I'd get from Barbara. She'd give me all kinds of shit. How about it?'

'You really want to go *now*?' The digital clock on the VCR showed 12:05.

'No time like the present. A midnight mission.'

The idea frightened Larry. It also excited him. He felt a vibration that seemed to hum through his nerves.

When was the last time, he wondered, that you did something really daring?

If you chicken out, you'll regret it. And Pete'll think you're a pussy.

A real adventure.

'Just like Tom and Huck,' he said.

'Huh?'

'Tom Sawyer climbed out his window in the middle of the night and went with Huck to a graveyard to cure their warts. I always wished I could do something like that.'

'You got warts, man?'

'Let's go for it.'

Grinning, Pete refilled the glasses. 'Fun and games,' he toasted. They clinked their glasses, and drank.

Pete took his glass with him. He turned on a lamp at the end of the sofa. Then, he removed the tape from the VCR, flicked off the television, and left the room. Larry sipped whiskey while he waited. It warmed him, but didn't ease the thrumming vibrations.

When Pete returned, he wore a gunbelt. His .357 hung in the holster against his right leg. Dangling by a strap around his neck was a camera with a flash attachment. 'I checked the bedroom,' he said in a low voice. 'Barb's out like a light.'

Pete set his empty glass down. He capped the whiskey bottle and handed it to Larry. 'You be the keeper of the hooch.'

'We shouldn't take it with us.'

'Fuck that. Who's gonna know?'

'If we get stopped . . .'

'We won't. Calm down, you'll live longer.'

They went to the door. Pete turned off the lamp.

They stepped outside. Standing under the porch light, Pete locked the front door with his key.

Larry, shivering, hugged his chest as he hurried toward the van at the curb. A chilly wind pushed at him. He thought about stopping by his house for a jacket. But Pete wasn't bundled up. Pete still wore his short-sleeved knit shirt and blue jeans.

If he can take it, I can, Larry told himself.

Besides, it'll be all right once we're in the van.

The van felt warm. It must've been like an oven before the sun went down, and it still retained a lot of heat. Larry settled into the passenger seat, and sighed.

'Pass it over.'

He handed the bottle to Pete, who took a swig and gave it back. Larry took a drink. 'Are you all right to drive?' he asked.

'You kidding? I don't hardly even have a good buzz on.'

I do, Larry thought. I'm buzzing, all right. But it isn't the booze. Just good old-fashioned excitement. And maybe fear.

Pete started the van. He kept the headlights off for a while. After turning the first corner, he put them on. They drilled into the night. 'Hey, this is something, you know that?'

'You think you can find the town?'

'No sweat.'

'We stay away from the hotel, though, right?'

'If you say so.' Pete drove in silence for several minutes. They were on Riverfront Drive before he looked at Larry and said, 'You know what I don't understand? How come you want to write about the juke box instead of the vampire?'

'Vampire books are a dime a dozen.'

'Not true ones. Don't get me wrong, I think your juke box story sounds pretty neat. But I'd think the true story of how you found a vampire in a ghost town would be . . . different, you know?'

'Different, all right.'

'Remember that movie, *The Amityville Horror*? That was supposed to be a true story.'

'It was supposed to be,' Larry said. 'But I've heard the whole thing was made up.'

'Maybe it was, maybe it wasn't. The thing is, they *claimed* it was true. And that's what made it. Would've been just another haunted house movie except for that. You're supposed to think it actually happened, right?'

'Right.'

'It was based on a book, wasn't it?'

'Yeah. And the book was pushed as nonfiction.'

'Did the book sell okay?'

'Are you kidding? It sold a ton.'

'So what's to keep you from writing up this vampire thing as nonfiction? Have a big bestseller, they make a movie out of it, presto! You're rich and famous.'

'Shit.'

'What do you mean, shit? You got something against money?'

'I'm doing okay.'

'Sure, you're doing okay. But how many bestsellers have you had?'

'You can do just fine without ever having a book on the bestseller lists. Those guys on the lists, they're making millions.'

Pete whistled softly. 'That much?'

'Sure. Some of those guys get a couple of million up front. Or more. That's before paperback rights, foreign rights, movie sales.'

'Christ, and you're not interested?'

'I didn't say I'm not interested. I just don't want to mess with any vampire.'

'Hey, let's not kid ourselves here. The thing's not a vampire. It's just some broad with a stake in her chest. But we don't *know* that. Not for sure. Neither will your readers. That's what keeps the story going. Wait till the very end, then you pull the stake. That's like the final chapter, you know? You pull the stake, and see what happens.'

'I don't know.'

They left the lights of Mulehead Bend behind. Pete turned off the main road, and headed west into the desert. There were no more streetlamps. The head-lights pushed paths of brightness up the lane in front of them. The moon cast a pale glow over the bleak landscape of boulders, scrub bushes and cacti, and the jagged mountains in the distance. It looked cold and forlorn out there. Larry suddenly wanted to turn back.

It was bad enough, driving through this bleak terrain on the way to a juke box.

But that obviously wasn't what Pete had in mind.

'What are we *really* doing?' Larry asked.

'Just what we planned. Bring the juke box back. Or just take some pictures, if we can't carry it.'

'Then what's this vampire business?'

'Just a thought. Hey, you don't like the idea, fine. I'm not trying to push you into something. But Jesus, why on earth would you want to pass up a chance to make a million bucks?'

'The thing scares me.'

'That's the point.' He reached over, took the bottle from Larry, drank from it, and handed it back. 'The point is, you're in the business of scaring people. Right?'

'Scaring them with fiction. Not the real thing. They want real scares, they can watch the TV news.'

'This wouldn't be all that different from your novels. Hey, we are talking about vampires, not homicides or nuclear war. The only difference is, this would be a true story. And it'd fit right in with your image, you know? This is the sort of thing that'd make publicity people drool. Get this, 'Renowned horror writer discovers vampire on weekend outing.' It's a natural. They'd put you on the tube, man. And here's the best part, you could *take her with you*.'

'Oh, wonderful.'

'Just let 'em *try* to say you made the whole thing up.'

'Great. You've got me carting a corpse around on the talk-show circuit.'

'We're talking about a million bucks, Lar. I'd sure do it.'

'Be my guest.'

'I can't write for shit. And you've got . . .' His head snapped around. 'I've *got* it! I'll be the main guy. You can be the guy who takes it all down.'

'Your Watson, your Boswell.'

'Yeah, whatever. God, I wish we had a recorder. We oughta have all this on tape for the book.'

'You're really serious.'

'Damn straight. Can you remember all this? Hell, we should've laid off the booze.'

'Right.' Larry took another swallow of it.

'I see this as a major book and movie. It's a natural.'

'It does have potential,' Larry admitted.

'Potential? It'll be a blockbuster.'

'It'd need a story, though.'

'Hey, man, we're living the story right now. You start it off with last Sunday when we found the thing. You write it just the way it happened. That's a few chapters worth, right there. Then you've got tonight. And how we go off to get the juke box, but I talk you into getting the vampire instead.'

'That's maybe fifty pages,' Larry said. 'Then what?'

'You just tell it like it happens. Describe us going into the hotel, taking out the corpse, putting it in the van and taking it home.'

'To whose house?'

'Have you got any good hiding places?'

'Nowhere that Jean wouldn't find it. Besides, I don't like keeping secrets from her.'

'How do you think she'd react?'

'To having a stiff in the house?'

'In the garage, say.'

'I don't think she'd be delighted by the idea.'

'Barb would just shit.'

'So much for the blockbuster,' Larry said.

Pete went silent.

Thank God, Larry thought. Good thing we're both married. That ought to nip the idea right in the bud.

He felt enormous relief. He took a drink of whiskey, and sighed.

'I've got it!' Pete blurted. 'That's part of the story! We need stuff to happen after we get the thing, right? You can put all the stuff in there about Jean and Barbara giving us grief about the thing. But we talk them into letting us keep it.'

'Now you're talking fiction.'

'We just explain to them, you know? It's not like we'll be keeping the thing forever. Just a couple of months, maybe, while you're working on the book. With a big jackpot at the end. I think the gals might go for it.'

'Where's the big jackpot for Barbara?'

'I'm getting a cut, right?'

'Yeah, I may cut your throat. Then I can do a book on that while I'm in prison.'

'What do you say, twenty percent? My idea, after all. You wouldn't do it at all if it weren't for me.'

'True enough. Not that I'm planning to do it at all, regardless. The whole thing's crazy.'

'That's what makes it so great. It's crazy. It's wild! You think Stephen King would pass up a chance like this? Hell, he'd probably do it for the fun of it.'

'Why don't you give *him* a try? I've got his address.'

' 'Cause you're my pal. I don't want to take this away from you. This is your big chance.'

'Thanks.'

'So, what do you say? Are you in?'

If you tell him no, Larry thought, he'll never forgive you. He's probably already calculated twenty percent of a million bucks. It'd be like robbing him. No more outings with him and Barbara, no more drinks and dinner with them. The end of all that.

He thought about the fun they'd had during the past year.

He thought about Barbara stretched out on the sofa, and the way she had tucked the back of her robe between her legs.

Wouldn't necessarily end the friendship, he told himself. But it would sure put a strain on it.

And Pete was right about the book. It *could* be big. It could be another *Amityville Horror*.

Doing it would mean spending a lot more time with Pete, too. With Pete and Barbara.

It would also mean bringing the corpse into your life.

Probably not so bad, once you got used to it.

'I think we'll have real trouble with the wives,' he said.

'Nothing we can't handle. What do you say, man?'

'I guess we could rent a room for it, or something, if they won't let us keep it around.'

'Sure. We'll figure something out. Are you in?'

'Maybe.'

'Ah-ha!'

'Let's just play it by ear, okay? We'll have a look at the thing. But I still want to do the juke box book, so let's take care of that first, and see how it goes.'

'Oh, man. Hey, this is the start of something big.'

'We ought to have our heads examined.'

Chapter Fifteen

When the reaching headlights found Babe's Garage at the east end of Sagebrush Flat, Pete killed the beams and eased off the gas pedal.

They entered the town, moving slowly.

Larry studied the moonlit street ahead of them. He felt trapped by their crazy plan, but he held onto a hope that something might intercede to stop it. They needed privacy. If a car were here . . . if light came from a doorway or window . . .

But the street looked abandoned. The buildings were dark.

The van rolled to a halt in front of the Sagebrush Flat Hotel. Leaning forward, Pete peered past Larry.

They both stared toward the doors. But the hotel blocked the moonlight, throwing a black shroud of shadow all the way to the sidewalk. The blackness looked solid.

Unable to see the doors, Larry imagined them standing wide open, imagined he was gazing deep into the lobby, pictured the cadaver on her withered feet beside the staircase, staring out at them.

His skin crawled. His scrotum shriveled, tingling as if spiders were scurrying on it.

'Drive on ahead,' he whispered.

'Right. The box.'

The van moved forward.

He lifted a hand to his chest and fingered a nipple through the fabric of his shirt. It felt like a pebble.

True of guys, too, he thought. You get goosebumps, your nipples get hard.

He remembered the way Barbara had looked as she told her story about the dark church. Focusing his mind on that, he lost the image of the corpse. But he felt guilty about using Barbara that way, so he thought about Jean. Jean on Sunday night after her nightmare. Slipping out of her gown, climbing onto him. But then he was kneeling above her and her slim body looked cadaverous in the shadows, and he was suddenly in the hotel on his knees beside the coffin, staring at the corpse. Dried brown skin, ghastly grin, flat breasts, pubic hair shining like gold in the flashlight's beam.

He shook his head to dislodge the images, and let out a shaky breath. 'I don't know if I can hack this,' he muttered.

'Never fear, Peter's here.'

Pete drove past Holman's, made a U-turn, and parked in front of the gasoline pumps. He shut off the engine.

They each took a drink of whiskey.

'Let's take it with us.' Pete said.

'Let's not. I want my hands free.' Larry capped the bottle and set it on the floor.

They climbed out. Leaning against the chilly wind, Larry trudged to the rear of the van. Pete met him there. He had his flashlight, but left it dark. Side by side, they walked past the corner of Holman's. The desert ahead of them looked gray, as if its rock-littered surface, boulders and bushes were painted with dirty cream.

They were almost to the rear corner of Holman's when a

vague shape darted in front of them. Larry flinched. Pete, gasping, crouched and snatched out his gun. The wind-tossed tumbleweed bounded on by.

'Shit,' Pete muttered, holstering his weapon.

'Good going, Quickdraw.'

I'm not the only nervous one around here, he thought. It pleased him to know that Pete was also feeling jumpy.

'Maybe you should turn on the flashlight,' he suggested.

'It'd give us away.'

'To whom?'

'You never know, man. You never know.'

They left Holman's behind and headed out into the desert, angling toward the faroff smoke tree that marked the edge of the stream bed. Another tumbleweed crossed their path, but Pete saw this one coming and didn't draw down on it.

Larry studied the landscape ahead. He wished it didn't have so many clumps of rock and brush. Hiding places. Each time he approached one, he tightened with fear. Each time he passed one, he quickly looked behind it, half expecting to find someone crouched and ready to pounce.

Nobody's here except us, he kept telling himself.

But he couldn't convince himself.

At last, they reached the rim of the embankment. Larry turned around. He scanned the area they had just finished crossing.

Pete did the same.

Then they faced forward. The area below them lay in shadow. Pete turned on his flashlight. He played its beam over the slope, and started down. Larry stayed close to his side. A few times, they stopped while Pete waved his light across the bottom of the gully as if to assure himself that no surprises were waiting down there. The stream bed didn't look familiar to Larry. He was sure it hadn't changed since Sunday, but it seemed very different in the darkness. He couldn't even tell for certain which was the rock that Barbara had been sitting on.

We might not be here now, he thought, if she hadn't wandered away from Holman's looking for a place to relieve herself. We wouldn't have found the juke box. Maybe the corpse, but I never would've started out tonight except for the juke box.

He realized that he had to urinate, himself.

When they reached the bottom of the embankment, he said, 'Hang on a minute. I've gotta take a leak.'

'Don't get any on you,' Pete said. 'Want the light?'

'Yeah, thanks.' He took the flashlight. Pete waited while he wandered to the left, stepping around blocks of stone. He clamped the light under his arm to free his hands. With his back to Pete, he opened his pants. The wind felt good against his penis. He aimed his stream straight out. The wind flapped it sideways, but not back at him.

When he was done, he zipped up his pants and started to turn around. The pale beam of the flashlight passed across a circle of black surrounded by rocks. 'Hey, Pete. Come here.'

'I don't want to get my feet wet.'

'Come here.' He took the flash out from under his arm while Pete came up beside him. He pointed it at the circle. 'Look at that.'

'A campfire.'

'Was that here before?'

'I don't know. Might've been, but I didn't see it.'

They walked toward it. The center of the fire circle was black with ashes and the charred remains of wood.

And bones. Larry saw half a dozen bones, intact among the dead cinders – gray and knobbed at each end.

'Holy shit,' Pete muttered.

'Rabbit, you think?'

Pete squatted. He picked up a bone that was nearly a foot in length. 'This sucker didn't come from any rabbit,' he said. 'A coyote, maybe.'

'Who the hell would eat a coyote?'

'The fuckin' Madman of the Desert, that's who.' Pete tossed the bone down. 'This'll go good in our book.'

'Great,' Larry muttered.

Pete pressed a hand against one of the sooty rocks. 'Still warm.'

'Don't give me that.'

'It is.'

Crouching, Larry touched one of the rocks for himself. It was cold. 'Asshole.'

Pete laughed. 'Had you going there, huh?'

'Prick.'

'Get out of the way. I'm gonna take some pictures.'

He backed off, but kept the light on the fire circle while Pete removed the lens cap, switched on the camera and its flash attachment.

'What if the guy who did this is still around here?'

'No sweat. He's already eaten.'

'A guy who eats coyotes isn't someone I want to meet.'

'He's probably long gone.' Pete raised the camera to his eye, bent over the remains of the fire for a close-up, and took a shot. The flash strobed, hitting the area with a quick blast of white.

He stepped backward. One stride. Two. Then another flash split the darkness.

In that blink of white, Larry saw something beyond the fire circle. He found it with the beam of his flash-light. 'Oh, my God,' he muttered.

Three rocks were stacked up. At the top rested, the head of a coyote, its gray fur matted with blood, a bone held crosswise between its teeth. It had bloody holes where its eyes should've been.

Pete lowered his camera and stared. 'Wow,' he muttered.

'Maybe we ought to get out of here.'

Pete flapped a hand at him and stepped closer to the thing. He raised the camera. He took a shot. In the stark flick of light, Larry saw *into* the empty sockets. He started gagging as Pete stepped right up in front of it, crouched, and snapped another picture.

He turned aside and vomited. When he finished, he backed away from the mess. He took out his handkerchief, blew his nose and wiped his lips. He blinked tears from his eyes. He rubbed them with the back of a hand.

'You all right?' Pete asked, coming up behind him.

'Christ,' he muttered.

'Feeling a little queasy myself. Bad scene. Guy that did that must be a fuckin' lunatic. You see the way he poked out its eyes? Wonder if he did that *before* he ate.'

Larry shook his head. 'Let's do the juke box and get out of here.'

'Give me the light. I want to check around, see what else we can find.'

'Are you nuts?' He kept the flashlight and started walking through the gully toward the place where they'd found the juke box.

'Aah,' Pete said. 'What the hell. Don't want to lose *my* supper. Wouldn't taste half as good on the way out.' His head swung around.

A shiver rushed up Larry's back. 'What is it?'

'Nothing, I guess.'

'Did you hear something?'

'Probably just the wind. Unless it's our crazy-fuckin'-coyote-muncher sneaking up on us.'

'Cut it out.'

'Wonder if he talked to the thing while he ate. You know? Like put the head up there for a dinner companion. Had a little chat with it. Talked to the head while he ate the body.'

It was an image, Larry realized, that had passed through his own mind while he was vomiting.

'Wonder if he ate the eyes.'

Larry *hadn't* thought of that. 'He probably just didn't like the thing staring at him.'

'Maybe. Guess we'll never know. Unless we get a chance to ask him.' Pete chuckled.

'Give me a break.'

Larry stepped around a large rock. He pointed the light at it. 'Is that where Barbara was sitting?'

'I think so.'

He swept the beam forward until it found a thick clump of bushes on the right. He glimpsed chrome and dirty red plastic through the foliage. 'There.'

They hurried the final distance.

Larry stared down at the machine resting smashed and bullet-riddled in the bushes. He imagined a photograph of it on the cover of his book. *The Box* by Lawrence Dunbar.

That's the book I'm going to write, he told himself. Not some damn thing about a vampire.

'See if we can lift it?' Pete asked, squatting down.

He saw them struggling to carry it up the steep embankment. He saw himself stumble, fall, roll down the slope. The box tumbled and crashed down on top of him. Pete lifted it off. *We'd better not try to move you, Lar. I'll go get help*. Pete left the revolver with him, and hurried away. He lay there, alone and half paralyzed. Soon, he heard someone creeping toward him. A ragged hermit dripping coyote blood, a knife in his hand. What makes me think there's only one of them? he wondered.

'What do you think?' Pete asked.

'Let's not try it.'

'Yeah, maybe you're right. God knows what's under the thing. Or inside it, for that matter. Don't want to go upsetting a rattler. Or a nest of scorpions, or something.'

'That's what I like about you,' Larry said. 'Adventurous, but not foolish.'

'My momma didn't raise no morons.' Pete got to his feet. He backed away from the box and lifted the camera.

Larry stepped aside. He faced the length of the gully and probed its darkness with the flashlight. The campfire and the grisly remains of the coyote were well beyond the range of the pale beam. He swept the light from side to side. None of the rocks or bushes in sight seemed large enough to conceal a person.

'You spot Ragu the Desert Rat,' Pete said, 'give us a yell.'

'I won't yell, I'll scream.'

Pete laughed.

Larry kept watch, his back to Pete. In his peripheral vision, he noticed four blinks of light.

'Why don't you get into the picture?' Pete suggested. 'We'll get a couple of you with the famous juke box.'

Though reluctant to abandon his guard duty, he stepped backward until he came to the box. He crouched beside it. A red light on the flash attachment beamed a ray at his face.

'Say "cheese".'

'Come on, get it over with.'

'Say "head cheese".'

'Screw you.'

White light hit his eyes. Pete took another photo, then stepped closer and fired two more. 'That oughta do it.'

'Sure did my night vision.' He stood up, shutting his eyes and rubbing them. Bright sparks and balls fluttered under his lids.

'We done down here?' Pete asked.

'I sure hope so.'

'Want to go back and pick up a souvenir? Take it home with us, put it in the freezer?'

'Yeah. Why don't you do that.'

'Hah! You think I'm out of my tree?'

'You want to take the corpse back,' Larry said, stepping past the bushes and starting to climb the slope. 'What's the big difference?'

'The corpse isn't all bloody and gross.'

'It looked pretty gross to me.'

'Well, the coyote head ain't worth a million bucks. For a million smackaroonies, I'd pick the thing up in my bare hands and *walk* home with it.'

'Would you eat it?' Larry asked, starting to feel almost cheerful as he approached the top of the embankment.

'Who'd give me a million bucks to eat it?'

'It's hypothetical.'

'Would I get to cook it up first?'

'Nope, gotta chow it down raw.'

'You're sick, man.'

'Me?'

They reached the top and the wind pushed against Larry. It seemed to be blowing much harder up here than in the gully. But he was glad to be out. He felt as if he had been an intruder in the lair of the coyote eater. Ragu the Desert Rat. He hurried forward, wanting to put as much distance as possible between himself and the madman's domain.

Now and then, he glanced back. So did Pete, but not as often.

At last, they reached the van. Larry flung himself onto the passenger seat, slammed the door shut and locked it. The warmth felt wonderful. And it was good to be out of the wind. The skin of his face and arms felt tingly from the buffeting. He opened the whiskey bottle, and took a couple of sips while Pete climbed in behind the steering wheel.

He offered the bottle to Pete.

Pete shook his head. He flicked a switch, and light filled the van. With a nervous glance at Larry, he slipped between the seats.

Larry watched him move in a crouch toward the rear of the van – head darting from side to side, fingers wrapped around the handle of his holstered magnum.

Christ, he's afraid someone might've gotten in.

Pete searched the length of the van and turned around. 'It's cool,' he said, coming back.

In his seat again, he shut off the interior lights. He started the engine. He reached out, and Larry put the bottle in his hand. He drank, then gave it back. 'Now, are we ready for the real fun?'

'I think I've had enough fun for one night.'

'You aren't going yellow on me, are you?'

'What'll we do with the corpse if we *do* take it home?'

'You write a book about it.'

'About what? Having a pseudo-vampire as a house guest?'

'Exactly.'

'It'll just lie there. That's if the women don't make us get rid of it.'

'You're right. We'll have to do something with it. Maybe we can find out who she is.'

'How would we do that?'

'First things first, Lar. Let's take her home, then figure out what's next.'

'Why don't we *not* take her home till we figure that out.'

'Hey, we're already here. When'll we get another chance like this? Come on, man, we agreed. Don't bail out on me now.'

'I'm not bailing out. I just don't see what we'll accomplish. Our book has to be a lot more than a couple of goofs taking a stiff home and freaking out their wives. Even a true story needs action along the way, drama, a climax. Especially a climax. We've got nothing.'

'Well, eventually we pull the stake.'

'And the damn thing *still* just lies there.'

'Maybe, maybe not.'

'Oh, come on. You said yourself she's not a vampire.'

'We don't know that for sure. Obviously, *someone* thinks she is.'

'Okay. Suppose we pull the stake and she *is* a vampire?'

'That'd be something, huh? Then we've got a best-seller for sure.'

'If she doesn't bite our necks.'

'We'll take precautions when the time comes. You know, have plenty of crucifixes and garlic handy. Maybe buy some handcuffs or tie her up.'

'So what happens if we pull the stake and nothing happens? Which is the way it's bound to go down. Then what?'

Pete started the van moving forward.

'A big dud, that's what,' Larry told him.

Pete eased the van onto the road. It rolled slowly toward the Sagebrush Flat Hotel.

'Let's just go home and forget about it.'

'You said we should play it by ear.'

'My ear tells me to forget it.'

'I've got a better idea.' Pete's head turned toward Larry. In the hazy moonlight, his teeth seem to glow as he smiled. 'You say we've got a dud if we pull the stake and she just lies there. Well, let's find out tonight if she's a vampire.' He eased the van to the other side of the street and stopped in front of the hotel. 'Let's go in there and pull the stake.'

Chapter Sixteen

Larry stood in front of the van, shivering, and aimed his flashlight at the doors of the hotel. They were shut. The padlock hung from the hasp, but nobody had repaired Pete's damage. The staple was still ripped from the right hand door.

Pete came up beside him. He held the tire iron.

'You won't need that to break in,' Larry whispered.

Nodding, Pete slipped the rod under his belt. He glanced up and down the street. Then he raised the camera and snapped a shot of the doors.

As he stepped onto the sidewalk, Larry clutched his shoulder. 'Wait a minute.'

'I'm going in there. If you're scared . . .'

'Aren't you?'

'Hey, sure. But I'm not gonna let that stop me. You can wait out here if you want.'

Larry let his hand drop. He followed Pete across the sidewalk. The muscles of his legs felt soft and shaky. His bowels ached. His heart thudded and he panted, trying to get enough air into his tight lungs.

Who's going to write Pete's book, he thought, if I have a heart attack and keel over dead?

Pete opened the door. Larry shone his light into the lobby. Its beam trembled on the stairs to the left, jerked past the banister and downward, sweeping over the empty space to the right.

They stepped inside. Pete shut the door.

I'm in, Larry thought. Good Christ.

The wind was gone. He heard it, but it no longer blew against him. The hotel was warm. Not as warm as the van, though. He couldn't stop shivering. His skin felt tight. He knew he was goosebumps from head to toe. An icy hand seemed to be squeezing his genitals.

He swung the flashlight back and forth. Over the sandy, hardwood floor. Across the registration counter. Along the walls. Turning slowly, he lit the boarded windows at the front. The closed doors.

The click and blink of the camera made him flinch. Its automatic film advance buzzed.

'Wanta get the general layout,' Pete whispered. He took several more photos, turning in a full circle to capture every foot of the lobby's empty interior.

While he reloaded, Larry squatted down to ease a cramped feeling in his bowels.

'You okay?' Pete whispered.

'Hardly.'

'Crap your pants, you'll have to walk home.'

'Ha ha.'

'I'm going up and get a couple of the landing.'

Larry stood, but didn't go with him. He aimed the light at the stairs. Pete climbed them, holding the camera in both hands. And stopped abruptly.

'Very interesting. Have a look.'

Grimacing, Larry forced his wobbly legs to carry him to the stairway. He made his way upward until he reached Pete's side.

Four dirty, weathered planks lay across the landing. They covered the hole left by Barbara when the boards gave out beneath her.

'You know what this means,' Pete said.

'Let's get out of here.'

'God, I hope he didn't take our vampire.'

God, I hope he did, Larry thought.

Hope he doesn't *show up*.

What if he's the coyote eater?

Larry shined his light up the stairs. It reached into the second floor corridor, threw a faint glow high on the wall. He stared, half expecting a wildman to shamble into the beam.

Pete's got a gun, he reminded himself.

But the scare will probably kill me.

He wished he could make himself look away from the upstairs corridor. But he didn't dare take his eyes off it.

Pete drew the revolver. 'Hang onto this for a minute.'

Larry switched the flashlight to his left hand, and took the gun in his right. He aimed both toward the top of the stairs.

The solid, heavy feel of the .357 was comforting.

Very comforting.

Almost like putting on a coat, the way it soothed his chills and calmed him. But better.

No wonder Pete's been so cool about most of this. He's had the pig-iron on his hip.

Pete snapped a photo of the landing. Then, letting the camera dangle by its strap, he crouched and lifted one of the boards. He propped it upright against the wall. When all four planks had been removed, he took two shots of the gaping hole.

No longer worried much about an intruder, Larry lowered his gaze to the break in the landing. He saw the splintered edges of wood that had gouged and scraped Barbara. He remembered the feel of her body when he'd wrapped his arms around her. The soft warmth of her breasts against his forearm. The way she'd looked later, standing in the sunlit doorway with her blouse open.

His mind came back to the present as Pete began setting the boards back into place. He realized he was no longer shivering at all. He wondered if it was having the gun or thinking about Barbara that had taken away the shakes. Probably both, he thought.

'Okay,' Pete said, getting to his feet. He held out his hand for the weapon.

'Let me keep it,' Larry said.

Pete was silent for a moment. Then he shrugged and said, 'Sure, why not?'

They turned around, and started down the stairs.

'We're gonna have a lot of good shots of this place. Did that *Amityville* book have photos?'

'Nope.'

'Great. We'll be going it one better.'

They reached the bottom of the stairway and stepped around the newel post, shoes crunching on the sandy floor.

The panel alongside the staircase was shut, just as they had left it. The body of Christ on the crucifix gleamed golden.

Pete took a few strides backward, and snapped a photograph to show the staircase enclosure.

Stepping up to it, he ran his hands along a seam in the paneling. He tried to dig his fingers in, then gave up and took out the tire iron. He pushed its wedge into the crack. Slowly, as if trying not to make a sound, he pressed the bar.

'Open, sesame,' he whispered.

With a soft groan and squeak of nails, the slab of wood moved outward half an inch.

Pete slipped the fingers of his left hand into the gap. He shoved the bar under his belt. Using both hands, he eased the panel toward him. Nails squawked. The gap widened.

At last, the panel came off completely. It was about four feet across. Pete stretched out his arms and grabbed both edges. He looked like a lifesize imitation of the body on the cross as he lifted the panel and carried it aside – the crucifix almost touching his cheek. He propped the slab against the staircase, rubbed his hands on the front of his pants, then moved backward and took a shot of the opening.

Larry waited until Pete was beside him. Together, they stepped under the staircase.

Let the thing be gone, he thought as he swung the flashlight to the left.

It lit the foot of the coffin. Raising the beam slightly, he saw the old brown blanket covering the body. The blanket was propped up like a small tent over the stake. Beyond the upthrust area of blanket was the corpse's dark face.

Pete nudged him with an elbow.

'What?' Larry whispered.

'Nobody absconded with it.'

'Too bad.'

'I'll get a shot from here,' Pete said.

A small patch of red light from the camera's flash attachment appeared on the blanket. It floated upward to the underside of a stair just above the corpse's head, then found the face. Over the pounding of his heartbeat, Larry heard the camera make brief, whiny buzzing sounds as its autofocus made adjustments. The red light trembled on the tawny forehead, touched a sunken eyelid, roamed down a hollow cheek and settled on the upper row of teeth.

Larry shut his eyes in time to miss the sudden shock of brightness. He saw it through his lids. Then another.

'Come on,' Pete whispered.

He opened his eyes. He followed Pete. Though he kept the coffin lighted, he avoided looking at it.

Crouching, Pete reached the end of the coffin and grabbed its edge. He gave it a yank. The coffin moved toward him, scraping on the floor. Larry stepped out of the way, and Pete dragged it past him.

Dragged it out from under the staircase and into the lobby.

Larry followed it out.

'What are you *doing*?' he blurted in a loud whisper.

'Don't like it under there,' Pete said.

'Christ.'

Larry, himself, was glad to be free of the enclosure. But this was going too far. Way, way too far. The thing didn't belong out here. It belonged under the stairs, for godsake, not in the lobby.

'We've gotta put it back.'

Instead of responding, Pete took a photo.

The white of the flash hit the sandy floor, the coffin, the feet and face of the corpse, its blond hair, the blanket.

The blanket.

Larry's chest tightened. 'Pete.'

'Stop whining, would you?'

'The blanket.'

'What about it?'

'We didn't leave it that way.'

'Hey, you're right.'

Sunday, Pete had flung the blanket carelessly onto the corpse, leaving it heaped on the chest and belly. Barbara had pulled a corner down to cover the groin. Now, the blanket was spread out smoothly, shrouding the body from shoulders to ankles.

'Must've been the same guy who did the landing,' Pete said. He sounded pretty calm about it. Even without the gun.

'That means he knows we found the body.'

'He doesn't know *we* found the body. Just that someone did.'

'I don't like this.'

'He's not here, is he?'

'He might be.' Larry pointed his light toward the top of the stairway. He saw no one.

'He shows up, we can ask him about this.'

'Right. Sure. What if he doesn't like the idea of a couple of guys messing with his vampire?'

'You got any idea what a .357 does to a person? Just wing him, he'll think he got hit by a Mack truck. So don't shoot unless you have to.'

'God,' Larry muttered.

'Keep me covered while I get some skin shots.' Pete bent down and tossed the blanket off the corpse.

Larry's eyes and flashlight went straight to the stake protruding from the center of its chest.

Pete wandered around the coffin, snapping half a dozen pictures. Then he faced Larry and lowered the camera against his belly. 'Okay, pal. Time to see if she's for real.'

Cold streaked up his spine.

'Don't.'

Pete grinned, raised his eyebrows. 'You said we don't want her if she's a dud.'

'For Christsake, it's *night*.'

Pete stepped toward him. He lifted the camera strap over his head. 'Maybe you should record this for posterity.' He slipped the strap over Larry's head. The weight of the camera pulled against the back of his neck.

Pete stepped to the far side of the coffin and sank to his knees. He wrapped a hand around the end of the stake.

'Don't. I mean it.'

'Don't be a pussy, man.'

Larry aimed the revolver at him.

Pete's smile fell away. 'Jesus Christ.'

'Take your hand off it.'

The hand jumped off the stake as if burnt. 'It's off, it's off. Jesus!'

Larry lowered the gun.

He shook his head. He couldn't believe he'd actually threatened his friend with the magnum. He felt sick. 'I'm sorry. God, I'm sorry, Pete.'

'Jesus, man.'

'I'm sorry. Look. We'll take it with us. We'll take it home. We'll do the book. Okay? And you can take the stake out, but not till the right time. We'll do it in daylight. We'll cuff her first, or something, like you said. We'll do it right, so nobody gets hurt. Okay?'

Pete nodded and got to his feet. He stepped around the coffin.

Larry met him beside it. 'Here, you'd better take this thing.'

Pete took the revolver from him. 'I ought a stick it in your face and see how you like it,' he said. 'God*damn*, man, you know?'

'Go ahead. I deserve it.'

'Nah.' He holstered the weapon. He clasped Larry's upper arm and looked him in the eyes. 'We're partners, man. We're gonna be *rich* partners.'

'I shouldn't have pulled down on you, Pete. I don't know what . . . I'm sorry. I'm really sorry.'

'No sweat.'

They shook hands. Larry felt his throat go tight. He knew he was close to tears.

'Okay, *compadre*,' Pete said. 'Let's haul this bitch out of here and head for home.'

591

Encounters

Chapter Seventeen

'Don't do it! I'm warning you!'

'Aah, don't be a pussy.' Pete started to pull the stake from the chest of the corpse. It slid slowly upward.

Larry fired. The slug punched Pete's forehead. A spray of blood and brains flew up behind him. As he tumbled backward, Larry saw that he still clutched the stake. It came all the way out.

'NO!' Larry shrieked.

Hurling the revolver aside, he ran toward the coffin, toward Pete sprawled on the lobby floor, toward the pointed shaft clenched in his dead hand.

You bastard! he thought. You bastard, how could you do this to me!

Gotta get the stake! Gotta shove it back in! Fast! Before it's too late.

But he couldn't run fast enough. The sand sucked at his feet. Moments ago, it had just been a thin layer. Now, the sand was thick, heaped like dunes on a beach. Had somebody left the door open? He looked back. The door was open, all right.

A man stood there, ankle deep in the sand, the wind at his back flapping his dark, hooded robe. A robe like a monk. The hood concealed his face. In his upraised right hand, he held a crucifix. 'You're screwed now,' the stranger called. 'Up shit creek without a paddle.'

Terrified, Larry turned his eyes away from the stranger and tried to run faster over the soft, shifting sand.

I'll never make it in time, he thought.

He was still far from the corpse. It still looked like a dried-up mummy. But he could hear it *breathing*.

Maybe that guy will lend me his crucifix.

He glanced back. The hood fell away. The stranger had the eyeless, bloody head of a coyote. The crucifix, now clamped in its maw, crunched as the thing chewed.

When he looked forward again, he gasped.

The coffin was empty.

But then he saw that Pete was sitting up. He suddenly felt so overwhelmed with relief that he nearly wept. *I didn't kill him, after all! Thank God! Thank* . . . He felt himself shrivel inside.

Pete wasn't sitting up because he was alive. He was being held by the brown hag on the floor behind him. Its withered legs were crossed around his waist. Its arms hugged his chest. Its mouth sucked and chewed on the exit wound at the back of his head.

Larry yelled and woke up.

He was alone in bed. The room was dark. Rolling onto his side, he checked the alarm clock. 4:50. He groaned as he realized this was Saturday morning and he'd been in bed less than an hour.

He remembered what they had done.

God, if only the whole thing had been a nightmare. What if I only *dreamed* that we went out there.

He knew it was too much to hope for.

They'd done it, all right.

At least I didn't shoot Pete, he thought. Thank God *that* was just in the nightmare.

He climbed out of bed. Naked, sweaty and shaking, he stepped to the window. The moon hung low over the roof of the garage.

He didn't want to think about what was inside the garage.

We've gotta call this off, he told himself. We've gotta take it back, put it back under the staircase.

He wondered if he could do it by himself.

No. Alone, he wouldn't be able to face the thing, much less drive it out to Sagebrush Flat and drag it into that damn hotel.

He returned to the bed, sat down on the edge of the mattress, slumped forward and rubbed his face. He felt wasted. He needed sleep. A lot of sleep. But he knew the kind of dream that waited for him.

Never should've done it, he thought. Never should've.

He wandered into the bathroom, turned on the shower and stepped under the hot spray. The water felt wonderful splashing against his chilled body. It soothed his shivers, eased the tightness of his muscles. But it didn't help the fog in his head. His mind seemed numb.

Won't be able to write today, he thought. Not unless I get some sleep.

Work on correcting the manuscript?

That's why you didn't go with Jean and Lane.

God, he wished he had gone with them. None of this would've happened.

He saw himself in the hotel again, aiming the revolver at Pete.

Hell, I wouldn't have shot him.

But even to aim at him . . .

That was the worst part. That was even worse than the damn corpse in his garage.

Just have to live with it, he told himself. It happened, you can't make it go away.

The thing is to do the book for him. Even if it doesn't hit the big time like he hopes, it ought to sell. Give him a chunk, he'll be happy. He'll figure it was worth having a gun pointed at him. Then, maybe I can stop feeling guilty.

So write the book.

Larry shut off the shower, stepped out of the tub and dried himself. He made his way sluggishly into the bedroom. He took a sweatsuit and socks from his dresser, dropped onto the bed and struggled into the soft shirt and pants.

Write the book, he thought. But not today. Too wasted.

In the kitchen, he made a pot of coffee. He carried his mug into the living room, settled down in his recliner, and started to read. His eyes moved over the lines of the paperback. But the words seemed disconnected, meaningless.

One hour of sleep, he thought. What do you expect?

He closed the book. He gazed into space while he sipped his coffee.

Can't just sit here like a zombie.

Work on *Madhouse*, he thought. Should be capable of that, just going through and changing it back to the way it was in the first place.

He pushed himself off the chair, picked up his empty mug and headed for the kitchen.

Damn copyeditor. Hadn't been for her, I'd be in LA right now. Wouldn't have gone out to that damn town. None of this shit would've happened.

He filled his mug with coffee, carried it into his work room, and gazed at the manuscript. He sighed. The chore seemed too great.

Maybe make some notes for *The Box* first. Work something in about the guys going out to bring it home, stumbling across the campfire . . . the coyote eater . . . what if he's a guy who's connected to the past somehow? Could be a character in the sixties section. One of the bikers? He's stuck around for some reason, mad as a hatter, living off the land.

Maybe a dumb idea, he thought. Who's in any shape to judge? Might as well put it down, though. Decide later whether it's worth pursuing.

He turned on the word processor and brought up the notes he'd made yesterday. He scrolled down to the last entry. 'But maybe there are some other "box" angles. Fool around with it.'

A coffin is a box. There's an angle for you.

He typed, 'Notes – Saturday, October 8.'

Spaced down, tapped out, 'Guys go to fetch juke box. In ditch nearby, they find campfire and disgusting remains of a coyote someone had eaten for dinner. Who? A crazy hermit who was the main badass biker in the sixties section. He's still around after all those years.'

Who *really* ate the coyote? he wondered. What if it's the same guy who fixed the hotel landing and straightened the blanket on the stiff?

What if he was watching us?

What if he followed us?

Larry downspaced a couple of times.

'Somebody,' he wrote, 'hammered a pointed shaft of wood through the heart of a woman. He left her inside a lidless coffin, and hid her corpse beneath the stairway of an abandoned hotel in the town of Sagebrush Flat.

'We found it there.

'My name is Lawrence Dunbar. I am a writer of horror fiction. This book is not fiction. You may judge for yourself whether it is horror.

'This is what happened.

'On Sunday, October 2, we left our home in Mulehead Bend for a day trip to visit an old-west town in the desert to the west. The morning was clear and warm as we started off. Pete drove his van. I rode shotgun. Our wives poured coffee from a Thermos bottle, passed the plastic cups to us, and gave us first tibs at the assortment of doughnuts I'd bought earlier that morning.'

Not bad for a space cadet, he thought.

And kept writing.

It flowed. He finished his coffee. He fired up his pipe. The words came so easily. As if a voice were speaking in his head, and he merely had to copy the dictation.

He introduced Jean and Pete and Barbara. He described the beauty and desolation of the desert they drove through on the way to Silver Junction. He told about the old-west town: the quaint shops they'd visited, the characters in cowboy garb, the gunfight staged on Main Street, their sandwiches and beer in the saloon. Finally, they were ready to leave the picturesque town. They climbed into the van. Pete said, 'How about a little detour on the way home?'

Larry returned to the start. He numbered the pages, then shook his head in astonishment. He'd written *fifteen*. He couldn't believe it. He looked at the wall clock. Eight-thirty. He'd been working for nearly three hours. That's about five pages per hour, he realized. Usually, he averaged two.

I should always write when I'm zoned, he thought.

Maybe it's garbage.

He read the chapter. Sure didn't *seem* like garbage. It seemed as good as anything he'd ever done. Maybe better. He felt as if he had transformed the somewhat mundane visit to Silver Junction into a sharp, colorful portrait, rich with incident, fast-paced.

The characters lived. Perhaps too well, in the case of Barbara. Her presence dominated the chapter.

That's as it should be, he told himself. Barbara is certainly a major figure in this tale.

But he worried that his infatuation with her might be too apparent. After all, Jean would eventually read the book. So would Barbara. Even Pete, the nonreader, was certain to plow through this one.

Can't let them get the wrong idea.

Better be careful, he warned himself. Watch out when you revise. Take out anything too suggestive.

Though eager to continue, Larry felt hot. He pulled off his sweatshirt and stretched, sighing with pleasure as his muscles drew taut and a warm breeze caressed his skin. He stood up, stretched some more, then went into the bathroom. He rolled deodorant onto his armpits. He urinated. Then, he entered the bedroom and tossed his sweatclothes onto a chair. He put on shorts and a T-shirt. The loose, lightweight garments let the air in. Feeling a lot better, he headed for the kitchen.

He found a hardboiled egg in the refrigerator. He peeled off its shell and started to eat it over the waste-basket. It was dry in his mouth. He knew it would taste much better sprinkled with salt. But he couldn't be bothered. He stood at the waste-basket until the egg was gone. Then he refilled his coffee mug and returned to the office.

The second chapter went nearly as well as the first. But he was more cautious with it. He censored the voice in his head, refusing to tap out several descriptions it provided of Barbara's appearance. When he came to the part about the ruin of the old stone house they'd passed shortly before arriving at Sagebrush Flat, he stopped himself. He lit a fresh pipe and stared at the screen. Should he omit Pete and Barbara's dialogue about screwing in that place?

This is supposed to be a true story. They *did* say those things.

It's already strayed from the truth, he realized. I've certainly tampered with my own side of it.

Hell, the conversation happened. Tell it like it was. Besides, it'll say a lot about their relationship, help to flesh them out, make them seem more real.

' "We spent too much time screwing around in there."

' "Watch it, mister."

'From the tone of Barbara's voice, I realized that Pete hadn't been speaking figuratively. I imagined what it must have been like, picturing myself with Jean inside the tumble-down walls of the ruin. Hard on the knees, probably. But exciting. I found myself wishing we were there, now, rather than riding with Pete and Barbara toward the remains of a dead town.'

Larry grinned at the screen.

Nicely done.

He kept on writing. It went smoothly until the time came for Barbara to answer nature's call. Should he put that in? Without it, how would he get her over to the stream bed behind Holman's?

Tell it like it was, he decided.

And he did: Barbara wandering away, Pete going in search of her, the waiting, the worry, he and Jean finally going to look for them. All four were down in the gully studying the juke box when the doorbell rang.

Larry looked at the clock. Ten to eleven. He groaned as he got to his feet. He made his way through the house on legs that felt nearly too weak to support him. He blinked sweat out of his eyes and opened the front door.

Pete, in a knit shirt and jeans, looked well-rested, alert, cool, chipper. 'You taken up exercise?' he asked as he stepped inside.

'I've been writing.'

601

'Didn't know writing was such hard work. You oughta turn the air on, man, it's hotter than hell in here.'

'Yeah,' Larry muttered. He peeled the seat of his shorts away from his rear. 'Want some coffee or something?'

Pete shook his head. 'Already had my morning dose.'

'You look so bright-eyed and bushy-tailed it makes me want to barf.'

He laughed. 'You look like death warmed over. How about cleaning up and coming with us? Barb and I are going across the river and checking out the casino action. You're welcome to come along.'

Larry felt the fuzz coming back into his head. 'You've gotta be kidding. I'd probably collapse.' He rubbed his face, yawned.

'Stay out too late last night?'

'Ha ha. I got about an hour of sleep.'

'Should've slept in like I did. I feel like a million bucks.'

'Speaking of which . . . I started on the book.'

'*The* book?'

'Yeah.'

'Fantastic! Man, you didn't waste any time.'

'Maybe I just want to get it over with.'

'You're actually *writing* it?'

He nodded. His head felt heavy. 'Almost done with the third chapter. It's . . . I'm on a roll, I guess. It's really moving.'

'Well, God, don't let me stop you. Forget I mentioned the casinos. I'll tell Barb I couldn't drag you away.'

'You didn't tell her about . . . the thing?'

Pete looked as if he thought Larry had lost his mind.

'She's gonna find out sooner or later.'

'The later the better. How much can you write before Jean and Lane get back?'

'I don't know.'

'You've got the rest of today and tomorrow. And the coffin's pretty well hidden. Might be a week or so before anyone catches on. Hell, by then, who knows? You might be so far along in the book that it won't even matter.'

'I don't know,' Larry said again.

'How many pages you got?'

He shrugged. 'Around thirty, I think.'

Pete's face lit up. 'All *right*! Thirty! That's incredible. You did all that this morning? No wonder you look like shit.'

'Thanks.'

'Hey, I'm getting out of here. Go back and pound out some more pages. This is terrific.' He stepped out the door and faced Larry again. 'If you feel up for drinks and dinner, stop by around five.'

'Okay. Thanks. I don't know, though.'

When Pete was gone, Larry staggered into the bedroom. He peeled off his wet clothes and flopped on the mattress.

Just a quick nap, he thought.

He woke up, gasping for air and drenched with sweat. The clock on the nightstand showed 2:15.

Chapter Eighteen

Larry toweled himself dry and stepped into his shorts. They were still damp, but they felt cool. In the kitchen, he poured himself a glass of iced tea. He put salami and cheese on a few crackers, and took them along with his drink to the work room.

Just stick with it for a couple of hours, he thought. Then have a nice, cool shower, get dressed and head on over to Pete and Barbara's.

It would be wonderful. Sit out in back with them like yesterday, have a few cocktails . . .

He read the last few sentences on the screen, and added a new one. Then another. Then, it was flowing again, the words in my mind rushing ahead of his typing fingers.

He was in the story. He was living it.

The iced tea and crackers disappeared. He smoked his pipe. He had another glass of tea. After that was gone, he couldn't force himself away from the story to get another. He wrote and wrote. He rubbed the sweat off his face with slick forearms. Drops dribbled down his chest and sides, tickling until they stopped at the waistband of his shorts. Later, a breeze cooled his wet skin. Dried him. His mouth was parched. He told himself he would quit soon and go over to Pete and Barbara's and drink up a storm. After this page. Or after the next.

Suddenly, he noticed that his room was dark except for the amber glow of the words on the computer screen. Dark and cold. A chill night breeze blew through the open window. He realized that he was sitting rigid, shivering, teeth clenched as the breeze scurried over his bare skin.

Feeling disoriented, he squinted up at the dim face of the clock.

Ten after seven.

Impossible. What had happened to the time? He knew he'd been deeply involved in the story, but he could hardly believe he'd been so immersed that he'd allowed himself to miss the cocktails and dinner.

He hadn't even been aware for the past hour that he'd been writing in the dark, nearly naked and freezing.

He read the final sentence.

'It was with a strange mixture of sadness and expectation that I watched the car vanish around the corner, carrying my wife and daughter away from me for the weekend.'

He muttered, 'Good God.'

He scrolled upward to the start of the chapter. It was labeled Chapter Six. No page number. How many pages *had* he written today? Seventy? Eighty?

His normal output was seven to ten pages.

The most he'd *ever* done before in a single day was thirty. That was on a piece-of-garbage romance novel a few years ago when money was short and his agent had lined up a lousy deal for two romances at a thousand bucks a whack.

This was more than twice his record.

And I'm not done yet, he thought.

Holy smoke.

He folded his arms across his chest for warmth, and shook his head.

Well, he thought, this is a true story. I'm just more or less reporting what happened.

It was astonishing, anyway.

If he'd gone over to Pete and Barbara's . . . He realized he ought to give them a call and apologize. He left his work room and wandered through the house, turning on a few lights. In the bedroom, he got rid of the shorts and put out his sweatsuit and socks. As if his skin resented the loss of cold, it tingled and itched. Larry rubbed himself through the soft fabric while he walked to the kitchen.

Tacked to a bulletin board beside the wall phone was a card on which Jean had written emergency numbers along with those of repair people and friends. Larry found the number for Pete and Barbara.

Do I really want to call them? he wondered. It had been an open invitation, not the kind of thing that required much of an apology. No big deal that I didn't show up.

They're sure to ask me over.

I'll probably go. And that'll be the end of today's writing.

For godsake, I've written enough for one day. Enough for a week.

But if I stick with it, I can bring the story all the way up to the present. And be done with it. Nothing more to tell, once I get to where we hid the coffin in the garage. Tomorrow, I'll be able to finish the corrections on *Madhouse*, get it into the mail on Monday, and spend next week finishing *Night Stranger*. Then start on *The Box*.

Only if I don't go over to Pete and Barbara's tonight.

He wondered if Barbara was in her nightgown. And he realized that he didn't much care.

He stepped away from the telephone and opened the refrigerator's freezer compartment. His eyes roamed its contents.

A lot to choose from. The lasagna would be easy. Just throw it in the microwave for a few minutes.

Too much trouble.

He shut the freezer door and checked the refrigerator. There, he found a pack of hot dogs. He opened it, slid out a wet frank, and poked it into his mouth. Holding it there like a pink cigar, he put away the package. He took out a bottle of Michelob beer, twisted off its cap, and returned to his work room.

He wrote. The hot dog and beer distracted him for a few minutes, but when they were gone he sank deeply into the story. He was there, over at Pete and Barbara's, first on their patio and then in their house, telling it all just as it had happened. Almost. Censoring, as if by reflex, every mention of Barbara's appearance and his own reactions to her. Then he was in the van with Pete. Then in the gully behind Holman's.

As he tapped out, ' "I've got to take a leak," ' he realized that he did need to do exactly that. He went into the bathroom. As he urinated, he thought about what would come next in the story.

Finding the campfire of the coyote eater.

Shivers crawled up his back.

He flushed the toilet, walked to his work room and stared through the doorway at his waiting chair.

I'm not sure I want to write about that tonight, he thought. Not about the coyote eater, not about what happened in the hotel.

He turned away from the work room. He wandered into the kitchen and looked at the clock. A quarter past ten.

That's no time of night to be writing scary shit, he told himself.

I'm so close to the finish, though.

Hang in there for a couple more hours, you'll be done with it.

Right, hang in there.

With a little help.

He dropped a few ice cubes into a glass, filled the glass with vodka and added a touch of Rose's Lime Juice. He took a sip. Sighed with pleasure. Drank some more. Then carried the glass to his room, slumped against the back of the chair, and gazed at the screen.

Once this stuff hits the system, you won't be *able* to write.

Hell, this isn't writing. This is typing.

The beer had been enough to turn his typing a trifle sloppy. This should really mess it up.

Who cares? he asked himself. Just fix it when you revise. Or don't. Give the copyeditor something constructive to do for a change. If she has to correct real errors, maybe she won't mess with the good stuff.

He took a few more swallows, then set the glass down and faced the dead campfire, the bones, the severed eyeless head of the coyote.

He was glad to have the vodka in him. Though the words flowed, he felt slightly disconnected, more an observer than a participant. He described the Larry character's fear and revulsion, but hardly felt them at all.

Then, they were out of the ditch. Then in the van. Then about to enter the dark lobby of the hotel.

His glass was empty. He took it into the kitchen. This time, he didn't bother adding lime juice to the vodka. He felt very fine as he sauntered back to his computer. He took a drink. He filled a pipe and lit it. He looked at the last sentence on the screen.

'Side bu side, we stoppped across teh threshold and entered the black mouth og the hotel.'

Grinning, he shook his head.

'Take care of that later,' he muttered.

He puffed his pipe, checked the keyboard to make sure his fingers were positioned correctly, and continued.

He wrote, and sipped vodka and smoked his pipe.

Somehow, a while later, the stem flipped over between his teeth and the briar bowl turned upside-down, dumping ashes down the front of his sweatshirt and onto his lap. Luckily, no embers fell out. Larry brushed the gray dust off his clothes, put the pipe aside, and took another drink.

When he looked at the screen, he saw double.

'Oh, am I fucked up,' he muttered.

With a little effort, however, he was able to line up his eyes and read the amber print.

' "Take you're hand offf that steak!" '

'Pete let go teh thing real fast. "If's off! Christ! Don]t shoot1" '

Larry muttered, 'Oh, shit.'

Concentrating hard, knowing he could lose a lot if he messed up, he fingered the save key and followed his usual procedure for exiting the computer. He put the disks away, then turned off the machine.

'Better hit the ol' sacko,' he mumbled.

Larry woke up, but couldn't bring himself to open his eyes. He felt as if the back of his head had been split open with an axe. His dry tongue was glued to the roof of his mouth. He was shuddering with cold, and his bed felt like concrete. As he struggled to free his tongue, he reached down. He found the blanket near his waist and pulled it up. That helped a little, but not much. The real coldness was under him.

I am on concrete!

Larry forced his eyes open.

Though the light was faint, he knew that day had come and he knew where he was.

In his garage.

His heart suddenly pounded hot spikes of pain up the back of his neck and into his head.

He was curled on his side, the coffin near enough to touch.

Oh, Jesus H. Christ!

Turning his face away from the coffin, he bolted up. The pain in his head brought tears to his eyes. As he staggered backward, his bare foot landed in a mat of vomit. It flew out from under him. His bare rump smacked the garage floor.

Sitting there, he clutched his head with both hands and blinked his eyes clear.

He saw that he was naked.

He saw that the blanket heaped on the floor near the coffin, the one he had used to cover himself, was the same old brown blanket that had shrouded the corpse.

It was on me! Touching me!

A whiny noise started coming from Larry. He slapped a hand across his mouth and gazed down at himself. Nothing on his skin.

What'd you expect? he thought. Cooties?

'Oh Jesus,' he said, his voice coming out high and girlish.

He moved his left foot out of the glop and stood up.

The withered cadaver was still inside the coffin, the stake still in its chest. Thank God.

At least he hadn't pulled the stake.

What *had* he done? What was he doing here?

He didn't know. But he knew that he had to get out. He had to shower, and fast, to rid himself of the horrible crawly feeling left by the blanket.

His left foot was caked with vomit. Not wanting to spread the mess, he hopped through the cluttered garage until he reached the side door. It was open. The sunlight made his eyes ache. Squinting, he held onto the door frame. From the coolness of the air, he guessed it was still early morning. Maybe seven o'clock.

What day? He struggled to concentrate. Saturday night was when he got himself bombed. So this was Sunday.

It sure better be, he thought.

Jean and Lane shouldn't be home till tonight.

What if they came home early?

What if this is Monday?

Shit, he thought. You've got enough problems without inventing more. If they were home, they would've found me.

Naked in the garage with a goddamn corpse.

That would've been . . . don't think about it. Didn't happen.

The yard was fenced, so at least he had some privacy.

He hopped across the walkway. When he reached the lawn,

609

he wiped his foot on the dewy grass. There was still vomit between his toes. He went over to the garden hose, turned it on, and sprayed his foot clean.

Then, he hurried down the driveway and entered his kitchen through the sliding glass door. The house was silent except for the soft hum of the refrigerator.

His damp feet left bits of grass on the floor as he made his way to the bathroom. He would have to clean that up, later.

He would have to clean up a lot.

Later.

The blanket. It was on me.

But it has two sides, he told himself. Fifty-fifty chance the side that touched the corpse was up . . .

Fifty-fifty it wasn't.

If I took the blanket off her . . .

Did I touch her?

Horrified by the thought, he gazed at his trembling hands.

I wouldn't have.

How do you know?

Oh God! I could've done *anything*!

He lurched into the bathroom, threw the door shut, and staggered to the tub. Falling to his knees, he reached out and turned the faucet handles. Water gushed from the spout. He held his hands under it.

All the perfumes of Arabia . . .

'I didn't touch her,' he said.

It's bad enough I used the blanket.

He turned the knob to activate the shower, then climbed into the tub and slid the glass door shut. The hot water pounded against the top of his head. It ran down his body, soothing the chill, easing some of the tightness out of his muscles. When he stopped trembling, he lathered himself with soap. He rinsed the suds off, then soaped his body and rinsed again before shampooing his hair.

By the time he stepped out, he felt a lot better.

If only he could remember what happened!

Maybe just as well that you don't, he thought.

After drying, he took Alka-Seltzer. Then he washed down two aspirin for good measure.

He left the steamy bathroom. In his bedroom, he found his sweatclothes heaped on the floor. His side of the bed had been turned down, the pillow dented, the bottom sheet mussed.

So you *did* go to bed last night, he told himself. But you got up again, and went out to the garage. Must've decided to take a look at the corpse, God knows why.

Must've had a reason.

Maybe she *willed* you to do it.

'Terrific,' he muttered.

He sat on the edge of the bed and rubbed his face.

Never should've had that vodka.

Keeping his back to the coffin, Larry used paper towels to clean his vomit off the garage floor. He put them in a plastic garbage bag, then dropped the bag into the bottom of his trash barrel and covered it with a heap of debris from the grass-catcher of his lawn mower. Satisfied that Jean would never find the evidence, he returned to the garage. He filled a bucket and scoured the area with a wet sponge. Afterward, he cleaned the bucket and sponge carefully.

All that remained, now, was a patch of wetness on the concrete. The heat of the day would soon take care of that.

He slid the bay door open to let in fresh air and sunlight.

From here, the garage looked perfectly normal. The damp area, the blanket and coffin were safely out of sight behind standing shelves and stacks of boxes.

He shook his head. Whatever his condition last night, he'd been aware enough to negotiate a virtual obstacle course in order to reach the corner where the coffin was hidden. In the dark, apparently.

What do you write about this? he wondered.

You don't.

I've got to. It's part of the story.

And you need to fill up more pages if you're going to make a book out of this thing.

Just leave out the business about being naked, he thought. Write it like it happened, but keep your clothes on. Otherwise, people might start thinking you . . .

I didn't, he told himself. No way.

What were you doing in there?

Suddenly, he realized that he needed to take a close look at the corpse.

Besides, I've got to cover it up again.

He entered the garage. His heart started thudding, stirring the remnants of his headache.

He made his way among the shelves and trunks and boxes, and soon he reached the dim corner where the coffin rested. The wet spot on the concrete was nearly gone. He stepped over the blanket and stared down into the coffin.

The body looked ghastly, as usual: shrunken and bony, its skin dried out and brown, its breasts flat, its mouth open and lips twisted in an awful, toothy grin.

The body didn't look as if it had been disturbed. It lay flat on the bottom of the coffin, the stake jutting upright in the same position as usual, one withered hand on its hip.

Larry frowned.

The left arm, on the far side of the corpse, was bent at the elbow. The hand rested, palm down, against the hip bone. Its fingertips lay among dull blond curls of pubic hair.

Before, (Larry was almost certain) both hands had been out of sight in the dark, narrow gap between the body and the sides of the coffin.

He was sure that he would've noticed, if a hand had been in plain view.

Especially since this one wore a ring.

He bent down for a closer look.

A school ring? Surrounding the garnet stone was a tarnished silver border that appeared to be engraved.

'Holy Toledo,' he muttered.

This could give a clue to the corpse's identity!

But how did the hand find its way onto the hip? Obviously, she hadn't placed it there.

I must've done it last night, he thought.

I did touch the damn thing.

Larry heard himself groan.

Disgust mixing with his excitement, he hurried to the section of the garage where he kept the yard tools. Maybe he *had* touched the corpse last night, but he sure didn't intend to do it again. He found some old gardening gloves, and put them on as he hurried back to the coffin.

On his knees, he reached over the body. With his left hand, he gently held the bony wrist. With the thumb and forefinger of his right hand, he slipped the ring off.

Pete, he realized, was bound to visit the corpse sooner or later, and was sure to notice the new position of the hand. It had to be put back down where it belonged.

Wrinkling his nose, Larry tightened his grip on the wrist and gave it a slight push. It resisted him. He pushed a little harder, forcing it. This time, the hand moved. Larry cringed at the quiet crackling sounds that came from the arm. Sounds like dry leaves being crumbled. His eyes darted to the cadaver's face. It looked as if it were grimacing, teeth bared in pain.

'Christ,' he whispered.

Has to be done, he told himself.

Letting go, he switched the ring to his left hand and clutched the corpse's wrist with his right. He shoved down hard, jamming the arm toward the floor of the coffin. The shoulder lifted. The head began to rise. He yelled. Then came gristly snapping sounds, a pop. The arm went limp in his grip and the body sank back into position. He tucked the arm against its side, then lurched away.

He dashed through the garage, dodging his way through the maze of clutter, and didn't stop running until he reached the safety of the house.

He shoved the sliding door shut. He locked it.

He pressed his face to the glass and stared at the open garage.

Acting like an idiot, he thought.

But *God*!

After catching his breath, he opened his trembling hand. He lifted the ring close to his face.

Engraved in the silver that surrounded the garnet were the words, 'Buford High School,' and the date, '1968.'

He looked into the middle of the loop.

Inside the band was a name.

'Bonnie Saxon.'

Chapter Nineteen

'I gazed at the ring, dumbfounded. The hideous corpse in my garage now had a name. Bonnie. A pleasant, rather cheerful name.

'Perhaps she is a vampire. Somebody thought so, killed her with a stake and used a crucifix to seal her makeshift tomb. But a vampire by the name of Bonnie?

'She seems, to me, less frightening than before.

'The gruesome, mummified thing in the coffin may indeed be a demonic beast that would drink my blood if unleashed from death. But it was a girl once. A "bonnie" lass.

'She attended the same high school as my daughter, Lane. She walked the same halls, perhaps sat in the same classrooms, may even have had some of the very same teachers as Lane. She was a girl who ate lunch in the school cafeteria, who probably struggled against dozing off during her afternoon classes, who worried about pop quizzes and homework and zits.

'A teenager. Who studied school work. Who watched television. Who listened to the latest music with the volume blaring. Who went to movies, to the school's football games and sock hops and the prom. Who had boyfriends.

'The vile thing in my garage was once a teenaged girl named Bonnie . . .'

The doorbell chimed. Larry flinched. He scrolled up to remove his words from the computer screen, then hid the class ring under the matchbooks and scraps of note paper scattered on his desktop. He hurried into the living room.

He half expected the person at the front door to be Pete. He was right.

'Hey, bud!' After a glance toward his house, Pete gave Larry a sly look. 'Barb's off grocery shopping. Thought I'd drop by and see how our bestseller's coming along.'

'Not too bad.'

He entered, and Larry shut the door.

'I guess you really whaled on the thing yesterday,' he said.

'Yeah, it went pretty well. Sorry I didn't make it over for supper. Time just got away from me, and . . .'

'No sweat. So how many pages you finish?'

'I don't know. Quite a bunch.'

'Terrific. Gonna let me read 'em?' he asked, flopping onto a chair.

Larry hoped his alarm didn't show.

'They aren't printed up yet,' he said.

'Well, go do it. Don't let me stop you.'

'It'd take hours,' Larry said. He sat on the sofa, rested his elbows on his knees, and shook his head at Pete. 'Besides, I'll have to make a lot of corrections. It's pretty much of a mess right now.'

'So when'll I get to read it?'

'How about when it's all done?' Larry suggested, trying to smile.

'Hey, come *on.*'

'No, really. I think it'd be best if you don't read any of the thing while I'm still working on it. It'd make me too self-conscious.'

'Oh, bull.'

'I mean it.'

'What about my input? Maybe you forgot some stuff.'

'I'll give you a copy when it's finished. If there's anything you want added or changed, I can revise it then. Okay?'

'That's kind of late in the ballgame,' he said, frowning slightly.

'You want me to write the thing, don't you?'

'Yeah, sure. But . . .'

'I can't do it if I have to pass every chapter along to you for inspection as I go along. I'll quit right now . . .'

'Jeez, don't get in a huff. Do it your way. I'm just curious, is all.'

'Well, that's all right,' Larry said, relieved that he had backed off. 'I didn't mean to get testy about it.'

'What's a testie between friends,' Pete said, and smiled. 'Anyway, it's going pretty good?'

'I think so.'

'What's next on the agenda?'

'Well, I need to do those revisions.'

'I guess we've gotta start thinking about how we break the news to the women,' Pete said. 'Jean'll be home tonight, won't she?'

'Yeah. Tonight.'

'Should we just walk her and Barb out to the garage and show them? Or work up to it more gradually?'

' "Guess what we brought home Saturday night?" '

'Something like that.'

'Suppose we just keep the whole thing secret?'

'Are you kidding?'

Larry shook his head. 'They won't let us keep a body around. No way. I don't care what we tell them, they'll make us get rid of it.'

'They've *got* to find out sooner or later.'

'Let's wait. We can tell them about it when everything's set to pull the stake. By then, the book'll be almost done.'

'Yeah. Course, they might give us shit about pulling the stake.'

'Good point.'

'No pun intended,' Pete said.

Larry frowned for a moment, thinking. 'Okay. Let's pull the stake and *then* tell them what we've done. After the fact. By that time, it'll be too late for the gals to screw things up for us.'

Pete grinned. 'Man, will they be pissed!'

'That's for sure. The book's bound to find a publisher, though. Bestseller or not, I'm sure we'll be seeing a pretty good chunk of money from it. That should get us out of the doghouse.'

'Maybe they don't have to find out about it,' Pete said, 'until you make the sale.'

'If we work it right. What we have to do is hide the thing better. Right now, anybody wandering into the garage might stumble onto it.'

'We *use* our garage.'

'I know, I know,' Larry said. He was well aware that Pete and Barbara often parked their cars in it, while he and Jean only used their garage for storage.

'There's a crawlspace under our house,' Pete said. 'I suppose we could shove the casket under there. If we do it quick before Barb gets back from the store. We'd have to lift it over the fence. Wouldn't wanta be seen lugging it around the front.'

'Not necessary,' Larry said. 'I know just the place to stash the thing.'

Should've put it there in the first place, he thought. Maybe I wouldn't have ended up spending the night with it.

'Where?' Pete asked.

'Come on. We'll take care of it right now.'

They went out the kitchen door, and walked up the driveway to the garage. Its bay door was still open. As they entered the shade, Larry hoped that the wet spot on the floor had dried.

Must've, he told himself.

A few yards beyond the door was a square wooden platform half a foot high. Larry stepped onto it, reached up, and caught hold of a dangling rope. He pulled the rope's knotted end. A plywood ceiling panel swung down on hinges.

'All *right*'. Pete said. 'A trap door.'

Fixed to its top was a ladder folded into three sections.

Larry lowered the ladder until the shoes of its side rails rested firmly against the platform.

'Gonna be a bitch getting our stiff up there,' Pete said.

He was right. Though the ladder stood at an angle like a flight of stairs, it was much steeper than a stairway.

'It's the perfect place,' Larry told him. 'Nobody's going to find her.'

He stepped aside. Pete climbed to the top and looked around. 'Yeah,' he said. 'Great if we can manage it.' He started down. 'How come you don't use it for storage?'

'Never got around to it.'

'Pretty neat up there. Floorboards and everything. Hotter than shit, though.' He grinned. 'Guess our friendly local vampire won't mind, huh?'

'Probably not.'

They stepped off the platform. Larry led the way toward the far corner of the garage.

'Almost need a map to find the thing,' Pete said.

I can find it in the dark.

'We're almost there.'

Larry slipped through a passage between stacks of boxes, and entered the small open area near the corner.

The concrete had dried.

The blanket lay heaped on the floor beside the coffin.

No!

He'd raced from the garage, near panic after dealing with the arm, and had totally forgotten to cover the body.

Now, it was too late.

Pete appeared at his side, stepped forward and picked up the blanket.

Larry felt as if his skin were on fire.

'Been checking her out, huh?'

Deny it?

Pretend you don't know how the blanket got on the floor?

Pete's no idiot. He'd spot that lie in an instant.

'Yeah,' Larry said, trying to sound lecherous. 'Just had to. She's such a doll I just couldn't help myself.'

618

'Can't blame you. What a mug. What a bod.'

'Gives a new definition to feminine pulchritude.'

'Gives a new definition to ugly,' Pete said.

'Seriously, though, I *did* have to take a look at her yesterday. Research. Came time to describe her for the book, and I wanted to get it right.'

'Right, sure.' It was apparent from his tone that Pete believed the story. He shook open the blanket and spread it over the corpse, covering Bonnie from her shoulders to her ankles. Then, he bent down again and pulled it up to hide her face. 'That's better,' he muttered.

'Why don't I take the front?' he suggested.

They lifted the coffin, and carried it back through the garage.

'I'll go first,' Pete said. 'Should work better that way, since you're taller. Try to keep your end high.'

He started up the ladder backward, moving slowly. As the box tipped upward, Bonnie slid toward Larry until the casket stopped her feet. The blanket dropped away from her face.

Larry raised his end of the box. Bracing it against his chest, he stepped closer to the ladder. The front kept rising. The blanket slipped down. The stake caught it, and the blanket hung from the wooden shaft like a cape tossed over a wall hook.

When Larry reached the base of the ladder, he realized he wouldn't be able to climb with the coffin pressing against his chest. 'Wait,' he called.

Pete stopped.

Larry lowered it to his waist.

'Okay.'

Pete resumed climbing.

Larry mounted the ladder's first rung. Bonnie stood almost vertical inside the coffin.

'Oh, boy,' Larry muttered.

'You okay?'

'So far.'

'I'm just about there.'

Larry shoved the casket upward with his knee, planted the toe of his shoe on the next rung, and tried to rise. His foot slipped. As it dropped to the rung below, he lost his grip. The bottom edge of the casket pounded the ladder.

'Shit!' Pete yelled.

Larry grabbed the box's sides.

Something moved above him. He looked up.

He shouted, 'NO!'

Bonnie, standing rigid, teetered forward and plunged straight down at him.

It seemed to happen very slowly. The blanket fell from the stake and drifted toward her feet. Her dull blond hair flowed behind her head. Her right arm stayed tight against her side, but her left arm swayed down from the elbow as if reaching for him. Her mouth seemed to be stretched into a delighted grin.

He heard himself squeal.

He heard Pete shout, 'Watch out!'

Hurling himself off the ladder, he staggered away and flung up his hands. He caught Bonnie by the sides, just under her armpits, and tried to shove her away. But her weight drove him backward. He stumbled off the edge of the platform.

He seemed to fail for a long time.

His back slammed the concrete floor.

His hands lost their grip, and the body crashed onto him, the blunt end of the stake ramming his chest. He twisted his head aside. Dry teeth struck his cheek. Hair floated down, tickling his face like spider webs.

Larry bucked, throwing her off, and rolled away and scurried to his feet. He stared at her. He gasped for breath. He felt as if a horde of ants were crawling on his skin, but he looked down at himself. Except for a snag and a smudge of dirt on the chest of his T-shirt, he saw no evidence of the encounter.

'Are you all right?' Pete asked.

Larry moaned.

'Right with you,' Pete said, and dragged the empty casket up through the opening. Larry heard it scoot along the attic floorboards. Then, Pete rushed down the ladder. 'Guess maybe we should've tied her in.'

'Yeah.' Larry wanted to rub his crawly skin, but not with hands that had touched the body. 'I've gotta shower,' he said.

'Don't blame you. Gross-out. Let's take her up, though, huh?' Pete crouched over Bonnie's head and slipped his hands beneath her shoulders. 'Take the legs, buddy.'

Larry shook his head. 'I . . . uh . . .'

'Come on, don't be a pussy.'

He looked at his hands. 'Don't wanta touch . . .'

'For God's sake, Lar! She was all *over* you. Come on, grab hold. We can't just leave her here.'

Pete lifted. The rigid body didn't bend. Bonnie slanted down, straight as a plank, from her head at Pete's waist to her heels against the garage floor.

'Guess I can just drag her,' he said. 'Save you from messing your hands. You can bring the blanket, can't you?'

'Yeah.' Relieved, Larry crouched and picked up the blanket.

He watched Pete turn the corpse around and walk backward. Bonnie's heels sounded like newspapers sliding along the concrete.

Pete backed onto the platform. When he stepped onto the first rung of the ladder, Bonnie's feet rose off the floor. Her Achilles' tendons scraped the edge of the platform.

And left flakes of brown skin behind.

Larry winced.

He didn't want to touch her. But it pained him to see her getting hurt.

She's *not* getting hurt, he told himself.

The backs of her feet pounded the ladder rungs as Pete climbed higher.

Larry rushed forward. He tucked the blanket under his right arm, grabbed Bonnie's ankles and raised them. Holding both feet against his left side, he started up the ladder.

'Good man,' Pete said.

Larry climbed carefully. He kept his eyes away from the corpse. At the top, the heat was stifling.

They lowered Bonnie into the coffin. He spread the blanket over her, then hurried down. Pete came after him. They folded the ladder. A yank on the rope sent the trap door swinging upward on its springed hinges. It slammed shut.

As they headed for the house, Larry realized that he felt guilty about leaving Bonnie in such a dark, hot place.

Don't be ridiculous, he thought. She's dead. She doesn't feel a thing.

'When do you think we oughta pull the stake?' Pete asked when they reached the living room.

'The sooner the better, I guess. I'll want to do some research on Sagebrush Flat, though.'

'Right, good idea. Maybe they had some vampire troubles. Maybe that's how come the place was abandoned.'

'We'll see. Anyway, I need to fill up more pages somehow.'

'Right. And I need to pick up a video camera before the big event. I want to tape the whole thing, you know? It'll be great.'

'Yeah.' Larry opened the front door for him.

'See you later, bud. Going good, huh?'

'Well, at least we don't have to worry about the women catching on.'

Grinning, Pete slapped his arm. 'See you later. Don't let your meat loaf.'

When Pete was gone, Larry hurried to the bathroom. He threw his clothes into the hamper and rushed to the tub.

As he stood under the hot spray of the shower, he wondered why he hadn't mentioned finding the ring. He *should've* told Pete about it, told him that the body was a girl named Bonnie Saxon who graduated from Buford High in 1968.

How come I didn't? he asked himself.

Pete'll find out sooner or later. He'll realize I kept it from him.

So what?

Chapter Twenty

'Good morning, ma'am.'

Lane swung her locker shut and turned around. 'Well, hi, stranger.'

Jim's hands were pushed into the front pockets of his jeans. Smiling, he drew them out for her to see, and slipped them in again. 'Keeping 'em to myself,' he said.

'Good for you. You're learning.'

'Did you have a nice trip?'

'It was okay. I missed you. How was Candi?'

'Oh, she was grateful. She'd like you to go away more often.'

Lane tried to hold onto her smile, but she felt it being tugged down. Her arms tightened around the binder and school books clutched to her chest.

'I was *kidding*.'

'I know.'

'*You* brought her up.'

'I know. Dumb, huh?'

'I wouldn't go out with Candi. Or anyone else. Not as along as I've got you.'

Lane's smile came back. She lifted an eyebrow. 'Think you've *got* me, do you?'

'Hell, you know what I mean.'

'Yeah. Give me one of those hands.' She moved to his side, dropped one arm away from her load of books, and squeezed his hand when he offered it. 'Want to walk me to the library?' she asked.

'The library?'

'I've got an errand.'

'It's only ten minutes before the first bell.'

'Shouldn't take very long.'

Holding hands, they made their way through the crowded hall.

'Is it still on for Friday night?' she asked.

'Sure. I hope so. Rather go out Saturday, but . . .'

'*Hamlet.*'

'I know. What a drag.'

Outside, they cut across the quad. Jim opened the library door for her. 'Guess I'll make myself scarce,' he said. 'Ol' lady Swanson and me don't exactly hit it off. See you at lunch?'

'Fine. See you.' Lane gave his hand another squeeze, then let go and entered the library. She headed straight for the circulation desk. There, Miss Swanson was busy checking out books to several students.

'Ol' lady Swanson' was probably no older than forty, an attractive woman with very short red hair and a freckled face. But Lane knew what Jim meant. Though the woman was hardly ancient, her rigid posture and high, thin eyebrows suggested a severity that made her seem older than her years.

She'd always been nice to Lane, but she seemed to enjoy visiting grief upon students who acted up. Kids usually referred to her as 'the bitch.' She was also known as 'the dyke' and 'the shithead.' Henry, perhaps the most literate of her detractors, preferred to call her 'the Scarlet Pimple.'

After the last student wandered off, Lane stepped up to the desk.

'Good morning, Miss Swanson.'

'Lane? How are you?'

'Fine. I was wondering if you could help me. Are old yearbooks kept around somewhere?'

'Indeed they are. We're missing certain years, of course. Books *fly* out of here if I'm not constantly on the alert. The students are a pack of thieves. And several of the teachers are just as bad, if I do say so myself.' Her left eyebrow climbed her forehead. 'What year would you be interested in?'

'Nineteen sixty-eight.'

'That's long before I took over. Matters were an absolute shambles back then. I'll take a look, but don't be at all surprised if sixty-eight is among the missing.'

Lane smiled politely and said, 'Thank you.'

Miss Swanson entered the office behind the circulation desk and stepped out of sight.

Lane leaned forward. She propped her elbows on the desk and crossed her feet. She waited.

'And how are you this fine morning?'

Before she could turn around, Mr Kramer appeared beside her. 'Oh, hi!' she blurted, and felt the warmth of a blush.

'All rested up and rarin' to hit the books?'

'Sure. I managed to re-read *Hamlet* over the weekend,' she said, hoping he would be pleased by the news.

'Wonderful.'

He smelled wonderful. After-shave lotion? His cheeks looked smooth. They had a faint bluish hue where his beard would be if he grew one. She wondered if he ever had trouble shaving the deep cleft in his chin.

She met his eyes for a moment. They were *so* blue. She looked away and said, 'It's really amazing. I get more out of the play each time I read it.'

'Well, old Billy Shakespeare was no slouch.'

She laughed, then faced forward as Miss Swanson returned to the desk. The librarian held the tall, thin volume of a yearbook. Seeing Mr Kramer, she smiled and color came to her face. She suddenly looked softer, more feminine, younger.

'Good morning, Shirley.'

'Mr Kramer. May I help you with something?'

He shook his head. 'Just visiting with one of my ace students, here.'

Miss Swanson nodded, and turned her smile to Lane. 'You're in luck, young lady.'

'Terrific. How long can I check it out for?'

'I'm afraid you won't be *able* to check it out. Rules of the house. You may peruse it to your heart's content, but it remains in the library.'

Lane wrinkled her nose. 'Not even overnight?'

'I'm afraid not.' She glanced at Mr Kramer as if seeking approval. 'If we allow the yearbooks to leave the library, we soon won't have any at all. You understand.'

'Yeah.' Lane shrugged. 'Well . . .'

'Now please, those are the rules.'

'This is my fault,' Mr Kramer said. 'I asked Lane to pick the book up for me.'

'Oh?'

He reached out, and slipped it from Miss Swanson's hands. He nodded. 'Yes, this is it. Sixty-eight. Is there a problem with *me* checking it out?'

'Why, no. Of course not. Let me write up a card.' She slid open a drawer, took out a blank card, and jotted down, 'Buford Memories, 1968.'

'I really appreciate it,' Mr Kramer said as he signed the card.

Miss Swanson blushed even more. 'Quite all right. Will you be able to return it tomorrow?'

He glanced at Lane. She nodded. 'I should be done with it by then.' Lifting the book, he said, 'Thanks again, Shirley.' He tucked the book under his arm, gestured for Lane to follow him, and walked out to the quad. 'Here you go.' Handing it to her, he gave his face a silly, terrified expression. 'For heaven's sake, don't lose it.'

Lane laughed. 'I'll be careful.'

They walked together. 'How come you're interested in a yearbook that old?' he asked.

'Oh, it's for Dad. He's planning a novel that has stuff happening in sixty-eight. He wants to check out the hairstyles, clothes, that kind of thing. Thanks an awful lot for handling Miss Swanson.'

'That's what friends are for.'

Lane felt a pleasant glow spread through her. 'I wish there was something I could do for *you*.'

'Well, if you mean that, I can always use an able hand to help me correct papers.'

'Great. When?'

'Can you spare half an hour after school? I still have those spelling tests from Friday that need to be marked.'

'Sure.' The bell rang.

'Uh-oh. We'd better get to first period. See you later.'

Nodding, Lane watched him hurry away. She took a trembling breath, then forced her weak legs to carry her forward.

She set her lunch bag and drink down on the table beside Jim, then peered across the cafeteria. Henry and Betty weren't at their usual table. Someone else must've beaten them to it. But she spotted her friends at the other side of the crowded room. 'Back in a minute,' she told Jim.

'Forget something?'

'I have to see Henry and Betty.'

Jim rolled his eyes upward, suffering.

Lane patted his shoulder, then hurried away.

She found them sitting across from each other, Betty ripping open a bag of taco chips with her teeth while Henry lifted a brown paper sack out of his briefcase.

'Hiya, guys,' she said.

Henry twisted around and grinned up at her. 'Salutations, my darling.'

'Eat road apples,' Betty told him.

'I have to stay after school today,' Lane said. 'I guess you'll need to get home under your own power.'

'No pro-*blem*,' Henry said.

'Detention?' Betty asked.

'Ha! Me? Don't you wish.'

'So what gives?'

'I'm staying late to help Kramer grade papers.'

Betty pounded a chubby hand against her chest. 'Be still, my heart. How'd you wangle that?'

'Just lucky, I guess.'

'He's not Tom Cruise, you know,' Henry pointed out.

'You wouldn't know a hunk if one fell on you,' Betty said.

'They fall on me every time I go to PE. It's among their favorite sports.'

'Anyway, I'd better get back to Jim. I just wanted to let you know.'

Betty leered, advised, 'Keep your shorts on,' and jammed a taco chip into her mouth.

'Degenerate,' Lane said.

The girl nodded eagerly as she chewed.

Lane made her way back to Jim's table and sat down beside him. 'See? Back already.'

'Have a nice chat with Tweedle Dee and Dumb-dumb?'

'If you aren't going to be nice, I'll scram.'

'Okay, okay. Just kidding. So what gives?'

'Aren't you the curious one?'

Shrugging, Jim turned away and took a bite out of his apple. For lunch each day, he ate two apples and a chocolate bar, and washed them down with Pepsi. He was on his second apple. Only a core remained of the first. It was turning brown. Glad that she had *real* food, Lane unwrapped her salami-and-cheese sandwich. She bit into it, and sighed.

Jim glanced at her. 'You're eating poison, you know. All them preservatives.'

'I'm counting on them preserving me.'

'Ha ha.'

'Cheer up.'

'So what's the big deal with Hen-house and Betty Boob?'

'I'm staying after, that's all. I had to let them know.'

'How come you're staying after?'

'I'm helping Kramer mark tests.'

Jim wrinkled his face, baring his upper teeth. They were caulked with white mush from his apples. 'Judas priest. Grades slipping, or something? Isn't enough, you giving up Saturday night for that bozo? Now you're doing slave labor? Shit! All of a sudden, you're sure into some major league brown-nosing.'

'If you don't know what you're talking about,' Lane said calmly, 'you ought to keep your mouth shut. Besides, it's disgusting me.'

He opened his mouth wide and shook his head at her.

'Real cute. God, you can be so juvenile sometimes. To think I've actually kissed you.'

'And will again, no doubt.' He closed his mouth and commenced chewing with a blissful smile on his face.

Why do I even bother with him? Lane wondered. She took

another bite of her sandwich, looked at the cafeteria clock, and wished sixth period would hurry up and come.

In her fifth period physiology class, Lane had to scribble notes furiously to keep up with the lecture. The time sped by. When the bell rang, it took her by surprise.

She hurried into the hall and ducked into the smoky rest room. There, she leaned close to a mirror and checked her teeth for remnants of her lunch. They looked fine. She brushed her hair, then opened her denim skirt and tucked in her blouse so that it slanted down, smooth and taut, from her breasts to her waist. The straps and lacy pattern of her bra cups showed faintly through the blouse's white fabric. She fastened her skirt, turned around once to make sure of every angle, then left the restroom and headed for class.

You'd think you were going out with him, she thought, feeling a little foolish. He's just a teacher. He's not interested in a *kid*.

So? It doesn't hurt to look nice.

Lane entered the classroom by its front door. Mr Kramer wasn't there yet. She sat at her front row desk, put away the books she wouldn't be needing, and waited.

Just before the bell rang, Riley Benson and Jessica came in. Jessica's left arm was still in a cast, but her right arm was around Benson. She glanced at Lane as she sauntered by. Her face looked better: though she still wore bandages on her chin and left eyebrow, the swelling had gone down; her lips no longer bulged; her bruises had faded to a sickly greenish yellow; some of her scabs had come off, leaving patches of shiny pink flesh.

She stepped to the other side of her desk. Benson rubbed her rear end, then ambled down the aisle. Jessica sat down.

'How are you doing?' Lane asked.

The girl sneered at her. 'What do you think?'

'Just asking. Sorry.'

'Blow it out your ass,' she said, and turned away.

Woops, Lane thought. Obviously, Benson had told her about

the quarrel. Why'd she wait a whole week to sound off about it?

Bitch, she thought. Never should've bothered trying to be nice to her.

'Keep outa my way and keep your fuckin' nose outa my business,' Jessica suddenly added, 'or I'll let Riley go ahead and ream you out.'

'Okay. Jeez!'

Lane slumped in her seat and stared straight ahead.

She imagined herself telling Jessica to take a flying leap, but realized she'd better keep quiet. It wouldn't take much, she thought, to set the girl off. Jessica, alone, could probably take her apart. Not to mention what her scumbag boyfriend might do.

Mr Kramer entered the room.

Lane sat up fast, pulling in her legs and swinging her knees together. She straightened her back. She folded her hands on the desk top.

Kramer took off his sport coat. He draped it over the back of his chair, and began rolling up his shirt sleeves as he stepped to his usual position at the front of the table. His forearms were tanned under thick, black hair. He sat on the edge of the table.

Lane smiled when he met her eyes.

He acted as if he didn't see it, picked up his roll book and gave the classroom a quick scan. 'Mr Billings is apparently having himself another holiday,' he said, and marked the student absent.

'Okay. This week's spelling words. Who'll volunteer to write them on the board?'

Lane raised her hand. He chose Heidi.

No big deal, Lane told herself. But she couldn't help feeling a small letdown. First, he hadn't returned her smile. Now, he'd called on someone else to go to the board. Was he ignoring her?

Don't be ridiculous, she thought. I'm not the only kid in the room.

But as the class went on, Kramer continued to ignore her. He rarely gave her a glance. He called on other students to read from the poetry book, to answer questions about rhythm and meter, to offer interpretations.

Lane's uneasiness grew.

Is he mad at me, or something? What did I do? Maybe he thinks I took advantage of him at the library. But hell, I didn't ask *him to check out the book. That was his idea.*

She began wondering whether he still wanted her to stay after class.

Go on, get out of here.

He wouldn't say that.

Lane imagined herself sitting alone in the room, humiliated. 'But you asked me to stay and help you.'

'I don't care. Leave me alone.'

Maybe I should go ahead and leave when the bell rings, she thought. *But I* said *I'd stay. I can't just walk out. He'd think I'm nuts.*

'Lane?'

Startled, she looked up at Kramer.

'Would you like to read the next stanza?'

'Uh . . .' She felt herself shriveling inside. 'I'm afraid I've lost the place.'

A few sniggers came from the back of the room.

Kramer shook his head slightly. He looked amused. 'You *should* try to follow along in the book.'

'Yes, sir.' She lowered her eyes to the page.

'Aaron, will you read the next stanza?'

Aaron began to read. Lane hunched over her book, shielded her eyes with one hand, and studied the page.

Where the hell are we?

Shit!

She couldn't find the stanza.

Dipstick, you wanted *him to call on you. And he did. He sure did.*

Why don't I just die now, and make it easy on myself?

Aaron finished.

A hand appeared beneath Lane's face. Kramer's hand. It turned the page for her, pointed to a middle stanza, and went away.

'Thanks,' she muttered.

Everyone else in the classroom seemed to find this quite amusing.

Lane kept her head down.

'Would you care to favor us with a rendition?' Kramer asked.

She nodded against her sheltering hand, and began to read aloud.

She was halfway through the stanza when the bell rang.

'That'll be fine,' Kramer said. Raising his voice, he announced, 'Don't forget your spelling sentences for tomorrow. In *ink*, please. Class dismissed.'

Lane shut her book and stared at it. Kids walked past her. Someone rubbed the top of her head. She looked up. Benson grinned down at her. 'You gotta pay *attention*, babe.'

She sneered at him.

He sauntered out with Jessica, a hand on her rump.

Soon, the room was empty except for Lane and Kramer.

Lane forced her head up. Kramer stood behind his table, busy stuffing books and folders into his briefcase. He seemed unaware of her presence.

I should've left with the rest of them, she thought. God, how did I get into this?

Dad and his yearbook. Thanks a bunch, Dad.

She wondered if she should say something.

'Do you have a red pen?' Kramer asked, and finally looked at her.

The tension spilled out of her. 'Uh . . . no. I don't think so.'

'No problem. Let me get you one.' He stepped over to his desk and opened the top drawer. He found a pen, shut the drawer, and searched through a stack of folders on the corner of his desk. 'Here we go. I'll give you first period. How does that sound?'

'Fine.'

He came toward her. 'If you get done with these and want

some more, I've got plenty. Don't want to keep you all afternoon, though.'

Lane nodded.

I don't believe this, she thought. He's acting as if nothing happened.

What do you want, a lecture?

She cleared her desk. Kramer set the folder and pen in front of her. 'It's five points a word,' he said. 'But I guess you know that.'

'Yeah.'

'Any questions, just ask.'

'All right.'

He turned away.

'Mr Kramer?'

He turned to her again, a pleasant smile spreading across his face.

'I'm sorry about losing my place.'

'Daydreaming?'

'I guess so.'

'Well, no harm in that. I hope you weren't too embarrassed.'

'I was pretty embarrassed.'

'You're the best student in the class, Lane. Don't let one little lapse of attention throw you. Happens to everyone.'

'Okay. Thanks.'

'Of course, I had to give you an F for the day.'

'Oh.'

Laughing softly, he squeezed Lane's shoulder. 'That was supposed to be a joke.'

'Oh.'

His hand stayed there. Lane felt as if its warmth were spreading down through her. He rubbed her shoulder gently, then let go.

'I really appreciate your staying after to help like this. It takes some of the pressure off.'

'Glad to help.' She could still feel where his hand had been.

'Teaching ain't all it's cracked up to be. Sometimes, I feel like I'm being consumed by paperwork. All I seem to have time for is grading papers, preparing lessons.' He shook his head. 'A real drag.'

'If you'd like me to, I'll stay more often and help you out.'

Her heart thudded. She couldn't believe she'd said that.

He'll think I've got the hots for him.

Kramer's head tilted slightly to one side. He pressed his lips together and raised his eyebrows. 'Well, I sure appreciate the offer. You must have better things to do with your time, though.'

'I wouldn't mind. Really.'

'It's up to you. I'd certainly be glad to have the help.' Smiling, he knuckled the folder on her desk. 'Now, get cracking. Talk's cheap, and time's a-wasting.'

Lane laughed. 'You're a real slave-driver.'

'Start correcting those papers, or I'll give you a taste of the lash.'

'Yes, sir.'

He turned and headed for his desk. Lane's eyes stayed on him.

His sport shirt tapered down from his broad shoulders to his slim waist. The tail, just a bit untucked, puffed out over his belt. His wallet made a bulge over his left buttock. There seemed to be nothing in his right rear pocket. That side of his slacks was smooth against his rump, and Lane watched the way it moved as he walked.

Chapter Twenty-one

Jean, peeling potatoes at the sink, looked around at Larry as he entered the kitchen. 'Quitting a little early, aren't you?' she asked.

He glanced at the clock. Almost four. He usually worked until four-thirty.

'I finished the damn corrections,' he said. He took a beer from the refrigerator. 'Too late to get started on anything else.' He twisted the cap off the bottle. 'Where's Lane?'

'Not home yet.'

'I know *that*. Did she have some kind of plans for after school?'

'Not that she mentioned. Maybe she stopped over at Betty's, or something.'

'Yeah.' He poured the beer into a stein, sucked off the head of white froth, and emptied the bottle. 'What're you going to do with the potatoes?'

'French fries.'

'All *right*!' He dropped the bottle into the trash. It landed with a thunk.

He carried his beer into the living room, sank into his easy chair, and started thumbing through the new issue of *Mystery Scene* that had arrived in the day's mail. Jean had probably already looked it over. She would've told him if she'd found any mention of him. So he went straight to Brian Garfield's 'Letter from Hollywood.'

He tried to read it.

But the day was mild. The air conditioner was off, the windows open. Each time Larry heard a car on the street, his eyes shifted to the window.

Where is she?

Patience, he told himself.

They might not even *have* the sixty-eight yearbook.

They've got to.

He wished he'd asked Lane to phone him from school. Then, he wouldn't have spent the whole day worrying. But he didn't want her to think it was any big deal.

'Try for the sixty-eight.' he'd told her. 'That's the year I'll be working on. If they don't have it, though, sixty-seven or sixty-six will be okay. Even sixty-five. If fact, if you could get the annuals for each of those years . . .'

'You've got to be joking,' Lane had said. 'I'll be lucky if Swanson lets me check out *any* of them, much less four.'

'Just go for sixty-eight, then, okay?'

He heard another approaching car. He knew the Mustang's sound – a low grumble – and this wasn't it. He looked out the window, anyway. A station wagon swept by.

He drank some beer, finished the Garfield piece, and looked for Warren Murphy's 'Curmudgeon's Corner'. This issue didn't seem to have one.

He muttered, 'Shit.'

Probably a story behind its absence. Have to ask Ed next time we talk.

At least de Lint's horror reviews weren't missing. Larry scanned the columns. Half the books were by writers he couldn't stand. But he spotted reviews of new books by Daniel Ransom, Joe Lansdale and Chet Williamson. He'd already read the three books under discussion. Good. That way, the reviews couldn't spoil anything for him.

He took a drink of beer.

Started to read.

Heard the Mustang.

About time!

The shiny red car appeared on the street, slowed down, swung into the driveway and vanished from sight. The engine went silent. A door thumped shut. When he heard Lane's boots scraping on the walkway, he tossed the magazine aside and hurried to the door.

'Hi ho,' he said, opening the door. Lane had her keys in one hand. Her other hand was empty. 'How was your day?'

'Terrific.'

Must've been, Larry thought. She looked even more chipper than usual.

He stepped out of her way and shut the door. Lane slung her book bag off her shoulders. Trying to keep his voice calm, Larry said, 'So, did you have any luck with the yearbook?'

'Swanson didn't want to check it out to me. You really lucked out, though. Mr Kramer was there, and she let him have it.'

'But you've got it?'

'But of course.' She dropped her denim bag on the sofa, unstrapped its top, and slipped out a tall, thin volume. 'It has to be returned tomorrow morning.'

'No problem.' Larry reached for it.

Lane clutched it to her chest and shook her head. 'You owe me.'

'What do you want?'

'Well, that's open to negotiation. I've had to make considerable sacrifices on your behalf. In particular, I'm obliged to help Mr Kramer grade papers after school every day this week to pay him back for the favor.'

'You're kidding.'

'I wouldn't kid you.'

'He shouldn't make you do that.'

'Well, I kind of made the offer, and he didn't refuse.'

'Ah. Well, that's different.'

'It's still because of this,' she said and, grinning, rapped her knuckles against the back of the yearbook.

'Okay. What do you want?'

Her eyes rolled upward. 'Let me think. My services don't come cheap, you understand.'

'They never have.'

'Daaad!'

'Laaane.'

'You make me sound absolutely mercenary.'

'But you're not.'

'Of course not. However, I just happened to notice an absolutely radical pair of denim boots a while back.'

'And you didn't buy them?'

'I didn't think I should. I'd already made a few purchases that day.'

'If you're talking about the day your mother and I went on our last outing with Pete and Barbara, I remember it well.'

'I *really* wanted those boots. But I held back. For your sake.'

'I'm touched. Truly.'

'So, can I have them?'

'Sure, why not?'

'Oh, Dad, you're great!' She thrust the book at him. As Larry took it, she threw herself against him and gave him a quick kiss. Then she hurried toward the kitchen.

Larry retrieved his beer.

He heard Lane call out, 'Yo! Mom! What've we got to eat around here? I'm dying.'

In his office, Larry shut the door. He placed his beer on the coaster beside his word processor. He leaned back in his chair and rested the bottom of the book against his stomach. The blue cover was embossed with gold lettering that read, BUFORD MEMORIES '68.

This is it, he thought. My God, this is it.

His heart was racing. His stomach felt tight and shaky.

He opened the book. A quick riffle revealed glossy pages of black and white photographs. At the back was an index. The final page of the index listed students with S names. Larry slid his eyes down the column:

> Sakai, Joan
> Samilson, Pamela
> Sanders, Timothy
> Satmary, Maureen
> Schaefer, Ronald

No 'Saxon, Bonnie'.

Come on! Larry thought. She *has* to be in here.

Despairing, he flipped pages toward the front of the index. And spotted a subheading: 'FRESHMEN'.

'Thank God,' he muttered.

In 1968, Bonnie was a senior, not a freshman.

He thumbed the pages over, passing the lists of sophomores and juniors. Just above the heading 'JUNIORS' was the name 'Zimmerman, Rhonda.' Tail end of the senior class. He lifted his eyes to the left-hand corner. A senior named Simpson, Kenneth.

Simpson. An S!

Larry clamped his lower lip between his teeth. He turned the page and worked his way up from the bottom:

> Simmons, Dan
> Seigel, Susan
> Sefridge, John
> Sclar, Toni
> Schultz, Fred
> Schmidt, Dennis
> Saxon, Bonnie

Just another name in the index. 'Saxon, Bonnie.' Not printed in red. Not in bold lettering or italics. But it seemed to explode off the page and slam through Larry's head.

To the right of her name were page numbers. Six of them.

Six pages with photos of Bonnie Saxon.

God Almighty!

Larry scanned the column. Plenty of the names were followed by a single page number, several by two or three. Few had more than three.

Bonnie had six.

She must've been busy, Larry thought. And popular.

Popular girls are almost always pretty.

The first page number after her name was 34. Larry slipped a match book into the index to mark his place, turned to the front of the annual and thumbed through its pages until he found 34. Blocks of small, individual photos showing members of the senior class. Boys in sport coats and neckties. Girls in dark pullover sweaters, each wearing a necklace.

The first name in the upper left-hand corner was Bonnie Saxon.

Larry shifted his eyes to the photo.

He moaned.

She was lovely. Radiant, adorable. Her gleaming blond hair swept softly across her brow, flowed down to her shoulders. Her eyes seemed to be directed at something wonderful just beyond the camera. They looked eager, cheerful. She had a small, cute nose. Her high cheeks curved smoothly above the corners of her mouth, as if lifted and shaped by her smile.

This was Bonnie.

She looked quite a bit like Lane.

She looked very little like the corpse in the attic of Larry's garage, but her hair and teeth and the general shape of her face convinced him that he had made no mistake: the body was Bonnie Saxon. No doubt about it.

The hideous cadaver had once been the girl in this photo – beautiful, glowing with youth.

Larry gazed at the picture.

Bonnie.

He felt very strange: excited by his find, enthralled by her beauty, depressed. When the photo was taken, she must've thought a whole, wonderful life waited in her future. But she had only months, and then someone ended it all by pounding a stake through her chest.

This was no vampire.

This was a sweet, innocent kid.

Probably a real heart-breaker. Every guy in school must've longed for her.

Had one of them killed her? A jealous boyfriend? She'd broken his heart, so he drove a stake through hers? Possible, Larry thought. But the stake in her chest and the crucifix on the staircase wall sure made it seem that somebody believed she was a vampire.

Larry gazed a little longer at the photo, then checked the index and turned to page 124. There, he found group pictures of the Public Relations Committee, the Program Committee, and the Art Club. He didn't bother studying the lists of names. He wanted to search for Bonnie, to pick her out, to enjoy the surprise of recognition.

The Public Relations Committee photo was overexposed. Most of the faces were little more than pale blurs, their features washed out and faint. Bonnie didn't seem to be in this group, but Larry glanced at the names to make sure.

Then he went on to the Program Committee photo. He

half expected to find her here. Though he wasn't sure about the functions of the Program Committee, Bonnie looked like the sort of girl you might find in charge of decorating the gym for a dance. He studied the face of each girl in the picture. No Bonnie.

He found her with the Art Club.

In the front row, second from the left, between a couple of gals who looked fat and dumpy.

Bonnie looked grand. She stood straight, arms at her sides, head up, smiling at the camera. This wasn't a close-up like the senior photo, but it made up for that by showing her from head to foot. She wore a short-sleeved white blouse, a straight skirt that hung to the tops of her knees, white socks and white sneakers.

Larry lifted the book, watching her grow as the page neared his eyes. He studied her face. In spite of the distance from which the photo had been taken, it had very good definition. All her features were clear. The collar of her blouse was open. He looked at her neck and saw the hollow of her throat, the faint curves of her collar bones. Lower, the rise of her breasts was no more than a hint. Larry followed her arms down to her hands. Her hands were open, fingers curled slightly inward against the fabric of her skirt. His gaze lingered on the slender curves of her bare legs.

One of her white socks was slightly lower than the other. If she'd known that, she probably would've fixed it. Larry could almost see her bending over and pulling up the sock. The image gave him a little ache, as if he'd missed something important by not being there.

He lowered the book and read a short description of the Art Club's activities. Bonnie, he learned, had been the secretary.

Must've been smart. You don't appoint someone secretary unless she's intelligent and responsible.

Probably a straight-A student, he thought. One of those kinds who has everything going for her – looks, a terrific personality, brains.

He checked the index again, and discovered that the next

photo was on 126. He turned back to the Art Club, flipped the next page, and immediately recognized Bonnie in the top photo. She'd been in the school's Legislative Assembly, whatever that was. A quick scan of the small print informed him that the group was responsible for 'passing school laws and putting them into action.'

Bonnie was seated on risers, feet on the floor, legs together, hands cupping her knees. She was dressed just the same as in the Art Club picture. In this one, her socks were even. Larry smiled. She had a bemused look on her face. Her bangs hung a little crooked, showing a V of uncovered brow.

Larry brought the book closer to his face. Her head was turned slightly. Her hair was swept back behind one pale ear. She seemed to be leaning forward. Her blouse looked snug against her belly, and her breasts cast a vague, horizontal shadow across the white fabric.

He was about to turn to the index when he spotted Bonnie on the opposite page. She was in the top photo, front row, third from the right. A member of the Social Activities Committee.

'Ah ha!' Larry whispered.

So she decorated the gym for dances, after all.

'I knew it.'

In this photo, she wore a crew-neck sweater with a large B on its chest.

A cheerleader?

Figures, he thought. I should've guessed.

Bonnie looked different, somehow. Larry stared at the picture. She had been caught without her smile. The glimmer was gone from her eyes, and her lips were pressed together in a soft, straight line.

Something was obviously troubling her.

Maybe she was feeling sick, that day. Maybe she'd messed up a test. Maybe her boyfriend had dumped her.

Something had happened. Something, at least for a moment, had robbed her of happiness.

It didn't seem fair. Bonnie's life should've been perfect – there'd been so little of it left.

Larry felt a tightness in his throat.

He turned quickly to the index, then searched out page 133.

Bonnie stood in line with six other girls. 'Songleaders,' not cheerleaders. They all wore light-colored sweaters with the huge B in front, and dark, pleated skirts. They stood with pompoms raised in their left hands, right hands on hips, right legs thrown high.

Bonnie looked as if she were having the time of her life. Her head was tossed back. The shutter had caught her laughing. She'd kicked up her leg higher than any of the other girls. Not straight toward the camera, but a little to the side. The toe of her white sneaker seemed about to collide with her left armpit. Her skirt hung down from the upraised leg. She wore no socks. Larry gazed at her slim ankle, the curve of her calf and the sleek underside of her thigh. He saw a crescent of underwear not quite as dark as the skirt, rounded with the slope of her buttock.

He fought an urge to bring the book closer to his eyes.

He looked away from the picture. He picked up his stein and took a sip of beer.

Glanced again.

It's not actually her panties, he told himself. It's part of the outfit.

But still . . .

He turned his attention to the second picture on the page. Same girls. Same costumes. In this one, they were all facing the camera and leaping, pompoms thrust overhead with both hands, backs arched, legs kicked up behind them. Bonnie's sweater had lifted slightly. It didn't quite meet the top of her skirt. A narrow band of bare skin showed. Larry glimpsed her flat belly, the small dot of her navel.

He shook his head. He took another sip of beer, but had a hard time swallowing. He turned to the index.

Only one more page number after Bonnie's name. He turned to 147.

And sucked in a quick breath.

A 3 × 5 close-up of Bonnie filled more than half the page.

'Jesus,' he whispered.

He glanced at the caption. 'Bonnie Saxon, 1968 Spirit Queen.' On the same page were small photos of four other girls – princesses. Her court.

He postponed studying her picture. It was the last. He wanted to savor the anticipation.

On the opposite page was a photo of a tackled football player smashing to the ground. The heading beneath it read, 'SPIRIT WEEK HIGHLIGHTS FALL SEASON'. Larry scanned a description of the festivities, which were apparently marred by Buford's loss of the game. Then, he came to the part he'd hoped for. 'Sherry Cain, Sandy O'Connor, Julie Clark, Betsy Johnson and Bonnie Saxon were presented as homecoming princesses at half time. Bonnie Saxon was crowned queen at the Homecoming Dance that night. In spite of the defeat of the varsity, tremendous spirit was shown.' Nothing more about Bonnie.

Fantastic, Larry thought.

Homecoming queen.

'Good going, Bon,' he muttered.

Then he turned his attention to the photo.

And flinched as someone knocked on his door. 'Time to eat,' Lane called.

'Okay. I'll be right there.'

Larry glanced at the Spirit Queen, then shut the book.

He lay motionless in bed that night, staring at the ceiling. When the sounds of Jean's breathing convinced him that she was asleep, he crept out of bed. The air was chilly. He shivered with the cold and nervous excitement. At the closet, he pulled his robe off a hook. He put it on as he stepped into the hallway. The soft velours felt warm on his bare skin.

In the living room, he found Lane's book bag propped against the wall beside the front door. He opened it, searched inside with one hand until he felt the annual, and slipped the book out.

He carried it to his office. He shut the door, flicked on the light, and eased himself down onto his chair.

In spite of the warm robe, he was shaking. His heart felt like a pounding fist.

I must be crazy, he thought. What if Jean wakes up? Or Lane? What if one of them catches me at this?

They won't. Calm down.

With the book on his lap, he turned to the Spirit Queen.

God, so gorgeous.

She wore a dark top that left her shoulders bare.

He could look at her later.

He took an X-Acto Knife from his desk drawer, pressed the open book flat against his thighs, and drew the razor-sharp blade down the annual's gutter, neatly slicing off the page where it joined the spine.

He cut out every page that showed a photograph of Bonnie.

When he was done, he hid them in his file cabinet, sliding them into one of over fifty folders that contained copies of short stories he'd written over the years.

His pictures would be safe, there, from Jean and Lane.

He sat down again and riffled through the yearbook. A few pages were loose. He touched their edges with glue and carefully inserted them.

He shut the book and peered at its top. Along the spine, tiny gaps were visible where the pages had been removed. But only an extremely close inspection would reveal the damage. And if someone did notice, who was to say when the desecration had been performed? Maybe years ago.

Larry shut off the light and left his office. He returned the annual to Lane's book bag, fastened the straps, and went to his bedroom.

From the doorway, he could hear Jean's long, slow breaths.

He hung up his robe. He crept to the bed and slipped cautiously between the sheets. He sighed. He thought about the pictures.

They were his, now. His to keep.

He remembered the way Bonnie looked in each of them. But his mind kept returning to the songleader shots.

Then, she was alone on the football field. She thrust her pompoms at the sky and twirled, her long golden hair floating, her skirt billowing around her and rising higher and higher.

Chapter Twenty-two

Larry woke up in the morning and remembered cutting the pages from the book. He was suddenly certain that the librarian would notice the damage. Lane would catch hell. It would be his fault.

He realized that he'd done a lot of things, lately, that left him feeling guilty: threatening Pete with the gun; bringing Bonnie home and keeping her presence a secret; wandering out to the garage, apparently in a drunken stupor, and not even knowing what he did out there; and now, defacing the library book, maybe getting Lane into trouble.

Before finding Bonnie out there in that ghost town, he'd never done much to be ashamed of. About the worst, he thought, was having a few lustful thoughts about other women. That seemed pretty harmless.

But all this.

What the hell's happening to me?

Too hot, he flipped onto his back and tossed the blanket aside. Jean was already up. Good. He didn't want any company, just now. Especially not Jean's. She might sense that he was upset and start asking questions.

Oh, nothing's wrong. I've got a corpse hidden in the garage and you know that library book? Well, it had these terrific photos of the dead gal . . .

I had to have those pictures, he told himself. Nobody was about to let me keep the book. Photocopies wouldn't have been any good: they're fine for printed stuff, but the pictures would've look awful.

I bet nobody's even opened that book for the past twenty years.

Nobody'll notice the pages are gone.

You hope.

So if they give Lane shit, I'll pay for the book.

Lot of good that'll do. She's never been in trouble. It'd kill her.

Nobody will notice a damn thing. She'll return the book, and that'll be it.

No point in worrying, anyway. The damage is done. You can't put the pages back in, even if you wanted to.

They're mine, now.

He closed his eyes and let his mind dwell on the photographs. The memories of them soothed him. He filled his lungs with the mild, morning air. He stretched, savoring the solid feel of his flexing muscles, the softness of the sheet against his skin, the images of Bonnie.

He stayed in bed until he heard the soft grumble of the Mustang's engine.

He spent the day on *Night Stranger*, closing in on its finish. The writing was hard. His mind kept wandering. It slipped away from the story and tortured him with miserable thoughts about Lane being confronted by an outraged librarian. It tantalized him with thoughts of Bonnie.

Frequently, he looked away from the computer screen and stared at his filing cabinet. The drawer where he'd hidden the yearbook pages was within reach. He longed to pore over them. But Jean was in the house. What if she came into his office while he had the pictures out?

Shortly after two o'clock, Jean knocked on his door and opened it. 'I thought I'd run over to Safeway. Anything you want me to pick up while I'm there?'

'Not that I can think of,' he said. 'Have fun.'

'See you later.'

She closed the door.

Larry stared at the computer screen. He heard the faint thump of the front door shutting. He rubbed his moist hands on the sides of his shorts.

He waited for a while, then rolled his chair back, left the office, and reached the living room in time to see Jean's car pass the windows.

Gone. She's gone!

He glanced at his wrist watch. A quarter past two. Give Jean ten minutes to reach the store, at least ten inside, and another ten to get home.

He had at least half an hour.

Stomach trembling, he hurried to his office, shut the door and pulled out the steel drawer of the file cabinet. He'd slipped the pages into the folder for his short story, *The Snatch*. He took out the entire folder, left the drawer agape, dropped onto his chair, flicked open the cover and Bonnie smiled up at him.

The 'Spirit Queen' photo.

'God,' he whispered.

Bonnie seemed even more beautiful than he remembered. Lovely, fresh, innocent.

No wonder she was voted queen.

He gazed at her flowing blond hair. It swept softly down her forehead, slightly longer on the right so that it brushed the curve of her eyebrow. It didn't quite touch her left eyebrow. The sides of her head were draped by shining tresses. Her eyes sparkled. Larry supposed that their gleam was a reflection of the camera's flash. Her lips were together, and curled upward just a bit at the corners with the mere hint of a smile. She looked serious, but pleased and proud.

Her jaw cast a shadow that slanted across her neck and puddled in the hollow above her right collar bone. Her shoulders sloped down gently, bare to the borders of the photo. The top she wore looked black. Only its upper edge showed. It eased downward to a point in the center of her chest. Not quite low enough to show any cleavage.

Larry placed an open hand across the bottom of the picture. With the garment covered, she might have been naked.

He gazed at her face, at the smooth, pale flesh of her chest. Faint shadows revealed the hollow of her throat, the curves of her collar bones.

If the picture extended downward, his hand would be resting across her breasts. He imagined firm mounds with skin like warm velvet, nipples erect and pressing into his palm. He moved his thumb downward. It would reach to the golden curls between her thighs.

Suddenly shocked at himself, Larry jerked his hand away from the picture. He slapped the folder shut.

God!

What's wrong with me?

Face burning, he lurched out of his chair. He stuffed the folder back into the cabinet, and shoved the drawer shut.

He returned to his chair. He stared at the computer screen. The sentences there seemed empty, meaningless. No point in trying to write more of this novel. Not today.

He signed off, and replaced the disk with the one labelled 'Vamp'.

'Vampire,' he muttered. 'No way. Not Bonnie.'

He brought up the directory, then the last chapter he'd written on Saturday night.

A lot of catching up to do.

He exited that chapter.

He gazed at the blank screen.

Good luck, he thought. How in hell do I write about ending up in the garage with her? Say I was wearing pajamas, for starters.

Any way you slice it, you're going to look like you're losing your grip. Like you're obsessed, or something.

And what about the annual? Tell the world you cut a library book to pieces? Figure out some kind of lie, maybe.

No matter what you write, Lane will know the truth. She'll read the damn book.

The photos *have* to go in it.

Shit.

Cross that bridge when you come to it.

And be *really* careful when you write, about seeing the pictures. Understate it. For godsake, don't let it look like the things turned you on. The girl's dead.

She wasn't dead when the pictures were taken.

She was so alive then. So glorious.

And now . . .

In his mind, Larry saw the way she looked now. Hideous. A withered mummy with a stake in her heart.

That wasn't done by any jealous boyfriend. Some bastard actually thought she was a vampire.

Murdered her.

Hid her body under the hotel stairs and hung a crucifix on the wall for good measure.

And padlocked the front doors?

That was a brand new padlock, Larry reminded himself. And someone had placed boards across the broken landing.

Bonnie's killer?

Someone was certainly watching over the hotel. The coyote eater? Had he been hanging around Sagebrush Flat for more than twenty years – a mad sentry guarding the tomb of his slain vampire?

Still there.

By now, he knows she's gone.

I've got her, you bastard.

How could you do that to her? How could you take my Bonnie and drive a stake through her heart?

Larry stared at the computer screen.

His fingers went to the keyboard.

They jabbed the keys, and amber words appeared.

'SOMEBODY OUGHT TO RIP YOUR HEART OUT, YOU MOTHERFUCKER.'

Somewhere in the house, a door bumped shut. Larry quickly backspaced, erasing the words.

* * *

Larry managed to write four pages after Jean's return from the store, and was busy describing his clean-up of the garage when footsteps approached his office. He scrolled up quickly to clear the screen. A knock on the door. The door opened.

Lane stepped in.

His stomach shriveled, but he managed a smile.

'Hi ho,' he said. 'I thought you were staying late.'

'So did I.' She shrugged. 'Mr Kramer had a parent conference, so I came on home.'

One hand was hidden behind her back.

Probably holding a gun, Larry thought.

But she didn't seem upset.

'What've you got there?' he asked.

Her hand come forward. It held a chocolate chip cookie. 'Fresh from the oven,' she said. 'Want it?'

'Sure.'

He reached for the cookie. His hand was shaking. Lane noticed. 'Are you feeling okay?'

'Hard day at the office,' he said, and took the cookie. 'How was your day?'

'Okay, I guess.'

'You returned the yearbook?'

She frowned. 'You said you were done with it.'

'Yeah. I am. Thanks a lot for the help. I owe you.'

Smiling, she said, 'Right, you owe me. One pair of boots.'

'I don't have to pick them out for you, do I?'

'Just lend me your credit card. I'll take care of the dirty work.'

Larry laughed softly. 'My wallet's in the bedroom. Help yourself.'

When she left, Larry ate the cookie. It was soft, still warm from the oven. But his mouth was dry, and he had a hard time swallowing.

Chapter Twenty-three

When the public library opened its doors at nine o'clock Wednesday morning, Larry was waiting.

He felt nervous, approaching the librarian. She was a young, attractive woman with a cheery smile. But he half expected to be shunned, thrown out on his ear.

She's not psychic, he told himself. She has no idea I cut up the high school's annual.

'I'm doing research on 1968,' he explained. 'Would you have copies of the *Mulehead Evening Standard* going back that far?'

Minutes later, she produced a box of microfiche. She showed Larry to the reader-printer.

Yes, he knew how to use it.

The librarian told him there was a charge of ten cents per page for hard copies, and he could pay at the desk before leaving. Her name was Alice. She would be around and more than glad to help if he needed any assistance.

He thanked her.

She left.

Larry began his search at the June 1, 1968 edition of the newspaper. High school graduation had probably taken place around the middle of the month. Because of the ring, he assumed Bonnie had graduated. But he might be wrong.

The paper from Saturday, June 22, settled the question. Graduation ceremonies had occurred the previous night, and the list of eighty-nine matriculating seniors included Bonnie's name. Photographs of the festivities showed the school principal, the head of the Board of Education, and two students who had given speeches. No Bonnie.

But he had found what he needed: evidence that she was alive and well as of June 21.

He pushed a button at the base of the machine. Seconds later, a copy of the page slid out.

He went on.

He watched for Bonnie's name. He watched for stories about murders and disappearances. But he kept his mind open, hoping to notice any story that might have a bearing, no matter how remote, on Bonnie's fate.

The story he found in the July 16 edition wasn't remote. Larry saw the headline, and gasped. His heart thudded as he devoured the paragraphs.

TWO SLAIN IN SAGEBRUSH FLAT

Elizabeth Radley, 32, and her daughter Martha, 16, were brutally murdered last night in their rooms at the Sagebrush Flat Hotel. Their bodies were discovered by Uriah Radley, the husband and father of the victims.

According to a county sheriff's spokesman, Uriah had yesterday driven into Mulehead Bend for supplies. During the course of his return in the evening, his truck broke down 15 miles outside Sagebrush Flat. He traveled the remaining distance afoot, and arrived at the hotel at approximately midnight to find his wife and daughter murdered.

The nude bodies were discovered in their beds, both apparently having sustained multiple wounds of a fatal nature. The nature of the murder weapon, or weapons, has not been disclosed. Nor has it been revealed, as yet, whether the deceased were victims of sexual assault.

Uriah Radley was questioned by authorities, but is not being held in connection with the murders.

No suspects are in custody at this time.

Larry read the article again. Incredible. Two murders at the same hotel where they'd found Bonnie.

There's *got* to be a connection, he thought.

He copied the story.

In the next day's *Standard* was a follow-up.

SAGEBRUSH HOTEL MURDERS

Authorities remain baffled by the brutal double-homicide which occurred sometime before midnight this past Monday in Sagebrush Flat. Autopsies of the victims, Elizabeth Radley and her daughter, Martha, revealed that both died from exsanguination, or blood loss, as a result of multiple wounds.

Authorities have few leads, and no suspects at this time.

According to County Sheriff Herman Black, 'We're of the opinion that they were victims of opportunity. That is to say, they were in the wrong place at the wrong time. Sagebrush Flat was no place to be living. I'd warned the Radleys on several occasions about the dangers of staying there, now that the town's as good as dead. For the past couple of years, we've had lots of troubles with undesirables vandalizing the place and generally raising Cain.'

The Sheriff went on to point out that biker gangs had frequently used the town as a site for wild parties. During the past 12 months, no fewer than three rapes and half a dozen beatings had been reported as occurring in the town's abandoned buildings, either at the hands of bikers or other transient types.

'It would be my guess,' said Sheriff Black, 'that Elizabeth and Martha Radley ran afoul of some bikers. That's a rough lot, and two women alone wouldn't stand much chance.'

Uriah Radley, along with his wife and daughter, had continued to reside in Sagebrush Flat during the town's decline and eventual abandonment following the closure of the Deadwood Silver Mine in 1961. In the resulting economic chaos, businesses shut their doors and the citizens migrated to greener pastures, many of them settling in our own Mulehead Bend.

By early 1966, only Holman's general store and Uriah Radley's hotel remained in operation. Later in that year, the fate of the town was sealed when Jack Holman died as the result of an apparent suicide. In an ironic twist of fate, his body was found hanging by a rope in his general store by Martha Radley, then 14 years of age, who was murdered along with her mother on Monday night.

Though Holman's went out of business following the demise of its proprietor, the Radley family continued to reside in the Sagebrush Flat Hotel. The hotel ceased operations last year, but the Radleys remained. Uriah made weekly visits to our town for supplies, and he is known to be well liked.

Elizabeth and Martha were active members of our own First Presbyterian Church.

Martha attended Buford High School, where she completed her sophomore year this past June. She was a member of the school band, and the Art Club.

Services will be held Sunday at First Presbyterian.

Larry copied the story.

He felt as if he'd discovered a treasure. The town had a grim history: suicide at Holman's, a pair of grisly murders at the hotel, 'rough' types using the abandoned buildings for their fun and games. Great material.

To top it off, Martha had been in the Art Club. Like Bonnie. They must've known each other.

They'd been in the same club. And Martha had lived, and finally died, in the very hotel where Bonnie's body had been hidden.

That made two connections.

Larry knew he was onto something.

He suddenly realized he had a picture of her. Probably. If Martha wasn't absent on the day the Art Club's photograph was taken, she would be standing in the group with Bonnie.

Fantastic luck, he thought.

Hell, it's more than luck. It's no coincidence. Somehow, all this is related: the hotel, Martha's death, both girls in the same club, Bonnie's death. All linked.

He kept on searching.

Monday, July 22.

SERVICES HELD FOR SLAIN
MOTHER AD DAUGHTER

Funeral services were held Sunday at the First Presbyterian Church for Elizabeth Radley and her daughter, Martha, who were murdered last Monday night at the Sagebrush Flat Hotel.

The ceremony was attended by numerous friends and by the husband and father of the deceased, Uriah Radley, who accepted the ashes of his wife and daughter following the service.

That was all.

Larry made a copy.

He wondered if Bonnie had attended the funeral.

He thought about the ashes. The two women had been cremated. Not unusual, but interesting. Larry knew plenty of vampire lore. The wide belief was that a vampire's victims would become vampires, themselves. Burning their bodies would prevent the women from coming back. Was *that* the reason Uriah had his wife and daughter cremated? Did he have some reason to think they'd been killed by a vampire?

The paper had been vague about the nature of the wounds and murder weapons. More than likely, the cops kept that information to themselves. A common practice. You don't tell the press everything.

Suppose the wounds were bites, the weapons teeth?

The women had died of blood loss.

Uriah, discovering the bodies, certainly saw the wounds. And maybe he noticed that there wasn't much blood on the beds. He might conclude that they'd been murdered by a vampire.

Right, Larry thought. If he's crazy.

But what if he *did* believe a vampire'd killed them? What if, for some reason, he thought the vampire was Bonnie? And he went after her. And he pounded the stake through her heart. And he hid her under the stairs of *his* hotel. And he's still out there, after all these years, living in the hotel and standing watch over the remains of the vampire who murdered his loved ones.

It works, Larry thought. My Christ, it works.

Which doesn't make it true, he told himself.

Flights of fancy were his way of life. He'd built his whole career on daydreams, constructing them into a semblance of reality. You make up an unlikely situation, you make up characters and motives and causal links, and pretty soon the situation takes on a certain kind of sense.

Real life, he knew, didn't work like a book. People acted out of character. Motives were often murky. Chance and coincidence could make a shambles of looking for a neat chain of causes.

Maybe bikers killed Elizabeth and Martha, just as the Sheriff speculated. Or maybe a serial killer, passing through. Or maybe Uriah himself.

Whoever killed them, vampires might've been the furthest thing from Uriah's mind when he requested the cremations.

It might be pure coincidence that someone had selected Uriah's hotel as the hiding place for Bonnie's corpse.

On the other hand . . .

Everything fit together so neatly if Uriah blamed Bonnie for the killings and put her out of commission.

Pounded a stake through Bonnie's chest.

The crazy bastard.

How could anyone think that Bonnie was a vampire?

I did, he reminded himself. Just a little bit, maybe. At the start.

But Larry knew better, now. She was a beautiful, innocent girl, murdered by some deluded human garbage who obviously believed in the most outlandish superstitious nonsense.

Very likely Uriah Radley.

* * *

657

After eating a hamburger at a cafe down the block, Larry returned to the library. He smiled a greeting to Alice, took the box of microfiche off the circulation desk, and returned to the machine.

He resumed his search where he'd left off, at July 24, 1968. In the July 27 edition, he found this:

LOCAL GIRL DISAPPEARS

Foul play is suspected in the disappearance of 18-year-old Sandra Dunlap, daughter of Windy and William Dunlap. The young woman was discovered to be missing from the bedroom of her parents' Crestview Avenue home early this morning.

According to authorities, the front door of the house showed evidence of forced entry, and traces of blood were found on the bedsheets of the missing girl.

Sandra, a recent graduate of Buford High School, was last seen Friday night when she attended a movie with her boyfriend, John Kessler, and two other friends from high school, Biff Tate and Bonnie Saxon. The three youths, interviewed early today by police officials, all indicated that Sandra was dropped off at home shortly before midnight and that she was seen to enter the house without mishap.

Windy and William Dunlap stated they were asleep at the time of their daughter's return from the double-date.

The disappearance is believed to have occurred between midnight Friday and sunrise today.

Anyone who may have noticed unusual activity in the area near the Dunlap residence during that period, or who has any knowledge about the present whereabouts of Sandra Dunlap, is urged to contact the Mulehead Bend Police Department immediately.

The story was accompanied by a small, grainy photograph of the girl. It showed the head and shoulders of a pretty, smiling brunette. She wore a dark sweater. Larry guessed that this was her 'senior picture', the same one that probably appeared in the school yearbook.

If he still had the annual . . .

Forget it, he told himself. You got away with cutting out Bonnie's pictures. Pressing your luck to try the same thing with Sandra. Pressing Lane's luck.

No way.

He went back to the part of the story about Bonnie. She and her friend were actually the last people to see Sandra.

Incredible.

Okay, he thought, maybe not 'incredible'. It's a small town, only eighty-nine kids in the graduating class. Bonnie was 'Spirit Queen', without question one of the most popular girls in her class. It would be strange if she *didn't* know every other kid her age. She was probably close friends with several of them.

Sandra must've been one of her very best friends, though. You don't go double-dating with just anyone.

What about this Biff Tate? Bonnie's boyfriend, obviously. Stupid name. He was probably a football star, or something.

Bonnie was probably making it with the guy.

A goddamn jock. Larry could just hear him bragging in the locker room. 'Sure, I slipped it to her. Had her begging for more.'

Come off it, he told himself. It's stupid to be worrying about her boyfriend. Kids Bonnie knew were getting nailed. Two down in less than two weeks.

Had to be tough on her.

Yeah, and I bet good ol' Biff was more than eager to comfort her in her grief.

Larry muttered, 'Shit,' then glanced at Alice across the room. Her back was turned as she shelved books. She didn't react, so Larry assumed that she hadn't heard him.

He copied the story about Sandra Dunlap and returned to his search of the newspapers.

A brief piece in the July 31 edition indicated that the girl was still among the missing, that her parents feared the worst,

659

that the police were again asking witnesses to come forward with information.

On August 10, 1968, Linda Latham vanished.

The photo showed a cheerful, blond girl with freckles and a cute, uptilted nose. This didn't look like a school picture. She wore a T-shirt, and a ball cap with its bill turned sideways. Larry gazed at the girl's young, innocent face. It saddened him, stifled the excitement he felt about discovering another victim.

TOWN STUNNED BY KIDNAPPING

Linda Latham, 17-year-old daughter of Lynn and Ronald Latham, was apparently abducted late Friday night while walking home from the house of a friend, Kerry Goodrich.

At approximately midnight, Linda's parents grew concerned about her absence and telephoned the Goodrich residence, only to learn that their daughter had left more than an hour earlier. The walk, a distance of four blocks, should have taken the girl no longer than ten minutes.

Alarmed, her parents searched the area between the two homes. Finding Linda's handbag near the curb approximately a block from the Goodrich house, they promptly called the police.

Though the area was canvassed by authorities, no information about the apparent kidnapping was obtained.

Linda Latham is the second teenaged girl to disappear under suspicious circumstances in recent weeks. On July 26, Sandra Dunlap vanished from her home on Crestview Avenue, and her fate remains unknown to date.

Police point out that there is little similarity in the circumstances of the two disappearances. 'The M.O.'s are completely different,' according to police spokesman, Captain Al Taylor. 'It would be premature, at this point, to speculate that both crimes were the work of the same perpetrator. In spite of that, we do need to recognize that two teenagers have been abducted over a short period of time. There certainly *is* cause of concern. I would advise parents to keep a close watch on the activities of their adolescent children, particularly females. The youths themselves should exercise extreme caution until the perpetrator or perpetrators have been apprehended.'

Captain Taylor went on to suggest that teenaged girls refrain from going out alone, that they carry whistles in case of an emergency, and that they report any encounters of a suspicious nature.

Authorities are conducting an all-out search for the two missing girls. Anyone with information about either disappearance is requested to contact the police immediately.

Nothing about Martha Radley, Larry realized. Didn't the police see a connection there? Obviously not, or they'd be even more concerned.

One murder, two disappearances. That's three down.

Larry removed the bottom page from his small stack of copies – the list of 1968 graduates from Buford High School. He found the names 'Dunlap, Sandra' and 'Latham, Linda'. The Radley girl wasn't there, of course: she was only sixteen.

But she'd been in the Art Club, and Sandra and Linda had both been Bonnie's classmates.

Bonnie knew all three.

God, she must've been devastated. And scared.

Something like that happens, and you've got to start wondering who will be next.

Maybe you.

He copied the story.

He continued searching. He copied three follow-up stories, none of which provided any new information. The girls were still gone. The police had no suspects.

Bonnie *was* next.

He found her picture and story on the front page of the *Mulehead Evening Standard*'s August 14 edition.

He stared at the screen with a horrible feeling of loss.

What did you expect? he told himself. You knew she was dead, you've got her body. This shouldn't come as any great blow.

But it was as if part of his mind had held onto a wild hope that Bonnie's story would have a happy ending, after all. Somehow.

The newspaper crushed that hope.

He moaned as he stared at the photo. He knew it well. It was her senior picture. He had it in his filing cabinet.

Reluctantly, he read the story.

BONNIE SAXON VANISHES

Bonnie Saxon, voted Buford High School's 'Spirit Queen' during the fall 1967 homecoming festivities, disappeared during the night from the Usher Avenue home where she lived with her mother, Christine.

The 18-year-old girl was last seen by her mother when she returned home following a date Friday night with her boyfriend, Biff Tate. The next morning, Bonnie was gone. Her bedroom window was found to be broken, and blood was noted on her sheets.

This marks the third disappearance, since late July, of local teenaged girls. On July 26, Sandra Dunlap, 18, vanished from her home. Like Bonnie, Sandra was apparently taken during the night from her bedroom. In both cases, there was evidence of forced entry, and blood was found on the bedsheets. The second disappearance occurred on August 10, when Linda Latham, 18, was the victim of an apparent kidnapping while she walked home after visiting a friend.

According to Police Chief Jud Ring, 'It looks now as if we have a definite pattern, especially between the Dunlap and Saxon cases. It's reasonable to conclude that all three girls were abducted by the same perpetrator. This is a very nasty situation. We still hope that the girls will be found alive, of course. But we just don't know what has become of them. What we do know is this: there is every reason to believe that such crimes will continue if we fail to apprehend the person responsible for these outrages.

'Our department,' he went on, 'is conducting a full-scale investigation of the matter. No avenue is being overlooked. I have every confidence that we'll soon have the perpetrator in custody. Until then, however, it's imperative that all our female citizens exercise the utmost caution in their daily affairs.'

Bonnie Saxon is a graduate of the Buford High School Class of 1968. In addition to being voted 'Spirit Queen,' Bonnie was on the honor roll, and was active in numerous school activities. She and her mother are members of the First Presbyterian Church, where Bonnie sang in the Youth Choir. This energetic and beautiful young woman is a familiar figure to a great many citizens of our town, and it is hoped that her widely recognized appearance may prove useful in locating her.

Anyone with information about the abduction or present whereabouts of Bonnie Saxon, Linda Latham or Sandra Dunlap is urged to contact the authorities at once.

She was gone.

Dead.

Whoever wrote the story didn't know it, but somebody had pounded a stake through her chest. Killed her.

Larry knew he should go on, but he didn't have the heart.

He checked his wristwatch. Three o'clock. It was early to quit. If he stopped now, he would need to come back tomorrow.

He didn't care.

He made a copy of the story and shut off the machine.

Chapter Twenty-four

When the bell rang, the students began to file out of the classroom. Lane slowly gathered her books from the rack under her seat so it wouldn't be obvious to the others that she was remaining.

No point letting the whole world know she was staying to help. Some of the kids would think she was brown-nosing. Not that I *care* what they think, she told herself. Still, it seemed wise to keep a low profile.

Jessica stopped in the doorway and looked back at her.

Lane slid her stacked books toward her chest as if preparing to stand.

'You're leaving?' Mr Kramer asked.

'No, huh-uh. Not if you have something for me.'

Nodding, he smiled. 'I have a job, if you don't mind a little manual labor.'

'No, that'd be fine.' She glanced toward the door. Jessica, frowning, turned and walked away.

'Come on up here,' Kramer said. He reached into his briefcase, but kept his eyes on Lane as she approached.

She hoped she looked all right. Jim had certainly thought so. During the lunch period, he'd snuck his hand under the loose bottom of her blouse several times before she finally lost her temper. 'If you don't like it,' he'd said, 'you shouldn't wear that kind of thing.'

The white pullover blouse had a cowl neck, short sleeves, and a hem that reached just to her waist. It wasn't meant to be tucked in. Neither, however, was it meant as an open invitation for Jim to explore the bare areas just out of sight above her belt.

That morning, when Lane chose to wear the blouse and her short denim skirt, she hadn't been thinking about Jim's reaction. Her mind had been on Mr Kramer. She'd wanted to look good for him. And maybe just a little sexy.

664

If Kramer appreciated her outfit, he gave no sign.

He turned his attention to his briefcase as she stepped around the back of the table. He pulled out a file folder, turned toward her, and opened it. Inside was a stack of 8 × 10 pictures.

'Whitman?' she asked, peering at the upside-down face of the top portrait.

'Very good.'

'I used to play "Authors" a lot when I was a kid.'

'How would you like to hang these up? Give the kids something worthwhile to gaze at while they're daydreaming.'

'Great,' Lane said. 'Where do you want them?'

He pointed out a strip of corkboard high on the front wall between the chalkboard and the ceiling. 'Think you can manage that? You'd have to stand on the stool, I'm afraid.'

'No problem,' Lane said.

'Fine. Just fine. I'd give you papers to correct, but all I've got are essays. I really have to do those myself.'

'Oh, this'll be okay.'

He took a clear plastic box of thumb tacks from his desk drawer, and gave it to her along with the folder of pictures.

'Any special order you want them in?' Lane asked.

'Doesn't matter.' He brought the stool from the corner of the room.

It was as high as Lane's waist, with metal legs and a disk of wood for a seat. Each room seemed to have just such a stool. Teachers often perched on them, but Mr Kramer never used his, preferring to sit on the front table when he addressed the class.

He carried it to the far end of the chalkboard. 'Maybe I'd better hold something.'

Lane handed the pictures and tacks to him. He stood beside her, watching, frowning slightly.

'Don't worry, I'm not planning to fall.'

'I'm sure you know what Burns said about the best laid plans and schemes.'

'Promise you'll catch me if they "gang a-gley"?'

'I'll give it my best.'

She stepped onto a rung, planted her other knee on the seat, and braced herself against the chalkboard as she got to her feet.

'You okay up there?'

'Yeah, I think so.' She looked down at him and managed to smile. Her position *did* feel precarious. There was little room for her feet and nothing to hold onto. But the corkboard was just in front of her face, so she wouldn't have to stretch for it.

'Try one, see how it goes.' He passed the Whitman picture to her. Lane took it in her left hand. She reached her right arm across the front of her body, and Mr Kramer dropped two tacks into her palm.

She raised the picture and pressed it flat against the corkboard. Holding it in place with one hand, she shoved a tack into its upper right corner.

And knew what her blouse was doing. She knew that she'd made a mistake when she selected it. But she'd thought she would be correcting papers, not climbing onto a stool and leaning forward with both arms extended and Mr Kramer below her.

The hem was brushing the skin of her back at least an inch above the top of her skirt. Lane couldn't see the front. She didn't have to. She could well imagine the way it must be hanging away from her body. If Mr Kramer happened to be looking in the right direction, he could probably see all the way up to her bra.

The knowledge gave her a hot, crawly feeling.

She pushed the other tack into place, lowered her arms, and looked down at the teacher.

He nodded. 'So far, so good,' he said, smiling. He gave her a photograph of Mark Twain.

'I can probably manage,' Lane said, 'if you want to go ahead and correct the papers. Just give me the box of tacks and set the pictures on the chalk tray.'

'Sure you don't want me here as a spotter?'

'I think I'll be okay.'

He handed the tacks to Lane, then removed the short stack

of pictures from the folder and propped them up on the chalk tray. He didn't leave.

The hell with it, Lane thought. No big deal.

She went ahead and lifted Mark Twain up to the corkboard.

'Get him right there next to Walt. Maybe overlap the edges a little. You could use the same tack for both.'

He isn't paying attention to *me*, anyway, she told herself.

Yeah? Don't bet on it.

If he's like most guys, he's probably staring straight up my blouse. Or crouching for a peek at my panties.

She tucked the plastic box under her chin to free her right hand, and pried out the tack at the corner of the Whitman picture.

By now, she thought, Jim would have a hand sliding up my leg.

Mr Kramer's not Jim, thank God.

Besides, I'm a student. He wouldn't dare touch me, even if he wanted to.

She overlapped the edges of the pictures, and pushed in the tack. It held Mark Twain in place while she took the box from under her chin, crouched down, and lifted a portrait of Charles Dickens off the chalk tray. As she straighted up, she looked around at Mr Kramer. He nodded with approval.

'Looks as if everything's under control,' he said.

'Yeah.'

'Just give a whistle if you need me,' he told her, and headed for his desk.

He sat down. He bent over a stack of papers and picked up a red pen.

Thank goodness, Lane thought.

She felt strange, though – not just relieved that he no longer stood below her, but a little disappointed, a little abandoned.

Guess he wasn't all that impressed, she thought.

She rammed a tack through the corners of Dickens and Twain.

I didn't *want* him looking up my clothes!

Maybe he didn't even take advantage of the opportunity.

She climbed down from the stool, adjusted its position, and saw Mr Kramer turn to watch her mount it. 'Careful,' he said. She smiled and nodded.

And a terrible thought struck her.

What if he thinks I dressed like this to turn him on?

Fire spread over Lane's skin.

He must think I'm a slut.

As she tacked up a picture of Tennyson, beads of sweat slid down her sides.

I did want to look nice for him, she told herself. But I had no idea . . .

She wished to God she had worn jeans and a long-tailed blouse. A blouse she could have tucked in tight.

I would've, she thought. So help me, I would've if I'd had any idea . . .

I'm not a slut.

What if he thinks I did it for grades?

A lot of kids were known to flirt with their teachers in hopes of getting higher marks. Some probably even offered sex. Though Lane didn't know of anyone who'd done that, she supposed it sometimes happened.

I'm already getting an A from him, Lane told herself. He can't think I dressed like this for a better grade.

For that matter, why should he even suspect I wore this stuff for *him*? He probably just thinks I'm just trying to look good for a boyfriend.

Lane began to feel better as the sickening heat of embarrassment subsided.

Sure, she thought. He can't suspect I dressed for him. He's no mind reader.

She continued to put the pictures up, balancing on the stool, bending over for new ones, reaching out, tacking them to the corkboard, frequently climbing down and moving the stool closer to Mr Kramer's desk.

Often, she glanced at him. Usually, he was busy reading the essays. A few times, however, she found him looking over his shoulder at her. When that happened, he never tried to turn away and pretend he wasn't watching. He never acted guilty. He usually just smiled or nodded, and made a comment: 'You're doing a good job,' or 'Glad it's you and not me up there,' or 'Don't push yourself if you start getting tired.'

Lane finally began to suspect that he didn't care about the way she was dressed.

I might as well be wearing coveralls, she thought.

She wondered if he might be gay.

Give it a break, she told herself. What do you want? He's a teacher.

She stepped down to the floor once again, and moved the stool a couple of feet nearer to his desk. Swiveling his chair around, he scanned the high row of pictures. 'Terrific,' he said. 'They add a nice touch to the room, don't you think?'

'Be nicer if they weren't all *dead* guys.'

'Well, unfortunately, the literary community doesn't hold much stock in living writers. You can't be a "major author" till you're dead.'

Lane thought he was wrong about that. Though she felt reluctant to question his views, he usually seemed to enjoy discussions with his students. Besides, if she stopped talking, he would return to the essays.

'Dad says that's a myth,' she told him, and climbed onto the stool. She lifted a picture of Hemingway from the chalk tray and raised it to the corkboard. 'Most of these guys were enormously successful and famous in their own time.' She punched a tack through its corner. 'Only a few weren't recognized till after they died. Like Poe, for instance.'

Bending down for a picture of Steinbeck, she looked over her shoulder. Mr Kramer was smiling, nodding his head.

'And Poe was *all* screwed up,' she added.

Mr Kramer laughed. 'I suppose he had to be, to write the way he did.'

'I don't know.' She straightened up and pressed the picture into place. 'Dad writes worse stuff than Poe, and he seems fairly normal. I've met scads of horror writers – going to conventions and stuff?' She pressed in the tack, then turned carefully atop the stool to look down at Mr Kramer. 'Some are even really good friends of Dad, guys I've known forever. Almost none of them are weird. In fact, they seem more normal and well-adjusted than most people I've known.'

'That's hard to believe.'

'I know. You'd think they'd be raving lunatics, wouldn't you?'

'Or at least slightly weird.'

'You know what *is* weird? Nearly all of them I know have this incredible sense of humor. They're always cracking me up.'

'Strange. Maybe their humor is a reflection of their somewhat off-kilter world view.'

'More than likely.' Lane climbed down from the stool, moved it closer to Mr Kramer, and mounted it again. As she rose, she lifted a picture of Faulkner from the chalk tray. She pressed it against the corkboard and tacked it into place. Hearing a squeak, she glanced back. Mr Kramer had turned his swivel chair around. He was looking up at her.

He didn't say anything.

Lane crouched for another picture. As she raised it, she said, 'You know how we were talking about dead writers and fame?'

'The myth.'

'Right. Well, you want to know something odd? The reverse is actually true. At least nowadays.' She tacked the picture of Frost to the cork. 'When a writer kicks the bucket, he's screwed.'

She heard her teacher laugh. Turning around, she smiled down at him. 'Publishers want to *build* a writer. Once he's dead, they don't want to touch him.'

More laughter.

'It's true. Unless he's a real biggy. With most guys, they just lose interest. I know about an agent, and one of his best writers died, and he *kept it a secret*. She was a big writer of romances, you know? He stood to lose a fortune. So what he did, he actually got some hack to start writing imitations, and he sold them using the dead writer's name. Do you believe it?'

'Gives a new meaning to "literary immortality".'

'Yeah, I'll say.'

Lane turned away, and took a picture of Sandburg off the tray. Rising, she realized she should have moved the stool. Frost was already some distance to her left. Sandburg would mean a stretch. She supposed she could manage it, though.

Easing herself forward, she braced her right forearm against the chalkboard. She leaned to the left. She reached way out with the picture of Sandburg and pressed it to the wall and the stool flipped.

Lane heard herself gasp, 'Oh shit!'

Part of her mind seemed to disconnect, to step back and observe this ridiculous and embarrassing event. She saw herself dropping sideways, arms waving in the air beyond her head, her right leg high as if the overturning stool had thrown it toward the ceiling. Her skirt was up around her hips. Her blouse was halfway up her chest.

Wunnerful wunnerful.

She heard a crash, but it wasn't her. Not yet. Maybe Kramer's chair slamming against his desk.

He coming to the rescue? she wondered. Or just trying to get out of the way.

Coming to the rescue, she realized as one of his hands jammed under her armpit and another clapped the bare skin of her upraised leg, high against her inner thigh. She felt the hands thrust upward. Then she slammed the floor, grunting at the impact.

The hands went away.

'My God, are you okay?'

Nodding, gasping, Lane rolled onto her back. Mr Kramer was kneeling over her. His face was red, his eyes wide, his lips twisted in a grimace.

'Guess I'll live,' she muttered. She started to sit up.

'Don't.' He gently pushed her shoulder. She eased back down. 'Don't try to get up. Just rest a minute.' He kneaded her shoulder. 'That was a nasty fall.'

'Thanks for catching me.'

'Well, I tried. It happened so fast.'

'You broke my fall some.'

'Not much.'

'I feel like such a dork.'

'These things happen.' His other hand patted her belly. 'I just hope you're all right. You really gave me a scare.' His hand settled there, big and warm against her bare skin just above her belt. 'Where do you hurt?' he asked.

'My side, I guess.'

He leaned farther over her. His hand slid across her belly to her hip. 'Here?'

She nodded. 'And my ribs.'

'Hope nothing's broken.'

'I don't think so.'

Lane closed her eyes. Gently, Mr Kramer rubbed her hip bone and the side of her rump. His other hand brushed her blouse upward. 'Pretty red,' he murmured. 'You'll probably have a whale of a bruise.'

'Moby bruise,' she said, then sighed as he began to massage the side of her ribcage.

'Tender?' he asked.

'Yeah. A little.'

His hand roamed higher, fingers kneading, soothing the soreness.

'Any sharp pain?' he asked.

'No.' She moaned when his wrist brushed against the underside of her breast.

'It hurts here?' he asked, pressing her ribs. The wrist moved slightly, rubbing her.

'Just kind of an ache,' she murmured.

He massaged her side, his wrist staying against her breast, caressing Lane through the thin fabric of her bra.

Doesn't he realize it's there? she wondered.

She hoped not.

If he realized, he would stop.

His other hand eased lower. Lane's skirt was no longer in its way. She felt him stroking and squeezing the side of her leg, high up.

'Better?' he asked.

'Yeah.'

He continued to rub her.

Doesn't he know what he's doing to me? she wondered.

Lightly, he patted her leg. 'Okay,' he said. 'Why don't we get you to your feet, now?'

Lane considered telling him she wasn't ready. Any more of this, though, and it might become all too obvious that his touch was doing more than just soothing her injuries.

He took a firm hold on her upper arm, placed his other hand at the base of her neck, and helped her sit up.

Her blouse unrumpled and drifted toward her waist. Her skin was as high as she had suspected. She glimpsed glossy blue between her legs, and dropped a hand to conceal it.

A little late for modesty, she thought.

Mr Kramer held onto her arm until she was standing.

'Thanks,' she murmured.

When he let go, she looked down and straightened her skirt.

'Are you all right?'

'Yeah. I think so.' She raised her eyes. 'At least I was wearing clean undies,' she added, and smirked, and couldn't believe she'd said that.

'Always should,' Mr Kramer said, a smile spreading across his face. 'You never know when you might be in an accident.'

'As Mother says.'

'As all mothers say.'

'Shit,' she muttered, and lowered her head.

He put his hands on her shoulders, rubbed them. 'I'm just glad you're all right. I feel responsible, you know.'

'I'm such a klutz.'

'You're a terrific young lady. Don't ever think otherwise.'

Lane looked into his eyes. They were clear blue, gentle, knowing. 'Thanks.'

'I mean it. Now, you'd better run along.'

'But I haven't finished putting up the . . .'

'I'll take care of the rest. If I were you, I'd take a long, hot bath. Really soak. That'll help the soreness.'

'I will.'

Lane waited until after dinner that night, then went into the bathroom. She still wore her school clothes. She lay down on the floor. There, she hitched up her skirt and blouse so they were just as they'd been after the fall. She arranged her legs to match her earlier position: left leg straight and flat against the carpet; right leg raised a little, bent at the knee, angled outward. Bracing herself up with her elbows, she stared down at herself.

This is how I looked to Mr Kramer.

Holy cow.

Then she noticed that her right leg had a faint purple hue. The imprint of Mr Kramer's hand? That must be where he grabbed me to break my fall, she realized. It was just below her groin.

'Man,' she whispered.

She thought she could still feel his hand there, as if it had left a ghost of itself.

If Jim had grabbed me there . . .

Forget Jim, she told herself.

She got to her feet, stepped in front of the mirror, and again lifted her skirt. Her panties were tight and clinging, the blue fabric nearly transparent.

She grimaced at her reflection. Her face was very red.

'He sure got an eyeful,' she whispered.

But he never got funny. He acted like a perfect gentleman. That's the difference between a mature, sensitive man like Mr Kramer and a horny teenager like Jim.

Lane stoppered the tub and ran water for her bath. While the tub filled, she took off her clothes. She returned to the mirror. There were bruises over the jut of her left hip bone and low along the side of her ribcage.

She stared at her left breast. Leaning backward, she studied its underside where Mr Kramer's wrist had rubbed it through the bra. The skin looked smooth and white.

What did you expect? she asked herself.

But it didn't seem right for there to be no visible evidence of his touch.

Shaking her head, Lane turned to the tub. She crouched and shut off the faucet. Then she climbed over the side.

She settled down into the hot water. She sprawled beneath it, squirming under the fluid caress, and once again arranged her body to match its position on the classroom floor. She closed her eyes.

She remembered the feel of Mr Kramer's touch. In her mind, the teacher stopped massaging her ribs. His hand closed gently over her breast and he sank down onto her and covered her mouth with his. She wrapped her arms around him. She squeezed him hard and sank into the moist heat of his kiss.

Chapter Twenty-five

Jessica woke up. Keeping one eye shut, she squinted at her bedside lamp. Then at her alarm clock. Almost three. In the morning?

What is this? she wondered. What's the lamp doing on?

She rolled onto her back and sat up.

Kramer, naked, stood with his back to the closed door of her bedroom. His left hand rested against the switch plate. His right hand, down at his side, held a straight razor.

Jessica felt as if her heart had been stomped.

'Aren't you glad to see me?' Kramer asked. He spoke in a normal voice, not a whisper. It was very loud in the stillness.

Jessica struggled for a breath, then whispered, 'My folks'll hear you.'

'Think so?' he said, speaking even louder than before.

Maybe not, she told herself. Her door was shut. Her parents' room was at the other end of the hallway, and they were sound sleepers.

Kramer let his hand fall away from the light switch. He stepped slowly toward the end of the bed.

Jessica gazed at the razor swinging near his side.

Why did he have that?

He'd warned her that he might come back with a razor.

She panted. She couldn't seem to get enough air into her lungs. 'I didn't tell,' she said. 'I didn't . . . tell on you. What do you want?'

He said nothing. A corner of his mouth curled up. He stopped at the foot of the bed. Eyes on Jessica, he reached down with his left and dragged the covers toward him.

She didn't move.

The blanket and top sheet slid off her lap, down her legs, and dropped off the end of the mattress. Her short nightgown, rucked up and twisted while she slept, left her bare below the waist.

'Nice,' Kramer said. 'Now, lie back and relax.'

She shook her head. She lifted her left arm and rested its cast against her thigh, her hand blocking the teacher's view.

'That's no way to behave. You'll get low marks for cooperation.' He lifted the razor close to his face and shook it in a scolding gesture.

Jessica moved her arm aside. She lay down.

The mattress shook as Kramer crawled onto it. He knelt between her legs. He lifted her nightgown and slit it up the middle until it parted between her breasts. With the end of the blade, he flicked the fabric aside.

'Don't cut me,' she whispered. 'Please.'

'I'm not happy with you, Jessica.'

'I didn't tell.'

'I know.'

She whimpered as cold steel slid down her belly. Raising her head, she saw that it was the blunt side of the blade.

'But you might,' Kramer said.

'I won't. Never.'

'I saw how you looked at Lane this afternoon. You were thinking about it, weren't you?'

'No.'

'Thinking about warning her.'

'No. I wouldn't. Why should I care what you do to her? I don't even like the bitch.'

He flipped the blade and cut her. A quick, curling slash. It didn't hurt much, but she flinched rigid and sucked in her belly. A red S appeared above her navel. Its curving line thickened. Dribbles spread out from it like tendrils. They blurred as tears filled Jessica's eyes. Her sobbing made them shimmer and wiggle.

'Please!' she gasped.

'Shouldn't have called Lane a bitch.'

'I am *sorry*!'

Kramer hunched down. Braced on his elbows, rump high, he lapped up spreading blood. With the tip of his tongue, he probed the shallow cut. Jessica shuddered as his tongue spread the raw edges.

She crashed her cast against the side of his head, crying out as pain lanced up her arm.

The blow knocked his head sideways.

Twisting, she rammed a knee into his hip.

He toppled, and the edge of the bed wasn't there to catch him. He dropped out of sight, slammed the floor.

Jessica rolled, grabbed the side of the mattress and looked down at him. He was flat on his back, an upraised knee resting against the box springs, his other leg straight out, one arm against his side, the other flung out limp against the carpet, its hand open, the razor a few inches beyond his fingertips. His jaw drooped. His open eyes were rolled upward as if gazing at something beneath his upper lids.

He's out, she thought.

She knew out when she saw it; she'd seen enough boxing matches with Riley.

Gasping for air, trembling and nauseous, she swung her legs down. She rose from the bed, and stepped over him. With one foot, she pinned his right wrist to the carpet. She crouched and picked up the razor. Once she had it, she ground her heel against his wrist.

He groaned.

Coming to! Jessica's heart lurched. Her stomach seemed to shrink and go cold.

She stepped off his wrist, turned around and looked down at him. His eyes were squeezed shut, his teeth bared.

She had to do something fast!

She took a deep breath, about to cry out, 'DAD!' But she stopped herself.

Kramer would talk. If he lived, he'd talk. Everyone would find out she'd been sleeping with him. Everyone. Her folks, all the kids at school, Riley.

Can't let him talk.

A chill swept up Jessica's body. Her skin prickled with goosebumps.

Nobody'll blame me. It's self-defense. He broke into the house and attacked me.

She looked down at her wound. Blood still spilled from the S-shaped slice. The skin below it was slicked with shiny red. Her pubic hair was matted and drops trickled down her thighs.

That's my proof, she thought. He cut me. He came to rape and murder me. I had to defend myself.

Kramer opened his eyes.

Jessica rushed to his side and rammed her foot down, driving her heel into his belly. Breath whooshed out of him. His eyes bugged. He half sat up. She dropped onto him, knees landing on his chest and stomach. As his back struck the floor, she swept the razor down at his throat.

His left arm shot up faster than she could imagine. It met her descending forearm just above the wrist. Pain streaked to her shoulder. The razor flew from her tingling fingers.

Kramer's other hand punched her in the spine. As she jerked rigid, he grabbed her hair. He yanked it and bucked beneath her knees, hurling Jessica backward. She crashed against the floor. The impact jolted her, knocked her breathless.

Kramer had one of her legs. He raised it, dragged her by it, propped it high.

Jessica lifted her head and saw her right leg stretched upward, heel on the edge of her mattress. Before she could move, Kramer stomped her knee. As if her leg were a branch. She heard the sharp *crack*, watched her leg cave in beneath his foot, felt an explosion of agony that turned her vision bright red, then black.

When she woke up, she was on her bed. Kramer was on top of her, in her, grunting and thrusting. Her right leg felt as if it were burning from the inside, as if her bones were ablaze. The pain was so fierce that Kramer's ramming penis seemed incidental. She just wished he would get it over with and stop bouncing on her leg.

When she tried to move her outstretched arms, she realized they were tied at the wrists. Probably to her bed posts.

No chance of fighting him.

At last, Kramer finished.

But she knew he wasn't done.

It didn't seem to matter much. She knew it ought to matter, she ought to care. But her mind was fuzzy, couldn't seem to focus on anything except the pain.

The pain couldn't get any worse.

But it did.

It got a lot worse when he started with the razor. So bad that she screamed, and wondered why she hadn't screamed earlier. Dad would hear it. Dad would save her.

Kramer stuffed a rag into her mouth.

He kept on cutting.

Where's Dad?

She passed out.

When she came to, Kramer was hunched over her, licking and sucking on her wounds. He raised his face and gazed at her. Except for his eyes, his face was smeared with blood. Even his teeth were red.

He pulled the rag from Jessica's mouth. He tossed it aside, dropped flat and squirmed up her body. His penis pushed into her. His tongue filled her mouth. He rode her hard as if trying to pound her through the mattress.

Later, she saw him standing beside the bed. He was clean. He was dressed. He had a bundle of newspapers under one arm. He crouched out of sight.

She heard the crackle of papers being crumpled.

She heard the snick of a match.

Kramer stood over her.

'Sleep tight,' he said, 'Don't let the bedbugs bite.'

On his way out, he turned off the light.

But the room wasn't dark for long.

Chapter Twenty-six

Bonnie came to him. She stepped silently toward his bed. She looked lovely, glorious, her blond hair floating around her face. She wore the pleated blue skirt and golden sweater of her songleader costume, but her feet were bare.

Stopping beside Larry's bed, she gazed at him with solemn eyes. 'I've been waiting for you,' she said, her voice as soft as a caress. 'Why haven't you come to me?'

'I . . . I don't know. I've *wanted* to, but . . .'

'Don't you know that I love you?'

Her words quickened Larry's heart.

'You do?' he asked.

'Of course. Why wouldn't I?'

'Why *would* you?' he asked. 'We don't even know each other.'

A sweet smile lifted the corners of the mouth. 'We know each other with our hearts. I love you so much, Larry. And you love me, don't you?'

'Yes,' he said, and felt a hot rush of joy. 'Yes, I love you.'

Then a thought came to him that seemed to crush his heart. 'But you're dead, Bonnie.'

Her laugh was a quiet rush of breath. 'Don't be silly. Do I look dead?'

'You look . . . so beautiful.'

Bonnie stepped closer. She bent over him, her hair drifting down until its tresses brushed against Larry's cheeks. Then her lips met his. They were soft, warm, moist. They parted, and he felt her breath enter his mouth.

He lifted his arms out from under the covers. He placed his hands on Bonnie's sides, caressed her through the sweater, felt the heat of her flesh, the gentle curves of her ribs.

She eased her lips away. 'Do I feel dead?'

'You sure don't,' he murmured through the tightness in his throat. 'You feel wonderful.'

'I've longed so much for you, Larry.'

'I've longed for you, too.'

He slipped his hands under the bottom of her sweater. A tremor swept through him as he touched the velvety skin above her hips.

Then he remembered something else, and again his joy sank into anguish. Though he ached for her, he pulled his hands out from under the sweater and let them drop to the mattress. 'I'm married, Bonnie.'

'Do you love her?'

He wanted to say, 'No.' But he couldn't. 'Yes,' he said. 'I'm sorry. God, I'm sorry. I love Jean, but I love you, too.'

'That's all right,' she whispered, her warm breath touching his lips. 'You can have us both.'

'I don't think Jean would like that.'

'She'll never know. I promise. It'll be our secret.'

Larry felt the covers glide down his body, felt the cool

morning air chill his skin. Bonnie kissed the side of his neck. She kissed his shoulder, his chest.

'No,' he whispered.

'You don't mean that, darling.' Her soft lips pressed his nipple.

He moaned with an agony of desire and loss.

'It wouldn't be right,' he said.

'Love is always right.'

'I don't know.'

'Yes,' she whispered. 'Yes, my love.' She crawled onto him. She straddled him, upright on her knees, her light cotton skirt draping him and keeping out the morning chill. The heat of their bodies seemed to mingle in the air beneath it. Larry knew, somehow, that she wore no panties. He ached for her to sink down, to impale herself, to let him plunge high up into her slick, hugging warmth.

But she didn't. Not yet.

Smiling down at him, she drew her sweater up. He watched it rise slowly, unveiling her sleek belly, the rise of her ribcage, her breasts. They were twin, creamy mounds with pink nipples standing erect. They lifted slightly as she pulled the sweater up past her face. Keeping her arms high, she slipped out of the sleeves. She tossed the sweater to the floor.

Larry raised his hands to her breasts. Lightly, he caressed them. He thought that he had never touched anything so fine.

Smiling down at him, Bonnie guided one of his hands to the smooth valley between her breasts. She moved it up and down, stroking herself with his fingertips. 'Not even a scar,' she whispered.

He remembered the stake.

'Oh,' he said. 'That's right.'

'I'm as good as new. And I'm yours. I'm yours forever.'

She began to ease herself down.

Larry groaned.

This is wrong, he thought. I can't do this. Even if Jean never finds out . . .

But Bonnie was moving slowly lower, lower. He squeezed

her breasts. Lower. He felt as if his penis were being sucked toward her dark, waiting center.

The alarm clock blared.

Larry's eyes flew open.

Bonnie was gone.

A dream. It had only been a dream, and the alarm had cheated him out of its best moments. His chest ached. He felt as if he might weep.

But he felt lucky, too. A few more seconds, and there would've been a mess.

He was sprawled on his back, covered only by a sheet. The sheet jutted up like a tent over his groin.

If Bonnie had slid down onto him . . .

He rolled onto his side. Jean was braced on one elbow, her back to him. As the alarm went silent, she flopped face up and closed her eyes.

Larry reached out and put a hand on her belly. Her skin felt hot through the thin fabric of her nightgown. Her head turned toward him. Her eyes opened a bit, and she made a lazy smile. 'Morning, fella,' she whispered.

He said, 'Mmmm,' and moved his hand up the slick nightgown to her breast. Not like Bonnie's. No fire coursed through him when he touched it. But Jean's breast was soft and warm and familiar, and he felt a fresh stir of arousal as her nipple rose stiff against his palm. He brushed the strap off her shoulder and slipped his hand inside the loose pocket of fabric. Jean moaned. She squirmed as he caressed her. Then, she rolled toward him.

'We're sure feeling our oats this morning,' she murmured.

'Yeah.'

Her fingers curled around his erection. 'You'd better shut the door. Lane'll be getting up any minute.'

On his way back from shutting the door, he watched Jean kick the sheet down to the end of the bed and pull her nightgown up. When it covered her face, Larry's mind flashed an image of Bonnie taking off the songleader sweater.

Their bodies looked very much alike.

Don't think about Bonnie, he told himself. That was just a dream.

And it's crummy to think about her. It's like cheating, like adultery.

But he couldn't stop.

He didn't want to stop.

He closed his eyes as he made love with Jean, and the woman under him ceased to be his wife. She was Bonnie, the Bonnie of the yearbook photos, the Bonnie of his dream: eighteen, beautiful, innocent, eager and gasping and writhing with lust, ramming up against him to meet his thrusts. His Bonnie. His Spirit Queen.

He seemed to explode. He flooded her.

When they were done, she hooked her legs around Larry as if to keep him inside forever. She hugged him hard. He opened his eyes.

Jean gazed up at him, looking haggard and happy.

He kissed her mouth.

He felt like a total shit.

'Something wrong?' she asked.

He shook his head. 'Just that I've gotta go back to the library today. I hate wasting time with research.'

'Why don't I fix you a nice big breakfast before you go?'

'Great.'

Lane smelled frying bacon as she struggled into her jeans.

They're having breakfast? she wondered. What's the big occasion?

She left the zipper down to give herself breathing room, sat on the edge of the bed, and pulled on the new, blue denim boots she'd bought after school yesterday.

Standing up, she admired the way they looked with her white jeans.

Too bad I didn't wear this stuff yesterday, she thought. A blush spread up her skin as she remembered standing on the stool in her short skirt and loose blouse, Mr Kramer standing below her, and the disarray of her clothes after the fall. Then

she remembered his touch. She still felt warm, but her embarrassment turned to pleasure.

Known he'd play doctor, she thought, I would've fallen
sooner.

Lane smiled and shook her head at herself as she stepped
past the closet mirror.

She took a bright blue and yellow plaid blouse off its hanger,
stepped back in front of the mirror, and started to button it.

And stopped.

What if I take off my bra?

The idea made her stomach flutter.

Don't be a dork, she thought. Nobody'll even realize except
Jim, and he'll be wanting to paw me. Mr Kramer probably
wouldn't even notice the difference.

Mr Kramer doesn't have anything to do with it, she told
herself. It'd feel good, that's all.

Besides, my ribs are sore.

Good enough reason.

She took off her blouse and checked herself in the mirror.
Sure enough, the side panel of the bra was pressing against her
bruised ribs.

She reached back, unclasped the bra, and pulled it off.
Holding it between her knees, she slipped into her blouse
again. She buttoned it, tucked it in, and fastened her jeans.

She smiled at herself.

Aren't you the daring one?

The soft fabric, taut against her breasts, felt very good.

Should do this all the time, she thought.

Noway. With most of her blouses, it would show. But this
one had dark, bright colors, and a pocket over each breast.
With the double thickness of the fabric there, it was hardly
even noticeable that her nipples were erect.

Nobody'll know the difference, she thought. Just me.

It sure does feel good.

She turned in a circle once for a final check, then returned
her bra to the dresser drawer. Grabbing her handbag, she
headed down the hallway.

What if Mom and Dad notice?

They won't. Ease up.

The aromas of bacon and coffee made her mouth water as she entered the kitchen. Her parents, still in their robes, were seated at the table, bacon and fried eggs on their plates. 'What's with breakfast?' she asked. 'This doesn't *feel* like Sunday.'

They both looked at her. Neither seemed interested in her chest.

'I'll be spending the day at the public library,' Dad said. 'Mom figured she oughta fill me up.'

'Yeah, I'd hate for him to perish among the tomes.'

Stepping up beside her father, Lane said, 'You could sustain yourself with bookworms.'

'Come on, I'm eating.'

'Mind?' she asked, and reached for a strip of bacon on his plate.

He jabbed his fork at her hand. He stopped just short of poking her.

'I wish you wouldn't fool around like that,' Mom complained. 'You might slip.'

'I might indeed,' he said.

Lane took the bacon and bit it in half.

'There goes my nourishment.'

'Hey, I'm a growing girl.'

'I could certainly start making breakfasts for you,' Mom said. 'Just say the word.'

'The word is "yuck." Who can stomach food at this ungodly hour?'

'You seem to be stomaching my bacon all right,' Dad said.

'Gotta go.' She bent down and kissed his cheek. He swatted her rump. She hurried around the table, kissed her mother, then grabbed her lunch bag out of the refrigerator and hurried from the kitchen. 'See you guys later. I'll probably be late again.'

'Have a good day, dear,' Mom called after her.

From Dad, 'Have fun.'

'I'm going to *school*, guys,' she called from the living room.

She checked her book bag, dropped her lunch inside, then took the car keys from her purse and rushed outside.

The sun felt warm on her shoulders. The mild breeze stirred her hair. A gorgeous day.

The back of the car seat was cool through her blouse, reminding Lane of the missing straps. As she waited for the engine to warm up, she squirmed against the upholstery, savoring how it felt against her back.

Nice.

She cranked her window down and eased slowly out of the driveway.

She headed for Betty's place. On the radio, Anne Murray was singing 'Snowbird.' Lane joined in. She swung her arm onto the window sill and felt the blouse pull snug against her left breast.

Very nice.

Steering with one hand, she swung the car around a corner. 'Snowbird' ended.

A jingle came on signaling the start of a news break.

'This is Belinda Bernard with the top local news stories of the hour.'

'Top of the morning, Belinda,' Lane said.

'. . . died in a fire early this morning in their Cactus Drive home.'

Lane glanced at the radio. Cactus Drive? Died in a fire?

'The deceased were identified as Jerry and Roberta Patterson and their seventeen-year-old daughter, Jessica.'

'My God,' Lane muttered.

'Flames were first noted by neighbors at approximately 4:30 a.m. Firemen arriving at the scene were unable to enter the house to attempt any rescue. Due to the heavy conflagration, however, it's believed that the family expired from smoke inhalation some time prior to the arrival of the fire department. This was confirmed later, when the bodies of the three family members were found in the rubble, still in their beds. The cause of the fire is under investigation, but it is believed that it started in the bedroom of the daughter, Jessica.'

Smoking in bed? Lane wondered.

'The Board of Education met last night . . .'

She turned off the radio.

She felt cold and numb inside.

Jessica dead.

The girl'd been a royal pain, but God! Dead.

How could something like that happen?

Jessica smoked like a chimney. Spent half her life in the girl's john, puffing away. She must've fallen asleep with a cigarette.

Didn't they have a smoke alarm?

Lane rounded a corner. Betty was waiting beside the street. Lane stopped the car, stretched across the passenger seat, and unlocked the door.

'Did you hear?' Betty asked, swinging the door open.

'Yeah.'

'Holy smoke!' She hurled her book bag into the rear, and dropped onto the seat. The car shook. 'I knew that bimbo'd come to a bad end.' She slammed the door.

'She's dead,' Lane muttered.

'Well Jesus, I guess *so*.'

Lane stepped on the gas. 'She didn't deserve that.'

'Smoking in bed, it'll get you every time.'

'God, I can't believe it.'

'I can. Boy, I sure can. Good riddance to bad rubbish. Know what happened yesterday? I went to take a leak after third period, and there she was, sitting on a john with the door wide open, sucking on a butt. I go, "Those things'll give you cancer, you know." And she gives me this look.' Betty demonstrated, wrinkling her nose and curling up her lip. 'And she goes, "Fuck you and the horse you rode in on, lardass." So like I can't say I feel any great amount of sympathy, you know? She did it to herself.'

'And her parents.'

'Yeah. Too bad Riley Benson wasn't sleeping over. That piece of greasy-haired shit would be improved considerably by a good dose of smoke inhalation. Know what I mean?'

Lane nodded. It seemed wrong, knocking Jessica and Benson. But she didn't feel like defending them. They *were* creeps.

She wondered if Benson might actually have been in love with Jessica.

Hard to imagine him loving anyone.

But maybe he did.

'That babe did have some rotten luck,' Betty went on. 'First she gets herself creamed, next thing you know she's a crispy critter.'

Lane turned the radio on, volume high. Willie Nelson and Ray Charles were singing 'Seven Spanish Angels.'

'A hint? A subtle but effective hint?'

'I just don't think we should be bad-mouthing her.'

Ahead, Henry waved from his perch on the boulder in front of his house. He hopped down and picked up his briefcase. 'Salutations, merry-makers,' he said as Lane stopped the car.

Betty climbed out. She held the seat-back forward while Henry scrambled in behind it. Following him, she pulled the door shut.

Lane glanced back at them. Betty had an eager look in her eyes. 'You haven't heard,' she said.

'Heard what?' Henry asked.

Lane started driving.

'Jessica got toasted last night.'

'Huh?'

'Burnt, char-broiled, cooked, incinerated.'

'You mean she's dead?' He sounded perplexed.

'Dead dead dead. She bought the farm. She bit the weenie. Dead.'

'Holy shit,' Henry whispered.

'It would appear that Miss Congeniality fell asleep smoking a cigarette.'

'We're talking about Jessica *Patterson*?'

'Who else, numbnuts?'

'Holy shit,' he said again. His hand clamped over the corner of Lane's seat back. 'Is she shitting me?'

'No,' Lane said. 'It's true. Jessica and her parents were killed in a fire last night.'

'Oh, man.'

'Good riddance,' Betty said.

'Hey, cut it out.'

'Oh, and like she's suddenly a saint now that she's cooked?'

On the radio, Belinda Bernard's voice said, 'We now have an update on the fire that rushed through the home of . . .'

'It just isn't . . .' Henry began.

'Quiet,' Lane said. 'News.'

They were silent.

'. . . are now indicating that a preliminary examination of the charred remains has revealed that all three members of the Patterson family sustained massive, possibly fatal injuries, prior to the fire. Details are still sketchy, but it appears that an intruder may have slain the trio, after which the fire was deliberately set in order to destroy evidence of the crimes. We also have word that a youth seen entering the house earlier last night has been taken into custody for questioning. The identity of the underaged suspect has not been disclosed.'

'Benson,' Betty said. 'Betcha.'

'We now return you to . . .'

'Holy shit,' Henry muttered. 'They were *murdered*.'

'I bet it *was* Benson. Wouldn't put anything past that slime-bag.'

'This is awful,' Lane murmured.

'Speak for yourself.'

'Cool it,' Henry said. 'It's not funny.'

'Maybe not funny, but . . . somehow, deeply satisfying.'

Chapter Twenty-seven

Alone as he drove to the public library, Larry at last had time
to himself, time to ponder what he'd done that morning and
try to relieve himself of the shame.

He'd betrayed Jean.

Not really, he thought. It wasn't that big a deal. You had a
little fantasy, that's all.

You really wanted Bonnie.

Jean didn't know that. She thought it was great.

The girl's dead, for godsake.

I must be nuts, having a dream like that.

Hell, it's perfectly natural. I've been *studying* the poor kid –
looking at pictures of her, reading about her – *I've got her in the
garage*! Who wouldn't start dreaming? I ought to just be glad it
wasn't a nightmare. What if she'd paid her visit the way she
looks now!

Maybe better if she had. Might have scared the shit out of
me, but at least I wouldn't have ended up with a hard-on and
all this damn guilt.

Take it easy, he told himself. It was your subconscious. You
can't control your subconscious.

Bullshit. It was a wish-fulfillment dream. I *wanted* her to
come to my bed. And it wasn't my subconscious that made me
take out my lust on . . .

The radio news interrupted his thoughts.

A family of three murdered here in Mulehead Bend. Their
house set on fire.

One of them, a seventeen-year-old girl.

He wondered if Lane knew the girl. The name didn't sound
familiar, but she must've been a senior at Buford High. Lane
almost had to know her.

691

They couldn't have been very good friends, he thought, or I would've heard the name before. Jessica. No. It didn't ring any bells.

Even if they're just acquaintances, it'll be a shock to Lane. A girl in her own class murdered.

Isn't *anywhere* safe?

Of course not. What are you, an idiot?

You know damn well Mulehead Bend hasn't been exactly a haven. Bonnie, Linda and Sandra are pretty good indications of that. And don't forget Martha Radley. She was over in Sagebrush Flat, but that's right next door.

All high school girls.

Jessica, too.

Larry felt a small tremor of excitement in his belly as he wondered if there might be a connection between Jessica and the others from so long ago.

Didn't seem likely.

What if we triggered something? What if taking Bonnie's corpse . . .?

That's ridiculous.

Besides, the radio'd said that a young man had been taken into custody. More than likely, this was some kind of a lovers' quarrel. Most murders come down to that, or an argument between friends, or robbery.

Maybe this Jessica jilted a guy and he flipped out.

Nailed her parents, too.

In a way, he supposed, that was fortunate. Better they should be dead. Easier on them.

If someone ever did that to Lane, *I'd* rather be killed on the spot than . . .

No, I'd want to kill the bastard first. Cut him up *real* slowly. Make him feel it. Make him . . .

STOP IT!

Larry shook his head sharply, trying to jar apart the idea of Lane being killed.

It won't happen! It can't happen!

It could.

Christ! Why do I do this to myself? She's fine. We're *all*

fine. Forget it.

He swung into the library's parking lot, shut off the engine, and slumped back against his seat. He felt as if he were suffocating. He took deep breaths, trying to calm himself. The armpits of his shirt felt sodden. He wiped his sweaty hands on his pants.

He sighed.

'Me and my damn imagination,' he muttered.

Didn't have that, he thought, wouldn't be an infamous and semi-successful author of horror tales.

Might be happier, though.

He sighed once more, then climbed from the car and headed for the library entrance.

Alice smiled a greeting at him from behind the circulation desk.

'Morning, Alice,' he said. 'Back for another look at those sixty-eight *Standards*.'

'Oh, I think that can be arranged.'

She vanished into her office, and returned with the box of microfiche.

After thanking her, Larry settled down in front of the reader/printer. He searched through the box until he found the fiche labeled *Mulehead Evening Standard*, August 15, 1968 – the day after the story of Bonnie's disappearance. He slipped the plastic card out of its envelope, inserted it into the viewer, and brought the newspaper's front page onto the screen.

Pictures of the three missing girls.

The headline read, 'URIAH RADLEY SOUGHT IN DISAPPEARANCES OF MULEHEAD TEENS'.

'Oh, man.' Larry muttered. He'd expected followup stories, but nothing like this.

> Uriah Radley, whose wife and 16-year-old daughter were mysteriously slain at the Sagebrush Flat Hotel on July 15, is being sought by authorities in connection with the recent disappearances of three Mulehead Bend teenagers.

This startling development was revealed early today by Police Chief Jud Ring, who stated that a witness has identified the former hotel proprietor as the man he saw sitting in a pickup truck near the residence of Bonnie Saxon shortly before the girl vanished.

An attempt to apprehend Uriah Radley ended in failure early this morning when a party of Mulehead Bend police officers, together with County Sheriff's deputies, raided the Sagebrush Flat Hotel but failed to locate the suspect.

It is believed at this time that Uriah Radley has fled the immediate area. A bulletin for his arrest has been issued throughout California, Nevada and Arizona.

Bonnie Saxon, 18, former 'Spirit Queen' of Buford High School, disappeared from her Usher Avenue home on Friday night. The broken window of her bedroom indicated forced entry, and blood was found on her bed. She was the most recent of three local girls to vanish under mysterious circumstances.

On August 10, Linda Latham was abducted while walking home from a friend's house. Prior to that, on July 26, Sandra Dunlap vanished from her home under circumstances nearly identical to those surrounding the disappearance of the Saxon girl.

The information that Uriah Radley had been seen near the Saxon residence Friday night is considered to be a major break in the matter of the three abductions.

'We're very interested in having a chat with Mr Radley,' commented Chief Ring. 'He may or may not have committed the crimes, but we'd certainly like to find out what he was doing in front of the Saxon place at that hour.'

Authorities have speculated that all three teens were the victims of the same perpetrator. It is now believed that the apprehension of Uriah Radley may lead to information regarding their fates and present whereabout.

While the suspect has so far eluded the law, police and deputies are carrying out an exhaustive search of Sagebrush Flat in hopes of locating Radley and/or the missing teens.

A side-bar story told of Christine Saxon, Bonnie's widowed mother, issuing a 'tearful plea' over a local television station. In a 'choked voice,' she begged the kidnapper to release her daughter unharmed. Reading it, Larry's throat tightened.

God, he thought. The poor woman.

The story pointed out that her husband had died in a car accident. Now, she'd lost her only daughter.

He wondered what had become of her. She would probably be in her sixties now, if she was still alive.

Check the phone book?

What would I tell her? I've found your girl's body?

I can't do that. No way.

He knew it would probably be a consolation for the woman to learn, at last, what had happened to Bonnie. She would want to give her a proper burial.

She'll find out, one way or another, when the book comes out.

Hell, she might be dead.

Larry hoped so, then felt guilty for wishing such a thing, then told himself that the woman was probably better off dead, at peace, spared from her endless grief.

But maybe she's still alive, he thought, clinging to the fragile hope that she might someday be reunited with her daughter.

The book will destroy her.

Worry about it later, he told himself. Who knows, she *might* be dead. Or she might be somewhere out of touch and never hear about the book. For that matter, the book might never even be published. What's the point in stewing about her now?

Trying to forget about her, Larry copied the two stories. He put away the microfiche and slipped the next day's *Standard* into the machine.

BIZARRE FINDINGS AT SAGEBRUSH
FLAT HOTEL

Though yesterday's search of Sagebrush Flat failed to locate either Uriah Radley or any clues as to the whereabouts of the three Mulehead teens who disappeared in recent weeks, authorities have revealed the discovery of several strange items in a hotel room which apparently served as the suspect's residence.

The door and windows of the second floor room were found to be decorated with strands of garlic cloves. In addition, no fewer than four crucifixes were said to be in evidence, though it is believed that the Radleys were of the Presbyterian faith, and not Roman Catholics.

By far the most startling discovery, however, was the presence of a hammer and half a dozen shafts of wood which had been whittled to sharp points.

Commented Chief Ring, 'I saw enough movies when I was a kid to know this looks like a man who was in the business of killing vampires. I realize it sounds crazy, but why else would a fellow surround himself with garlic and crucifixes, not to mention making himself a batch of wooden stakes? Uriah always was a strange sort. It could be that the loss of his wife and kid unhinged him completely.'

The Chief went on to speculate that Uriah Radley may have believed vampires were responsible for the slaying of his family. 'Somehow, he just might've gotten it into his head that Sandra Dunlap, Linda Latham and Bonnie Saxon were the guilty ones and that they were vampires. We're operating on that assumption, right now, in our search for the girls.'

Asked about the prospects of finding the three teens alive, Chief Ring responded, 'I can only say that we'll continue searching and hope for the best.'

Larry sat back in his chair and stared at the screen.

My God, he thought, I was right!

He remembered his own speculations, yesterday, after reading about the cremations of Uriah's wife and daughter. He'd wondered, then, if the crazy bastard had vampires on his mind when he ordered the bodies burnt. The possibility had seemed remote.

But the guy had garlic, crucifixes and stakes in his room.

He *did* go after the girls thinking they were the vampires who murdered his family.

Incredible!

Larry frowned, wondering why he hadn't heard of all this before. After what was found in Uriah's room, the news media should've gone wild. You'd think there would've been nation-wide coverage.

Probably did get a lot of attention in rags like *The National Inquirer*, along with the usual array of stories of UFO visits, disemboweled cattle, men giving birth, that kind of thing.

The legitimate media may have covered it in some small way, but Larry couldn't recall anything about the situation. There *were* bigger stories in the summer of 1968: the assassination of Robert Kennedy; the capture of James Earl Ray for the April shooting of Martin Luther King; rioting in the streets because of Vietnam and the King assassination. Hardly surprising if little or no attention was paid to a crazy man running amok in a desert town and kidnapping three teenagers he thought were vampires. Especially if the bodies were never found, if Uriah never got picked up.

Larry copied the story, then continued his search.

A small article in the August 17 issue of the *Standard* indicated that a thorough search of Sagebrush Flat and 'its environs' had failed to turn up the missing girls. Uriah Radley was still at large.

A piece in the August 22 issue indicated that there were no new developments in the matter.

On Sunday, September 1, a service was held at the First Presbyterian Church for Sandra Dunlap, Linda Latham and Bonnie Saxon. Families and friends of the missing girls were present. The girls were remembered. Prayers were offered for their safe return and for the comfort of their loved ones during this terrible ordeal.

Larry noted that the service wasn't called a 'memorial'. The girls were 'remembered', not 'eulogized'. Prayers were said for their return.

He supposed they all knew the poor kids would never be seen again, but they were still clutching onto the small, frail shadow of a hope.

Larry copied the story, swept the other pages across the screen, found nothing of interest, and went on to the next fiche in the box. He scanned one after another, but finally came to the end of September without finding more stories about Uriah or the missing girls.

Neither was there news of any further disappearance. The series had ended with Bonnie. It came as no surprise. After that, Uriah had fled the area.

He'd been gone by the time the cops arrived at Sagebrush Flat. He must've known he'd been recognized while he waited in front of Bonnie's house.

Larry guessed he had taken her back to the hotel and hidden her body under the staircase before striking out for parts unknown. But what about Sandra and Linda? He wouldn't have been in such a hurry with them. Maybe he took their staked bodies out into the desert and buried them in unmarked graves.

On the other hand, maybe he hid them in town the same as Bonnie. All those abandoned buildings. He might've boarded them inside walls or under floors.

I wonder if we could find *them*, Larry thought.

The cops didn't have any luck. Hell, though, they weren't able to find Bonnie and she was right under their noses when they searched the hotel.

Under their noses.

Well, the area under the stairs was enclosed. Hot and dry. She didn't decompose so much as she mummified: that was obvious from looking at her. So maybe there wasn't much to smell.

Larry remembered the smell under the staircase. Dry, dusty, a little bit like the odor of old books with their pages turning brown.

And the aromas from his dream came back to Larry. There was the cozy wool odor of her sweater. Her hair, drifting against his face, had smelled like a fresh morning breeze. Her skin had a faint cinnamon scent. Her breath had been like mint, as if she'd recently brushed her teeth.

Larry leaned back in his chair. He closed his eyes. He could almost smell Bonnie now.

You didn't smell a thing, he told himself. It was all a figment of your imagination.

So real, though.

So real that the memory of it made him long for her.

Had she smelled that way, he wondered, when she was alive?

Would she smell that way if she *came back to life*?

She's not a vampire, Larry told himself. But just suppose she is. Just suppose I pull out the stake and she really is a vampire. Would she be just the same as the Bonnie who came to me this morning?

Would she smell the same? Look the same?

Would she *act* the same?

Would she love me?

Chapter Twenty-eight

With a minute to spare before the start of sixth period, Lane entered the classroom. About half the seats were still vacant. Including Benson's. Including Jessica's.

Walking toward her desk, Lane gazed at Jessica's empty seat.

The girl would never sit there again.

The idea of that seemed black and vast, and Lane felt a hot sick feeling in the pit of her stomach. She sat down and slumped forward, elbows on her desk top, hands on her cheeks, eyes straight forward.

Mr Kramer, she saw, had finished tacking the author pictures to the corkboard. She'd fallen while reaching out with Sandburg, whose calm and solemn face, white hair draping one eye, was now in place next to Frost. After Sandburg, Mr Kramer had put up T. S. Eliot, F. Scott Fitzgerald, and Thomas Wolfe.

I only had four to go, she thought.

The fall had seemed like such a major deal: her clumsiness in letting it happen, her embarrassment at the way so much of her body was revealed to Mr Kramer, the thrill she felt when he touched her. Now, none of that mattered very much. Jessica's death seemed to shrink the importance of everything.

She'd hardly known the girl. She hadn't even liked her.

But ever since hearing the news of the murder, Lane had felt small and insignificant – as if her own life were nothing more than a performance. She was acting in her own stupid little play. And while she dwelled on her petty problems and hopes and desires, safe on her tiny stage, *real* things were happening in a real world nearby. A frightful, alien place full of darkness and violent death.

She didn't like the feeling, not at all. It made everything she did seem so trivial. Even worse was the nagging worry that somehow, sometime, she might *herself* be dragged into the same real world where Jessica and so many other people (everyone, maybe, sooner or later) got crushed.

It scared the hell out of her.

All day, whenever she was reminded of Jessica, Lane had broken into a sweat. Stopping in the restroom on her way to sixth period, she'd sniffed her armpits. They'd smelled okay, thanks to her deodorant, but her blouse was damp under there. Right now, it felt sodden. Perspiration was sliding down her sides, tickling slightly. With no bra to soak up the droplets, they kept going until they were absorbed by her blouse just above her belt.

She wished, again, that she'd worn her bra to school. Not because of the sweat. Because of Jessica. Because leaving it at home seemed like part of her own little drama, childish and coy in light of the real world's horrible intrusion.

Also, she would've liked the security of it. Earlier, she'd savored the loose, free feelings. But after hearing about Jessica, she'd stopped feeling free. Just vulnerable.

The bell rang, startling her.

She sat up straight as Mr Kramer entered the room. He put down his briefcase, took out a small brown book, then stepped to the front of the table. He sat on its edge, resting the book on his thigh. The room fell silent. He scanned the rows. His face looked grim, a little haggard.

'I'm sure you're all aware, by now, of the tragedy that occurred last night. Everyone's talking about it. I imagine some of your other teachers have spoken to you about the situation.'

Pressing his lips together, he shook his head. He frowned at the empty desk.

'Jessica was my student. She was your classmate. Obviously, her death is a shock to all of us, and we'll miss her.'

He looked up from her desk. His eyes briefly met Lane's, then turned away and roamed from face to face.

'I don't have any magic words,' he said, 'to ease the grief we share. But I'm a teacher, and there is a lesson to be learned from this. *The Bible* tells us that, in the midst of life, we are in death. But the reverse is also true. 'In the midst of death, we are in life.' We need to keep that in mind. Life is a precious gift. We should never forget that, or take it for granted. We should savor every moment that is given to us.'

Lane felt her throat tighten.

'We have the present, and that's all we can ever really be sure of. So many of us – and I'm as guilty as anyone – allow our present moments to pass us by, unnoticed, unappreciated, while we occupy our minds with other thoughts. Certainly, we need to work and plan to help things turn out right in our futures.

But we even lose our futures if we spend them worrying about what may come next. When the future arrives for us, it comes as single moments, present moments.

'So if we're to learn anything from what happened to Jessica and her parents, it's this – we need to live life now. We need to notice each second, and fill ourselves with its wonders and mysteries . . . and its joys.'

His final words brought tears to Lane's eyes. She blinked and wiped them away.

He's so right, she thought. Each moment is precious.

This moment is precious, sitting here, listening to Mr Kramer. She realized that she had never felt closer to him, not even yesterday when he was touching her.

'I want to share a poem with you. Then, we'll get on with class.' He lifted the slim volume off his leg and opened it to a bookmark. 'This is by Allan Edward DePrey. It's called, "Grave Musings".' He lowered his eyes and began to read, his clear voice low and solemn:

> If I should sleep, this moonless night,
> Nevermore to rise,
> I'll keep with me the shimmering light
> Of the love in my lady's eyes.
> I'll keep the touch of dewy grass
> Wet on my feet at dawn,
> And how it smells, so sweet, alas!
> After the rain is gone.
>
> I'll keep the flavors I have known
> Of bread and meat and wine,
> And cherish them when I am bone
> Because they taste so fine.

A few of the kids tittered. Mr Kramer looked up from the page. 'If you'd rather not hear the rest of this . . .'

'Go on,' Lane urged him.

'Maybe I *should* skip over some of this,' he said. 'It gets pretty long.' He took a few moments to search the poem, apparently trying to decide where he should resume reading. Then he continued:

> Into the grave with me I'll take
> Each sight and smell and sound
> And pray that they will not forsake
> Me in my sleep beneath the ground—
>
> If memory, in truth, survives,
> The reaper's savage knife
> I'll keep with me my golden prize
> Of what I loved in life.
>
> But if an empty darkness waits
> Bereft of all I've known,
> I shall not curse the cruel Fates
> That cast me there alone.
>
> For I was given years to taste,
> To smell, see, feel and love.
> Though doomed, at last, to charnal waste,
> I had my glorious days above.

Someone in the room said, 'Yuck,' and a few kids laughed.

'I admit the poem has its grim aspects, but I think DePrey's point is well taken – "I had my glorious days above." We have to always keep ourselves aware of those glories.' He shut the book and set it aside. 'Okay,' he said, nodding. 'Let's take out our textbooks and pick up where we left off yesterday.'

When the bell rang, Lane stayed in her seat. The other students filed out. She remembered how, yesterday, Jessica had stopped in the doorway and scowled at her.

The girl should've been enjoying the time she had left, Lane thought. Not giving me crap.

Hell, she didn't know.

703

None of us knows. Any one of us could die tonight.

Instead of striking fear into Lane, the thought reminded her again of Mr Kramer's advice to savor every moment.

She watched him step behind the table and load his briefcase. He met her eyes. He smiled. 'How are you feeling today?' he asked.

'A lot better, thanks.'

'Bruised up?'

'Yeah, some.'

'Well, you'll have to stay out of bikinis for a while.'

Lane felt the warmth of a blush spread over her skin. 'Good thing summer's over,' she said.

'I promise not to make you stand on any more stools.'

'Do you have some papers or something for me?'

'So happens, I do.' He walked to his desk and began searching through stacks of file folders. 'Ah, here we go. Spelling sentences.' He came toward her with the folder and a red pen. 'Make sure you check for everything: spelling, punctuation, grammar. Five points off for each mistake.'

'Right.'

Stopping in front of Lane, he set the folder and pen on her desktop. 'If you have any questions . . .'

'I really liked what you said at the start of class,' Lane told him. She felt daring and embarrassed. 'About appreciating each moment. It was very . . .' She shrugged, and felt her blouse brush softly against her nipples. 'I don't know. It made me feel a lot better about things.'

He looked down at her, sorrow in his eyes. 'I'm glad if it helped. This was a terrible thing. I guess everyone's pretty shocked about it. I know I am, even though Jessica was a bit of a problem in class. Were you friends?'

A corner of Lane's mouth curled up. 'Hardly. But even still . . . When something like that happens . . .'

'I know. It makes us aware of our mortality. If it can happen to her, why not to us?'

'Yeah. I was feeling . . . *little*. Like everything in my life is so petty and trivial compared to the big stuff.'

'You shouldn't.' His hand reached out and stroked Lane's hair. 'You shouldn't feel that way at all.'

'I guess I know that now,' she said, feeling slightly breathless as his hand slipped down to her shoulder. It moved from side to side, sliding the blouse against her skin. 'Each moment is something . . . to be treasured.'

'Exactly.'

Did he notice there was no strap on her shoulder?

'Nothing is trivial,' he said. 'Everything counts.'

'Yeah.'

He rubbed the side of her neck. 'You're one very tense young lady,' he said. 'Your neck muscles feel like rock.'

'Yeah. Hasn't been exactly a banner day.'

'Same here.'

The gently kneading hand sent warmth flowing through her body.

'Does that feel better?'

She nodded. Her head felt heavy.

Mr Kramer stepped behind her. She heard a desk squeak against the floor as it was pushed out of his way. Then, both his hands were on her shoulders, rubbing, squeezing.

'How's that?'

'Wonderful,' she murmured. His fingers moved up and down. The front of Lane's blouse moved with them, caressing her breasts. She took a shaky breath. She lowered her head.

He swept her hair out of the way so it hung past the side of her face. Then he rubbed her neck just below her cars. She felt drowsy, felt as if he were squeezing warm fluid into her head. She shut her eyes. She sighed.

'Nothing like a neck rub to make things right,' he said. His hands moved lower, his gently plying fingers easing down inside the collar of her blouse. They were warm and smooth on her bare skin.

She wondered how she could feel so lazy and so excited, both at the same time.

She felt powerless to move.

Her head wobbled as he massaged her.

The top button of her blouse popped open. Lane knew where his hands were. He hadn't unfastened the button. It had simply pulled out of its hole because of the way he was spreading her collar.

She wished he *had* done it.

She imagined him unbuttoning her blouse, spreading it open, taking her breasts in his big, powerful hands.

'I'd better call it quits,' he said, 'before you get too relaxed to mark the papers for me.'

'Just a little more?' she asked, her voice a quiet murmur.

His hands went away from under her collar. They squeezed her shoulders. 'Some other time. Hey, someone might come in and get the wrong idea.'

She supposed that was true. She couldn't expect Mr Kramer to risk his job for the sake of giving her an innocent massage.

He patted her shoulder in a coach-like fashion. 'Now let's see you grade those papers.' He stepped out from behind her and started walking toward his desk.

'Mr Kramer?'

Looking around at Lane, he raised his eyebrows. His face was slightly red.

'I feel a whole lot better now. Thanks.'

'Glad to help.' He continued to his desk, sat down, and started shuffling through papers.

Lane began to check the spelling sentences. Her neck and shoulders seemed to keep the warmth of his touch. She felt as if she were glowing inside.

She realized that the neck of her blouse was still spread apart. Hunched over the desk, she looked down at herself. Below where the button had pulled open, she saw the shadowy side of her right breast.

Had Mr Kramer noticed?

Probably not, she decided. After all, he'd been standing behind her.

She didn't fasten the button or straighten her blouse, and she remained pleasantly aware of the small gap as she went on correcting the papers.

706

She hoped Mr Kramer was aware of it, too.

Each time she looked up, however, she found him bent over his papers.

Finally he stood up and carried a folder to the far side of the table. He slipped it into his briefcase. 'How's it going, Lane?'

'I've just got a few left.'

'Well, I'm afraid it's time to close up shop. I'll finish them off tonight.'

'Fine.' She arranged them neatly inside the folder, eased out of her seat, and approached the table. Stretching across its top, she handed the folder and pen to her teacher.

As he took them, she saw his eyes lower briefly. A glimpse, then he was looking at her face. 'I sure appreciate that help, Lane.'

'Glad to be of service.' Bending over, she placed her hands on the table and stared at the small book from which he'd read 'Grave Musings'.

She could feel the way her blouse was hanging, its front not touching her chest at all. I can't believe I'm doing this, she thought. Why don't I just rip it open instead of being so tricky?

She felt as if she were blushing from head to toe. But she couldn't bring herself to straighten up.

She opened the book's cover and flipped to the title page. '*Collected Poetry of Allan Edward DePrey*,' she said. 'I've never heard of him,' she added, keeping her eyes on the book.

'Few people have,' Mr Kramer said. 'He's a rather obscure poet from upstate New York, lived around the turn of the century. I happened onto that little volume in a second-hand store when I was a teenager. For a while there, he was my favorite poet.'

'Is everything in here as grim as "Grave Musings"?' Lane asked, turning to the table of contents. Though she glanced at the listed titles, none of them registered.

'Oh, that's one of his more pleasant pieces. He had quite a morbid turn of mind.'

'I wonder if Dad's ever heard of him. Sounds like DePrey might be right up his alley.'

'I tell you what. Why don't you take the book home tonight, let him have a look at it.'

'Could I?' she asked, finally looking up at him.

He smiled. He had tiny speckles of sweat in the whiskers above his lip. 'Just don't lose it.'

'Oh, I won't.' She lifted the book and stood up straight, feeling her blouse pull against her breasts. 'Maybe I'll even read it myself, since he's a favorite of yours.'

He laughed softly. 'Hope you enjoy it. Now, you'd better run along. Thanks again for your invaluable services.'

'My pleasure,' Lane said.

She returned to her desk, gathered her books and binder, and headed for the door. Stopping with one foot in the hallway, she looked around. Mr Kramer was staring at her. 'Hey,' she said, 'thanks again for the neck rub.'

'My pleasure,' he said.

'Bye.'

'Have a nice evening, Lane.'

My evening, she thought, will be a drag after this. But she said, 'Thanks' before leaving the room.

In the corridor, she fastened her button.

Chapter Twenty-nine

The alarm clock startled Larry awake, Friday morning. As Jean stopped the noise, he rolled over and pressed his face into the warmth of his pillow. The bed shook slightly. Jean getting up. He heard her quiet footsteps on the carpet, then the door latching shut.

Alone in the room, he wondered whether he'd dreamed of

Bonnie. If so, he couldn't remember it. He felt a little disappointed. Mostly, though, he felt relieved.

His stomach tightened as he remembered last night's decision.

After supper, Pete had phoned.

'Hey, man,' he'd said, 'What's going on? You freezing me out, or something?'

'No, huh-uh. I've just been busy, that's all.'

'Yeah, well you could've let me know what's going on. You still working on our book?'

'It's coming along fine.'

'Can you talk? Anyone in earshot?'

'No. Okay here.' He'd grabbed the extension in their bedroom. Jean, he knew, was in the kitchen cleaning the dishes. Lane was in the living room, reading the poetry book her English teacher had lent her.

'I've got a little privacy myself,' Pete told him. 'Barb's taking one of her marathon baths. So look, I think we've gotta talk about this thing. You were going like gangbusters over the weekend. Are you all caught up, or what?'

'Pretty much.'

'Well, what's next? Seems to me like we oughta get this show on the road. I've been shopping. I got a good deal on a VHS camcorder. Set me back about thirteen hundred, but I figure it'll be worth it so we can make a video when we pull the stake. Which we oughta *do*. How about tomorrow night?'

'Tomorrow night?' Larry hadn't been able to keep the shock out of his voice.

'Why not? That's what this is all about, right? Why delay it?'

'There are some loose ends.'

Silence. When Pete spoke again, the pushy edge was gone from his voice. He sounded excited. 'What do you mean? What kind of loose ends?'

'I know who she is. I think I know who killed her.'

'Holy shit.'

'It's a long story. Look, why don't we meet tomorrow during

your lunch break. I'll tell Jean I'm going to the library. I'll tell you everything then. How about Buster's?'

They agreed to meet there at noon.

Now, lying in bed, Larry wondered if he should go through with it. He'd made the suggestion, mostly, as a delaying tactic. Pete had taken him off guard, demanding that they pull the stake tonight.

Larry wasn't ready for that. He wasn't sure he would *ever* be ready for that.

What do you want to do, he asked himself, keep her up there forever?

The stake's the mystery, he thought. Once we take it out, Bonnie won't . . . she'll just be a corpse.

She *is* just a corpse.

No. As long as she has the stake in her heart, she's more than that.

What, a vampire?

Uriah thought so.

And Larry knew he was clutching a faint hope that she *might* be one. It was a ridiculous hope, of course. But pulling the stake would take it away. Bonnie would just lie there, a dried up cadaver with a hole in her chest, and it would be over.

He would lose her.

He wouldn't even be able to pretend she might come back to life, fresh and young and beautiful – and his.

So you're stalling Pete, he thought, trying to keep your stupid dream for at least a while longer.

What's the harm in that?

Larry climbed out of bed. He stepped to the window and gazed out across his sunlit yard at the garage. He imagined Bonnie in the dark of the attic, lying in the casket, the end of the stake jutting upright from her chest. He seemed to hear her voice, as clear and sweet as it had come to him in yesterday's dream. *Free me, Pull the stake, and I'll come to you. I love you, Larry. I'll be yours forever*.

Sure, he thought. Fat chance.

* * *

Shortly before noon, he told Jean that he needed to check on a few things at the library. He took a large manila envelope with him when he left the house. He drove to Buster's, a diner near the south end of town, not far from Pete's shop.

He found Pete waiting in a booth at the rear, and scooted in across the table from him.

'Long time no see, *compadre.*'

'Yeah, sorry about that.'

A waitress came, set places for them, and asked if they would like to see menus.

Pete shook his head. 'I'll have the Buster-Burger with the works, chili fries and iced tea.'

'Guess I'll have the same,' Larry said.

'Making it easy on me, huh fellas?' she said. Then, she went away.

'So what's the story?' Pete asked.

Larry dug into his pants pocket, took out Bonnie's ring, and set it down in front of Pete. 'It's hers.'

'What?' Pete picked up the ring and squinted at it.

'I found it on her hand.'

Pete frowned at him. 'And you didn't tell me?'

'I'm telling you now.'

'Well shit, when did you find it?'

'Sunday morning. Before you came over. I know I should've told you about it, but . . .'

'Damn right . . .'

'I wanted to check on a few things first.'

'Why you been holding out on me?'

'I don't know, Pete. I just wanted to see where it would lead. I figured I'd lay it on you once I got the whole story.'

'My pal,' he muttered, then studied the ring again. 'Bonnie Saxon.'

Hearing Pete speak her name, Larry felt an ache of loss. She was no longer his alone.

'You think that's her name?' Pete asked.

'I know that's her name. She was graduated from Buford

711

High in sixty-eight. Like I said, I did some checking.' He opened the manila envelope.

I don't want to do this, he thought.

But he was already committed. Besides, Pete would find out everything, sooner or later. Best to get it over with.

He slid out the Spirit Queen photograph of Bonnie. It fluttered in his trembling fingers as he passed it to Pete and took the ring back.

Pete's eyes widened. He pursed his lips. 'This is *her*?'

'Yeah.'

'Man!'

'Yeah.'

'She's a fuckin' *knockout*.'

'I know.'

He shook his head. 'So this is our babe.'

Our babe. I shouldn't have done it. Should've kept her to myself.

'Where'd you get this?'

'A school yearbook.'

'Man, you *did* do some checking. What else have you got?'

'Let me have it back,' Larry said, holding out his hand. 'Somebody might see it. There could be people in here who knew her.'

Pete stared at the picture for a few more moments, then gave it back to him. Larry slipped it inside the envelope. He pulled his stack of photocopies halfway out. 'There's too much here for you to read right now. I'll make copies of them, if you want.'

'What do they say?'

Larry let them slide out of sight, and set the envelope down beside him. 'It's a long story. I had to spend a couple of days searching back-issues of the town paper.'

'Come on, man. Give.'

Larry waited while the waitress approached with their meals. She set down the plates and drinks. 'Enjoy, fellas,' she said. Then, she was gone.

'It started with two murders in the Sagebrush Flat Hotel.'

While they ate, he told Pete how the town had been abandoned after the mine failure; how the Radleys had remained, living in their hotel, after everyone else had left. He told about Uriah's trip to Mulehead Bend, the trouble with his pickup, and how he'd walked the final miles only to find his wife and daughter slain in the hotel. He gave Pete the official speculation that bikers or other transients were responsible.

'But Uriah thought they'd been killed by vampires,' he said.

'That wasn't in any newspaper,' Pete said.

'He had his wife and daughter cremated so they wouldn't come back to life.'

'You guessing, or what?'

'Just let me go on.'

'Well, how about sticking to the facts?'

'Okay. Facts. The Radley women were murdered on July 15. On July 26, a teenaged girl named Sandra Dunlap was abducted from her parents' home right here in Mulehead. Blood was found on her bed. On August 10, another girl vanished. This was Linda Latham. She was apparently kidnapped on her way home from a friend's house. Bonnie Saxon . . .'

'That's *our* gal . . .'

'Right. She was taken from her mother's home on the night of August 13. Blood was found on her bed the next day.'

'Just like the other one, huh? Dunlap?'

'That's right. All three girls were about the same age. They all disappeared within a month after the Radley murders in Sagebrush Flat. The police had absolutely nothing to go on. Until Bonnie was taken. That night, a witness spotted Uriah Radley waiting around in front of her house.'

'The guy from Sagebrush?'

'Right. So the cops went looking for him. They searched the hotel. They didn't find him or the missing girls, but they found some pretty interesting stuff in one of the rooms: crucifixes, garlic cloves, a hammer and some pointed wooden stakes.'

'Holy shit. So you're telling me this Uriah guy is the one

who snatched the teenagers?'

'It sure looks that way.'

'And he's the one who staked our gal.'

'Probably the others, too.'

'Man, this is *far* out.'

'You're telling me?'

'Were the other two found?'

'Not that I know of. Neither was Uriah, apparently.'

'So what do you think?' Pete asked. 'You think this Uriah guy went off his rocker and thought he was killing the vampires that nailed his family?'

'It sure looks that way.'

'Jesus, our book's gonna be a blockbuster for sure! Now, if we just pull the stake tonight and she *is* a vampire – gangbusters!'

Larry's heart quickened. 'Not tonight.'

'Why the hell not? We've got the whole story. Everything but the finish.'

'There's still a loose end.'

'Okay. Your famous "loose end." What is it?'

Larry didn't know. But he had to find a reason to delay the pulling of the stake.

Suddenly, he saw the loose end. It was obvious.

'Who put the brand new lock on the hotel door?' he asked. 'Who covered the break in the stairway landing? I think it might be Uriah. I think he's returned to Sagebrush Flat.'

Pete, wiping his mouth with a napkin, stared at Larry. He lowered the napkin. He stroked one side of his thick mustache. His eyes narrowed. 'God almighty,' he muttered. 'I bet you're right. Maybe he's our friend the coyote eater.'

'What if we can find him?'

'What if we can *bust* him! A citizen's arrest! Jumping fucking Judas, the *publicity*! Lar, you're a genius!'

A genius? He felt as if he had just stepped off a cliff.

'We'll go out there tomorrow,' Pete said. 'We'll tell the wives we're going target shooting. They didn't want to come along last time, they'll be glad to get rid of us. And we'll drive out to Sagebrush Flat and nail us a killer.'

714

Chapter thirty

'I asked Henry and Betty to come with us tonight,' Lane said.

Jim, chewing a mouthful of apple, suddenly looked as if he'd gnashed a worm. His voice came out muffled.

'You gotta be kidding.'

'You don't mind too much, do you?' she asked.

'Mind? Shit! You *are* kidding, right?'

'I think it'll be nice.'

'How could you do this to me? We haven't been out together in *weeks*, and now we've gotta take along those two rejects?'

'They're my best friends, Jim.'

'That doesn't mean you've gotta take 'em everywhere you go. Shit. They'll ruin everything.'

'No, they won't.'

'Oh, right. Sure. *Damn*. Can't you just tell 'em you changed your mind?'

Lane shook her head. 'I knew you'd cause a stink about this.'

'Then why you do it?'

'I felt like it, okay?'

Scowling, Jim turned away from her and bit out a chunk of apple with an angry snap of his teeth.

Lane gazed at the remains of her ham sandwich. She thought she might choke if she tried to eat any more.

A rotten trick to pull on the guy. Maybe I *should* tell them I changed my mind.

Damn it, though, she didn't want to be alone with him. Asking Henry and Betty to come along had been a way to squirm out of the situation: either Jim would call the whole thing off, or the presence of her friends would keep him in line. At least as long as they were in the car. Once Jim dropped them off, she'd be on her own.

I can handle him, she told herself.

But maybe I won't have to.

'Would you rather skip the whole thing?' she asked.

Jim faced her. His scowl was gone. There was a look of hurt in his eyes. 'Is that what you want?'

He does care about me, she reminded herself. Maybe he even loves me.

Lane knew she didn't love him. Maybe once. Not any more. She'd seen too many samples of his juvenile behavior: his pettiness, his meanness toward her friends, his constant preoccupation with sex as if all he really cared about was her body, as if his whole aim in life was to score with her. Why couldn't he be kind and sensitive? If he were only more like Mr Kramer, there wouldn't be a problem.

But they'd been very close. She supposed she still cared about him. She knew she didn't want to hurt him.

She put a hand on his arm. 'No. Let's go out tonight. I want to.'

'I guess I can stand those two for a few hours. If I have to.'

'Who knows? You may even end up having a good time.'

'Sure,' he muttered.

'Let's see a smile.'

He bared his upper teeth.

'A smile, not a snarl. You look like an old hound with a burr up its ass.'

That brought a real smile, and a small laugh.

'Much better,' she said.

She realized that her appetite had returned. She bit into her sandwich. As she chewed, she said, 'Just wait and see. We'll have a great time.'

Jim reached behind her. He rubbed the middle of her back, sliding her blouse against her bare skin. 'Nice,' he said softly. 'Nothing in the way. You'll leave it off for me, won't you? Tonight? I'll be real nice to your pals.'

'We'll see,' she muttered.

'Oh, come on. You been coming to school without it, you won't need it for the movies.'

'In school, you have to keep your hands to yourself.'

'Don't *have* to. I'm just too much of a gentleman to take advantage.'

'Sure.'

He grinned. 'Besides, I'm no idiot. If I got cute, you'd start up wearing the damn things again.'

'You better believe it.'

He continued to caress her back. 'I love it,' he said, 'just knowing you got nothing on in there.'

'Cool it, huh?'

When Lane entered the classroom just before the sixth period bell, she found Riley Benson in Jessica's seat. He was slumped low, legs stretched out, ankles crossed. He didn't look at her.

Why's he at Jessica's desk? she wondered.

It came as no surprise that Benson was back in school. She'd learned from news reports that 'the suspect' had been released by the authorities, and she'd already seen him a few times today in the hallways and cafeteria.

But it seemed pretty weird to plonk himself down at Jessica's desk instead of his own.

Lane could only think of one reason for that: he missed her. Sitting where she used to sit, maybe he felt closer to her.

She looked at him.

Poor bastard, she thought.

His head turned, and he glared at her. 'What're *you* staring at?'

'I'm sorry about Jessica,' she said.

'Yeah? Well, fuck you.'

'I was just trying to be nice,' she muttered.

'Yeah? Who needs it?'

In a soft voice, she said, 'You don't have to be such a tough guy all the time.'

'You don't have to be such a fuckin' goody-two-shoes.'

'Did the police treat you okay?'

'Cram it, huh?'

'Why won't you let anyone be nice to you?'

'*You* wanna be nice to me?' He suddenly drew in his legs and lunged sideways, leaning out over the aisle and grabbing Lane's arm. He tugged her from her seat. As her rump hit the floor, he dragged her closer.

'What're you *doing*?' she cried out. 'Stop it!'

She heard other kids in the classroom suddenly shouting: 'Leave her alone' and 'Benson, you turd!' and 'Somebody *do* something!'

Benson released her arm. Clutching her hair and chin, he twisted her face upward. 'Wanta be nice to me, huh?'

'Somebody stop him!' a girl yelled.

Benson spit. The saliva spattered Lane's tight lips. He let go of her chin and rubbed the spit around her mouth and cheeks.

'What's going on here?' A shout. Mr Kramer's voice.

Benson thrust Lane away. She caught herself with an elbow, and winced as pain shot up her arm. With the back of her other hand, she wiped the spittle from her face. The stuff had a sweetish, sickening odor like the smell of a sneeze.

'Benson, you son-of-a-bitch!'

'Fuck you, man!'

Sitting up and holding her elbow, Lane watched Mr Kramer stride toward the front of the desk where Benson sat.

'Hey, man, you better not touch me!'

The teacher leaned over the desk, clutched the long hair on top of Benson's head, and jerked him into the other aisle. His right fist smashed Benson's face. The boy's head snapped sideways. Lane saw spit fly from his mouth. Mr Kramer released the hair, and Benson slumped to his knees.

'Apologize to Miss Dunbar.'

'Eat shit, fag.'

'Cream him!' a guy advised from the rear of the room.

Benson looked up at Mr Kramer. The way the boy's face was red and contorted, Lane thought he might start to cry. In a shaky voice, he said, 'You're gonna get it. You hit me, you fag bastard. I'm gonna have your job.'

Mr Kramer picked him up by his shirt front, glared in his face and shook him. 'Apologize to my student.'

'It's all right,' Lane said, getting to her feet. 'Please. Can't we just forget it?'

'Say you're sorry, Benson.'

'Okay, okay, I'm sorry.'

'Tell her.'

Benson turned his face toward Lane. He said, 'Sorry.' He looked as if he wanted to kill her.

'Very good,' Mr Kramer muttered. 'Now get the hell out of here.' He shoved the kid backward and let go. Benson stumbled, tripped over his own motorcycle boots, and fell sprawling.

A few kids laughed, but most watched in silence.

Benson scurried to his feet and ran for the rear door. 'You're gonna be sorry!' he shouted back, his voice high-pitched and trembling. 'Both of you! Just wait!' Then he darted into the hallway.

When he was gone, Heidi began to clap. The rest of the class joined in, and in seconds the room was thundering with applause.

'Stop it,' Mr Kramer said. 'Everybody settle down.' He stepped over to Lane. 'Are you all right?' he asked.

She nodded. 'I'd like to wash my face.'

'Maybe you should see the nurse.'

'No, that's okay. I'm not hurt. Really. I just want to wash off the spit. If I could have a restroom pass . . .'

'I'll escort you there myself, then drop by the principal's office to have some word about our friend.' Turning to the class, he said, 'I'll be out of the room for a few minutes. Take out your books, and make good use of the time. When I come back, I want to find everyone quiet and busy. Understood?'

He followed Lane into the hallway. She looked both ways. No sign of Benson or anyone else.

Side by side, they walked toward the restroom. Her leg felt weak and shaky.

'What started off Benson, anyway?' Mr Kramer asked.

'I don't know. I told him I was sorry about Jessica, that's all.

I was trying to be nice to him, and all of a sudden he grabbed me.'

'Some people are best just left alone.'

'Guess so. Thanks for coming to the rescue.'

'I'm just sorry I wasn't quicker about it. Seems like I'm never quite on time when it comes to helping you out of jams.'

Oh yeah, she thought. My fall, too.

'Sorry I keep causing you all this trouble,' she said.

'No trouble. But I'm starting to wonder if you might be accident prone, or something.'

'Didn't used to be.'

'Just in my room, huh?' He smiled.

'Looks that way.'

They stopped at the double doors of the girls' restroom. 'I'll wait here while you go in and take a look around.'

'You don't think Benson . . .?'

'Never hurts to be careful, Lane.'

She pushed open one of the doors and entered. The air reeked of stale smoke. Though the place appeared deserted, she checked each of the stalls. About half the toilets were unflushed, all the seats looked wet, and so did the tile floor around each fixture. But Benson wasn't lurking about. Feeling a little disgusted, she returned to the door and opened it.

'Nobody here, Mr Kramer.'

'Fine. I'll see you back in the room.'

As he walked away, Lane let the door swing shut. She stepped to a sink, turned on the hot water, and pumped greenish-yellow liquid soap into her palm. Though her face was dry, she could still smell Benson's saliva. She started washing.

Sure isn't my day, she thought.

The crud. Why would he want to do something like that?

I should've known better than to mess with him. Now he'll really want to get me.

Even worse, Mr Kramer might get into trouble for slugging him.

Lane wished she had stayed home. If she'd been absent, none of this would've happened with Benson. She even would've had a good excuse for breaking off tonight's date. Should've just stayed in bed this morning and pretended to be sick.

It'll be all right, she told herself. It isn't the end of the world.

And Mr Kramer was terrific.

She dried with paper towels. When she finished, she saw in the mirror that her skin was a little red around her mouth and chin. Her eyes had a weird, dazed look. She shook her head as if to wake herself up. Then she tucked in her blouse and left the restroom.

Arriving at the front door of the classroom, she glanced in. Mr Kramer hadn't returned yet. She heard quiet murmurs and laughter. Sounded like everyone was behaving – sort of. But she didn't want to step inside until the teacher was there. Everyone would stare at her, ask questions, offer comments. So she stepped away from the door and leaned back against a locker.

Finally, Mr Kramer came strolling up the corridor. She stood up straight when he stopped in front of her.

'Are you feeling all right?' he asked.

'Yeah. How did it go in the office?'

'I explained the situation. It looks as if our friend Benson will find himself transferred to Pratt.'

Pratt was the 'alternate school,' mostly designed as a holding pen for students with chronic behavior problems.

'God, I feel like it's all my fault,'

'Benson already had one foot in Pratt's door. This just nudged him the rest of the way. My only regret is that you had to be one of his victims. It makes me sick when something like that happens to a sweet kid like you.'

His words set a pleasant warmth flowing through Lane.

'Come on,' he said. 'I've got a class to teach.'

She followed him into the room.

With a minute remaining before the final bell, Mr Kramer read off the names of the four students chosen to accompany him to the City College production of *Hamlet*. 'Are all of you still planning to make it?' he asked.

They nodded, muttered 'Yes' and 'Sure.'

'Okay. Jerry and Heidi,' he said to the alternates, 'it looks like you're out of luck. Sorry. Maybe there'll be another opportunity later in the year. I want you others to stay in your seats for just a second after the bell rings, and I'll fill you in on the situation.'

Class ended. Everyone filed out except Lane, George, Aaron and Sandra.

'Okay,' Mr Kramer said. 'Curtain is at eight thirty tomorrow night. I'll pick each of you up in my car between about seven and eight, so write your address on a piece of scrap paper and hand it to me before you leavet the room. Any questions?'

'What should we wear?' Sandra asked.

'I think a sports coat and tie would be appropriate for the guys. As for you two young ladies, this isn't the prom, but I'd like you looking good. After all, you'll be representing Buford High. Anything else?'

There were no more questions.'

Lane took out her binder. She wrote her address on a sheet of loose-leaf paper, and waited at her desk while the other students gave their slips to Mr Kramer. When they were gone, she approached him.

'Thank you,' he said, taking her paper.

'Do you have some work for me?'

Smiling, he shook his head. 'This is Friday, Lane. Why don't we both knock it off early? Besides, after what Benson put you through, I'd think you might want to get out of here.'

'Oh, I kind of enjoy helping you.'

'There's always next week, if you're that eager.'

'You're sure you don't want me to stay?'

'I'm sure. Thanks, though.'

'Well, let me get the poetry book for you.' She returned to her desk, and crouched to take it from the rack under the seat. 'Dad read quite a bit of it,' she said, looking over her shoulder.

'He'd never heard of DePrey. He thought the poems were pretty neat.'

'Glad to hear it. I'm looking forward to meeting him tomorrow night.'

Lane stood up, turning, and handed the book to her teacher. 'I read the whole thing, myself.'

'Terrific. I hope you didn't have any nightmares.'

She smiled. 'None that I remember.'

'Why don't you get your things together?' he said. 'I'll walk you out to the parking lot. I'm sure Benson's long gone, but . . .'

'Never hurts to be careful,' she interrupted, repeating what he'd told her in front of the restroom.

'I couldn't have put it better, myself.'

'I'll have to stop by my locker,' she said.

'No problem.'

It took Mr Kramer a few minutes to get ready. Finally he said. 'All set,' and they left the room. Several kids were still in the hallway, standing in front of open lockers or heading out, some talking with friends, some laughing. Lane wished they were all gone, the school deserted except for herself and Mr Kramer.

'Right. And what would you do, throw yourself into his arms?'

They walked in silence. Lane searched her mind for something to say – something that might force him to see her as a woman, not just as a student.

Ask about his love life, she thought, and rolled her eyes upward. Sure thing. That'd be subtle. Besides, what if he *is* gay? No way. He couldn't be. Not Mr Kramer.

She arrived at her locker. 'I'll just be a second,' she said.

'No rush.'

She shifted her load of books to her left arm and hugged them against her chest.

'Here, I'll hold them for you.'

'Oh, I can . . .'

'Chivalry ain't dead yet,' he said, setting down his briefcase. His left hand braced the bottom of the stack. His right hand slipped between the top book and her breast. It pressed against her, warm through the blouse. A knuckle rubbed her stiff nipple. She felt a warm, trembling rush. Then, his hand was gone.

She turned to her locker, bent over, and began to spin the dial of its combination lock.

Did he touch me there on purpose? she wondered. No. It was just an accident. But there was no possible way he could've not noticed what was against his hand.

She got the combination wrong.

She got it wrong again.

'You're sure this is the right locker?' he asked.

'Yeah. I'm just not thinking straight.'

'Rough day.'

She smiled at him. 'It's getting to be the story of my life. If I'm not falling off astool, I'mgetting attacked.'

She tried the combination again. This time, it worked. She opened her locker. Mr Kramer didn't touch her at all when he returned the books. She put some away, kept others, struggled to concentrate on which of those in her locker she would need for homework. Finally, she took out her denim book bag. When it was full, she buckled it shut and closed her locker. She lifted the bag by its shoulder straps.

'All set?' Mr Kramer asked, picking up his briefcase.

'Yeah. I'm sorry it took so long.'

'I assure you, I have nothing in my immediate future more important or enjoyable than the task of escorting a beautiful young lady to her car.'

Lane felt herself blush and smile. 'I bet you do,' she said, and started walking beside him.

'To be honest, I don't have much of a social life.'

'Oh, sure.'

'It's true, I'm afraid.'

'Well . . . what do you do with your spare time?'

'I read. I go to movies and plays.'

'Don't you . . . see anyone?' Lane grimaced. She couldn't believe she had asked that.

'No,' he said. He glanced at her, then looked quickly away. 'I was engaged to be married. Her name was Lonnie. She was a lot like you, Lane: lovely, intelligent, cheerful, quick to poke fun at things, including herself. But . . .' He shook his head sharply. 'Anyway, I guess I'm still not over her.'

'I'm sorry.'

She wanted to ask what happened to Lonnie, but didn't dare. Already, her probing may have opened a wound.

'Well,' he said, 'I guess we all have our crosses to bear.' He pushed open the heavy exit door, and followed Lane outside.

The sun was warm on her face. A stiff autumn wind was blowing. It tossed her hair, fluttered her blouse, pressed her skirt against her legs, caressed her. She took a deep breath, savoring the fine feel of walking with Mr Kramer on such an afternoon.

He thinks I'm just like Lonnie, she told herself. The woman he loved.

'It's the red Mustang, isn't it?' he asked as they entered the parking lot.

She turned to him, smiling, and the wind flung wisps of hair across her face. 'How did you know?'

'I notice things,' he told her.

The way he said it, Lane knew he had more in mind than her car. Did he want her to realize that he'd noticed the feel of her breast when he took the books from her? Or maybe that he was aware of her feelings for him? Could he sense that she'd fallen in love with him?

I'm not in love with him, she told herself. Good God, he's a teacher. He's probably ten years older than me.

Ten years isn't such a big deal, she thought. And he won't be my teacher after I graduate.

Dream on, stupid. Don't kid yourself. He's not interested.

She stopped beside her car, and took out the keys.

'Well,' Mr Kramer said, 'I guess you didn't need a body guard, after all.'

'I'm glad you walked me out, anyway. Thanks.' She opened the door, swung her book bag onto the passenger seat, and

725

climbed in. While she folded the sun shade, she said, 'You won't be in trouble for hitting Benson, will you?'

'I doubt it. He had it coming.'

She twisted around and tossed the cardboard shade onto the back seat. Then she smiled out the open door at Mr Kramer. 'You know, you'll be a legend around here once it gets around that you cleaned his clock.'

'Well, that would be unfortunate. It's a shame when people are admired for acts of violence. I'd much rather be known as someone who is caring and sensitive.'

'You already are that,' Lane said. 'At least as far as I'm concerned.'

'Thank you, Lane.' For long moments, he stared into her eyes. Then, he swung the door shut.

She cranked the window down. 'Do you need a ride or anything?'

'My car's just in the other lot.'

'I could give you a ride over to it.'

Dumb! Can't you be a little more obvious?

'That's all right. Take it easy, now. I'll see you tomorrow night.'

'Okay. Bye, Mr Kramer.'

Lane watched him walk away, the wind mussing his dark hair and making his shirt cling to his back. She gazed at his broad shoulders, the curves of his shoulder blades, the way his shirt tapered down to his waist. Today, he didn't have the wallet in the back pocket of his slacks. The fabric was tight against his rear. The mounds of his buttocks took turns flexing as he walked.

I notice things, too, she thought.

Then, Mr Kramer stepped behind a parked car.

Lane slid her key into the ignition.

Chapter Thirty-one

Lane knocked, opened the door, and leaned into her father's office. 'Jim'll be here any minute,' she said. 'Do you want to come out and harass him?'

'I'll give the kid a break tonight,' he said, pushing a key to make his computer screen go blank as she stepped into the room.

'Writing more dirty stuff?'

'Yep.'

Lane lowered a finger toward the 'page down' button on his keyboard.

'Ah-ah!' He swatted her hand away.

'Aw, come on. I'm a big girl.'

He looked up at her, smiling. Then his smile slipped away. 'You'll be careful, won't you?'

'Yes, Daddy.'

'I mean it. I'm not at all sure you should be going out tonight, what with this Benson character and everything.'

'This isn't one of your books, you know.'

'I know. It's real life, and that's worse. Look what happened to that Jessica girl.'

'Benson didn't do that.'

'What makes you so sure?'

'Well, the cops let him go.'

'Cops have been known to make mistakes, honey. And even if he had nothing to do with it, he showed himself to be violent in class today. And he threatened you. So don't pretend there's nothing wrong. I want you to be very careful.'

'I will be. And it's not as if I'll be alone. Nobody is going to attack me with Betty around.'

Larry laughed. 'Nasty.'

'Inherited it from you, along with my allergies.'

She heard the doorbell ring. 'He's here,' she said. Bending down, she kissed her father. 'See you later.'

'Have fun. And I mean it, keep your eyes open.'

'Righto,' she said, turning away. '*Adios*.'

She pulled the door shut, and hurried into the living room. Jim was talking to her mother. He smiled at her. He looked handsome in his tan chamois shirt, corduroy pants and sneakers. She realized she was glad to see him in spite of their frequent quarrels.

'Hi ho,' she said.

'Lane,' he said. A red hue colored his face. She wondered what had brought that on. Jim wasn't a guy who often blushed. 'You look very nice,' he said.

She said, 'Thanks.' If he was disappointed, it didn't show. But Lane knew he couldn't be very happy that she'd worn tight blue jeans instead of a skirt, and a thick v-neck sweater over her blouse.

She kissed her mother.

'Have a good time, you two,' Mom said. 'And don't stay out too late.'

'We will and we won't,' Lane told her.

Mom shook her head, rolled her eyes upward.

'Have a nice evening, Mrs Dunbar,' Jim said.

She thanked him. As they walked across the yard, Lane heard the front door bump shut. She glanced back. The porch light came on, lighting the entrance with a yellow glow.

Jim's car was parked at the curb. He opened its passenger door for Lane, then strode around the front of the car and climbed in behind the steering wheel. He inserted the ignition key but didn't start the engine. He turned to Lane. 'You really do look terrific,' he said.

'I figured it's too cold for a skirt.'

'That's okay.' He was silent for a moment. Then he said, 'Are you wearing it?'

'Wearing what?'

'You know.'

Lane grinned. 'Aren't you the guy who can spot that sort of thing a mile away?'

'Yeah. But the sweater.' He reached out. His hand curled

around the back of Lane's neck. She scooted across the seat, turned to Jim, kissed him. The hand on her neck slid upward, fingers pushing into her hair and easing her head forward, pressing her lips harder against his open mouth. His other hand closed on her right breast. 'Yeah,' he said into her mouth.

'Happy?'

'Yeah.'

It was nothing like the gentle, accidental touch of Mr Kramer's hand. Jim rubbed her breast hard through the sweater and blouse. His tongue thrust into her mouth. He squeezed her nipple. The pain made her squirm. She forced his hand away and freed her mouth.

'That's enough,' she whispered. 'Come on. We've got to pick up the others.'

'Yeah, okay. Shit.'

'You promised to be nice,' she reminded him.

'I know. Just watch. I'll be great. I love you so much, Lane.'

'Or at least my boobs, huh?'

A mean thing to say, she realized. Jim couldn't help it if they turned him into a sex maniac. After all, she thought, he's just a horny teenager.

'I love everything about you,' he said, not sounding offended by her remark. 'And I'd like to kiss you everywhere.'

'Oh, man. Cool off, huh?'

'I'm cool, I'm cool,' he said, and started the car.

Lane scooted across the seat and fastened her safety harness. As he drove, she gave him directions to Betty's house. 'Henry'll be there, too,' she added.

'I can hardly wait.'

'You promised.'

'I'm a man of my word,' he said. 'Do we have to sit with them at the movies?'

'Yep.'

'God, the things I do for you.'

'I'm worth it, right?'

'You know it.' He reached over and squeezed her thigh. His hand stayed there, rubbing her through the denim. It felt good.

But when he moved it higher, she guided the hand down to her knee.

'Behave,' she said. 'And make a left.'

He made the turn onto Betty's street, and Lane saw her two friends standing together in front of the mobile home.

'Here goes nothing,' Jim muttered. He stopped.

Lane twisted around in her seat and unlocked the back door for them. 'Greetings, good folks,' Henry said as he scurried in. 'James, Lane. Sounds like a picturesque London road. James Lane.'

'Hi-ya, guys,' Betty said, squeezing into the car.

'Hello,' Jim said. He sounded pleasant enough.

'How's it going?' Lane asked, looking back at them.

'We're fine,' Betty said. 'What about *you*?'

'Great.'

'Really?'

'Yeah,' she insisted.

'Why wouldn't she be?' Jim asked, sounding a little annoyed as he made a U-turn.

'Oh, I don't know. Unless maybe it has a tad to do with a certain Riley Benson.'

Lane felt her skin go hot.

'What about Benson?' Jim asked.

'Oh, nothing. Just that he jerked Lane out of her seat in English class today and hocked on her face.'

'What?' Jim blurted.

'Christ, Betty.'

'That's what Heidi told me, and she was there.'

'Did he really spit on you?' Henry asked. He sounded concerned.

'Yeah.'

'*Benson spit on you?*'

'It's no big deal,' Lane said. She had realized everyone would find out about it, sooner or later. But she wished it hadn't happened this soon.

'I'll kill the cock-sucker!'

'I'll help,' Henry said.

'Mr Kramer already punched him out,' Lane explained. 'And he's being sent to Pratt.'

'*I'll* send the fucker to Hell.'

'Take it easy, Jim. Okay? My God, his girlfriend was just murdered. He's having a tough time.'

'It'll get a lot tougher . . .'

'It's no reason to take it out on you,' Henry told her. 'That guy's such a rectum. He always has been.'

'That's right,' Betty said. 'He was a shit-chute long before Jessica got her ticket canceled.'

'Look,' Lane said, 'I'm the one he messed with. I'd like to just forget about it, all right? It's over. It's finished. Now, why don't we talk about something else and enjoy ourselves?'

'I'm gonna kill him,' Jim said.

'Shut up about it!' Lane snapped.

He did.

There was a long silence.

Finally, Lane said, 'I guess I'm lucky to have friends like you guys. I don't want anyone trying to nail Benson because of me, but it's nice to know you care enough to be pissed at him.'

'I'll piss *on* him,' Jim said.

'Hey!'

'Okay, Okay, I won't.'

'Besides,' Henry put in, 'Benson would probably enjoy it. He'd be right in his element.'

'Hen,' Jim said, 'I'm starting to like you.'

'You're not so bad yourself.'

'The jock and the nerd,' Betty said. 'What a pair.'

'You got a nifty pair yourself there,' Henry said, and Betty squealed as he did something to her.

Jim glanced back and grinned.

'Keep your eyes on the road,' Lane warned.

Betty cried out, 'Don't you . . . ! Ow!'

'Oh, that didn't hurt.'

'Did too.'

'But this might.'

'Don't you *dare*!' She shrieked, then giggled.

731

'Are we having fun yet?'

'No! Yes! No, *stop* that!'

'Hope they don't act like this in the movies,' Lane said. 'They'll get us all kicked out.'

'Oh, I'll be a model of decorum,' Henry assured her.

Betty yelped. It was followed by a smack, and Henry said, 'Ow! You didn't have to slug me.'

'Want another one, four-eyes?'

Jim looked at Lane and shook his head.

It was Henry's idea that they sit in the last row of the movie theater. 'That way,' he explained, 'you don't have to worry about who's behind you.'

'The dink won't sit anywhere else,' Betty said, following Lane into the row. As they sat down, she added, 'He's paranoid.'

Leaning forward, Henry looked past Betty and said, 'Did you read *Curtains*?'

'Dad's book? Yeah.'

'Remember he had that lunatic sitting behind people in the movies and slashing in their throats? Makes a person think, you know?'

'Makes *me* think you shouldn't read that kind of book,' Lane told him.

'Better a wall at your back than a stranger. You just never know. Until it's too late.'

'Spare me,' Betty muttered.

'I may be sparing us all. You'll thank me for it when nobody rips open your jugular.'

The theater darkened and Previews of Coming Attractions started. 'Want some?' Betty whispered, lifting her tub of popcorn toward Lane.

'No thanks.' Though it smelled good, the popcorn would make her thirsty and she had no drink. She and Jim had decided to wait for the intermission before getting snacks.

Jim stretched an arm across her shoulders. As he caressed her upper arm, she leaned closer to him. He tried to push his hand under her arm, but she pressed it tight against her side.

'No funny stuff,' she whispered, 'or I'll trade places with Betty.'

'Anything but that,' he said. He brushed his lips against the side of her forehead, then turned his face toward the screen.

About ten minutes into the feature attraction, he stopped stroking Lane's arm. The film was *Night Hunt*, about a young woman being stalked through the woods by a heavily armed killer. Jim seemed engrossed by it. The heroine was beautiful and running around in torn clothes. Lane suspected that had something to do with grabbing his attention. But the suspense was terrific. Soon, Jim took his arm away and sat up straight. As Lane shifted in her seat, she noticed that Betty had stopped eating, though her tub of popcorn was still half full. She glanced past Betty at Henry. The boy's eyes were fixed on the screen, the lenses of his glasses reflecting the light. Betty gasped, and Lane jerked her eyes back to the film.

It seemed to be over very fast. When the lights came up, Jim gave her a look as if he'd been blown away.

'Pretty decent,' she said.

'Man.'

Henry said, 'Was that totally awesome, or what?'

'Must've been,' Lane told him. 'Betty couldn't even finish her popcorn.'

'Small oversight,' Betty said, and stuffed a handful into her mouth. To Henry, she said in a muffled voice, 'I could go for a hot dog.'

Henry and Jim headed for the lobby to pick up refreshments. They returned with loaded arms just as the lights dimmed. Lane took her Pepsi and nachos from Jim. He sat down beside her.

Leaning close to him, she whispered, 'How are you and Henry getting along?'

'He's not so bad for a twerp.'

She elbowed Jim gently in the ribs. The wrapper of a straw shot past her face and landed on Jim's far shoulder. She grinned at Henry.

'Sorry,' he said. 'Aim was off.'

'He was trying for my eye,' Betty explained.

As the movie began, Lane clamped her drink between her thighs and poked her straw through the X on its lid. She sipped her drink. She ate her nachos, leaning forward and keeping the cardboard dish under her chin, careful not to drip any of the melted cheese on her white sweater.

From the start, it was obvious that this film, *Dance of the Zombies*, was a turkey. Henry started talking back to it. Once Jim was done with his nachos, he drew Lane closer to him. He caressed her arm and kissed the side of her face while she tried to eat the last of her chips.

'Pay attention to the movie,' she whispered.

'It sucks,' he said, and kissed the corner of her eye.

She stuck her last nacho chip into his mouth. 'Suck on that,' she told him.

As Jim chewed, she took the Pepsi from between her legs and drew the cold, watered-down soda into her mouth. She didn't expect his other hand. It had been resting on the far arm of his chair. But now it suddenly pressed tight against the crotch of her jeans. She flinched and shoved it away and choked on her Pepsi. The drink shot up her throat, sprayed from her mouth, burned inside her nasal passages and spilled out her nostrils. Hurling her cup to the floor, she hunched over and flung both hands under her face to catch the mess.

Jim pounded on her back as she coughed.

'Jesus, gal,' Betty said, and joined in the pounding.

'Is she all right?' Henry asked. 'What happened?'

Finally, Lane could breathe again. She wiped her tearing eyes. With a napkin from Betty, she dried her face. The legs of her jeans felt damp. So did the front of her sweater.

'What happened?' Henry asked again.

'Went down the wrong pipe,' she muttered. 'I'm going to the john.' Without a glance at Jim, she squeezed past the knees of Betty and Henry. She lunged into the aisle and shoved through the swinging door to the lobby.

In the restroom, she used damp paper towels to clean the faint spatter of stains on her sweater.

Second time today, she thought. First Benson, now Jim. I'm spending half my life cleaning up after getting messed with by shitheads.

Why'd he *do* that?

My hands were full, that's why. Figured he'd get in a grab when I couldn't stop him. Rotten bastard.

Betty came in. 'Are you okay?'

'No. And I'm not going back in there.'

'What's the matter?'

'Jim. The bastard.'

'What'd he do?'

'Never mind. I'm gonna call my dad and have him pick me up.'

'Well, Jim's waiting right outside the door.'

'Yeah?' Lane wadded the paper towels, tossed them into the trash bin, and shouldered open the restroom door. It missed Jim, but not by much. Henry was standing nearby, staring at the floor as if embarrassed to be a part of all this.

'Are you okay?' Jim asked, frowning, all concerned.

'What do you think?'

'I'm sorry. Jesus, Lane. I didn't mean for you to choke.'

'Yeah, sure.'

'I'm *sorry*.'

She turned away from him and strode toward the pair of public phones beside the drinking fountain. Jim rushed after her. 'Hey, what're you doing?'

'Calling home. Go on back in and enjoy the movie.'

'Hey, come on.'

'Get lost.'

'I didn't *do* anything.'

'Right.' She dug into her handbag, searching for change.

'You don't have to call anyone,' Jim said. 'I'll drive you home, if that's what you want.'

'I'm ready to leave,' Betty said.

'Me, too. The movie stank, anyway,' Henry said.

'How about it?' Jim asked her.

'Okay,' she muttered. 'But you'd better just keep your fucking hands to yourself.'

Jim grimaced.

Henry's head snapped toward him. Glaring, he snapped, 'What did you do to her?'

'What's the trouble over here?' the manager asked, approaching.

'We're just leaving,' Jim said.

They hurried for the exit doors. Henry, in the lead, kept glancing back at Jim with furious eyes. He held the door open for the group.

Outside, he grabbed Jim by the arm. 'What'd you do to Lane, you rotten scum?'

'Don't you touch me, asshole.'

'You want to make me?'

'Henry!' Lane snapped. 'Quit it. Let go of him.'

'Better do like she says,' Jim said, 'before I wipe up the sidewalk with you.'

'Oh yeah?' Though Betty tried to pull him away, he kept his grip on Jim's arm. 'I've been beat up by tougher guys than you.'

Jim cocked back his arm.

Lane kicked him hard in the rear. Crying out, he jerked rigid, freed his arm from Henry's grip, and grabbed his rump. He started hopping up and down as if that somehow helped the pain. He turned around as he hopped. His face was bright red under the streetlights.

'That *hurt*!' he blurted, his voice high-pitched and accusing.

'It was supposed to. You want to beat up on somebody, try me. Better yet, why don't you team up with Riley Benson? You're no better than him. Maybe the two of you'd like a try at me.'

'Oh yeah?' He stopped hopping. He stood there, gasping, clutching his seat with both hands. 'Well, fuck you.'

'Not in your lifetime.'

'If you think I'm gonna forget this . . .'

'I sure hope not. Do me a favor and get lost.'

'Yeah! I'll get lost, all right! You and your asshole friends can *walk* home, see how you like it.'

'We'll like it just fine, thanks.'

He turned away from her and hobbled past Henry and Betty.

'*Ciao*,' Henry said, and Betty thumped the side of his head.

Jim scowled back at them, then turned his head more until his eyes met Lane's. 'I wouldn't take you back if you begged me. Not a chance. It's over.'

'I'm already eating my heart out,' she called to him.

'Who needs you? You're a pain in the ass.'

'Literally,' Henry said.

Betty thumped him again.

'Try Candi,' Lane suggested. 'I'm sure she'll appreciate your finer traits.'

Jim flipped her off, then vanished around the corner.

Joining her friends, Lane said, 'Let's walk over to Antonio's and get a pizza. My treat. Then I'll call home and get Mom or Dad to pick us up.'

'Spectacular,' Henry said.

'I could go for some pizza about now,' Betty said. 'All this excitement sure stirs up the ol' appetite.'

They started walking. Lane, stepping between Henry and Betty, put her arms across their backs. 'You were great,' she said to Henry.

'The nerd showed hair,' Betty agreed.

'Our Henry's not a nerd.'

He beamed.

'You almost got yourself creamed,' Betty told him.

'That was sure some kick,' Henry said. 'Any harder, you would've knocked his ass out his mouth.'

Lane laughed. 'Well, I tried.'

'Did you see the look on his face?' Betty asked. 'I mean, that crud didn't know whether to shit or go blind.'

'He'll wish he'd gone blind when he tries to shit,' Henry said. 'Spectacular. You ought to try out for the football team.'

'Anyway,' Lane said. 'That's over. I should've dumped that creep a long time ago.'

'That's what we've been telling you,' Betty said.

'I'm a slow learner.'

'You're lucky to be rid of the slime-bag,' Henry told her.

'Yeah.' They waited for a car to pass, then stepped off the curb and started across the road. 'He wasn't *all* bad, though. Sometimes, he could be . . .' A lump suddenly closed her throat. Tears filled her eyes. '. . he could be nice,' she finished, her voice trembling.

Betty rubbed her back. 'Hey, it's all right. You're better off without him.'

'I know. I know.'

'If you get desperate,' Henry said, 'there's always me.'

'You ready to die, Hen-house?' Betty asked.

'Just a suggestion.'

Lane squeezed both of them closer against her sides. 'Quit it before I kick your butts.'

Chapter Thirty-two

'Do you want to talk about it?' Larry asked after dropping off Henry and Betty.

Lane, slumped in the passenger seat with her arms folded, turned her face toward him and said, 'I kicked Jim in the butt. So he advised us to walk home.'

'You *kicked* him?'

'You wouldn't believe what he did to me.'

'Oh, I might.'

'Guys are such pigs.'

'Thanks.'

'Not youuuu. But I mean it. Honestly. All they want to do is grab grab grab. They've got sex on the brain.'

'And you don't, huh?'

'I don't go around grabbing . . . their private areas.'

'Happy to hear it.'

'You weren't like that, were you? When you were a teenager?'

He was glad there wasn't enough light coming into the car for Lane to see his face go red. He'd been in his office with the door shut when she phoned from the pizza parlor. Gazing at his pictures of Bonnie. Remembering all the details of his dream. Longing for her. A girl nearly the same age as Lane. Who even *looked* quite similar to her.

'I guess every teenager has sex on the brain,' he said.

'But you didn't go around always trying to cop a feel, did you?'

'When I was your age? No. I dated sometimes, but I wasn't especially interested in the girls I went out with. So I didn't try much funny stuff with them.'

'You weren't *interested* in the girls you dated?'

'We're talking about my high school days, right?'

'Yeah.'

'Well then, no. Not much. I basically just went out with dogs.'

'Dad!' She sounded shocked but amused.

'It's true. And I didn't want to get fleas, so . . .'

'Really, that's not nice.'

'Okay okay. Seriously? I wasn't exactly dashing, and I knew it. So I never even tried to go out with any of the girls I really thought were neat. They scared the hell out of me. If a girl looked like you, for instance, I'd just admire her from afar and maybe daydream about her. I sure wouldn't date her.'

'Jeez, Dad.'

'Weird, huh? Now I've got a kid who's one of *them*.'

He looked at Lane and smiled. She shook her head. Then she reached out and patted his shoulder. '*I* would've gone out with you.'

'A pity date.'

'No way. I'll bet *you* would've been a perfect gentleman.'

'A lust-crazed maniac!' He shot his hand under Lane's outstretched arm and thrust it into her armpit.

'Don't!' she cried out. Giggling, she clamped her arm down and squirmed.

He pulled his hand free, got it under her elbow, and tickled her side.

'Dad! Stop!'

He returned his hand to the steering wheel. As he eased the car to the curb in front of their house, Lane grabbed *his* side and dug her fingers in.

'Don't!' he cried out, mimicking her and laughing. 'Please. Stop!'

'You can give it but you can't take it,' she said.

Writhing as she tickled him, he shut off the engine. Then he grabbed her forearm and pushed up the sleeve of her sweater. 'Indian burn,' he announced.

'No!' she gasped, breathless with giggling. 'Don't! I mean it! I'll tell Mom!'

'Tattletale.' He gave her the Indian burn. Gently. Then let go.

'Is that the best you can do?'

'Oh? You want me to give you a good one?'

'I think I'll pass, thanks,' she said. She patted his arm. 'Maybe some other time. Maybe . . .' She suddenly clutched Larry's forearm with both hands and twisted, wringing its flesh.

'Yeeeoow!'

'That'll teach you, tough guy.' Laughing, she hurled herself at the passenger door and scurried from the car. She ran to the house. But instead of using her keys to let herself in, she waited on the porch for him.

Larry rubbed his arm as he walked toward her. It stung.

'I didn't really hurt you, did I?' she asked.

'I'll live. With luck.'

Lane held out her arm. 'Want to give me one?'

'No.'

'Come on, I'll feel better if you get me back.'

'You'd just scream and wake up your mother,' he said, and unlocked the door. They entered the house quietly.

Lane looked toward the sofa. 'Where is she?'

'In bed.'

'Ah-ha. Gosh, I hope I didn't interrupt anything when I phoned.'

Jean, complaining of a miserable headache, had gone to bed nearly an hour before the call, giving Larry his opportunity to be with the pictures of Bonnie. He said, 'You'll never know.'

'Ho ho ho.'

'Well, it's time for me to hit the hay.'

'Time for me to hit the shower,' Lane said.

'Didn't you just have a bath before supper?'

Her smile fell away. 'I'm feeling kind of grubby.'

'Oh.'

'Yeah. Everything that . . .' She pressed her lips together. Her chin began to tremble and tears glimmered in her eyes.

Larry's throat suddenly tightened. 'I'm sorry, honey.'

She wrapped her arms around him and hugged him. 'Why do things . . . have to get so fouled up?'

'I don't know. It's life, I guess.'

'Life's a bitch, then you die.'

'Don't say that, honey,' he whispered. 'Everything will turn out fine.'

'Yeah, sure.'

'Jim isn't the only guy in the world. Just wait and see. You'll run into some fellow, one of these days, and fall head over heels for him.'

'Good way to break your back,' she muttered against the side of his neck. Relaxing her hold, she kissed his cheek. 'Anyway, thanks.' She stepped back and wiped her eyes on a sleeve of her sweater.

'You'll feel better in the morning,' he told her.

'At least until I wake up.'

Larry stretched out between the sheets of his bed. They were cool and felt good.

'Lane back?' Jean asked in a husky voice.

'Yep.'

She sighed, and seemed to fall asleep again. Larry listened

to her deep, slow breathing. Soon, he heard the distant windy sound of the shower.

He wondered if Lane would go right to bed when she was done.

You don't need to look at those pictures again, he told himself. Go to sleep and forget it.

What if Lane caught you looking at them? A girl her own age. A dead girl, to boot. She'd think you're no better than Jim. Worse. *Guys are such pigs.* Including Dad.

Just explain you're writing a book about her. She was murdered, and tomorrow . . .

Tomorrow.

Larry had struggled, ever since lunch, to push that out of his mind. Whenever he thought about returning to Sagebrush Flat, a sick hot feeling swept through him. It came now. He kicked free of the top sheet and blanket.

Call it off?

What do you tell Pete? Sorry, I changed my mind. Right. We've got to go through with it.

What if we find Uriah?

We won't. We were there twice before, and he didn't put in an appearance.

Maybe he just happened to be away the other times. Taking a stroll in the desert. Killing coyotes.

Or right there, hidden, watching us.

Terrific.

Now I'll never get to sleep, he thought.

Think about something pleasant. Think about Bonnie.

No! I've got to *stop* thinking about Bonnie. It's crazy. It's wrong.

He heard the shower go silent.

Lane was done. Give her fifteen minutes, he thought, to make sure she's asleep. Then it'll be safe to take out the pictures.

Might as well, if I can't sleep anyway.

No.

Besides, what's the point? She's dead. She won't come back.

She might. When I pull the stake.

Bullshit.

But what if she does?

She won't. There's no such thing as vampires.

'Pull it and find out,' Bonnie said, her voice soft and teasing in his mind.

'You'd like that, wouldn't you?' he told her.

'Very much.'

'I suppose it can be arranged.' He straddled the coffin and smiled down at her.

It was confusing. He hadn't pulled the stake yet, but she was already alive, naked and beautiful and talking to him.

'How come you're already alive?' he asked.

She gave him a playful smile. 'Vampire magic.'

'So you *are* a vampire?'

'Never said I wasn't.'

'I don't know.'

'You want me, don't you?' Her hand reached up from inside the coffin, and stroked him.

'It's not as simple as that, Bonnie.'

'You want me, don't you?'

'But if you really are a vampire . . .'

Bonnie lifted her legs, spread them apart and hooked her knees over the sides of the coffin. 'You *do* want me,' she said.

'I know, but . . .'

'And I want you.' Her hands went to her breasts, caressed them, squeezed them. 'Take out the stake, and I'll be yours.'

He didn't want to pull the stake. He ached for her, but she had as good as admitted that she was a vampire. If he freed her, what would she do?

'I won't feed on you or your family,' she told him, as if reading his mind.

'How do I know that?'

'Trust me. Pull it.' Then her head lifted. It came up off the bottom of the coffin. As she writhed and massaged her breasts, her neck grew longer. Slender and white and curving forward. It lowered her head toward the jutting stake. Her tongue slid out, long and pink, dripping. It curled around the wooden shaft. Slid down to where the wood entered her chest. Cheek resting against the smooth skin above her breasts, she looked up at Larry and smiled. 'Pull it,' she urged him, somehow able to talk in spite of her extended tongue.

Larry watched, breathless, his heart slamming.

Bonnie's tongue, wrapped around the shaft, wound its way to the top. Her head followed. She drew in her tongue. And then she stretched her lips wide and lowered her mouth over the blunt end of the stake. She sucked on it.

She's going to suck it right out of her, Larry thought.

It's okay if *she* does it. As long as I'm not the one . . .

'Cop out!' A stranger's voice.

Bonnie's head jerked up, fluid spilling down her chin, her eyes furious. With her long neck, she reminded Larry of a cobra rising to the tune of a snake charmer. Her head swiveled toward the sound of the voice.

Larry looked, too.

The stranger wore the dark robe of a monk. Its hood hung low, hiding his face.

'Uriah?' Larry asked.

'Do not be deceived by the evil one,' the stranger said.

'Kill him, Larry,' Bonnie said, her voice low and calm, coaxing. 'That's Uriah, all right. He's the one who did this to me.'

'Get thee back to Hell, demon!'

'He's a madman,' Bonnie said. Her voice sounded farther away. And different. There was nothing sly or seductive about it. She sounded very much like Lane. Larry felt his chest tighten. 'He *murdered* me. And it hurt. It hurt so much.'

Larry looked away from the stranger.

The coffin was empty.

For a moment, Larry thought, *It's too late! She sucked the stake right out and she's alive!*

Then, he saw her. She stood on the other side of the coffin. Tears gleamed in her eyes. Her chin trembled slightly. There was no stake in her chest. Somehow, she now wore Lane's white sweater, jeans and boots. But she was Bonnie, beautiful and innocent and weeping softly.

Larry suddenly realized he was naked. He looked down at himself, and sighed with relief. He now had his robe on.

'He killed me,' Bonnie said, her voice trembling.

'Vampire!' Uriah bellowed. 'Hideous slut!'

'Shut up,' Larry snapped at him.

'I'm no vampire,' Bonnie said. She sniffled. 'Uriah's crazy. He . . . he murdered my friends and me. We never did anything.'

Larry scowled at Uriah.

'She's lying, you fool.'

'Oh yeah?' Larry snapped. 'You goddamn maniac, you . . .' And he was suddenly rushing the man. 'I'll kill you, you fucking maniac!'

Uriah hurled the severed head of a coyote at him.

The eyeless head tumbled through the air, blood spraying from the stump of its neck, its maw wide, fangs dripping. Larry flung up his arms to block it. The teeth snapped shut on his forearm. He yelped and flinched and woke up.

The house was dark and silent. He lay uncovered on the bed, trembling, his skin tingling with goosebumps and bathed in sweat. He sat up. The bottom sheet peeled away from his wet back. Looking past the vague form of his sleeping wife, he squinted at the alarm clock. Almost one. He couldn't have been asleep for more than half an hour.

Not even *close* to morning.

He ran his hand through his drenched hair. The muscles along the sides of his neck felt tight and cold. They seemed to be squeezing pain into his head.

He climbed out of bed, stepped quietly to the closet, and put on his robe. It clung to his damp skin. Knotting the belt, he went into the hallway.

He passed Lane's open door on the way to the bathroom. Her light was off, but he wondered if she was asleep. He didn't stop to check.

745

It doesn't matter, he told himself. I'm not going to look at the pictures.

What *will* I do? he wondered.

He knew what he wouldn't do – go back to bed. Not right away, at least. He felt wide awake. Besides, there was no point in trying to sleep until the headache subsided. And he didn't want to risk another dream. Not like that one.

At the end of the hallway, he entered the bathroom. He shut the door, but left the light off, knowing it would hurt his eyes. The mellow glow from the nightlight was enough. As he stepped toward the medicine cabinet, he breathed deeply of the scents that still lingered after Lane's shower. Feminine, flowery aromas from her soap or shampoo or body powder . . . who knows what? But they filled the bathroom with her presence, and Larry felt himself relax a little.

He took two aspirin, washing them down with cold water.

He returned to the door. He took hold of its knob.

He realized that he didn't want to face the dark, silent house beyond the door. He didn't want to lie in bed and waitforsleep. Hedidn't want to sleep. He didn't want to sit alone in the living room and try to read or watch television. He didn't want to sneak into his office and slide open the file cabinet and take out his pictures of Bonnie.

I'm just fine right here, he told himself.

He thumbed down the button in the middle of the knob. The door locked with a loud ping.

He lowered the toilet seat and sat down. Leaning forward, he rested his elbows on his knees. He stared at the bathmat. Even in the faint light, he could see where Lane's wet feet had matted down the nap.

He breathed through his nose, savoring the comfortable, familiar mix of aromas.

Bonnie can't get to me here, he thought.

A knock on the door startled him awake. The bathroom was gray with morning light. 'Dad, my teeth are floating.'

'Just a minute.' He pushed himself off the floor, picked up

the bath towel he'd used to cover his legs, hung it on the rack, and straightened his robe. He flushed the toilet. Then he lifted its seat and stepped to the bathroom door. 'What's the secret password?' he asked.

'I'm gonna pee on the floor!'

'That's it.' He opened the door.

Lane rolled her eyes upward. 'About time.' As she side-stepped past him, she stopped and frowned. 'Are you okay? You're looking kind of weird.'

'Rough night,' he said.

'Case of the trotskis?' she asked.

'Just a headache.'

'Good. So you didn't stink the place up.'

'Smells fine in there.' It smells like you, he thought. He rubbed her mussed hair. She stepped past him and shut the door.

In the bedroom, he found Jean still asleep. He closed the door, hung up his robe, and crawled into bed. The sheets on his side were cool. He rolled, and curled himself against Jean's back. He slipped an arm down across her belly. She was warm and smooth. He eased his face against her hair. The smell of her was like those that had kept him company through the night.

She and Lane must use some of the same stuff, he thought, snuggling against her.

'Time to get up?' she mumbled.

'Not yet.'

'Good. Hold me for a while.'

Chapter Thirty-three

'Try not to shoot each other,' Barbara said through the van's open window. She gave Pete a kiss, then stepped backward.

Jean, by the passenger window, frowned at Larry and said, 'Are you sure you're all right?'

'I'm okay.'

Ever since getting up, he'd been plagued by stomach cramps and loose bowels. Jean had suggested he phone Pete and cancel the outing. He'd been tempted. But he knew that his problem was caused by nerves. If he called off the trip to Sagebrush Flat, Pete would insist on trying it again tomorrow. Better to get it over with.

'What's the problem, pardner?' Pete asked.

'A little indigestion,' he said. He didn't want to discuss his runs. Not with Barbara standing there. 'I'm fine now.'

'Okey-doke. We're off.'

Jean kissed Larry, and moved out of the way.

Pete turned the ignition key. *Click-click-click.* He twisted it again. Nothing. 'Shit!'

'Must be the battery,' Larry said.

Pete tried again. Again, he said, 'Shit.'

Larry felt like celebrating.

'Do you want to jump it?' Jean asked, approaching the passenger window.

'No. Damn it!' Pete whacked the steering wheel with his palm.

'Calm down,' Barbara told him. 'It's not the end of the world. Why don't we jump it, and you can stop by the service station on the way out and have the problem taken care of?'

'Its probably gonna need a new battery.' He pounded the wheel again. 'There goes the rest of the morning.'

'It's not that big a deal,' Barbara insisted.

748

'Maybe we weren't meant to go shooting today,' Larry said.

'We'll take your car,' Pete told his wife.

'Oh? Terrific. And how am I supposed to get to the grocery store?'

'You can walk, for all I . . .'

'Oh, sure thing. Why don't you . . .'

'Wait,' Jean interrupted. 'Hold it. Why don't you guys just take one of our cars?'

Thanks a heap, Larry thought.

'I don't know,' he said. 'I'd hate to take a chance on the Dodge overheating . . .'

'Take the Mustang.'

'Maybe Lane has plans.'

'Don't worry about it. If she wants to go someplace, she can take the Dodge.'

Larry nodded. Why argue? We're meant to go after all, he thought.

They climbed from the van. They transferred the VCR camcorder, their firearms, food, and beer to the red Mustang. Larry settled in behind the steering wheel. Pete harnessed himself into the passenger seat.

'Let's hope this one works,' Pete said.

'Yeah.'

He knew it would work. Nothing was going to save him from his rendezvous with Sagebrush Flat.

He turned the key. The engine grumbled to life.

The wives stood side by side, smiling and waving as Larry backed the Mustang onto the road.

'Is this exciting, or what?' Pete said, grinning.

'Or what.'

'Should be just around this next bend,' Pete said.

Larry hoped he would find the town occupied. This was a Saturday, after all. Maybe some folks on an outing had stopped to explore the 'ghost town.' Maybe some kids had dropped by to decorate the walls with graffiti or shoot the place up. Even a biker gang would be a welcome sight. Anyone would do. Just

Richard Laymon

so the town wasn't deserted and they had to give up their hunt for Uriah.

But he rounded the bend, and the broad main road through Sagebrush Flat stretched in front of him, glaring in the sunlight, empty except for a tumbleweed rolling lazily past the saloon.

'Stop the car,' Pete said. 'I'll get us some footage.' He climbed out with his video camera. Standing in the middle of the road, he turned slowly from side to side, panning the area ahead. Then, he stepped closer to Larry's window. 'I'll get you driving in. Head on up there and park at the hotel.'

'Seems kind of dippy to me.'

'Hey. Did Doug MacArthur complain when he had to wade ashore at Bataan?'

'I don't think it was Bataan.'

'Wherever. This is *us* returning, pardner.'

'Right,' he muttered.

He drove the rest of the way alone, swung off the road in front of the hotel, and got out. Pete, still about fifty yards away, was walking slowly forward, the camera to his eye.

'Open the trunk!' Pete called. 'Strap on your shootin' iron.'

He opened the trunk, lifted out his holstered Ruger .22, and strapped the belt low around his hips. Squinting at Pete, he tugged the brim of his battered old Stetson down across his eyes.

'Terrific!' Pete called. 'Now, slap some leather!'

'Get real,' he said.

'Well, at least *load* it.'

He supposed that wasn't a bad idea. If they somehow did manage to run into Uriah, he didn't want to be standing there with an empty gun.

He sat on the rear bumper, dumped some .22 magnums into his hand, and started feeding them into the cylinder. By the time he finished, Pete was only a couple of yards away.

'Gimme an Eastwood sneer.'

'If Uriah's watching all this, he'll think we're clowns.'

'Good. Give him a false sense of security.'

750

'False, huh?' Hedropped a handful of cartridges into the pocket of his shirt, and set the box down inside the trunk. 'Should we have a beer before we start?' he asked.

'Not yet. Here, take this. I don't want to be left out.'

He gave the camera to Larry, and showed him how to work it. Larry stepped away from the car, picked up Pete in the viewfinder and recorded him strapping on his gunbelt.

'A couple of real *hombres*, huh?'

'Yup,' Larry said.

It felt good, he realized, to be dressed up in his boots, faded jeans, old blue workshirt and cowboy hat. It especially felt good to have the holster against his leg and know it held a real six-shooter with live rounds in the cylinder. Like playing cowboys for real.

Pete, though smaller than Larry, looked twice as tough. He wore scuffed and dusty combat boots. The cuffs of his jeans were frayed. The sleeves of his plaid shirt were turned up, revealing his thick hairy forearms. The shirt, too tight across his chest, bulged with the push of his muscles. His dirty straw hat, sides curled up and front swooping low, looked like something he might've swiped off a drunken old-timer in an alley behind a saloon. But the best part was the black handlebar mustache, sprinkled with flecks of gray. The mustache was more than dress-up. It was real.

Leaning back against the car, Pete fed ammo into his revolver. His bullets looked about three times the size of Larry's.

'I'm gonna have to get me a forty-five or something,' Larry said.

'Yeah. Get yourself a piece with some real stopping power.' Pete bolstered his magnum. Squinting into the camera, he poked a cigarette into the corner of his mouth. He lit it with a Bic. 'Ready to go after our man?' he asked.

'How about a beer before we start?'

'Reckon that'd hit the spot.'

They leaned against the side of the car while they drank. Larry kept looking up and down the road, hoping someone might show up and ruin their plan.

Pete finished his cigarette. He tossed it down and mashed it under his boot. 'This'll be great in our book,' he said 'The two of us coming out here to kick ass.'

'Yeah. We probably won't find him, though.'

'Hey, man, think positive.'

'I am.'

'Get outa here. You mean to tell me you came all the way out here *hoping* we won't find the guy?'

'I'm not exactly looking forward to it.'

'You're not gonna chicken out on me, are you?'

'Came this far.'

'That's the spirit.'

'The thing about Uriah, though . . .' He stopped, shook his head, and drank some more beer.

'Yeah?'

'Nothing.'

'Come on, man. Spit it out.'

'Well, he's *real*.'

'No fooling.'

'You've been to Vietnam and everything. It's different for you. The closest I ever came to real trouble was when some neighbors got shot up back in LA. I just hit the floor and prayed none of the bullets would come our way. I've never actually *gone after* anyone.'

'Me neither. I wasn't a grunt, you know.'

'You've never shot anyone?'

'Nope. Or been shot *at*. Closest I ever came to getting plugged, ol'hoss, was when you drew down on me last Friday.'

'Oh.'

'Yeah, oh.' He laughed. 'Hey, buck up. It showed you had balls. If you can stick a gun in my face, you'll do it when it counts.'

'Hope so,' Larry muttered.

'Don't worry, you will.' Pete stepped away from the car, tossed his beer can high, and went for his gun.

'No!' Before he could clear his holster, Larry grabbed his wrist.

The can clinked on the street and rolled.

'Hey, man . . .'

'Are you out of your gourd? That cannon . . .'

'We didn't exactly *sneak* into town, Lar. If Uriah's around, I reck on he knows we're here.'

'Well, jeez.'

'Okay okay. You done, there? Let's get this show on the road.'

While Pete retrieved his can, Larry finished his beer and stepped to the trunk. They dropped both cans inside. 'What about the camera?' Larry asked.

'It'll betoo dark in the hotel.'

'Better take this, then.' Larry searched a corner of the trunk. Along with the jack, tire iron and flares was a flashlight he kept there for emergencies. He took it out, and started to shut the trunk.

'Whoa there. We might need this, too.' Pete reached in. He lifted out the tire tool.

Looking over his shoulder, Larry saw that the hasp on the hotel doors still dangled loose. 'Think we'll need the bar?'

'We're gonna check the rooms, aren't we?'

He hadn't thought of that. He realized, in fact, that he'd avoided thinking about what they would actually do once they were here. 'I don't know about breaking into rooms.'

Pete shook his head and chuckled. Tire iron in his hand, he closed the trunk. 'You really *don't* want to find this guy, do you?'

'I sure don't want to shoot him,' Larry said as they approached the front doors.

'I don't aim to shoot anyone, either. But it's nice to know we've got some protection.' He patted the handle of his revolver. Then he slipped the tire iron under his belt, swung open one of the doors, and stepped into the hotel.

The light from the doorway swept across the lobby floor and faded, leaving the far areas of the room in darkness. Larry could barely make out the vague shape of the registration counter, could only see halfway up the stairs to his left. As he tried to see more, the light was squeezed out. The door bumped shut.

'Let's get our eyes used to it,' Pete whispered.

Larry felt as if a black hood had been dropped over his face. But when he turned around, he found strips of sunlight coming through cracks in the boarded windows and a glowing band across the bottom of the doorway.

Pete stood beside him, silent.

Larry faced forward again. Soon, he was able to make out the faint shapes of things: the long counter, the cubby holes behind it, the banister and stairs. They were almost invisible, but there. Soft around the edges. Flowing. Melting into the blackness. He saw some shapes he wasn't sure about. Something above the distant counter that might be a face. Something partway up the stairs that might be a man standing motionless, staring down at them.

It was better, he thought, when I couldn't see at all.

'The lair of the madman,' Pete whispered.

'Cut it out.'

'That'd be a good title for you, huh?'

'Shhh.'

'You're gonna get a lot of good material from all this.'

He wished Pete would hush. He wanted silence so he could hear if anyone . . .

'Go ahead and turn on the flashlight,' Pete said.

He thumbed the switch. Swept the light up the stairs. His breath snagged as shadows from the banister squirmed on the wall. But nobody was there. The beam reached all the way to the top. It cast a dim glow into the second floor hallway. Larry quickly swung it away, and darted it across the top of the registration counter. Nobody there, either. Breathing more easily, he probed each corner of the lobby.

'Let me have it,' Pete said.

Larry was reluctant, for a moment, to give up control of the light. Then he realized that it should belong to the one leading the way. He preferred Pete to be the leader. He passed the light to him, and rested his hand on the grips of his revolver.

They started forward, their boots making gritty sounds on the sandy hardwood floor. Larry watched where the flashlight went. It stopped briefly on the crucifix. It moved around the edges of the panel, which was flush with the other sections enclosing the area under the stairway. It swept along the length of the counter and lingered on a closed door near the far end.

'Let's check that out,' Pete said.

They climbed over the counter and dropped into the space behind it. Pete led the way to the door, eased it open and leaned in. Larry peered past his head. The pale shaft of light revealed an empty room with a boarded window on its far wall.

'The hotel office,' Pete whispered. 'Let's try upstairs.' He pulled the door shut.

They swung themselves over the counter again, and crossed the lobby to the stairway. Pete aimed the light at the top as if to make sure nobody was waiting up there. Then he lowered it to the steps just above them. He started to climb.

The landing was still covered by loose planks.

Seeing them, Larry wished to God that Barbara had never broken through.

How can you wish such a thing?

The voice was Bonnie's, sad and accusing.

I thought you loved me.

'Think I'll take a peek,' Pete said. He sank to his knees and carefully lifted two boards out of the way. Ducking low, he lowered his head into the gap. The flashlight followed. 'I don't see anything,' he said.

'What did you expect?'

'Who knows?' He straightened up, replaced the boards, and got to his feet. Again, he shined the light at the top of the stairs. Then, he began to climb.

Larry took a long stride to avoid stepping on the planks.

Just above him, Pete switched the flashlight to his left hand. With his right hand, he drew the revolver from its holster.

'Be careful,' Larry whispered. 'I mean, don't go blasting anything that moves. There might be a bum living here, or something.'

'Don't worry, huh?'

'We're the ones trespassing, you know.'

'Yeah, yeah.'

One stair from the top, Pete leaned forward and glanced both ways. He stepped into the corridor. Larry followed. The corridor ended just to the left of the stairway. To the right, it stretched long and dark with doors on both sides.

They stopped in front of the first door. Pete pressed his ear to it, shoving his cowboy hat crooked. After listening for a moment, he moved back. 'You wanta do the honors?' he whispered, pointing the flashlight at its knob. 'I'll cover you.'

Heart thudding, Larry gripped the knob. He tried to twist it, but there was no give. 'Locked.'

Pete tapped the muzzle of his revolver against the end of the tire iron in his belt.

Larry pulled the bar out. Holding it with both hands, he forced the wedge into the crack between the lock plate and the door frame. He looked at Pete.

'Well, go on.'

'I don't know.'

'Well, shit.'

'We shouldn't be here.'

'Don't go pussy on me now.'

'Maybe we ought to just go shooting like we told the gals.'

'The book, man. The book. Uriah's the missing piece, remember?'

He murdered me. Bonnie's voice again. *You can't let him get away with it. He's got to pay.*

'Okay,' Larry muttered.

He put his weight against the iron bar. He felt it move a bit sideways, digging into the wood. There were soft crunchy sounds.

Then came the blare of a car horn.

He froze.

'Uh-oh,' Pete said.

Larry jerked the bar free and spun around. 'That was *our* car!'

Chapter Thirty-four

Pete in the lead, they raced down the stairs. The wood clamored and creaked under their pounding boots. The loose planks across the landing jumped and clattered. If the horn was still honking, Larry couldn't hear it.

His stomach was a ball of ice. His chest ached. He could barely breathe. There was a tightness in his throat like a scream trying to force its way out.

Somebody was out there. Uriah? Curious strangers? A gang? Cops?

'Don't go running out with a gun in your hand,' he gasped as he rushed after Pete to the front doors.

Pete stopped. Larry, at his back, grabbed his shoulder.

'Take it easy,' Pete whispered, and eased the door open a crack. A strip of daylight jabbed Larry's eyes. 'I don't see anybody.'

'A car or anything?'

'Just yours.' The daylight spread. Pete stuck his head through the gap and looked from side to side like a kid getting ready to cross a busy road. 'Nope. Nothing.' He holstered his revolver, swung the door wide, and stepped onto the sidewalk.

Larry, just behind him, squinted at the bright red Mustang. He saw no one. He looked both way. The street was deserted.

'The horn didn't honk itself,' he muttered.

'Tell me something I don't already know.'

'I don't like this at all.'

'Join the crowd.'

'You think he's behind the car?'

'Let's find out.' Eyes on the car, Pete sidestepped his way to the middle of the street. There, he saw something that made him scowl and shake his head. He dropped to his knees, set down the flashlight, and peered beneath the car. Rising, he stepped close to the driver's side and glanced through the windows. He took a deep breath. He looked at Larry. 'Nobody here,' he said. 'But we've got a flat.'

'Oh no. Jesus.' His head seemed to go numb inside. His legs felt wobbly as he staggered into the street.

The Mustang's left front tire was mashed against the pavement.

Crouching, Pete fingered its sidewall. 'Slashed.'

'He doesn't want us to leave,' Larry said. His voice sounded far away.

'Either that, or he's just pissed off. You've got a spare, don't you?'

'Yeah.'

Pete stood up and turned his back to the car. Eyes narrow, he scanned the store fronts across the street. 'He's probably over there laughing at us.'

'Let's change the tire and get out of here.'

'This is our chance to get him.'

'It might not even be Uriah.'

'Bet it is.'

'Well, I'm gonna change the damn tire.' Larry dug the car keys out of his pocket and stepped toward the trunk. 'Keep an eye out, huh?'

'Uriah, all right,' Pete said. 'And I'll bet he knows we're the guys who took his stiff. That'd explain why he slashed the tire. Wants to keep us here and nail us.'

Larry moaned. He opened the trunk, leaned in, and took out the jack.

'Maybe he thinks *we're* vampires.'

'Jesus, Pete.'

'I'm serious. What if he thinks we already pulled the stake and she bit us?'

'It's daytime, for one thing.'

'So?'

Larry lifted the spare tire, swung it away from the trunk, and lowered it to the pavement. As he rolled it toward the front of the car, he said, 'Vampires can't survive in the sunlight.'

'Maybe that's just movie crap.'

'It's in all the books.'

'You believe everything you read?'

'Of course not.' He let the tire fall and hurried to get the jack. 'I don't believe in *vampires*, for godsake.'

He imagined Bonnie laughing at that, shaking her head, her golden hair swaying.

'But Uriah believes in them,' Larry went on. 'He believes in using crucifixes and garlic and stakes.' Setting down the jack beside the spare, he reached up. Pete handed him the tire iron. 'So he must know that vampires can't be out in the sunlight the way we are.'

'Unless he knows different.'

Larry pried the hubcap loose. It fell and clanked on the pavement. He covered one of the nuts with the lug wrench. He yanked on the bar. It slipped off and he stumbled backward.

'I'd better do it,' Pete said. 'You keep watch.'

Larry gave him the tire tool, turned his back to the car, and scanned the buildings across the street. A few of the doors stood open. Some of the windows were boarded, but others weren't.

'One down,' Pete said.

The hubcap rang as a nut dropped into it.

'Besides,' Larry said, 'if he thinks we're vampires, he'd have to kill us with stakes.'

'Good point. No way, right?' Another nut rang into the hubcap. 'He must *think* he has a chance, though, or why the flat tire?' Pete grunted. Seconds later, a third nut hit the hubcap. 'Three down, one to go.'

'Maybe it *wasn't* Uriah. Could've been anyone. A hermit, or somebody. Maybe doesn't like strangers, did it to teach us a lesson.'

The last nut clanged into the hubcap.

'You got the emergency brake on?'

'Yeah.' Larry looked around. Pete, on his knees, was putting together the jack. He dropped lower to study the undercarriage, then shoved the jack beneath the car and started pumping it up with the tire iron. The car began to rise.

The arrow missed Pete's hat, skimmed above the hood of the Mustang, flew across the sidewalk and thunked into the hotel wall.

'What the . . .?' Pete blurted.

Larry whirled, crouching and drawing his gun. Nobody. Just shadows beyond the doors and windows.

'Shit! That's a fuckin' *arrow*!'

Then Pete was on his knees beside Larry, arm out, sweeping his revolver slowly from side to side.

'Where'd it come from?'

'Over there someplace.'

'You were supposed to keep *watch*, man. Thing coulda *killed* me!'

'What're we gonna . . .?'

Larry still saw nobody. But he saw the next arrow. It shot out of the gloom beyond a window directly across the street. The big display window of a shop, partly criss-crossed by weathered boards, mostly open.

'Pete!' he shouted as he threw himself at the pavement and the arrow hissed by. A moment later, he heard it punch into something.

Then his ears pounded. He felt as if they were being slapped hard by open hands determined to destroy his eardrums.

Huge, horrible explosions.

Pete's .357 magnum.

Pete was on his knees, eyes narrow, teeth gritted, arms straight out and jerking upward as another blast struck the air. Larry fought an urge to cover his ears. Facing forward, he was hit by another explosion and saw a hole get punched through the wall below the window. There were three or four other holes nearby, spaced about a foot apart.

He started firing, aiming to the left of Pete's holes, making new ones he could barely see, stitching a line toward the open door. His gun made sharp, flat bangs that seemed insignificant compared to Pete's thundering weapon. But he knew the .22 magnums were strong enough to penetrate the wood. If the walls inside weren't lined with plaster or sheet rock, his bullets would be flying through the room.

His hammer clanked on a spent round.

'Reload, reload!' he heard Pete yell through the ringing in his ears.

He rolled onto his side and started to eject the casings.

Pete, still on his knees, was shoving fresh cartridges into his cylinder. Then he was rising, rushing the window.

'Wait!' Larry shouted. Though his gun was still empty, he scurried up and ran for the door.

Lot of use I'll be, he thought.

He half expected Pete to dive through the window and come up inside firing like a movie cowboy. But his friend proved more cautious, and ducked below the window sill and peeked in. Larry slammed his shoulder against the door frame. Pressing his back to the wall, he flicked the last two shells from his revolver.

'I don't see him,' Pete said.

'Think we got him?'

'I don't know.' Pete dropped lower, turned around, and squatted, seeming to sag against the wall as he stared into the street.

Larry fumbled fresh cartridges out of his shirt pocket. He started thumbing them into the chambers. The cylinder made quiet clicking sounds as he turned it. Done, he snapped the loading gate shut.

Pete looked at him. 'All set?'

'For what?'

'We're going in, aren't we?'

'Are we?'

'We're not going anywhere *else*, I'll tell you that much. I'm not changing any fuckin' tire with Tonto talking potshots at me.'

'You want us to *go in*?'

'That's the idea.' Pete started duck-walking toward him.

'I don't know about this.'

'What don't you know?'

'What if he's waiting?'

'If you're chicken, I'll go first.'

'I'm not chicken, but . . .'

Pete dropped to his knees, crawled past Larry, and eased his head past the doorframe. 'I think he's gone.'

'If you catch an arrow in the face, Barbara's gonna kill me.'

Pete rose slowly until he was standing in the middle of the doorway. Larry turned around and stepped up close beside him. The room was brighter than he'd expected. Light not only poured in from the front door and display window, but also from a smaller window at the rear.

'Bet he took off out the back,' Pete said.

'What about over there?'

Over there was an L-shaped counter with a few bullet holes near its top. Behind it was the closed door of a room that occupied the shop's right rear quarter.

'If you're in here,' Pete said in a loud voice, 'show yourself right now.'

Nothing happened.

He fired three times, the explosions slamming Larry's ears as bullets crashed through the counter at knee level.

'Christ! Did you have to do that?'

'Yep.' Even as the word left Pete's lips, he raced at the counter. He vaulted it. His kick sent the door flying open. He rushed into the back room, then came out shaking his head. 'Like I said, he beat it out the window.'

Larry joined up with Pete and they reached the window together.

He yelled, 'SHIT!'

He shoved Pete. The force of the push sent them both stumbling, separating them, and the arrow sizzled between their sides.

As he fell to one knee, Larry's mind held a frozen image of the man he'd seen an instant ago. A man standing in the desert about hundred feet beyond the back of the building, letting an arrow fly. A savage with wild gray hair, a bushy beard, and a black patch over one eye. Wearing a necklace of garlic cloves, a crucifix that hung in the middle of his chest, and open vest and skirt of gray animal fur with a knife in the belt at his hip.

'Did you see *that*?' Pete asked.

Getting up, Larry said, 'Uriah?'

'Fuckin' wildman of Borneo!'

They both peered out from the sides of the window.

The man was running away, hair streaming out behind him, the bow pumping up and down in his right hand, a quiver of arrows and some kind of cloth bag bouncing against his back.

Pete crouched. He braced his arms on the window sill and took careful aim.

'You can't shoot him in the back!'

'Watch me.'

Larry was ready to knock the gun aside, but an image of Bonnie filled his mind. He saw her alive, sleeping in her bed, the weird old man creeping toward her with a hammer and stake.

Pete fired.

His bullet kicked up a puff of dust a yard behind the sprinting lunatic.

His next shot chopped through the bow. The weapon was ripped from the man's hand, its string flinging the broken ends high, whipping them together.

'All *right*!' Pete cried out. 'Now we've got him!'

As they climbed out the window, Larry saw him leap and drop out of sight.

'He's in the ravine,' Pete said.

'Yeah.' The ravine. The stream bed where they'd found the old jukebox and the campfire with the remains of the coyote.

They started walking toward it, Pete reloading.

'We won't have to shoot him now,' Larry said.

'Right. We'll take him alive, ask a few questions. This'll be great. We'll take him to the cops. Man, we'll be the guys that solved the disappearances.'

'Yeah,' Larry muttered. He knew he should feel good. They'd come here for Uriah. Pretty soon, they'd find out whether this was him.

Certainly wasn't the Uriah of his nightmares.

Probably him, though.

The guy who murdered Bonnie and the other two girls.

They'd have him. Alive. He could tell them everything.

But Larry didn't feel good. He felt as if he were being strangled by fear.

Pete grinned at him. 'You look like shit, pardner. You okay?'

'Yeah.'

'Nothing to be scared of, man. What's he gonna do, *throw* arrows at us?'

'I don't know. But I don't like this.'

'I do. Fantastic!'

Maybe we won't be able to find him, Larry thought. This is a guy who eats coyotes down there. Probably knows the ravine like the back of his hand. Maybe has special hiding places.

Or, once at the bottom, he might've taken off running in either direction. By the time we get there, he could be long gone.

God, I hope so.

Get him for Bonnie. He killed her. Make him pay.

When they were thirty or forty feet from the rim of the gap, Pete waved toward the left. 'You go that way.'

'Huh?'

'We'll split up and box him in.'

'*Split up?* You outa your mind?'

Halting, Pete scowled at him. 'Just do it.'

'No! If we split up, one of us'll get nailed. Happens in every shitty splatter film I've ever seen.'

'This ain't a fuckin' movie.'

'We stick together, and that's final.'

Looking disgusted, Pete shook his head. 'Okay, okay. Shit.'

'Besides, if we aren't together down there . . .'

In the corner of Larry's vision, something moved. He jerked his eyes toward the ravine. Glimpsed the head and arm of the one-eyed wildman, the face leering, the arm snapping forward as it hurled a rock. 'Watch out!' he shouted.

Ducking, he looked at Pete.

Pete ducked as he brought up his revolver. The rock caught the bridge of his nose, knocked his head back, and bounced to the side. His hat flew off. He stumbled backward a few steps like an out fielder going for a high flyball. Blood spilled over his mustache, dribbled into his open mouth and spread down his chin. The gun fell from his hand. He flopped to the ground. The back of his head thumped a flat slab of granite.

Larry cringed, watching all this, as if he could feel the sharp impacts himself.

Then he remembered Uriah. Or whoever it was.

He snapped his head sideways.

The man was gone.

He dashed for the edge of the ravine.

I'm gonna kill you, you rotten bastard! his mind shrieked. *Look what you did! What'm I gonna tell Barbara? Shit shit shit! You piece of shit, I'm gonna blow your fucking brains all over the desert! Wasn't enough you had to kill Bonnie, you goddamn fucking lunatic!*

He teetered on the rim and gazed down. The embankment below was steep, cluttered with boulders and scrub brush. But nobody was on it. Nobody was running along the flat bottom of the stream bed.

'Where are you, shit!' he yelled.

Then he was scrambling down, dodging the rocks and bushes in his way, arms waving for balance, digging his heels into gravel, skidding over the hardpacked earth. Halfway down, he slipped. His rump pounded the slope. He slid on the seat of his jeans, throat going tight and tears filling his eyes. A boulder stopped his descent. He pushed himself up, stepped onto the outcropping, blinked his eyes clear and scanned the area below him.

No trace of Uriah.

But a lot of hiding places: boulders, thickets, deep cuts eroded into the walls of the ravine.

The bastard might be anywhere, Larry thought.

Or not even down here, at all.

Instead of heading for the bottom after he threw the rock, he might've gone *across* the slope.

A chill swept up Larry's spine. He twisted around.

Nobody there.

But he felt exposed, vulnerable.

Might be anywhere. I've gotta get out of here.

The walnut grips of his revolver felt slippery. He switched the gun to his left hand, rubbed the right dry on a leg of his jeans, and wrapped it around the revolver again. Then, with quick glances all around him, he began to climb the embankment.

Might be anywhere.

He snapped his head from side to side. He glanced behind him. He squinted at the top. Behind him. To the left. To the right. Whenever he looked one way, he imagined Uriah leaping up from the opposite direction.

It's like backing out of a tight space in a parking lot, he thought. A busy lot. Other cars backing out of other spaces.

Exactly the same.

You don't know where to look first.

I'll have to remember that and use it sometime, he told himself.

Christ, this is no time to think about your damn writing!

Took my mind off Uriah, though. At least for a while.

Long enough to get me the rest of the way to the top!

His head almost even with the rim of the embankment, he felt a great surge of relief.

You're not there yet, he told himself. This is when he gets you – when safety's in easy reach.

He looked to the sides. He looked back. No Uriah.

I *made* it!

He chugged for the top.

Uriah was kneeling beside Pete.

Holding a stake against the middle of Pete's chest. Swinging his hammer down.

Chapter Thirty-five

Larry didn't take aim. No time for that. He pointed and fired.

The man's head jerked sideways. Dropping the stake, he grabbed his cheek, glared at Larry with a single, mad eye, twisted on his knees and flung the hammer at him. Larry jumped out of the way. The hammer tumbled by, just missing his shoulder.

'Freeze!' he shouted.

Though he aimed his cocked revolver at the wildman, he held fire. His first shot had been lucky. He didn't want to risk another. Not while his target was kneeling beside Pete.

But Uriah didn't freeze.

He didn't seem to care that a gun was aimed at him. Nor did he seem to care, any more, about his wound. Blood spilled down both sides of his shaggy gray beard as he snatched the stake off the ground and leaped up and charged.

'Stop or I'll shoot!'

'VAMPIRE!' he yelled, spraying blood from his mouth. He dashed straight at Larry, the stake raised in his right hand.

Larry fired.

The metal belly of Jesus caved in and the upper corner of the big wooden cross gouged Uriah's chest.

I hit Jesus! Christ saved Uriah.

Larry thumbed back the hammer, but he couldn't pull the trigger.

As Uriah bore down on him, he flung up his left arm to ward off the stake, and whipped the barrel of his gun against the man's temple. The gun discharged. Hair and flecks of bloody flesh flew off the side of Uriah's head.

Larry was slammed to the ground by the man's limp weight. As his breath was knocked out, he drove his knees up. They jammed into Uriah's belly.

The vampire killer tumbled over Larry.

From the sound of him, he kept on tumbling.

Larry crawled to the rim and saw Uriah plummeting down the slope – rolling, twisting, bouncing over rocks, smashing through bushes, arrows flying from his quiver, his limp arms and legs flapping. Near the bottom, he skidded on his back, head first until his shoulder struck a knob of granite. The impact jarred him to a stop that sent his legs swinging up. He did a backward somersault and landed face down on the floor of the ravine. He lay there motionless.

Larry gazed down at him.

Finish him off. It seemed to be Bonnie's voice. *Do it for me. If you love me, kill him.*

I can't.

If you don't care what he did to me, look at your friend Pete. Look what Uriah tried to do to you. He tried to kill you, too.

It would be easy, he realized. So easy to raise the revolver and empty it into the sprawled body.

Do it, the voice of Bonnie urged him.

But he thought about the way his bullet, fired point blank at Uriah's chest, had been stopped by the crucifix. As if God Himself had intervened to protect the man.

God had nothing to do with it. Uriah was just lucky, that's all. Finish him off, or you'll be sorry.

I've gotta get back to Pete.

Kill Uriah.

'No!' he blurted. Holstering his weapon, he turned away from the ravine. He snatched up his hat and hurried toward Pete.

You'll be sorry.

He dropped to his knees and sagged with relief when he heard Pete's raspy, gurgling breath. Out cold, but alive! Probably a broken nose. He looked like hell. The bridge of his nose was split and swollen. His eyes were swollen. Below his nostrils, his face was sheathed with blood. A string of red saliva hung from the corner of his mouth.

Larry shook him gently by the shoulder, wobbling his head. 'Pete. Pete, wake up.' Nothing.

Straddling him, Larry grabbed the front of his shirt and pulled him into a sitting position. As his head came up, bloody drool flowed from his mouth. He coughed softly, spraying out more, but didn't come to.

Now what?

I'll have to carry him. There's no other choice.

What about his stuff?

Sighing, Larry eased him farther forward until he hung slumped over his own legs. He seemed fairly steady that way. Letting go, Larry gathered the nearby revolver and hat. The gun went into Pete's holster. Larry shoved the hat down on top of his Stetson.

He crouched over Uriah's canvas bag. It contained six wooden stakes, their ends whittled to points.

Bring it along?

Just an extra burden, he decided.

Straddling Pete, he again tried to shake him awake. Then he gave up and grabbed him under the arms and hoisted him. He crouched, wrestling with the body until it flopped over his shoulder. Hugging the backs of Pete's legs, he forced himself upright and started to walk.

He made his way forward, eyes on the distant row of buildings. There seemed to be no passageways leading to the street. He would either have to lug Pete all the way around the end of town, or take him through a window. His legs were already straining and shaky under the weight. It would have to be a window.

Might as well be the one they'd climbed through when they went after Uriah.

Suddenly imagining Uriah rushing at him from the rear, he swung around and looked back.

Nobody there.

Probably still at the bottom of the slope, Larry told himself, and continued trudging toward the window.

He wondered if he *had* killed the man. The first bullet, he was pretty sure, had gone in one cheek and out the other. Certainly not fatal. The second bullet had buried itself in the crucifix or ricocheted off it. But the gun had discharged when he pounded Uriah with it. The bullet from that shot had struck the man's head. No telling what kind of damage it might've done. Maybe it only sliced across his scalp. Or it might've gone into his head. That one could've killed him.

At least I didn't finish him off, Larry told himself. If the guy died from that last shot, it was an accident. And self-defense.

Not that the cops are going to find out about any of this, he thought. Not if I can help it.

He was nearly to the window when Pete moaned and squirmed a little. He took another step, another.

'Uhhh. Put me down,' Pete mumbled.

'Hang on.' Larry staggered the final distance to the wall. Crouching, he pressed his friend against it.

'Look out, man.' Pete shoved him away, sank to his knees, hunched over and heaved bloody vomit. Then he hocked and spit out gobs of red mucus. When he finished, he stayed down, his head hanging. 'Fuckin' A,' he mumbled.

'Are you all right?'

'Ohhh shit. You gotta be kidding.' With one hand, he fingered his face. 'What happened?'

'Uriah clobbered you with a rock.'

'I think my fuckin' nose is busted.'

'Yeah.'

'Feel like my head's split open.'

'You hit a rock when you fell, too.'

He moaned again. He touched the back of his head. Larry didn't see any blood in the hair.

'We'd better get you to a doctor.'

'Fuck that. Take me to an undertaker.' He pushed himself up and leaned against the wall. Holding the sides of his head, he squeezed his swollen eyes shut.

'So what happened to Uriah?'

'He's down in the stream bed.'

'Did one of us get him?'

'Sort of.'

'Huh?'

'It's a long story. Let's get to the car. I'll tell you about it later.'

'Yeah, but is he dead, or what?'

'He might be. I don't know. Think you can get through the window okay?'

'Sure,' he muttered.

Larry climbed into the building. There, he clutched Pete's arm and held him steady while he clambered over the sill. Keeping his grip, he led Pete through the shadowy room and out to the street.

The car was still resting on its jack.

The feathered shaft of an arrow jutted from the wall of the flat tire.

'Good thing we hadn't finished changing it.' Larry said.

'Our lucky day,' Pete muttered.

'It *has* been lucky.'

'Trade heads, you won't think so.'

'Could've been a lot worse.'

'Yeah, sure. Get the trunk open, huh? Get me a beer.'

'I'm not sure you should drink any alcohol. A head injury like that . . .'

'Who died and made you a neurologist?' Pete slapped the trunk. 'Come on!'

Larry opened it, removed the lid from the cooler, and took out two cans of beer. He popped their tops, and gave one to Pete. Instead of drinking, Pete poured beer onto his handkerchief and started cleaning the blood off his face.

Larry stepped to the front of the car. The can was wet in his hand. He took a drink. The beer was cold and good. Squatting, he yanked the arrow from the tire.

'Let's see it,' Pete said, tossing the sodden handkerchief to the pavement.

Larry gave the arrow to him.

'Just like I thought, Apache.'

'Right.'

'Nice souvenir.'

'Good thing it didn't end up in one of us.' Larry drank some more beer. 'We're out here playing cowboy and a lunatic starts shooting arrows at us.'

'Why don't you take off my hat? You look like a dork. If I laugh, it's gonna hurt.'

He plucked Pete's hat off the crown of his own, and held it out.

'On this head? You've gotta be kidding. Just toss it in the car.'

He sailed it through the open window. It landed on the passenger seat. Taking another drink of beer, he squatted down and started pumping the jack handle.

'You sure we don't have to worry about that bozo jumping us again?'

'I shot him three times,' Larry said.

'Holy shit.'

While he worked on changing the tire, he told Pete about rushing down the embankment after Uriah had thrown the rock, being unable to find him, returning to the top just as the old man was about to hammer a stake into Pete's chest, and putting a bullet through his face. He told about Uriah yelling 'Vampire!' and attacking him with the stake. About the bullet that was stopped by the crucifix, about the accidental shot and throwing Uriah down the slope.

When he finished, he looked around. Pete blew, softly through pursed lips and muttered, 'Are you shitting me?'

'Nope,' Larry said. 'It got pretty wild there for a minute.'

'And I missed it.'

'Sorry about that.'

'The bastard was really gonna do a Van Helsing on me?'

'That's right.'

'Sure glad you're good with that shootin' iron, old hoss.'

'Me, too.'

Pete tipped his can high and emptied it into his mouth. 'I'm having another. How about you?'

Though Larry's can was still half full, he said, 'Yeah.' He used the lug wrench to tighten the nuts while Pete went for the beers.

Pete set the fresh one down beside him.

Larry started lowering the car.

'Sounds to me like the old buzzard might still be alive,' Pete said.

'If he is, he's not feeling too spry. And his bow's busted, so he can't do us any harm.'

'Wish you'd polished him off, though.'

'I thought about it.'

Pulling the jack out from under the car, he waited for Pete to suggest they go back and finish the job.

It didn't happen.

Instead, Pete said, 'What'll we do about him?'

'Leave him.'

'I've got half a mind to go back there and put a bullet in his head. But the other half hurts too fucking much.'

'Let's just get the hell out of here. We can worry about him later.'

'Come back in a few days, maybe.'

'Maybe,' Larry said. He had no intention of returning. But why argue about it now?

He didn't feel like fighting with the hubcap, either. Instead, he took it and the jack to the trunk. Then he rolled the flat tire to the rear of the car, and lifted it in.

Pete showed up beside him with the flashlight and arrow. 'We're gonna keep this quiet, right?' he asked. 'You aren't thinking we should tell the cops?'

'No way,' Larry assured him.

'Or the wives.'

'What'll we tell them?'

'We went target shooting, right? I tripped and smashed my face on a rock.'

'Sounds good to me.' He shut the trunk. He returned to the front, picked up his two beers, and climbed in behind the steering wheel. He finished the first can as Pete moved his hat out of the way and lowered himself gingerly onto the passenger seat.

He started the car.

'It's all gotta go in the book, though,' Pete said. He made a U-turn and sped for the end of town. Pete grinned at him. 'It's gonna be great in the book, huh pardner?'

'Yeah. Great.'

'Who would've figured it? We come out here looking for the bastard and we wind up in a fuckin' battle. Fantastic. Gonna have us a bestseller, for sure.'

'And a lot of explaining to do.'

'Hey, the guy's a homicidal maniac. What's to explain?'

'Plenty, I should imagine. The wives'll find out everything. The cops'll find out everything. We'll be up to our ears in crapola.'

'Hey, you're not gonna pussy-out on me, are you?'

Larry shook his head. He took a drink of beer as he sped past Babe's Garage and out of town, 'After all this, nothing in the world could stop me from writing that damn book.'

'My man.'

Chapter Thirty-six

Uriah got slowly to his feet. He stumbled over to a boulder and sat down on it, wincing as his rump met the hard surface.

He knew he'd lost a lot of skin on his way down the slope. But the abrasions were nothing compared to the bullet wounds.

Leaning forward, he spit out some blood and bits of tooth. With his tongue, he gently probed the hole in his left cheek. The pain made him cringe. The hole was pretty small, though. A lot smaller than the wound in his right cheek. Not only had the bullet exited there, but so had one of his molars.

Lucky that bloodsucking son of Satan just had a twenty-two, he thought.

Hurt like crazy, though.

Spitting out some more blood, he fingered the furrow in the scalp above his left ear.

I've been hurt worse, he reminded himself.

This was bad, but he figured nothing could ever hurt as much as the time one of the vampires stabbed the stake into his eye. Talk about a world of pain!

Uriah rubbed the bleeding gouge in the middle of his chest.

He saw the crucifix.

The gold-plated body of Jesus was broken in half at the stomach.

He stared at it for a long time.

My Savior, he thought.

You know I still have work to do.

That's why You helped me escape from the boobyhatch. That's why You brought me back home. That's why You saved me today from the hands of the evil ones. You knew I still had work to do.

Confined in the Illinois hospital for the criminally insane, Uriah had thought his mission was over. He hadn't destroyed every vampire, but he'd done his share. He'd whittled the army down some. He'd lost his eye. He'd been caught. Though they didn't know all he'd done, they knew he'd tried to kill that Charleston vampire, which was enough to get him put away. He'd hated to admit it, but he'd been glad it was over.

When he escaped, he'd had no intention of going after any more vampires. All he'd wanted was to make his way back to Sagebrush Flat, and live in his hotel where he belonged.

But God was behind it, after all. God had led him back here, knowing in His infinite wisdom that trouble was afoot.

Uriah had been in town no more than a month before those people came and found the hiding place. He'd been out in the desert, hunting up supper. They were gone by the time he returned. When he spotted the broken floor of the landing, he'd prayed that they hadn't discovered the vampire. But his prayer was in vain. The panel enclosing its tomb was loose. The blanket was disarrayed.

He knew, then, that Satan had sent them to undo his work.

But why hadn't they pulled out the stake, then and there? It didn't make sense. Had God intervened, somehow, to prevent it?

For days afterward, Uriah had kept a vigil. He never left the hotel. At night, instead of retiring to his second floor room, he'd slept in the lobby. It puzzled him that the intruders didn't return to resurrect the foul thing under the stairs. Perhaps they hadn't been sent by Satan, after all. Maybe pure chance had led them here, and they had no intention of coming back.

But if they were innocents, why hadn't they told the police about finding a corpse?

Day after day, Uriah waited and pondered these things. He left the hotel only to relieve himself and to fetch water from the old well out back. He ate jerky from the small supply that he'd set aside for emergencies. When the last of the jerky was gone, he fasted for two days rather than abandon his watch to go hunting.

Finally, gnawed by hunger and knowing he would need all his strength to combat the evil that was sure to come, he'd set out into the desert. Not until after dark did the Lord provide him with a meal. He'd cooked up the coyote. It had spoken to him as he ate. It told him to beware. While he'd been guarding the vampire under the stairs, the intruders had found the other two and set them free.

He'd been sure it was the voice of God that had warned him. Terrified that the evil had been unleashed, Uriah had hurried back to the hotel. With candles and a rusty old spade from his room, he ran to the east end of town. The front door of King's Liquor had long since been broken open. Entering, he made his way to the rear of the empty shop. Holding a candle close to the floor, he was able to find the trap door.

It had been Ernie King's pride and joy – a secret entrance to the cellar where he kept his most precious bottles of wine. In the old days, Ernie used to brag that nobody knew about the trap door except for his own family and his best pal, Uriah. They'd spent many fine evenings down there, sampling, before

Ernie upped and left town along with nearly everyone else.

A thin layer of sand blown in from the desert covered the wooden hatch.

Sure didn't *look* as if anyone had opened it up recently.

But maybe the intruders had sprinkled sand around, afterward, to make the area look undisturbed.

Uriah took out his knife. He pried up the trap door and eased it down against the floor. Lifting his shovel, he descended the stairs.

The dirt floor didn't appear to have been dug up. That should've been another clue. But Uriah was not about to question the words of the Lord. By the light of the candles, sweating in spite of the cellar's chill, he'd dug for the bodies.

These had been buried deep. With these, he'd had plenty of time. He would've put the last vampire down here, too, but he'd been in too much of a rush. He'd been seen. So he'd just hidden it under the hotel stairs and fled town as fast as he could.

Digging in the hard earth of the cellar, he wished he hadn't put these two down so far.

Hours seemed to go by, and his last candle was down to a tiny stub before the blade of his shovel struck wood. He had buried the coffins next to each other. He wasn't sure which he'd found. But it didn't matter.

Standing in the shoulder-deep hole, he worked feverishly to clear the coffin's lid. The candle was guttering as he scooped out footholds on each side.

He straddled the coffin. He rammed the blade of his shovel under its lid. The nails squeaked. The candle died.

A chill of dread squirmed through Uriah as he worked in total darkness.

The Lord had told him that the vampires had been set free. Not that they were gone.

There might be a living vampire in the coffin below him.

My crucifix and my garlic will protect me, he told himself.

But his terror grew as he wrenched the top of the casket loose. He tossed his shovel out of the hole, bent down and lifted the lid. He brought it up between his spread legs. He hurled it out of the hole.

Carefully, he eased himself down until his knees came to rest on the narrow wooden edges of the casket. Gripping an edge with his left hand, he bent lower. He reached through the darkness.

His fingers slipped into soft, dry hair and he felt as if a thousand spiders were rushing up his back.

He touched the parched, crusty skin of the vampire's face. When his fingertips met the edges of her teeth, he gasped and jerked his hand back.

'The Lord is my shepherd, I shall not want,' he whispered, and forced himself to touch her again. He felt her neck. Her collar bone. 'He maketh me to lie down in green pastures.'

He touched the smooth roundness of the wooden stake.

He curled his hand around it.

The stake was still buried in her chest, just as it ought to be.

Uriah knew, then, that the coyote had lied. Its voice hadn't been the Lord. Satan had spoken through the beast to trick him.

Throwing himself out of the hole, Uriah scurried through the darkness. He stumbled up the cellar stairs and rushed out to the sidewalk.

In time to see two men come out of the hotel carrying the coffin.

Angry, miserable with fear and guilt, he watched them slide the coffin into the rear of a van. They climbed into the front seats. Without headlights, the van sped up the moonlit street. For a wild moment, Uriah considered rushing out and trying to stop it.

But the Lord held him back.

Bide your time, He seemed to say. I won't fail you.

So Uriah had ducked out of sight within the store until the van was gone.

He had bided his time.

Today, the Lord had brought the men back to Sagebrush Flat. They had come to kill him. Of that, he was certain. They had set the vampire free and become its undead brethren. They had come here to destroy the only man worthy of laying them to rest.

But they had failed.

Uriah touched his tongue against the raw inside of his cheek, and winced.

They failed, he thought. But I didn't.

No, he hadn't succeeded in putting them at peace. But he would.

He would get them *and* the vampire who had slaughtered his family. All together.

He smiled. It sent fire through his cheeks and made his eyes water.

Reaching, down, he plucked a slip of folded paper from between his belt and the skin of his belly.

Before honking the horn of their car to draw them out, he had searched the glove compartment. He had found what he knew must be there.

The vehicle registration slip.

Unfolding it, he blinked the tears from his eyes and gazed at the paper.

The car was registered to Lawrence Dunbar, 345 Palm Avenue, Mulehead Bend, California.

Mulehead Bend.

Uriah used to know that town very well.

It's where the vampires had come from before – when they came in the night to murder his Elizabeth and Martha. It's where they were gathering again, growing in numbers.

Some fifty miles off.

It'll take me a couple of days, he thought. I'd better get started.

He tucked the registration slip under his belt, and began to climb the wall of the ravine.

Chapter Thirty-seven

Lane's hand trembled as she applied eyeliner. It's not a date, she told herself. Just a school function. Nothing more than a glorified field trip, really.

She'd been telling herself that all day, but it never seemed to help.

I probably won't even have a chance to be alone with him.

The doorbell rang, and her stomach gave a sickening lurch. *He's here.*

Lane took a deep breath, trying to calm herself, then brushed mascara onto her lashes. She put the make-up away. She took her purse off the dresser, and stepped back in front of the closet mirror.

I can't go dressed in this! she suddenly thought, and saw her face turn red. No, it's okay; He doesn't want us in evening gowns. He said it's not the prom.

Besides, she'd worn this outfit to mass a few times. If it's good enough for mass, it's good enough for *Hamlet*.

And I do look good in it, she thought. And it's *me!*

Lane lifted her arms. Though her armpits felt wet, no moisture showed on the tie-dyed blue denim. Probably because the blouse fit so loosely. Most of the perspiration just ran down her sides.

'Lane!' Mom called. 'Mr Kramer's here.'

'I'll be right out!'

Quickly, she popped open the top snaps. She plucked some Kleenex from a box on top of the dresser, reached inside the blouse, dried her armpits, and applied a fresh coating of roll-on. Pinching the snaps shut again, she hurried from the room.

I *am* too casual, she thought when she saw Mr Kramer in the foyer. He wore a necktie with a white shirt, blue blazer and gray slacks.

'Good evening, Lane,' he said. Then he turned back to her

father and raised the copy of *Night Watcher* in his left hand. 'Thanks again for the autograph, Larry.'

'Thanks for buying the book,' Dad said. 'I'm glad you could find a copy.' His face was a little more red than usual, his voice a little thicker. But at least he didn't slur his words. He'd had a *lot* to drink before dinner. Lane hoped Mr Kramer didn't realize he was pretty well polluted.

'And I can count on you for October thirty-first?'

'I'll be there.'

'That's terrific. The kids'll get a great kick out of having a speaker like you on Halloween.'

'I'll read 'em some *really disgusting* stuff from my books.'

'I'm sure they'll love it.' He nodded at Lane. 'Well, I guess we'd better be on our way. Are you all set?'

'Am I dressed okay?' she asked. 'I could put on something more . . .'

'No, no, you're perfect.'

Mom, smiling, nodded in agreement. 'You look just fine, honey.'

'You shore do, little pardner,' Dad said. 'If'n you run into Hoot up the trail, be sure'n tell him 'Howdy' for me.'

'Oh, Daaaad.'

Mr Kramer laughed. 'It was very nice meeting you, Larry,' he said, and extended his hand.

Dad shook it. 'Nice to meet you, too. And I'll see you on Halloween.'

Shaking hands with Mom, Mr Kramer said, 'A real pleasure meeting you, Jean. I can see where Lane got her looks.'

She blushed. 'Why, thank you.'

As he opened the door, Lane kissed her parents. 'See you later,' she told them, and they wished her a good time. Then she was on the walkway with Mr Kramer. His station wagon, parked at the curb, looked empty.

He *did* come here first!

Lane hoped it wasn't just a matter of geographical convenience, hoped he'd chosen to pick her up before the others so they could have some time alone.

'Are you warm enough in that?' he asked.

Did he realize she was trembling? 'Oh, I'm fine,' she said. Her shivers, she thought, had little to do with the chilly night air. 'I'm just excited,' she added.

He smiled at her. 'It's great to have a student actually excited about going to a play.'

That isn't it, at all, Lane thought as he opened the passenger door. She climbed into the car. He shut the door, walked around the front, and got in behind the steering wheel.

'Excuse me,' he muttered. Leaning sideways, he reached in front of Lane to open the glove compartment. 'Don't want anything happening to the book.' For just a moment, as he slipped the paperback into the compartment, his shoulder pushed against her upper arm. 'There,' he said. 'Safe and sound.' He sat up straight and started the car.

'Have you read it yet?' Lane asked.

'No, unfortunately.' He pulled away from the curb. 'I should be able to get to it next week, though.'

'After you read that, you may want to reconsider having Dad speak to the class.' She grinned. 'You may not want him anywhere near a group of high school students.'

'That bad, huh?'

'That nasty.'

'He seemed like a very nice man,' Mr Kramer said.

'Oh, he is. You'd think he was a monster, reading that stuff, but he's awfully sweet. He had kind of a bad time today, though. In case you thought he was acting a little . . . weird. See, he went out shooting in the desert. With our neighbor, Pete. 'I'm running off at the mouth like a kid, she thought. He doesn't care about any of this. 'Anyway, Pete had some kind of an accident.'

'Not shot, I hope.'

'Oh, no. Nothing like that. But he fell off some rocks and got knocked out cold. He actually broke his nose. Dad had to take him to the emergency room. So anyway, he wasn't exactly himself after he got done with all that.'

'It doesn't sound like much fun.'

'No. It wasn't. So, how have you been?'

'No complaints. How about yourself? You haven't had any more run-ins with Benson, I hope.'

'No.'

'He'll probably leave you alone. But let me know if he causes you any trouble.'

'I think you put the fear of God into him.'

Mr Kramer shook his head. 'You never know, a guy like that. You'll have to keep your eyes open. Don't let him catch you alone. There's no telling what he might do, and I'd sure hate for anything to happen to my best student.'

'I'll be careful,' she said.

'Speaking of which, maybe you'd better buckle up.'

'Planning to crash?' she asked, and reached up for the safety harness.

'I'll sure try not to. But you may have noticed, you keep getting hurt when you're around me.'

'Yeah. Guess you're bad luck.' She drew the strap down between her breasts and snapped its metal tab into the buckle by her left hip.

'Now you won't have to worry about a rendezvous with the windshield.'

'Yeah. I'd look lousy at the play with blood all over my clothes.'

'I do like that outfit,' he said, glancing at her. 'You haven't worn it to school, have you?'

'Not this one.'

'I've seen you in something similar, though. A blue denim jumper with white lace. A mini, as I recall.'

'Oh, that.' She felt a warm stir, pleased to find out that he actually remembered what she wore to school, but slightly embarrassed that he recalled the jumper. 'Probably too short,' she said.

'I wouldn't say that. You've got the legs for it.'

'Thanks,' she said, heat rushing to her face.

He swung the car to the curb and stopped. Lane gazed at him, her heart pounding. *Why'd he stop?* He turned on the overhead light. He smiled at her. Then he reached inside his blazer and took a sheet of paper from his pocket.

Just checking directions, she realized.

'Okay,' he said. 'Aaron's at 4980 Cactus. Should be just on the next block.'

Lane felt a pull of disappointment. Their time alone was almost done.

She hoped she would get to sit with him in the theater, but it didn't work out that way. Sandra, bending his ear about something, followed him down the aisle and into the row. There was no way for Lane to get past her without making a spectacle of herself.

Mr Kramer took a seat beside a college student. Sandra sat beside him, and Lane found herself between Sandra and George, with Aaron at the other side of George.

She felt cheated.

I'm here to see *Hamlet*, she reminded herself. Not to be with Mr Kramer.

He likes me, though. He really does. He likes me a lot.

George, squirming in his seat, brushed against her arm. 'Excuse me,' he whispered.

'That's okay,' she said without looking at him.

'I didn't mean to do that.'

She looked at George and nodded. 'I know. It's okay.'

'I guess guys are probably always bothering you, you know? It must be annoying.'

Lane shrugged. 'It all depends on the guy.'

'Yeah. I guess it would. That makes sense. Well, you don't have to worry about me. These seats are kind of close together. That's the problem.'

'You shouldn't worry about it.'

'I just don't want you to get the wrong impression.'

'I won't.'

'It was nice talking to you, though.' George turned his face forward, leaned the other way, and scanned the audience ahead of him. His lips were pressed together. With his far hand, he adjusted his glasses and brushed some stray hair off his forehead.

'George?'

He jerked his head toward her so fast that Lane feared he might've hurt his neck.

'If it makes you so nervous sitting next to me, maybe you should trade places with Aaron.'

For a moment, he looked hurt. Then he said, 'Sure. If you want me to.'

'I don't.'

His eyebrows lifted. 'You don't?'

'Not unless you want to.'

'Me? No. I mean . . .'

'You sit way in the back of the class. I don't think we've ever even talked to each other.'

'No, we haven't.'

'You're really good in English.'

'You, too. You're the best in the class.'

'When I don't lose my place?'

He smiled. 'Oh, that was nothing. I lose my place all the time. I get to daydreaming, and that's all she wrote.'

'I'll bet you want to be a writer, don't you?'

His head tilted. He frowned. 'How did you know?'

'You have that look about you.'

He wrinkled his nose, making his glasses rise slightly. 'The look of the nerd.'

'Don't let my dad hear that. He's a writer.'

'A *real* writer?'

'He likes to think so. You've probably never heard of him. Lawrence Dunbar.'

George's frown deepened. 'No. I don't think so.'

'He writes penny dreadfuls. Or, as he likes to say, three dollar ninety-five dreadfuls.'

George laughed. 'That's a good one,' he said.

'I really liked the story you read in class. The guy whose bones dissolved?'

His face went bright red. 'You did? Thanks.'

'Have you got any more?'

'Are you kidding? I've got piles of them. My parents think I'm doing homework all the time, but I'm actually up in my room writing stuff. Boy, would they be pissed.' He cringed. 'Excuse me. That just slipped out.'

'I say it all the time.'

The theater lights went dark.

Lane leaned toward George. 'I want to read some of your other stories, okay?'

'Do you mean it?'

'Sure.' The curtain started to rise. 'If you want, I'll even have Dad take a look at some of them.'

'Jeez, I don't know.'

On the stage, it was night and two sentries stood on the parapet of Elsinore, looking very cold.

George settled back in his seat. When his shoulder brushed against Lane, he leaned away to break the contact. Lane swept her elbow up past the arm of the chair and nudged him. Again, he snapped his head around.

'I don't bite,' Lane whispered.

She tried to pay attention to the play. But her mind kept drifting.

She felt good about her talk with George. He seemed nice. A little like Henry. Not as weird, though. Those two should really hit it off.

Awfully shy, but he would get over that once they knew each other better.

And we will, she thought.

Maybe it was Fate that she ended up sitting with him. And Fate that she'd broken up with Jim last night.

George would never act like Jim. He probably never even would've had the nerve to talk to me, she thought, much less ask me out. Probably *still* won't ask me out. I can ask him, though. Why not?

I never would've gotten anywhere with Mr Kramer, anyway.

Thinking that, she felt a hollow ache.

He's a teacher, she told herself. He can't get involved with me even if he wants to.

But her mind dwelled on him, lingering on the way he looked, the things he'd said to her, the way he'd handled Benson, the way he'd caught her when she fell from the stool, how his hands had felt when he touched her bare ribs and leg, when he'd accidentally touched her breast as he took the books from her yesterday.

He remembered her denim jumper, though she hadn't worn it for nearly two weeks. He recognized her car in the lot yesterday. Didn't those things prove that he cared for her?

Maybe he likes me as much as I like him.

She wondered how it would feel to kiss him.

The lights came up for intermission, and she realized she'd hardly paid any attention at all to the play. Not that it mattered. She'd read it a few times, and seen both the Olivier and Burton movies.

Mr Kramer stayed in his seat and talked to Sandra. Aaron went off, probably to find a bathroom since he couldn't be going for refreshments – the theater had no snack counter. Lane turned to George. He was looking around the auditorium, but not at her. Intentionally not at her, she suspected.

'How do you get to school?' she asked.

'Me?' Now, he looked. Straight into her eyes.

'Yeah, you.'

'Oh, my mom drives me.'

'Your place is just a few blocks from Henry Peidmont. I usually give him and Betty Thompson a lift to school in the mornings.'

'Oh, yeah, I know.'

She smiled. 'Spying on me?'

'No! Huh-uh.'

'I was just joking.'

He kept staring into her eyes. For a few moments, he was silent. Then he smiled. 'Me, too. I mean, I don't *spy* on you, exactly. But I notice you a lot. All the time. Whenever you're around, anyway.'

'Really?'

'If you want to know the truth . . .' Grimacing, he shook his head. 'Never mind.'

'No, what?'

'You'd think I'm a dork.'

'No, I wouldn't. Come on.' She elbowed him gently. 'Spill it.'

'It's stupid. Never mind.'

'All right. Anyway, what I was going to say is you can ride with us if you'd like. I could pick you up Monday morning on my way to Henry's. I've got room for one more passenger. It'd save your mother a trip, and we'd be glad to have you along.'

George looked confused. 'Why?' he asked.

'Why what?'

'Why would you want me along?'

'Why wouldn't I?'

'We don't even know each other.'

'We do, now. And I want to know you better.'

His face went crimson. 'You do?'

'Yes.'

'Jeez.'

'How about it?'

'Sure. Fine. I'll have to check with my parents, but . . .' He shook his head.

'Why don't you give me your telephone number?'

'Yeah. Sure. Okay.'

Lane opened her purse. She took out a pen and a small notepad. George told her the telephone number. She wrote it down, then wrote her own number on the next page, tore off the sheet and gave it to him. He stared at it.

'You find out if it's all right with your folks, and I'll give you a call tomorrow.'

'Yeah. Okay.'

'You don't *have* to ride with us.'

'No, I think . . . that'd be neat. Henry's a cool guy, and . . .'

'I've never heard him called that before.'

George grinned. 'Well, yeah, he is. I think so, anyway.'

'Me, too.'

'Betty's kind of obnoxious.'

Lane laughed. 'Ah, you know her.'

'To know her is to fear her. But you're not so bad.'

'Why, thanks. You're not so bad, either.'

Chapter Thirty-eight

'Would you mind if we stop at the marina for a minute?' Mr Kramer asked after he'd dropped off the others. They were back on Shoreline Drive, still a mile from the turnoff to Lane's house. 'It'll save me an errand in the morning.'

'That's okay with me,' she said.

'Great. It won't take long. I just need to pick up a couple of things I left on my boat.'

'You have a boat?'

'She isn't much, but she's mine.'

'Jee, that's neat.' Neat, Lane thought. Dumb. Stop talking like a kid.

He pulled the station wagon into the parking area in front of a hardware store, turned around, and headed back the way they'd come. Lane was well aware that they had passed the marina shortly after leaving the Community College. Either Mr Kramer hadn't wanted the rest of the kids to know about his boat, or he'd just remembered whatever it was that he needed to pick up. Either way, she was glad. This would give her a little while longer to be with him. And it made her feel special that he was willing to take her along, to let her have a glimpse of his real world.

I'm more than just a student to him, she thought. He wants me to see that he's not just a teacher.

789

'So,' he said, 'I guess you made a new friend tonight.'

'George? Yeah. He's nice.'

'He's a good student. He seems like quite a young gentleman. Did he ask you out?'

'No, not hardly.'

'Well, then, he missed the boat. No pun intended.'

'George is pretty bashful. But I might start giving him rides to school. He has to check with his parents.'

'Always a good idea. Speaking of parents, it's almost midnight. I don't want to get you into any trouble.'

'Well, they know it's a long play. I don't think they'll mind if I'm kind of late. Especially since I'm with you. Since you're my teacher, and everything.'

'Good. That's good. This won't take long.' Soon, he turned into the marina parking lot. A few other cars and pickups were there, but Lane saw no people. 'Come on down with me,' Mr Kramer said. 'I'll show you the pride of my fleet.'

'Great.' She climbed out. She met him in front of his station wagon. Side by side, they walked toward the dock. A chilly wind, blowing in off the river, swept her hair back and pressed the front her blouse and skirt against her skin. She leaned into it. She folded her arms across her chest.

'Cold?'

'A little.'

'Here.' He started to remove his blazer.

'No, no. I can't take that. I'm fine. Really.'

'I insist.' Turning to Lane, his white sport shirt flapping, his necktie whipping this way and that, he draped the jacket over her shoulders. She clutched its lapels to keep it from blowing away.

'You're gonna freeze,' she warned, her voice trembling.

'Naw. I'm of hearty, sea-faring stock.'

'If you say so.'

He unlocked a chainlink gate, and held it open while Lane stepped onto the dock. When he came toward her, his shoulders were hunched.

'You *are* freezing.'

'Me?' Arching his back, he threw his chest out and pounded it with his fists.

Lane laughed. It felt strange to laugh with her lungs feeling so tight and shaky. It left her breathless.

'You can shield me,' Mr Kramer said. He turned her around. Holding her by the shoulders, he pressed himself against her back and steered her forward. She twisted her head to look at him. Their faces nearly collided. 'Careful,' he said. 'Or we'll have *still another* accident.'

The dock swayed under her feet. The boats moored along both sides bobbed and pitched on the rough surface of the river. Most were dark, but lights glowed from the cabins of a few. She wondered if there were people inside the lighted boats. She didn't see anyone. And hoped that no one saw her.

What if it got back to Mom and Dad that I was out here fooling around like this with Mr Kramer?

'Hard to port,' he said into her ear. Turning Lane to the left, he pushed her along an arm of pier. Past a rocking, dark sailboat. Past a catamaran. He halted her at the bow of a powerboat that must've been at least twenty feet long. Moonlight gleamed on its foredeck and cabin windshield.

He hurried ahead of Lane, and she followed him up a narrow strip of pier that reached alongside the boat. Near the stern, he stepped onto the gunwhale and hopped down. 'Watch your step,' he said. He held out a hand to her. She took it, hung onto his jacket with her other hand, and planted a foot on the rail. As she thrust herself up, he pulled. She dropped, landed on the pitching deck, and staggered against him.

Mr Kramer wrapped his arms around her. He squeezed her tightly against him. He said, 'Brrrrr.'

His face felt cool on her cheek. His chest was solid against her breasts. His hands moved up and down her back. She could feel him shivering.

'Why don't we go below for a minute?' he gasped. 'Warm up.'

Lane nodded.

He turned away, unlocked the cabin door and slid it open. 'Go on first. And watch your step.'

791

She climbed down into darkness. Away from the wind. At the bottom of the stairs, she found herself in narrow, cozy quarters. Moonlight came in through the portholes, casting a gray haze over cushions to both sides and in front of her.

She heard the door skid shut. It cut off most of the wind's noise.

'Sleeps three,' Mr Kramer said. 'If they're munchkins.'

'Nice,' Lane whispered. She turned around, careful not to lose her balance, and saw the dim shape of Mr Kramer coming toward her.

'A haven from the tempest,' he said.

'That's for sure. You might as well have this back.' She slipped the blazer off her shoulders.

'Just toss it down anywhere.'

She folded the jacket. As she bent down to place it on a cushion, a hand stroked the back of her head and she flinched.

'Sorry. Did I startle you?'

'A little.'

She stood up straight. The hand slipped down to her shoulder. Then both Mr Kramer's hands were on her shoulders, gently rubbing them through the heavy denim. Her mouth went dry. Her heart thudded.

'Does that feel good?' he asked.

'Yeah. But . . . I really can't stay.'

'I know. We'll go in a minute. But you like this, don't you? I know you liked it after school the other day. Really eases the tension.'

He kept on massaging her, squeezing her shoulders, moving to the sides of her neck.

We shouldn't be doing this, she thought. Not here.

Her head felt heavy. She could hardly hold it up,

His hands eased down along her neck. Under her collar. The top snap of her blouse popped open. And his hands were inside, kneading her shoulders.

'Mr Kramer,' she murmured.

'Hal. Call me Hal.'

'Hal. I'd better go now. Honest.'

'It's all right,' he said. 'We're not doing anything wrong.'

It *felt* wrong. But it felt good, too. Incredibly good.

His big, warm hands curled over her shoulders and down her upper arms. She realized they had taken her bra straps with them. Something low in her belly, something cold, seemed to jump.

'Now, you're smooth,' he whispered, massaging her shoulders.

'We shouldn't. This isn't . . .'

He brushed his mouth against hers, and the words got lost. 'Oh, Lane.' His breath caressed her lips. His hands drifted over her cheeks as softly as a mild breeze. They went away. He kissed her again, his mouth open and warm and tender.

Lane had daydreamed about this. And this was much the same as her daydream. But more exciting. And more frightening. And somehow shameful. She hadn't expected the feelings of fear and guilt.

It's already gone too far.

But she felt helpless, trapped by the pull of his moist, warm mouth.

While he kissed her, he popped open the next snap of her blouse. And then the next.

Jesus, she thought.

After the last snap came apart, Hal slid his tongue into Lane's mouth and spread her blouse open.

She turned her face away. His tongue came out of her mouth and spread a wet path across her cheek. 'I have to go home,' she gasped. 'Right now.'

'This is what you've been waiting for,' he said, slipping the blouse off her shoulders. She tried to raise her arms, but he pressed them down and pushed the sleeves off. 'It's what we've both been waiting for. You know that.'

'No.'

Embracing her, pinning her arms to her sides, he kissed her wet cheek and unclasped the back of her bra.

'No! I mean it!' She squirmed, but he hugged her hard against him.

'What's the matter with you?' he asked. She heard no anger in his voice. He sounded confused, even hurt.

'It's just not right. You're a teacher.'

'You've been trying your best to seduce me. Well, I'm only human. You've won. You've got me.'

She struggled in his embrace, but he held her fast.

'There's no reason to be frightened. Just calm down.'

Lane stopped struggling.

'That's better. That's much better.' He relaxed his hold. His hands roamed gently over her bare back. 'Doesn't this feel good?'

'I guess so.'

'You're a very lucky young lady,' he said. 'They *all* want me. You know that, don't you?' His hands slid lower. They rubbed her buttocks. 'Every female in that school has the hots for me. But only a lucky few actually *get* me.'

'I want to go home,' Lane said, trying to keep her voice from shaking. 'Please.'

'I'll take you home.' He found the button at the hip of her skirt. He opened it, and slid the zipper down.

'No!'

'I'll take you home as soon as we've finished.'

The skirt dropped around her feet. He slipped his hands inside the seat of her panties. His fingers kneaded her rump.

'Mr Kramer, don't.'

'It's Hal. Remember?'

He peeled the panties down around her thighs.

'Damn it!' She shoved him.

He stumbled backward and dropped onto a cushion. Sprawled there, he said, 'You're a real disappointment, Lane.'

She bent over. The bra fell away from her breasts, its straps sliding down her arms. She tugged her panties up. Bending lower, the bra drifting down to her wrists, she reached for her skirt. Before she could lift it, Hal stretched out a leg and pinned the skirt to the deck. 'Take your foot off.'

His leg jerked back. The skirt, hooked by his heel, tugged sharply at Lane's boots. Her feet skidded. With a gasp, she lurched up straight and waved her arms, flinging her bra through the darkness. Just as she found her balance, Kramer ducked, grabbed the skirt with both hands, and yanked it toward him.

Her feet flew out from under her.

'NO!' she cried out as she fell.

The edge of a cushion caught her across the rump. Her back slapped the cool surface. She jammed her hands down and pushed herself up.

Kramer stepped between her knees. He grabbed her throat and shoved her down against the pad. With his other hand, he punched her just below the sternum.

Pain blasted through Lane's body. Her breath whooshed out. She wheezed, trying to suck in more, but her lungs didn't seem to work. Nothing seemed to work. She felt as if her body had exploded apart from the center.

Kramer let go of her throat.

She tried to lift her head, but couldn't.

'You'll be okay in a minute,' Kramer said, his voice faint through the roaring in her ears. 'I hit you in the solar plexus. It's a nerve ganglion, in case you're not up on your physiology. Somewhat the equivalent of a man catching one in the nuts. I'm sorry you made me do that to you.'

Lane realized the agony was fading and she could breathe, taking small, painful gulps of air.

'But I'll do worse,' he said, 'if you give me any more trouble.'

She felt one of her boots come off. Then the other. Kramer's hands moved slowly up her legs.

'We'll have a long, wonderful relationship, though. In spite of this rather shaky beginning. You'll see.'

She felt his mouth against the crotch of her panties. She felt his lips and teeth, his squirming tongue. Then his mouth went away. He ripped apart each side of her panties and tugged the remnants of fabric out from under her rump.

'This is what you wanted,' he whispered. She heard a tremor in his voice. 'This is what we both want.'

* * *

795

'You're home,' he said. 'Safe and sound. And it isn't even all that terribly late.'

His words seemed to come from far away.

'Look at me.'

Lane turned her head. Vaguely, she realized that Kramer was smiling.

'You had a wonderful time, didn't you? I know I did. We'll do it again, won't we? Maybe Monday or Tuesday. We'll work out where and when later. And you'll be there. Won't you?'

She managed to nod.

'I didn't hear that.'

'Yes,' she murmured. 'I'll be there.'

'And you'll never tell a living soul about our little party, will you?'

'No.'

'And what happens if you do?'

'The razor.'

'That's right.' Kramer patted the pocket of his slacks. 'And who gets the razor?'

'My parents. And me.'

'Very good. You're an excellent student. Now, go on inside your house. Your folks are probably waiting up for you, so you'd better look lively. You'd better put on a good show. If I so much as suspect that you've betrayed me, you know what'll happen.'

'I know.'

'And don't think the cops can save you. They can't. Even if they take me in, I'll be out. You know what bail is.'

'I know.'

'And you know what'll happen when I get out.'

'I know.'

'Okay. Goodnight, now, darling.'

She concentrated on her hand, and watched it pull the door lever. The door swung away from her shoulder. She felt a cool wind.

'Sweet dreams,' Kramer said.

Then she was standing on the curb, watching Kramer's car

until it disappeared around the corner. She turned slowly until she was facing the house. Its porch light was on.

How can I pretend . . .?

She took careful steps toward the house. She felt as if Kramer had shoved a thick branch deep inside her, a branch of embers that any quick motion would set ablaze.

They'll know something's wrong, she thought.

I'll say I got my period.

At the front door, she halted under the light and looked down at herself. Her skirt was crooked. She straightened it. She supposed she looked as if nothing had happened. As long as they couldn't see under the skirt.

Kramer had kept her panties.

A souvenir of our first date, he'd said.

What am I going to do?

She tried to focus her mind.

All that matters right now, she told herself, is getting past Mom and Dad. I can't let them suspect.

She found her keys, unlocked the door, and stepped slowly over the threshold.

The television was on.

Dad lay on the sofa, snoring.

Mom wasn't in the room.

Thank God.

Silently, Lane shut the door. She crept past the sofa, out of the living room and into the hallway. 'Is that you, honey?' Mom called. Her voice sounded groggy as if she'd been asleep.

'Yeah.' Fixing a smile on her face, she stepped to the doorway of the master bedroom. Her mother was propped up in bed, an open book resting on her lap.

'How was the play?'

'Pretty good.'

'Did you go somewhere after?'

'Yeah. Mr Kramer took us all out for pizza.'

'Oh, that was awfully nice of him.' Mom yawned, patted her mouth, and squinted at Lane. 'Are you feeling all right?'

'I've got a miserable headache. And cramps.'

'Oh, I'm sorry. Hope it didn't ruin your time.'

She shrugged. 'I'll be okay after I've had a shower and some aspirin.'

'What's your father doing?'

'Snoozing on the sofa.'

'He overindulged.'

'Yeah. He was upset about Pete's accident.'

'Whatever. I think I'll just let him stay there.'

'Okay. Night, Mom.'

'Sleep tight.'

Lane went to her bedroom. When she came out with her robe, light no longer spilled into the hallway from her parents' room.

In the bathroom, she turned on the light and locked the door. She took off her clothes. Sitting on the toilet, she removed the tampon.

Don't want you ruining your nice skirt, Kramer had said before pushing it into her.

He actually kept a supply on his boat.

The tube was sodden with blood and semen.

Lane knew she shouldn't flush it down the toilet, but she couldn't leave such evidence in the waste basket. She had never used tampons. If Mom noticed it . . .

She flushed it away.

Leaning back, she looked down at herself. Her skin was red where he had punched her. Red where he'd squeezed her. Red where he'd sucked her. She thought she could smell his saliva. A sickening, sweet odor. But not as sickening as the taste in her mouth.

Groaning, she leaned forward and peered down. Her blond curls were matted flat, dry now but sticking to her skin. Under the sparse hair, her skin had a reddish hue like her breasts. She saw no blood. Or anything worse. Kramer had licked her clean.

Her vulva looked like a raw wound, the lips crimson and shiny.

Lane winced when she eased her legs together. She stood

up, hobbled to the sink, and started to brush her teeth. The toothpaste had a minty flavor that overcame the taste of Kramer.

She stared at herself in the medicine cabinet mirror as she brushed. Her hair looked windblown. Her eyes were pink where they should've been white, and had a strange, dazed look about them. They hardly seemed to be her eyes at all.

This *isn't* me any more, she thought. It's somebody else. Somebody who got fucked.

Really fucked.

I'm ruined, she thought. Wrecked, fucked.

And I'm dead meat if I tell. Dead meat if I don't let him do it to me again.

Like hell I'll let him do it to me again.

A thick foam of toothpaste spilled over Lane's lower lip. In the mirror, she watched it roll toward her chin. She suddenly gagged. Eyes going blurry, she whirled away from the sink. She dropped to her knees in front of the toilet, grabbed its seat with both hands and heaved into the bowl.

When she was done, she crawled to the bathtub.

Chapter Thirty-nine

Lane patted herself gently with the towel, taking care not to awaken hurts. Then, she draped it over the bar and put on her robe. The soft fabric stuck to her skin where she'd missed wet areas.

Her toothbrush lay in the sink, its bristles and handle still coated with white goo. She rinsed it off. Knowing she could never put it into her mouth again, she dropped it into the waste basket.

I'll say it fell on the floor and got hair on it, or something, she thought.

In a cabinet under the window, she found her leather traveling case. She took out her spare toothbrush. She brushed her teeth again. When the paste thickened inside her mouth, she gagged once and her eyes watered. This time, however, she didn't throw up. She spat out the paste, rinsed and put her brush into the holder.

She took aspirin, washing down three caplets with cold water.

After checking the toilet and finding no traces of vomit, she gathered her clothes and left the bathroom.

The hallway felt cool. Light still glowed at the far end. She wondered if her father was still snoring on the sofa.

Mom always got pissed off when he drank too much.

It's not such a big crime, Lane thought.

Mom ought to be glad she's married to someone like him, and not give him crap about little stuff like that.

She stepped into her bedroom. With an elbow, she nudged the light switch up. She carried her denim boots to the closet and set them down.

And stared at them.

Her present, her reward for getting Dad the yearbook.

God, she thought. If Kramer hadn't helped me get the yearbook, I wouldn't have started staying after class. None of this might've happened.

You got me raped, Dad.

Bullshit. It was all my fault.

Grievously did she sin, and grievously did she pay.

What's that, Shakespeare?

Kramer rigged that coin toss for *Hamlet*, she suddenly realized. He had it all planned.

She stepped over to the bed with her clothes. She tossed her skirt and blouse down, and lifted her bra close to the lamp. It didn't appear to be soiled.

Soiled enough, she thought. The bastard touched it.

As she inspected her blouse and skirt, her mind went back to the coin toss. When was that? Before Mom and I went to Grandma's last weekend. Friday. He did it on Friday, and it wasn't till this last Monday that he got the yearbook for me.

If he rigged the coin toss, he must've had it all planned by Friday to get me tonight. *Before* the yearbook. *Before* I started staying late and fell off the stool and started acting like an idiot and leaving my bra home and *everything*. It had nothing to do with all that.

The bastard picked me like a target.

Lane brought her mind back to the present task. Her blouse and skirt were okay. She might never wear them again, but they weren't spoiled by stains.

She tossed her garments into the hamper.

She stared at her bed.

She didn't want to get in it. She wouldn't be able to sleep. She would lie there, thinking. All her worst thoughts came when she was trying to sleep, and she didn't want to face those that were waiting tonight.

Did he get me pregnant? Did he give me AIDS? Is he going to sneak into the house with his razor, some night, and murder us all?

Shit.

Who needs to be in bed to think about that shit?

He probably didn't get me pregnant, not with my period due so soon. What about AIDS, though? Even if he's got it, the chances . . .

There I go, thinking about it.

And it'll be *worse*, lying there with the lights out.

Be nice to just sit up all night and watch television.

The TV's *on*, she remembered. And poor Dad's an outcast on the sofa.

She left her room, uncertain what she planned to do. Maybe sit down and stare at the tube. Or maybe turn it off and wake up Dad so he could have a good night's sleep in the bed where he belonged.

At any rate, the TV and lamp shouldn't be left on all night.

Lane made her way toward the living room, walking slowly.

Though she ached all over, the pains seemed rather mild. Maybe the aspirin had helped. Certainly the shower had helped. And the long, hot bath she'd taken after cleaning herself under the spray.

The virus could've gotten in when he busted the old maidenhead. Wouldn't that be ironic? I died because I was a virgin. Shouldn't have been so fucking chaste.

I'll be all right, she told herself. I'll be all right.

The television was still on, its screen fuzzy with snow. The lamp at the end of the sofa was still on. But Dad was gone.

Lane heard the soft rumble and thump of a door sliding shut.

What's he doing? Going out back?

She went into the kitchen and cupped her hands against the glass. Dad was out there, all right. Walking funny as if he wasn't completely awake – awfully soused. He made his way toward the garage with a lurching, staggering gait, weaving a little.

Lane slid open the kitchen door. She almost called to him, but realized that a shout might wake up her mother. Whatever Dad might be up to, Mom was sure to interfere and give him some grief about it.

As Dad opened the garage door, Lane stepped outside and eased the kitchen door shut.

'Dad?' she called, not too loudly.

He didn't seem to hear her. He vanished into the darkness.

Lane frowned. Maybe I should just go back in, she thought. But what if he isn't okay?

What's he doing in the garage, anyway?

The wind parted her robe below the cloth belt and swept it away from her legs. She liked how caresses felt, supposed that the cold didn't bother her because she was still heated from the bath.

What if Dad can see me?

Reluctantly, she pulled the robe shut. She clamped its soft fabric between her thighs.

Something suddenly glowed white inside the darkness of the

garage. The light seemed to be moving. Lane realized it must be the battery lantern that she'd given Dad for Father's Day. It had a fluorescent tube instead of a regular flashlight bulb.

Is he looking for something? she wondered.

Because of her bare feet, Lane stayed off the grass. She walked across the concrete sundeck. She was nearly to the garage door when she saw him.

He had the lantern in one hand. He was standing on the small wooden platform beneath the trap door to the attic, his head tilted up, his back to Lane. His other hand waved overhead in an attempt to catch the dangling rope.

The wind tossed Lane's hair across her eyes. It bared her right side, curling gently over her skin. As she halted to close her robe again, she saw her father grab the cord and pull the trap door down. He set the lantern on the platform at his feet. He unfolded the ladder.

'Dad?'

Acting as if he didn't hear her, he picked up the lantern and began to climb.

Is he deaf?

She hurried toward him, afraid he might fall.

It wasn't like Dad to ignore her. Something was definitely wrong with him. Either drunk senseless or . . . *sleepwalking*?

She stopped beneath the ladder. He was almost to the top.

Maybe I'd better get Mom, she thought. If he's walking in his sleep, this is serious. What if he finishes whatever he's doing up there and doesn't know he's in the attic and falls right through the opening?

He could do that while I'm going for Mom, she realized.

Dad scrambled off the ladder and crawled out of sight.

Lane started to climb.

What'll I do?

Somewhere, she'd heard that sleepwalkers often dropped dead if you woke them up. Probably just a stupid myth. What if it's true, though?

I'd better just keep an eye on him, try to keep him from getting hurt.

Through the opening above her, Lane saw the garage's slanted roof, its crossbeams casting bands of shadow against the ceiling planks. The lantern had to be nearby, but she couldn't see her father.

She climbed higher. The rungs pressed into the bottoms of her feet. She noticed that her legs were shaking.

When she stepped onto the next rung, her head lifted above the attic floor. She stopped. Not much more than a yard in front of her face was a long, wooden box.

A coffin?

No way. That's ridiculous.

But shivers crawled up her back. Her heart began to thud, pumping throbs of pain through her body. She felt as if her muscles, already sore and trembling, were melting into warm mush. She clutched the ladder's top rung in case her legs should give out.

And gazed at her father.

He was standing at one end of the box.

It can't be a coffin!

Standing there, staring down into it. The lantern, held close to the side of his chest with his one hand, left smudges of darkness on his face.

'I know,' he said.

The words seemed to suck out Lane's breath. She knew he wasn't talking to *her*.

'I've missed you, too,' he said. 'So much.'

He nodded as if he heard a voice in his head. Then he straddled the box and sat down on its end. He rested the lantern on his left knee.

'Forever?' he asked. After a moment, he said, 'That would be so wonderful, Bonnie.'

Lane forced herself to climb higher. Dad didn't seem to notice.

She knelt on the attic floor.

She saw over the edge of the box.

She went numb.

It *was* a coffin and it wasn't empty and the thing inside

looked like a fucking Egyptian *mummy* that someone had unwrapped – a *girl* mummy with a horrible grin, a stub of wood jutting out of her chest between breasts that look like oblong flaps of leather. She didn't wear a stitch. And Dad was sitting above her feet where he could see *everything*, and he was staring at her and *talking* to her!

This can't be happening, Lane thought. I must be sleeping, and . . .

He's the one sleeping.

'I know,' he said, but not to Lane. 'But I'm afraid.'

He nodded.

He scooted forward on the edges of the coffin. Just above the mummy's pelvis, he stopped. If Lane reached out, she could touch his left leg.

'I love you, too,' he said. There was agony in his voice. 'But I love my wife and daughter. I won't give them up, not even for you.'

Those words seemed to scatter the fog in Lane's mind.

'Do you promise?' he asked.

He's talking to a corpse! About me and Mom!

'If you do anything to hurt them . . .'

Again, he nodded. 'All right. I'll do it.' Leaning forward, he reached down toward the chest of the mummy with his right hand. His fingers wrapped around the stake.

'DAD!' Lane punched the side of his knee. The impact shot his leg inward. The lantern tumbled off. Dad's leg slammed the coffin. The lantern struck the attic floor. It went out.

Black fell across Lane's eyes. She scurried forward.

'Huh?' Dad's voice. Confused. Then he bellowed, 'Yeeeeeahhhh!'

Lane found his leg. He flinched rigid and his yell turned into a shriek. She wrapped her arms around his waist. 'Dad,' she gasped as he tried to twist free. 'Dad, it's me. It's Lane. You're okay.'

He stopped screaming, stopped trying to struggle free. He made choked, whimpering noises.

'It's all right,' she whispered. 'It's all right.'

She felt a hand press against her back. Another hand touched the side of her head, moved forward and stroked her face, the fingers fluttering against her cheek. As he caressed her and sobbed, he slowly seemed to calm down.

He started to murmur, 'Oh, my God,' over and over again.

Lane kept whispering, 'It's all right.'

After a while, he said, 'I don't know what I'm doing here.'

'I think you were walking in your sleep.'

'She made me. She brought me here. Oh, my God. Did I pull the stake?'

'I don't know.'

'Oh, God.'

The hand went away from her face. She felt him lean forward.

'What're you doing?'

She felt a shudder pass through him.

'Dad?'

'It's still there. Thank God.'

'Come on, let's get out of here.'

'How could I *come* up here?' he blurted.

'It's all right, Dad. Let's just try and get down without breaking our necks.' She let go of him and turned around. Dad kept a hand low on her back.

'Be careful, sweetheart.'

'You, too.'

The opening was a gray rectangle. His hand went away. She heard him moving, climbing off the coffin as she sat down and swung her legs toward the dim gap. 'Why don't you wait up here till I can turn on the garage light?'

'You've got to be kidding,' he said.

He sounded almost like Dad.

Lane scooted forward. She lowered her legs until her heels found a rung of the ladder.

'You okay?' Dad asked.

'Yeah.' Gripping the side rails, she pushed herself off the attic floor. She climbed down slowly, her back to the ladder, rungs rubbing against her buttocks and dragging open her robe until nothing covered her front except the cloth belt loose against her belly.

She hoped Dad couldn't see her.

For a moment, she pictured herself lying naked in the coffin up there, Dad sitting above her with that light.

Who is she?

Lane's feet found the wooden platform. She thrust herself away from the ladder, stood up straight and tied her robe shut before turning around.

Dad came down facing the other way. When he reached the platform, he folded the ladder, took hold of the dangling rope, and swung the trap door up. It shut with a soft bump.

He stepped down. Lane went to him and put an arm around his back. He hugged her against his side.

Together, they walked to the house.

'I guess we need to talk,' he said.

'What's that thing doing in our garage?'

'It's a long story. Why don't you make a pot of coffee? I'll go and get your mother.'

'You're going to tell Mom?'

'Yeah. I think I'd better.'

'If you're afraid I'll snitch . . .'

'No, it isn't that. I've gotta tell her what's going on.'

He left the kitchen. Lane threw out the used filter, put a fresh one into the machine's plastic basket, added coffee grounds, and slipped the basket into place. She poured water into the top of the brewer. She thumbed the 'ON' switch. A red light came on. She gazed at it.

The times are out of joint.

Understatement of the fucking year, she thought.

Chapter Forty

He sat on the edge of the bed and shook Jean gently by the shoulder. Groaning, she rolled over. She squinted up at him. 'Huh? Wha's . . .'

'You need to get up,' Larry said.

Suddenly, she looked alarmed and wide awake. 'What's wrong?'

'It's not a fire or anything. Nobody's hurt. We just need to talk.'

'Oh, my God. What? Tell me!'

'Lane's waiting in the kitchen.'

'Is she all right?'

'She's fine. This is about me. I'll explain everything in a few minutes.'

Jean sat up. She had a strange look in her eyes. A look of pain and fear. She caught her lower lip between her teeth.

'Don't get all upset,' Larry said.

'Are you leaving us?'

'No, no. God, no.' A strap of her nightgown had slipped off, baring her shoulder and right breast. Larry curled his hand over the breast and kissed her mouth.

Pulling her head back, she stared into his eyes. 'You're having an affair?'

'No. I love you, Jean.' He lifted the strap onto her shoulder and kissed her again. Her arms went around him. She hugged him fiercely. 'Come on, now. Lane's waiting.' She released him.

Larry stood up. He waited while she climbed out of bed and put on her bathrobe. Then he took her hand and led her from the room. As he entered the kitchen, he smelled the comfortable aroma of coffee.

'It'll be ready in a couple of minutes,' Lane said. She exchanged a rather sick-looking smile with Jean.

'Do you know what this is all about?' Jean asked.

'Not really.'

They both faced Larry. 'Go ahead and sit down,' he said.

They sat at the table. Larry stood behind his chair and gripped its back. To Jean, he said, 'Do you remember that body we found?'

'What about it?'

He looked at Lane. 'When your mother and I were out exploring in the desert with Pete and Barbara, we found a body in an abandoned hotel in Sagebrush Flat. That's a ghost town about fifty . . .'

'That's where you found *her*?'

'Yeah.'

Jean frowned. 'I thought we agreed not to tell Lane . . .'

'I didn't tell her.' He felt a grimace twisting his face. Here goes, he thought. He took a deep breath. 'Lane saw it. Tonight. It's up in our garage attic.'

Jean gaped at him. The color drained from her face. In a low voice, she said, 'You're kidding.'

'Pete and I went out and brought it back with us. While you two were in Los Angeles.'

'You're kidding,' she said again.

'He isn't,' Lane told her.

Larry turned away from the table. Coffee had stopped streaming into the pot. He opened a cupboard. 'We're doing a book about it. *I'm* doing the book.'

'A book,' Jean muttered.

'A vampire book,' he said, taking down three mugs. 'Non-fiction.' He started to fill the mugs. His hand shook, slopping coffee onto the counter.

'You're telling me . . . you and Pete *took* that hideous *thing* out from under the stairs and brought it *home* with you, and it's out in our garage?'

'That's right. I'm writing a book about it.'

'A vampire book,' Lane murmured. She sounded as if she were talking to herself.

Larry brought the mugs to them. Lane seemed to be

staring at the center of the table. Jean looked up at him as he set the mug in front of her. 'You're out of your mind,' she said.

'I know.' He sat down. 'I knew you'd be upset . . .'

'Upset? Me? Why would I be upset? My husband brings a goddamn *stiff* home and hides it in our garage.'

'Boy, Dad.'

'I'm sorry. I know it was a stupid thing to do. But Pete and I figured . . .'

'Pete.' Jean's eyes narrowed. 'I'll just bet it was his idea.'

'Well, it was. But I went along with it. We're talking about a major book. It could make us rich.'

'So would robbing a bank,' Jean said. She put her hands on the table. She pushed her chair back. She got up and walked to the phone. 'Does Barbara know about this?'

'No. What're you doing?' Larry asked.

She didn't answer. She jabbed buttons on the handset.

'Oh, boy,' Lane muttered.

Larry groaned. He wished he hadn't mentioned Pete. But it *was* Pete's idea.

Now we'll have two wives going apeshit.

It would be nice, though, to have Pete here for some moral support.

'This is Jean.' Her voice sounded calm. 'I'd like to speak to Barbara . . . No, I'm not kidding . . . Yes indeed, "uh-oh" . . . Hi, Barbara, Jean . . . Yes, I'd say no. Something is quite wrong. I'd like you and Pete to come over here right away . . . Let's just say our dear husbands pulled a certain stunt. Bring something sharp. We may want to kill them.'

At least she hasn't lost her sense of humor, Larry thought.

Jean hung up. 'They'll be right over,' she said.

'Wonderful.'

She sat down, took a sip of coffee, put down the mug, scowled at Larry, and said, 'What were you doing out there with it tonight?'

The question made his heart lurch. He felt heat rush to his face. 'Nothing.'

810

'What do you mean, nothing? You were out there with it, weren't you?' She faced Lane. 'Wasn't he?'

'He walked in his sleep,' Lane said. 'He didn't know what he was doing.'

'What *was* he doing?'

Lane looked at him. She pressed her lips together.

'Go ahead and tell,' he said. 'Then we'll both know.'

'Dad was talking to . . . the body. I guess he was dreaming or something, and they were carrying on a conversation.' She turned her eyes to Larry. 'I think she was trying to talk you into pulling out the stake.'

'*Oh*-for-godsake,' Jean gasped.

Lane's head jerked toward her mother. 'He didn't do it,' she said very fast. 'I mean, I didn't realize that thing was supposed to be a vampire, but . . . I woke him up before he could take the stake out.'

'And what were *you* doing out there, young lady?'

'I was worried about him. I didn't think Dad should have to spend the whole night on the couch just because he had a couple of drinks too many.' She gave Jean a frown. 'So after I finished my bath I went out to wake him up so he could go to bed, and he wasn't there. He was on his way to the garage. So I followed him. I was afraid he'd get hurt. You could tell something was wrong. He was walking in his sleep. He didn't know *what* the hell was going on.'

'You followed your father into the attic and saw him talking to a corpse.' She looked at Larry. 'I hope you're proud of yourself.'

'I couldn't help it, Jean. I was asleep.'

'He really was, Mom. You should've heard him scream when I woke him up.'

The doorbell rang. Without saying a word, Jean got up from the table. She stepped closer to Lane. Shaking her head, she slid a hand gently down the girl's hair. Then she hurried from the kitchen.

'I'm really sorry,' Larry said.

'That's okay. Mom's really pissed, isn't she?'

'I'm afraid so. It's a big shock. For both of you.'

'I'm just glad you didn't take that stake out.'

'So am I. I was going to do it, huh?'

'Yeah. You had your hand on it when I woke you up.'

'Jesus.'

'You don't really think it would've . . .' She shook her head.

'Come back to life? I don't know. Probably not. But I'm still glad you stopped me.' He managed a smile. 'And I also do appreciate the way you stuck up for me.'

'That's all right.'

'You're a good kid, no matter what everyone says.'

She laughed softly and winced. Her eyes widened as if she were surprised by a sudden pain. Color drained from her face.

'What's wrong?'

She gave him a very strange look. For a moment, Larry thought she was on the verge of telling him something terrible. But she said, 'Nothing. I'm just not feeling very swift. Cramps. You know.'

'Are you sure that's all?'

'Isn't it enough?'

'You could go to bed. You don't have to stick around for the fireworks.'

'I wouldn't miss this.'

Pete was first to enter the kitchen. He wore a blue bathrobe over white pajamas, and had moccasins on his feet. His nose was bandaged. From the look on his face, he might've been a fourth-grader caught red-handed putting a tack on his teacher's chair. Meeting Larry's gaze, he mouthed 'What's happened?' but didn't utter a sound.

Larry felt his lip curl up. He shook his head.

'I don't know what you boys did,' Barbara said as she followed her husband through the doorway. 'But I've got a feeling you're both neck deep in runny shit.' She leaned back against the counter. Her hair was tangled and sticking out in odd places. Though she obviously hadn't brushed it, she must've taken time to dress. She wore white sneakers, tight red sweatpants, and a loose gray sweatshirt with an emblem on the front that read, 'Alcatraz Swim Team.'

Any other time, Larry thought, I'd be wondering if she had anything on under the clothes.

He realized he *was* wondering.

Guess I'm not totally out of it, he thought.

As Pete sat down, Jean came in with an extra chair from the dining room. She placed it near a corner of the breakfast table. 'You'd better be seated for this,' she told Barbara.

'That bad?' She pushed herself away from the counter and stepped toward the chair. Larry watched her breasts jostle the front of the sweatshirt. Obviously no bra, he decided.

He imagined Bonnie in her cheerleader outfit, the sweater jiggling just a bit with her movements. He saw the sweater rising above her belly as she leaped. When she came down, her pleated skirt billowed high.

'Larry.' Jean's voice. 'Are you with us?'

'Huh? Sure.' He felt a rush of guilt.

Jean was already sitting down. To Barbara, she said, 'It appears that our two geniuses, here, decided to do a book about the body we found in Sagebrush Flat. So they snuck back and brought it home with them. It's in our garage.'

'Holy shit,' Barbara said.

Pete gave her a lopsided grin that lifted one side of his moustache.

She cuffed him high on the arm and Larry watched the Alcatraz emblem swing.

'Hey! No need to get physical. It's a brilliant idea, honey. I'm in for twenty percent of the take.'

She socked him again.

'Cut it out, huh? I've got a broken nose, for Christsake.'

'I oughta smack it for you. Shit! Are you outa your fucking *gourd*?'

'We knew it'd upset you ladies,' Larry said. 'That's why we tried to keep it a secret until the book was finished and we could get rid of the corpse.'

'Lane caught him in the garage with it tonight.'

Now *Pete* looked angry at him. 'Jesus, man.'

'It wasn't his fault,' Lane said. 'He was walking in his sleep.'

'Oh, sure. Jesus, man.'

'You were sleepwalking?' Barbara asked. 'That's wild.'

Sensing an ally, Larry said, 'Yeah, it was weird. Ever since we brought that body back with us, I've been having all kinds of strange dreams.' He decided not to mention the other sleepwalking incident. 'It's almost as if Bonnie's been trying to *communicate* with me. Like it's telepathy, or something.'

'Bullshit,' Pete said. 'You're just obsessed, that's all.'

'Bonnie?' Jean asked.

'That's her name,' Larry explained. 'Bonnie Saxon.'

'You know who she is?' Barbara sounded excited.

'She was wearing a school ring. She went to Buford High, graduated in 1968.'

'The yearbook,' Lane muttered.

'Yeah. I found pictures of her. She was a cheerleader and the Homecoming Spirit Queen.'

'Holyshit,' Barbara said. 'That yucky corpse . . .?'

'And she was murdered the summer after graduation,' he went on. 'Somebody thought she was a vampire.'

'Uriah Radley,' Pete added. 'The guy who broke my nose.'

'*What?*' Barbara blurted.

He grinned at her, settled back in the chair, and folded his arms across his chest. 'We lied about target shooting.'

She didn't punch him. She gazed at him. She looked astonished.

'We went out there figuring we might take him in for the murders,' Pete explained. 'He also killed two other high school girls. Right, Lar?'

'It looks that way.' He turned to Jean. 'You know all that time I spent at the library this week? I was studying up on her.'

'God, you've been lying about everything.'

He grimaced. 'Not about everything. Just about this vampire stuff.'

'You went out *gunning* for the guy?' Lane asked. She sounded just as intrigued as Barbara.

Larry nodded.

Pete said, 'Yep. And we almost got him. Should've seen the bastard slinging arrows at us. He thought *we* were vampires.'

'He *shot* at you?' Barbara asked.

'This is mad,' Jean muttered.

'He was about to pound a stake into Pete, but I managed to stop him.'

'Saved my ass. Or at least my heart.'

Barbara's lips moved, but no words came out. Pete gave her a martyred look. She stretched an arm toward him and rubbed his shoulder. 'Oh, honey.'

'This is incredible,' Lane said.

Larry smiled at her. 'Make a good book, huh?'

'*Yeah.*'

'The thing about the book, it'll all be true.'

'It'll sell *millions*,' Pete said. 'Just like *The Amityville Horror*. We'll be rich and famous.'

'*In*famous, Jean corrected him. 'People read something like that, they'll think you're a couple of assholes. Like that guy who got "beamed up" by space monsters.' She glared at Larry. 'You want to be the laughing stock?' In a dopey, hick voice, she said, ' "Hey, there goes Larry Dunbar. Him's the dork that believes in vampires. Yassir." '

'It won't be like that,' he said. 'It's just an account of what happened. I've got a lot of it written already, and . . .'

'God, I've gotta read it!' Barbara blurted, her hand going motionless on Pete's shoulder.

'When it's done,' he said. 'It'll just be a couple more weeks. But the thing is, I make it clear in the book that I *don't* believe in vampires. I tell it exactly the way it happened . . . how Pete and I thought it'd be a neat idea for a book. Neither *one* of us really believes it's a vampire.'

'Not me,' Pete said.

'But it's not really a vampire story any more. It grew into a lot more than that. Now, it's a murder mystery. Those three girls disappeared in 1968, and nobody knows what happened to them. Nobody but us.'

'And Uriah,' Pete said.

'We know who killed them, and why, and we've even got one of the bodies.'

'In our garage,' Jean muttered.

'And you almost got yourselves killed,' Barbara said.

'But we've got the story,' Larry said. 'We've got it. I didn't think we had anything, at first. It's like you said, Jean. I thought we had nothing but a couple of nuts cart a body home 'cause it might be a vampire, and they've got nothing else to do but pull out the stake to see if she comes alive. And then they do it, and she just lies there. Zip. Big deal. The whole thing falls flat. But it doesn't *matter* if she's a vampire. She's a *homicide*, and we can name her killer.'

'Killed her because *he* thought she was a vampire,' Pete put in.

'Uriah's wife and daughter were murdered,' Larry said. 'Somehow, he got it into his head that they were the victims of a vampire. He had their bodies cremated so they wouldn't come back. Then he went hunting. He got Bonnie and two other girls.'

Frowning at him, Jean said, 'You guys didn't make any of this up?'

Larry realized she had actually been listening. Though she didn't seem fascinated like Lane and Barbara, her anger had melted. She was interested.

'Some of it's speculation,' he admitted.

'More than some, I should imagine.'

'Not all that much,' Pete said. 'Lar's got a whole stack of newspaper stories.'

'This is big,' Barbara said, her voice low.

'Big?' Pete said, 'Enormous. Now, if we just pull the stake and it turns out she *is* a vampire . . .'

'She'll suck all our blood and there won't be any book,' Lane said.

Everyone looked at her.

'Just kidding,' she muttered, blushing.

'There's no such thing as vampires,' Jean said to her.

'I know. I know that.'

'We all know that, don't we?' she asked. Her gaze roamed the group. She was met by nods of agreement. She looked at Larry. 'You've got that thing here just so you can pull the stake?'

'Yeah. I guess so.'

'That's all you need it for? Once you've taken out the stake and proven she isn't a vampire, that's it? You'll be done? We can get rid of it?'

'Yeah.'

Pete scowled, apparently recalling his plans to take the body on the talk show circuit.

Larry said to him, 'We'll have to turn her over to the authorities.' To Jean, he said, 'They can take up the investigation from there, and go out and try to pick up Uriah.'

Jean nodded. 'Okay. Let's go out to the garage and do it.'

He stared at her.

She raised her eyebrows. 'I mean it. You want to pull out the stake, we'll do it right now. I want that thing off my property. Tonight.'

'It might be better to wait for daylight,' Pete said.

Jean sneered at him. 'Get real.'

'Just in case,' Larry said.

Her sneer turned on him. 'In case of what?'

'Yeah!' Barbara pitched in, her voice loud and cheery. She was beaming. 'What *are* you guys, a couple of pussies? Let's yank the fuckin' stake, see if the babe sits up and says "hi."'

'What the hell,' Pete said.

'Okay,' Larry said.

'Oh, boy,' Lane said. She looked scared.

Chapter Forty-one

Pete went home for his video camera. Jean and Lane left the kitchen to get dressed. Barbara, still seated in the extra chair from the dining room, had her arms folded beneath her breasts and kept shaking her head.

Larry, trembling and wondering if his teeth might begin to chatter, took a sip of coffee. It was luke warm. He realized they'd neglected to offer any to their guests. 'Want some coffee?' he asked.

'Thanks, but I don't think so. I'd probably wet myself. God, this is exciting.'

'Yeah,' he muttered.

'It *is* like something from a book. One of your books.'

'Hope it doesn't turn out like one.'

'You and me both, buster.' She let out a nervous laugh. 'I'll be in it, won't I?'

'Sure. You already are.' He managed a smile. 'You're the one who found the body.'

'Pete found it. But I'm the one who busted the landing, right?'

'Yeah.'

'You don't describe me as a big lummox, I hope.'

'No way. You'll like it.'

Her head nodded, bobbing slowly up and down a few times, then switched directions and shook from side to side. 'I can't believe you guys actually *did* all this.'

'Neither can I.'

'Jean can, though.'

He groaned. 'Don't remind me.'

'She'll be okay,' Barbara said. 'Once it's all over and she realizes what's going on. You know, the fact that it's true. It's gonna be hot.'

'Hope so.'

'I bet there'll even be a movie. De Niro'd be perfect for Pete. They'd need someone big for me. Not big famous, necessarily. Big big.'

'How about Susan Anton?'

She beamed. 'Hey, that'd be great. Now, what about you and Jean? Somebody kind of small and cute for Jean. What about that gal with the husky voice from *An Officer and a Gentleman*?'

'Debra Winger.'

'Yeah. She'd be perfect for Jean. For you, we've got a choice.'

'Really?'

'Nick Nolte or Gary Busey.'

He chuckled and felt his face heat up. 'Thanks a bunch.'

'No, they'd be great. Either one of them.'

'At least you didn't suggest George Kennedy.'

Larry heard slow footsteps coming toward them. Lane stepped into the kitchen, dressed in sneakers, jeans and a heavy plaid shirt. The shirt was very large. It wasn't tucked in.

In her right hand, she held a crucifix.

The one that belonged on the wall of her bedroom.

It looked identical to the crucifix that Larry had seen hanging around Uriah's neck. The one that had stopped his bullet.

'Don't let your mother see that,' Larry warned.

'You're probably right.' She slipped it underneath the front of her shirt and worked some of the long end down inside the waistband of her jeans. When she finished, the loose shirt showed no trace of the crucifix.

'You wouldn't happen to have a spare?' Barbara asked.

Lane spread the shirt's neck and lifted out the small golden cross. The cross, on its thin chain, had come from Larry's parents. They'd given it to her as a first communion present. He hadn't noticed Lane wearing it in a long while.

'Bring a vampire around,' he said, 'people start discovering religion.'

'You're sure prepared,' Barbara told her.

'Here, you take it.' Lane started to fool with the clasp behind her neck.

'No, no. Hey, I'm not worried about vampires.'

'Take it anyway,' Lane said, and held the necklace out to her.

'Well . . .' She looked at Larry.

'Why not?'

'Right. Why not?' She slipped the chain around her neck and fastened it. Then she dropped the golden cross down the front of her sweatshirt. 'Thanks, hon. If it looks like the babe might start chomping on me, I'll just whip this out and send her packing.'

'That's the idea,' Lane said. 'Mom always wears hers, so she's protected.'

They're all protected, Larry thought. He told himself that he didn't believe in vampires. He told himself that the crosses wouldn't protect them from squat. But still, he was glad they had the things.

Barbara patted her hair. She curled her upper lip. 'You wouldn't have a brush handy, would you? Since Pete's gonna record this for posterity . . .'

'Sure,' Lane said. 'I'll get one.'

Barbara stood up. Saying, 'I'll need to use a mirror,' she followed Lane out of the kitchen.

Larry sat alone at the table.

Oh, man, he thought. This is it.

At least we'll get it over with. No more wondering.

God, Bonnie. So what's it gonna be?

'*I'll be yours*,' she seemed to tell him.

Sure thing. Right. You'll just lie there dead.

Don't count on it.

What if she kills all of them but me?

He pictured himself pulling the stake. And Bonnie suddenly changing. Very suddenly. One second a dried-up grinning hag, the next second a gorgeous teenager, the next second throwing herself out of the coffin with a mad shriek and attacking. Hurling bodies, breaking necks, ripping open throats with her teeth. And Larry stands there helpless, watching the slaughter, too stunned to feel the pain of losing Jean and Lane, Pete and Barbara.

When they're all dead on the garage floor, Bonnie comes to him, her naked body sheathed with gleaming blood. She raises her dripping hands toward him. *Now we'll be together forever.*

Come off it, Larry told himself. My goddamn mind. It's not going to happen that way. Not a chance.

But he started to imagine himself back in the scene, so he shoved himself away from the table. He hurried into the living room. Barbara was standing in front of the fireplace, watching herself in the mirror above the mantle as she brushed her hair. Lane, beside her, seemed to be gazing into space. He put an arm across her back. She flinched, then looked at him and settled against his side.

As a toilet flushed, off in the distance, the front door swung open and Pete came in. He wore boots and jeans and a blue turtleneck sweater. A leather strap crossed his chest like a Sam Browne belt. He held the video camcorder on his shoulder. In his right hand was a bow.

'All set 'n rarin' to go?' he asked.

'We're just waiting for Jean,' Larry said, staring at the bow.

'Man, I can't believe we're finally gonna do it.'

'Me neither,' Larry told him.

'At night, no less.'

Barbara turned away from the mirror and looked at him. 'What are you doing with *that*?'

'This?' He raised the bow. 'Got the idea from Uriah.' To Larry, he said, 'I used to hunt deer with this baby.'

'Oh, give me a break,' Jean said, coming in from the hallway. 'You're not serious.'

'Wooden arrows, darlin'. Just as good as a stake when it comes to dispatching vampires. Better. You don't have to get up close and personal.'

'I thought we all agreed we didn't believe in any of this nonsense.'

'It can't hurt to take precautions,' Larry told her.

'God, you guys really take the prize.'

'If it bugs you,' Pete said, 'just consider it a stage prop. There'll be a video of this, you know.'

Jean obviously knew that, all right. She had not only brushed her hair, but put on lipstick. She'd dressed in her blue velours jumpsuit and white boots. She'd even knotted her Anne Klein silk scarf around her neck.

Larry realized that two of them – Jean in her scarf and Pete in his turtleneck – had chosen to wear garments that covered the region traditionally preferred by thirsty vampires. He wondered if they'd done it on purpose.

Pete raised the viewfinder to his eye, and the camera began to purr. He pivoted slowly to get everyone. Then he kept the camera on Jean as she crossed the room to join Larry and Lane. She smirked at him and shook her head. Stopping beside Larry, she put her arm around him. Barbara got into the picture, moving in close to Lane.

'Here we are,' said Pete as he panned the group. 'The dauntless, intrepid team as it prepares to go outside and remove the stake from the heart of the cadaver.'

'Does that thing have sound?' Jean asked.

'Yes indeed,' Pete said. 'Any famous last words before we embark on our adventure?'

Larry shook his head.

'Say something,' Barbara urged him.

'Well . . . None of us actually believes in vampires. I want to make that clear. But the body we found . . . a girl named Bonnie Saxon, was murdered by a man who very much believed in vampires. He believed *she* was one, and killed her by pounding a stake into her heart. In just a few minutes, we're going to pull out that stake. We'll see what happens.'

'Terrific,' Pete said. 'Anybody else?'

Nobody offered to speak.

'Okay,' Pete said. 'Let's do it.'

They went out back through the kitchen door. Jean was first to reach the garage, and turned on the overhead light before the others arrived.

When they were all inside, Pete said, 'Why don't we close the door?'

'Let's not,' Larry said.

'Yeah,' Barbara said. 'You never know, we might have to run for our lives.'

'Give me a break,' Jean muttered.

Larry left the garage door open. He stepped onto the platform and reached up for the dangling rope.

'Just a minute,' Pete said. 'Here, Barb.' He handed the camera to her.

'What am I supposed to do with it?'

'Get us bringing the coffin down.' He showed her how to hold the camera. 'You look through this. What you see is what you get. Just hold this button down, and that's all there is to it. Okay?'

'I think so.'

Pete set his quiver and bow on the concrete floor. Joining Larry on the platform, he glanced around at Barbara. 'Okay, get her going and keep her going till I say to stop.'

'Yessir.'

Larry caught hold of the rope. He pulled the trap door down, and Pete helped unfold the ladder. 'Be my guest,' Larry told him.

Pete started to climb. Halfway up the ladder, he looked over his shoulder and waved. 'Famous last wave,' he said.

'Quit screwing around,' Barbara told him.

Larry smiled at her. Jean and Lane were standing close to Barbara. Jean's hands were stuffed into the front pockets of her jumpsuit. Her shoulders were hunched and she looked as if she were gritting her teeth. Lane's teeth were bared. Her arms were wrapped tightly across her chest. She met his eyes and said, 'Be careful. Don't fall or anything.'

Murmuring 'Thanks,' he turned to the ladder just as Pete's boots disappeared beyond the edge of the floor.

'NO!' Pete cried out. 'IN THE NAME OF GOD, NO!'

Larry's heart kicked.

He heard gasps from the women.

'Watch out!' Jean's voice.

From above came the sound of Pete laughing.

Behind Larry, something crashed. He heard glass break.

Pete's grinning face appeared at the top of the ladder. 'Just kidding,' he said.

'You bastard!' Larry yelled. Turning around, he saw Barbara sprawled on her back. The crotch of her red sweatpants was dark, the patch growing, urine seeping out and dribbling onto the concrete floor between her legs. The camcorder lay about a yard beyond her head.

'What's wrong?' Pete asked.

Larry scowled up at him. 'You idiot! You scared Barbara so bad she fell down. I think your camera bit it.'

'NO!'

This time, the outcry was real.

'Yes,' Larry told him.

As Pete hurried down the ladder, Jean and Lane helped his wife up. She rose to her feet, grimacing, rubbing her rump as she stared down at herself. 'Oh shit,' she said. Her voice was pitched high and trembling. 'I don't believe this.' She started to sob.

Pete halted in front of her. 'Don't hit me,' he said.

She stared at him and wept. Then she rushed from the garage, leaving dribbles on the concrete, and hobbled down the driveway bow-legged.

'I did it this time,' Pete muttered.

'You sure did,' Jean said.

'Oh, man.' For a moment, he looked as if he might go after Barbara. Then he shook his head. He glanced at the small puddle on the garage floor, shook his head again, then stepped over it and crouched in front of his camera. He picked it up. He picked up a few pieces of plastic and glass. He stood and raised the viewfinder to his eye. 'Oh, man,' he said.

'Serves you right,' Jean said.

'I'm sorry. Man, am I sorry.'

'Save it for Barb,' Jean told him.

'Yeah. I really blew it, huh?'

'Now what?' Lane asked.

Pete frowned at Larry. 'Can we call this off for now? I mean, we've just *gotta* get the whole thing on video. I bought this camera especially . . . God, why did I have to fuck around?'

'Do you think it can be repaired?' Larry asked.

'I don't know. I'll have to check it out. Even if I can fix it, I wouldn't be able to buy any parts tomorrow.'

'You mean today?' Lane asked.

'Yeah. Sunday. Can we put this off till Monday? I'll either have it fixed by then, or get a new one. Okay?'

'It's up to Jean,' Larry said. 'Can you wait till Monday?'

She sighed. 'I don't want to be the one to ruin . . . Yeah, I guess it's okay. You've waited this long.' She shook her head with disgust. 'On one condition. We lock the garage doors till then. Padlock them.' She peered up at Larry. 'I don't want you coming out here again, sleepwalking or otherwise.'

'Neither do I,' he told her.

'That's great,' Pete said. 'Thanks.'

'You'd better go home,' Jean said, 'and look after Barbara.'

'If she'll let me in the house. God, she's probably on the phone trying to get a divorce lawyer. Or busy loading my magnum.'

Larry, somehow pleased by Pete's agony, patted him on the shoulder. 'If we hear shots, we'll call an ambulance.'

'Thanks a load, pardner.'

Chapter Forty-two

When Lane woke up, her bedroom was full of sunlight. For just a moment, she felt good. Then the memories of last night with Kramer crashed down on her. Sickened with shame and terror, she threw her covers aside, sat up and hugged her belly. She couldn't think straight. Her mind was a torrent of horrible images that kept her heart racing, her skin burning, her stomach knotted.

She fought the images. Like trying to shove dozens of writhing snakes down inside a box. Their heads kept popping up, striking at her, sinking in their fangs. But at last she got them all shoved down and slammed the lid. Though they were out of sight, she still thought she could hear them hissing and thumping around, eager to escape and hurt her.

She sat on the bed gasping, sweat trickling down her face, nightshirt clinging to her skin.

I'll kill the bastard, she thought.

Oh, sure I will.

What am I going to do?

Last night hadn't been enough for him. He'd made that very clear. And if Lane gave him any trouble about it, he'd get her with the razor. Her parents, too. He would kill them all.

The same way he killed Jessica and her family.

My God, she thought. Where'd that idea come from? Kramer certainly hadn't told her any such thing.

But he'd killed them. Lane was suddenly sure of it. Jessica's been in his sixth period class. He must've been getting it off with her until she gave him trouble. He was the one who beat her up, who broke her arm. Not Benson, after all. Kramer had taught her a lesson about cooperating, but that wasn't enough. Maybe she wouldn't have any more to do with him. Maybe he was afraid she might talk. So he crept into her house last week and slaughtered the whole family and set the place on fire.

He'll do the same to us.

Dad gave her a sheepish smile when she entered the living room. He was in his easy chair, a paperback in his hands, a mug of coffee on the lamp table beside him. 'Good afternoon,' he said.

She kissed him on the cheek. It was scratchy with whiskers. 'Where's Mom?'

'She went to the twelve o'clock mass.'

'Glad she didn't wake me up for it.'

'Figured you needed your sleep. How's it going?'

'Okay, I guess.'

'Hope you didn't have any vampire nightmares.'

'I don't think so,' Lane said. If I had nightmares, she thought, they wouldn't have been about vampires. 'How about you?'

'Your mother and I were up till after sunrise.'

Lane managed to smile. 'Having a little discussion?'

'It turned out okay. Better than I deserved, I guess. When you see her, just don't bring up the subject of our guest in the garage.'

'I wonder how Pete fared.'

'We didn't hear any gunshots.'

'That's a good sign.'

'I don't think your mother would've been quite so forgiving if *she'd* been the one who wet her pants.'

'Daaaad.'

He chuckled softly and shook his head. 'Anyway, there're some sweetrolls in the kitchen.'

'Yuck. Maybe I'll eat something while I'm out. I've got to pick up a few things at the drug store. And maybe I'll drop by the mall. Need anything?'

'I'm getting a little low on pipe cleaners.'

'Okay.' She headed for the front door. 'See you later.'

'Have fun,' he said.

Outside, she took the keys from her denim shoulder bag. She locked the front door and hurried to the Mustang. She slid in behind the steering wheel and swung her heavy bag onto the passenger seat.

As she drove away from the house, her stomach began to flutter. The car was hot inside, but she kept the windows up and didn't turn on the air conditioner. Though the heat didn't stop her from shivering, she found it comforting.

A block from home, she stopped the car. She reached into a pocket of her blouse. She took out a folded sheet of paper and opened it. While she studied the first of the two addresses she'd copied from the telephone book, she eased her hand between the buttons of her blouse and gently rubbed her left breast. Both her breasts were sore, but the left hurt more than the right. It had been purple with bruises when she looked at herself before dressing.

She finished memorizing the address, took her hand out of her blouse, folded the paper again and tucked it gently into her pocket.

She drove to the address.

She parked at the curb and stared out the passenger window at the mobile home. It was on a foundation some distance back from the road, a battered pickup truck near one end, a motorcycle in front of the pickup. There was no driveway, no lawn. Just the home and the vehicles sitting on a patch of desert.

It looked like the kind of place where you'd expect to find throw-backs.

It looked exactly like the kind of place where Lane expected to find Riley Benson.

I must be out of my mind.

She grabbed the strap of her bag and dragged it behind her as she climbed from the car. She lifted the strap onto her shoulder. On wobbly legs, she made her way around the front of the car, stepped onto the curb, crunched over gravel, and climbed a few stairs to the front door.

She thumbed the doorbell button, but no sound came from inside. So she knocked.

'Yeah?' A woman's voice. 'Who is it?'

'A friend of Riley's,' she called.

The door opened. The woman standing on the threshold looked too young to be Riley's mother. Maybe in her late twenties. Her blue eyes seemed too pale for the deep tan of her face. Her blond hair, neatly brushed, hung to her shoulders and draped her brow. Her tank top, tye-died pink, was cut off to leave her midriff bare. Lane could see her nipples through the fabric. She wore cut-off blue jeans low on her hips. Her feet were bare.

She doesn't look like *anybody's* mother, Lane thought. Maybe Benson's sister. Or maybe he'd already found himself a replacement for Jessica.

'Don't just stand there gawking,' she said. 'Come on in.'

'Is Riley home?' Lane asked, climbing the steps.

'You say you're a friend of his? You sure don't look it.'

'Well, I knew Jessica.'

'That poor thing.'

Inside, the mobile home smelled good – a coffee aroma blended in with hints of perfume and maybe floor wax.

'Have a seat, darling. I'll tell him you're here.'

Lane sat at a table in the kitchen area and watched the woman stride down a narrow passageway. The jeans were frayed where the legs had been cut off, and strands of ragged denim dangled against the backs of her thighs. Her right thigh was smudged with a nasty bruise that reminded Lane of those she'd seen on herself today.

Near the far end of the corridor, she rapped gently on a door. Then she rolled it open and stepped out of sight.

'You've got a visitor, honey.' Though she spoke in a hushed voice, Lane easily heard her.

'Huh?'

'Well, take the blessed headphones off.'

'What?'

'You've got a visitor.'

'The cops?'

'No, it's not the cops. It's a nice young gal who says she's a friend of Jessica's.'

'Oh, Jesus.'

'You watch your tongue.'

'I don't wanta see nobody, Mom.'

She *is* his mother?

'Put on your shirt and go on out and talk with her. And try to keep a civil tongue in your head.'

As Riley's mother came out of the room, Lane turned her eyes away. The salt shaker on the table was a little plastic dog, the pepper shaker a red fireplug.

'He'll be right along,' she said. 'I ought to warn you, though, he's been in a mighty foul mood lately. First it was Jessica's murder, then the police bothering him, and then he got into trouble with some gal at school and got himself expelled. This has been a mighty bad week for him, the poor kid.'

'I'm really sorry,' Lane said. 'Some of it's my fault, I guess. I'm the one who got him kicked out of school.'

Riley's mother frowned. 'I hope he didn't hurt you. I heard what he did, and . . .'

'*You!*'

His mother looked around. 'Be nice, honey.'

Riley stepped around her. 'What're you doing here, Dunbar?'

'I just want to talk a minute.'

'Whatever you've gotta say, I don't wanta hear it.'

The mother turned on him, scowling and shoving her fists against her hips. 'Did you hear what I said about being nice?'

'Mom, for godsake!'

'I just want to talk to you a minute,' Lane said. 'It's really important.'

'Maybe the two of you should step out front. There isn't much privacy in this place.' She fixed her eyes on Riley. 'You be a gentleman, or you'll be sorry.'

He wrinkled his nose. Glaring at Lane, he said, 'Okay. Let's go out. But make it quick.'

Lane stood up. 'It was nice to meet you, Mrs Benson.'

'Nice to meet you, honey.' She held out her hand. 'The name's Melanie. You can call me Mel.'

'Lane shook the woman's hand. 'I'm Lane Dunbar.'

'Hope to see more of you around here.'

'Don't hold your breath,' Riley told her.

He led the way outside. Lane followed him to the road. He sat down on the hood of her car. 'Okay, what's the fuckin' idea?'

'Your mom's nice.'

'Yeah, sure, a sweetheart. She's probably got an eye on us, or I'd take you apart, you fuckin' cunt.'

'I came here to tell you who killed Jessica.'

He sneered. 'Yeah, sure.'

'Kramer did it.'

The sneer fell away. He stared at Lane. He said nothing.

'Kramer got me alone last night. He beat me up and raped me.'

Riley's eyes narrowed. 'You don't look beat up.' His voice came out quiet, uncertain.

'He didn't hurt my face.'

'How do I know he did *anything* to you?'

Lane checked the area ahead. On the other side of the street was empty land, a barren hillside. Keeping her back to Riley's home, she fumbled open three buttons. She spread the front of her blouse wide enough for him to see her breasts. 'That's just some of it,' she muttered, closing the blouse.

'Kramer did that to you?'

'And plenty more. And he had a razor with him. He said he'd use it on me if I talked. He said he'd kill me and my family. I think that's what happened to Jessica and her parents.'

Riley slumped forward and clutched his knees. His head lowered. For a while, he just sat like that on the car's hood, staring down. Then he raised his head and met Lane's eyes. 'Jessica looked like that. After she got herself pounded. She said it was a gang of spics got her behind the mini-mart.'

'It was Kramer.'

'I'm gonna kill him,' Riley said.

'I'm gonna help you.'

Lane swung the denim bag forward. Clutching it to her belly, she reached inside and took a revolver. 'It's my dad's,' she said. 'It's just a twenty-two, but . . .'

'That'll do just fine,' Riley said.

Lane waited in the car while Riley went back inside his home. A few minutes passed. Then he came out and climbed into the passenger seat. 'I told the old lady we're going to a matinee.'

Lane took the paper out of her blouse pocket. She checked the second address.

'What's that?'

'It's where Kramer lives.'

'All *right*.'

She put the paper away and started to drive.

'I've got something for him,' Riley said. He tugged up a cuff of his blue jeans, reached down, and came up with a knife. Lane glanced at it. The thing looked wicked. Its blade must've been eight inches long.

'Here's how we're gonna work it,' he said. 'You keep the motherfucker covered with the gun. *I'll* do him. Don't you go shooting him up unless he makes a break for it.'

'We'll be each other's alibis,' Lane said, her voice shaking.

'Fuck alibis. I don't care if they get me for it.'

'I do. And I'm sure your mother does. If we're caught, we might not get charged with anything, or end up with suspended sentences. I mean, I don't think jury's going to put us away for this. But let's try to work it so the cops don't come looking.'

'Oh yeah? How do you figure we can manage that?'

'Why don't we make it look like suicide?'

'Fuck that. I'm gonna cut his dick off. I'm gonna cut his head off.'

'Maybe we can make him write a suicide note. Make him confess what he did to Jessica. On paper. Then we hang him. Right there in his house.'

'You read too many fucking books.'

'It's worth a try.'

On Kramer's street, two blocks from where his house should be, Lane swung the car to the curb. She faced Riley. He had the knife in his right hand, rubbing its blade along the leg of his faded jeans.

'Why don't we walk from here?' she said. 'That way, nobody's likely to connect the car with what happens to Kramer.' She paused and tried to catch her breath. She hadn't been *doing* anything, but she felt as if she'd just finished dashing up a few flights of stairs. 'I'll go on ahead first. Give me a couple of minutes headstart.'

'You'll be alone in there with him.'

'Don't I know it,' she muttered. She lifted the bag onto her lap and dropped the keys inside. After a quick look around to make certain no one was in sight, she took out the revolver. She set the bag on the floor. Leaning back against the seat, she untucked her blouse, lifted its front, and slid the muzzle under the waist band of her skirt. It only went down an inch before pushing against her pubic mound. Lowering the blouse, she held the gun against her belly. She opened the door and climbed out.

'Goodluck,' Riley said.

'Thanks.' She shut the door. Facing the car, she slipped the revolver farther down until it was snug between her skirt and body. She glanced down at herself. The hanging front of her blouse concealed the bulges.

The back of the blouse was glued to her skin. She peeled it away, but as soon as she let go it stuck again.

There was no sidewalk in this neighborhood, so she walked along the edge of the road. The barrel pressed her groin. The front sight sometimes scraped the inner side of her left thigh, so after a while she nudged the gun butt sideways. Then the muzzle was stroking her right thigh with each step she took. But it was smooth, and didn't scratch her the way the sight did.

She remembered last night with the bottom of the crucifix stuffed in her jeans.

Last night, a cross. Today, a revolver.

It's a weird damn world, she thought.

She glanced back. The Mustang was a block away, Riley still in the passenger seat.

She kept walking.

A mortal sin, she thought. I'll be risking Hell, murdering Kramer. Even if it's Riley who does the dirty work. I'll be just as guilty as him in the eyes of God.

What am I supposed to do, let Kramer go on raping me? Let him kill Mom and Dad?

It's self-defense. Lane didn't know a lot about Church policy, but it seemed like allowances were made for killing people in self-defense, war, that kind of thing. She sure hoped so.

At the next corner, she took the paper out of her pocket. She unfolded it. Squinting as the white paper glared sunlight, she read the address again.

838.

She looked back. Riley was out of the car.

She put the paper away. She rubbed a sleeve across her face to dry the sweat. She continued walking. The sun felt like a hot blanket on her back. She wanted to reach around and pluck at the seat of her panties, but Riley was sure to see her do it.

The house to her right was 836.

Next door was Kramer's. A small, adobe house with a picture window. Its driveway was empty.

Gasping for breath, heart slamming, leg muscles feeling as soft as pudding, she walked up the driveway.

No garage. A car port, instead.

The station wagon wasn't in the car port.

It wasn't anywhere in sight.

He's not home!

After all this, she thought, he *has* to be.

She mounted the front stoop. She rang the doorbell, and heard quiet bells from inside the house.

She waited.

She wished she could catch her breath.

She slipped a hand under the front of her blouse and wrapped sweaty fingers around the grips of her father's revolver. The barrel moved, nudging her groin. She thought about Kramer's mouth down there.

'Come on, you bastard,' she muttered.

They found his station wagon fifteen minutes later in the crowded parking lot of the marina.

The chain link gate, which had been locked last night, now stood open. Lane didn't pass through it. She stood there, alone, and peered at Kramer's deserted slip.

Then she went back to the car. She opened the door, pulled the revolver up high enough so its barrel wouldn't dig into her, then slid into the driver's seat.

'He's out in his boat,' she said.

'Shit.'

'God, I don't know. Maybe it's just as well.' She took the gun out of her blouse and stuffed it into her denim bag.

'Just as well, my ass.'

'Would've been tough getting away with it here. Awful lot of people around.'

'Yeah, but we could've deep-sixed him in the river.'

'I know.'

'Shit,' Riley said again.

'There's nothing we can do about it. We'll have to figure out something else.'

'Like what?'

Shaking her head, Lane backed up the car. She drove toward the parking lot exit. 'He's gonna want me again. He said Monday or Tuesday. He'll probably want me to meet him someplace. Someplace where we'll have privacy. Maybe I can let you know ahead of time. You can be waiting.'

'Sounds good.'

Lane steered onto Shoreline. 'Want to go to the mall?'

'Okay with me.' He gave her a strange look. 'Do you?'

'Yeah, I think so. It'll give me time to calm down.'

'You forgetting who you're with?'

She glanced at him. 'Riley Benson. Tough guy. Just don't try getting tough with me, okay?'

'Not with you,' he said. Then he added, 'Lane.'

Chapter Forty-three

During the day, Uriah stayed in a dry wash some distance from the road.

He had tried to eat jerky, that morning, but found that he couldn't chew it without sending horrible pulses of pain through his jaw and cheeks. He was able to drink water, though some dribbled out through the holes in his face. And he was able to sleep.

He dreamed the vampires got him. He recognized all of them. All were demons he had slain, but they were slain no longer. They came shrieking at him through the desert sunlight. They brought him down. They stripped off his animal skins. They took the hammer and stakes from his pack. Holding him down, they pounded the wooden spikes through his hands and feet. They nailed him to the ground. Crucified him. As he writhed in torment, one ripped the patch off his eye. He looked up out of the depths of the socket, thinking, *How strange!* He could see with both eyes. The vampires were all around him, down on their knees, hunger and delight in their eyes, drool spilling down their chins. Their hands moved over his body as if trying to awaken his lust. Horrified, he realized they were succeeding. *I must resist*, he thought. *I am God's warrior.* The faces lowered onto him. He felt their mouths all over. Sucking him. Instead of pain, he felt ecstacy. *This is wrong!* Lips pressed against his mouth. A tongue thrust in. Other tongues slithered through the holes in his cheeks. Another pushed into his anus. As he wondered how that was possible, flat on his back the way he was, a tongue entered the tip of his penis and snaked in deep and he squirmed. Another slid into his empty socket. He realized he was not pinned to the ground by stakes. The wooden shafts had turned into vampire tongues that writhed inside the holes in his hands and feet. Then tongues were sliding into his body where he had no openings, melting in through his flesh, filling him.

Uriah twisted and bucked in an agony of exquisite pleasure and woke up as pain flared in his right cheek. He found the tip of his forefinger inside the bullet hole. Wincing, he eased it out. He sat up, and gently held both sides of his face.

Night had come.

In the frenzy of his dream, he'd tossed his blanket away. He dragged it toward him and clutched it around his shoulders. But he couldn't stop shaking.

Satan had visited that dream upon him. Trying to tempt him. Trying to weaken his resolve.

I *am* God's warrior, he told himself. *I won't fail.*

He got to his feet, picked up the satchel that held his weapons and useless food, wrapped the blanket around himself, and climbed the loose gravel wall of the wash.

Soon, he came to the road. He looked both ways. There were no headlights.

During the whole of the night, as he made his way toward Mulehead Bend, Uriah encountered no headlights. Not once was he forced to flee from the road and hide. He made good time.

When the horizon began to go pale, he climbed to the top of a bluff. From there, he could see the Colorado River in the distance – a broad, twisting ribbon of slate bordered by lights like hundreds of stars that had fallen to the desert near its shores.

Street lights. A few slowly moving headlights. Porch lights. Maybe even lights from the windows of homes where people had already started their day or spent a sleepless night.

Uriah wondered which of the lights might be glimmering from the lair of the vampires.

Maybe none.

Tomorrow night, he would be in among those lights. He would sneak into the lair and put Satan's children to rest.

Chapter Forty-four

A hand gently shook Lane awake. 'Time to rise and shine, honey,' her mother said.

Monday morning.

Her stomach clenched.

'Okay,' she muttered. When she was alone, she rolled onto her side, hugged her belly and drew her knees up.

I can't go to school, she thought. I just can't.

I've got to.

Yesterday, she'd told Riley that she would talk to Kramer after class and arrange to meet him.

But that was yesterday. It was easy to make brave plans when you were safe with someone else and talking about tomorrow. Now she was alone and this was the day she had to do it. Not quite the same. Not the same, at all.

Curling up more tightly under the covers, Lane pictured herself in sixth period. Sitting at her desk. Right next to Jessica's empty desk. Right in front of the table where Kramer always perched when he talked to the class. He would be sitting up there, all smug and handsome, acting as if nothing had happened. But sneaking glances at her. Calling on her, sometimes. And all period long, he would be thinking about how she looked naked, remembering the things he'd done to her, daydreaming about what he would do the next time he got her alone.

I can't go, Lane thought. I can't sit there in front of him. Not for an hour, not for a second. I'd go crazy.

So don't.

Right away, she felt better.

Uncurling, she rolled face down. The mattress pushed against her bruised body, but didn't hurt very much.

The pressure against her breasts reminded Lane of opening her blouse for Riley, yesterday. She felt the heat of a blush spreading over her skin. She hadn't been embarrassed at all when she did it, but now she could hardly believe she'd shown herself to him. Right by the street in broad daylight. It seemed as if someone else had done that. A different Lane.

The same, different Lane who'd walked up to Kramer's door with a gun shoved into her skirt.

I must've been crazy.

What if Kramer'd been home? What if we'd actually murdered him?

Didn't happen, she told herself.

Her breasts were starting to ache now, so she rolled onto her side, pushed away the covers, and sat on the edge of the bed. She'd worn a jersey nightshirt instead of a nightgown, just in case Mom or Dad should see her without a robe. The gowns were either low cut or diaphanous, or both, and no good for concealing her injuries. The crew neck jersey hid everything. Though not at the moment. Her rump was bare from scooting across the mattress, and the nightshirt was rumpled on her lap.

Lane glanced at the closed door, then peered down at herself. Her thighs were bruised, but some of the areas that had looked chafed and red now seemed okay. She pressed the gathered fabric to her belly and leaned forward. The edges of her vulva no longer looked raw. She lifted the nightshirt above her breasts. They were looking better, too. The bruises weren't so dark. They'd changed from deep purple to a greenish-yellow color.

A few more days, Lane thought, I'll be good as new.

On the outside.

Next time, maybe he won't hurt me.

There won't be a next time!

She let the nightshirt drift down to her waist, raised herself off the bed for a moment while she pulled it beneath her, then sat again and spread the fabric snug against her thighs.

There has to be a way out of this, she told herself.

Yeah, kill him.

Yesterday, she could've done it. Or helped, at least.

But now the idea of murdering Kramer seemed so much

bigger. Enormous. She felt as if it would cast a black cloud over her life that might never go away.

I can't kill him. I can't tell on him. I can't let him get me again.

I could kill myself.

The idea shocked Lane, sent a sickening flood of heat rushing through her body.

If I kill myself, he won't have any reason to go after Mom and Dad. But it'd ruin *them. I'd burn in Hell, for sure. And everything . . .*

Fuck that.

She stood up quickly, walked to the closet and put on her robe.

There has *to be a way out.*

Yeah, stay the hell home from school. That's a way out, at least for today. Worry about tomorrow tomorrow.

Maybe Riley'll take care of him without me. If I just stay out of it long enough. If Kramer doesn't come after me in the meantime.

Lane stepped into her slippers. She left her bedroom, made a quick trip to the toilet and relieved herself, then headed for the kitchen. Mom, unloading the dishwasher, looked around at her. 'You're not dressed.'

'I'm really feeling rotten today,' she said, giving her voice a low, groany tone.

'What is it?'

'You name it. Cramps, a headache, the trots. I've got it all.'

'Oh, I'm sorry, honey.'

She shrugged and frowned. 'I'll live, I guess. But I don't think I'm up for school.'

'What about Henry and Betty?'

Lane grimaced. She'd forgotten about them. About George, too. She'd phoned George yesterday after coming back from the mall, and he'd sounded eager to ride with them. 'I guess I could go ahead and take them, and then just come home.'

'No, if you're not feeling good enough to go to school . . . I suppose I can pick them up. Just this once. Since they're expecting you.'

'That'd be great.'

'They have other ways of getting home, don't they?'

'Oh, yeah. They can always work something out. There's a guy named George, too. We got to know each other at the play. I was going to give him a ride, today.'

Mom nodded. 'All right. Well, get me their addresses and I'll take care of it.'

'That's wonderful. Thanks a lot, Mom.'

'Would you like me to make you something before I go?'

'I don't feel much like eating. I'll come out when I get hungry, okay?'

'Well, suit yourself. You'll feel better, though, once you have some food inside you.'

Lane poured herself a mug of coffee, then went into the living room. Dad was in his usual chair, dressed in the sweat-clothes he usually wore after getting up, a mug in one hand, a paperback in the other.

'Morning, sweetheart,' he said. 'How's it going?'

'Not so hot. I'm staying home sick. Mom said it's okay.'

'A touch of the flu?' he asked.

'Something like that, I guess. Anyway, I feel rotten. I'm going back to bed pretty soon.' She took a sip of coffee. 'Are you all excited about tonight?'

He wrinkled his nose. 'I don't know whether I'm excited, or just scared.'

'If it bothers you, why not skip it?'

'Not that simple,' he said. 'What would I do about the ending of my book?'

'That can be the ending. You make an ethical choice, or whatever, not to meddle with the thing. Let sleeping dogs lie. That could be the theme of the book.'

Nodding, he laughed softly. 'Not a bad idea. Do *you* think we shouldn't take the stake out?'

'Hell, I wouldn't have brought any corpse home in the first place.'

'I *wish* we hadn't. God knows.' He shrugged. 'But now that she's here . . .'

'I don't know, Dad. You've always warned me not to mess with weird stuff like ouija boards and fortune telling . . .'

'Yeah.'

'Remember when I bought that voodoo doll in New Orleans?'

'It still holds,' he said.

' "You don't want to monkey with the supernatural." That's what you always told me. And now you're planning to pull a stake out of a dead person to see if she's a vampire?'

'No good can come of it,' he said, sounding like the voice of caution from an old mad-scientist movie.

'So why do it?' Lane asked.

His smile came back. 'Because it's there?'

'Try again, Pops.'

'You don't sound so sick to me.'

'Maybe you *should* forget it. I'm serious. Make up your mind not to pull out the stake, and you'll be amazed how much better you suddenly feel.'

'Will it make you feel better?'

'Maybe. I don't really care. I can always stay in my room when you do it, and you'll have to be out there. You know? This isn't my thing, it's yours. I've got my own problems.'

'What kind . . .?'

'I'm just saying,' she hurried on, 'you shouldn't let Pete or anyone else push you into doing something that you're against. You're the one who'll have to live with it.'

'You think it's morally wrong to pull the stake?'

'It is if she's a vampire.'

'Of course, we know she isn't.'

' "There are more things in heaven and earth, Horatio, than you've dreamt of in your philosophies." '

'Hey, pretty good!'

She smiled. 'I'm off to bed.'

' "Goodnight, sweet Princess. And flights of angels sing thee to thy rest." '

'Oh, thanks. I'm not dying, I'm just going to take another nap. I hope.'

She left the room, wrote down the addresses of her friends, gave them to her mother in the kitchen, thanked her again for taking care of the matter, then returned to her bedroom.

Propped up against pillows, she tried to read. Though her eyes moved over the sentences, her mind kept straying, tormenting her with thoughts of Kramer. After a while, she set the book aside. She snuggled down beneath the covers.

She *wished* she had her father's problems. He doesn't know how lucky he is, she thought. How nice it would be if the biggest worry in her life was whether or not to pull a piece of wood out of a corpse.

Dad had said the girl – Bonnie? – was the Homecoming Queen. She must've been beautiful. Maybe just Kramer's type.

Drifting toward sleep, Lane imagined getting all her friends together: Betty and Henry and George and Riley. *I need your help*, she told them. She explained her plan, and they all seemed eager to join in. So they crept into the garage and sneaked out with the corpse. They tied the coffin to the roof of her Mustang. They drove through the night across town to Kramer's house. His station wagon wasn't there. He was still out on his boat. While her friends waited on the front stoop, she broke a back window and entered the house. She opened the door for them, and they brought the coffin inside. They took it to Kramer's bedroom. They lifted the body onto his bed, and hid the empty coffin in a closet.

Lane volunteered to pull the stake. *I'm not scared*, she said. And she wasn't. Not of Bonnie. Bonnie was not the enemy. Bonnie was her ally, her weapon. She drew the stake out of the girl's chest. The hole melted shut. The cadaver began to expand like an inflatable rubber doll with air being blown in. Its dry, leathery skin uncrinkled, took on a healthy glow of life. Except for the bruised places.

Lane was startled when she realized that Bonnie looked like her own twin. No, she thought, she's not a twin. She's me. This is even better than I hoped. Kramer'll think I came to him.

The Lane on Kramer's bed opened her eyes. *Don't worry*, she said. *I'll take care of him*.

Lane woke up feeling as if a terrible burden had been removed. She didn't know why, but she felt good. Then she remembered the weird plan of her daydream. It had only been a fantasy. Nothing was changed. Her spirits sank, and dread returned to its nesting place in the pit of her stomach.

She looked at the clock beside her bed. Almost one.

She'd been asleep for a long time, and she was glad. If only she could just *stay* asleep.

But she was hungry. So she got out of bed, put on her robe and slippers, and left the room.

The house seemed deserted.

But the door to her father's office was shut. She knocked. Opening it, she glimpsed a page of black and white photos as Dad swept a folder shut. He smiled at her, but he looked startled and his face was red.

She wondered what he'd been looking at. Whatever it might be, he seemed ashamed of it. She decided not to ask. 'Sorry to bother you,' she said.

'No problem. Feeling any better?'

'A little. Hungry, though. Have you already eaten?'

'Yeah. We had lunch an hour ago. Do you want me to make you something?'

'No, that's okay. I can manage. Where's Mom?'

'She went to the store. We decided to ask Pete and Barbara over for dinner, so she had to pick up a few things.'

'Barbara's recovered?'

'Apparently. Your mother dropped in on her. Sounds as if she's a little embarrassed about her accident, but she's eager to resume the adventure. Pete's already picked up a new video camera.'

'Let's hope Barbara doesn't break this one.'

'She probably won't get her hands on it.'

'If Pete's smart. What time are they coming over?'

'Around six.'

'If I'm not around, make sure you get me up. I wouldn't want to miss anything.'

'You're sure about that?'

'Absolutely. See you later.' She pulled the door shut, and went to the kitchen.

While she made herself a grilled cheese sandwich, she thought back to the folder that Dad had shut so quickly. She tried to remember the look of the paper inside. Glossy, with two or three pictures on it.

Like a page out of *Buford Memories*.

'Oh, boy,' she muttered. He must've torn it from the 1968 annual. And there had appeared to be more than one in that folder.

Pictures of Bonnie. He'd been studying pictures of Bonnie.

God, if ol' lady Swanson ever found out . . . I would've been in such deep shit . . . How could he do that to me?

Pete had called him 'obsessed.' Right here in the kitchen, when Dad was talking about his weird dreams.

Obsessed, all right.

Lane slid her sandwich on to a paper plate. She took it to the table and sat down.

Dad just wanted the pictures for his book, she told herself as she started to eat. Nothing weird about that. He looked so guilty in there because he stole them from the yearbook, doesn't want me to find out. That's all.

Maybe that isn't all. He's been dreaming about her. Walking in his sleep. He went out there to pay her a visit.

Lane remembered the way she'd found him staring at the naked corpse. What if he *is* obsessed with her? Maybe he *wants* her to be a vampire, wants to see her change back into a beautiful girl, wants to . . .

Come on. This is Dad, not Kramer. Dad wouldn't . . .

The things he was saying to her. But he was asleep. He was talking to her in his dream. Awake, he wouldn't . . .

Awake, ten minutes ago, he was staring at her pictures. What was he thinking? Was he wondering what it might be like if she comes back to life tonight?

845

He's just a man.

No, he's not. He's Dad. He's doing this for his book, not because he's horny over a high school girl.

Lane couldn't finish her sandwich. She threw the remains away, took a drink of water, and hurried back to her bedroom. She shut the door. She tossed her robe across the chair. She kicked her slippers off. She drew the covers up around her neck, curled on her side, and hugged her belly.

Dad isn't like that, she told herself. He's not a pervert. He loves me and Mom.

He even told Bonnie that he loves us.

The way someone might say it to his mistress.

He claimed he loved us, but he went ahead and started to pull the stake.

He was asleep, for godsake!

But what if I hadn't been up there?

The girl is dead, Lane told herself. She's dead. She's not a vampire. She wouldn't have come back to life. That's bullshit, and Dad knows it.

That's the end of it.

But maybe . . .

She started to recite an 'Our Father,' softly mumbling the words. To stop herself from thinking. To calm herself down. She did another 'Our Father,' not speaking this time, going through it in her mind. And then another.

A gentle rapping on the door woke her up. She rolled onto her back as the door eased open. Dad looked in. 'Are Pete and Barbara here?' she asked.

'Not yet. But you have a visitor.'

'Was she asleep?' came a voice from the hallway behind Dad.

Lane lost her breath.

'She's awake now,' Dad said.

'Really,' Kramer said, 'there was no need to disturb her.'

'That's all right,' Dad said over his shoulder as he entered the room. 'It was time to get her up, anyway. We're having some other guests pretty soon.' He gestured for Kramer to come in.

'Daaaad.'

'What's the matter?'

'I'm in bed.'

I'm dreaming this.

'If she'd rather . . .'

'It's fine. She's just doing her shy routine.'

Kramer came into the room.

He's in my bedroom. The bastard's in my bedroom.

Lane tried to force herself to smile.

Kramer's smile looked tentative and concerned. 'I just dropped by to see how you were doing. I hope you didn't catch a bug, or something, while we were at the play Saturday night.'

Wasn't a bug, she thought.

He stepped around Dad and approached the bed. He had a manilla folder in one hand. Like the one in which Dad kept his pictures of Bonnie. 'Just in case you might be down for a while,' he said, 'I thought I'd bring you this week's assignments.'

'Thank you,' she muttered.

'That's very nice of you, Hal,' Dad told him.

Kramer smiled back at him. 'Wouldn't want my ace student to fall behind.' He set the folder down on her nightstand. 'How are you feeling?' he asked her.

'Not very swift.'

'I'm sorry to hear that. Do you think you'll be up and around . . .?'

Far away, the telephone rang.

'I'd better get that,' Dad said. 'Jean's taking a bath.'

He left the room.

I don't believe this, Lane thought, *It's a nightmare.*

Kramer sat on the edge of the bed and smiled down at her. 'Obviously, you've kept our little secret.'

She nodded. She didn't think she *could* talk.

'That's very good, darling. But I'm not happy about you staying home today. I missed you.' He slipped a hand beneath

847

the covers. Staring into her eyes, he gently squeezed her right breast. 'You missed me, too, didn't you?'

Lane gasped for breath. She shuddered.

Kramer laughed softly. He glanced toward the open door, then fixed his gaze on her face and moved his hand down the front of her nightshirt.

She choked out, 'Don't.'

'Shhhh. I've got a sharp friend in my pocket.' His hand found her bare skin below the rumpled jersey. Lane pressed her legs together. But his hand pressed between them. She started to whimper. 'I could easily slash your throat in an instant. And then do the same to your father. And your mother. She's taking a bath. That might be fun.'

Kramer took his hand away.

'See you later,' he said. He went out to the hallway and shut the door.

Chapter Forty-five

After hanging up the kitchen phone, Larry went into the living room and found Hal in front of the book-shelves, looking at the collection of his works.

'You've got quite an output,' Hal said.

'Seventeen novels, so far.'

'That's fantastic.'

'Well, things have been going okay. I'm not as successful as I'd like to be, but who is?'

'What are you working on now? Or is that a secret?'

'No big secret, I guess. Would you like a drink?'

'Oh, I don't want to impose. I just came by to check on Lane, and . . .'

'You don't have to rush off. I was about to fix myself a vodka tonic. What can I get you?'

'Sounds good to me,' Hal said, and followed him into the kitchen.

'That was a friend who called,' Larry said as he started to prepare the drinks. 'Another writer. Quite a coincidence. He's putting together an anthology of vampire stories, and asked me to contribute.'

'Well, congratulations.'

'Thanks. It's nice to be at the point where they're *asking* for stories. I don't even write short stories any more unless I'm asked for one. That's a big step from the old days when I used to send them out to magazines and collect rejection slips.'

'Must be very gratifying. You mentioned something about a coincidence?'

'Oh, yeah. Pretty weird. He wants a vampire story, and I've been up to my neck in vampire stuff for the past few weeks.'

'So, you're working on a vampire novel?'

'Not exactly.' He handed a cocktail to Hal, picked up his own, and led the way back to the living room. He sank into his easy chair. Hal sat across from him at the end of the sofa. 'Here's how,' he said.

They drank. Hal smiled and said, 'Hits the spot.'

'I'm doing a book about vampires, but it's not a novel. Non-fiction.'

'A study of some kind?'

'Actually, it deals with personal experiences.'

Hal shook his head, smiling as if he thought Larry was putting him on. 'You've had personal experiences with vampires?'

'Yep.'

I'd better quit talking about it, he thought. Then he thought, why? The guy's certainly in no position to steal my story. And it might be worthwhile to get an outsider's reaction.

Everybody will know about it, anyway, after tonight and we turn Bonnie over to the police.

'Want to hear about it?' he asked.

'Sure!' He took a sip of his drink, and leaned forward like a kid eager for a spooky tale.

'Well, it all started a few weeks ago when Jean and I went out in the desert to explore a ghost town with some friends. Pete and Barbara. They'll be coming over for dinner in a little while, so you'll have a chance to meet them.'

'Great.'

'In fact,' Larry said, 'how would you like to join us for dinner?'

He hoped Jean wouldn't object. Probably not. She had a roast in the oven. There was undoubtedly more than enough to feed an extra guest.

We'll get him to stay for the big event, if he wants. Have an objective observer.

'I hate to impose,' Hal said.

'We'd be glad to have you. This is a rather special occasion. You'll see why, once you've heard the whole story.'

'Well, I'd be delighted to stay. If it's all right with Jean.'

'She'll be happy to have you.'

Hal shrugged. 'If it's okay with her . . .'

'Great. Okay.' Larry took another drink. 'So, the four of us went to this ghost town about an hour's drive from here. It's called Sagebrush Flat.'

As he told the story, Hal watched him and drank. Sometimes, the teacher shook his head as if he couldn't believe his ears. A few times, he murmured his astonishment. After finishing the part about bringing the body home, Larry left the room briefly to refresh the drinks. Then he sat down again and resumed his tale. Carefully leaving out the details of his infatuation with Bonnie. Concentrating on the facts. He enjoyed Hal's reactions. The man was clearly fascinated.

'And so,' he finished, 'tonight's the night we finally pull out the stake. Right after dinner.'

'Holy shit,' Hal muttered.

'You're welcome to stick around for it. You can play the role of the disinterested observer.'

'Get myself killed?' He laughed. It sounded a trifle nervous.

'I don't imagine it'll come to that.'

'No, I don't either. I may be superstitious, but I don't think I'm ready to believe in the existence of vampires.'

Grinning, Larry nodded. 'If she comes to life, I guess we'll all be in for a shock.'

'I'd certainly hate to miss it, though.'

'No reason you should.'

Excusing himself, Larry went down the hall to his bedroom. He found Jean putting on makeup. She wore her jumpsuit, boots and scarf.

'Are they here?'

'Not yet. But Hal Kramer is. He came by to see Lane and bring her some assignments.'

'That's certainly above and beyond the call of duty.'

'I think he felt a little guilty. He was afraid her absence might have something to do with Saturday night.'

'He did keep her out awfully late.'

'Maybe he thought she got sick on the pizza. Anyway, it was nice of him. I've asked him to stay for dinner.'

Jean frowned in the mirror. 'Won't that kind of put a damper on things?'

'I told him all about it.'

'You told him about the *vampire*?'

'Sure. Why not? It's no big secret. Or it won't be, once we've called the police.'

'Still, you shouldn't have . . . You're always *blabbing*, Larry. God.'

'What's the big deal?'

'I'm not saying it's a big deal, just that I wish you'd be more careful about what you say to people. Everybody doesn't need to know our business.'

'I just wanted to get his reactions.'

'Now, he'll probably think we're all nut cases.'

'Hardly. He was blown away.'

Jean sighed. She glanced at her wristwatch. 'Well, what's done is done. I just wish you'd . . .'

'I know, I know.'

'Right, you know. Anyway, Pete and Barbara should be arriving any minute. Would you like to make sure Lane's about ready?'

'I shouldn't leave our guest abandoned . . .'

'It'll only take a minute.'

Wishing Jean wouldn't be so negative about everything, he left the room and went to Lane's door. He knocked.

'Yeah?' she called.

'Are you decent?'

'Yeah.'

He opened the door. Lane was still in bed, hidden under covers except for the back of her head. She didn't look at him.

'I thought you'd be up and dressed by now.'

'I had a relapse.'

'Do you feel good enough to have dinner with us?'

'I don't know.'

Concerned, he went to the bed. He sat down on its edge and stroked Lane's hair. She looked up at him with solemn eyes. Her face was slack and pale. 'Are you okay?'

'If I was okay, I wouldn't be lying here.'

'I mean, do you think it might be something serious? Maybe we'd better get you to a doctor.'

'I don't need any doctor. I'll be fine.'

'I really hate to see you like this, honey.'

'I'm sorry.'

'Look, if you're not up to having dinner with us, we could bring it in for you.'

'Are Pete and Barbara here yet?'

'Not yet. But Hal's still here. We've asked him to join us. For dinner and for the big event.'

Closing her eyes, Lane muttered, 'Wonderful.'

'What's the matter?'

'Nothing. I just feel awful, that's all.'

He gently caressed her cheek, then stood up. 'It'd be nice if you can join us. It's up to you, though. Wouldn't want you barfing on the table.'

Lane didn't crack a smile.

She *is* sick, Larry thought.

'Like I said, we'll bring you something.'

'Thanks.'

He went out to the hallway and closed her door, feeling depressed. It's probably nothing serious, he told himself. But he thought. What if it's spinal meningitis? Or bone cancer? Or . . . Knock it off!

Jean was no longer in the bedroom.

He found her in the living room, sitting on the sofa near Hal, saying, 'I know the whole thing sounds crazy, but . . .' She looked up at Larry.

'Lane's feeling worse. She might not make it out for dinner.'

Jean scowled. 'I'd better go see her. Larry, why don't you get Hal another drink?'

Her mother shut the door when she left the room. A few minutes later, Lane heard the doorbell. That would be Pete and Barbara arriving.

She heard faint, cheerful voices. Some laughter.

It all seemed too weird to be real: the group drinking and eating and having a merry old time while they prepared to conclude their business with the 'vampire,' never suspecting they had a *real* monster in their midst.

The Devil hath the power to assume a pleasing shape.

Kramer hath a pleasing shape, all right.

God, if only they knew what he was really like.

Lane imagined herself getting out of bed and going into the living room. 'Hey, guess what Kramer did to me.' Then he gets out his 'sharp friend' and has at them all. Maybe Dad and Pete could nail him, but he was sure to cut someone.

She pictured the straight razor slashing a quick gash across her father's throat.

I'm not going to risk Mom and Dad, she thought. Better to let him keep on messing with me, than . . .

Lane suddenly realized how vulnerable she was, lying in bed with nothing on but her nightshirt, and Kramer in the house.

853

They're probably all drinking. Kramer says, 'Mind if I use the facilities?' Somebody points out that the john is just at the end of the hall. Of course, nobody escorts him. He excuses himself from the group and comes straight to my room for another round of threats and feelies.

Lane climbed out of bed. She turned on the lamp. At her dresser, she took panties from a drawer and put them on. Though flimsy, the snug fabric felt shielding. She pulled off her nightshirt and stuffed it into a drawer. Shivering, she slipped into a bra. As she fastened its hooks, she remembered the times she'd gone to school without one, hoping to attract Kramer's attention.

You attracted it, all right.

Had nothing to do with that, she reminded herself. Kramer picked me before I started anything.

For additional protection, Lane put on a T-shirt. At the closet, she took a pair of thick corduroy pants off a hanger. She stretched the T-shirt down to her thighs, drew the pants up over its tails, and fastened the waist button and closed the zipper. Now, to get at her skin, Kramer would have to yank the shirt up out of her pants. She slipped a belt through the loops and cinched it tight. Then she put on her big, plaid shirt. She buttoned its front, but didn't tuck it in.

She glanced at herself in the mirror.

Not exactly armor, but a lot better than the nightshirt. If Kramer paid another visit, he would have a tough time finding any bare skin below her neck.

Lane climbed into bed. She pulled the top sheet and blanket up to her chin. It felt strange to be completely dressed beneath the covers.

Not only strange, but hot.

Better a little discomfort, she thought, than to let that slimy bastard put his hands on me again.

She listened for his footsteps. She *knew* he would come.

Suppose he comes, and I've got Dad's gun under the covers and I blow him away? They'll find the razor on his body.

Lane's heart began hammering as she thought about it.

I'll get it.

She climbed out of bed. When she eased the door open, voices and laughter flooded in. They're having one hell of a party, she thought.

The hallway was clear.

She rushed to her parents' room. Leaving the light off, she made her way toward the closet where Dad kept his revolver.

In the dim glow from the hallway, she saw the telephone on the nightstand.

And felt a rush of relief.

She turned on the bedside lamp, phoned directory assistance, and got the number for Melanie Benson. She tapped out the number.

As she listened to the quiet ringing, she watched the door. 'Come on, come on,' she muttered.

After the fourth ring, someone picked up.

'Yeah?' Riley, sounding annoyed by the interruption.

'It's me, Lane.'

'All *right*! What's up?'

'Kramer's here. He's at my house.'

'No shit?'

'He's having *dinner* with us, for godsake.'

'What the hell . . .?'

'Never mind. Look, he's probably going to be here for a couple more hours. I can't get away, but . . . I don't know, I just thought I oughta let you know. He'll probably be going back to his house afterwards, you know? Maybe you want to be waiting for him.'

'Fuckin' – A.'

'What do you think?'

'Fucker's gonna be in for the surprise of his life. The *last* surprise of his life.'

'Be careful, okay? He carries that razor with him.'

'When they autopsy the fucker, they'll find it up his ass.'

'Good luck, Riley.'

'Yeah, sure. See you around, Lane.' He hung up.

Lane cradled the telephone. She rubbed her sweaty hands

on the legs of her corduroys, turned off the lamp, and hurried to the bathroom. She locked herself in.

Sitting on the toilet, she hugged her belly and hunched over and tried to stop shaking.

Chapter Forty-six

'Well, here she is,' Pete announced, lifting his cocktail as if toasting Lane as she came into the living room.

'Can't keep a good woman down,' Hal said.

Larry felt a surge of relief, but it was mixed with apprehension. 'Feeling better, honey?' he asked.

'A lot better.'

'That's terrific.'

'The gang's all here,' Barbara said.

Now I can relax, Larry told himself. While everyone else had been drinking and munching snacks and apparently having a good time, he'd been drinking and worrying about Lane.

But she must be okay. Thank God.

In a way, though, he'd been comforted by the knowledge that she would be staying in her bedroom away from the action when it came time to pull the stake.

The way she was dressed, she obviously intended to go out there with them. She even wore the same shirt that she'd had on the other night – the one she'd used to conceal the big crucifix from her bedroom.

Barbara seemed to notice the same thing. Smiling at Lane, she patted her belly and said, 'You got it?'

Lane looked perplexed for a moment.

'You know.' She patted her belly again.

'Oh, that.' Lane glanced around.

'Jean's in the kitchen,' Barbara told her.

'It's on my wall. I'll get it when the time comes.'

'What's that?' Hal asked her.

Lane glanced at him and looked away, her face going red as if she were embarrassed to admit such a thing to her teacher.

Barbara leaned sideways and put a hand on Hal's knee. 'We're discussing our protection.' With her other hand, she lifted the gold chain out of her sweat-shirt and showed him Lane's cross. 'She loaned me this for the big event. She's got a giant one for herself. Has to hide it under her shirt so her mom won't know about it. Jean's superstitious about being super-stitious.'

'Better eighty-six, Barb,' Pete said.

'I'm fine,' she protested.

'Must be fine,' Larry said. 'Anybody can say "superstitious" twice in one sentence without messing up . . .'

'You're the one who'd better watch it, buster,' Barbara told Pete. 'You go pulling another stunt like last time and you'll . . .'

' "This little piggie went wee-wee-wee-wee all the way home."'

Barbara's face went crimson. 'You shut up.'

'Chow time,' Jean called from the dining room.

'Saved by the bell,' Pete said.

Hal laughed. 'Is that b-e-l-l-e?'

'Good one, Hal. The belle of the ball.'

Barbara showed Pete her teeth. 'Here's one belle you won't ball till Hell freezes over.'

'Oooo, the lady's pissed. No pun intended.'

'Come on,' Larry said, getting quickly to his feet. 'Let's put on the nose bag.'

'Let's *muzzle*, Peter.'

When they were all seated at the dining room table, Pete raised his glass of wine and toasted, 'To Bonnie. Will she or won't she?'

'Only her hairdresser knows for sure,' Barbara said.

Larry took a sip of his wine. He felt more than a little light-headed. We've all been drinking too much, he thought. Joking around too much. Doesn't anyone realize . . .?

Going out to fool with a dead person.

'Let me say something,' he said. They all looked at him except Lane. She was sitting beside Hal, frowning at her empty plate. 'Bonnie Saxon was a sweet and beautiful young woman, murdered. She was just a little older than Lane, and she would've had a whole life ahead of her if some goddamn nut hadn't . . .' Larry's voice started to tremble, and tears filled his eyes. 'It shouldn't have happened. It was a cruel . . .' He sobbed. He shook his head. 'I'm sorry,' he muttered.

'You'd better lay off the stuff,' Jean warned.

'Eighty-six, Lar,' Barbara blurted.

'I think what Dad said is right.' Lane sounded upset. She looked angry. 'This isn't a movie, you know. That corpse out in the garage wasn't put together by a special effects department. She was a real girl. Some damn bastard . . .'

'Lane!'

'I'm sorry, Mom, but *really*. You're all kidding around about this thing like it's fun and games. Will she or won't she sit up and say "Boo!"? Well, it's real, and she's really dead. Just because she's got a stake in her chest, it's a Halloween party. How do you think her parents would feel if they were here listening to all this shit?'

'Watch your language, young lady.'

'What if that was *me* out there? Would you all party it up and go out with a video camera . . .?'

'Stop it!' Jean snapped.

Lane lowered her head. 'I just think you should leave the poor girl alone. It's not right.'

'Nothing good can come of it,' Larry muttered.

'Well, I'm in agreement with that,' Jean said. 'I just want the body gone.'

'Now, hold on a minute,' Pete said. 'None of us are ghouls, here. Me and Larry know this is serious business. God knows, we faced down her murderer Saturday and damn near got ourselves wasted. So maybe we're all a little edgy about this business, and maybe we're carrying on a bit too much. But that's no reason to call things off. Somebody's gonna take that stake out of her. If it isn't us, it'll be people from the cops, or the coroner's or someone. It might as well be us. Our book depends on it, right Lar?'

'Yeah,' he muttered.

'We've gone this far. We've gotta see it through.' Looking at Lane, he added, 'It's not like we'll be desecrating the body. The girl's already been desecrated by that lunatic Uriah. We pull out the stake, we'll be un-desecrating her. It'll be doing her a favor.'

'Especially if she's a vampire,' Barbara said.

Jean, groaning, rolled her eyes upward.

'What do you think, Hal?' Barbara asked.

Solemnly, he shook his head. 'I'm just here as an impartial observer. But I have to say that Larry and Pete won't have much of a book if they don't go ahead with pulling out the stake.'

'My man,' Pete said.

'I think we should eat before the roast gets cold,' Jean said.

Nobody spoke much during the meal. Larry felt ravenous. As he forked beef and mashed potatoes into his mouth, he noticed that the others were also gobbling their food as if they'd been starved. Everyone except Lane. When the others were done, her plate looked as if it had hardly been touched.

'Are we ready, pardner?' Pete asked.

'As we'll ever be,' Larry said, his heart suddenly thumping so hard he felt dizzy.

'Hang on, I'll get my camera.'

'Think I'll pay a visit to Mr Toilet,' Barbara said.

They both left the room.

'That was a delicious dinner, Jean,' Hal said.

'Well, thank you. I made some Black Forest pie for dessert, but I think we should wait and have it afterward. Let the boys get this nonsense out of their systems, first.'

Pete returned with the camcorder he'd left in the living room. 'Let's hope this one survives the night,' he said.

'Just don't pull any cute tricks like last time,' Jean told him.

'Not a chance.'

When Barbara came back, she said, 'All set.'

They went to the kitchen door. As Larry slid it open, Lane said, 'I think I'd better pay a visit, too. Go on ahead. I'll be out in a minute.'

'Right,' Pete said. 'Let's not have any more accidents.'

The others followed Larry outside. He started to shudder as he strode toward the garage. Hunching over, he hugged his chest. He clenched his teeth.

Oh Bonnie, he thought. Here we come, ready or not.

Stopping at the garage door, he dug into a front pocket of his pants. He brought out the keys. The padlock felt like ice in his hand as he tried to hold it steady. The key shook, but finally he got it in. He twisted it, and the lock dropped open. He removed it, flipped away the latch, and tugged the door sideways a few feet. He dropped the padlock into his pocket, where it pressed heavy and cold against his thigh.

Jean entered ahead of them. Seconds later, the overhead bulb came on and the others stepped into the garage.

Larry was surprised to see the ladder down. Had someone been in here?

Then he remembered that they hadn't put it up again after the last try.

He stared at the dark opening to the attic.

'What's this?' Hal nudged Pete's bow, which lay on the concrete floor beside the quiver of arrows.

'Our insurance,' Pete told him. 'Just in case she gets lively after we take out the stake. Hey, maybe you'd like to keep her covered with that. I'll be busy filming. Any good at archery?'

'I used to be pretty fair,' he said as he picked up the bow. 'I'm no William Tell, but . . .'

'It'll be point-blank.'

'It won't be necessary,' Jean said to Hal. 'Just more of their foolishness.'

'Well, I'll be happy to play along.' He left the quiver on the floor, but slipped an arrow out.

860

'Good man,' Pete said. 'Just go for the heart if she turns out to be Dracula's daughter.'

Hal chuckled softly and nodded.

Pete took a step toward his wife and raised the camera toward her.

'No way, Jose.'

'Hey, come on.'

'And break this one?'

'Don't be such a pussy.'

'Screw you.'

'Come on, Barb! This is no time to be . . .'

'I'll do it,' Jean offered. 'Show me how it works.'

'Great. Just get us coming down with the coffin. Then I'll take over and get Larry when he unsticks the babe.' He gave the camera to Jean, showed her how to hold it, and pointed out the viewfinder. 'It's all set,' he said. 'Automatic focus, the whole ball of wax. Just push this button here, and you're rolling.'

He turned away from her. He grinned at Larry and rubbed his hands together. 'Anything you want to say for our home viewers?'

'Let's just do it,' he said. His voice came out shaky.

Pete slapped his upper arm, then hurried past him to the ladder. As he started to climb, he glanced back at Jean. 'You getting this?'

'Yeah.'

Larry waited until Pete crawled onto the attic floor. Then he began climbing. Though he didn't feel especially cold, he couldn't stop shaking. His bowels ached. His legs seemed so weak that he feared they might give out.

In a few minutes, he told himself, it'll all be over.

I'll be yours forever, Bonnie seemed to whisper in his mind.

What if it's true? he thought.

It's not. She's dead. Her 'voice' is nothing more than my damned imagination trying to mess with me.

What if she *does* come back to life?

As Larry's head rose into the gloom of the attic, he saw

861

himself in bed, Bonnie straddling him, naked and more beautiful than any woman he'd ever had.

What if it could be that way?

He paused, his mind full of her. He could feel her warm hands roaming over his skin, feel the moist softness of her lips, her breasts brushing against his chest, and then her slick tightness sliding down as she slowly impaled herself.

'What're you waiting for?' Pete asked. 'Losing the ol' nerve?'

'I'm okay,' he muttered. Clambering onto the attic floor, he realized he *was* okay. His dread had melted in the warmth of his fantasies.

It can't turn out that way, he told himself. But wouldn't it be nice?

No! It *wouldn't* be nice. What's the matter with me?

In the faint light from below, he saw Pete kneeling at the head of the coffin. He made his way toward the other end. His hand came down on the fluorescent lamp he'd brought up the night Lane caught him here.

Lane.

Wanting Bonnie was a betrayal of her. Even worse, it was a betrayal of Jean.

He moved the dead lamp out of the way, crept over the floorboards to the foot of the coffin, and put his hands on its corners.

Inside, the coffin looked black.

He couldn't see Bonnie in there, at all.

In a whisper, Pete said, 'Hey, wouldn't it be something if she *does* come back to life?'

'Yeah,' he murmured.

'She was one fabulous babe, wasn't she?'

'You're married to a fabulous babe.'

'Yeah, but *Bonnie*. I haven't been able to get that picture out of my head, you know?'

'She doesn't look like that now,' Larry said, and he was glad that he couldn't see her corpse in the black depths of the coffin.

'In the movies, they come back good as new.'

'This isn't the movies, Pete.'

'Too bad, huh?'

'Yeah.'

'What are you guys doing up there?' Barbara called from below.

'We're on our way,' Pete called. Speaking softly, he said, 'Ready?'

'Yeah.' Clutching the wooden corners, Larry began to crawl sideways, looking over his shoulder and scooting the foot of the coffin toward the lighted gap in the floor. He stepped down onto the ladder. Left hand gripping the top rung, he braced the end of the coffin with his right.

'Let's hope she doesn't fall out this time,' Pete said.

The panel tilted against Larry's hand and the coffin eased forward.

'Got it?' Pete asked.

'Yeah.' Larry stepped slowly downward, holding the end high. It didn't seem to weigh much.

Just as he wondered if it might be empty, Pete said, 'Ugly mother.' She was in there, all right. The box probably felt light because Pete was supporting most of the weight.

When it started to tip, Larry released the ladder and grabbed it with both hands.

'Be careful,' Barbara said.

'I think I'm . . .'

'I've got you,' she told him, and clasped the sides of his legs just above the knees. She held him steady, her hands moving up his thighs as he stepped lower. Then they were on his hips. They pressed against his back, and she said, 'Okay, one to go.'

He stepped onto the platform, and her hands left him. He backed away from the ladder.

'Watch it,' she warned as he approached the edge of the platform.

'Thanks.' He stepped down to the concrete and slowly lowered the coffin to keep it level while Pete descended the remaining rungs of the ladder.

The edge sank beneath his chin. He glimpsed the corpse's brown, withered legs and quickly looked away. The box nudged his chest. He backed up until Pete was off the ladder, off the platform.

They set the coffin on the garage floor.

Hal hurried forward. 'Good God,' he said. 'You people weren't kidding.' Holding the bow and an arrow at his side, he bent over for a closer look.

Barbara came up beside him. 'Yuck,' she said. 'I'd forgotten just how disgusting . . .'

'It's like she's mummified,' Hal said.

'Jerky,' Barbara said.

'Let's everybody quit admiring her,' Jean said, 'and get this over with.'

Hal reached in. His fingertips prodded Bonnie's thigh. 'Though,' he muttered. Then he rubbed the leg with his open hand.

'Cut it out,' Larry told him.

'Sorry.'

'Come on, everyone,' Jean said.

'Yeah,' Pete said. 'Let's get this show on the road. Larry, get on the other side of the coffin.'

Larry stepped around to the other side. Pete took the video camera from Jean, raised it to his shoulder, and peered into the viewfinder. 'Everybody clear away,' he ordered. 'Hal, get ready with the bow.'

Larry crouched beside the coffin. The others stood together a few yards away, gazing at him. Hal raised the bow and nocked his arrow.

'Okay,' Pete said.

'Hold it,' Barbara said. 'Shouldn't we wait for Lane?'

Do it now while she's not here, Larry thought.

He lowered his gaze to the body in the coffin. He looked at its straw-colored hair, its sunken eyelids, its hollow cheeks and horrible grin. Then he stared at the stub of wood protruding from the hole in its chest.

Take it out and I'll be yours.

He wrapped his right hand around the stake.

Closing his eyes, he saw Bonnie alive. He saw her striding

toward his bed, hair drifting around her face, her eyes innocent and loving, the tip of her tongue moist at the corner of her mouth. Her flawless skin gleamed. Her breasts jiggled just a bit. Her nipples stood erect. Her pubic curls glinted like filaments of sunlit gold. Kneeling on the mattress, she swung a leg over Larry. On hands and knees, she hovered above him.

Pull the stake, she whispered. *We'll be lovers forever*.

Larry's hand tightened around the wooden shaft.

He opened his eyes and looked at Jean. Her fists were planted on her hips. She was scowling at him. 'Well, go on,' she said.

Shifting his gaze toward Pete, he looked into the camera lens. 'Forget it,' he said. 'I'm not going to do it. *We're* not going to do it. None of us. It's over. Forget it.'

Lane moved in from the darkness beyond the garage door. She halted. She looked at Larry. Then at Hal.

'NO!' she yelled, and ran at her teacher.

Chapter Forty-seven

Once the others were out of the house, Lane waited at the kitchen door and watched until they were inside the garage. Only then was she convinced that Kramer wouldn't break away from the group and come in for a visit.

She went into her bedroom. There, she removed her crucifix from the small nail on her wall.

Pushing the bottom end of the cross under her waist band, she thought about the revolver.

She could take the gun instead of the cross.

And do what with it? Blow Kramer away? Make him confess, first. It'll all be on video tape.

I can't.

I don't have to, she suddenly realized. She'd made the phone call to Riley. Right now, he was probably waiting in Larry's house eager to nail the bastard for murdering Jessica.

I'll be in the clear. He'll be dead, and nobody will ever have to find out what he did to me.

If Riley doesn't botch it.

He won't.

Leaving her room, Lane decided to go ahead and use the toilet. She went to the end of the hall, turned on the bathroom light and shut the door. She locked it just in case Kramer might decide to come back, after all. She took out the crucifix, set it down by the sink, lowered her corduroys and panties, and sat on the toilet.

Maybe I should just stay here, she thought.

She finished, dried herself, and didn't get up.

Just stay here, and I'll never have to see Kramer again. I can read about him tomorrow in the newspaper. Buford High School English teacher brutally slain in his home.

Nobody will ever know what he did to me.

Unless they get Riley for it. Then I'd have to testify for him.

Maybe that won't happen. Maybe it'll just go unsolved forever, and Mom and Dad will never have to know.

Lane wondered if they were waiting for her. They might not pull the stake until she was there. Maybe they would send someone in to get her. Maybe Kramer would volunteer.

He can't get me with the door locked.

Hell, *anybody* could unlock the damn thing. All it takes is something that'll fit into the keyhole. You could almost do it with a fingernail.

Besides, I should be there for Dad.

With the crucifix tucked into the front of her corduroys and out of sight under the draping shirt, Lane left the bathroom. She walked slowly down the hallway. No need to hurry. The longer she took, the less time she would have to spend in the presence of Kramer.

Not that it had been too bad, being around him tonight.

With all the others in the same room, he didn't seem very threatening. Or maybe he didn't seem so threatening because she knew what was waiting for him.

He was a dead man. He just didn't know it yet.

In the kitchen, Lane rolled open the sliding door. She stepped outside and pulled it shut. The wind swept her hair back. Though it fluttered the front of her shirt, the T-shirt underneath kept her from feeling much chill. She walked toward the driveway.

The garage door had been pulled back no more than four or five feet. Light spilled out onto the pavement, but she couldn't see anyone inside until she stepped through the opening.

Dad was squatting on the other side of the coffin, his hand inside, gripping the stake. The others were watching him. Pete had the camera on him.

Hal had an arrow aimed at him. At Dad.

'NO!' she yelled.

Dad looked confused. Everyone else whirled around as she ran at Kramer, shouting, 'You bastard!' Even as the words left her mouth, she realized her mistake. Kramer hadn't been about to shoot Dad; the arrow was meant for the vampire. *You blew it*, she thought.

She saw shock in Kramer's eyes. He yanked back the bowspring. Barbara rammed an elbow into his side at the same instant he released the string. The arrow zipped past Lane, missing her right arm by less than an inch.

Almost on him, Lane hunched down. The top of her head struck the bow, knocked it aside, and rammed Kramer in the chest. He staggered backward. She wrapped her arms around him. She heard shouts of alarm. A knee punched into her belly, striking the crucifix and driving it against her skin, lifting her off her feet. Kramer's arms went under her. He swung her sideways and let go.

She hit the floor rolling, the concrete pounding her bones, the crucifix falling out of her shirt. She came to a stop on her back. Breathless, she struggled to sit up. Kramer's knee had blasted out her strength. She could lift her head, but that was all.

Dad, a look of shock on his face, still squatted behind the coffin as if frozen. Barbara was down on her back. Mom was behind Kramer, an arm clamped across his throat, riding him, swinging as he spun around and slashed at Pete with his straight razor. Pete thrust the camera out, blocking the blade.

Lane shoved at the floor. This time, she managed to sit up. She got to her feet.

'STAY PUT!' Dad's voice boomed.

She looked at him.

Their eyes locked. Lane had no breath to tell him what Kramer had done to her. But Dad seemed to know.

His eyes lowered.

And Lane saw him begin to rise from his crouch, his face twisting with rage, lips peeling back from his teeth, left hand shoving down against Bonnie's chest as he rose, right hand drawing out the stake. It came out, a long shaft of wood, stained dark just below his grip, tapering to a point. Like a madman with a butcher knife, he bounded over the coffin yelling and rushed Kramer.

Mom had lost her chokehold. She was on her knees behind Kramer, hugging his thighs. Barbara was scurrying toward the quiver of arrows. Pete took a slash across the chest as he brought the camera down with both hands, crashing it against Kramer's face.

The blow knocked the teacher's head back. He waved his arms, fighting for balance, about to topple over Mom.

Dad punched the stake into his throat.

Kramer's knees folded. His rump hit Mom's back, driving her to the floor. Dad, still clutching the embedded stake, went down to his knees. Snarling, he put his other hand to work. He used them both, shoving down and working the stake deeper into the man's throat.

Kramer kicked and twitched and flapped his arms. Blood gurgled up around the stake. His eyes bulged as if they might explode from his head. His mouth gaped, tongue stretched out and jerking as he made gagging noises.

Then came a violent spasm that seemed to shake the last of

Kramer's life out of his body. He sagged. Lane heard a soft fart. A stench of excrement came, and she covered her nose and mouth.

Dad, using the stake like a handle, dragged Kramer's body off Mom.

He left it in the man's throat and straightened up, gasping for air. He looked at his dripping hands. Then he looked at Pete. 'Are you okay?'

Pete was holding his bloody chest, staring down at himself, shaking his head.

Barbara held an arrow in each hand. She let go, and they clattered against the floor. She put an arm around Pete's back. 'God, honey.'

'Are *you* okay?' Pete asked her.

'Just had my wind knocked out.'

'Jean?' Dad asked.

Mom was on her knees, staring at the body. Instead of answering, she got up. She lifted her arms toward Lane. She had tears in her eyes and her nose was runny, but she didn't look hurt. Lane stepped closer, and they embraced.

'What did he do to you?' Mom asked.

'He hurt me,' Lane said, making sure her voice was loud enough for everyone to hear. 'He raped me. After the play Saturday night. He's the one who murdered Jessica Patterson and her parents. He said he'd kill us, too, if I told on him.'

'Oh my God,' Barbara murmured. 'You poor kid.'

'Fuckin' bastard,' Pete said. Lane heard a quick thud. Someone kicking Kramer?

She heard footsteps. Then Dad pressed against her back. His arms went around Mom, and Lane was enclosed between their bodies. She felt Dad's breath stirring her hair, warm against her scalp.

'Our pal Bonnie didn't come out of it,' Pete said.

Turning her head, Lane saw the dark cadaver stretched out motionless in its coffin, a hole where the stake had been.

Pete said, 'Guess she wasn't a vampire, after all.'

'Thank God,' Dad muttered.

Chapter Forty-eight

'I don't wanta leave you holding the bag,' Pete said from the back seat of his car where he was stretched out with a towel hugged to his chest.

'Don't worry about it,' Larry said through the driver's window.

'We'll come back,' Barbara told him. 'It shouldn't take more than an hour or so . . .'

'If they don't have to send out for more thread,' Pete said.

'The cops'll probably still be here.'

'I wouldn't be at all surprised.' Barbara took a hand off the steering wheel, gently patted Larry's cheek, and said, 'Don't worry. Nobody's gonna throw you in jail for killing that maggot.'

'If they do,' Pete said, 'you can write a book about it.'

'Thanks a bunch, partner.'

'Come on, babe. Let's move it. I'm turning into vampire dessert back here.'

'Take care,' Larry said. Then he stepped back from the car. Jean held his hand, and they stood side by side while Barbara steered out of the driveway.

Lane, sitting on her parents' bed with the phone book open on her lap, picked up the handset and punched in Kramer's number. She listened to the first ring, and imagined the phone suddenly blaring in Kramer's dark house, probably startling Riley, making his heart jump.

Two more rings, then the line opened.

Before she could speak, Kramer said, 'I'm not available to answer your call, right now. At the sound of the tone, please leave your name, number, and message, and I'll get back to you as soon as possible.'

'Like hell you will,' Lane muttered over the sound of his 'Thank you.'

She heard an empty, windy sound like the desert at night.
What if Riley isn't there and the cops end up with this?
The beep came.

'Hey, pick up. It's goody-two-shoes. You know? Goody-two-shoes with the spit on her face. Pick up. It's urgent.'

She heard a click. 'Lane?' Riley's voice.

'Yeah, it's me. Take the tape out of the machine and put it in your pocket.'

'Sure. What's up?'

'Do it now, okay?'

A few seconds later, he said, 'Okay, I've got it. What's going on? Is he leaving?'

'He's dead.'

'*What?*'

'My dad killed him about ten minutes ago. I don't have time to tell you about it now. The thing is, you can go on home.'

'Damn it!'

'You oughta be glad.'

'I wanted to . . .'

'I know, I know.'

'Maybe I'll burn the fucker's house for him.'

'No, don't do that. There might be some kind of evidence.'

'Oh yeah, there's plenty of that, all right.'

'Really?'

'Hey, the fucker's got a regular museum here in a closet – pictures on the walls. You, Jessica, half a dozen . . .'

'*Me?*' Lane asked, feeling as if her breath were being sucked out.

'Sure as shit. Must be thirty, forty of 'em. He's got a darkroom here, all kinds of cameras, telephoto lenses, you name it.'

'My God.'

'A lot of girl's stuff, too. Panties, bras, nightgowns. Fuckin' pervert. Looks like he used 'em to . . .'

'Just leave everything the way it is. For godsake, don't burn the place. The cops've gotta find that stuff. It'll help keep my dad out of trouble.'

For a few moments, there was silence. Then Riley said, 'I don't know. Some of the shots he got of Jessica . . . I don't want a bunch of cops seeing her like that.'

'They have to know what Kramer was doing.'

'Yeah? Bet you wouldn't be saying that if you saw what he's got on *you*.'

'He couldn't . . .'

'He was following you around, Lane. He was out to your house, too, from the looks of it. You better start learning to shut your curtains better.'

'Jesus,' she muttered.

'Still want me to leave everything?'

Squeezing her eyes shut, she groaned.

Pictures of me on his walls. Taken through the windows? Her skin went hot and crawly.

'Leave everything,' she said. 'Please. You've got to.'

More silence. At last, Riley said, 'I'll leave some of it. Enough so the cops get the idea. Okay? I'll take the worst ones of you and Jessica and burn 'em.'

'All right. Thanks.' She heard the front door bump shut. 'Look, I've gotta hang up. My folks just came in. I'll be in touch. You get out of there.' She hung up the phone and hurried to the hallway.

From his hiding place behind a cactus cluster across the street, Uriah watched the lair of the vampires and wondered what had happened there.

Everyone else in the neighborhood must've been wondering, too. He counted more than twenty rubber-neckers wandering around the street and sidewalks, all of them strange in the flashing lights of the police cars and coroner's van.

After a long time, a couple of gurneys were rolled down the driveway. As they were being loaded into the coroner's van, Uriah caught glimpses of bulky dark bags.

A lot of the gawkers cleared out, once the meat wagon was gone.

One by one, the police cars left. The last of them stayed for quite a while. Only a few neighbors were still hanging around by the time a pair of cops stepped out of the front door, went to the remaining car and drove away.

Uriah sat down on the gravel behind the cactus, wrapped the blanket around himself to keep off the chill, and waited.

Whatever had gone on across the street, he still had to go in and carry out his mission. The cops hadn't taken care of any vampires, he was sure of that. Cops might be good at some things, but they didn't know beans about Satan's blood-thirsty children.

That's where I come in, he thought.

'Guess that's that,' Pete said, and yawned. He was reclined in the easy chair, wearing one of Larry's shirts over the bandages that had been applied in the emergency room. 'Score one for the good guys.'

'I just wish you would've told us,' Jean said, looking at Lane with weary, sad eyes.

'Let it go, honey.'

'I was just so scared,' Lane murmured.

'It's all right,' Larry told her, and stroked her hair. 'It's over, now.'

She nodded, her cheek rubbing against his shoulder. 'Is it okay if I go to bed now?'

'Sure, go on.'

Lane got up from the sofa. She told Pete and Barbara goodnight, kissed Jean, came back to Larry, whispered, 'Night, Dad,' and kissed him. Then she walked out of the living room, moving slowly, her head hanging.

When she was gone, Barbara said, 'Poor kid. The hell she must've gone through . . .'

'You got the bastard, Lar.'

'With a little help from my friends.'

'Man, you nailed him good.'

'Let's not talk about it any more,' Jean said. She slumped forward until her elbows met her knees, and seemed to stare at the carpet.

'Come on Pete,' Barbara said, getting up. 'Let's go before you pass out.' To Larry, she said, 'They doped him up pretty good at the ER.'

'I'm fine.'

She took his arm, and helped him out of the chair.

'I'm okay, I'm okay.' Pulling away from her, he staggered toward the sofa. He shoved a hand toward Larry.

Larry reached up and shook it.

Pete held on. 'So I guess we did good, huh pardner?'

Larry shrugged. He didn't feel as if he'd done good. He felt dazed, sick and weary and sad.

'Too bad old Bonnie didn't perk up for us.'

'Just as well,' Larry said.

'Still got us a hell of a book, though, huh?'

'No book,' Larry said. 'Not about this.'

'Hey, man . . .'

'We never had a vampire, anyway. Even if we did, I couldn't write the truth. I couldn't write about Kramer. About Lane. I won't.'

Pete stared down at him, eyes still blackened from his encounter with Uriah's rock. He stared for a long time. Then, he sighed. His grip on Larry's hand tightened. 'Good man,' he said.

'You, too. We'll do a different book together.'

A corner of Pete's mouth tilted up. 'All *right*. I'm full of ideas. We'll . . .'

'You're full of Darvon,' Barbara broke in, putting an arm around him. 'Now, come on. Let's go home and get some shut-eye.'

When they were gone, Larry turned off the lights and walked with Jean toward their bedroom. At the end of the hallway, a glowing band showed beneath the bathroom door. He heard water running.

'I've gotta take a shower, too,' he mumbled.

'Don't be long,' Jean said. 'I don't want to be alone.'

'I'll hurry,' he told her. They entered the room. He went to the master bath, turned on the light, but left the door open.

He took off his clothes. When he lifted the lid of the hamper to drop them in, he saw the wadded, bloody shirt he'd been wearing when he killed Kramer. The sweatsuit covered it. He shut the lid, stepped to the tub, and turned on the water.

Under the hot spray, he thought of Lane in the other bathroom. Like him, trying to cleanse herself of Kramer.

He was weeping when the shower curtain rattled open. Jean stepped into the tub. She slid the curtain shut and put her arms around him. Her face pressed against the side of his neck.

They didn't speak. They held onto each other hard.

Lane draped her towel over the bar and slipped into her nightshirt. Where she had missed a patch of water, low on her back, the soft fabric hugged her skin.

She left her clothes hanging in the bathroom, and stepped out.

The house looked dark except for light from the open door of her parents' bedroom.

She went to her own room, flipped on the light, and stared at her bed. As weary as she felt, she knew that sleep wouldn't come easily or soon. She would lie in bed, wide awake, remembering.

No, I won't, she told herself.

She was in her room just long enough to pick up her pillow and blanket. Holding them to her chest, she turned off the light and walked silently down the hallway.

She glanced into her parents' room. They weren't there, but she heard a windy sound of rushing water from their bath.

Moving through darkness, she made her way to the sofa. She dropped her pillow and blanket onto it, stepped to the television and turned it on.

A Christopher Lee movie. She changed the channel, recognized Jimmy Stewart in some kind of Air Force story, and returned to the sofa.

There, she lay down and covered herself with the blanket. Curled up cozy on her side, she watched the show. When Kramer forced his way into her mind, she made herself remember the people zipping the rubber bag shut around him, taking him out to the van along with Bonnie.

They're both gone now. Kramer can never touch me again. And I don't even have to worry about Bonnie. They're gone. I'm safe. Mom and Dad are safe. Everything's okay.

She wondered if she should go to school in the morning.

They'll have a substitute in English.

It would be nice to see Henry and Betty and George.

Not tomorrow, though. It's so late. I'd be a space case.

The Jimmy Stewart movie ended. Lane wondered what would come on next. Before she could find out, however, a warm fog seemed to fold itself over her mind, and she closed her eyes.

Chapter Forty-nine

In the first light of dawn, Uriah left his hiding place. The neighborhood was silent. He crossed the empty street, and glanced at the red Mustang of the vampires as he walked by.

Getting his hands on its registration had made things so easy. The first time he'd gone after Bonnie, he didn't have that. All he knew, then, was what kind of car she drove.

One of those Volkswagen bugs had gone by on the road while he was hiking back to Sagebrush Flat after his pickup broke down. It had a pale color in the moonlight, and he'd glimpsed enough of the driver to see she was a girl.

Not much to go on. He couldn't even be sure the bug was on its way to Mulehead Bend, though that was the first town to the east, the direction the car had been heading. So that's where he went looking.

It took him a while, but he found the girl vampire who had

a yellow VW. He put her to rest. But then another turned up, and then another. They were all girls, all about the right age, and they all had light-colored Volkswagens. They were all vampires, too.

During his search was when he came to learn they didn't behave like vampires should. They didn't sleep in coffins. The sunlight didn't burn them up. They could go around in daytime, just like regular girls. All the sun did was weaken them.

The sun would've made them easier to kill, but he'd been so headstrong, back then, that he'd gone after them at night. When he thought about it afterwards, he figured it must've been a kind of deathwish on his part. He'd wanted his revenge, all right, but he hadn't really cared whether he kept on living.

That had been a fool way to go about it. But the Lord stood by him, and kept him from harm.

The Lord had a mission all set up for Uriah. He planned to send His warrior all across the nation to hunt out the legion of vampires doing Satan's work in every corner of the land. So He'd let Uriah slip by, even though he went about killing the first three vampires in such a foolhardy fashion.

Uriah hoped the Lord would allow him to retire after today. If he survived.

Going up against five of Satan's children would be no easy task. He figured his chances were slim, especially since he didn't have his bow and arrows.

But if the Lord stuck with him, he planned to stake them all, and cart them back to Sagebrush in the van that belonged to the vampire he'd almost put to rest on Saturday. It was in the driveway of the house on the right. He would go to that house after finishing here.

Uriah tried the front door. He found it locked, so he made his way around to the side. He let himself in through a gate. Up ahead was the garage. It had a yellow plastic ribbon across the front – the kind of thing police put up in places where there'd been a crime.

That's where the vampires must've killed those two people,

last night. What kind of story had they told, anyway, to make it all right?

The police couldn't have kept them long, anyway.

Only one thing will do the job on those creatures, and that's what I've got.

At the rear of the house, Uriah found a window that was open just a crack at the bottom. He set his satchel down on the concrete, pulled his knife, and cut an opening in the screen. He tried holding the knife in his teeth to keep it handy, but clamping his jaw shut tight just hurt too much, so he sheathed the knife at his side. Then he reached through the split screen and pushed the window up.

He slung a strap of his satchel over his shoulder, and climbed in.

A bathroom. It smelled flowery and nice.

The door was open. Beyond was a hallway, dim in the early morning light.

Before leaving the bathroom, Uriah took off the bag. He removed his hammer and one stake, then slipped the strap onto his shoulder again and crept into the hallway.

He stopped at an open door. A bedroom. But he saw nobody in it.

He kept moving, and came to another bedroom. There, he found the vampire who'd shot him. Uriah tongued the hole in his right cheek. It made him wince, and his eyes watered up.

This one's chest was exposed. He was sprawled on his back, bare to the waist where the covers were rumpled up.

A woman vampire slept next to him. She was covered to the shoulders, lying on her side with her face toward the other. She wasn't Bonnie.

As much as Uriah wanted to kill the one who'd given him such hurt, he'd already decided to take care of Bonnie first. She'd made these two into vampires after they brought her here. So they were new at it. They wouldn't be near as dangerous as Bonnie.

Besides, Bonnie was the demon that killed Elizabeth and Martha.

The two girls he'd staked before Bonnie were vampires, but she was the one who killed his family. The Lord had told him that. So she needed to be the first, here, to be struck down.

Silently, he stepped past the bedroom. As he continued down the hallway, he heard a quiet sound of voices. His heart almost stopped. But then he heard music, too, and realized the noises must be coming from a radio or television.

He paused to catch his breath. Then he went on.

In the front room, he found the television. Some kind of news report was on, the volume very low.

On the sofa, he found Bonnie.

She looked just as Uriah remembered her. Satan's vermin, disguised as a beautiful young woman. She lay on her back, her golden hair spread out against her pillow, a blanket up around her neck.

Uriah gazed at her. She looked so peaceful, so innocent, so lovely.

He lowered his satchel to the floor, then stepped between the coffee table and the sofa. He slipped the stake under his right arm. Holding it against his side, he bent over and slowly drew the blanket down. Bonnie didn't stir. Uriah, though trembling and breathless with the sight of her, didn't rush. He eased sideways, taking the blanket with him. At last, it no longer covered her at all. He left it heaped on the end of the sofa.

Satan took such beautiful ones for his own.

The leg closer to Uriah was stretched out straight. The other was bent a little, heel against the cushion, knee resting against the back of the sofa. Slim, bare legs, softly tanned, but bruised up around the thighs.

In her sleep of the undead, her red nightshirt had slipped up around her hips. Uriah stared between her legs. He licked his dry lips. His heart pounded so badly he feared the sound of it might wake her up. He felt his hardness rising against the coyote hide of his skirt.

She's a vampire, he reminded himself. She's a vile daughter of Satan, a blood-thirsty demon.

Get on with it! he told himself.

He stepped sideways, but he couldn't help himself from looking back. From here, he could see her fine golden curls, but not the tempting region lower down.

He rubbed the back of his hand across his lips. Then he took the stake out from under his arm.

He looked at her chest.

I've got to look, he told himself. Have to see where I want to plant the stake.

He stared at her breasts, smooth mounds under the night-shirt, nipples pushing at the fabric.

The cloth was so thin that Uriah knew the stake would poke right through it – almost as if it wasn't there at all. Still, having it out of the way would be better.

She'll wake up, sure as hell.

But Uriah had to do it.

He set the hammer and stake on the floor at his feet. He drew his knife. Ever so slowly, starting at the neck, he sliced his way down the nightshirt. Bonnie stirred, once or twice, but she didn't wake up.

At last, he sheathed the knife. He carefully spread the severed edges.

She was mighty bruised up. Someone had used her in a rough manner. It surprised Uriah to see injuries. He'd thought such demons couldn't be damaged except by the stake.

Her breasts looked smudged with faint shadows. So did much of the skin around them. He saw a bruise the size of a fist just below her rib cage.

And a shape like a cross on her belly. A cross, for sure. It looked just like the one on Uriah's own chest after he'd been saved from the bullet. The beams of the cross had bruised her, and its edges had gouged her skin. The scraped places looked raw and shiny.

A wound from a cross on the vampire's belly. Uriah wondered what it could mean.

Had someone else come after her? Someone armed with a cruficix?

Those bodies the police took away last night . . .

Are there more of us? Had the Lord sent a couple of other warriors, afraid I might fail?

Well, they're the ones that failed.

Uriah picked up his hammer and stake.

She had no bruise at all where he had planted the stake the last time. There, her skin looked flawless, a silken cream in the gloomy light.

He let his eye roam once more down her slim, smooth body. Then he eased the stake forward. He brushed its point against her left nipple and wished he could put his mouth there, wished he could kiss it and suck on it – but she would wake up for sure if he did that, and kill him. Besides, his mouth was in no shape to suck on anything.

He guided the stake to the place where he'd put the other one in. It shook slightly, its tip trembling half an inch above her skin.

Then he raised his hammer.

Chapter Fifty

The alarm didn't go off, that morning. When Larry awoke, he found Jean still asleep beside him. He sat up, and looked past her at the clock. Eight-fifteen.

Lane's going to be late for school, he thought.

Then he realized she probably wouldn't be going, today. Not after all that had happened.

All that had happened. Kramer raped her. Oh Jesus. Oh God. My girl.

I killed the rotten son-of-a-bitch.

Good. Good good good good.

881

Larry started to cry, and quickly got out of bed before his sobbing could wake up Jean. At the closet, he took down his robe. He used it to rub the tears off his face, but more came. He put the robe on, and went to Lane's room.

Her bed was empty.

He felt a rough grip of panic.

She's okay. Kramer's dead.

What if she's done something stupid?

He rushed through the house, trying to choke back his sobs, trying to tell himself that Lane's a strong girl, a brave girl, she'd had something terrible happen to her, something terrible beyond words, but she was a survivor.

He found her in the front room.

On the sofa.

Asleep, covered to the neck by her blanket.

'Thank God,' he whispered.

Bending over the sofa, he caressed Lane's cheek. It felt very warm, as it always did when she slept.

He went into the kitchen to start the coffee.

His breath flew out as if he'd been kicked. He dropped to his knees.

He thought, it's a good thing I can't breathe. If I can't breathe, I can't scream. Don't want to wake up Lane. Don't want her seeing this.

Uriah Radley was sprawled belly down on the kitchen floor beside his canvas bag. He wore his vest and skirt of coyote skin, but the skirt was held up by the handle of a hammer that jutted from between his buttocks.

His head was twisted around so he wore it backward.

Much of his neck had been eaten away.

The blunt end of a wooden stake filled his mouth, and he had a stake in each eye. The eyepatch hadn't been removed first. It must've been pushed right in by the stake. The broken side of its black band lay across Uriah's forehead, but the other side was there at the corner of the socket like a bloody worm that had tried to creep out between the stake and bone.

Larry staggered into the living room. Lane was still asleep.

Did she . . .?

No, that was impossible.

Someone turned his head around.

Stepping closer to her, Larry stubbed his toe on a leg of the coffee table. He grunted at the sudden pain, and Lane opened her eyes.

She frowned. 'What happened?' she asked, her voice husky.

'Bumped the table,' he said.

'You look awful.'

'Lane, somebody . . . Let me have your blanket.'

'What's going on?'

'I'm not sure.'

As Lane sat up, the blanket slid to her lap. She reached down for it and gasped. Larry glimpsed her bare chest and belly. She jerked the blanket up again. She looked at him, eyes wide, mouth hanging open. 'Daaad?'

'Oh, my God,' he murmured.

'What's happening?'

'Uriah got into the house last night, honey.'

'Uriah?'

'It's okay. He's dead. He's in the kitchen.'

'The guy that killed Bonnie?'

'Somebody got him. Somebody . . . he's really messed up. Go to our room, honey. Stay with your mother, and don't either of you come out until I say it's all right.'

Hugging the blanket around herself, Lane rose from the sofa. She faced Larry. She looked haggard, frightened. 'Who killed him, Dad?'

'I don't know. I just don't know. But I don't think we're in any danger.'

She stared at him, lower lip caught between her teeth. Then she turned away and headed for the bedroom.

Larry returned to the kitchen. He crouched beside the body, being careful not to look at it, and took a stake out of Uriah's bag. He left Uriah's hammer where it was.

Outside, the morning was sunny and still. He broke the police seal, opened the garage and stepped into the shadows.

The concrete floor was cool on his bare feet. Casting a glance at the attic ladder, he felt gooseflesh scurry up his back. He hurried on. At the workbench, he found his hammer.

'You're the one, aren't you?'

He went numb. The hammer slipped from his fingers and thudded the top of the workbench. He snatched it up again. He whirled around.

In front of him stood Bonnie.

Larry knew he was gazing upon a monster. Only a monster could've done such things to Uriah. Only a monster could be standing before him now, radiant and beautiful, though she'd been dead two decades, though last night she'd been a hideous, withered hag.

But she was Bonnie, the girl of the yearbook pictures, songleader and Spirit Queen. Bonnie, the girl who had haunted his dreams.

Her eyes flitted from his right hand to his left, from the hammer to the stake. A smile lifted a corner of her mouth. 'You won't need those, will you?'

He struggled to breathe.

'Hey, calm down. You'll give yourself a coronary.' One of her hands reached toward him. There was no blood on it. There was no blood on her at all that Larry could see.

Her hand caressed the side of his face. It felt smooth and warm.

'This can't be. It can't be.'

'Hey, come on.' She pulled his ear. The way she did it seemed playfully affectionate. 'Are you okay?'

'No. Jesus.'

'Look, I'm sorry.' Frowning, she put both hands on Larry's sides. They rubbed him gently through the robe. 'I thought you'd be glad to see me. I didn't mean to freak you out or anything.'

'You . . . you did that to Uriah?'

She lowered her eyes. 'Yeah,' she murmured. 'Pretty gross, huh? You must think I'm awful.'

'How could you do something like that?'

She looked up at him. 'Hey, I'm a vampire. Remember? Besides, he had it coming.'

'But what you did to him . . .'

'I know, I know. Look, you don't have to rub it in. But he was all set to do a number on the girl.'

'What do you mean?'

'He was going to kill her. The girl on the couch.'

'God,' Larry muttered. 'You saved Lane?'

'Is she your kid?'

'Yeah.'

'I'm extra glad I saved her, then.'

Moaning, he eased forward against Bonnie. Her arms slipped around him. He dropped the stake and hammer to the floor and embraced her.

'What's your name?' she asked.

'Larry. Larry Dunbar.'

'I'm Bonnie.'

'Yeah, I know.'

Her face pushed against the side of his neck.

It passed through his mind that she might sink her teeth in. But he wasn't frightened.

Nor was he aroused.

This wasn't like his dreams, at all. He caressed the smooth skin of her back. He felt her breasts pushing against his chest. He knew that only his loosely belted robe kept their bare bodies from meeting. But he felt no heat in his groin, just a mellow warmth in his chest and belly.

'You saved my girl,' he whispered.

Bonnie squeezed him hard, then kissed the side of his neck. 'It was the least I could do for you. I'm just glad I got here in time.'

'How . . .?'

'No sweat.' Tilting her head back, she gazed up at him. 'I just came back to say thanks. I figured . . . hell, you're the guy who took the stake out of me. I wanted you to know the truth, too. You would've found out, anyway, I guess. I mean, you were bound to hear about my disappearing act at the morgue.

But I wanted to thank you in person. You mean a lot to me, Larry. A hell of a lot. Anyway, I just happened to get here in time to nail that bastard. He's the same guy that murdered me. A real lunatic.'

'He knew you were a vampire.'

'Oh, he didn't know shit.'

'But you *are* one.'

'Yeah, but I didn't touch his wife and kid. That was Linda Latham, not me. Hell, you don't go around ripping people up. Not if you want to last long. You just give 'em a little kiss while they're asleep. A little suck. Take a pint, maybe. They wake up the next day, and half the time they don't even know anything happened. You don't go around *wasting* people. Linda did that 'cause her boyfriend dumped her for Martha Radley.'

'A jealous vampire?'

Scowling with indignation, Bonnie dug her fingers into his sides.

He squirmed. 'Don't. Hey.'

'What do you think, we've got no feelings?'

'I don't know what to think. I can't even believe you're here right now.'

Bonnie put her arms around him again. 'I'm here, Larry. And everything's okay. Everything's just fine. The dirty bastard's dead, and Lane's alive.'

'Because of you,' Larry murmured.

'You gave my life back to me, or I couldn't have done it. You pulled that damn stake out of me. I'm so . . .' Her voice trembled. She looked up, and Larry saw tears glimmering in her eyes. 'I'm so glad to be back. I'll always love you for that, Larry. I'm so happy I could . . . could go something good for you.'

Lowering his head, he kissed each of Bonnie's eyes. They were wet. Her tears tasted salty.

She sniffed. 'Look, I'd better amscray.'

'You can't leave,' he said. 'It's morning.'

She rubbed her face against the front of his robe, sniffed again, then sighed. 'I'd like to stay, but . . . too much has happened here. I'll go off somewhere, start over.'

Bonnie eased away from him, but he caught her by the shoulders.

'You'll burn up,' he said.

'You've seen too many movies, Larry. I love the sun.' She spread her arms, tilted back her head and closed her eyes. 'It's like warm hands. Warm hands caressing me.' She sighed. 'I think I'll go to the ocean and be a beach bum.'

'I don't want you to leave.'

Her eyes met his. She smiled a little sadly. 'Want to keep me in your garage?'

'We could figure out . . .'

She touched a finger to his lips, silencing him. 'I can't stay. You know that. But I'll always love you.' She curled her hands over his shoulders, drew him down, and pressed her lips gently to his mouth. Then she kissed his cheek. Then the side of his neck.

There, her lips parted and her teeth slid into his flesh.

A cold stab of panic quickly melted away. He felt the pull of her mouth, heard the soft sucking sounds. A pleasant, warm langour spread through him. Closing his eyes, he saw Bonnie standing naked on a beach, arms spread out, face raised toward the sun, a mild breeze stirring her golden hair.

She stopped sucking. Her teeth eased out of him, and he felt a harsh ache of loss. She licked the side of his neck. She kissed the wounds. Tilting back her head, she gazed up at him with such tenderness and love that he thought his heart might break. Her lips gleamed with his blood.

'Now you'll always be with me,' she said, her voice husky.

'You mean . . . you made me a vampire?'

A smile trembled on her red lips. 'Nooo.' Stepping away from him, she placed her open hand between her breasts. 'From now on, you'll be with me here.' She lifted the hand. She tapped her fingers against the side of her head. 'And here. If you ever need me, I'll know it.'

'I need you now.'

'No. Not now, but maybe someday. And if that ever happens, I'll come back.'

'But . . .'

She was gone. She didn't turn and walk away. She didn't vanish in a puff of smoke. She didn't dissolve. Suddenly, she was simply there no more. Larry stared at the daylight glaring in through the garage door.

'Oh, Bonnie,' he whispered.

As tears filled his eyes, he lowered his head.

There on the garage floor, between the hammer and the stake, stood a pure white seagull looking up at him.

Larry crouched down.

With a quick flap of wings, the seagull perched on his knee. It cocked its head to one side.

'You've got to be kidding,' he murmured.

The bird pecked his knee. But not very hard. Then it took flight. It circled his head once, buffeting him with the soft breeze of its wings, then flapped its way to the garage door and soared into the sunlight.